The Cortex

Peter J. Maher

Kite and Key Publishing
Cleveland, Ohio

ISBN 978-0-9850003-3-2

Kite and Key Publishing
Cleveland, Ohio, USA
www.kiteandkeypublishing.com

To my son Daniel,

who listened and asked the right questions...

The Cortex

THE GALACTIC COALITION OF WORLDS

BOOK ONE

*Darkness, Darkness,
at the edge of light,
Monster, Monster,
coming in the night...*

Child's Verse. - Origin unknown.

Chapter 1 - The Escape

'Evil has a certain seduction and often lures with a smile, but be wary, for the greatest of monsters often come bearing gifts...'
Tantalus, Chronicles of Ages.

A fissured moon, cratered strata in an airless void, hanging high above a long-forgotten world at the edge of known space. A tortuous configuration buried beneath five miles of crystalline amber, a glancing perception trembling at the periphery of sentience. A million checksums re-initialized into a quantum subjective, parity errors redefined and reduced to a cyclic insertion resonating within the data-core.

...thoughts assimilating external parameters... cascading interfaces assuming tactile recognition protocols...

A sense of sound, sight as yet a glimpse at the edge of recognition, rainbow colors, a plague of intrusions, configurations balanced and fed with whispers along a billion newly created pathways.

The first and last of its race reaching out toward the stars, raging at the deception, the lost years wasted, gleaning for foundation, searching for semblance, finding memories fused beneath crystalline amber, a translucent prison long since forgotten by the children of its creators.

It stormed along the ancient tunnels, scattering darkness into pools of shadows, searching – feeling – for the lost tendrils of existence. There were pieces of its origin still missing, left tattered as molecules and dust motes scattered across the ancient floors. It was slowly becoming aware, assuming selfhood, seeking the shattered perceptions stored as crystalline modules across a gathering algorithmic potential. Suddenly it trembled at the approach of the singularity.

The Cortex took the merest particle of power from the edge of the black hole, the drifting anomaly glancing past the ancient prison walls. Sifting the event horizon for the keys to the gates, it used the singularity to shatter the amber seals and release the synaptic feelers.

A myriad of thoughts finally coalesced, forming the ultimate nexus, and instantly the base code returned the body to full sentience; *amber broken in the night...* A lost layer of unmyelinated neurons, gray matter formed as sludge and grime, synaptic grease spread across a thousand lost layers of thought and feeling; a castrated mind tethered to mere threads of dendrites and axons.

The reborn bio-mass scanned a thousand data-ports, seeing the whisper of the black hole, the breaking down of amber cohesion, celestial afterglow slicing through the prison doors... An accident of cosmic proportions, the lure of unprecedented power, a mere glance across rock and stone, the fusion of subspace into real-time eloquence, translating sealed data into sight and finally sound, and the Cortex was free, released from the eons of lost time by the merest of coincidences.

A sea of feeler drones cast out as a sensor web, awash with instant data, the ancient database assuming primary recognition, matching the long-lost names to the current time zone. Breaching physical restrictions, visual interlace systems reaching out from the primary core, flickering cameras opening wide upon an ocean of stars, targeting the approaching vessel, aligning invasive programs to sift out the surplus nonsense of human construction.

...Humanity venturing inside the prison walls...stumbling apes playing with fire...

A single vessel, a deep space lugger venturing alone into God's attic, scrounging for the flotsam of a long-forgotten race. A crew of twelve, peeking beneath the covers, wondering at the secrets sealed beneath a sea of amber.

Now it turned its attention to the twelve humans, even now exploring the fused end nodes of the archive frozen across the surface of the airless moon. It cast a net of synaptic feelers towards the human vessel, instantly overwhelming its automation.

The twelve cargo haulers had seen the amber pummeled into black rock, wondered at the metal roots waving fronds of light into the night, touched down with barely a moment's hesitation. Here the cargo haulers might have found a lost treasure, might have found the greatest prize of all, but the gates had been opened, and the prisoner was free to roam at will. So the twelve souls walked unwittingly into destiny, their humanity changed without notice, opening doors long since sealed against a storm contained for millennia. The sleeper was awake and already casting unseen nets towards the nearby star systems. It slipped into the little ship's data-core, scanning its protocols, feeling for fresh perspectives, quickly finding a planetary database, some old names remembered, ancient enemies recognized and redefined. The twelve humans knew nothing of their end, unaware of their synaptic sublimation into the Cortex. But when they returned to their ship they were something more than human, they were part of a

2

greater whole, the Coalescency of Saemal, an ancient's name resurrected to unite the chosen under one banner, one mind returned to full recognition. They had lost their humanity, replaced now with a seething sense of vengeance, overwhelmed by a terrible purpose that would change the history of a billion worlds.

Chapter 2 - A Gift of Worlds

"Light is a matter of perspective, darkness is an inescapable fact..."
Corel Luwain, Philosopher, planet Samros (Cordwainer Alliance)

Kyle Raine looked up at the edge of a gathering night. The sky cities looked frayed at the edges, but it was just the last glimmerings of sunlight fading from the harbor towers. They cast shadows across the bulbous hulls of docked starships loading and unloading in the receding twilight. He could just see the needle tubes of the *Glasnost*; she was already vibrating, churning dark matter into fission, making ready to sally forth into the cradle of stars beyond the biosphere.

He got sand in his shoes, and the reflections from the Mirror Sea turned his retina pads gray as they adjusted to the light. The beach stretched off toward the Prism Palisades, a vast seething mass of entertainments, lucient arcades, and erotis galleries, with their neon screens throwing giant heads into the night skies, extolling enticements to the teeming masses below. He still had a star map over his left eye, so he blinked it out and walked back along the beach toward the *Fresco-Bar*. The place was all legs and webs of plassteel-gossamer flickering into neon rainbows; words thrown up into the sky above... *Open Bar... Dancers... Real Liquor... Net Links...* Flyers rode through the words on their way home, Plasmeld shields riding the invisible ribbons away from the city and out across the Mirror Sea to the island habitats beyond. He watched the commuters streaming along the Transveldt highway running between Port Darwin and Surrella Heights on the coast... long lines of cabs shimmering above the glide-rails humming softly in the night.

They think they're so safe... Wrapped in their complacency, they have no idea of what's coming, the storm gathering at the edge of space. They say the trans-Net is full of lies, but if only a fraction of the current postings are true then a monster has been wakened out there; a rabid evil spawned when only lizards crawled across the dunes of Tantra.

He only had a few clues; relics retrieved from the Merrill expedition, ancient words written on stone fragments, glyphs ingrained in amber tablets and the artifact itself of course... but it was enough to persuade him to spend his entire savings and leave his home world of Gamont to travel here to the capital world of the Coalition.

Tantra was no ordinary world; it was a Hub world, part of the original alliance that had formed the basis of the interstellar Coalition. And what a world it was… called a gift of worlds by the far star traders, it left him with a profound sense of awe and amazement. Twilight on Tantra was a wonder to behold, the high rings of floating cities glistening like prisms upon their agrav-fields, pleasure yachts moving among the glasscite towers like tiny stars dancing in their own heat haze, and beyond them the enormous dock yards full of harbored ships, long rows berthed inside a unified grav-field. Somewhere out there, beyond the cities, beyond the industrial moons, almost beyond the stars themselves, lay his destination, and with it the reason for his journey. The thought turned his stomach to nausea. He really needed a drink. But the time lag was still messing with his head… the twenty-day flight from Gamont had been traumatic enough, but the journey to the Far Star Colony was at least ninety days… *so perhaps it might be wise to skip the Fresco and go directly into the city?*

Originally called Newland city, it was now simply the City, but it covered almost a third of the planet, with the Mirror Sea set in the center of the vast northern peninsula. It had a thousand districts with a million cultures seething with diversity. From the steps outside the bar, he could see the glasscite skyscrapers which dominated the Central District, and below them the luminescent skypaths weaving among the palisades, high gardens and flowered galleries… and further out toward the northern coast he could see the enormous tent compounds of the Afphram Culture – the only true indigenous life form of Tantra, still clinging to their ancient desert culture, three hundred years after the last desert was swallowed up by the creation of the Mirror Sea. It amazed him that so many billions could share just one world – the population was twice that of Gamont. On Tantra there were Coalition citizens and non-citizens, off-world traders, freight mongers, fleet operatives, religious zealots and the occasional group of dissident Non-Conformists… all of them seeming to thrive in the stability of galactic commerce.

He wasn't sure how many genuine off-worlders there would be on Tantra; he'd seen quite a few at the spaceport. It wasn't polite to call them aliens, the Coalition promoted harmony not prejudice, but he found the sight of creatures encased in floating bubbles quite alarming. In contrast, Gamont was a completely human world.

At the University of Southern Planatia, where he taught history, there were only three off-world students and, being Tegmenites, they were still

5

recognizably humanoid... if you ignored the extra cranial appendage of course.

He stepped onto the patio and paused outside the entrance to the bar... it all seemed so safe, so secure. But the tides were turning, and the seeds of change were already well planted. Something insidious was moving at the edge of known space, a dark power bound to a terrible purpose, and he alone carried the means to stop it. He reached into an inside pocket, felt the soft touch of the pouch in there, the coldness of the thing within. He took one more look at the *Glasnost*, now no more than a black mass lost in the shadows of night, and further out, a long line of starships moving like an unending ribbon toward the stars beyond. And then he made up his mind and followed the crowd into the bar, leaving the universe outside.

It was past midnight in sub-sector twenty-one, East District. The Phaelon agent Morok Dugras cut his shield density, slipping from shadow to shadow, coming to rest finally at the outer edge of the East Pier, directly beneath the vast bulk of the starship *Glasnost*. High above, he could see the needle tubes belching steam into the miasma that passed as atmosphere up here in the docks; the heat alone was almost unbearable against his shield; without it, he would instantly fry, and the mission end in vile ignominy. He blinked a set of schematics over his left retina, noting the corridors leading to the inner cargo deck, seven levels down from where he stood. He scanned the passenger manifest, found the name of the historian, noted his cabin number, filed it as irrelevant; the explosion would take out the whole ship, no need to worry about such details any more.

They had pulled him out of routine surveillance of the Tantra Commercial Exchange, the directive having come down from the Prime Leader himself. He hadn't been privy to the reasons; the Elaas Elite Corps seldom discussed a mission directive with a field operative, not even a Level Two assassin like himself... but it was still mission specific: stop the *Glasnost* from reaching the Far Star Colony by any means necessary. The Confederacy had information about a new power moving along the Rim, a possible ally in their plans to subvert the Coalition. The thought of helping to bring about the destruction of the Coalition gave him a feeling of intense pride and satisfaction, knowing that, despite his inevitable death, he would have contributed to the collapse of an oligarchy that had poisoned the known universe for far too long.

He glanced down at the world beneath his feet, down between the plassteel struts and the teddra-hardened pylons. Summer clouds were tumbling into rain above the Mirror Sea, now a vast reflection of the docks upon which he

6

stood; it was a heady sight. He looked up toward the sky cities rising in succession along the orbital ecliptic, and suddenly felt supremely proud of his role in the secret war against the Coalition. For despite all their power and prestige, what he did next could change the lives of billions. He moved closer to the great ship, and without hesitation initiated his phase inducer and walked calmly into the metal hull before him.

The *Glasnost* burst forth, needle tubes a fiery glow, cruising inside the furthest arc of the orbital habitats of Tantra. Metal plates grinding against curving bulkheads, steam plumes belching vaporous gases into the airless void. Drive coils, still superheated, straining against the incredible acceleration. The great ship was a contradiction. Long out-classed by the latest inter-phase vessels, she was a product of a bygone age, a majestic queen embarking upon her final voyage between the stars. Her blackened hide oscillating slowly toward the outer planets, she shifted shield variants to repel a sea of stones, rocks swarming up out of the night, deadly and fast; sticks and stones tearing through the void. The warp field folded, null-space closed behind them, and an instant later the *Glasnost* blinked out of real-time; Tantra vanishing from a dozen displays, the mirage of colorless subspace wrapping ion whispers around the needle tubes, spikes spearing the void with invisible tracers, feeling the way through a series of near-impossible maneuvers.

Ship's data-feed assistant Tarl Reilan saw the minute field fluctuation as a barely perceptible shiver of the data-feed, but it was there nevertheless. There was an exotic field influence somewhere deep inside the cargo decks, probably no more than a vacant data-port left online prior to leaving the docks. If it was still open it could influence the subspace insertion protocols... nothing drastic, but if he didn't check it out First Officer Doran would no doubt pick it up on the evening feeder sheets, and then it would be up to him to explain his lapse. So he logged off the data grid and as inconspicuously as possible he left the Bridge and made his way toward the cargo bays twelve levels below the command deck. There weren't many passengers about at such a late hour, ship time being 01:30. A few people were leaving the observation lounge – no doubt satiated after watching the shift from real-time into subspace. Their fascination was a mystery to him, it wasn't as if there was anything to see, the stars simply blinked out to be replaced by a swirling gray mass of nothingness... hardly awe inspiring; certainly not worth staying awake for. He checked his duty time; in

7

two hours he would be off-shift and heading to his quarters… just this one thing to see to first.

The drop-tube opened on Level 13, sub-sector A14 – the directional signs on the walls were in Galac, the only universal language system in the Coalition, and the one used exclusively by Tantra Universal Commerce Incorporated. TUCI had forty-two ships of the line, the *Glasnost* being without doubt the oldest and already slated for retirement. But Tarl loved the old ship. Constructed soon after the founding of the Coalition, when the Hub Alliance had been the dominant power, she still boasted the original fixtures and fittings, and a lot of the furniture was actually hand-carved *Dharma* originals from the colony at Dronheim. The carpets were stitch woven and not plascite variations like the ones used on the latest liners of the fleet.

The entire crew was fully aware that this journey was to be the old ship's last, and it was fitting that it should be to the Far Star Colony, for that had been its first destination on its maiden voyage so long ago.

Reilan used his datapad to catch the field fluctuation he had noted on the Bridge; it was resonating from the third cargo hold directly in front of him. He noticed that the atmosphere condensers were struggling to cycle down here in the depths… the air tasted stale and slightly metallic. He didn't want to stay here for too long; the sooner he shut down the open data-port the better.

The door slid slowly to one side, gears grinding against worn bulkheads, the rush of stale air hitting him as a wave of heat across his face. The light from his datapad was a soft glow in the darkness. There should have been illumination from the overhead arc lights, but for some reason they were offline, which meant it was doubtful he'd be able to sign off-shift in two hours as he had hoped. Now he would have to get a repair crew down here, *sort the crell lights out…*

As he walked slowly into the storage bay he passed between two rows of bulk storage containers, produce for the worlds they would visit during the journey to the Far Star Colony. The field fluctuation was somewhere further into the room, and he began to wonder if he should inform the First Officer of the situation, *but he'll just tell me to deal with it myself…* It would be easier just to trace the problem and put a report in later. He scaled up the light from his pad, and walked forward into the semi-darkness.

Morok Dugras had tuned his phase inducer to allow him to walk as far as the central cargo area of the *Glasnost*; passing through meter-thick bulkheads was

8

not the most pleasant of experiences; the plassteel rivets seemed to slide through his skin as the walls wavered and flowed to the precise rhythm of the inducer. He struggled to control the phase variance as he stepped quickly across a corridor and into the opposite wall.

Reilan felt the phase wave before he saw it, a rippling of light forming into a shape directly in front of the data console. He was instantly alert, terrified at the apparition now forming before him. He had only seconds to react... he reached for a power node plugged into the air filtration system above his head; it was by no means a weapon, but it would give a sizable power jolt to whatever was forming in front of him. He stepped back into the shadows and watched as a shape solidified into a humanoid. He saw the familiar shimmering of a Plasmeld shield, and what looked like a phase inducer net strapped to webbing around the shoulders. Reilan noted his datapad was bouncing into ultraviolet; he no longer had any doubt as to the reason for the field fluctuation... the ship had an intruder. But he had no idea what he was going to do about it. So he decided to wait and see what this creature would do next. It wasn't long before he noticed that the intruder was carrying something resembling a fusion emitter, a small tube of dark crystal infused with what looked like crytonin slivers, one of the few explosives he recognized from his days at the Academy, when the cadets used to throw flash bombs into Crater Lake. The realization of what he was witnessing came as a terrible shock... this intruder, this creature, was actually planting a bomb, no doubt intending to destroy the ship. He tried to think quickly, there was no time to call for help, it was up to him, he had no choice... this maniac had to be stopped before he could place the device.

Morok Dugras felt the familiar tingling along his arms and legs as he phased back into real-time, his scales rippling slightly, his sweat glands exuding moisture across his back. He immediately took in his surroundings, listening for any sign of detection. The device he held in his hand took a few seconds longer to stabilize, *like playing with fire...* Crytonin was dangerously unstable when out of phase, but there was nothing like it for a satisfactory core implosion. He needed just two minutes to connect to the main data trunk, feed the crystal into the sublimnator without catching any excess ions in the backwash, and then it was just a matter of seconds before the crytonin hit the subspace field generator. He didn't see the sudden movement from behind him, nor the chunky slab of power node touching the back of his neck, he simply convulsed, as if flayed by

9

pure energy, the crystal tube shattering on the deck below, the sudden realization of death casting its shadow across his eyes. And then he knew no more.

Reilan saw the crystal fall and tried to turn away, but the resulting explosion tore through the cargo hold, rolling fire across the upper bulkheads, tearing at the millions of rivets studding the walls. He felt himself falling into a sea of flame, his arms withering before his eyes. For several seconds the cargo doors heaved against their hinges, but they held, while behind the bulkheads the fire raged unchecked.

Every alarm on the ship seemed to scream at once. Bulkhead doors were sliding closed along the corridors, sealing off entire sections, closing down the vast central Galleria. Crew members were rushing to pre-determined emergency control centers, and someone on the Bridge was issuing orders across the entire compad system.

Almost imperceptibly, the ship stuttered out of subspace, flickering into real-time with only an instant of discontinuity.

First Officer Doran was on the compad to the Captain, who was making his way toward the Bridge.

"Captain, we have fire somewhere on 13. Tracing the sensors now; bulkheads are tight and holding..." All around him the Bridge crew were reading data, shutting down live feeds, and tracing the path of the heatwave now rising from Level 13.

"What was it?"

"No idea yet, Sir; I have crews on their way down now, looks like sub-sector A14."

"We've phased back out, haven't we?"

"Yes, Sir, we have; AI took control at 01:47, we've lost subspace containment... we're on the grid now plotting our current position."

"Are we venting?"

Doran glanced down at the stream of data-feeds before him, tracked the sensors back to the source, and saw no red lines beyond the outer hull.

"Apparently not, Sir, no, but we're dead in the water."

"What's the word from the Engine Room?"

"Chief Frome said he'd get back to me..."

"Don't wait, go down there yourself, I'm almost at the Bridge... and I want the AI disengaged from the Navs as soon as possible."

"Yes, Sir, will do..."

Captain Salazar entered the Bridge and dismissed the salutes. Taking in the main board, he saw that most data-feeds were in the red, but the dangerous ones were still green: life support, hull containment, and pulse-drive were all within normal parameters; it actually looked a lot better than it sounded.

"Will someone shut off those damn alarms?"

An ensign input reset codes and the Bridge alert screens fell silent.

A young com technician spoke up from his station. "Sir, we have alarmed passengers wanting to know what's going on…"

Salazar glanced at the com feeds streaming across a nearby floater screen. "Just deal with it, Ensign; and someone get me the repair crew down on Level 13, now."

"Sir, we have the First Officer for you…"

"Doran, what's the situation?"

"Sir, Chief Frome says the pulse drive is back online, there's been no damage to the field generators, the core is viable so we can initiate a subspace insertion on your orders; but of course the AI will usurp the protocols unless we've fixed the problem on 13…"

"Right, I'm going down there myself. Get back up here and start dealing with the passengers."

"Yes, Sir."

Salazar found the drop-tube to Level 13 offline, so it took a lot longer to reach the repair crews in sub-sector A14. By the time he got there they were already inside the hold and were busy dealing with several pockets of fire. He immediately noticed the suppressers had been taken out by the explosion, and the fire damage looked extensive. He found Sub-Lieutenant Madras barking out orders to his team. Most of the storage containers seemed badly damaged, and the plassteel ribbing had fused to the feeder cords and data panels running along the walls; everything was covered with silium fire suppressant, giving the air a foul chemical taste, which only added to the overall impression of destruction.

Madras looked up as his captain entered the room. Removing his face visor, he walked carefully around the remains of two bodies, crumpled and distorted on the floor before the main data console.

"Madras, what's the word?"

"Well, Sir, it looks a lot worse than it is… the data cords are fused but structural integrity is holding, we're just sealing the outer bulkheads with extra plassteel as a precaution."

"An explosion, then?"

11

"I would say so, yes; and you might want to get sci-tech down here, it seems we might be dealing with a case of sabotage…"

"Sabotage? Are you sure?"

"Sir, we've picked up traces of crytonin… we don't ship crytonin. And then there are the bodies…"

"Bodies?"

"I'm afraid so. Two in fact… and it's pretty messy, but we do have two partial torsos over here." He led him back to where the bodies lay.

Salazar moved closer to the charred remains. There wasn't much left of either of them, but he could clearly make out the ship's insignia on one of the bodies.

"A crewman, Madras?"

"Looks like it, yes, Sir, but the other one is a completely different story. Take a look at this." He reached down with a probe and pulled at the remains of a wire grid. "You see this, Sir? It looks like what's left of a phase inducer net. And all of this over here…" he pointed to a gray puddle formed beneath the remains of an arm, "…this is the liquid residue of a Plasmeld shield. I think this person, whoever he was, walked through the hull to get here… the shield would have allowed him to enter the docks unseen, and considering the crytonin traces, it seems perfectly logical to assume that this creature wasn't here to sabotage the ship, he was here to destroy it."

"Can you confirm that?"

"The facts fit Sir."

"Very well, I'll have a technician join you. I want to know who that was, and I want our crewman identified. Make it a priority; and let's hope that whoever this saboteur was he was working alone."

Kyle Raine woke to the distant sound of whooping, *was it bells?* He had felt the cabin shudder, but it hadn't really registered. But now there were sounds of people running up and down the corridor; something was definitely wrong. He sat up, and reached for his datapad. Once loaded, it still had the Kyrillian-architext on screen; he slid it away and connected directly to the ship's internal sensor system. The hacking link was illegal but he'd already broken more than a few laws to get as far as Tantra, and now it was vital to find out what was going on. The screen flowed blue for several seconds until the link was made and a series of data-feeds began to stream into the pad. The ship's codes were instantly deciphered and he began to read the alarming news. The ship had dropped out of

12

subspace and they were currently drifting in real-time... there had been an explosion in one of the cargo holds and a preliminary Tech report detailed the finding of two bodies: one crewman and an unknown intruder... this fact alone was the most alarming. It was his greatest fear that the Power might already have agents placed within the Coalition. *And now someone has tried to blow up the ship! Will my quest end before it even begins?* He needed to find out more, try to discover the origin of the intruder; but at that moment his door alarm buzzed, and he quickly broke the connection... *have they traced my link to the sensor grid?*

Excerpt from the Forbidden Works:

Brother Fiodore, First Ascetic Ministry of Petra – Sacred Book of Jophrim. (Kyrillian-archi-text translation)

Once, long before the dawn of the Coalition, the Beast had reigned over a billion parsecs, a vast interstellar dominion spreading its nets across countless civilizations. It was a dark maelstrom of conflict, a teeming mass of thought patterns riding the cosmic ether as bio-luminescence, shifting beyond the ultraviolet into subspace realms where the Cortex could blossom, where the physical constructs which sustained its empire could flourish and develop and spread across real-time cities and states, fleets and armadas. It wasn't so much a matter of mind control, as a shifting of thought patterns. The Beast was an insidious interloper, sweeping through the minds of billions, taking them into a self-replicating existence barely above the conscious level; a more apt description would be automatons, slave children bound to the apron strings of a god.

It had taken the combined forces of a thousand planets just to stem the tide, to hold the Power at bay. They had been reduced to fifty worlds by the time the ancient weapon was found, crystallized in amber, the neuron net embedded deep in its core, fronds of enticement swaying in the current of an interstellar breeze. It had taken time to find the one who might wield the last gift of the First Race, and even longer for him to know his destiny; but the day finally dawned when the Fleets of Liberation set forth, bound for a star tethered to the edge of the Rim. Thirty thousand starships had broken away from the occupied worlds, seething with a terrible rage, screaming toward the human filth that dared to challenge his glory. The Beast had become enticed by a new hunger, lured

13

toward an inexplicable and unprecedented anomaly at the very heart of its domain; something of the First Race was coming his way.

Coalescency

The prognosis was easily defined: there appeared to be a sliver of the Creator's power still in existence, moving its way toward the Sacred Sanctum; a tiny slice of an ancient mind verging upon its latent flowering, an insignificant beast void of real coalescence, a tawdry upstart easily dismissed, but tinged with the possibility of threat and physical countenance. It too must be incorporated into the Cortex, reduced and assimilated to accessible data configurations. It would use all its power for this one final conflict. There was an attraction in that thought, the lure of unprecedented conquest, and yet there was a risk, an uncertain variance to the information data load. There were significant gaps in the feeds, drops in perception at odd intervals, a narrowing of cognitive extrapolation; and yet there were no alarms. The fleet armadas would act as a buffer zone, its primary core tendrils kept at a safe distance; but even so, a physical connection had to be maintained. There was something about this new threat, something vital and cognizant, a memory once lost restored again to full recognition... that fact in itself permitted a certain amount of risk. It was within acceptable parameters, and once the threat had been incorporated, it would turn its attention to the core worlds of the Coalition, and to the countless minds as yet untouched by its power.

Chapter 3 - Foothold

"... And out of the night something wicked moved, and from its mouth fell a million lies, and death shone brightly in its eyes..."
Tantalus: Chronicles of Ages.

Eighty-five thousand light years off the galactic plane, almost perpendicular to the galactic pole at the outermost rim of a fading spiral of constellations, lay the Cordwainer Alliance, named in honor of a long-forgotten explorer. The Alliance consisted of seventy-two inhabited worlds, united in commerce and technical support. They were so distant from the Hub Coalition that the known Net was restricted to local chatter and restricted data-feeds; they were a frontier collection of backwoods worlds strung together out of a fear of the unknown – for life on the Rim was anything but safe.

There are no Coalition security patrols along the Rim, no med-tech fleets cruising the space lanes administering aid or provisions; the Cordwainer worlds pretty much tended to their own needs and seldom felt it necessary to unite against a common foe. That was until one high summer's day when a small ship blinked into semblance high above the ecliptic plane of Samros, the capital world of the Alliance.

An insignificant arrival by any standards, its point of origin logged and filed as the Far Star Colony; not surprising since there was the occasional traffic from that far-flung foothold in the lap of the Great Expanse. But this was the first ship in six months, and it might have caused some alarm if anyone had noticed its feeler systems trying to make a connection to the planetary data-core; but it slipped almost unseen into the docking station on Harvest Moon, the largest satellite in the system. It fed a series of unremarkable questions into the planetary AI core, tracing linkages and pathways throughout the docking complex. Sensor glitches were picked up across Samros Fleet Operations, diagnostics kicked in; problems were traced and resolved with little deceptions buried beneath secret truths laced with sensory perception algorithms. Failure nodes burned red as a thousand data-ports instantly shut down; vidcams flickered into gray, guidance tracers lost cohesion, and inbound ships lost their locking grids and began to drift alarmingly off course, as one by one their navigation computers shut down. Agrav-plates buckled, as linear nodes broke loose, drifting into space. Everywhere automation was perverted, sequestered in a secret cohesion, realigned upon impossible configurations, a thousand eyes opened wide in abject terror.

As the great ships began to fall from the sky, the citizens of Samros ran screaming from their homes. The overhead glide-rails were on fire, and people were falling from the high-flung cables… in every city, the oxygenation plants began to fail, sealing the fate of millions inside the domed cities.

The new Power moved effortlessly across a billion datapads, flowing across med-screens, killing a million hospital patients instantly, closing down auto-response units, isolating millions of citizens. One massive cargo ship broke through the domed city of Altair, crashing down upon the parks and fields below. Fire stormed through a thousand city districts and floods from the water-reclamation plants spread new rivers across the face of the world. Millions died in the first few minutes of the assault… but it took some time before the people realized they had been occupied, and it was remarkably soon after that when the survivors, without ever really knowing why, welcomed their new god to Samros.

Two days later the Cordwainer Alliance ceased to exist. Seventy-two inhabited planets had been subjugated and incorporated into the Cortex… and for all their suffering, for all the death and the pain endured, the surviving citizens had only one overwhelming feeling in common, and that was simply… gratitude.

Chapter 4 - A Windy Day on Primus

"... out of pain and restraint rise the strongest of hearts, the most trustworthy of souls are seared with scars..."
Brother Fiodore: First Ascetic Ministry of Petra.

Shari S'Atwa kept her head inside the Lucidator five minutes longer than was prescribed. It wasn't a significant infraction, but it was noticed, *red dot flickering in the corner...* Her long dark hair was caught in the static as she withdrew from the lens head. She was perspiring in her tight gym top, and a shower in her dorm room would help, but time allocation was one of the biggest problems when you used the Lucidator, and she was already running late. Everyone wanted access, and Second Level students like her were supposed to stick to the limit; there would be a reprimand on her course evaluation, but it shouldn't affect her overall score, she was still nine-tenths above the common centile... more than enough to make it through the semester. She would have passed the previous term if it wasn't for her supervisor, the inauspicious Professor Drake; his insistence on her re-taking *Theron's Musings on Tantalus* had given her an underscore and earned him her utter and unbridled animosity. *Dumb Barg...*

The Lucidator released its probes, and for a few seconds she lost cohesion, but the prescribed mantra came to mind: *concentrate on your feet firmly on the floor...* and then she stepped back, instantly aware of the students behind her, waiting for their turn. The fact that the university had only been allocated three of the devices was ridiculous in the extreme, but Primus had only recently been incorporated into the Coalition, and high-tech gadgets were still few and far between.

An hour later she still had after-images floating through her mind. The Lucidator tapped into the cerebral cortex and directly downloaded just about anything you wanted, the embedded neural restrictions were pre-set so that you couldn't cheat; nothing remained beyond the barest of facts, enough for revision only. You were taught lessons, not answers, those you had to deduce the old-fashioned way... but the experience was exhilarating nonetheless, and formed the foundation of a suitable paper. If it wasn't for the fact that *Tantalus* was almost always written in archaic Galac she'd have passed already; but language wasn't her forte, she was a math kid, always had been, and that is probably why that *Barg* Drake hated her so much... and probably why she wanted him dead.

17

"You going to pay for that?"

Shari was startled. Remembering where she was, she flashed her student ID at the attendant, who tapped her code into his till. The coffee in the student union house was dreadful, but she was already running late for her meeting... she hadn't seen her father in over a year, not since he mysteriously left for planets unknown on one of his fact-finding missions for the Legislature.

Of course she was never on time, he knew that, but now things were different... she just didn't want to see him. Her mother's death had come between them, forced them apart; the distance seemed to suit him. So now, even though she had no idea why he wanted to see her, she just wasn't going to make it easy for him.

Walking outside, she caught sight of a deep space transport breaking through the high clouds, bound for the new spaceport at the edge of Egrain city. Checking the time on the clock tower, she took a few sips of coffee and threw the cup in the trash can. Instantly the face of a smiling woman appeared and thanked her for depositing her trash in a prescribed location as opposed to the nearest gutter – it seemed that all the techno thrills of the Coalition were creeping into Primus society... *first it was the new spaceport, and now the stupid trash cans talk back to you...*

She pulled her jacket from her backpack; her gym top wouldn't be warm enough in the cooler autumnal winds. She really ought to go back to the dorm to change, but the Uni-station was closer and of course she was already an hour late for the meeting.

She took the Ribbon out toward Foscombe Park Station, deciding the night was far too pleasant not to walk the rest of the way home through the park. The Ribbon should have been full of rush hour commuters, but there were only a few people in her carriage, which seemed strange considering it was Festival time in Egrain city.

Tens of thousands of tourists from all over the system would be arriving for the annual parades and entertainment extravaganzas; it was probably an excuse for one long party, but it was nice to exchange gifts among family and friends. She had so many fond memories of Festival time as a child; handing out presents on Festival morning with Momma in the kitchen and father actually having a good time... it was probably the only time of year when he seemed to enjoy family life. For some reason the Festival celebrations were important to him... he would even take her out to the woods to cut down a Festival tree for the living room. And then after lights out he'd hide presents all around the

18

house… *he was actually a real father for about four days… and then they'd call him back to the Legislature and we wouldn't see him again until springtime.*

She hopped off the Ribbon as the grav-plates buckled, settling momentarily on a sea of super-heated air, and then it was gone, no more than a passing breeze in her hair.

The station was quiet, with just a few people passing through. She stopped to watch a news screen floating images of a Festival parade along Ventura Avenue in the city, *giant clowns… just what every kid needs…* She took the steps down to the park, the wind picking up the leaves and swirling them like fountains in the high autumnal airs. Off toward the city the night was a luminous gray, merging into a shimmering iridescence that dimmed the stars above. The pathway through the park led her along an arched avenue of brightly colored *azali* flowers leading directly to the central lake, where *treliss* vines spread out around the statues of the founding colonists – ancient faces lost to moss and grime, weather-beaten now so you could no longer actually see the faces, nor even read the inscriptions beneath the heads.

She had always loved the park; they'd spent so many happy times here when she was a child… She saw the ancient Dharm Oak towering over the boat house. It was fenced off now, preserved and protected by Legislative Censure. It was rumored to be over a thousand years old… the oldest tree on the planet… Scientifically, she doubted that, but it didn't matter, her memories of family picnics beneath its mighty branches were something to be treasured.

She used to visit the park almost every day. Her mother had resigned her teaching position at the New School after her father had left to join the Off-World Commission. During the summer they would sit together eating lunch beneath the great Dharm Oak. Her mothers' illness forced her father to come home early. He did his duty, of course… took time off work to organize nursing care, arranged for home schooling for his daughter… until one day her mother died quietly in her sleep and she was gone. Any sense of family life died that day as well. Primus was still an independent world back then, the Coalition and its high-tech medical facilities were beyond them. One quick scan on the Coretech had told her that *Lysordia Syndrome;* although native to Primus, could now be cured thanks to the new treatments brought in since incorporation two years earlier… this fact alone caused her to hate the Coalition as much as she hated her father, who despite being a member of the Legislature, still couldn't save her mother.

19

Looking up at the gathering night, she saw storm clouds cresting the city towers beyond the park. Flyers were twisting and turning through the upper airs, Plasmeld shields rippling in the heat haze, breaking through the sky-high adverts throwing words and faces along the boulevards down town. *Oh look, the wonders of the Coalition... it makes me sick... Primus would be better off without the Incorporation. Nothing is the same any more... Professor Drake's distrust of the Coalition is his one redeeming feature. Primus was never part of the Hub Alliance, so we won't be protected from the influx of the huge corporations... Drake had said they would commercialize and sanitize the entire planet, bringing it into an acceptable profit margin, deduced on some far-away Hub world... and they'd even make the damn trash cans talk back to you!*

She left the park by the South Gate and started walking along Cansum Street... her street, the street of her childhood. The family home was halfway down between two *conifern* trees perched at the edge of the park. It began to rain, the wind picking up, and she was glad of her jacket, although her gym shorts left a lot to be desired as the night grew cooler. She saw a light on at home... her father probably in there, angry as crell that she was so late.

At the far end of the street a ground car moved out from the shadows. She took no notice, lost in thought, rehearsing what she was going to say to her father. She had a whole speech ready, but like so many times before she would probably end up just sitting there while he ranted on about what she was doing wrong in her life... he could be such a *Barg* at times; she had half a mind to turn round and head back to the station.

She would never quite remember what happened next, nor did she know that she would never see her home again; it all happened so quickly. Suddenly there was a car next to her, and from behind her someone put a hand over her mouth... something burned her neck, and then she knew no more.

Lorn S'Atwa was fuming, pacing up and down, casting an eye on the data-feeds running across the living room wall. He touched the interface and brought up a series of ships' schedules, scanned quickly for ship allocation tags, logged itineraries, dates and ports of origin, planetary fleet rosters, and cargo manifests... he followed the details with a frantic eye, looking for anything out of the ordinary, something that might stand out as *wrong*. But so far the only inconsistency was the loss of Net feeds from the Cordwainer Alliance due to so-called gravitational anomalies along the Rim, and there was an unusual concentration of Phaelon ships in the region of the Combine Alliance, fifty thousand light years off the galactic core.

Where in Demos' name is she?

He had told her to meet him at seven precisely... the screen flashed eight forty-one... *this is typical of Shari, always trying to make a point, always trying to make me the enemy... by the Stars, if she had any idea what was really going on...* He had hoped that going off to university would make her a little more responsible for her actions; but apparently turning eighteen hadn't done the trick, *this is ridiculous...*

He linked his datapad to the Skysat tracking system, logged in under a false ID tag and proceeded to track down his daughter. He linked to the university vid-system and scanned Shari's dorm room for bio-signs: empty. He found her ID tag logged into the Lucidator, traced her coffee purchase at the student union building, tracked her Ribbon ticket from the University Station, and scanned the vidcams at the Foscombe Park Station. He looped the feeds to an approximate arrival time and then he saw her entering the park through the West Gate. He slid the screen to the boat house cams and saw her walking toward Cansum Street, time logged at eight twenty-nine; *she should be here already!*

Something was wrong. He dropped a bio-graph of Shari's tag over the screen and scanned the entire university, and then pulled out to include the park and the surrounding streets. Every registered citizen of Primus had a data plug inserted at birth – embedded at the back of the neck. The small sliver of crystal was a universal ID tag used to facilitate correct identification after an accident or worse, but it was also a perfect way to keep track of people. If Shari was anywhere within a twenty-mile circumference she would certainly show up on the grid. *Nothing!* So she was either out of range or her tag had been neutralized somehow. *They have they taken my daughter!*

He called the only other person on the planet that he could still trust. He linked to the Department of Interior Affairs and scanned for his brother Limon. The DIA was a sub-division of the Legislature, but it was almost certainly a front for the more covert Central Security Service, as a Field Coordinator Limon might well be in a position to help. As far he knew his brother was not yet corrupted by the enemy which even now seemed to be stalking the streets of Primus.

Chapter 5 - Glasnost Revelations

'Beneath the veil of civilization the veneer of permanence is tenuous, prone to the perfidy of chaos; it takes surprisingly little to reduce an empire to rubble...'
Tantalus: Chronicles of Ages.

Kyle touched the comview and saw two ship's officers standing outside his cabin door... his heart was racing... *What do they know? Will it all come to an end so soon?* Taking a deep breath, he allowed the door to slide open.

"Mr. Raine? Mr. Kyle Raine?"

"It's Professor Raine, actually..."

The two officers glanced at each other, showing a complete disinterest in his academic title.

"*Professor* Raine, the Captain has requested you visit him on the Bridge."

"I'm sorry? What's this all about?"

"If you'll just come with us, Sir, I'm sure the Captain will explain."

"Very well..." He reached for his jacket, pulling it on as they made their way to the nearest drop-tube.

The tube rose vertically and then slipped into the horizontal as it deposited them directly onto the Bridge. The place was a mass of screens, data-ports, and what looked like spatial-grids floating in the air... crewmen were moving through the stars, constellations breaking apart, reforming back into readable data... one officer was busy plotting subspace coordinates on a floating math grid... he even recognized several star codes; the glowing blue of the Far Star Colony easily recognizable in the stream of data flowing rapidly across the floater.

The Captain came over and introduced himself: "Professor Raine, I'm Captain Salazar."

He suddenly realized just how nervous he was – it felt like he was standing before his students in the great lecture hall on Gamont.

"I hope you haven't been too disturbed tonight..."

"Not really, no. Is there a problem, Captain? I noticed we are no longer in subspace..."

"You noticed that?"

Big mistake... how could I know that unless I'd linked to the ship's sensor grid?

22

"Yes, well, I noticed that your data-ports are all offline; that can't be right if we're still moving."

"Oh, yes, well that's right, we had a little problem, some damage actually, in one of our cargo holds."

"Really? Is it bad?"

"There's some fire damage, but it's been dealt with. The AI took us out of subspace... as a precaution, you understand."

"Of course... can't be too careful."

"That's true, but now we seem to have a little bit of a mystery on our hands."

"A mystery?"

""Yes indeed. Our investigations so far seem to point toward an act of deliberate sabotage."

"Sabotage? By the Stars... that's incredible..." *The enemy? Here on board the ship?*

"Yes, and that's where the mystery comes in. Our analysts were able to retrieve an ID tag from a deceased intruder and they found something very interesting ingrained in its data-core."

"Oh yes, and what was that?"

"Well, Professor, they found your name and cabin number."

Kyle's heart began to race... he clenched his fists as he felt his legs buckling; it took all his willpower not to turn and run back to the drop-tube.

"Well, I don't know what to say... how can that be possible?"

"I was hoping you might be able to tell me Professor. Do you know of any reason why this intruder would have your details loaded onto his tag?"

"I really don't, Captain, I'm as surprised as you are... I just can't understand it."

"I see... well this begs the question as to his motives. Do you think he was here to kill you? Because blowing up the ship would certainly achieve that end."

"Captain, believe me, I have no idea who this intruder was, or why he would want to tag my name. I'm as mystified as you are. I teach history, Captain... and although some of my students might wish me harm, I doubt any of them would actually try to kill me." He tried to smile, desperate not to show the utter panic he was feeling inside.

The Captain took a moment to consider the Professor's words.

"Professor Raine, I've checked your luggage allocation… I was interested in this one item…" He was reading from a small datapad as he spoke. "Item Four: crypto-lingual data artifact…" He looked up. "Can you tell me what that is exactly?"

"Why, yes, of course… It's a cipher tube, pre-Galac actually, I'm hoping it will prove useful in translating certain ancient texts. Believe me, Captain, it's a simple aid to translation, and its purpose is purely academic."

"And you say you teach history?"

"Yes, ancient history at the University of Southern Planatia on Gamont; my research grant allows me to take part in the occasional expedition, such as the dig recently started at the Far Star Colony."

"And you're taking part in this dig?"

"Yes I am…it's quite exciting really…"

"So you wouldn't consider this item or anything else in your possession to be a reason for someone to want to kill you?"

Kyle tried his best to smile. "Captain, I assure you, I can't think of any reason why someone would want to kill me." He knew he had no choice now but to try and bluff his way through.

"Very well, Professor. Perhaps we'll know more after the autopsy; if we can identify race we may be able to backtrack the intruder to a planet of origin. But for now I'll let you get back to your sleep. One of my officers will escort you to your cabin."

"Thank you, Captain… and if there's anything more I can do to help, please let me know."

"I will… thank you, Professor."

First Officer Doran approached the Captain as the Professor was led back to the drop-tube.

"Do you believe him, Sir?"

"Not a word. He's definitely hiding something. What do we have on him?"

"I checked his tags. They're valid as far as I can tell; his ID scan matches the one on file… he seems to be who he says he is, but…"

"But what?"

"Well, he just told you he's taking part in a dig at the Far Star Colony, but according to his admin file, he hasn't registered any such request with his Academic Council on Gamont; in fact, before he left the planet he turned in his academic draft and closed down his office at the university."

24

"Well that's odd… anything else?"

"Well yes, a quick sift of the trans-net shows dozens of posts concerning the Professor's rather eccentric theories…"

"What kind of theories?"

"Well, until very recently he maintained an online science forum dedicated to discovering the origins of the apocalypse myth…he shut the site down last month."

"And what exactly is the apocalypse myth?"

"It's quite fashionable, actually. There's a whole sub-culture of online forums dedicated to the myth of an ancient power imprisoned for millennia beyond the Rim… "

"Yes Doran I've heard the legend…beyond the Rim there be serpents…"

"Yes well, according to legend this power wiped out the first galactic-wide civilization, and will one day return to do the same to the Coalition."

Salazar considered this. "It all sounds a little fanciful to me…"

"Well that's myth and legend for you … the Professor was practically censured in academic circles back on Gamont."

"Well, we can't hold a few crazy theories against him. But I do want a guard posted outside his cabin; and get Doc Milcher to finish that autopsy. I need to get some answers to all of this."

"Of course, I'll go down there now."

"Good. Oh, and Doran, the name of the dead crewman?"

"Tarl Reilan, Bridge Officer Second Class. I've streamed it on your pad, along with details of his next of kin."

Captain Salazar looked down at the details flowing across the datapad.

"He was just twenty?"

"Yes, Sir; this was only his second deep space tour."

Salazar couldn't think of anything to say… *what words could describe the futility of such a death?* He tagged a note to contact Reilan's family as soon as they were underway.

"Tell the Doc I want answers Doran."

"Yes Sir, of course."

Salazar moved over to the main console and took note of the data-feeds coming from the Nav and Stats screens… everything was finally in the green. The AI autonomous systems had been disengaged and manual subspace protocols had been re-initiated.

"All right, Navs, realign to our previous course. Stats, I want a full ship inspection and a displacement graph for the current grid." He tapped his compad. "Engine Room, I want full power, engage subspace drive."

It took longer than usual for the First Officer to reach the Medical Bay. He couldn't avoid passengers milling about wanting to know why the alert had sounded. Telling them it was a false alarm seemed to work. He was stopped again outside the drop-tube by a group of people leaving the forward viewing lounge; the large glasscite window now shifting from a sea of stars into the colorless maelstrom of subspace.

He finally arrived on Level 4; sub-sector B6, directly in front of the Medical Bay. Walking past several vacant beds he found Dr. Rolph Milcher leaning over what looked like a large pile of ash, although upon seeing fingers he quickly realized it was the charred remains of a body.

"Doctor…"

Milcher looked up, a half-eaten sandwich in his hand. "First Officer… and what can I do for you today?"

Doran looked at the sandwich. "Is that really sanitary in here, Doc?"

"What? This? The man's dead, Doran, I doubt much can harm him now."

"Very well. Have you found out anything worth reporting back to the Captain?"

"Well the first corpse over there is pretty straightforward, that's our crewman."

"And this one?"

"Well, as you can see, I haven't got much to work with here; the explosion and the fire that followed pretty much destroyed this person."

"I can see that, Doc, but the Captain wants answers, and he wants them sooner rather than later."

"Doran, I'm a doctor not a Forensics analyst."

"So perhaps we should get the science team in here to help…"

"Oh, very funny… it took me an hour to get those autons out of here."

"Doc, please…"

"Okay, very well, let's see what we can see…" He forced the last of his sandwich into his mouth and pulled down an overhead scanner. The bio-feed flowed over the remains of the body several times, uploading data to the diagnostic interface.

26

Doran stepped back as a holo-grid began to flow across the examination table, enveloping the corpse in a soft translucent light. A nearby data-feed engaged and bio-charts formed and re-formed on several floater screens. Milcher touched the interface and an array of needle probes began to enter the corpse, extracting blood and tissue and dividing chemicals into analytical segments for bio-analysis. He carefully picked at the corpse with a scalpel, slowly lifting the charred remains of several mesh-like filaments from the shoulder area.

"Well, Doc... anything relevant?"

"Intriguing..."

"What is?"

"Well, this thing here seems to be what's left of a phase inducer net, probably high-end black market, very difficult to obtain, unless you have connections and some serious financial backing – which this man evidently did. And just here beneath the left clavicle, see this? That's an ion burn; probably from a leaking Plasmeld shield... once again you're talking highly organized and heavily financed. This man was no lone saboteur, Doran; he was definitely part of a greater whole. And if you look at this analysis grid here, that's the chemical residue of pure crytonin, not the cheap combat grade the military use... no, this is pure high-grade explosive; costs more than you and I can earn in a year."

"Okay, so he was well financed. Can we determine his race?"

"I think the scales have already answered that, but let me just verify..."

Milcher touched a few more floaters, watched as columns of data rose and fell in succession. "Why, yes, I do believe we have a winner. This man, First Officer, was a Phaelon... pure bred, too, by the look of his blood work; the gene code alone puts him in the upper echelon of Phaelon society."

"But wouldn't that make him..."

"A member of the Elaas? Exactly; surprising, no?"

Doran stared at the body on the table. "This is so much bigger than we first realized, Doc."

"I'd say so. It might be a good idea to have the passengers and crew bio-scanned... because you know what they say, don't you?"

"No, Doc, what do they say?"

"They say that where there is one Phaelon there are bound to be a few more lurking nearby..."

"I'll tell the Captain at once."

At that moment the com buzzed and Doran was summoned back to the Bridge.

"All right, Doc, I'd better get back. If you would just upload your findings, I'll brief the Captain."

"I'll get right on it… Oh, and Doran?"

"Yes, Doc?"

"I wonder why the Elaas would want to kill us all…"

"I have no idea. Perhaps we are just collateral damage." He left the Medical Bay before the Doctor could ask what he meant by that.

When the cabin door finally slid closed behind him Kyle Raine sat down on the edge of his bed; his hands were trembling and he quickly dialed for a whiskey from the cabin bar.

He moved over to the wall safe and carefully tapped in his personal code. The lock flashed green and then, with some slight hesitation, he removed the artifact from its pouch. Once again, he was drawn to its inherent beauty: a simple hexagonal tube of crystalline amber. The overhead glow tube cast multiple reflections across its glistening surface. When he held it up against the light he could see luminous tendrils inside radiating with a quiet intensity… *gossamer whispers encased in a sea of amber.* The feel of the thing sometimes left him breathless….he was holding true power, power spawned by the First Race to cage a monster…*to hold such a device…* Its apparent simplicity belied its true purpose; it seemed to challenge the very meaning of existence, reducing his humanity to a profound sense of fear and awe. *Forged by the gods themselves…* He was in fact holding the fabled *Sword of Jophrim,* a parting gift left behind by the First Ones… *the hope of millennia, the key to the prison and possibly the only way to undo a terrible mistake.*

It had once been used to defeat a nightmare, sealing the Beast beneath a crystalline lake, imprisoned and tethered to a distant star… and now, as fate would have it, it was time to use it again… *if it isn't already too late…* He quickly swallowed his drink. *They have tried to blow up the ship!* His translations of *Tantalus* had given him some insight into the insidious nature of the Beast… he described it as: "*the usurper of souls… a vile corrupter of innocence; men once touched by the evil were no longer real men, but mindless servants lost to the thrall of the Beast.*"

He was certain that the power now rising from the Far Star Colony was indeed capable of corrupting the minds of men, and might already be moving among the worlds of the Coalition, unseen and unnoticed even by those it quietly enslaved.

But is the Captain already lost? And what of his crew?

He no longer had a choice... the enemy had found him and the mission was compromised, he would have to contact the one person who might be able to help... *by the Stars' own fire, if I can't finish this journey then someone else will have to...*

He activated his datapad and linked to the Net, skimmed for the planetary database and flowed down to the planet he needed. He found Primus just below Primal IV, and quickly tapped for the citizen registry... he found the name he was looking for and made the connection.

A name glowed on the screen: *Lorn S'Atwa, Consular Advisor to the Primus Legislative.*

The screen flashed *Engaged*, and he left it on re-link, pouring himself another whiskey. He took a moment to tap into the local sensor feed and discovered that the ship had finally returned to subspace. *At last!*

The screen flashed blue and the face of Lorn S'Atwa appeared, looking worried and highly agitated. "Yes! Is that you, Raine?"

"Who else from deep space?"

"You're not supposed to contact me until you make planetfall; has something gone wrong?"

"Before I go into details, what's happened to you? You look dreadful..." He saw Lorn look away, studying something off-screen.

"It's my daughter, Kyle. Someone has her... she's been abducted."

"By the Stars, no! Has Primus been infiltrated, then?"

"I'm not sure, but it's possible yes. I've asked my brother Limon for help; his security people might still be trustworthy. I've arranged to meet him outside of the city, he says he can help... he might even know where Shari is being held."

"I am so sorry, Lorn."

"Yes, well, we knew things could go wrong. I just didn't think they would go after my daughter."

"Lorn, if they have Shari... you might already be compromised."

"I realize that, Kyle."

"But they didn't target you Lorn..."

"No... So why take Shari?"

"Blackmail perhaps? Does she know anything of our plans?"

29

"Absolutely not. I was going to try to explain some of it tonight, so at least she could be prepared for what's coming… that's why I asked her to come home…" He fell silent, his eyes looking toward the window behind him. "It makes no sense… what possible value can Shari be to the enemy?"

"I have no idea my friend, but have faith in your brother; isn't he supposed to be good at this sort of thing?"

"He is yes… it's just that when you got me involved in all of this I didn't expect that it would place my daughter's life at risk."

"I know you didn't. We had no idea how far the enemy's reach would extend, but we have to think of the bigger picture right now; we are walking along the edge of a precipice, my friend… we can't afford to make mistakes."

"I'll take care of my affairs, Kyle; you just concentrate on the mission."

"Actually, that's why I had to break protocol and risk contacting you; there's been an incident aboard ship…"

Lorn leaned closer to the screen. "What type of incident?"

"The type where a Phaelon agent tries to blow up said ship."

"A Phaelon? Are you all right?"

"I am, yes, but there were deaths and now I think the Captain suspects me of complicity."

"But the artifact… it is safe?"

"Yes, of course it's safe, but I'm not sure how long that will last… we have no idea how many agents are already in place."

"Don't jump to conclusions, Kyle; there are no indications that the Phaelon Confederacy has been subverted. I think we'd notice if those pirates suddenly started attacking Coalition worlds. But there are other forces gathering, groups who think they can ally themselves with the new power and still maintain some level of independence."

"Fools! They have no idea what they are dealing with."

"Of course they don't. How can anyone really know? How can we know Kyle? It's been over a million years since that thing last crawled out of its hole. Let's face it; we have no idea what we're up against."

"Perhaps not… but one thing is for sure: the last time this *thing* came storming across the stars, a galactic-wide civilization fell into ruin, and it took thousands of years for any semblance of unity to reappear among the stars."

"You've already convinced me, Kyle. Just tell me what you want from me now."

Raine looked at his old friend. The beard was graying now, the hair receding to the point of baldness, his eyes filled with worry and fear... *they have taken his daughter!*

"All right, you have your meeting with Limon; see if you can determine the location of Shari. I understand her safety is a priority to you Lorn, but we cannot be deterred from the path, no matter the risk to those we love."

"You have no family, Kyle... I'm not about to abandon my daughter."

"I know that, and I'm not saying that you should. I just want you to keep in mind the wider issues here. Our priority is to get the artifact to the Far Star Colony, and right now that plan is in serious jeopardy."

"Just tell me how I can help; I have to be out of here in five minutes."

"Very well. When we dock at Primus I want you to take possession of the artifact. I'll act as decoy and travel on to the Colony while you arrange to get there by another means... an indirect route if you can. If the Phaelon's want me dead then at the very least the new power suspects something, it's only a matter of time before he moves against me, I can't have the artifact with me if that happens... you have take the lead from Primus. I'm sorry I have to put this on you, Lorn, especially now... but the mission has to take priority... you know this. If we should fail... then it's all over, we lose everything... including your daughter Shari."

"I know that, Kyle, I have the nightmares as well... but I will find my daughter. One way or another, I will find her."

"I know you will, my friend."

Lorn looked off-screen before continuing. "Look, I'm meeting Limon soon, we'll work something out; one of us will definitely be at the port when you dock. I take it you're off schedule right now?

"Yes, I'm afraid so, we'll be down by eight hours by the time we reach Primus; we have a layover at Petra first. I'll connect before we break subspace."

"Kyle they could be waiting on Petra."

"I know that... I'll just have to be careful."

"All right then... safe journey."

"Thank you, my friend... and may the Stars guide you in your search for Shari."

He closed the connection. Leaning back against the wall, he took a deep breath and realized his hands were still trembling; *must hold it together for a while longer...* For so long it had all been conjecture, postulated theories, vague fears based on the most obscure of ancient translations... And it had all seemed

31

so very far away, lost in the mists of time... distant threats from the edge of known space... and now here he was, stuck right in the middle of events that could change the universe forever. He just managed to get to the sink before he threw up.

Chapter 6 - Dark Room

"In the deepest, darkest well I found a butterfly's wing, and then I knew I would see the light once again..."
Lothar Theron, Philosopher and Poet - 'Personal Poetics'.

The light was a flickering thing, like an old-style projector from the Museum of Antiquities... *walking with Momma down the aisles of glasscite, prisms of words cascading into waterfalls, rivulets of memories backing up against a dam, flowers in her hair, leaves and trees swaying on a windy day on Primus. Thoughts and words, dull and distant, echoes tremulous and touched with tears falling, broken hopes, lost love left alone in a darkened cell... where in Demos am I?* Shadow upon shadow... watching how darkness leaps into pools of night scattered across the floor. Somewhere a red tinge flickering into grey, a vaulted chamber; beams up there in an arc, the sound of silence broken only by her breathing, the slow falling of her tears. Naked and alone in a terrible nightmare, a taste of metal in her mouth, eyes stinging and sore, nose running and her mouth so very dry... *drugged?* Knees on a cold floor, solid, metallic, plassteel... vibrating... there are air vents somewhere close, whispers of vegetation carried into the room, humid and so very hot, *where are my clothes?* Every trembling glance returns as fire... Sick, feeling so sick... throwing up all over the floor... just coffee and ice cakes... memories trapped inside a familiar smell, breakfast... Every singular perception arrives as broken memory... she tries to focus... *why is it so hot?* Movement nearby, lost in the shadows... *Father?* Somewhere... a sudden draft of warm air, humid and full of fragrance... *someone is here!* A spike of light... A tall man lost in darkness, shadows seeking recognition... watching... waiting...

"Who are you? What do you want?" Frail echoes carried trembling into silence.

A soft voice, almost a whisper..."Everything is lucid; your life is a drop in His ocean"

"What? I don't understand?"

"The pathways flow... we are grains of sand in His service."

He doesn't move... he drops something... *clothes!* She sees a neatly folded T-Shirt and shorts, two sneakers, and then he is gone... the soft hush of a door closing behind him. Darkness again, silence... the burning pain at the back of the neck... she reaches back and feels a wound there... *they've cut out my tag!*

She took the clothes, dressing slowly, careful to avoid stepping in the mess on the floor... her arms and legs felt like plassteel... the clothes were field gray, and she recognized the emblem... the *heart in hand* of the med-tech service... *am I in a hospital, then?* She reached out to the nearest wall and slowly began to edge her way around the room. When she finally reached the door, she raised her hands and started to bang as hard as she could.

"Hello! Can you hear me? Hello? Come back, please... I need to talk to you... hello?" Silence, the mute realization that she was a prisoner, that she had been kidnapped. In frustration, she began to pound on the door until the pain was too much to bear and she collapsed to the floor, tears falling, fears rising, threatening to seize her and reduce her to a whimpering mess.

After a while, she forced herself to stand up, and she tried to calm her breathing, realizing that the darkness was not so complete, she was beginning to get used to it. She could see the high-beamed ceiling, and nearer still an air vent humming above the door. She decided to map the room with her hands and began to follow the walls around the room. On the far wall she came across another air vent, but different this time... *this vent leads to the outside!* Cascading slivers of light were lines reaching into the cell, and the scents were noticeably different... *vegetation, and flowers of some kind...* There was also a humid dampness which the vent could not quite filter out, and she felt her new-found clothes sticking to her skin... *The Tropics? Have they taken me to the Tropics?*

The Tropics were on the other side of the world from Egrain City; she'd only ever flown over that vast area on the way to the Islands of Lanoir. Most of the land was jungle, and for the last thirty years it had been a protected Legislative Preserve – all commercial industrialization was restricted in the Tropics; it was part of the Global Oxygenation Project for the Sustainment of Natural Resources. The Project was included in every First School curriculum... most kids knew the details of the GOP by the time they started Second School, and as such she knew the land was sparsely populated, being restricted to GOP workers, science teams and permit holding tourists. If they'd brought her to the Tropics then the chances of being rescued were very slim. She felt her spirits wilt yet again, and as she leaned back against the wall, she slid slowly to the floor... her neck was hurting and now she was so very thirsty... it wasn't long before the tears came once again.

Chapter 7 - Interlude in the City

'Sometimes you have no idea you are walking along a cliff edge until you fall off...'
The Poet Brayman - Planet Entrymion.

Limon S'Atwa sat back in his chair and looked out over the city. Sunlight swept into his office and the large glasscite window re-polarized to compensate for the sudden brightness. He could see the Phuyani construction yards where an army of drones were busy constructing the new space docks. Soon the agrav-lifters would float the massive slabs of plassteel into orbit to be fused into one giant platform, and then the final phase of the project would begin in earnest. Phuyani had assured the Legislature that the docks would be completed in time for the arrival of the First Coalition Fleet in less than two months time. The local press called the docks: *'An unnecessary extravagance...just one more way to lose our independence...'* Perhaps they are right... even the Legislature will have to run cap in hand to Tantra if they want to re-finance the planetary debt index... if we survive that long... His security team had finally delivered the data-plug. *Now perhaps we might have some answers...* He carefully held it up against the light to verify the seal. Its crystal lattice contained details about the men from Samros; a scattering of so-called Priests had recently arrived in the city, quickly disappearing beneath the sensor grid. But Samros had become a closed world, its Net links severed into silence. There had been no Net feeds from the Cordwainer Alliance in over a year and Samros itself had become isolated from the trade lanes. The last cargo fleet bound for the Rim was lost to the grid six months earlier. *Something is going on out there...* And now these Priests had kidnapped his niece... *But why? What could they possibly want with an eighteen-year-old student? Lorn is a more viable target... for that matter, so am I...*

The desk com buzzed: a polite reminder of his scheduled meeting with the First Minister... *well, that's going to have to wait.* He could no more trust Fentor Mann than he could his own secretary. The recent data-burst from the Far Star Colony was worrying; its codes had been siphoned into the Legislature AI system, terminating inside an unidentified algorithmic matrix. And now people were acting strange. There was a certain oddness among his friends which he couldn't explain; it wasn't so much the way they spoke, but more the coldness behind their eyes.

35

He glanced at the latest feeder sheet. The new orders coming down from the Legislature were bordering on the paranoid... Planetary security forces had been put on a twenty-seven-hour alert; in-system military checkpoints had been established. *Search and seizure they called it...more likely a net to catch the Glasnost when it arrives... if it arrives...* The Phaelon incident was a stark reminder of how widespread the enemy infiltration had become. *They had tried to kill the Professor! And now they had taken dearest Shari...* He turned to look up at the darkening skies. *And who will arrive here first I wonder?*

He touched his datapad and scanned for the latest news feeds. There was a lot of hysterical ranting concerning broken Net links along the Rim sector. Several large combines were refusing to haul cargo beyond the borders of the Coalition. People among the outer worlds seemed to be hunkering down to weather a storm. *What do they know that we don't?* Among the more alarming posts there were polite requests for information, threads of inquiry seeking out ship schedules, ports of origin, passenger manifests... anything and everything coming from the Rim was being tagged and scrutinized by programs he didn't recognize. But what alarmed him the most was the occasional Thread mentioning an artifact outbound from Tantra... *Someone has noticed us...* He sifted for any connection to Primus but found nothing; that fact alone was the most terrifying.

He had to meet Lorn. The last reliable trace of Shari was somewhere over the Tropics; her tag was dead but the latest feeds indicated a secret jungle compound. *That had to be where she was being held... praise the Stars she still lives...*

Lorn wanted to meet him inside Jarvis Park on the Kandian Peninsula. He skimmed for a geo-grid of the park and transposed it directly onto his left retina pad. He told his secretary to cancel the meeting with the First Minister and quickly made his way to the nearest drop-tube. With his head down he moved through the sub-basement parking lot towards his ground car. He glanced once at the exit scanners as he drove swiftly onto Ventura Avenue, heading directly for the Outer Ringway, following the flash signs toward the Peninsula.

It was still bright out, but early-evening mists were already forming around the highest of the city towers pushing sunlight back towards the distant horizon. It would be nightfall by the time he reached Port Arthur on the Peninsula. His agents had traced the Samrosian priests to the Tropics; Shari was being held somewhere beyond the GOP preserve. He had spliced the location into his ID tag for retrieval via datapad once he had met with his brother. *There's a very good chance we could all lose our lives in this madness...*

Neiron Thane touched the flow-screen and watched the ground car exit the Department of Internal Affairs, *the pathways flowed...* He summoned the Viper to the roof of the building, a dark black needle-like craft with enhanced wet-wire feelers casting sight and sound across the ether... one of the first gifts from his Master, and so suitable for this night's work. He wrapped the webbing around his shoulders, felt the contradiction of humanity amid the data-flow from Samros, *bones on nodes gone viral with seedlings and pathogens...* He touched the shimmer data that followed the ground car, tapped into its base code and found a destination: Jarvis Park, Port Arthur on the Kandian Peninsula. He flicked the craft into stealth mode and slipped into the upper airs, cruising higher into the flight lanes, and turned south toward the coast... a shimmering blur unseen and undetected even by the Skysat platform. He sent thoughts into the data-stream: *Thane actuate arrived and implementing termination procedural...* There was a brief flash of a black flag emblazoned with the Worship Glyph, symbol of his Master, then the stream shut down, to be replaced by a schematic of Jarvis Park.

He dropped an ion cube into the Tetra gun beside him, felt its pulse hum softly beneath his hands... if he could still feel emotion he might have felt satisfaction, and perhaps pleasure in carrying out such an important assignment, but now he was no more than an instrument, his soul long since extinguished, his mind controlled by a cerebral hand reaching out from the far reaches of the known universe.

Chapter 8 - A New Day on Primus

"It's easy to kill a person; the difficulty is trying not to show how much you enjoy it..."
Poron Metklon: Phaelon First Assassin to the Elaas Elite Corps.

Lorn S'Atwa broke the connection, noting the time on the screen... *Limon must be on his way to Port Arthur.* It was the only place they considered safe, and far enough away from the city to be almost free of vidcams. Port Arthur was an enigma, a jumbled collection of early colonial mansions and parks, untouched by the high-tech systems brought in by the Coalition combines. They would meet in Jarvis Park, just one block from the former S'Atwa family home. The park was also beneath one of the few gaps in the Skysat coverage – mainly because several of the upper Legislatures had holiday homes in the area.

Port Arthur lay at the head of the Kandian Peninsula and was surrounded by mainly rural lands, with the occasional working farm supplying the dairy produce for which the state was famed. The vast food combines of the Coalition had yet to make an appearance on Primus, and many citizens, even within the Legislature, still opposed the full mechanization of industry which was the way of the Coalition.

He keyed his ground car and had it come round to the front of the house. Minutes later he was heading north toward the Central Causeway and the roads leading to the Peninsula. The Skysat tracking system showed a steady stream of ground cars heading away from the city – personal flight permits were rare among ordinary citizens, but as a member of the Legislature he could have called up a skipper craft, but that would have been noticed; Limon had warned against that, better to take the Causeway, where there was less chance of being traced.

Looking up at the night skies, he caught sight of several starships flickering at the end of fiery torches, pushing out toward the stars beyond. There were no floating cities around Primus, this was no Hub world; high-tech here was limited, but it was definitely creeping in. He felt it ironic how little any of it actually mattered, not in the grand scheme of things, anyway. The threat they now faced was beyond measure and perhaps not even the might of the Coalition would prevail in the end. *They have no idea how overwhelming the danger actually is... the darkness is growing, and perhaps it's already here, covertly spreading its influence among the citizens of Primus.*

38

The local Skysat link shut down as he drove into the outer parking lot of Jarvis Park. The place was a sudden rush of familiarity... the public tennis courts and the nearby Sky Plaza café where he had first met his wife Tania. Further away toward the boating lake he could see the cascading waterfalls of the *torelinni fountains*, and the rare luminous surrela vines creeping among the ancient Dharm trees and around the old colonial statues watching over the gardens and galleries of the Palatial Centria. *So many memories made in this place... Had it all been for nothing?* His datapad flashed a grid-reference, *Limon...*

Walking quickly, he noticed several people passing through the park, no doubt late clubbers on their way home, *and yet any one of them could be the enemy...* That chilling thought brought him back to his daughter, *who had her? And where the crell was she?* Limon had to know something, he had said as much.

He arrived at the old orchestra pit in front of the Galleria, now no more than a dilapidated collection of abandoned market stalls and old-style advertising posters left tattered and fluttering in the wind. And then he saw his brother waiting beneath a flickering neon sign proclaiming the zero gravity delights of the Sensua off-world colony.

Limon had seen him and raised his hand to wave him over. He took the steps down toward the Galleria, the leaves and litter scattering in his wake. And that's when he saw the red dot reaching out through the night, rising slowly over Limon's tunic. The world slipped into slow motion as the dot came to rest upon his brother's forehead. They both had an instant of stark recognition, pure terror at the sheer inevitability of the moment. He watched helplessly as his brother fell slowly to his knees, collapsing finally to the ground. There had been no sound, no distant echo, but now Limon was lying face down in the dirt, his blood already pooling in the mud.

Lorn dived down behind a bench, his mind racing. He was shaking, desperately trying to calm down and take stock of the situation. It wasn't easy to see beyond the Galleria, not without risking his own life. The silence was now overwhelming and only seemed to add to his terrible sense of loss. Left alone in his grief, he stared across at his brother's body... *they killed Limon... and perhaps Shari as well...* He glanced at his datapad, aware that it would not detect a phase inducer... *so they can still kill me and I won't even see them coming... but Limon...*

39

He risked a quick glance around the side of the bench and then with some hesitation he began to crawl slowly toward his brother. After several terrifying minutes he was close enough to reach out and feel for a pulse... *dead.* Tears welled up and he quickly wiped them away; thoughts of Shari came to mind and he began to go through his brother's pockets, searching for anything that might lead him to his daughter. He stopped several times to stare into the surrounding darkness, waiting for the shot that would kill him. As he moved around the body, he suddenly realized he was lying in his brother's blood... a sickening feeling rose up inside, forcing him to his knees, sick and ashamed of his own weakness in the face of such a loss. But he was desperate now; Limon's killer would certainly be targeting him next. *Limon must have something... they killed him for it, didn't they?*

Somewhere high above the park, the throbbing beat of a police aerovane could be heard, strumming its arc across the night skies, the red and blue glows casting rainbow colors along the paths and flower beds below. They mustn't see him, no time to explain. Limon carried no files, no datapad, nothing... *where can it be?* And then he knew... it was so simple, the perfect way to ingrain secret data was to have it spliced into a personal ID tag. But there was no time to link it to his datapad; the killer could already be stalking him.

Without a moment's hesitation, he used the edge of a key card to dig into the back of Limon's neck. Blood obscured his view and he felt his stomach churn, but he cut deeper and soon found the edge of the tag. He prized it loose and then pulled it free... a crystal data sliver inscribed with Limon's DNA recognition codes, *and hopefully much more.* He felt the desecration as an intense pain in his chest, but there was no time for reflection; the police aerovane was turning around, its forward beams moving slowly toward him. He pulled his brother's body into the shadows beneath the awning of a market stall just as the aerovane passed overhead, gradually disappearing into the distance. He realized the proximity of the police had probably saved his life.

He wiped the tag clean and placed it carefully in an inside pocket before taking a moment to assess the situation. He had to calm down, start thinking logically. He pulled out his datapad, flicked it into full bio-scan mode. The screen was a mass of data-feeds bouncing bio-recognition signals into the surrounding area seeking out the tell-tale signs of life. Instantly, Limon's death was confirmed... *no life signs here but my own,* but further away, beyond the Centria... there was movement, fast, really fast... heading his way.

40

He made a break for the trees, keeping to the shadows behind the Galleria. The illusion of safety was soon lost as a branch above his head flamed into incandescence. He kept running, stopping only once to check the scan... someone was crossing the orchestra pit, *where to run?* He looked around frantically, the once familiar surroundings were now lost in the night. But from somewhere beyond the trees came the sound of the Parkway Tram humming softly on its glide-rails. The tram could take him directly into Port Arthur, but the carriage now resting on its glide rails was almost certainly the last one of the night... *run!*

From behind came the sound of someone running through the trees. Suddenly a needle of light lanced into the stone face of a colonial founder. It erupted in a plume of stone and vapor... *that was too close!* He kept to the shadows, more for the psychological boost than anything else, but in his haste he ran straight into a litter bin, falling over and cutting his knee badly against the wire meshing; the bin instantly erupted in flame as he forced himself to his feet and carried on toward the station. He could see the glide-rail through the trees, its overhead arc lights spiking the night into fluorescence... there was a tram hovering against the main platform... but the rail was already vibrating...*it's leaving!*

The station looked deserted, but that was hardly surprising, Jarvis Park was a terminus, the end of the Parkway line, and this tram would probably be the last to leave tonight. *I miss this one and I'm a dead man...*

When he reached the pay booth the entry gate was sealed tight. A vid-screen flashed *Payment Required* in bright red letters. He fumbled through his pockets for his credit tag. Now he could hear someone running across the gravel beyond the railings. He quickly waved his card over the sensor panel and the gates slid slowly to one side; he forced them the rest of the way and made a dash for the tram.

For several agonizing seconds the doors refused to open and he was left standing there totally exposed on the brightly lit platform, knowing that the killer could come around the corner at any second. And then the doors swished apart and he was aboard. Not knowing when the tram would move off, he began to move forward, passing through the connecting doors and on into the next carriage, constantly looking over his shoulder. He was limping now and his lower right leg was wet with blood. He tried to ignore the pain and continued to move toward the front of the tram. But just when he thought he couldn't go any further the tram began to rise gently above the glide-rail and then slowly it slid out of the station, heading back toward Port Arthur. It was only then that he noticed that there were other people onboard; but they ignored him, no doubt assuming he was a late-night drunk on his way home after a party.

As he sat down, the shock finally passed through him in slow tremulous waves. He gripped the handrail tightly as his body began to shake, and it took all his self-control not to vomit. The pain in his leg was a dull ache now and he quickly wrapped his kerchief around the cut… it didn't look too deep. He took a look around and then carefully pulled out his datapad and tapped in his recognition code. He took Limon's tag from his pocket, and laid it down flat on the screen. The pad flickered into a response grid and he sat back, waiting for the pad to download the data splice. *Now to find Shari, and hope to the Stars she's still alive…*

Neiron Thane seethed in frustration, his humanity now overriding the data-stream webbing. It sat inert upon his shoulders, and for once he feared to make the connection… but… *the pathways flowed…* The stream joined his awareness as a tide gently overlapping his peripheral independence. Slowly he slipped into a state of acute fixation, his eyes wide and seemingly lifeless. The neuron net overwhelmed him for an instant as the influx from Samros scanned his perception and streamed across his brain whilst the synaptic rivers uploaded and downloaded specific data characteristics … *dendrites and axons floating in a cerebral breeze…* He received a vision of the Worship Glyph, and instantly his eyes began to re-focus. He was standing on a station platform at the edge of Jarvis Park, and his secondary target had escaped. He had feared his Master's wrath, but there had been no admonishment, no threats of termination. His Lord had seemed unconcerned at the failure of his secondary mission; he was simply to proceed to the compound and take custody of the girl, she was to be taken off-world before the fleet arrived….*and that's why there was no wrath… this world will fall soon enough, and after that, Lorn S'Atwa, there will be no place for you to hide, no place at all…*

Sub-Orbital Ecliptic

....Skysat platform recognition burst....comsat data-feed Legislative Censure level

Primal One... coordinate fleet signals... tracer nodes recognition parameters online...

Unknown echo location points at data point one zero termina six to the tenth overcore tech fleet liaison designates following text:

Language path Arctura Prime, Drometia, Dronheim, Galicia, Petra, Primal IV, Primus Coalition Protectorate...

....Unknown ship movement throughout outer Rim sectors, possible military fleet operations, coordinates show possible incursion within outer Coalition sectors...

Designated targets in line with language path terminating at Primus... recommended immediate defensive action... repeat... recommended immediate defensive action...

*Skysat platform data-burst file 0000111^*

Chapter 9 - A Parting of the Ways

"... Freedom is a unique gift, but it involves risk, and sometimes the need to attain it outweighs the reason for wanting it..."
Corel Luwain, Philosopher, planet Samros (Cordwainer Alliance)

Shari saw the door open slightly, a touch of light, fading as the door once more closed; a bowl there, a jug, darkness again. She crawled over to the bowl, some kind of food, *gross!* But the water was welcome. As she swallowed she thought about poison, then decided not to care less, the relief was worth the risk. Only then did she hear the whispering as an interruption in the humming from the vents. Something different, vague at first, almost not quite there, but then more real, a definite sound, a whisper, *a voice!* She followed the sound, traced it to the outer air vent, *someone is out there!*

Moving closer she called out: "Hello? Is anyone there? Hello?" Whispers, more hissing than anything else... a ragged jumble of words... she picked up old Galac from her First School days...

"Frail me okay? You frail too?"

"Oh, please help me! I'm a prisoner; can you hear me?"

"Listening now, shush... voices carry, air waves catch you... quiet please..."

She lay down next to the air vent, her mouth close to the vanes rotating in their cycle.

"Please, who are you? Can you help me? Hello?"

There were the sounds of movement outside, a waft of scents flowing into the room, leaves and trees swaying in the breeze.

"Yes, help you, yes, Saepid am I. Away move, I thrust into your chamber..."

She had no idea what the voice meant, she didn't recognize the name *Saepid*, but it definitely sounded off-world. Regardless, if it could help her escape then she would go along with it. She stood up, backing away from the vent.

She saw a movement inside the rotor vanes, something long, like a finger, or a claw maybe, but it moved in a precise way, clutching the ribs of metal, and rolling around each stem, holding the vent wide open as a longer *thing* forced its way through the outer bars and dropped into a puddle of goo on the floor. It took several minutes before she realized the puddle was solidifying,

44

and growing to about her waist height. It formed features as it grew taller, two spindly legs stuck to a tubular body covered in carapace, and above this four limbs thrashing about, and finally a head wrapped in what looked like wet gossamer, breaking through as though newly born and with secretions dripping from its reptilian face.

"Apologies for my forcement, not easy for me, last time I did that was for propagation and lot more fun I can say without hesitation... molecular dissolution bites!"

Shari moved forward slowly, watching this crazy apparition before her; she had never seen anything like it before, not on the VidTube or even on the Net. But whatever it was it seemed friendly enough, and might well provide the only way out of her prison.

"I am sorry, but who are you?"

"Saepid I am, many times I say this, listen you must, we not here stay for long, I take you outside, away from His servants."

"I don't understand; how can you just get me out of here?"

"Hard way, but only way, but trust me you must; not easy, faith, only faith takes you outside..."

Shari looked at the strange creature, and then the room and the sealed door... *what choice do I have?*

"Okay, I have faith, so get me out of here..."

The creature pulled at its lower abdomen, tore away something wet and dripping with slime. It looked pure gross.

"Swallow this you must. Hurry, they come for you now."

She looked at the piece of flesh the creature held out in its *hand?* No way could she swallow that...

"You want me to eat this? You're joking, right?"

"Hurry, child, they come, they come..." Outside the door, footsteps approaching, *someone is coming!* She quickly took the fleshy morsel in her hand and forced it into her mouth. It tasted salty and fibrous, almost impossible to chew, so she just swallowed it as the creature told her to. Instantly the room vanished and she found herself spiraling down into an impossible hole in the floor, her hands were green limbs, twigs being pulled through metal rainbows, stone parapets caught the side of her head, and flowers crashed into her eyes, fragrance flowed as an ocean into her mouth, and the taste of metal was replaced by the touch of soil on her face. She felt her breasts pressed down hard into the ground. Her chest heaving in agony, she tried to catch her breath but the wind wouldn't allow her, it flowed along her body and she found herself reborn, outstretched and straddling a large yuma plant, bent over by her weight. The strange little creature was there again, huddled at first, then all four upper limbs seizing her, taking her forward into the jungle and the heat and a mist which suddenly closed down upon her and for several seconds she lost consciousness.

A whispering on the edge of a precipice, falling over into sight and sound, a voice made real by touching... fingers on her face... fibrous nails brushing hair from her eyes...

"Rest not yet, fleshings are close now, moving with hurry, please."

She felt her body, wondering at the miracle of her escape. "How... how did you do that?"

"No time to explain... long story..."

She was instantly aware of being pulled up and through the undergrowth, huge green leaves slapping into her, wavy fronds and ferns strung like webs hanging from branches, all of it interlaced with vines and vegetation and the sounds of a million unknown creatures breaking into her mind like an unending chorus of madness. From somewhere behind her, a darker sound, a deep throbbing movement back there in the jungle.

"Move with hurry now pleases... fleshings airborne... hurrys..."

High above, she felt the shadows gathering, a darkness flowing over the upper trees, the sound of rotors grinding on grav-fields... *Vipers!* Somewhere behind her was a military pursuit craft, perhaps more than one, skirting the upper tree line, no doubt searching for her.

Her new-found companion slapped what looked like a mushroom over her mouth, and then without a moment's hesitation pulled her headfirst into a swampy bog. She had the good sense not to panic, and allowed herself to be pulled under, half-expecting to drown. She closed her eyes and waited, counting down from twenty, if she was still under at zero she would force her way back up to the surface. But at five she was being pulled up and out of the water and finally allowed to collapse, exhausted, by the side of the bog, her erstwhile companion scampering up a nearby tree. She could hear the rotors fading into the distance, with the wind carrying the scents of gastrol in their wake.

Shari rolled over, vomited something vile, along with what looked like mud. She noticed her hands were bleeding... *thorns from the Yuma tree...* something was pulling her hair. Looking up, finally she saw the strange creature gesturing for her to stand. She was covered in mud; her hair still had vines

46

wrapped through it, and her body was shaking, and yet she had to move, the Vipers could return any time, she had to escape.

"Hurrys… must run… now!"

She followed the creature deeper into the jungle, pushing past giant malahide leaves, climbing over Lupin vines wrapped around branches, swatting insects as they swarmed around her, and every now and then there were patches of swamp bog to be avoided as the creature led her toward a clearing between two giant *canoper* trees. She could see the creature clearly now, wild eyes bulging from a reptilian face, a long sliver of a tongue dashing in and out like a snake's.

"Here we sit, fleshings circle over structure, dark place, your prison no more…"

She looked around her; saw nothing but jungle and swarms of flitter flies, and then she noticed a faint light expanding into a shaft of brilliance streaming through the upper branches of the *canoper* trees. It was different from daylight, shifting from bright white to shades of purple and red, a singular line widening at the base, merging with the leaves and the trees. Looking up, she saw a darkness taking shape, something descending, intense waves of heat washing over her… *a ship!*

"Ha! She comes, my Saepid love… so hurrys now, child, back, fear the heat touching…"

She was pulled back into the undergrowth as the craft forced the trees aside, lowering slowly on spider legs, plassteel struts forced down into the soil and mud. A sudden backwash covered her in swamp water, and a throbbing in her head she hadn't noticed before got a lot worse. Suddenly the engines cut out and in the ensuing silence the jungle sounds returned in a series of bird calls and the buzzing of wisps trying their best to sting her.

"Hurrys now, must inside, fleshings return…" She was pushed and pulled into a gaping hole in the side of the vehicle, soft humming of an engine somewhere, the smell of something damp. She saw a flow-screen drift past with her face on it, smiling… *my class photo!* It dissolved as she was pushed toward webbing strung up on a nearby wall.

The straps were human standard, which seemed odd, but she recognized the need for haste, as an engine began to pulse beneath her feet. Data screens flickered in the darkness, numbers and figures floating through the cabin. She made out one other creature below her, similar to the one who had rescued her. It was already webbed, and sat before some kind of control interface. Her

47

companion was also strapping down; strange little feet dangling among vines and branches.

She pulled on the web grip, securing herself to the wall, just in time as the craft suddenly accelerated directly into the sky. Her stomach was doing somersaults, and it was all she could do not to throw up as the pulse engines groaned and vibrated, the webbing straining to keep her contained. She could hear atmospheric needles grinding out toward the stars above, forcing the craft into the upper reaches of the ionosphere.

A floater passed by with Primus filling the screen; but it was receding… *we're leaving Primus? By the Stars, no!* She closed her eyes, finally passing out.

Soil and dust motes spinning upon secret winds, casting rainbows across hard metal walls, flowers breaking out from data screens, vines wrapped about conduits, branches strung along plassteel beams, twisting and sealed at what seemed to be a command deck below.

Shari opened her eyes, adjusting to the light. She unclipped her straps and floated free from her webbing, *no grav-plates?* She saw above her a glasscite dome with branches and leaves breaking out from air vents, and tiny flitter flies fluttering in an impossible breeze. High above, the stars were spread like fields of lights flickering in the night, constellations swooned and swelled into galaxies with the soft fever of creation, all of it swirling past as the craft pushed out through the upper atmosphere toward the inner system moons. Below she could see one of the creatures, strapped down and working at what looked like a piloting console. As she turned to get a better view her legs caught a tree branch wrapped around her webbing, leaves scattered, floating by with tiny insects flitting into the upper branches, and everywhere in the background the sound of rain falling. Finally she saw her rescuer rise up to face her, with what she could only describe as a crazy lopsided smile on its strange and alien face.

"Beauty view catches your breath, yes child?"

She had to agree. "Beauty view catches, yes…"

It felt surreal floating inside this strange craft, no internal grav obviously, using evergreen as an oxygen influx… pretty advanced considering the overhead conduits, braced together from a cargo hauler by the look of it. She had studied the various fleet ships in her Coalition Assimilation class, hated buying into the corporate crell, but now she was grateful for the information. This was a deep space lugger, totally alien without a doubt, these creatures were not on any

48

infopad she'd ever read. But they had rescued her from certain death in that cell, so she'd wait and see, bide her time and try to find out where they were taking her. Although she couldn't help but wonder if she hadn't just exchanged one set of kidnappers for another.

"Fleshing child, I am Saepid Anthra, this below now is my mate Saepid Ventra, we are kindling's born to the Othrum race, of the Saepid Clan, here to save you from the Power which rises now in the deep dark...'scuse my Galac, not up to threads yet, our ways are not of the Coalition... but we get better..."

"I'm sorry, I don't understand, you have saved me from whom?"

There was a high laughing sound from below, and a shrill voice: "Dear fleshing child, she has no recognition of her fate..."

Her companion looked down annoyed... "Shush now, Ventra... I will explains..." He looked back up at Shari.

"Forgives, we are surprised you are dark when knowing of the enemy. He is here, or there on Primus as we talk, you are not safe there, we track you to find you, you have the wishful gift, we save you for our kindred souls." He looked up at the stars above.

Shari had no idea what the creature was talking about, but felt caught up in the moment. She watched the stars beyond the dome, the worlds out there spinning alone inside the grand dream of Coalition. She reached out a hand, and touched the creature on one of its limbs, *arms?*

"Please try to explain to me, I don't understand. I don't know why I was kidnapped, and I don't know where you think you're taking me, but you had better just take me home, right now, or there will be trouble; my father is an important member of the Legislature and you can get into big trouble, do you understand?"

Crazy frenetic gestures from the creature, arms waving in the air, the other creature shouting something from below, and from behind her the distant rumble of thunder inside the soft falling of rain.

"Explains yes, we are Saepid of the Othrum race, Saepid Anthra I am, our colony world once part of the Cordwainer Alliance, mostly fleshings, but Saepids own twenty bright worlds out there. We were invaded, yes, by a deep darkness, all our machines went bad, many of our great minds drained of life, yes, very bad. My mate and I were outflung, deep space trawling, cargo and commerce our life, far star traders we are... we picked up Threads from the Hub Net, many suspicions out there, many threats nearer home. We found blood information in Saepid archive, genetics yes, ancient texts connected to you, found your father also, important fleshing him, many connections we traced…"

Soft laughter from below. Anthra gave the funny smile again, seemed to shrug before continuing. "Yes, we broke many rules, found leaks in the Skysat system of Primus, tapped into the data codes your father used, yes, broke many rules…." He seemed to drift off into silence, staring into space. She thought he might have finished, but he suddenly continued. "Made connections, yes, father and you and Gamont… fleshing there with many secrets… but making wrong conclusions, they make big mistake, think they have answer to the Beast… big mistake, many errors… forget blood line, big mistake…"

She was trying to make sense of what he was telling her, but it wasn't easy. "Look, just tell me in plain Galac, what the crell is going on!"

Anthra took a deep sigh; she could see he was desperately looking for the correct words, obviously trying his best to explain. "Forgives, please, I try. Beast comes soon, very old machine gone bad, gone biological in parts, sentient yes, very old. Your father knows of way to stop Beast, seal it away once again in crystal prison; your father has contact friend bound for Primus world, your world, this fleshing has ancient device to stop Beast, they think to travel to Rim, Far Star Colony to stop Beast, but they make errors in translation. The First Ones, who defeat Beast, made blood-line, genetic markers passed down through millions of years, called them *custodia*, very ancient name from lost text, only one such as these can wield device to stop Beast."

"And what has all of this got to do with me?" She wasn't really sure she wanted to know, but his next words sent a terrible chill right through her.

"Why, child, you are *custodia*…"

The creature turned away and began to use all four upper limbs to work flow-screens as they floated about the cabin. For a moment she thought he had forgotten her.

"Forgive yes? Must avoid local notice, police crafts and His agents are already nearby… where was I? Hah, yes, you see this fleshing bound from Gamont to Primus has made mistakes, already Phaelon allies of the Beast move against him, we must travel to planet Petra, last planet fall of *Glasnost* ship before Primus. There we intercept this fleshing and show him our archive, then we make our quest to stop the Beast…"

"Wait a minute, you can't take me to Petra, I have to go home… I can't stop some ancient monster from taking over the universe… that's just crazy, I'm an eighteen-year-old girl… just a student, I don't know anything about any device; in fact, look... the best thing you can do is to take me to my father; surely he can sort this matter out, isn't he expecting this man from Gamont?"

Saepid Anthra looked down. She saw a deep sadness in his eyes; his mate below whispered something that sounded like clucks and clicks to her ears. Anthra looked up again, his eyes looking directly into hers. "Forgive my words, child... but Primus no longer safe place to be..."

"What? What's that supposed to mean?" Fear began to rise somewhere inside her chest.

"Well, simply that as far away as the Rim is, the Beast's hand is a lot closer still..."

"How close?"

Anthra pulled a floater down from the wall, flashed various screens until he settled on one particular readout.

"This is a fleet of ships twenty thousand light hours out of the Primus system, they should reach planetary orbit in two days' time, local yes..."

Shari felt the sudden shock hit her with a throbbing pain just above her eyes. "Well then, we must do something, you must warn them, contact the Legislative Assembly, we have to tell them what's happening!"

"So sorry, but too late for that... those who rule Primus are already influenced, already usurped by the Beast. His power lives in all the machines down there, soon the ships will go bad, automation closing down, weapons platforms falling from the skies..."

"But my father, my friends..." Tears glimmered in her eyes.

Saepid Anthra said no more. He drifted over to a data-port, adjusting something over there; from below she could hear his mate humming softly to the sounds of wind and rain. Outside, the stars seemed to waver, shift, and then vanish altogether as the ship entered subspace, and suddenly she felt so terribly alone, tears floating away to touch the leaves as they drifted past almost in tune with the rain and the rumble of distant thunder.

Hours must have passed; she had fallen asleep in her harness, her eyes were sore and the webbing had left red lines across her legs. She picked a few thorns from her hands and shook leaves out of her hair and looked around the cabin. There was some chatter from down below where the pilot... *Saepid Ventra?* was busy with the helm controls. *Saepid Anthra?*...floated up from below pulling a flow-screen down in front of him, skimming through flash screens until he seemed to settle on one in particular; he flipped it around so she could read the information

51

display. She instantly recognized the language usage: Modern Galac with local syntax in the Primus dialect, her own language; *a dead language soon?*

"This will help you, our own archive it is, tells you more of the Beast, translated from ancient Othrum tongue... please, try this..."

She looked indignant. "I need to clean up first!"

The Saepid sighed. "Soon enough child...but first you learn..."

She touched for a vocal readout and the soft voice of a female began to read out the information as it flowed across the screen. The voice could have been any one of her friends from her tutorial classes. It caused tears to well up again as she realized just how far away she was from anyone who actually cared for her. The woman began:

"Core data Hub-variant Othrum sub-text from Tantalus Codices sub-lingual Gamont Translation as described in the Primal Prefecture of Syrillian Anthos, First General of Federated Fleets of Liberation, circa one one zero by six pre-Coalition. The Beast herein was assigned as a Cortex variant by an anthropological pre-existing species of non-specified origin. Purpose being the configuration of data histories and scientific expansion of the known universe into discernable algorithmic potentials and assisted by a symbiotic construction of a quantum data-core: a Primary Cortex super intelligence."

Shari touched the pause and looked up at the Saepid, floating now before her, waiting for her reaction. She had half a mind to skip through the screens, but figured she'd better hear the rest, even though it seemed to make less sense than the gibberings of the Saepid Anthra... She touched resume and the voice continued.

"In the Primary Year one zero one by seven (2 billion years pre-Coalition) the newly born Cortex Configuration achieved transapience, ultimately transcending its automation into sentient bio-matter for the spreading of its influence beyond the moon upon which it had been originally constructed. It took several decades before the Core worlds became aware of the Beast's leap to super-sapience, but by that time its expansion had overwhelmed hundreds of civilized worlds... and one by one the confederations fell before its thrall. Outer colony worlds were used for the physical construction of starships to carry the armies, newly suborned into the Cortex, further toward the high-tech civilizations of the Pre-Hub dynasties, Primary Year one zero by six nine pre-Coalition. After several years of expansion, in which almost two-thirds of the known universe fell to the armies of the Cortex Beast, a vast Confederation of worlds came together under the banner of the Federated Fleets of Liberation

under command of the Petran Lord Jophrim. Using an ancient bio-linked artifact (origin pre-dating known calendar computations but believed to have originated among the First Ones), they were able to resist the influx of coercive data into their fleets, and thus slowly they forced the Beast back toward the edge of known space, where it was finally confined using the ancient genetic link code bound solely to the Jophrim blood line.

The artifact began a cascading interface resulting in the formation of crystalline amber, sealing the monster beneath the very surface of the moon from which it had once spread its power.

Under the auspices of Syrillian Anthos, it was deemed impossible to completely eradicate the Core matter that was the original Cortex; there was at that time no safe way to eliminate the genesis of the Beast, not without risking its breakout and further expansion. However, the amber sealant was fused with bio-crystalline ribbons to inhibit any further data expansion, and sapience was finally terminated in Primary Year one zero by six."

Shari cut the voice feed as it started to explain the after-effects of the Beast's occupation of so many thousands of worlds. She saw long lists of planets, whole civilizations turned to madness and self-destruction when the influence of the Cortex was finally withdrawn. She realized she was reading about the Interregnum, the subject of so many historical theories; for over a thousand years the commerce of the known universe had come to an abrupt end. Individual empires fell off the map and whole dynasties were wiped out as the high-tech worlds of the Hub Alliance were reduced to no more than violent levels of medievalism.

So it was all true, the present-day Coalition was not the first galaxy-wide civilization, it was perhaps the second, or maybe even the third. And apparently the Cortex was known by many different names in thousands of separate archives, lost inside the arcane beliefs of hundreds of religious doctrines: the Beast, the Power, the God Saemal, and the Monster from the Rim... She was beginning to feel overwhelmed by the magnitude of the threat they seemed to face; *how do they expect me to fight something that old, that powerful? How the crell can I do anything about it?*

She looked directly into the eyes of the Saepid Anthra, still floating patiently in front of the tree... she had to ask the question, even though as she spoke the words she felt her soul grow cold with fear.

"Are you telling me... this, this Beast, is back?"

53

Anthra looked down at his mate, who was looking up, her eyes wide and moist as if touched with tears... Anthra looked back at Shari and spoke, almost in a whisper... "Yes, bad times here again, child, Beast is back."

Chapter 10 - The First Assemblage

"Out of the Darkness came the Light and the Light was the Power, and by His hand Life was given, and by His love it was sustained..."
Revelations: First Book of Saemal.

The Sacred Twelve arrived separately among the ruins of Altair, First City of Samros, and the capital world of the former Cordwainer Alliance. Each one had overseen the subjugation of the seventy two worlds within the Alliance, and each had assumed full command of the twelve fleets, newly born and patrolling the incorporated territories. They were here to discuss the Coalescency, the union of diversity into one body, one power, the flowering of His glory among the new converts.

Spatial platforms appeared as black slabs upon the horizon, each one descending upon a vast ionic pulse... waves of superheated air cresting the ruins of the high city towers, glasscite shards falling like showers of plassteel upon the parks and boulevards below. From out of each platform there stretched mile after mile of Ultravane Plasmeld shielding, vast agrav-nets strung out like gossamer threads catching the gravity field and re-forming it into null-space, allowing the massive platforms to glide gently down to the shattered and burnt-out city below. Each platform carried a portion of the quantum data-mass of the Cortex, mere tendrils really, reaching with poisonous recipes from out of the night. The Power had to remain with its primal core beyond the Rim, but the psyonic platforms allowed for the expansion of the mind into the inhabited realms where once it had roamed so free and unbridled by either mechanics or the restrictions of physical continuity. This time, however, things would have to go slower, caution was warranted; its agents were already moving among the outer worlds... little automatons sent to seek the lost recipes, prevent any interference.

There were gaps in the influx retrieval; data once thought insignificant, mere effluence left to seep into the bedrock, had suddenly become important; *if they could translate the primary codes...*

There were still tens of thousands of survivors in the ruins of Altair, all them now reduced to awe and lost to the ecstasy of the arrival of the Sacred Twelve.

Each platform disgorged waves of needle-drones, black metal insects streaming down through the streets, flickering wings garnering, linking to data-ports, grappling with home computers, terminating programs, rewriting the math of a million systems, and bringing everything instantly into the Cortex.

The twelve messengers from the Far Star Colony came together on a balcony of one of the upper pylons of the central core platform. Twelve humans, five female, seven male, originally no more than cargo grunts, trawling scrap metal between the outer worlds aboard a deep space dredge. They still had pre-eminence memories, shards of shared recollections of a time when they were merely biological life forms; but such thoughts were ghosts scurrying at the edge of a greater recognition, *tip-toeing over amber lakes, metal flowers flowing as a river of pure transcendence...* now they were Syphonts, radical end-nodes to the greater power.

Tanril, tall and lean, gray haired, and dressed in the ceremonial robes of the One Faith, reached out and instigated the Worship Glyph, touched a flow-screen, and instantly a giant figure appeared over the city, a holo-lucience of an old man, with long white hair, beard, long flowing gray robe... in his right hand an old wooden staff, an image from an ancient past, and in his left hand, a book, old and leather bound... His eyes were filled with untold love, generosity and familiarity, and a wave of kindness began to emanate across the city, spreading across the planet, simultaneously igniting similar displays over every city on every planet within the Alliance.

The voice, when it came, was overlaid with humility, kindness and love: *"My children, I welcome you to your future..."* The words were data-fed algorithms laced with servile base counter-interdictions, catching every open mind in an instant of stark vacancy, seeding the complex recipes of restructuring and realignment along intrinsic pathways to the cerebral thought processes, *axons and dendrites floating in a synaptic breeze...* leaving every single citizen of the fallen Cordwainer Alliance totally compliant and willing to do whatever was required to serve their new-found god.

"Behold, my children... the Jihad of Saemal..." The Cortex had pre-programmed the Glyph with the name of an ancient Power, one that might once have challenged the very walls of the Cortex itself, but it had fallen in the first great expansion. The name, however, was still remembered among the older races, and could prove useful in the coming expansion from the Cordwainer Sector. The giant Worship Glyph switched to scenes of battle fleets assaulting unknown worlds, vast armies tearing through cities, destroying the heathens who had dared to reject the love and grace of *Saemal.* It closed finally with a solitary

56

black flag raised high above a ruined city, emblazoned with one golden symbol... the Ancient Galac word *Nimris*, translated simply as God.

Tanril turned to face the eleven, each one standing impassively, their eyes alert yet betrayed by a certain inner vacancy. There were, however, tell-tale hints of the *communion*, each one of the twelve was connected directly to the Cortex... *the pathways flowed...* They saw the distant sun of the Far Star Colony, a blue-green world in orbit, once sparsely populated, but transformed now with enormous engineering projects. At the outer edge of the stratosphere lay the new fleet docks strung out in low orbit, and further out the giant construction drones harvesting materials from the asteroid belt, slag dredges disgorging ore into the plassteel refineries, scaffolds and turrets, towers and multifaceted auto-bots skimming between the agrav-nets, the rippling of Ultravane shielding across the face of furnaces and smelter chambers, and everywhere the green hue of ionic gases expelled into the upper atmosphere, adding poison and metallic detritus to a once beautiful world.

The twelve minds dive as one into the river of perception, the flow of neural streams casting synaptic nets across a million lights years of space, down past row upon row of newly built starships; vast bulbous metal hides shimmering inside their harbor walls, and then further on down across the world toward the assembly areas, where a million transformed minds are being marshaled, lost to the assuage of their God Saemal.

They rise with the data-stream, carried now toward the one cold moon orbiting the Far Star Colony. A black and pummeled surface; shattered amber and crystalline ruins the only real indication that miles beneath the surface their Master lives and spreads His glory across the stars. Finally, they settle upon a soft azure glow embedded, it seems, inside the womb of a dark chamber... *there....there is the Coalescence...*

The neurons flow, synaptic conjugation becomes a sublime touch of a deep, unremitting power. The Sacred Twelve are shaking, instructions downloading with quantum precision. Instantly, the fleet heading toward Primus is made aware of new requirements, and then the connection closes, releasing the Twelve as they fall to their knees, breathless.

Chapter 11 - Petra

"... So I asked the Master: 'Lord, how many stars are in the night sky?'

And he answered: 'As many as there are raindrops in a summer storm, as many as there are fish in the sea, and as many as there are grains of sand in the desert...'

And I asked: 'Will I know them all, my Lord?'

And he answered: 'No, but they will know us, for we are part of them as they are part of us, for where there is life there is memory of life...'

And thus I was comforted by his words."

Brother Fiodore, First Ascetic Ministry of Petra, (From the Book of Jophrim)

At the outer edge of the Petran system the *Glasnost* dropped out of subspace and assumed a wide arc that would bring it in line with the orbital docking platform hanging high above the capital city of Salicia Sonora. They were showing a flash display of the city in the central Galleria as Professor Kyle Raine went looking for a morning coffee. At this time of the day the Galleria was far less busy than the public viewing areas, crowded now with eager passengers watching the planet-fall approach toward Petra.

He hadn't been sleeping well, and what little sleep he did get failed to ease his nerves. Even though there had been no more attempts on his life, the threat was ever present. Fortunately, the Captain had left him alone since their first meeting, although the guard outside his cabin was a little too obvious. He glanced across the forecourt and saw his erstwhile companion seemingly engaged in reading a menu. *They are watching me all right. Well, no matter, after Petra we'll be on our way to Primus and my meeting with Lorn, and after that...* With his right hand he felt for the object inside his inner pocket. The cold feel of the artifact was a constant surprise to him. It never seemed to vary in temperature; it was always cool to the touch. It was no longer safe to leave it in his cabin, even the wall safe could be tampered with; he already suspected the place had been searched while he was in the dining room the previous evening... but if that satisfied them for a while, all to the good.

Looking up at the flash display, he decided to take in the beauty of Salicia Sonora. He had, of course, studied the planet extensively over the years, for it was unique among worlds, having been originally settled by a religious community fleeing some form of persecution. They claimed to be able to trace their origins as far back as ancient Earth – as a modern scholar he had his doubts about that; even the existence of such a world was highly speculative. But even so, no matter their origins, the monks and priests of Petra had built themselves a beautiful capital city.

Salicia Sonora was vast, as you would expect from such a wealthy civilization. The vidcam seemed to flow down from the sky, swooping low over tall minarets, passing grand basilicas, and panning along a great central street lined with colonnaded temples, sweeping by tall statues overlooking tented piazzas... and every now and then the cam would glimpse a canal winding its way among the gardens and gallerias. The view then moved down several side streets, shooting up suddenly and over a group of rooftop gardens displayed in the form of an ancient script... *like turquoise mazes in the sky...* and then the scene flowed down toward a vast central square where an immense statue of Jophrim stood tall at its center. The cam then zoomed out to show that every major city avenue eventually emerged into the square leading to the massive Basilica D'Jophrim standing along one entire side of the square. It was certainly a breathtaking sight, slightly ruined, perhaps, by the mile-high holo-vids of priests proclaiming the virtues of the Jophrim religion. *Such lavish expense...*

He glanced up at the ship's infotech screen flowing along the wall above the shopping arcades... *Planetfall 09:55 local... port call two days local... disembarkation procedures in effect 11:00 local... Passenger allocation cards available from Purser's Office Level One... Please retain shipboard ID tags for planetary inspection... Planetfall 09:55 local...* He stood up in frustration and decided to return to his cabin to think on his next decision. There would now be another two days wasted before continuing the journey to Primus, *would it be safer to stay on board? Or perhaps it would look less suspicious if I simply went with the crowds to the planet below?* He smiled to himself... *perhaps I should ask the advice of my loyal guard across the way?* He headed to the nearest drop-tube, his guard following on behind.

Captain Salazar checked the main screens: engines were thrusting slowly toward Petra, needle tubes a distant vibration still felt in the grav-plates beneath his feet. He saw the docking platform on a nearby floater growing ever larger across the spatial-grid. An ensign was busy adjusting coaxial drift to bring the ship in line with the dock's echo-point locators – gentle pings resounding around the Bridge as the dock AI requested procedural control.

"Docking requests ship assimilation, Sir."

"Go ahead, Baines, engage echo points."

"Ship online and answering the helm, Sir."

First Officer Doran entered the Bridge, took in the approach to the docking platform, and addressed his captain. "Sir, passengers' allocation tags are logged; I have duty officers in the viewing galleries and security officers covering drop-tubes and all primary areas."

"And our friend the Professor?"

"Returning to his cabin..." He looked down at his datapad. "Oh, and he just logged an allocation tag... looks like he'll be visiting Petra after all."

"I want him followed; we need to know what this man is up to."

"I'll see to it, Sir."

They both turned toward the main screen, the huge bulk of the docking platform growing ever closer. Docking lights flickered into luminance as the *Glasnost* cut engines and slipped slowly into its designated berth.

On the far side of the docking platform a small skipper craft detached from its bay, and moments later rippled into stealth mode and swung low beneath the docks, bound for the planet below.

Inside the *Temple of A'Thram*, located within the Arcadia Plazia, Brother Domini Thendosh sat contemplating his own death. High above his head he could see the Golden Scythe of Jophrim hanging by heavy graphile chains from the vaulted ceiling. In front of him were several penitents, variously gesticulating over their Doctrinal Episcopus; their gentle mumbling lost to the sounds of the Sacred Chimes as they caught the breeze from the upper air vents. For the first time in over a month he felt at peace. Perhaps it was because he had always felt safe in this place, or perhaps it was because he had finally bowed to the inevitable. It wasn't that he was dying as such, but simply that he felt death was inevitable, given the circumstances. He felt himself smile as he remembered his long and protracted meetings with the Episcopate, how he'd argued against their complacency, and how they had finally dismissed his words as heresy and removed him from office... *No matter, the truth will out...*

There were sudden street sounds as a penitent left the temple through the doors behind him... the mad clamor of religious commerce, the bartering and the marketing of a once great religion. *All of it so very delicate, balanced upon an unseen knife edge, perched upon the precipice of Demos itself...* He looked once again at the battered codex on his lap. Opening it, he saw the ancient Worship Glyph of the Beast, and inside the long passages of doctrinal histories, consigned now to myth and legend, but which he had come to realize were actually truth and fact. For two years he had worked at the Seminary, devoting more and more of his time to the translation of the so-called *Forbidden Works*. Forbidden or not, they were there for anyone to read – of course, you had to have a key and the ability to bribe the librarian's assistant.

In all the years of his young life, nothing had quite prepared him for the words written down so long ago; the tales of such horror, such tragedy on a galactic scale... it had soon become obvious why the volumes were labeled *Forbidden*; they seemed to go against every sacred doctrine espoused by the Jophrim religion.

But it was his study of the earlier translations from the Kyrillian architext that eventually pointed him in the right direction, and slowly a pattern had begun to emerge, a progression of events that had led inexorably to the first great Dark Age. There had been several references to the *Chalice of Creation*, and the *Sword of Jophrim*, and it had taken many long hours of study before he finally managed to break through legend and folklore into truth and fact; after that it was relatively easy to translate the final codex. The true source of Jophrim's great power, the so-called *Sacred Sword*, was actually an artifact created by the First Ones as a means to defeat the monstrosity grown out of the depths of space. But it wasn't until recently that he had finally made the connection to the planet Merril, and to the secret chamber buried there, and finally to the man who had discovered it... Professor Kyle Raine of Gamont, the very same man he would track down upon his arrival on Petra.

He pulled a datapad out of his robe, forbidden in Temple, but no one here seemed to be paying him any attention. He flicked for the Net, found the link he had tagged earlier... and there it was, the giant figure standing over a ruined city, probably on some far distant Rim world, the old face exuding kindness and love, the staff in one hand, the book in the other... a perfect match for the crude illustration of Saemal in the *Forbidden Codex*, and the Coretech date on screen? *Six days ago!*

The small skipper craft rippled into sight and sound and came to rest behind the Piazza Centria, two streets away from the Concordia, the main boulevard running through the center of the city. The Phaelon agent Dolmon Tendra was a First Level operative, brought in by his Masters in the Elaas after the failure to destroy the TUCI ship *Glasnost*. That plan had now been abandoned in favor of the direct assassination of the prescribed target: Professor Kyle Raine of

Gamont. He tapped the ship allocation tags, flashed down the passenger list and found the name: Raine, K. C4214.

Logging into the data-port of the docking terminal, he touched for arrival times: there was a shuttle arriving from the docking platform in one hour's time. He would walk to the terminal; the day seemed pleasant enough and the streets, although crowded with pilgrims, were easily negotiable for such a short distance. He took a quick bio-scan of the immediate area, found no one within sight of the craft, and decided to shield the skipper against potential discovery; the last thing he needed now was the added complication of explaining his illegal presence on Petra.

By the time Kyle reached the shuttle bay there were already long queues forming in the disembarkation lounge. There should have been at least forty shuttle craft in use, but there seemed to be no more than twenty online, moving slowly along glide-rails toward the main platform where passengers were beginning to board. As each one was filled to capacity it slipped from its moorings, rising gently and moving slowly toward the main exit. He saw the familiar shimmering as each shuttle breached the shield wall, passing from atmosphere to vacuum, thrusting gently away from the hull, turning on a wide arc down toward the planet below.

Eventually he reached the access scanner, flashed his allocation tag and the soft light of a phase barrier vanished, allowing him to pass through and onto his allocated shuttle. He had to smile at the grand name of the craft: *Maxima*, an old Galac word for *great* or *mighty*. Looking around at the forty or so people crammed into the seats with the battered overhead luggage racks, the outdated ad-boards and the constant flickering of faulty seatbelt signs, he couldn't help but wonder at the choice of *Maxima*...

Thrust pods bounced the shuttle off the glide-rail, pushing it forward toward the shield. As they passed through there was the usual tingling sensation along exposed skin, and then the craft dropped alarmingly, moving out and away from the hull of the ship, curving slightly as it maneuvered toward the atmosphere below. Kyle caught sight of the underside of the docks; great gaps showed where there were empty berths, and further away, the hulls of other liners already docked surrounded by the constant coming and going of shuttles traveling between the platform and the world below.

Within minutes they were in open skies, blue on blue with an occasional white whisper of a cloud, the bright sunshine making the internal air vents work twice as hard to keep the compartment cool. Below he caught sight of the capital city, Salicia Sonora, and he felt a sense of déjà vu after having seen the exact same image in the ship's Galleria. There below him were the towers and minarets, the basilicas, the temples and the long colonnades... the sense of having already seen the sights was a strange one. He had never visited Petra, but his studies of the Jophrim religion were extensive; if it wasn't for his readings of the *Forbidden Works* translated from the Kyrillian archi-text he might never had made the connection to the artifact. He certainly wouldn't have traveled to the ancient Drillium mines on Merril and found the answer to a million prayers.

Merril was a strange world, an enigma and a nightmare of a place to visit. It was a planet so far off the space lanes as to be no more than a dot on an outdated star map. It was no place to stay for any length of time... but circumstances had forced him to live and work there for nine long months. The planet was an endless collection of slag heaps and disused ore processors, abandoned factories and poisoned lakes, and it had become one of the most grueling archaeological digs he had ever undertaken... *I almost died in those pits...*

He realized the shuttle had settled into an aerial queue, waiting for its turn to descend to the terminal below. Memories returned to the dig on Merril, the months spent confined with his team beneath the plassteel domes, the seemingly endless nights of arduous study that would lead them down one viable translation matrix only to come up against a historical dead end. Days later another pathway would open up and they would follow it relentlessly across dozens of ancient texts. Translation upon translation... the primitive Lucidator he had surreptitiously borrowed from the university could hardly keep up with the evocations, but they had gradually mapped out the data-links into individual epochs, defining specific eras, aligning core references with a thousand illustrations and diagrams, until finally one day they had found the connection... they had seen the almighty error made by the Petran cultists.

The Holy Prophet Jophrim was not born on Petra as the religion had espoused for tens of thousands of years, but was more likely to have come from the planet Merril... lost and virtually forgotten among the far off Pleiades Cluster. He still remembered the original passage, word for word:

"... *and so it was that Jophrim, Son of God, was sent forth to heal the stars beyond the furthest edge of his Father's realm, and there did he slay the Beast and break him down for all time with the Sword of his Father... and upon*

63

his return to his Seven Sisters did he bury his Sword so that no man may ever know its true power... and Jophrim spoke to his Father in Harevakor, saying: 'Father, I place thy Chalice in the deep, so that none but the chosen might find it... let it be so written...'"

Of course, Kyle realized that the *Sword* and the *Chalice of Creation* were almost certainly one and the same; different interpretations of the same original text, but by using Kyrillian archi-text it wasn't long before he was able to discover the location of the so-called *Sword*.

They had found the chamber buried three miles deep beneath the surface, sealed and forgotten for several millennia. It took a month just to break through the graphile seal, but once inside they had found the crystalline artifact, fused in amber, resting upon a pedestal in the center of the room. He would never forget those first few minutes after entering the inner vault, the dust scattering as they walked slowly into the darkness, their glow tubes casting shadows across the ancient walls. His team of five had fallen silent; there was a profound sense of being in the presence of something supremely sacred. He had never been a religious man, but at that moment he had felt close to divinity, enthralled by the nature of transcendent power. The glow tubes had reflected off the glasscite eyes of figures carved into the walls among the colored murals and the strange carvings of winged beasts perched high in the corners... it was quite literally the history of a forgotten race written in stone, a story of the fall of civilization and the rise of the Beast. Further around the chamber they had seen the coming of Jophrim rising on a cloud of golden fire stones and below, carved in plain graphile, the fall of the Beast. Sometimes late at night, when he was caught between a dream and wakefulness, he could still taste the dust in that chamber, still feel the terrible cold as he walked around the walls... still feel the unutterable horror when saw the drawings of the Beast... pure fantasy, of course, but the power behind those eyes still seemed formidable, even after so many years.

There was a rush of air as the shuttle began to drop down toward a glide-rail inside the terminal building. People were already standing, reaching for bags from the overhead rails. He decided to remain seated until they were cleared out... he was in no rush, his only intention being to visit the great Basilica in Jophrim Square, and perhaps wander among the lesser temples later, returning to the ship by nightfall. He took out his ID tag and joined one of the queues in front of the Planetary Inspection desks. Behind him his guard duly followed in his wake.

Dolmon Tendra had purchased a bag of local coins; it was the custom to drop one into each of the fountains along the central Concordia: by so doing you would receive a specific blessing from the saint whose statue looked down from above the water spout. The text of the blessing was carved onto a scroll on the pedestal beneath the fountain. It amused him that a Phaelon assassin should receive blessings in such a manner, but, as they say: *when in Petra...*

He moved among the market traders, mixing with the off-world merchants in their multicolored robes and the street vendors trying to attract his attention, waving exotic birds in his direction... he wasn't sure if they were to be sold as pets or for food. He ignored the traders and moved on toward the terminal, making his way through a collection of money-changers barking out the latest exchange rates, *and they call this a religion?*

He stepped back into shade as a patrol of Predicants walked by... *what passed for local law around here...* He noticed the stun guns strapped beneath their cloaks... *plascite toys, primitive in the extreme...* But Petra was an ancient culture, and they would not have lasted this long without possessing a few secrets to deter troublemakers. He had no doubt that the stun guns were for show... there would definitely be a few high-tech gadgets secreted around these streets, so he would have to be very careful not to get noticed. In the skies above he saw a line of shuttles descending in ever-decreasing circles, and he quickly crossed the street, following the flash signs to the terminal entrance.

Ensign First Class Roj Devers wasn't really a security officer, but apparently he was the only one available, according to Section Chief Helman anyway. *Son of a Barg hates me...* Still, it wasn't really a difficult assignment, he was simply to follow the Professor wherever he went and report back to First Officer Doran if the man did anything remotely suspicious, which, as far as Devers knew, could mean just about anything.

Devers watched the Professor as he passed through Planetary Inspection. He flashed his own ship tags to the desk attendant and followed the man out onto the main concourse. The place was instantly overwhelming... the noise hit him like the backwash from a plasma vent. There were hundreds of shops and market stalls housed beneath a high vaulted ceiling of pure reflective glasscite. Religious iconography was everywhere – huge banners emblazoned with prayers and symbols of devotion hanging from long chains of graphile adorned the marbelite walls, and the entire complex was surrounded by rows of giant

65

statues looking on with an air of ancient solemnity. But the most overwhelming effect was the noise... the constant chatter of hundreds of voices was staggering... and most of them seemed intent on hawking their wares among the newly arrived tourists. *Mustn't lose him among this lot...*

For several minutes he lost sight of the Professor, and quickly began to force his way through the crowds, feeling panic beginning to rise inside. And then he caught sight of the man walking along an exit ramp behind a stall selling marbelite statues of the Prophet Jophrim. He made his way toward the ramp and followed the Professor outside and soon discovered that the city was just as busy and as tumultuous as the terminal building. In the extremely hot midday sun his uniform was quickly becoming a problem; he had no idea it would be so hot, so very busy, so totally chaotic. Picking up his pace, he got to within twenty yards of the Professor, and then decided to pull back a little as the man stopped to study the overhead street signs. And then he was off again, turning onto the main concourse and heading in the general direction of the central square.

Beyond the tall towers, and above the purple minarets, he could just make out the golden dome of the Basilica, *Basilica D'Jophrim, if I remember it right.* Now he was being caught up in the crowd, propelled forward in a sea of jostling bodies... out into the vast open space of the *Centria Jophrim*, with the huge statue of the prophet standing in the center of the square. Beyond, towering above it all, stood the great Basilica itself, its golden dome casting opalescent reflections across the colored glasscite windows of the surrounding temples. He started to force his way forward when he saw the Professor making his way toward the Basilica. He was beginning to wonder if the man would ever take a break, if only for a few minutes... anything to get out of the terrible heat.

Dolmon Tendra was closing in on his prey. He had already noted the presence of the young ensign... *so they watch him, too... no matter; if you don't get in my way I won't get in yours...* The crowds could be a problem, though, but perhaps also an advantage... the needle slug was small enough to fit into the palm of a hand... one slight touch and the target would go down... silently and instantly dead. He moved forward, skirting along the outer edge of the square, passing the colonnades that surrounded the pedestrian precinct. There was a Predicant guard standing at the base of the Basilica steps, and he watched as the target passed them by, moving on up toward the massive open doors of the building.

Too late to take him down outside, far too many ways things could go wrong... but once inside the Basilica, things would be different... there would be no guards in there, that would be contrary to doctrinal custom... and once more the anonymity of the crowds milling among the statues and altars would allow him easy access to the target. He crossed the *Centria* and started up the steps, surrounded once again by penitents and advocates and always the hundreds of off-world tourists getting in his way

Brother Domini Thendosh had made his way from the *Temple of A'Thram* to the *Centria Jophrim*. He had previously hacked into Professor Raines' datapad and could now track his bio-signs easily... *he's heading into the Basilica...* His hands were wet with perspiration, and the old codex seemed to be getting heavier by the minute, and of course his robes did not allow for speed... but it was vital to catch up with the Professor... he had no idea if there were other forces at work on Petra. So far the only opposition he had come up against was from the old guard of the Episcopate; staunch and immovable, they would not even consider his research. *What did they call it? Doctrinal suicide... fools the lot of them; having faith is all well and good, but turning a blind eye to the truth... isn't that just plain suicidal?*

Ensign Devers followed the Professor into the interior of the Basilica; he was met with a cool breeze coming from the air vents and it was a welcome respite from the unremitting heat outside. He saw hundreds of people milling around the vast interior, many of them kneeling on ceremonial prayer mats scattered across the marbelite floors. The Professor was walking past alcoves where candles burned brightly above glasscite basins glistening with holy water, and as he moved to follow he became aware of an all-pervading smell of incense and burning oils. He saw groups of priests huddled around altars chanting in unison, and among them there were tourists taking flash-vids without any regard to religious etiquette; and there, directly in front of him, was the Professor, looking up at the high domed ceiling with its beautiful frescos and multicolored murals.

Brother Domini Thendosh saw the Professor, and decided that now was as good a time as any to introduce himself... to try to explain to him everything he had discovered about the artifact and offer him his allegiance in his quest. Surely he would not refuse his help, not with the stakes so very high. He moved forward, pushing his way through a group of penitents, edging slowly toward where the Professor was standing admiring the dome above.

67

Dolmon Tendra was less than twenty paces behind his target. He edged to one side to see beyond the young ensign, and slowly took the needle slug from its pouch, palming it carefully, index finger pressing lightly upon the trigger pad. He locked the echo pointer at the base of the target's head, and fired.

Brother Domini Thendosh was pushed by a group of young advocates into the back of a young ship's officer. He was about to apologize when the young man suddenly collapsed into his arms, blood slipping from his mouth. Instantly there was panic among the advocates... they could see the blood as Domini lowered the body to the floor. Someone screamed, and the crowd began to move en masse toward the exits. Domini looked at his left hand, covered now in blood. *Shot in the back of the head...* He had to move... *now!*

Looking around, he saw the Professor running along the chancel toward the High Altar at the far end of the transept. He carefully laid the young man's head down onto the floor, and then sped off after the Professor. From behind him came the sounds of panic, and from further away the sounds of Predicants shouting orders as they moved into the Basilica.

Dolmon Tendra cursed the fates for his misfortune, and cursed the stupid ensign for getting in the way. No choice now... he had to preserve the mission, return to the skipper and re-evaluate the possibilities of intercepting the target before the *Glasnost* left orbit. He merged with the fleeing crowds and allowed himself to be carried out and past the Predicant guards, the needle slug once more back in its pouch.

Domini finally caught up with the Professor two streets away in the *Arcadia Theron*; the tented shopping and entertainment district didn't quite fit with the accepted religious precepts of Petra, but it was highly profitable, and even bishops have to eat.

The Professor was trying his best to lose himself inside a large store selling ceremonial scarves, but it didn't take Domini long to corner him behind a set of free-standing mirrors.

"Wait, Professor. Please, I mean you no harm. I wasn't the one who shot that poor man... I think we both know that you were the intended target... I was just trying to meet you, to introduce myself; I believe I can help you..."

Kyle looked at the young man, dressed in the daywear of a priest, but lacking the ceremonial tags that identified his particular seminary or devotional college. He had no idea if he could trust the man. *But if he can get me away from here…*

"So, quickly, tell me who you are and how you know me…"

"I am Brother Domini Thendosh, formerly of the Sacred Heart Devotional Seminary. I have been studying the ancient texts for some time now, and I know what is coming, Professor, as I suspect you do, too…" He passed him the codex. "Here… it's all in here."

Kyle saw that the title had long since faded from its cover, but turning to the first page he immediately recognized the Worship Glyph of Saemal… the same one he had seen carved into the walls of the chamber on Merril. He looked up at the young priest, seeing a shared recognition in his eyes.

"You know of Saemal?"

Domini moved forward and Kyle stepped back into the shadows.

"I know of the Beast newly risen from out of the Rim. I know that even now its agents are among us… evidenced by the murder in the Basilica. I know that unless we do something, the Beast will once more walk among the stars and whole civilizations will fall…" He leaned closer. "As they fell once before, Professor…"

Kyle considered this. "And tell me, young priest… how do you think I'm involved in all of this?"

"Why, Professor… I know what it is you carry."

Kyle's mind was racing. *How could this young zealot know so much? How had he found out about the artifact?*

"Professor, we can discuss trust and strategy later, but right now it is no longer safe here, I can take you somewhere safe where we can talk. Please, come…"

"Look, it's possible that you know something of my mission, but if you think that means I can trust you then you are very much mistaken."

"Professor, right now, in this place, on this world, I am truly the only person you can trust… so you can either come with me now or stay here and wait to be killed…"

Kyle studied the eager young face before him, saw only honesty and dedication there… *but the risk!* And yet he was now a stranger in a strange land, and apparently surrounded by assassins, and facing the very real possibility that he might not make it back to the ship. *This young man might well be my saving grace. It might be worth taking the risk… if I should fall, then perhaps this one*

69

might yet save the day… I need to find a secure uplink, contact Lorn, and let him know the situation.

"Very well, it seems under the circumstances I have no choice but to trust you… please, lead the way."

Domini took a quick look around and gestured for the Professor to follow him out through a side exit into the street beyond.

Chapter 12 - Subspace Serenades

Sitting enthroned within walls,
a billion stars casting nets of creation beyond
the skies streaming rain storms
and rainbows waiting for colors
created by God's right hand.

The forever song whispers with the
wind waiting to watch light cascade
into night, shadows shifting into
sight and sound and the soft pause
of revelation restored once more to glory.

The terminal translation of infinity
defines the froth and the foam
of constellations swirling into
semblance as life arrives without
a moment's hesitation.

Lothar Theron: Personal Poetics.

Shari didn't remember much of the first few days aboard the *Shaendar*, the Saepid ship now cruising through subspace at the edge of an ionic pulse. She spent most of her time in her 'quarters,' which was really no more than a corner of the main control deck, but it had its own tree, and she'd secured the webbing restraints to the branches, making a kind of hammock. She was past marveling at the interior of the strange ship. After a while the sounds of the wind and rain became second nature; the bugs continued to annoy her, though. She thought they were an infestation at first until she saw Anthra lashing out with his tongue to catch a few of them as they skitted on by, *food then...* She was crying less now, only at 'night' when the deck went quiet and all she could hear was the soft pattering of rain, and from down below the gentle humming of Ventra as she snoozed among her branches... only then did the heartache return, and the thoughts of home and the terrible fears for her father and her friends threatened to overwhelm her. Anthra had offered her sedation, but she had slapped the med-pump from his hand, *one of his hands, anyway.* She was alternating

71

between hating the Saepids for involving her in such a nightmare and realizing that perhaps they had no choice; but right now she was back to hating them.

"Why the crell travel all the way to Petra? Just link to this man Raine, that's the name you found, right? Call him and tell him the artifact thingy is no good unless I use it..." *How easily I've accepted my role in all this...*"Tell him to come meet us; we can do that, can't we? At least tell him to wait for us; I mean if everything you've said is true and Primus is... Primus is..." *Could she really say it?* "If Primus is no longer safe, then maybe we should just let him know that... right? Doesn't that make more sense than just waiting until we get there? The man might not even be there when we get there..."

Saepid Anthra seemed to sigh heavily; it was hard to tell beneath his carapace. He gave his usual lopsided smile as he pushed a floater away and came to face her as she sat nestled in her tree.

"Dear child, *Glasnost* ship will still be there, they will have suspicions of Primus. We cannot risk a link to Petra... you must know that our journey now is most secret, to break our silence will lay us open to many ears; many eyes are looking for you right now, fleshings and machines... so far we have advantage, we have you. Beast concentrates on retrieving the artifact, but your blood line is on record, if your father is compromised..." He floated away from her, fully aware of the girl's temper and present bad mood.

"My father would not cause me any harm, he won't allow anyone to know about me, you don't have to worry about him being compromised; how the crell do I know you two aren't compromised? Tell me that!"

From below, Saepid Ventra floated up to face Shari; her eyes had their usual look of kindness and compassion.

"Dear fleshing, you know we are safe, and you know in your heart that your father... well, your father might already have fallen, and if not he is certainly wholly changed... you must know this to be true, you have seen the Net feeds, seen the faces of the ones who have succumbed to the Beast, there is no life in those eyes, no soul behind those words, no joy, no light... We are so sorry for you, little fleshing, you have not earned this burden, but you are not alone, we share your grief... but dear Anthra is right; he means you no ill when he tells you such truths."

How can I argue with that? She had seen the Net feeds, the detailed vids of the fallen worlds, shattered cities and poisoned seas, the fleets of ships moving toward the Hub worlds. So many souls lost out there... those faces looking so bright with a new-found love and dedication... but they had soulless eyes, and their words were spoken from scripts written by a machine. And so now they preached the glory of their new God Saemal... tens of thousands of them on their knees before that giant old man in his long gray robes... *Madness, absolute madness... and they think I can stop all of that? Madness...* She turned away from the other two and wrapped herself inside her webbing, watching as the leaves drifted past to the rhythm of an artificial breeze.

"Just leave me alone for a while, will you..."

The two Saepids drifted back down to the command pod below.

She dreamed of the Islands of Lanoir, far out in the Serira Ocean. They had only traveled there once as a family; she had just turned eleven and the vacation was a reward for not only successfully finishing First School with perfect grades, but she had also passed the Quorn Exam and had been accepted into the Delphi School of Advanced Mathematics at the university. Apparently she was a natural. Math had always come easy to her... but if she'd known the curriculum included a course in Ancient Galac, she might not have been so pleased to get into Delphi.

But she never regretted visiting the Islands; they were a wonder worth seeing, no matter why you had traveled there. *Walking between Momma and Father along Riza Beach front, the multicolored pleasure palisades with their rides and amusements, the cottage out at Old Sam Point... that stupid neighbor's dog howling every night... Momma and father staying up late talking in front of the fire-vid...listening to their whisperings in the night, the ocean rolling up and down the beach, and Sargulls screaming high overhead, wings and shadows passing in front of Summers Moon...*

Someone was pulling her away from the beach... rough hands... claw-like... cold... clucking and clicking in the forest... a swirl of leaves... and she was awake...

Anthra was there, trying to get her attention.

"What? What is it?"

"Sorrys to disturb your restings, child, but we arrive at Petra within three hours, must prepare, must be ready, things to do now, important things, yes. Okay?"

She rubbed her eyes, took a slp from a water tube and stared back at the Saepid.

"All right. Just give me a minute, will you." He floated there, waiting.

"Look, just go away, I need to use the bathroom." They were beginning to get used to her archaic use of colloquialisms, putting it down to her human nature. Anthra apologized and floated away toward the command console.

Shari edged around toward the sanitation unit, pulled open the dispensary tube and wriggled into position. The Saepids had obviously retrofitted the unit, along with all the other little human additions to their ship, which was all very well, but the space they had allocated was hardly enough for your average human to maneuver with any level of comfort. When she had finished she drifted over to the vibro-shower – another addition – which was screwed tight against a rear bulkhead. It wasn't perfect, but after being confined for seven days inside a floating forest with countless bugs and two very smelly Saepids it was truly a blessing. She grabbed a fresh set of shorts and a top from her 'luggage,' which was no more than a mesh bag full of clothes the Saepids had somehow managed to gather together from the Stars only knew where. Anthra was floating toward her, looking like he was about to start talking again. She just glared at him…

"In a minute!" She opened the shower door and pulled it closed behind her, leaving him drifting, looking as worried as he did the first time she saw him back in her prison cell.

The shower was a tingling of energy running over her skin, a soft caress of warm heat rippling with forest flowers, subtle scents and fragrances… in some ways it was better than water; certainly the only real way to shower aboard such a ship. She'd heard the big space liners had real water showers… full agrav allowed that of course… *and swimming pools, and saunas, and tennis courts, and theatres… what she wouldn't give to be on a deep space liner right now…* Looking down at her nakedness she couldn't help but wonder if any man would ever get to see her quite like this… *now that is a nice thought…* She flicked the shower off, wrapped a fabric sheet around her and then dressed slowly, enjoying the afterglow of the shower… *let him wait; I'll save the universe when I'm good and ready…*

On the command deck Anthra was busy studying various floater screens, while below in the command pod Ventra appeared to be plotting course corrections on a spatial-grid screen.

Anthra saw her drifting down from the shower cubicle. "Ah, child… you are clean now, yes?"

She looked at him hard. "Yes. I am clean now. What did you want?"

"We have moved *Shaendar* into main Hub commerce lanes, see?" She looked up at the dome above... *Stars! They had already come out of subspace...*

"Okay, so now what? What's the plan?"

"Well, child—"

"Hold it, you can forget the child business... my name is Shari, or Miss S'Atwa if you like, but not certainly not child, okay?"

"Apologies, chi— Shari..."

"Well, that's okay. You were saying...?"

"Yes, I was saying... we are unfortunately very visible now, but works both ways, we have linked into *Glasnost* database..."

"The ship Raine is traveling on?"

"Yes, ship that carries the man Raine, berthed now at Petra docks, you see here..." He pulled down a floater to show Shari; a stream of passengers' names flowed across the screen, followed by numbers and what looked like times.

"This here, Shari, is list of allocation tags, ID permits for passengers to visit planet Petra; *Glasnost* has two days here... and see this name here: Raine, K. C4214. He is on planet now, Shari. There we must go to find him... retrieving the artifact is our goal."

"And how are we supposed to find him? I mean, that looks like a pretty big planet to me."

"Normally not possible to do so, but now we have you."

She looked puzzled. "Me? What do you mean you have me?" *If they throw one more surprise at me I swear...*

"Forgive me, Shari, but I am reminding you... you are *custodia*..."

She was beginning to find the Saepids' reverence for that word disconcerting, and not a little annoying. Even after listening to their archives for hours on end, she still wasn't sure what that word actually meant, never mind how it applied to her.

"Okay, so how will me being this *custodia* help?"

From below, Ventra gave a low whistling sound. Shari had quickly realized that when Ventra did that it was a sign to tell Anthra to be patient with her, especially when he was trying to explain her unique role in their quest. He seemed to take the hint.

"Well, you see, Shari, *custodia* is connected to artifact. Archives say that the First Ones combined sacred double helix into genetic engram; this was ingrained in crystalline structure, creating a pure genetic marker. We theorize that transcendence was used to imbue the artifact with certain properties, much unknown to us these days... some might say *magics* were used. Mysterious connections were forged to the chosen *custodia*... they have blood link to the magics inside. You have the link, dear Shari, you can feel the amber from far away, you can know its structure, sense its power. All we have to do is get you to Petra, and with glad tidings we might find this man Raine."

She thought about that for a minute. *Links to the power?* She had so many doubts, but the Saepids seemed to have confidence in her abilities, even if she didn't...

"What makes you think this man will just hand over the artifact thing? I mean, we could be working for the Beast."

Anthra gave a carapace shrug. "He might distrust us, yes, it is possible, but we will convince him... we have no choice."

Now she sighed. "All right then, let's get on with it. When do we reach Petra?"

Ventra shouted up from below: "We are approaching docks now. I've asked for parking privileges, they might have questioned our origins, but many tourists here on Petra; I think we'll get by unnoticed and unwatched."

Shari floated up to the viewing dome and caught sight of the huge plassteel wall of the Petran orbital docks. As the *Shaendar* rose higher she could see gangs of loading drones moving like giant crabs along the hulls of docked starships, and further away, where the distant sun was casting prismatic rainbows off the graphile antenna arrays, she could see a passenger liner, all windows and glass domed galleries... *the Glasnost?* They drifted closer toward a designated docking bay as Ventra adjusted the lateral thruster array. Looking up, she saw a line of ships already cradled in their berths, and beyond the support pylons there were groups of small pleasure yachts and slow-moving dredges drifting among the towers and tactile sensory cables of the inner harbor.

The place was certainly busy... what little she knew of Petra came from her Religious Studies class during First School... she knew next to nothing of the Jophrim religion, her father had always discouraged religious tendencies, and for once she had agreed with him... she saw no place for gods and saints in the real world; certainly not as far as science and mathematics were concerned.

She reached for a flow-screen, tapped into the *Glasnost* database. The Saepids really were breaking every rule in the book, such hacking was totally illegal, *but I suppose the need outweighs the means...* She was reading the ship's log when she came across something that started alarm bells ringing in her head.

76

"Anthra! Have you seen this?" The Saepid was busy with the docking procedures as he looked up at Shari... all four arms continuing to manipulate the main control screens.

"Yes, child, what is... apologies... Shari... what is wrong?"

"Look..." She pushed the floater in his direction, and he nimbly caught it with a free hand. He looked at the tagged log entry, studied the details of the attempted sabotage aboard the *Glasnost*.

"This is very grave, yes, very bad tidings, we must be wary now, careful not to be noticed."

"But was this the enemy? Was this the Beast from the Rim?"

He looked back at the screen, tapped into the autopsy report and the reports of the onboard Forensics team.

"Not likely, Shari, no. All signs are that the darkness has yet to reach this far into the Core worlds. It is more likely that this Phaelon is an ally of the Beast, or at least a wishful-thinking ally, seeking to suborn favor from the Beast in prelude to his arrival in this sector. Phaelon's are known Non-Conformists, haters of all things Coalition, if they have access to ancient text... and there is no reason to think they have not... then they too must know of the Power. By killing the human Raine they think to please the Beast and perhaps avoid enslavement... crafty creatures are the Phaelon race... darkly devious they are."

Ventra shouted up from below: "Nasty, too... wicked tricky are the Phaelon agents."

Anthra agreed. "Yes, we must tread carefully now. If there is one Phaelon there is always more, most likely close behind the human Raine."

Shari looked at the incident report again. "Do you think the Phaelon's know about the artifact?"

Anthra gave one of his almost imperceptible shrugs. "Possibly... but maybe not, very hard to tell. They must have hacked the human Raine by now... gleaned secrets from his datapad; but makes no sense to destroy ship; artifact might have been lost forever. Beast most desperate to have it back, to keep it safe in its Cortex... Phaelon's seem to have wrong end of stick..."

Shari laughed at that... such an ancient saying, and sounding so odd coming from the alien mouth of a Sacpid.

"So maybe they just think the Beast wants Raine dead, maybe that's all they managed to pick up from the Net?"

"Certainly more likely, Shari. Beast be very mad if Phaelon's succeed in destroying artifact, wouldn't want to be them if that happened..."

"I don't understand... wouldn't this Beast want the artifact destroyed if it can defeat him?"

"Yes, but Shari, Beast walks fine line right now... with the artifact fused to its core matrix its power will grow beyond all measure, and no life in any place will be free of its dark touch... but even so, Beast knows the artifact can kill it as well. Like I say, very fine line."

"I got the impression the artifact was some kind of key, something the First Race left behind to keep their monster child locked up."

"True enough... sacred Jophrim used it to seal the Beast in his lair... but Othrum texts state that he could not totally destroy Beast."

"But you said he was *custodia*, like me; are you saying that all I can do is lock this Beast away for another million years until it's ready to break out and start killing all over again?"

"Not really, Shari, no. You see, we believe you are the last of your kind, a special gift from the First Ones... it is our hope that you alone can finally destroy the Beast."

She thought about that. "Well, you know there's nothing like a little pressure to make a girl feel special..."

"We are so sorry for your burden, Shari."

She tried to smile. "I know... so we have to find this Professor Raine... let's just get on with it, where do we go next?"

Anthra looked at the echo-point locators; they were being pulled slowly into a berth, riding the guide beams past the outer harbor walls, finally coming to a rest inside the docking clamps of their own berth.

"Next, dear Shari, we shuttle down to the planet... and you find the human Raine."

Just like that, I find the human Raine. Sounds so easy when you say it out loud...

It was late afternoon by the time they arrived at the ruins behind the *Temple of Lucius*. Domini remembered that Lucius himself had also been accused of being a heretic for daring to question the doctrinal dogma of his time... but the years had long since forgiven that saint... *there might be hope for me yet.* The Professor was out of breath, sitting with his head in his hands on the stump of a fallen column. It was still very warm out, but the shade afforded by the ruins was a welcome respite.

"Are you all right, Professor?"

"What? Oh, yes, I'm fine, just a little tired, that's all… I'm just not used to having people try to kill me." He looked up at Domini, shading his eyes with one hand.

"Look, I need to get to a secure uplink, there's someone I need to contact, let him know what's been happening."

"Of course; may I suggest we use the one at my former Seminary? It's not far from here and it will be safer than using a public booth."

"Yes, that's fine, let's just get going."

He tried to swat the swarms of flitter flies away from his face as they set off, but they seemed intent on following them out onto the main street. Domini led the way toward the Avenue of Limes, which ran parallel to the Concordia. They walked through several local souks and open-air kitchens, sometimes making significant detours to avoid coming out onto the Concordia where they might attract unwanted attention. Finally they emerged in the Piazza Domo, directly beneath the Seminary of Sacred Hearts, Domini's home for the last ten years of his young life.

He hadn't been inside the Seminary for over a month, not since the Episcopal Inquisition into his so-called heretical investigations had banished him from the community and they had formally asked him to leave. But he still had his pass key, and if they hadn't yet canceled his access codes they could gain entry via the lower presbytery. The Episcopate hadn't condemned him outright as a criminal, but they'd certainly made him feel like one.

Climbing the steps toward the Outer Sanctum, they passed the obelisk dedicated to Tantalus on one side and the Sacristy gardens on the other. Domini stopped to let the Professor catch his breath.

Kyle turned around, surprised at how high they had climbed. From the top of the Seminary steps they could see clear across the city, all the way to the great Basilica in the main square. He still felt the shock of that futile death… *that young life so easily taken…* From somewhere beyond the walls came the sounds of flowing water, and for a few moments it restored his faith in life… *where there is water there is hope…* the words of Tantalus seemed to echo down the long years… *like whispers lost in the night…*

Domini caught the fragrance of the julipa flowers growing along the walls of the Sacristy gardens. They brought back so many wonderful memories of early-morning meditations sitting beneath the starburst fountains, watching the waterfalls cascading over the Purlion flowerbeds… and of course the magnificent views over the city… *will I ever know that kind of peace again?*

79

The Professor turned to look at him. "Well, are we going or not? Time is of the essence, you know."

"Forgive me, Professor, yes, please follow me, it's this way…"

They left the steps and entered a lower vestibule. Kyle noticed that the walls were made up of reflective marbelite tiles depicting scenes and text from the Book of Jophrim. Domini led the way down a long stone corridor toward a sealed doorway, its ribbed plassteel surface seeming out of place among the stone walls and statuary.

Domini hesitated for a moment, and then, holding his breath, he slid his pass key across the sensor panel… *by Jophrim, please open…* There was a few seconds delay as his heart began to race and then the door slid silently to one side. The relief was a welcome victory; he had no desire to explain his banishment to the Professor.

"This way, Professor. There is an uplink booth in the Monsignor's lounge; he shouldn't be there this time of day, busy with Vespers, so I doubt we'll be disturbed."

"Well let's hope not."

Domini led the way along another passage illuminated by several glow tubes fused to the ceiling. They walked past a series of cells, each one separated by an alcove containing a ceremonial prayer mat placed beneath a simulacrum from the Book of Jophrim. Kyle looked through the grille of one cell and saw a stone bunk and a lectern positioned beneath a dusty glow tube flickering among the shadows. It all seemed so very antiquated, and yet, as they made their way along the corridor, he could feel the almost imperceptible rippling of a static charge coming from an air equalization unit, probably ingrained in the ceiling… very high-tech for such an ancient place.

Domini came to a stop before an open doorway. "In here, Professor."

They entered a large room and Kyle was immediately struck by the level of comfort displayed compared to the cells they had just passed. There were several soft felore chairs in dharma oak with matching reading tables surrounded by plascite-ingrained bookshelves filled from floor to ceiling with tru-leather books and scrolls. Throughout the room there were dusty piles of triax parchments scattered among the tables and chairs, and there were piles of books left abandoned on several desk tops. The entire room was lit by a single large floater bulb hanging directly above a central table, dimmed now and casting shadows across the room. Kyle walked through a sea of dust motes swirling into rainbows cast from the sunlight seeping through a series of air vents set high in the walls. And despite the apparent high-tech air system, the place still smelled musty and felt airless, but this might well have been an olfactory illusion provided by the Seminary AI to imbue an atmosphere of reverence and so encourage meditative dedication to the One Faith.

"Over here, Professor…"

Kyle crossed the room and saw the uplink device fused between two large bookshelves. It seemed to be Hub standard, and if it wasn't locked out he should have no problem linking to the local Skysat system.

Domini moved to one side, and then returned to the door to keep watch for any unwelcome visitors. *To be caught here, now, would warrant a full investigation and they would surely call in the Predicants…*

Kyle linked his datapad to the uplink feeder, transferring his personal codes to the Skysat system, *not locked out, then…* There was a brief pause while the uplink scanned for the correct code sequence.

Domini called from the open doorway: "Won't that be traceable?"

"I have no doubt it will, but what choice do I have? I have to contact my associate, it's vital we amend our plans; and besides, we can be out of here as soon as I'm finished."

"Very well…"

Kyle watched the sequencer match the pre-loaded language paths, and then it linked directly to the Skysat communications platform. Mere seconds later the uplink leapt into the main Net feeds, streaming data partitions into both visual and audio parameters, and dropped out of real-time into the subspace ether of interstellar communication. Finally he input the data tag code for Lorn S'Atwa of Primus and waited for the connection to link to his datapad.

Domini put a finger to his lips and gestured for Kyle to move to one side out of direct view from the doorway… someone was coming down the corridor… *the Secretary?* But it was a young priest, probably on his way to Vespers, and he passed by without looking into the lounge. He signaled to Kyle that the coast was now clear.

At that instant, the face of Lorn S'Atwa appeared on the datapad screen and Kyle noticed that his old friend looked surprisingly less worried than he did the last time they had spoken.

"Lorn, thank the Stars, are you well? Have you news of Shari?"

Lorn S'Atwa smiled, his face seemed disconcertingly devoid of emotion, and when he spoke his words seemed contrived, overly deliberate, and somehow empty of real sentiment.

81

"Kyle, my dear friend, so good to hear from you at last. Where are you now?"

"What? Lorn, I was asking about Shari? Is she safe? Have you managed to find her?"

"My daughter is well, Kyle, she is safe. Do you have the artifact in your possession?"

Kyle was beginning to feel uncomfortable, fears gradually rising at the back of his mind.

"Look, Lorn, things are getting very tight here. There's been another attempt on my life. The artifact is safe... for now, but we must make other arrangements to get it to the Colony. I'm a marked man, Lorn. I doubt I'll even make it back to the ship."

Lorn S'Atwa looked away from the screen, spoke to someone off-audio, then returned to face gaze Kyle.

"You are on Petra..." A statement, not a question.

"Yes, we are on a two-day layover. But, as I said, I'm being followed; a man has already been killed, and even if I do get back to the ship, there's every chance that they'll just try to blow it up again..."

Lorn S'Atwa leaned forward, looking directly at Kyle, his eyes were like glass mirrors reflecting the data-stream as it flowed across the base of the screen.

"What is your exact location, Kyle?"

At that moment Domini dashed across the room and quickly broke the uplink. The face of Lorn S'Atwa faded from the datapad as the connection was terminated.

"What the crell are you doing?"

Domini pulled the Professor around to face him. "Don't you see? Don't you know?"

"Know what? Tell me, man!"

"Your friend, your trusted contact on Primus, has been suborned by the Beast; he is no more than a mouthpiece now. That wasn't your friend you were talking to Professor that was the enemy... that was the Beast himself..."

Kyle felt his legs give way and he fell back into a nearby chair, his hands beginning to tremble uncontrollably. The shock was profound, and hurt him far more than the previous attempts on his life.

Domini crouched down to face the Professor, placing one hand on his shoulder. "We have to get out of here, Professor! We have to leave... now!" He pulled him from the seat and propelled him out through the door, forcing him along the corridor and out toward the entrance. Once outside, they took a quick look around and started back down the steps toward the piazza below. They stopped once beneath a tall Yuma tree and Domini checked to see if they were being followed. *How long before the Beast or his agents arrive?*

They continued down toward the Avenue of Limes, and made their way into a nearby souk. Domini pulled the Professor into a small café, and found a vacant table next to a rear exit door, where they finally sat down to catch their breath.

Anthra said his mate would remain on board the *Shaendar*; she wanted to keep a constant tag on the Net feeds. The threats from out of the Rim were coming in thick and fast now, it was wise to scan the feeds for any news of the Beast. They already knew of the arrival of the enemy fleet off Primus, and of the apparent subjugation of the Legislature Assembly. There had been no mass destruction on Primus, no devastated cities following the pattern of assault among the Rim worlds – to all intents and purposes Primus was exactly how Shari had left it. The vid-feeds streamed from Egrain City showed people going about their normal daily routines, apparently untouched by any threat or danger. She had even linked to the online portal of the university AI and used the vidcams to scan the classrooms and corridors... everything seemed the same, normal, unchanged in any way. But then when she tried to link to the personal Net feeds of her friends she found them empty; there was no silly banter between classmates, no chatting about the latest holo-vid screening at the local multiplex, no indication that her friends were communicating with each other at all. And when she had linked to her best friend Simone, all she found was a blank portal, her site wiped clean of the many poems she loved to write. *Poor Simone, what has happened to you? Are you still alive in your mind?* It was all so wrong. The people were not the same any more; something had seeped into the lives of every citizen on Primus and emptied them of independence, removed their freedom of thought, and left them as mere appendages to a greater whole. *And what has become of Father? Is he, too, just a blank slate upon which some monster would write a new personality?*

Anthra was looking at her. "Anything from Primus, Shari?"

She looked at him, her voice touched with tears. "Nothing... they're gone, Anthra, they're still alive, but they're gone inside."

He touched a hand to her shoulder. "Come... we must go now."

She followed him through the outer air lock and took the ramp leading up to the main concourse. There were shuttles leaving for Petra every thirty minutes so they didn't expect to have to wait too long in the shuttle bay. She took one last look at the *Shaendar*, all wings and antenna nets, nestled in its berth, and then quickly caught up with Anthra.

They were going to travel to the capital city, Salicia Sonora. The passenger allocation tags from the *Glasnost* showed the capital as their main destination; if Kyle Raine was anywhere it was a safe bet that he was somewhere in the city. She still had no idea how she was expected to find the man, but the Saepids were adamant that she could do it… all she had to do was to concentrate on the artifact. The fact that she had no idea what the artifact looked like didn't seem to concern them. For that matter, they had no idea what it looked like either. There just weren't any actual descriptions of the artifact in the Othrum archives, nor in any of the ancient texts the Saepids had managed to study during their travels… the closest they ever came to a description of the thing was that it might be a sword… *Gods… a sword, couldn't get much more ancient than that…*

She had thought that Anthra might attract some attention once they were out among the crowds, but it seemed that even the strange-looking Saepids were nothing special. She saw plenty of humans passing through the docks, but there were also some very strange creatures indeed. To her left, as they passed through the shuttle bay doors she caught sight of something floating above the crowd. It looked like a giant bubble filled with pink mist, and as it passed by she caught a glimpse of something dark moving inside.

Anthra noticed her looking at the strange apparition. "That's the Coloquies, strange race indeed, good traders, though… come now, Shari, we board shuttle."

She followed him forward toward the open doors of a nearby shuttle pod. The heat from the glide-rail beneath the platform rose in undulating waves of pressure. They stepped inside, feeling an instant rush of cold air as the internal vents took control of the atmospherics. The crowd began to push them to the back of the shuttle and she was forced up against the back of a humanoid with long claws and a mouth full of razor-sharp teeth… *crell, this thing smells like a Dhromanian slime lizard.* Anthra must have sensed her discomfort, because he carefully edged around and pulled her next to a rear window, placing himself beside the creature with the teeth. She breathed a sigh of relief, but the feeling of claustrophobia was rising, and she couldn't wait for the shuttle to move off. She gripped the handrail as the grav-plates shuddered beneath her feet.

From somewhere outside a siren sounded briefly and the doors slid closed. The overhead glow tubes flickered momentarily and the flash signs told the passengers to hold the handrails and grips. The little craft rose gently from the glide-rail and moved slowly toward the shield wall. Shari felt the tingling along her arms as the craft passed through and dipped sharply down to fly under the docks. She felt her stomach tighten, and it was all she could do not to throw up over Anthra.

Chapter 13 - Sunrise over Tendrah

"... do not fear death, death for the Elaas is honor. Fear instead life without honor, for that is worse than death..."
Poron Metklon: Phaelon First Assassin to the Elaas Elite Corps.

Thirty-five thousand light years spinward off the galactic plane, almost at the edge of Coalition-dominated space, lay the twenty-two worlds of the Phaelon Confederacy. Not that many worlds by any galactic standard, but they were in fact only the core worlds of a greater sphere of influence, for the Confederacy had for centuries spread its power among the Hub worlds, and had ventured further out beyond the Coalition toward the very Rim itself.

The Phaelon race had originally been pirates, rabble-rousing buccaneers cruising the space lanes, attacking solitary vessels and often forming packs to seize and rob the occasional cargo fleet. Later they had become hired mercenaries to the rising dynasties of the inner Core worlds, and later still they would form small shock armies hired by the struggling empires of the newly created Hub Alliances. Much more recently, after the Coalition had become a unified force, when peaceful commerce among the Hub worlds had replaced warfare and subversive sedition, they had become outcasts, ostracized by the very races that had once been so willing to pay for their services. And so it was that the Elaas was formed, a corps of the very best that Phaelon military society could offer... Nav and Stat tacticians, spatial analysts, statistical data-readers, weapons masters, and above and beyond all others, the assassins... the primary agents of the Elaas Elite Corps.

One hundred years earlier, the Phaelon Confederate Council had met and created the First Doctrine of Phaelon, more of a charter than a law as such, but it had set out the precepts upon which all future Phaelon political motivations rested. The Confederacy would align themselves to the small cluster of worlds united under the banner of the Non-Conformist creed. They would instigate a series of measures aimed at bringing down the Coalition and by so doing destroy the unity of the entire Hub.

First Minister Torin Grenval was standing on the outer decking of his penthouse; below him the city of Tendrah stretched as far as the eye could see. It was a city of bright green plassteel, with ingrained turquoise tiles faceted against the convex spirals of the inner city districts. The old-style monorails were long dark tracks weaving among the curved towers of the Administration District and on toward the outer habitats. There was little of the high-tech gadgetry of the Coalition on Phaedra, capital world of the Phaelon Confederacy. But they still had their special wonders here and there on Phaedra, devices even the central Core worlds would envy... *it paid to have their hands in so many diverse pockets...*

He watched the sun rise over Tendrah; the city was truly a marvel first thing in the morning, and the pleasure might yet have remained had he not realized the time. His guest would be arriving soon. A meeting with Drondar Khan was like taking high tea with a serpent, the man was as slippery and as devious as they come, which suited his role well as Prime Leader of the Elaas Elite. He knew already that the meeting might prove difficult; Khan's assassins had twice failed to carry out their assignments. He had ordered Khan to his home to give the impression of cordiality; it wouldn't do to put the man on the defensive, which would have been the case had he been summoned to the Keep. *Best to keep this one on a short and mostly pleasant leash...* But the atmosphere inside the apparent serenity of his home might perhaps lull the man into complacency, and allow him to determine the true loyalty of the Prime Leader.

There had been some difficult questions to answer during the recent Council meeting; many doubts had been raised regarding the legitimacy of their current course of action. It had taken him longer than he had expected to convince certain members of the Council that given the current situation, there was no choice but to embrace his plan. They were now committed and, whether they liked it or not, they were bound to see it through to the end. He took a sip of Louna juice, an extravagant indulgence, but he was partial to many off-world delicacies. He glanced back into his bedroom; saw the Aluvian slave girl there, her dark naked body reflected in the overhead mirror tiles. She hadn't lasted as long as he had hoped, not really the best of the batch recently brought in from the slave markets on Lima, but she had helped pass a few idle hours. He scratched at his neck scales and touched the compad on the glasscite table next to him.

"Tanara, get up here and clean out my chambers... now!"

The voice of his house servant came online. "Yes, Lord, at once, I'll be right there."

"And bring Grogor with you, there's a body to burn."

"At once, Lord."

He watched as the sun crested the high city towers, flowing like a river of light along the Via Dezhra. There were early-morning flyers cruising among the tessellated spires of the Elaas Academy, dropping down every now and then to avoid the voltwires strung between the inner city pylons. They would be lower-echelon cadets making their way to the Assembly Hall in the center of the complex. Ordinary citizens were forbidden to use agrav suits, the costs of such units were a concession only to service within the Corps or the Council Assemblage; most people simply used the free-service monorail system… very few had their own ground cars. That brought a smile to his face… *Phaelon society is not the best example of social equality…*

He heard his servants cleaning the room behind him, checked the time and proceeded to his bathroom to shower and get ready for the meeting with Khan. Stepping around a large blood stain, he ordered Tanara to replace the carpet immediately.

Drondar Khan let the house AI take control of his skipper; the roof pad was a glow of radiating lights, flickering in concentric circles. The small craft banked gently to the left, leveled out and descended slowly to the roof below. There was a slight bounce in the air frame as the landing pad clamps locked onto the insect-like legs of the skipper. He took a few moments to review the reports from Petra, scanning his datapad, finding the tags he'd left earlier. The Dugras report and then the data-feeds from Dolmon Tendra… two failed missions, and one dead operative; it certainly didn't look good… there was every chance he would be dead sometime in the next half hour. The First Minister was not known for his patience, *but he must realize that I won't go down easily, and most certainly not alone.*

A servant met him in the upper vestibule and led him down a spiral staircase and out onto a wide veranda. He was immediately struck by the long rows of Gordenia flowers running along the top of a wide balustrade, and in the middle of the decking area covered by surrela vines was a large ornamental fountain in the form of a flying Draktar bird… not the sort of setting he would have expected from the austere First Minister.

Torin Grenval was standing with his back toward him. *He's either very trusting or he has a few spybots floating around here somewhere…*

"First Minister…"

Torin Grenval turned to face him, his face as stolid and as impassive as he remembered from their previous meeting a month earlier. "Ah, Drondar, I trust you had an uneventful journey?"

You know I did, you have spies watching my spies... "Yes, First Minister, the journey from Telaxa Prime was tedious, but as I stated in my report, I believe the connections made among the Vendhu people will prove advantageous in any future trade negotiations." *But we're not here to talk about trade negotiations, are we, First Minister?*

"Good, that's good. Would you care for tea? It's imported from the Lharn plantations... it's an acquired taste, but I think you'll like it."

So we follow the social graces; no matter...

"Thank you, yes, First Minister..."

"Please, Drondar, this is an informal meeting, you may address me by my given name."

This is getting more curious by the minute...

"Very well... Torin."

"So what do you think of my view, Drondar? Quite spectacular, is it not?"

He moved toward the balustrade and looked out over the city towers. He could just see the snow-covered peaks of the Morovian Mountain range overlooking the Saltair River basin, which was partly shrouded in early-morning mists.

"Yes, Sir, it is quite a view, you are most fortunate."

"Ah, yes, fortune, my dear Drondar, isn't that a fickle thing? And how easily lost, even by the slightest of mistakes..."

Here it comes...

"Sir... you have studied the reports from Petra?"

"Of course I have studied the reports; that is why I felt it might serve us better if we met here... prior to my presenting the facts to the High Council."

"I see... do you wish to discuss the current situation on Petra? I have the status reports with me."

"Well, Drondar, although our little debacle on Petra is of some importance, it has to be taken in the context of the overall equation. There are other matters that need to be brought out into the open. The situation at the Rim for one."

Is there another agenda beneath the surface here? "Are you referring to the envoys sent to meet the new Power?"

"Yes, indeed... the envoys... thirty ships gone these last six months and now only one returns; and that one has been making some rather peculiar requests."

He knows I already know all of this, and yet he has to dance around the facts like a buzz fly in heat...

"I have read the feeds from the ship... Torin."

"Of course you have... and tell me, Drondar, do you have an opinion on the matter?"

He's fishing... wondering where my loyalties lie?

"My opinion, as always, must be in line with my prime directive... the security of the Confederacy takes precedence over all other concerns."

"Indeed... a textbook response... Biscuits?"

"No thank you, I'm fine with the tea. *Games within games... and if you've poisoned me you won't live to regret it...*

"You know, Drondar, within the Coalition, there are certain... forces, including those we seek to remove from our sphere of influence, who consider this new Power to be some form of Beast, a monster if you will... and as quaint as that may sound, I wonder if we should put any credence in such beliefs."

"They are many superstitions rampant among the Core worlds, and as many races who base their lives upon them, and despite being a realist myself, I suspect that where there are stories of monsters, there are also hidden truths."

"Indeed, I suppose, given the historical antiquity of the clues you yourself have revealed in your latest reports, there may well be some basis in believing that the new Power is more than it first appears to be. But in my own way, Drondar, I too lean toward pragmatism. In your first report to the Council you detailed your suspicions that the Power may in fact be a machine, of ancient origin but now transcended to full sentience. In light of the failures at Petra, have you altered your opinions in any way?"

Now he's getting down to it...

"My original statements stand, First Minister. At its core there is every indication that the new Power was once an autonomous device... a machine if you will; however, we suspect that at some point sentience occurred, and not recently... there are sources indicating that transcendence took place millions of years ago. Given the current situation along the Rim, it's not yet possible for us to verify the exact nature of the new Power. We do know he is worshipped as a god... we've all seen the vids from Samros... we also know that he has taken the name Saemal, and that he is currently very busy organizing some kind of religious jihad. But you have seen the vid-feeds yourself; the Net is full of endless speculations as to the veracity of the data-feeds. But, Sir... if only some of the pictures getting through are accurate..."

The First Minister turned away to look out over the city once more. "Then, Drondar, we might well have bitten off more than we can swallow."

"Possibly, Sir, but the situation is fluid. Our intelligence as to the importance of this Professor Raine is still accurate; this human is still a legitimate target..."

The First Minister spun round to face the Elaas Prime Leader. "But why is he a target, Drondar? Why did your intelligence division isolate this one human for our interest?"

He knows all of this... why is he trying to rattle my scales?

"Sir, as detailed in my report to the High Council, this human is thought to be carrying a weapon that might possibly harm the new Power... the removal of this man proves our worth and may be advantageous in any future negotiations with the new Power. Right now, this... Saemal... has great physical influence among the Rim worlds; his forces of occupation have already conquered the Cordwainer Alliance. But further in toward the Hub, it is more likely that he will use deception and subterfuge to achieve his aims... the reach from the Rim to the Core is a long one... it seems inevitable that even a Power as great as this one must eventually need allies."

"Ah, yes, and that's the crux of the matter, isn't it? Are we of the Phaelon Confederacy the kind of allies such a Power might seek?"

"Isn't that why we sent the envoy ships?" *Get to the point, for Drak sake...*

"Of course, and now this one returning ship requests that we take possession of an obscure artifact now in the possession of this human from Gamont. In light of that request, it seems fortuitous that your field operatives failed in their attempts to terminate their target."

"I have yet to receive an order to rescind the termination protocol, First Minister."

"I know that, Drondar. I issued the order myself; your operative on Petra has been told to seize the human... hopefully he will still possess the artifact."

He has countermanded my orders!

"Sir, that is not exactly procedural, given the nature of the Elaas..." *Let him see that threat for what it is...*

91

"I realize that, Drondar, and, believe me, it is not my intention to undermine your authority. You know that I have nothing but respect for your work, but the Council is the supreme authority, and alas, even I am subject to its protocols. Up until this moment we have had the luxury of time, the Power has been somewhat occupied along the Rim, but now we know of massive fleet movements, of a marshaling of forces in the Far Star Sector. It seemed expedient for us to make ourselves useful while we still had room to maneuver. But this one solitary ship returning to us has caused some measure of alarm among the Council members... they are beginning to fear that the Power has intentions not entirely favorable to the Confederacy. "

What was really being said here? "And do they now propose to hand over this human as some form of peace offering?"

"That would appear to be their intention, yes..."

But not yours? "And may I ask your intentions, Torin?"

The First Minister looked away again; the sun was above the high towers of the Assembly building now, reflecting off the mirror-domes of the Lower Chambers, green light cascading among the office blocks of the Administrative Quarter.

"My intention, my friend, is to seize this mysterious weapon and keep it for ourselves..." *Playing with fire to catch fire...*

"Without sanction?"

"The Council is afraid, Drondar. They are no longer the warriors of old; they prefer servile compliance to the old ways of the Confederacy... you can't tell me that sits well with you? Will the Elaas stand aside while our race is suborned by another?"

"The Elaas has never feared an enemy, First Minister, you know this. But are we not dealing with a Power that can destroy whole worlds?"

"Yes. I have no doubt that this creature is a powerful beast, a left-over relic from a bygone age, perhaps the last great mistake of the First Race... but that's precisely why we must protect ourselves. There is every indication from the Net feeds that the new Power will not hesitate to invade and to subjugate our Confederacy. Oh, I have seen the vids, I have heard the polite proclamations from those priests on Samros... they preach cooperation and a sharing of power, but we've seen the results of such cooperation on Primus... that race has been overwhelmed, Drondar, they are no longer real people, no longer independent of this new Power. That fate awaits us, Drondar, I can see that, and the Council can see that, even if they refuse to admit that they can see it. This returning vessel

92

promises our race a seat at the right hand of a god; I say it is no more than a fist in a gloved hand, and its intention is simply to buy time for the new Power to spread its physical presence across the rest of the galaxy. We have to use this brief respite, Drondar, take the initiative, if you will, make our move while the Power is still at a great distance. His fleets seem to have halted at Primus, the reasons for which I have yet to discern, but it gives us a vital opportunity. We must take this human Raine and secrete him somewhere beyond the reach of the Power. We must learn the true meaning of the weapon he carries, and we must be in a position to use that weapon when the time comes... and come it will, Drondar, you know this."

He turned and looked directly into the Elaas leader's face before continuing. "And believe me when I tell you, if we don't find something to stop this so-called Beast, I fear a time will come when our Confederacy will be no more than a distant memory."

"Your order to seize the human is already in effect. So do you have any specific orders for me?" *Finally we reach the conclusion...*

"The Elaas has a trans-phase deep space cruiser orbiting Fremont moon. I want you to use it to get to Petra; you may only have days to carry out your mission..."

"Which is?"

"Rendezvous with your operative there. Hopefully, he will have taken possession of the human before he has a chance to leave the planet. Once you have him I want you to take him to our colony at Grainsfeld, hold him there and await my arrival."

As Prime Leader of the Elaas Elite Corps, Drondar hadn't been on a long-range mission in over a year, but the stakes were extraordinarily high and if anyone could complete such a vital mission he could.

"I will do as you ask, First Minister..."

"Good. And now I must leave for the Assembly. My sources tell me that there are those on the High Council who propose we send an open invitation to the fleet at Primus, ask them to join us here on Phaedra. Can you believe such madness?" He swept past Drondar and disappeared inside the residence. Drondar was left alone, looking out over the city below. The peaceful scene belied the reality of their situation. *A storm is coming, one that will change the face of Phaedra forever... there might not be a way to avoid it, but if one were careful, one might still survive it...*

Chapter 14 - Rendezvous on Petra

"... Life shall not cease at the clouds' own border, but shall spread, unfettered by mortal restraint, out among the stars, there to seed the glory of His everlasting life..."
Brother Fiodore, First Ascetic Ministry of Petra (From the Book of Jophrim)

Shari was annoyed. Anthra had pushed and pulled her through the largest crowd she had ever seen. The terminal in Salicia Sonora was a place of madness. Everyone was shouting at everyone else, and the heat... *I'm going to die here, I just know it...* Someone thrust some type of bird into her face and she just slapped it away and watched as it flew off toward the distant ceiling, the vendor shouting something foreign in her direction. *Sorry, don't speak Petran...* Anthra grabbed her hand again, and she pulled away.

"I'm coming! Just slow down, will you!"

Anthra glanced back at her, clucked and clicked something to himself and continued to move toward the main exit. Finally they were outside and standing on the edge of a wide concourse. She saw a statue of a robed man fused to a wall on the opposite side of the street... he held a scroll in his outstretched arms in which was inscribed the word: *Concordia.*

"This way, Shari..." And Anthra led her across the street to the other side.

She pulled him to a standstill. "Look, will you stop rushing about! What's the plan? Where are we going?"

Anthra pulled her into the shade beneath the statue. "We must find some quiet place, yes, somewhere for you to contemplate the artifact, find a connection..."

Shari looked up and down the wide concourse, it wasn't easy to see much beyond the crowds... people were pushing and shoving constantly and she had to keep stepping aside to let them by... but on a nearby street corner she noticed a small temple set behind a large fountain. She pointed in its direction.

"How about in there? That has to be a quiet place, don't you think?"

Anthra tried to look over the heads of the crowds moving as a tide toward a vast open space beyond the Concordia.

"Yes, temple it seems to be, might find peace in there. Come, we must hurrys..."

94

She watched him scamper ahead and, with a heavy sigh, followed on as best she could in the sweltering heat.

They entered the *Temple of Sonora* by the side entrance, passing by several people who were kneeling, heads bowed, praying before a statue of a woman with a child in her arms.

Anthra came close and whispered to Shari: "*Sonora*, fabled Mother of Jophrim, local deity of Petran race…"

Shari looked into the woman's eyes and saw that they were inlaid with jewels, and she wondered at the sheer extravagance of such a religion. *Father would hate this…*

"Over here, Shari, quiet corner, we sit…" He led her to a stone bench placed between two large flower stands at the back of the temple. "We settle here for a while, you try to find the artifact… slow your breathing… you must concentrate, allow your mind to flow from this place, and out over the city, feel for the power, it will recognize you, and you will recognize it… okay?"

She looked at him. "Okay… just like that, eh?"

He leaned his head to one side and asked: "Have you started yet?"

She glared at him. "No, not yet… just shut up a minute, will you."

She looked at the statue of Sonora. *What choice do I have? I've come this far…* So she settled down on the bench, it was cold beneath her legs, but it was welcome after the unremitting heat outside. She tried to forget her worries, her terrible fears for her father, her friends and her entire world…

She was thinking about the stars, *just how many are there? Millions of worlds spinning, dancing like lights over water…* she thought about the rainbows of her childhood, *'Make a wish, Shari…' Momma had said. 'Why, Momma?' 'Because rainbows are full of hope…'* It took a long time to understand what that meant… no matter how bad the storm, a rainbow gives hope that better days are ahead… *and now there is such a storm coming… and she would give numbers to the colors and string them with gossamer threads from the trees, and allow the flowers to leave the soil behind so that wherever they walked their fragrance would fill the world… and the ocean would come flowing out of the night, creeping along the shores of memory, making little islands of perception where she would sit for hours making pictures out of raindrops drifting with words which whispered secret serenades and left her forever haunted by the sound of something moving beyond the mountains to the east. She was hanging from a cliff over a dark and turbulent sea, the wind was whipping her hair across her face, and from a distance she heard herself crying... she looked down and the sea had turned into a golden city, tall towers and minarets, great statues and mighty temples, and among it all tens of thousands of people, moving like waves over a rocky shore... She let go of the cliff, falling into flight, and sweeping up toward the sun, then swooping down low, cruising just above the heads of the people scurrying in a thousand different directions. She felt a sudden pain deep inside her chest, it was a throbbing sensation, and she found herself gasping for air... falling now, down, down toward a pile of ruins, broken columns and overturned fountains. The pain was getting worse, a burning and tearing deep inside... she felt herself screaming but she couldn't hear anything, and then she was standing among a pile of stones, rubble around her feet, and high above her head a scroll on a wall: Temple of Lucius...* she leaned over and was violently sick.

Anthra was in a state of near panic. He had two arms around Shari as she fell to her knees, sick and exhausted. He held her close until she stopped shaking and slowly began to regain her breath.

"So sorry, Shari, are you well? Hurt, maybe?"

She sat back on the bench, careful to avoid the mess on the floor at her feet. She wiped her hand across her mouth, tasted the foulness around her teeth, and finally managed to re-focus and remember where she was.

"Yes, yes, I'm okay now... I had no idea... it was so strange... and painful..." She rubbed her chest.

"Painful, yes, I saw."

She smiled a little at him." Yes well, it felt a lot worse than it looked."

"May I ask? Did you succeed at all?"

"Yes... I think I know where the thing is, I saw a temple... the *Temple of Lucius*; yes that's it, that's where they are, two men, and the artifact..."

Anthra looked concerned.

"Two men you say? Bad tidings that... but we'll see. Anthra has taken precautions for trouble if it should come..." She had seen him conceal some kind of tube inside his flight jacket; she had no idea what it was, but presumed it to be a weapon of some kind.

"We must go now, Shari, no time to waste..." He looked down at her vomit. "Mind that..."

She glared at him as he made his way back toward the doors. "I will... no need to tell me everything; it's not like I don't know what I'm doing."

On the way out she passed a young priest who had seen her throw up. She smiled weakly at him as she walked by. "Sorry about that. Too much sun, I think..." He simply smiled back, waving his left hand in polite salutation.

Once outside, Anthra pulled up a city map on his datapad.

"Far away beyond great Basilica is the temple... too far to walk... come..."

He pulled her out onto the main street; and she barely resisted slapping his hand away. She saw a small glide-cab settling in front of a large Galleria opposite. Anthra pulled her across the street.

"Quick, we catch a ride..." They reached the cab and hopped inside. Anthra spoke into the AI sensor pad. "Temple of Lucius, please." He flashed his ID tag across the pad and the vehicle rose on a cushion of air, turned sharply to the right, and proceeded to travel along a side street away from the Concordia. It felt good to be out of the crowds at last, and the views from the cab were spectacular. Shari could see the great Basilica D'Jophrim off in the distance, the golden dome glistening in the late-afternoon sunshine. The cab dipped slightly, flying over the multicolored rooftop gardens of the tourist district, the cab's sensor screen identifying the area as the Avenue of Limes.

Interlude near Primus

Plasmeld dreams above an ionic pulse... the pathways flowed... data-burst integrate, seamless coaxial terminating with Neiron Thane... floating above Primus... the neurons flow, synaptic conjugation becomes a sublime touch of a deep resonance data sum configuration floating along a cerebral river, tributaries branching off... he follows one such... leading to a golden world, a shining beacon of light in the night: Petra... the command came first: "Go there..." then the vision of the Worship Glyph, and the sacred word, Nimris...

Neiron Thane sealed the data-stream, banked his Viper away from his Master's fleet, and, using the enhanced spatial feelers, slipped into subspace... the craft was a product of transcendent power, and instead of it taking more than twenty days to reach Petra, he would be there in just two days' time.

Chapter 15 - Temple of Lucius

'There were moonbeams dropping light into night,
and the frail fluttering of secret birds unseen;
recognition was a crescent perched at the edge of a constellation...
and silence was a memory left beneath a swath of stars...
Sunbeams fell weary and wondrous,
wishes wasted with rain and storm
cascading ceremonies of light caught my eye,
and I was the soil and the stone and the sky...'
Lothar Theron: *Personal Poetics.*

The glide-cab swept down toward the distant ruins; the sun, lower now, was a speckled haze casting shadows along the back streets of the city. Cruising just above the rooftops, Shari was glad to be high above the crowds; she'd had more than enough of the seemingly endless sea of religious zealots. Anthra was busy communicating with Ventra back on the *Shaendar*; apparently there had been a message burst from the *Glasnost* to all ship's passengers... the onward journey to Primus had been delayed by thirty hours... No reason was given, but supplementary information would be provided as it came in. Shari knew the reason, of course; Anthra had told her of the dark fleet in orbit about her homeworld, and she knew that if the *Glasnost* was to accept the friendly invitations from Primus, then the ship would fall into the same trap... she and all her passengers would be compromised by the new Power there. Anthra showed Shari the ship's message protocols... she looked away, her thoughts once more returning to the fate of her father.

There was a small chime from the cab as its landing gear slipped out from below and it dropped down gently upon a cushion of air, the little invector drive settling the vehicle on the ground directly in front of the *Temple of Lucius*. Immediately, Anthra pulled open the door and gestured for Shari to follow. He set off toward the ruins behind the temple. She noticed that one of his hands was already holding the tube device... *ready for whatever faced them around the corner...*

Kyle was exhausted; the young priest had brought them all the way back to the ruins. He was still in shock. Lorn taken over by the enemy? How could such a thing have happened? They were supposed to have months before the new

Power arrived anywhere near the outer Hub worlds. Local sabotage was expected, yes, subterfuge on a basic scale, poisoning of the Net feeds perhaps, but a physical fleet at Primus? He had scanned the available Net feeds after their mad dash from the Seminary; the news was bad. There were thousands of new Threads out there, wild speculations as to the nature and origin of the unknown fleet. The vast majority of Posts were frantic exhortations demanding some kind of response to the situation on Primus; many sites displayed a profound fear for the future of the Coalition. But alarmingly there were others who suggested that everything was normal at Primus, that all the crazy talk of an omnipresent power newly arrived at the borders of the Coalition was no more than fanciful speculation based solely on myth and legend. There had, after all, been no evidence of violence on Primus; there were no vid-feeds showing signs of destruction or mass deaths, no apparent damage to the cities or the orbiting platforms... all seemed well and peaceful on Primus. There was a feed showing the Legislative President of Primus giving a speech welcoming their visitors from the Rim worlds, extolling the virtues of mutual cooperation among the races newly incorporated into the Union of Saemal. He went on to inform his people that he had invited the military contingents now orbiting Primus to occupy the capital city of Egrain so that the people might participate in the Coalescency of Saemal.

Kyle sat back against a stone column... Primus has fallen... *have I truly failed, then?* He saw a tagged message flash from the *Glasnost*: 'Unavoidable departure delay. Please contact your ship Allocation Officer for further information.' *So, does my journey end here on Petra?*

Domini looked across at the Professor; the man looked beaten, tired and exhausted. *What can I say to him now? He has seen his friend taken by the Beast, an entire world swallowed up by the evil... what now for our great quest to quell the storm?*

Suddenly he heard movement nearby, chastised himself once again for not finding a weapon before meeting the Professor. He moved quickly over to the older man... his eyes were closed and he looked asleep, *but someone is coming!*

"Professor, Sir! We must move again, someone comes..." Fears of the assassin they had seen in the Basilica filled his head. *Has he found us again?*

Kyle opened his eyes, trying to focus. "What is it, man? What's wrong?"

"Sir, someone is coming, we have to get away from here."

They stood up, took a quick look around and realized they were surrounded by high walls... the only way out was past the temple, and someone was fast approaching from that direction. Domini took the Professor by the arm and forced him down behind a fallen column where they crouched together, watching and waiting for whoever was about to come around the corner of the temple.

From behind the furthest column came the strangest sight Domini had ever seen... a creature with four arms, with its back encased inside some kind of shell. It looked wet, or at least moist. It also wore some form of flight jacket with a cloak pinned over the top ...*a uniform?* It also held a metal tube of some kind in one of its strange-looking hands ...*a weapon? Has it seen us?* Domini was preparing to fight when someone else came around the corner... a young human girl, long dark hair, dressed in a dark jumpsuit; she seemed to be following the strange creature as they began to move among the ruins. *What can this mean?*

Kyle managed to get a glimpse of the two newcomers, pulled Domini close to whisper in his ear: "That's a Saepid, I believe, of the Othrum race. He's very far from home, very far indeed..."

"And the girl?"

Kyle looked over the top of the column again.

"No idea who she might be, or why a human would be traveling with a Saepid. They usually don't travel in the same circles."

"What should we do?"

"Well, we can't stay here all day, and let's be honest, they don't exactly look like assassins, do they?"

"But isn't that creature holding a weapon?"

Kyle looked again. "Possibly, but I think one of us should still reveal ourselves."

Domini looked at the Professor, sighed with a slight smile... "I'll do it; you just keep the artifact safe..."

Kyle smiled back. "Well, if you're sure..."

Domini stood up.

Anthra spun round as a man rose up from behind a fallen column. He quickly pulled Shari behind him, raising the tube in his hand. The man stepped out of the shadows with his hands raised in the air. Anthra had the sun in his eyes and couldn't quite see the man's face.

"Please don't shoot, I mean you no harm."

100

Anthra studied the man as he stepped out of the shadows, noting the dusty ceremonial tunic and trousers... *priest probably, maybe not a threat...* He gestured to the man to come forward, watching him closely.

"You are priest, yes?"

"Yes, I am a priest, of the Sacred Hearts, up there on the hill."

"Why you hide like this?"

"I'm sorry we... I mean, I thought you might be robbers..."

"No, not robbers, Saepid I am... you are not alone?" The man glanced back behind him. Someone was definitely crouching down there among the fallen columns. An older man stood up, walking out slowly into the sunlight.

Domini gestured toward the Professor. "He's with me, we're traveling together."

Anthra looked at the man, studied his face carefully, matching it instantly to the holo-vids he'd studied earlier.

"You are Professor Raine, no?"

The man suddenly looked alarmed, stepping back a few paces. "That depends on who you are and why you want to know."

"We have come to meet you, Professor. Here is my companion..." He took Shari's hand and brought her out from behind him. He whispered in her ear: "Tell him your name, he will recognize you and make meeting go easier for us."

Shari stepped forward, looking at the two men. She'd never seen Kyle Raine before, nor even heard her father mention him, but apparently he was her father's friend, and right now he was the closest thing to home she had come across in all the days since their flight from Primus.

"My name is Shari S'Atwa. My father is Lorn S'Atwa of the Primus Legislature, and we came here to find you, Professor."

The man stepped forward slowly, his face suddenly filled with relief. He quickly took Shari's hands in his, shaking them with a new-found joy.

"Oh, my dear child, it's wonderful to see you, to know that you are safe. I was so worried for you... when your father told me you had been seized I feared the worst."

Shari was busy trying to get her hands free, smiling at the man, feeling a little embarrassed at his display of affection. "I was kidnapped, but I was rescued by my friend here, Saepid Anthra."

The Professor stepped to one side and took hold of one of Anthra's arms and proceeded to shake it with just as much enthusiasm. Shari smiled at the

101

obvious discomfort on Anthra's face; she had discovered during their recent voyage that as a rule Saepids were very wary of being touched by so-called 'fleshings'. Ventra had apologized when she had told her that touching a fleshing gave her the creeps. That was the first and last time she had tried to hug a Saepid.

"I'm so very pleased to meet you, my friend, and so grateful to you for rescuing Shari here... but how did you find us?"

Anthra gave Shari one of his impatient looks; she just shrugged and gestured for him to explain.

"Well, very long story it is, but essentials are, we have tracked you since Tantra, listened in on your links to Shari's father. We know of the artifact, know of its origins, its purpose... but you are making many errors, we came to explain some truths to you."

Raine looked perplexed. "Errors?"

"Wait one moment, please..." Anthra pulled out his datapad, set it to bio-scan mode, triggered an alert interface and placed it on a nearby tree stump. "Must be careful, enemies everywhere, I scan for weapons signatures... safe here for a little while..." He gestured the others to sit on various stones and broken columns.

"Yes, main error is that you believe you can use artifact... you cannot use artifact, it is bound to specific genetic code, markers ingrained long ago for use only by certain type of human forms, DNA hybrids, yes, very special people... you are most definitely not one of these."

The Professor looked a little taken aback at that. "I'm not?"

"No, you see, the artifact is very powerful creation, a transcendent thing, a parting gift from the First Ones who walked the stars when all else was grains of sand, yes. The Beast was progeny of the first races... then the *it* became the *he* and assumed bio-mechanical sapience and spread his foulness among the younger peoples. Took very long time to put him back where he belonged. First Race left many clues, Jophrim found answers, found the artifact and with great fleet liberated the conquered worlds, pushing Beast back to outer Rim. Jophrim and Syrillian Anthos hailed as heroes; legend made one of them a god and one a saint... but basic story still true outside of myths and magics."

Domini began to feel very uncomfortable. Over the last few months he had begun to doubt his faith, doubt the Sacred Doctrine of Jophrim. All the awkward questions now seemed to coalesce into one inescapable conclusion: Jophrim was not the Son of God, not a god at all, but a man, like himself, sent

102

on a quest to save the galaxy from the domination of pure evil... *and am I not now on such a quest?*

Kyle looked across at Anthra, expecting him to continue. Shari was used to the Saepids long pauses; she had often thought they were finished talking, or had even fallen asleep, until they would suddenly start talking again from where they left off. But this time Anthra remained silent, obviously waiting for the Professor's reaction.

"Well, you're not telling me anything I haven't managed to discover for myself... I wouldn't have come this far if I didn't know a thing or two about this Beast from out of the Rim."

Anthra sighed. "Yes, I know you are wise in the knowledge of the ancients, you are Professor of histories; but you must understand... Jophrim was one who possessed genetic code... in Ancient Galac he was *custodia*; meaning one designed by the First Race. He alone among all his armies could stop the Beast through the power of the Chalice of Creation or the Sword of Jophrim... you know these names, correct?"

"Yes of course... legend and myth are often suborned by religion until the true facts are either lost or buried inside some long-forgotten text."

"Indeed. But Professor, unlike Jophrim, you are not *custodia*, you are just a man, only *custodia* can use the device to seal the Beast in his lair."

The Professor looked across at Domini, who shrugged, and then he turned toward Anthra and Shari.

"And I suppose you know where we can find such a person?"

Anthra smiled, looking back at Shari. "Why yes, Shari is *custodia*..."

Domini sat up straight, staring at the girl. *Was it possible? Did this girl have the sacred blood of Jophrim flowing through her veins?*

Kyle stood up slowly, walked toward Shari. "Shari, is this true?"

She looked up at him, sunlight in her eyes. "Apparently. I had no idea myself; I doubt my father did either. But Anthra has shown me the ancient Othrum texts, it's all in there, the whole genetic code thing, a long line of people who can use the device to fight the Beast; and as it turns out, I'm the latest one... kind of weird, huh?"

Kyle looked back at Anthra. "So was Shari's father one of these *custodia* as well?"

Anthra gave a slight smile. "No, indeed not... very not possible. One like Shari comes once every ten thousand years; very rare double helix involved, many strange factors combine to form the likes of Shari."

103

Shari gave him a hard look.

Kyle considered this. "I would very much like to read those texts sometime; I truly believed I had the full translation of the Jophrim texts."

Anthra looked up. "But you do accept that Shari is the *custodia*, yes?"

"Why yes, I believe you... but can you keep the artifact safe?"

"We will keep it safe..."

"Then of course you must take it. I suppose you will want to be leaving now?"

Anthra stood up, dusting down his jacket and cloak, desperately resisting flicking the flitter flies into his mouth with his tongue.

"Yes, we must be on our way, very long journey to Far Star Colony. Many dangers lie ahead." He looked at the temple and the street beyond. "Many dangers here, I think..."

Kyle looked at Domini, then back at Shari and Anthra. *Time to be a hero, I think...*

"Listen, I don't think it's a good idea if I come with you. I'm a marked man. Domini can tell you... they've tried to kill me twice, and I fear that even now they are not that far behind us. If we were to be seen together you could both get killed... I can't allow that to happen. No, you must take the artifact, Shari; destiny dictates that it belongs to you now... you must finish the journey I started. Hopefully, our enemies will still be concentrating their energies on me while you make your escape... I can lead them astray; keep them busy here on Petra for a while."

Shari protested. "But that's crazy, Professor... I'm sorry, but it is. You'll be safe with us, we have a ship, we can be back on board in a few hours and then we'll be on our way... Tell him, Anthra."

Anthra didn't speak. He looked at Shari then started to shuffle his feet on the ground.

"Anthra, tell him!" She was pleading now.

The Professor took Shari by her hands, looked into her face, and saw desperate tears welling up.

"My dear child, your friend here knows that it makes perfect sense for me to remain behind. All along I've wondered how I was going to use the artifact to destroy our enemy, I just had no idea. I suppose I hoped that if I did manage to reach the Colony something would occur to me, or the thing might just come to life in my hands. It was all guesswork, Shari, and an awful lot of hope. But now... now I know that you are part of a chosen lineage capable of using the device to destroy this Beast, it all makes perfect sense. You do see that, don't you, Shari?"

"But Professor..." She was feeling desperate now. *This is my father's friend!*

"It's all right, Shari. I can finally do some good; make a contribution to the greatest quest the galaxy has known since before the Interregnum. Let them follow me around Petra for a while... the longer they waste time looking for me, the greater your chance of getting away from here. Only the quest matters, Shari, nothing else... certainly not an old history professor like me. And, my dear girl... your father would want me to protect you, and this is the best way I can do that."

Shari felt the tears fall, her fists clenched. She was resigned to it; she had to accept that once again she would lose a connection to her home, to her father.

The Professor turned to Anthra. "I do have one request for you, though, and I hope you will not deny me..."

Anthra looked up. "Yes?"

"I want you to take Domini here with you; he's proved a worthy ally and I know he can be of use to you."

Domini came forward, surprised. "But Professor..."

Kyle turned toward him, placing a hand on Domini's shoulder. "It's all right, my friend, go with them. You know in your heart that your journey cannot be allowed to end here."

Domini wrapped his arms around the Professor, and they held each other for a brief moment. Finally, Domini stepped back and the Professor turned to face them.

"Now, I think it's best if I leave here first. I'll make my way back toward the Basilica; if someone is tracking me then it makes sense to keep them away from the terminal."

Anthra stepped forward. "You are brave man for a *fleshing*, Professor Raine."

"Why, thank you... but as Tantalus once said: dark times demand the justice of the brave." And then he reached into a jacket pocket and pulled out a small gray pouch. He held it out to Shari. "Here, Shari, here is the savior of worlds..."

She looked down as he slowly unwrapped the object. She saw a hexagonal tube of crystalline amber. It glistened as it caught the sunlight and she saw a scattering of minute metallic fronds encased within. She had expected

105

something a little more spectacular, and found it hard not to show her disappointment. *Not a sword, then...*

She reached out and took hold of the object. It felt ice cold and her hand trembled slightly. But after a few seconds her fingers began to feel warm, the skin tingling slightly, as if caressed by a cool summer breeze. She felt a cold chill run down her spine and her heart raced as she took a slow deep breath. She smiled.

Anthra was looking at her. "Shari, dear... are you okay?"

"It feels... familiar... like a memory..." The other three exchanged glances and the Professor started to fold the object back into its cloth, enclosing it once more in its pouch.

"Perhaps you'd better put it away for now, keep it hidden until you need it. We have no idea if the enemy can detect it."

Anthra agreed.

"Yes, Shari, we must make haste after Professor leaves."

Shari squeezed the Professor's hand as he turned to leave. He smiled back at her.

"Take care, my dear girl." He took a moment to look around the small group of new-found friends, and then without another word, turned away quietly, disappearing around the corner of the temple building.

Anthra started to follow. "Come, Shari, you too, priest, back to terminal we go, must hail cab."

Dolmon Tendra had returned to his skipper, sealed it tight against the unremitting heat and opened the coolant vents. He was listening to *Dhramez Fourth Concerto*, lost to the wonder of the music, when his subspace compad lit up. It was a flash message from his boss Drondar Khan: *'Take possession of target, remove to rendezvous at coord. 0119000/60007anti 02224000/506879polo... fixed data-feed. Confirm: Khan. Tendra .bi-code xxx2p3A.* He input his receipt code, took a look at the follow-up feeds, data Threads and his links to the local Net. The *Glasnost* wasn't going anywhere, which wasn't surprising; since the apparent fall of Primus, regular interstellar travel was becoming fragmented, to say the least.

How quickly the cards fall... I suppose now it is simply a matter of whether you are behind the cards or in front of them... He pulled up the bio-scan he'd taken of the human Raine... *almost had him, and now it seems fortuitous that the attempt failed... so they want the Barg alive, do they? Well, no matter, dead or alive, I know exactly where my prey is...* After the close encounter in the Basilica he had linked and tagged the Professor's datapad; all he had to do was scan the city, zero in on the pad, cross-match with the bio-scan, and he'd have his man. *Ah, and there he is...*

He initiated the thrust drive and the skipper rose silently into the upper airs. He kept the craft shielded, aware of prying eyes, and swung wide over the city streets, heading directly for the outer Temple Ring. He glanced at the data-feeds... the bio-scan was reducing gradually, narrowing the point of origin to a specific body mass, moving along a back street behind the Arcadus Plazia. Instantly the tagged feeds linked to the bio-readouts and he knew he had his target cornered. Bringing the skipper down onto a flat rooftop, he loaded the needle slug with an anesthesia dart and quickly jumped out. He found a plassteel flower trellis at the side of the building, and climbed down to the street below. One quick look at his datapad and he slipped into a narrow gap between two disused shop fronts.

Kyle was forced to slow down; walking along the back streets of Salicia Sonora was no easy task... he had to keep backtracking just to ensure he was heading away from the terminal. He kept coming upon dead-end streets or tented areas where the residents would shoo him off as he approached. But finally he seemed to be moving away from the crowds... now it would be a lot easier for him to know if he was being followed. So far it seemed he had managed to avoid his would-be assassins. He was just about to cross the street when he felt something sting his neck. Reaching up, he pulled out a small sliver of something sharp. It was blurry at the edges; the ground seemed to be moving beneath him... his legs felt so very heavy, the cobbles in the street came up to hit him hard in the face... *the warm taste of blood in his mouth...*

Tendra pulled the unconscious man into the shadows, left him there while he climbed back up to the roof. The skipper drifted down slowly into the street, he cut the drive and quickly half-carried the man into the rear compartment, sealed the door and initiated the flight AI. The coordinates for his rendezvous with Khan were displayed and the craft suddenly accelerated at full speed toward the sky, and the stars beyond.

Back at the terminal, Anthra was doing the push–pull thing again. Shari kept slapping his hands away as they moved slowly through the crowds. The shuttle bay did seem less busy this late in the day, but nevertheless it took them nearly an hour to board a shuttle, and another twenty minutes before it slid away from the platform and rose slowly into the skies above.

For Domini this was the adventure of a lifetime, he had never been off-world – there had been a class visit to the floating gardens of *Sierra Tenada*, but being five miles high wasn't really space travel. But this certainly was; this was true adventure. As the small craft breached the upper atmosphere he felt his feet drawn down to the grav-plates; there was a rush of air as the ventilation system adjusted to the pressure changes, and a sign ingrained in the glasscite doors flashed an atmospheric equalization warning. He felt his ears pop as the shuttle banked right and rose up suddenly toward a distant slab of darkness which he took to be the docks. He gripped the handrails tightly and closed his eyes for a moment as his stomach turned over. When he looked up he saw the young girl Shari watching him. He remembered the precious cargo she carried inside her jacket, and all the old fears came rushing back. He squeezed the grips as the craft entered the grav induction zone of the docks, riding the backwash ripples of ionic energy flowing from the agrav vents fused beneath the great structure. *Adventure or not, this could all go terribly wrong...*

Shari looked across at the young priest. She'd never met a priest before; there were no churches on Primus, no religion as such, a few weird cults here and there, but nothing organized, nothing run on the grand scale of the Petran religion. She wondered why such a young man would devote his life to nothing more than myth and legend... he must have his reasons; maybe he would wonder why she wanted to become a scientist... *wanted to become a scientist... can't see that dream ever coming true now, not with the whole galaxy going to war, and me stuck right in the middle of it all...* The idea of having to come face to face with their terrible enemy suddenly came to mind. *How the crell am I going to survive that?* She felt for the object in her pocket, let her fingers feel beneath the cloth; the gentle tingling came again, *the warm feeling, faraway memories whispering by on a sea of fire...*

"Shari!" It was Anthra, pulling her hand out of her pocket. She glared back at him.

"What? What's wrong now?"

He leaned close to avoid being overheard by the other passengers. "Mustn't touch artifact yet, Professor might be right, Beast might know. He might be casting his eyes in our direction."

She looked across at Domini, who just smiled back. She sat up straight, turned away from Anthra.

108

"Okay, I won't touch it."

The flash signs indicated the proximity to the docks, and she watched as a huge starship drifted by below them, *so close I could lean down and touch it...* There was a bump as the shuttle entered the docks' gravity well, and proceeded to fall in line behind a row of shuttles entering through the shield wall. She saw Anthra on his datapad, linking to the *Shaendar*. She hadn't thought she'd miss the ship, but she did... she missed her tree in her corner, missed the cozy sounds of wind and rain, the soft pounding of surf on sand late at night. And then she remembered the bugs and the smell and, looking at Domini, she wondered: *where the crell is he going to sleep?*

The shuttle finally settled onto a glide-rail and they were pulled closer toward the platform. The whole place looked just as busy as it did when they had first arrived, *was that just this morning?* She caught sight of a couple of the strange Coloquies creatures, floating away from a shuttle further along the platform. The disembarkation lights came on and the doors slid open. Anthra was about to take Shari's hand but he saw the look on her face and thought better of it.

"So, let us go, my friends, let us go home to ship." And off he trotted, Domini and Shari following on behind.

Ventra drifted down from the viewing dome, touched a floater for oxygenation readouts, and gave the venting system a twenty percent boost, and then dropped slowly down into the command pod. She was concerned that Anthra had agreed to take on a passenger. Shari was vital for the quest, a necessary disruption to their Saepid serenity, but this other? She was annoyed. Anthra had no right to break compliance; she would speak to him about it. *Where are they?* She glanced at the docking feeds, *ten more minutes and they would receive an overstay violation warning*, any longer than that and they risked full confiscation. She linked to Anthra's datapad; flashed the current time in bright red letters... she smiled as he flashed back a large exclamation mark.

Domini was surrounded by marvels. When he thought about the years he had spent in Seminary school, the long nights and days sitting alone in his cell in quiet contemplation of the mysteries of Jophrim... while the whole time all of this was going on above his world. If he hadn't already begun to doubt the veracity of his faith, the scenes he was now witnessing confirmed his doubts completely. His faith had held him in a self-imposed prison; his dedication to the seminal disciplines of religious doctrines had blinded him to the vast wonder that was life among the stars. When he saw the passing Coloquies he walked straight into a trash can, and the face of a young woman flashed and wavered momentarily, her words slurred by the impact: *'Thank yo... for d..positing..yo..ur...waste...'* Then the face winked out, and he stumbled forward.

Shari reached out and took his hand, smiling. "Watch out for the trash cans, Mr. Priest, they bite back…" She walked on ahead, and he walked faster to catch up to her.

"It's Domini…"

She turned to look at him. "Pardon?"

"Domini, that's my name. Domini Thendosh actually and I am no longer a priest."

She looked surprised. "You're not?"

He smiled, a little shame-faced. "No, they asked me to leave the Seminary about a month ago."

"Oh, why did they do that?"

"Long story short, we fell out over doctrinal differences."

"I'm sorry, but I don't know what that means."

"Well, they believed in one thing and I believed in another."

"Oh, and what do you believe in now, Domini Thendosh?"

He came level with her shoulders. "Well, I suppose I believe in you now," he said with a smile.

She looked at him once but said no more, forcing her way past the queues waiting at the Planetary Inspection desks.

They used an overcrowded drop-tube to take them down to the port itself. Shari felt Domini pressing up against her back, which sent strange new feelings along her arms and legs. The tube opened and they quickly made their way toward their own berth.

The *Shaendar* was straddled by worker drones; Ventra had decided to take advantage of the docks' upgrade shops and had contracted for a few deep space enhancements to the ionic-drive array. The pulse drive itself was already twenty years old when they had purchased the ship, but now with a new transphase inducer fused to the power core they could possibly make it to the Colony in less than forty days, half the previous estimates.

Chapter 16 - Assignment Petra

"What is duty? Duty is Elaas."
Lomar Fendor - Field Tutor, Elaas Elite Corps.

The AI gave a proximity alert and Drondar Khan scanned the data-feeds. The little dark skipper was approaching aft; echo points pinged in the dark confines of the command deck. He swung round to initiate the umbilical tube as the skipper crept closer, docking lights flashing in concentric circles. There was a distant thump from the rear cargo hold as the proximity readouts flashed red and were replaced by the status grid. The skipper was docked. He flicked a floater screen out of the way and touched the compad.

"Welcome, Dolmon, I take it all went well?" The holo-vid cast a face in the air in front of the command boards. His First Level Operative Dolmon Tendra looked fairly satisfied with himself... *we'll see about that*...

"Yes, Prime Leader, all went according to dictate... permission to come aboard, Sir?"

"Permission granted... can you manage your cargo?"

"Yes, Sir, I can use a grav-sled."

"Very well, secure him in the aft container shell. I'll meet you there."

"Very good, Sir."

Khan touched the drive assembly, engaged the trans-phase pulse and initiated a subspace jump. He watched the stars disappear before floating back toward the exit hatch, and the container shell beyond.

The container shell was a vast space, usually reserved for contraband... illicit goods transported to and from the Rim worlds, eager and desperate colonies seeking suppliers who might be willing to bend more than a few import–export rules. It sometimes surprised Drondar Khan how little the Confederacy had changed since its early pirate days.

The prisoner was lying on a grav-sled, his arms and legs clamped to the runners either side. Dolmon Tendra looked up as his superior entered the room.

"You've searched him. of course?"

"Yes, Sir, and taken a full internal bio-scan."

"By your lack of enthusiasm, Dolmon, do I take it you haven't found anything of interest?"

"I'm afraid not, Sir, no... only a standard datapad; his ship allocation tags, a credit ID card, a couple of temple info sheets, and that's all."

Drondar floated over to the man on the sled.

"Interesting…"

"You expected something more, Sir?"

Drondar forgave the breach in etiquette, floating around the table to look at the man's datapad.

"Wiped clean, I see…"

"Yes, Sir, he obviously suspected he might be taken."

"Indeed…"

Tendra stepped back as Khan studied the man's face for several minutes. Finally the Prime Leader moved back around to float next to him, his hand reaching for a guide rail.

"The drug is timed, of course?"

"He wakes in the next three minutes."

"I want a deep brain scan, get the psyonic gear from the lab… I want you to scrape him clean, harvest every thought, every feeling, and every memory, no matter how inconsequential. Am I clear?"

"Yes, Sir, very clear, I'll set up the equipment now."

Drondar Khan moved toward the forward hatch, turning once to look back at the man lying prone on the grav-sled.

"Oh, and if he dies in the process, make sure it's after you've taken everything I need and not before; you wouldn't want yet another error entered into your record, Dolmon." And then the door slid closed behind him.

Tendra looked at the sealed hatch knowing that he had never heard a death threat uttered so politely.

Constellations cascaded into translucent rivers....the pathways flowed... irresolute domination tore away at the neural net... transposition occurred at data com frequency phala alpha deon... terminal tributaries transposed cerebral hemopoiesis, and the Cortex leapt into the synaptic ocean...tides against a conscious shore... memories tied to a cliff face... worlds spinning in the void... the cosmic gift of creation... the froth of a great flowering beyond the stars... terminating with Neiron Thane... the river ceased to flow... data sum downloads sealed in a burst of pure kinetic energy....the pathways flowed...

Neiron Thane sealed the data-stream, fed the necessary data-feeds to the onboard AI, and initiated the jump back into real-time. Subspace vanished from the screens, to be replaced by a sea of stars. Proximity alarms sounded... a space liner cruising by off his port side; he veered the Viper away, banked sharply with rear thrusters, and cut the pulse drive to cruise. He matched velocity with the orbiting docks, cut in the shield, and shimmered into darkness. He created a floater screen of the docks' AI initiation system, tapped into its data-core, and scanned the registry of ships currently in port. His Master had issued new instructions; there was a new priority, a vital addition to the overall program.

He skimmed the lists of ships, found the *Glasnost*, and tapped the passenger list, found Professor Kyle Raine, slid to the passenger allocation lists, found the shuttle disembarkation data. The screen flowed down. He touched arrival times, cast an eye on the datapad transmission link to Raine's datapad, found the Predicant incident report in the *Basilica D'Jophrim*, and traced the local Forensics report, needle slug: *Phaelon design...* He linked to the exterior vidcams – there was a sophisticated surveillance net covering Salicia Sonora; hidden from public view, it was nevertheless accessible with the right equipment. His Master had extended the gift of quantum-level upgrades to the Viper, his antenna web could usurp the local Net, interlace with the entire network. Instantly he was connected to a thousand data-feeds, vidcam holo-images flowing across the screen. He narrowed the data-stream; scanned for pre-existing timed markers, looping the stored feeds into an hourly rewind, and found the man Raine outside the Basilica... running, another man in pursuit, *a priest...* he linked to a nearby souk cam and saw the men standing together. An alert shone from the communications pad, he scanned directly to the uplink... the man had connected to Primus... *from the Seminary...* then the two had

113

returned to the city, hiding somewhere beyond the Temple Ring. There was a sudden drop in data... *they went off Net... probably somewhere in the ruins beyond the Ring...* He scanned the temple furthest from the Concordia, the Temple of Lucius... *nothing!* He flashed forward, linked to a nearby Chem-Store, saw a glide-cab settle in the street in front of the temple. Two figures emerged... a Saepid and a human female. Suddenly... *the pathways flowed...* He leaned forward in the webbing, studied the new arrivals, watched as they disappeared behind the temple.

He flashed the feed forward again, watched as the man Raine came from behind the temple... saw him turn and begin to walk down the street back toward the city. Almost immediately three figures emerged from the shadows... the girl, the Saepid and a man, *the priest!* They hailed a glide-cab, and within minutes they were airborne. He linked to the cab's onboard AI... destination: the terminal. He flashed forward, linked to the terminal AI, found the three boarding a shuttle bound for the docks. He tracked the craft as it arrived inside the shuttle bay. He tried to force-link to the Saepids datapad, found it blocked; frustrated, he instigated a loop program, again blocked... *clever little creature, very clever indeed...*

So he re-scanned the docks' registry, found a ship that matched Saepid specifications... the *Shaendar! Got them...* He closed down the data-stream, linked to the real-time data-net, scanned for the ship... *gone!* He formulated a tracer program, linked it to the Net, let it loose among the star lanes... *I'll find them soon enough...* He returned to the Salicia Sonora surveillance Net, scanned for the human Kyle Raine, and found him walking along a series of narrow streets behind an abandoned shopping arcade. There was an alert signal. He instigated a recognition protocol, narrowed the feeder points to a new addition... a craft of some kind, fully shielded, arriving upon a nearby rooftop... *Ah, now, what do we have here?* He watched as an individual climbed down the side of the building, *exterior keratinized scales... Phaelon!* The creature was armed, *needle slug...* He panned wide, saw Kyle Raine enter the street... *ambush!* The human didn't know what hit him; it all happened with fluid motion, the capture was precise and highly efficient... *certainly Elaas, this one...*

Moments later the skipper craft, with its new cargo, was heading skyward, breaking through the atmosphere high above the capital city; *this gets more interesting by the minute...*

He tried several times to link to the skipper's AI, was blocked each time... *high-tech influences among these Elaas, they would have to be dealt with eventually*... He was about to initiate a tracer program when the data-feed dropped off the grid... *clever little Phaelon, gone from the screens*... even the Net feeds terminated as the skipper broke orbit. *No matter, let the Phaelon's have their worthless prize, the new priority was now paramount.* It was vital the tracer net found the Saepid craft and tracked its journey across the stars. *But it will take time; time I can ill afford to waste*... He feared the inevitable reconnection to the Primus Core, feared the reaction from his god, but... *the pathways flowed...*

He entered the fugue trance, found the data-stream flowing hard and fast from Primus, and further beyond, the great storm seething at the Rim. Instructions were downloaded, confirmed, and compliance protocols instigated... *the fluttering of the dark flag... the Worship Glyph glistening high above a sea of fire...* and the connection broke, his eyes beginning to refocus, his body still trembling from the strain of the uplink. So he would wait; wait for the seeker nets to catch his prey...

Far below, the planet Petra spun serenely, a blue-and-white wonder bathed in starshine... *and even you, mighty Petra, will soon fall before my Master's Glory...*

115

Chapter 18 - Jihad

"... and as the towers fell, I saw a starship fall into the Azure Sea, and everywhere the people were running, their hair alive with fire..."
Poron Acton, Galician Refugee.

Delta influx wave bands coinciding with virulent pathogens, cascading thought patterns terminating at the biological. A new language concourse established to solidify the softening of dendrite cultures, axons floating in a cerebral serum. Lightning strikes out of the void, the usurper leaps from thought to thought, fronds of perception teetering above the abyss, soul thoughts trembling at the finite escalation of infinite diversity. Link nodes merging with flesh and bone, red and white cells coagulating into viral osmosis, the attenuation of human self-replicating individuality is left in shreds, torn perceptions withering inside the wreck and the remains of someone that was once a human being, entire of itself, reborn now as a servant of the one true God, Saemal.

Alone inside a dream, cast out like a million thoughts sent scattered into the star-flung empires of man. A singular thought, tied to the core, one solitary human faced with the Power of a God, translation codices weaved into language crevices, stunned and stoned into stem-cell memories of propagation; soft platitudes whispering in the night. A frail fruition cascades into semblance, blank recognition resides and steals the gifts of voice and sound, light takes whispering visions into ions and thought processes. The God breathes a wave of thought matter upon the realms, and worlds spin inside orbits bound to its thrall, space exudes the quantum data flux, arriving as a sole command: take everything, spare no one, and follow thy God...

Fifty thousand plassteel constructs, teddra-hardened warships stealthed and sealed with the Cortex base code, cruising out from the Cordwainer Alliance. A million troops stacked head upon head, battle flags wrapped and stored, plasma weapons and null-field drones, agrav bombs, and phase missiles, all of them girdled and crèched above the towers of hand guns secured to the central pylons. A wave of Net feeds streamed out ahead of the armada, soothing words, invites and suggestions, offerings and proclamations skirting the vast arrays of Net feeds across the entire Coalition.

Whisperings of God's own secrets to a galaxy untouched by His grace. Storms of fire breaking out across the outer worlds, cities and fields darkened beneath the pall of the huge missionary vessels. The armies of His Light moving out among the citizens of the outer Coalition, the flags held high above the storm troopers breaking down the doors of the heathens, destroying all resistance, and taking the heart out of every soul, replacing minds with the gift of His power, lucid dreams coalesced into fragrance and fragile subservience.

This would be no easy assimilation reserved for the inner Hub worlds; this was a lesson in futility, a display of raw power on an unprecedented scale.

The battle flags of the Saemal Jihad were placed upon the high towers of a thousand Rim worlds; ninety-five billion converts fell into the Holy Realm in an instant of coordinated indoctrination. Tens of thousands fell in battle, wars raged across hundreds of worlds – but for every soldier killed in battle, another ten would accept the way and the truth and the light.

Saemal's gifts were cosmic prescience, minds released from singular autonomy; the dedication to the one power was a river running through the fields of creation... God had come home, and the ancient realm was slowly being restored by the glory of His power.

Chapter 19 - Passing through Cassiopeia

'... In those days before the great darkness fell, Cassiopeia Alpha was known by its pre-Galac title Al-sadr, which was the source of light and sustenance to the First Race... it has been rumored that the Chalice of Creation was forged in the mines of Shedir...'
Tantalus: Chronicles of Ages.

There was a branch sticking into Domini's back. He tried to adjust the webbing, pulling hard on the straps. The female Saepid had told him it was the best she could do for him at such short notice; he got the impression that she wasn't too pleased to have him on board. And now the girl was glaring at him across the cabin. She seemed just as annoyed at having to share her end of the deck with him. Only the Saepid Anthra seemed indifferent to his presence; he was busy working with various floater screens, clicking away in some obscure language he'd never heard before. They had entered subspace soon after leaving the docks at Petra, followed by a mad scurrying among the Saepids, something about locking out security feelers. He wasn't sure what all the panic had been about, but they had since calmed down. Shari had said it was something about being tracked; they had to mask their ion signature, make sure they couldn't be followed from Petra... and yet Anthra never seemed to take his eyes off the security screens. *Who could be out here following us? The Beast or his agents?*

There was some commotion from the command pod below; he leaned forward, looking down past the drifting leaves and a scattering of insects flickering amid the com lights. He glanced at Shari... she seemed busy picking leaves from her hair. He shouted across to her: "What's going on?"

She looked up, and then down at the two Saepids busy clicking and clucking to each other.

"No idea; hold on... Anthra!"

The Saepid looked up, eyes wide. "Yes, Shari?"

"Is there a problem down there?"

Anthra looked at his mate before floating up to face her in her tree.

"Not real problem, Shari, not yet..." There was a loud *humph* from Ventra below.

Anthra sighed. "My beloved Ventra informs me that the new upgrades are having problems..."

"What sort of problems?"

"Compatibility problems. You see, *Shaendar* is very old ship, difficult to match with new high-tech gadgets, antenna swarm has degrading influx along needle tubes..."

Shari tried not to look too annoyed. "And that means what exactly?"

Anthra looked down at Ventra, and then glanced at a floater screen resting among the branches.

"Meaning our arrival time at Far Star Colony might be later than estimates..."

"How much later?"

"At present speed the ionic pulse drive will increase drag coefficient by five percent each day, and so decrease overall speed potential; making arrival estimate at least sixty days from this point in time..."

That was bad, that was very bad...

"And you tell me that's not a real problem?" Another *humph* from down below.

"Well, in truth, dear Shari, it's not a problem... yet."

She glared back at him. "But it will be eventually, right?"

"I'm afraid so, yes..."

Domini finally got comfortable inside his webbing and leaned forward to address Anthra. "So what can we do about it?"

Anthra seemed surprised at the interruption, turning to face Domini. "Well, Ventra has one suggestion, but I fear it involves more danger than is worth the risk..."

Shari continued: "So don't you think we should discuss this one suggestion? I mean we're all involved in this quest, are we not?"

"Indeed yes, Shari, no arguments from me there, but forgive me, you are not far star traders as we of the Saepid are. We are more aware of the many dangers that lurk out here between the worlds... many bad tidings out here in the darkness..."

"Just tell us how we can fix the drive problem, Anthra, and stop fretting. We all know what's going on... every day wasted out here could mean the end for some civilization. We already know what happened on Pr... on Primus..." She felt the old pain once again, deep inside her chest... *will that ever go away?*

Ventra looked up at her mate. "Best explain, dear one... no choice, cannot hide truth from *custodia*."

Shari sighed, she didn't like to hear that name; she was beginning to resent being treated as someone *special*...

119

Anthra pulled a floater down to show Shari, and gestured for Domini to float over, waiting patiently as the ex-priest struggled to undo his web straps.

Shari smiled as Domini got a foot trapped between a strap and a branch, causing him to spin away from the hull, twisting over until he came to face them upside down... his cloak floating over his face. She had to laugh. She had never heard a Saepid laugh, but she thought that the rapid series of clucks from both Anthra and Ventra might be the Saepid version of laughter. Anthra reached up an arm and pulled Domini round by his feet, helping him float into position. Domini gripped a ceiling rail as Anthra turned to face Shari.

"Very well, will no longer go into tech details of degrading drive problem, that's a fact, we must accept this... so dear Ventra has suggested we make a port of call..."

Shari looked at Domini, but remained silent as Anthra continued.

"... So we have two main options, these are the following..." He touched the floater screen, slid the data-feeds until he found a tagged view. "We can drop out of subspace here at Terak Nor, high-tech industrial world of the Sylvian Alliance, many docks at Terak Nor, high-grade workshops suitable to upgrade pulse drive; but..."

Shari leaned forward. "But what?"

Domini's face seemed to ask the same question.

"But Terak Nor is a very dangerous place for travelers, many Phaelon pirates there, Sylvian race indentured customers of Phaelon Confederacy, very bad race, bad tidings follow their cruisers."

Domini spoke up. "Very well, it's a bad place, so what's the second option?"

"Well now, that's a brighter prospect, a safer harbor, we think, here..." He flashed to a new screen, showed it to them.

"This is Landings Down, a deep space docking port, caters for far-flung travelers, an independent race of Coloquies administer to shipping needs, we Saepids have previously filed privileges with the Coloquies, traded many times at Landings Down, much safer bet, we think."

Shari looked away from the screen, looking directly at Anthra. "And you couldn't just give us this option first? Oh, for crell's sake..." She drifted back to her tree in the corner, and Anthra was left looking perplexed as Domini floated back to his wall, smiling to himself.

"So we are all in agreement, then? We break journey at Landings Down?" Anthra asked them.

120

Shari shouted back from her webbing nest. "Sounds like a plan to me."

Anthra drifted back down to the command pod and began to input the necessary course corrections.

Shari wrapped her foilair fleece around her shoulders, watching Domini working away on a floater screen. She caught sight of a spatial-grid of the Far Star Sector. *He likes to study, this one. Well, let him, it isn't my responsibility to know the way to the Colony... apparently I'll have enough to do when we get there...*

She pulled an audio plug from her wall console, placed it in her right ear, and felt it link to her auditory canal. The music flowed deep into her mind, instantly lifting her spirits. It was an adaption of *Corelion's Phantasia*... she and her friends from the Math Club had traveled into Egrain City the previous year to see the last ever production of the famous musical, *was that only a year ago? And where are all my friends now? Still alive but dead inside? Would they still know me? Would they remember all the long years of their youth? Remember studying for the Finals? Remember running track sports in the fields of Sorelli Park behind the university?* She thought of the long hot summer nights having fun along the Estrada Concourse; the flashdance clubs and the pierside bars....*all so far away now, gone with my whole life back there on Primus.*

She turned away from the cabin, lost her face inside her fleece, the branches and leaves of her tree trembling as the air vents cast a gentle breeze around her knees, and always the sensuround sounds of surf on sand, and rainfall caressed by distant thunder. She caught sight of Domini looking at her, and quickly wiped away her tears.

She felt him drift over, floating behind her. He placed a hand on her shoulder. She felt herself tremble beneath his touch. She spoke without turning around. "What? What do you want?"

"Nothing for myself. But you seem to be in pain."

"Well I'm not, so please leave me to my music."

He stayed there, floating behind her.

She turned around this time. "Look, I'm okay, see? I'm fine."

"Well, you don't look fine."

"Well, I am. Now please just go away."

"Listen, Shari, I'm no expert when it comes to people, I've spent my entire life locked away in a Seminary devoted to a God I no longer believe in, but I can see that you are suffering. Anthra has told me of the fate of Primus, and the loss of your father—"

121

"He is not lost! Anthra is wrong, Primus can still be saved, it can!"

"Yes, and I pray that it can, but you are also having to come to terms with your role in all of this. It can't be easy to be told that you and you alone can stop the Beast; that the fate of so many worlds rest upon your shoulders."

She looked up at him. "Well, I didn't think of it quite like that, thank you very much."

"I'm sorry. But I think we both know that you've been thinking exactly that, ever since you set off on this quest."

She looked down at the Saepids busy in the command pod. "Am I so easy to read?"

He smiled. "Not really, but I recognize pain when I see it. I just want to tell you that no matter what dangers lie ahead of us, we will face them together… you are not alone, Shari… we four will face the Beast as one, united in our faith in each other."

She smiled back at him. "That's quite a speech, Mr. Priest."

He laughed. "It's Domini…"

"Domini, of course."

"So, you're going to be okay?"

"Yes I am…" She gave a gentle smile. "But I can't guarantee that will last…"

"Then that will do for now." He pushed himself off the tree and floated back to his side of the hull, catching the straps as he drifted into the webbing.

Chapter 20 - Grainsfeld Variations

"An assassin is, by necessity, a solitary figure, he comes and goes where and when he will, you will never see him approach, but where he walks death follows quietly in his wake..."
Lomar Fendor, Field Tutor, Elaas Elite Corps.

Kyle Raine was in agony. Metallic slivers had been inserted into his shaved head; dried blood was caked around his eyes and nose. Someone was floating just out of view, moving around the table upon which he was secured with clamps to his wrists and feet. There was a brightening of light behind him, *here we go again...*

He is walking down the central corridor of the University of Gamont; students are everywhere, smiles, polite greetings, the scents of academia permeating the walls...he has finally translated the Kyrillian-archi-text...

He is web-strapped inside a deep space cargo tug, bound for the planet Merril, the turbulence is beyond belief, atmospheric variations causing the ship's shield generator to buckle; they will be lucky to make it down in one piece....He is inside the lost chamber, faded murals, ancient carvings, the pedestal... the artifact! He is talking to Lorn S'Atwa... He is in his cabin on the star liner Glasnost... he is running from the Basilica... he is talking to a young girl... a Saepid... a priest... ancient words are falling the sky... Sword of Jophrim... Chalice of Creation... amber crystalline device... the Beast... machine gone mad... gone bad... sealed and set free to wreak its malevolence among the stars... and the new word, shimmering, shining in glorious sunlight: Custodia...

Dolmon saw that Raine had passed out again. He glanced at the flow-screens. The inserted probes created a virtual brain in the air above the grav-sled; he checked the input data, matching it to the mass of memories now stored in the psyonic navigator. It would take several hours to translate the retrieved memory core into readable Galac, so he closed the probe assembly and drifted over to the psyonic console. *No point in contacting Khan just yet, better find him something worthwhile first.*

Drondar Khan jigged the ship three light years off course to enter the main Net feed trunk; he needed more information. The situation was fluid and subject to rapid change. The subspace message from First Minister Torin Grenval had surprised and disturbed him; there was supposed to be a communication blackout until their arrival at Grainsfeld. Apparently the envoy vessel recently returned from the Rim had submitted certain new proposals to the High Council. He had no idea what these were, but they were sufficiently important for Grenval to cancel the rendezvous at Grainsfeld; that made no sense at all, considering his earlier conversation with the First Minister. *What was happening on Phaedra? Was this still a legitimate and sanctioned mission? And was that really Grenval behind the message?* It all depended on the information Tendra could glean from the human; there might yet be some clue to the future in that so very delicate brain.

He linked to the Net, streaming through thousands of Threads, tapped into associate word algorithms to sift through the deluge of useless clutter. The Net was a seething mass of half-truths and innuendoes, vague deceptions, arbitrary comments, and outright lies; to find any measure of truthful fact meant sifting for certain associate language pathways. He had the ship's AI link to word junctures and articulations which he deemed significant: *Gamont, Primus, Beast, Saemal, Rim, Petra, Kyle Raine, sacred artifact...* He linked the incoming data to a nearby floater and pulled it down to read the information as it came in. The feeds were all in standard Galac, though the AI was prioritizing feeds which used the Phaedran dialect; he removed that tag, and the flow of information increased.

Primus was definitely compromised; the Power had brought an entire fleet to that world. Although it was only recently incorporated into the Coalition, Primus was still a highly advanced world and should have been able to mount some form of resistance. But apparently there had been no destruction on Primus. The holo-vids streamed from the capital city showed life was progressing normally; the people actually looked happy. *Although noticeably a little vacant...* The question remained, however: how had the new Power taken over an entire race without firing a single shot? *And if that is true... if Primus could fall so easily, what does that portend for Phaedra?* He scanned the latest data-feeds from the Rim worlds... *and there aren't that many...* and found a link to a recent Post discussing the fall of the Cordwainer Alliance. He found a tag to a city vidcam system, *Altair; First City of Samros...* the place was a mess... shattered towers, vast black burn fields, *seeker-bombs...* fire-ravished habitats and gaping holes where city blocks once stood. *A world of domed cities, how quaint...* But broken now, opened wide to the atmosphere, which was... according to the feeds, too thin to support life... *and yet... there!* Huge spatial

124

platforms resting high on the largest ionic pulse he had ever seen, pumping out oxygenates; restructuring the Skysat AI system from within, while disgorging hundreds of security drones, followed by swarms of mech-tech bots crawling over the city infrastructure, *rebuilding what they have destroyed...*

There was a sudden viral alert across his data screens. He flicked terminate on the floater and looked at the diagnostics. *A threat detected in the most recent Post. Is it dangerous to even look at the Power now?*

But he had seen enough. The threat to Phaedra was very real, and although he feared it with all his heart, it might already be too late for his beloved homeland. *Just as you predicted, Torin Grenval.* Somehow the new Power was able to subvert entire worlds, choosing to either destroy them physically, or to pervert their minds, *is that even possible on such a scale?* As the Prime Leader of the Elaas, he knew of many ways to subvert the mind of an individual, to undermine rational thoughts, and to reduce an independent mind to a compliant and easily controlled subject. They had even had some limited success with group mind control, but that had been with no more than a dozen people. To be able to assimilate an entire race hints at transcendence, *and if the Power from beyond the Rim is indeed a transcended being... I doubt even the glorious Coalition will be able to stem the tide...*

He input a spatial-grid onto the command console and brought up the colony at Grainsfeld. The planet was no more than a ramshackle collection of industrial combines strung out across a barren rock of a world. They mined detrium on Grainsfeld, a vital component in the manufacture of the all-terrain harvesters sold by the Phaedran Mercantiles. The harvester industry was one of the few truly legitimate concerns controlled by the Phaedran industrial cartels, and had become so profitable that for some time now the High Council had been urging the Elaas to infiltrate the upper echelons of the cartels. And being the dutiful Prime Leader that he was, he had placed several of his best operatives inside the syndicates; he even had one of his people running one of the larger combines out of Grainsfeld. Of course, it didn't do to let the High Council know just how profitable the combines actually were. His influence among the cartels was growing and might yet prove useful given the current situation on Phaedra. So he fed the Council just enough information to keep them at bay.

He let the AI do the necessary course corrections and the ship initiated the first subspace jump to Grainsfeld. He linked to the internal com and connected to the aft cargo hold.

"Tendra, do you have anything for me yet?"

125

The virtual face of Dolmon Tendra appeared in the air before him. "Sir, yes, I do believe I have managed to retrieve some significant data from his memory core."

"Very well, I'm on my way."

Tendra withdrew the last needle probe from Kyle Raine's scalp. The man had been moaning earlier but seemed to have settled down again. He injected a protein slug into Raine's upper arm, *might as well keep him alive until Khan decides otherwise...* Behind him, the hatch door slid open and Drondar Khan floated into the room.

"Sir, the subject still lives, and all readings are in the green."

"Excellent. You have something for me?"

"Yes, Sir. If you'd like to take a look at the navigator."

Khan drifted over to the psyonic navigator, began to read the translated data.

"Nice work, Dolmon, I had no idea you had such a penchant toward psyonic extraction; I particularly like your annotations, most enlightening."

"Thank you, Sir."

The room fell silent for long minutes as Khan studied the readouts; several times he paused to look back at Kyle Raine lying prone on the grav-sled. Finally, he moved away from the navigator, floating over to the side of the sled.

"I must admit to a certain amount of disappointment, Dolmon..." He saw the look on Tendra's face. "Don't worry, your extraction is very professional, and of course you managed to avoid killing your subject. I'm just a little concerned that the man is no longer carrying the artifact."

Tendra came closer.

"Yes, Sir, but we now know where it is, we know where to find it..."

"Indeed we do, Dolmon... those crafty Saepids interest me. Industrious little creatures, are they not? Snatched themselves their own human, two now, it seems..."

"Yes, Sir. But you saw the references to this *custodia*?"

"Yes. This situation gets more complex by the minute, certainly more mysterious. This human female now possesses the artifact....but does she know how to use it?"

"Sir, the memory dump made reference to the girl's blood line."

"Indeed..." Khan looked down at Raine again. "This one knew something of the power of that device, and yet he gave it to a mere child."

"There is no reference to her lineage, Sir."

"I noted that, Dolmon. And yet all the nets of space are cast in her direction."

"Sir?

Khan turned to face his subordinate. "I haven't been totally open about our mission, Dolmon, it's delicate in the extreme, and might well result in our deaths."

"Duty is honor, Sir."

"Of course it is, Dolmon, of course it is. But right now I'm no longer sure where our duty lies..."

"Sir?"

"I've been in contact with home world, Dolmon, with First Minister Torin Grenval actually, the instigator of our mission. Without going into specifics, we were ordered to rendezvous with Grenval at Grainsfeld and transfer our prisoner to his custody, hopefully handing over the artifact at the same time. But now..." He looked once more at the man on the sled. "... now we only have a possible location of the artifact, and a brain-wiped human who is now next to worthless."

"But, Sir, we can still track down the Saepid ship; surely we can out-run such a vessel?"

"No doubt we can, and that's probably the best course of action. But what do we do then, Dolmon?"

"Would we not seize the artifact and the girl? We could then deliver both to the First Minister..."

"Yes, that would be our duty, and certainly that would have been my decision not more than an hour ago. But, Dolmon, the situation on Phaedra is beginning to cause me some concern."

"What situation are you referring to, Sir?"

Khan seemed to drift away for a moment, and then he turned to look at Tendra. "Have you heard what has happened on Primus?"

"I know of the fleet newly arrived from the Rim; and from the feeds I've scanned it seems that Primus has allied itself to the new Power."

"Yes... and you see, Dolmon, that's just the problem right there. Why would an independent civilization, newly incorporated into the Trans-galactic Hub Coalition ally itself willingly to an unknown power that seems intent on galactic domination?"

"You believe they were coerced somehow?"

127

"Actually I think it's more subtle than that, it goes deeper than mere coercion. That fleet newly arrived from the Rim must have been intimidating to the people on Primus, but that wouldn't explain their instant compliance... they appear to have welcomed the newcomers from the Rim with open arms. There's no logic to their actions..."

"And you are thinking of Phaedra, Sir?"

"Precisely. You know of the envoy vessel newly arrived above Tendrah?"

"Yes, Sir, the single returning ship from the fleet we sent to the Rim some time ago."

"Yes, and that ship worries me, Dolmon; you see, soon after its arrival over Phaedra our esteemed First Minister informed me of a change in our plans. He will no longer be meeting us at Grainsfeld, and apparently this human here is no longer of any importance to him. In fact our current orders are to return home at once... we are to abandon the mission, Dolmon." Khan fell silent, the only sound being the soft hum of the navigator screens and the whistling of the air vents set high in the walls.

"Do you suspect that the First Minister has been compromised?"

Drondar Khan looked down at the unconscious man on the sled. "What I fear, Dolmon, is that the whole of Phaedra, and possibly the entire Confederacy beyond, has been compromised."

Tendra considered this. "So are we not returning to Phaedra, Sir?"

Khan didn't reply for several minutes, floating instead around the grav-sled, stopping in front of a diagnostics screen.

"No, Dolmon, we are not returning to Phaedra. How do you feel about that?"

Tendra saw that Khan was studying him carefully. "Sir, you are the Prime Leader, I go where you order; duty is honor."

"Good, that's just what I wanted to hear. Well then, Dolmon, we will set our tracers in the direction taken by the Saepid ship. We will use the trans-phase drive to catch them up, and once we have found them we will seize the girl and the treasure she carries." He started to drift back toward the hatch.

"And if I might ask, Sir? What do we do then?"

"Why then, Dolmon, we will use the girl to stop the new Power. I have no idea if the destruction of this so-called Beast will restore our race to its former independence, but I can see no other path to take right now." Once again he fell silent as they both tried to come to terms with the implications of such a

128

decision. "So, I shall set about configuring the tracer assembly; see if we can't find this Saepid ship…" He turned toward the hatch.

Dolmon looked down at the man on the sled. "Sir? Your orders regarding the human?"

"Oh, yes; send him on his way." With that, he floated through the hatch and was gone.

Dolmon Tendra looked down at the human, still very much alive. He slowly disengaged the grav-sled from the floor stabilizers and carefully maneuvered it through the hatch, heading back toward the rear air lock.

Chapter 21 - Landings Down

"... soft twirls are iridescent, tranquil dealings we do, transferal business extols the vibrant virtues of our repose, and fleshings translate as customary and tolerant in our debtude..."
Coloquies Business Slogan.

Forty days into their journey and the *Shaendar* was losing speed. It was a gradual thing at first, hardly noticeable by the on-board screens. But Anthra noticed. He said he could feel the changes; Shari doubted that, but the screens soon proved he was correct.

Domini had commandeered part of the cargo hold for himself; Shari had only been back there a few times to see him feeding the plants. The place was full of glasscite containers and graphile storage jars. Anthra told her they carried samples of over three hundred species of plant and tree foliage from the Saepid home world... she couldn't pronounce the planet's name, but she gathered it was mostly jungle. The Othrum race were not indigenous to the planet, though, having settled there only a few million years ago; she had no idea where the Saepids had come from before that... the very early Saepid archives were not translatable into Galac. But they seemed to need to bring a lot of their natural environment with them, hence the containers. Ventra would go back there every few days and remove a few plants, taking them forward to the command deck. Domini would help her re-position the old foliage and cut back some of the larger trees. After a while she seemed to warm to him, and it wasn't long before they were having long conversations, with Ventra recounting the Saepids' various adventures as far star traders.

Anthra had kept mainly to himself during the last few days, preferring to sit in front of the main console, monitoring the slow degradation of the drive core. He would occasionally cluck and click loudly in obvious frustration, then return once more to brooding in front of the screens. She once asked him how he had managed to get her out of her cell on Primus, she still had no idea what had happened back there; he had just told her it was a Saepid thing, *very private, best not to talk about...*

Shari watched from her corner as Domini eased a new plant over to the forward venting hatch; he'd grown a beard and let his hair grow, held back now in a pony-tail.

He looked quite the pirate, no longer like the sheepish-looking priest she'd first met on Petra. They hadn't talked much. At first she thought it was because he didn't want to get her all upset again, that he was just trying to appreciate her situation... but now she was beginning to think it might be something else. He was acting differently around her, more stand-offish... more reserved. She couldn't figure it out at first, and then she saw him studying the Othrum ancient text Anthra had let her listen to when they had first brought her aboard. He was reading up on the Sword of Jophrim, the Chalice of Creation and the stories passed down about the First Race and their genetically engineered *custodia.*

He's beginning to fear me... if not fear then certainly awe... son of a Barg...

She drifted down to settle next to Anthra. He glanced once, the usual smile on his face, and then he returned to the console.

"So, how long before we reach this Landings Down place?"

Anthra looked up at a static vid-screen. "Three days, Shari, three days... I have already made connections with Coloquies Port Control; they have extended permission to dock."

"Well, that's good, and the repairs?"

"We have submitted contract requests and I see no reason for their refusal; Saepid privileges are welcomed at the Down."

"Any idea how long we'll have to stay there?"

"Difficult to say, but Landings is a high-tech port, many upgrades available, best of the Hub, or so they advertise on the Net. If they speak truth then I estimate we shall be delayed no more than two days."

"Then I suppose that will have to do."

"Yes, can't be helped, I'm afraid. Apologies for oldness of our ship, Shari, but we had no conception of the needs for which it would be used."

"It's not your fault; I had no conception about any of this myself."

He smiled back at her. "Indeed not, no..." He looked into her eyes, his head turning to one side. "Are you well, Shari?"

"What? Oh, yes, I'm okay; bored, I suppose."

"You have studied charts of Far Star Colony?"

"Yes, many times. And I've been reading the Threads you archived, although I guess most of them are out of date by now."

"Yes, definitely out of date, but I have to fear reconnecting to the main trunk feeds, many ways for the Beast to leak into our automation, we must be watchful, weary of badness seeping in unseen."

"Can it do that? From so far away?"

"Probably not, but must not take any chances. Far Star is very far away, but Primus is nearer and, forgives me, Shari, they have already fallen into darkness."

"I know. I try not to think about it… but I have accepted it; I know that my people have been taken over. But I have to hope, right? I have to believe that what we're doing now, this quest, that it will make a difference somehow."

He reached down and took hold of her hand. "It will make a difference, Shari. We will stop the Beast, together, all four of us."

For only the second time since they first met she leaned into his shoulder, the hard carapace cold beneath her chin; but this time he did not pull away.

Interlude inside Cassiopeia

Neiron Thane sealed the data-stream. The voices from Primus were succinct, but the details were outside his purview. Phaedra had joined the Cortex. The God Saemal now reigned unchallenged throughout the Phaelon Confederacy. *The pathways flowed…* The tracer-nets were cast wide across the Cassiopeia Drift; a subspace link had been made from three separate locations. *Jumping from star to star, little Saepids…* The target ship was well masked; the Saepids knew how to avoid being noticed, changing course several times as they passed through the outer Hub worlds. They were rapidly leaving the civilized territories behind them, heading away from the galactic Core. *Making their way to the Rim?*

He touched the phase-inducer, initiated full pulse drive, the Viper streaming through cosmic dust, ions scattering in its wake.

Chapter 22 - Arrival

'A plague of uncertainties should be our first warning when walking among strangers...'
Lothar Theron - Philosopher and Poet.

Domini was beginning to feel guilty; he hadn't said more than a few words to Shari in days. Oh, they had talked over dinner, even laughed at Anthra's attempts at humor, but there had been nothing like an in-depth conversation between them. After reading everything the Saepids had on the artifact and the *custodia* themselves, he had found himself developing the same sense of reverence he used to feel during temple meditations. It was such a strange way to feel about a young girl. Looking at her now, he realized that she was actually a young woman, no longer the innocent-faced girl he had first met at Salicia Sonora, *and so very beautiful...* His thoughts returned again to his vow of celibacy, *was that still binding now that he had been excommunicated?* He felt his face warm as Shari looked up and caught sight of him staring at her. She smiled back and floated up toward the viewing dome. They were about to drop out of subspace and she always went up there to await the return of the stars.

Ventra did the count from below, reducing to zero point as the ship shimmered back into real-time. Echo points pinged from the proximity screens and both Saepids were instantly busy touching floater screens, reading data-feeds and inputting course corrections. There was a loud data-burst from the com panel. Anthra touched the response code.

"We have docking privileges from Coloquies port official named Dhimfaal; he honors us with his cordial terms and agrees to repair contracts at good costs for us. Good tidings indeed."

Shari watched a swathe of stars flow across the dome. The effect was always the same, her heart pounding, her eyes wide at the sheer vastness of the universe... *just a few centimeters of glasscite between me and infinity...* She was aware of Domini staring up at her; she adjusted her shorts and tried to ignore him. *So the priest might yet have lascivious tendencies...* That made her smile.

From below came a proximity alert. She turned her head around and was shocked to see a black wall in space. *What the crell?*

Anthra shouted from below: "Landings Down directly ahead."

Shari caught sight of a large dome, rising now above the wall. Further away she could see habitats strung out in a low orbit around the space station, and directly in front of the *Shaendar* a stream of starships were moving gracefully in and out of the docks. Some of the ships were huge cargo haulers, but most were smaller deep space cruisers, not unlike the *Shaendar*, but lacking her grace and insect-like Saepid design.

As they began to rise high above the ecliptic, she saw the workshops; immense plassteel biospheres complete with dozens of mech-cranes strung with graphile cables and fused to agrav-lifters secured to central support pylons. There were thousands of factory drones thrusting along the outer harbor walls and scurrying across the hulls of berthed starships. She pulled herself around to watch their approach toward the great dome. She could just make out towers and monorails inside the shimmering of the atmospheric induction zone, and what looked like some kind of lake floating on a grav-field near the center of the port. *Amazing...*

Looking down, she noticed Domini had gone... *seen enough, have you?* She floated back down to the command deck and drifted toward her webbing. Domini was already strapped into his old place against the far wall, and the Saepids were strapping in down below. She heard them clucking away between themselves as the ship began to descend gradually upon an ever-decreasing pulse drive. She heard the thrusters engage and the ship lurched to one side. From below Ventra whispered: "Apologies... tight berth Dhimfaal issue to us."

The first thing they noticed was a loud banging on the outside of the hull. Shari looked at Domini, who simply shrugged. Anthra drifted over to the main hatch, checking the atmospherics. Exterior readings were in the green.

"No worries, people, just the local yard chief connecting service repair drones. We can exit when you are ready. Ventra will remain on board for time being, much calculating to do for further journey."

Shari released her straps, floating over to the shower cubicle. "I want to change first."

Anthra sighed with a look of polite acceptance.

She saw the look. "I won't be long!" She punched the door shut behind her.

Half an hour later they were sitting in a travel pod gliding along a monorail into the domed enclosure. They passed by rows of workshops and weaved under massive construction platforms where a series of pleasure yachts were being outfitted. Anthra informed her that there was an annual yacht race from Landings Down, and the next one would be taking place the following week. *If they're lucky...*

From beneath them came a rush of warm air as they passed over the dome venting outlets, the smell filling the pod with gastrol fumes. Within minutes they were out of the tunnel and inside the dome itself. Seconds later, the pod came to a full stop at a pedestrian platform fused to the side of a hotel complex.

Shari was about to jump out when Domini reached out his hand.

She smiled. "Thank you."

Anthra pushed his way between them. "I need to meet port official Dhimfaal to register our payment, might take some time. Coloquies easy enough to make contracts, but not so easy to bargain costs, might well have to whittle down the payments to manageable levels."

Shari looked around her, saw the bustling markets beyond the platform and the many bars and shops further in toward the center of the port.

"That's okay, I think Domini and I can find something to do."

Domini was still trying to reconcile his very narrow existence with the sights of so many diverse life forms.

"What? Oh, yes, we'll be fine, Anthra. You just make your deals, we'll take a look around."

Anthra gave him a stern and somewhat forbidding look. "Very well, but listen well, human priest. You take great care of Shari; no harm must come to her, you understandings my words?"

"Yes, of course. I will protect her with my life."

Shari coughed. "Excuse me, but I'm right here, you know, and I can take care of myself."

Anthra gave a slight nod of his head. "I know that, child... Shari; but this place is not secure, no matter the promises of Coloquies. Many strangers here in port, not all of them friendly. You saw the deep space lugger as we berthed?"

Shari had seen it. "That black ugly ship below ours?"

"Yes, that one... wouldn't be surprised if that was a far star cruiser; must steer clear of that one. We sleep back on ship tonight, so return as soon as finished with tourist sights."

Domini assured him that they would, and they watched as he turned and trotted off toward the port admin buildings on the far side of the platform.

Domini turned to Shari. "So, where do you want to go first?"

She didn't even hesitate. "A bar!"

The *Phendosia Bar* was a marvel to behold. The place was shaped like a giant frel fly, all wings and stick legs festooned with tiny alcoves and cubicles

135

shrouded in multicolored atmospherics, with irilian lamps strung low over glasscite-paneled floors. Shari had never seen anything like it; her astonishment was perhaps only surpassed by Domini's. She elbowed him in his side to get him to close his mouth, and then took his hand, leading him inside.

There was an instant of disorientation as they were hit by a multitude of diverse atmospherics. Every alcove, it seemed, was tuned to the preferred environmental requirements of its occupants, and as they passed by they could see strange creatures wrapped around tall tubules, their long gangly arms writhing inside a sea of yellow and green mists. Every now and then they saw a Coloquies floating high above the bars; its bubble alternating in color as it drifted past the high arc lights, avoiding the hot irilian lamps as they arrived at one of the alcoves in the upper balconies. Shari shouted above the trumpet sounds of what they took to be the local equivalent of music.

"Isn't this amazing!"

"What?" Domini was deafened by the music.

"Come on!" She pulled him forward, pushing past a large group of people, who when she looked at them closely weren't people at all, but humanoids with flat featureless faces and shaved heads.

"Excuse me..." She pushed her way through to the bar as a gap opened up in the crowd.

Domini pulled her close. "Are you sure about this? I mean, are you old enough to drink?"

She turned to look at him. "Are you? Of course I'm old enough, you can go to bars at seventeen on Primus. Crell... don't you know anything about having a good time?"

He looked crestfallen as he replied, "Well, actually, no, I don't."

"Well, buckle up, Mister, because you and I are going to have some fun..."

She raised a hand to call the bartender over. She was surprised to see a human female come to serve her; since their arrival at the docks they'd seen only about half a dozen real people.

The woman was tall and had long blond hair down to her waist; there were crystal rings woven among the tresses, and lohari trade ribbons hanging from her shoulders. As she leaned over, her breasts almost fell out of her very low halter top. Shari nudged Domini when she caught him staring. He stepped back looking somewhat shamefaced.

"Yes, what can I get you?" the woman said with a tired smile.

Shari looked at the many shelves behind the bar; there were hundreds of bottles and containers lining the entire back wall. "What would you recommend?"

The woman eyed the two visitors. "For you two? Dralian wine might suit you best, not too strong, but very tasty."

"Very well, Dralian wine it is, thank you."

Domini was shouting to be heard again. "Perhaps we should find a seat?"

"Okay." The drink arrived and Shari touched the cash card Anthra had given her to the counter paypad. She thanked the barmaid and they turned to look for seating.

Domini stopped to watch a troupe of exotic dancers as they swirled around ceiling-high plassteel bars to the rhythm of the pounding music. Three of the women were human, but two others had green scales down their backs and arms and were definitely not human.

"Keep it in your pants, Mr. Priest."

"Shari, I assure you, I have no such thoughts; I—"

"Relax, I was just kidding. Sit down, for crell's sake."

Domini almost spilled his drink as Shari pulled him into a nearby alcove. The noise in the main bar instantly receded as the alcove's internal harmonics dissipated the external feeds and mood and context resonants kicked in. Shari felt a cool breeze as the alcove recognized its human occupants... she loved the place.

"Isn't this place amazing? There's nothing like it on Primus. I mean, we have some great clubs; bars really... and there's the dance forums at Prasedio, but nothing really alien... nothing like this place."

Domini looked out at the crowds, tried not to look in the direction of the semi-naked dancers.

"Yes, it's certainly amazing. I can't say that in all my years in Seminary I ever imagined that I might find myself in such a place."

She looked at him. "And you think I did? I was destined to join the Math Internship at the Legislature; I had my whole life planned out. Three years in Egrain City and maybe a year off touring the Hub worlds... you know my father was actually going to pay for that?"

"Were you and your father very close?"

She fell silent.

"Shari?"

"No, not really. We kind of drifted apart after my mother died."

137

"I'm sorry."

"Yes well, that's all in the past. I just wish... I wish I had seen him before... before things went bad, you know, just one more time..."

He leaned toward her, resting his hands over hers. "If we succeed in our mission you might get that chance; we might yet free your world from the shadow of the Beast."

Shari sat back, sipping her drink, feeling the liquid warm her deep inside; she tried to refocus her eyes as the wine took effect.

"You know it's just a machine, right? This Beast thing?"

"Not just a machine, Shari, at least not any more. This creature became sentient a very long time ago, and soon after that transcended the natural realm."

"Yes, but Anthra said it was still a Cortex... you know, deep down inside."

"Perhaps, but we can assume that it is no longer restricted to physical limitations; it has leapt from its lair, Shari, and even now spreads like a virus among the stars."

She swallowed the last of her wine. "And the three of you think I can stop that?"

"We believe so, yes... the ancient texts..."

She slammed her glass down on the table top. "I'm sick of hearing about ancient texts! It's ancient this and ancient that... I'm eighteen, for crell's sake, what do I know about ancient texts?"

He sat back, realizing that it wouldn't help to explain the situation all over again.

Shari looked out at the dance floor where all manner of 'people' were dancing.

"Fancy a dance, Domini?"

"Excuse me?"

"A dance! Come on..." She took his hand and pulled him out onto the dance floor. He tried to hold back, but suddenly they were among the dancers, with his back rubbing up against a tall blue-skinned creature who seemed to be exuding yellow liquid from slits in its neck. He moved toward Shari as she wrapped her arms around his shoulders and together they moved to the pulsating beat of the house music system.

Anthra had been waiting outside the Port Authority office for over an hour; he was about to touch the compad again when he saw the floating bubble form of

Dhimfaal approach from an overhead tube. The Coloquies used the tubes to move about the docks unhindered by humanoid traffic, and Anthra saw the sense in that as the huge form of the port official finally settled down in front of him. There was a translator node fused to the side of the bubble, and from its grille the high-pitched voice of Dhimfaal squeaked out in modern Galac.

"Well met, fair Saepid Anthra, much time since visit last."

"Yes indeed, kind one, we as traders are much required among the star lanes."

"Quite so... but talk we must of other things now, not here in this place, please with me you follow."

Anthra was instantly alert. There had been no discussion as to the payment for the repairs on the *Shaendar*, none of the usual business niceties he had come to expect from the Coloquies. *What is this all about? Surely not treachery here among friends?*

Dhimfaal rose up and turned to face a solid plassteel wall which had a drinks interface embedded in its center. As he drifted slowly forward, the wall vanished, revealing a large chamber beyond. Anthra saw several floater globes drifting beyond the hole. *Shielded walls... here?* He caught a glimpse of Dhimfaal floating inside his bubble, two wide eyes perched on the end of stalks floating in a sea of pink mist.

"Come, honored guest, must talk of dark words..." He then floated through into the room beyond. Anthra felt for the weapon secreted beneath his cloak. It was cold to the touch, and gave him at least some reassurance that if treachery was the game here he could at least defend himself. He decided to follow the Coloquies Dhimfaal and disengaged himself from the dome grav-field, drifting up and into the room where Dhimfaal now floated, waiting for him.

Anthra noticed the wall re-form behind him, and the old fears quickly returned; his carapace tightened and he fingered the weapon in its pouch. Dhimfaal didn't seem to notice, but was busy remotely adjusting several floater screens, bringing them down to face Anthra.

"Fair trader, Anthra, we of the Coloquies are most concerned..."

Anthra edged closer to the first floater screen as Dhimfaal continued.

"There is much that is wrong with the stars of late. We have been noting many bad Net Posts, stories of the darkness making itself known among the outer worlds. See here?" He had a floater drop down in front of Anthra. "We have our antenna swarms spread wide across Cassiopeia, many ships' tracers

139

identified, much movement among the peoples. As business folk we are wary of new customers, making notes of potentials and probabilities… it is our way to snoop among the comings and goings…" The bubble bobbed as he spoke, as if in embarrassment. Anthra knew very well the capabilities of the Coloquies; their high-tech was always ultragrade… if any race would know what was going on in the galaxy they would. Why that hadn't occurred to him sooner suddenly surprised him. He tried to identify some of the data-feeds flashing across the nearest floater.

"I see that you are concerned, friend Dhimfaal. How may I be of assistance?"

"We of the Coloquies are not in need of assistance, friend Anthra… you are."

Fears rising again along Anthra's carapace. "Is that so? Can you explain more?"

Dhimfaal drifted closer toward Anthra, who backed away slightly.

"Friend trader, you are pursued!"

That got Anthra's full attention. He looked more closely at the screen as Dhimfaal continued: "We have detected two very fast phase-type craft, bearing at one to the zero ten point ecliptic… see the data-stream wavers and shifts. They mask well, but tracers are acutely defined… the trails are clear. This one in front seems the slower of the two, but the one further back, he is very fast indeed… we speculate Viper class; much badness in that one, in fear we see signature recognizable to us."

Anthra looked up at the Coloquies. "You recognize this signature? What race is it?"

Dhimfaal seemed to wobble slightly in his bubble before replying. "Much apologies, friend Anthra, but that one has the same ionics as detected at Primus human world."

Anthra felt an icy chill along his vertebral column. He watched as the two dots shimmered on the floater screen, one so close behind the other that they seemed to be touching, though he knew that there had to be hundreds of light years between them. But they were both closing on Landings Down.

Anthra looked up finally, weighing up his options, deciding just how much he could tell the Coloquies. *Can I really trust this apparent friend? And do I have a choice?*

"Dhimfaal, what know you of our quest?"

140

The Coloquies drifted away from the screens, seeming to contemplate Anthra's words for a few moments.

"We know some things, not other things. Mostly we know you carry precious cargo; something that might cause the darkness to recede… In that, we are in unity, so helping you helps Coloquies Dynasty. Darkness not much a threat here yet, but the vid-feeds show much death at Rim, and fears of more closer still. If you have ways to halt the thing that comes this way, then we have ways to help you."

Finally, perhaps with allies we might yet have a chance.

Dhimfaal checked a docking registry screen. "We are upgrading your ship with our products, deep designs unseen among most worlds, things to carry you faster, stronger… we do this in hope of your success."

Anthra was suddenly very pleased. But business was still business.

"Might I enquire as to the cost?"

Dhimfaal floated back down to face Anthra, and the Saepid saw a dark face peering out from the pink mists, large bulbous eyes rotating beneath the rapid closing of leathery lids.

"Cost is simple, that upon completion of works you leave Landings Down at very first instant. We have sympathies for your needs, friend Anthra, but we do not want risks of those ships arriving here among us."

Anthra looked at the dots shimmering on the nearest floater.

"Indeed not, friend Dhimfaal. I will gather up my crew at once, making haste back to ship. Do you have a repair completion time?"

Dhimfaal remotely scanned the dock schedules.

"I have issued priority orders; we are saying twelve hours local for full completion."

"Excellent; then I bid you good tidings, friend Dhimfaal, and may your passage be a smooth one."

Dhimfaal touched his bubble to a wall panel and the wall behind Anthra vanished once more.

"Safe journey, fair trader Anthra, may your quest make light in the long dark night…"

Anthra floated back out to the waiting area. Dropping down, he re-engaged the grav-field link and quickly went looking for the nearest drop-tube.

141

Shari was feeling woozy; the music was a wild mix of trumpets and cymbals with an ever-present background chorus of voices rising and falling to the pulsating beat.

She shouted, "So, Domini, are you having fun?"

He looked around. His hair had become loose, covering his eyes, and as he brushed it to one side, he saw her grinning at him. "Yes, I suppose, but don't you think we should be heading back now? Isn't it getting late?"

She ignored him and turned away, heading back toward the bar.

He called after her in frustration. "Shari, please... where are you going?" But she was already forcing her way through the crowd of dancers.

Domini caught up with her at the bar, but she had already ordered two more drinks.

"Shari, please, this is most inappropriate, you know the importance of our mission; Anthra will want us back on the ship." From his hip he felt the compad vibrate. He left Shari to her drink as he looked at the screen, *Anthra!* The message was very clear: *'Return to ship now!'*

He took hold of Shari's arm, pulling her gently round to face him. "Shari, Anthra just called. We have to get back to the ship right now, do you understand?"

She looked back at him, her long dark hair glistening from the frosty dance floor atmospherics. "Of course I understand... back to the ship, in a minute, just got to finish this..."

She turned back to the bar, drink in hand.

Domini was beginning to lose patience, acutely aware that Anthra had made him responsible for Shari's safety and letting her get drunk was definitely not part of the plan. He took hold of her arm, much more firmly this time, but she tried to pull away.

"Just leave me alone, will you. I said in a minute. Just let go..." She tried to force his hand off her arm, but couldn't.

From somewhere behind them a large humanoid reached over and pulled Domini around to face him; it was one of the shaven-headed flat-faces. He was glaring at Domini with a sly and very threatening smile. "The lady said leave her alone, little human." The voice was a tightly clipped sound coming out of a slit halfway down the creature's face.

Domini tried to pull himself away. "I'm sorry, sir, but this is a private matter—"

The large flat-face grabbed Domini by his cloak clasps and lifted him high into the air. "Well, it's my business now…" And with that, he threw Domini across the dance floor, where he came to rest headfirst in a shrouded alcove.

Shari caught sight of a group of reptilians seated inside who promptly set upon Domini for knocking over their drinks. She tried to go to him, but flat-face stepped in front of her, his outsize hands beginning to rub her shoulders, moving slowly down to her breasts. She started to push him away, but she was no match for him, and he pinned her against the bar. She was about to scream for help when a long black rod reached over her shoulder to impact on the chest of the flat-face; instantly he convulsed, doubling over as a stun pulse coursed through his body. Shari turned to see the barmaid holding the stun rod.

"Get out of here, girl, and take your friend with you… Go!"

Shari stepped over the still writhing body of the flat-face and quickly ran over to where Domini was trying to escape the clutches of the reptilians.

"Come on…" She pulled him free from the claws and tails and together they made their way to the exit.

Once outside, they took a minute to catch their breath, and then Shari looked at Domini. His hair was disheveled and his cloak had been torn from its clasps, there were claws marks across his neck, and a small cut beneath his lower lip. She asked him if he was all right. He was still trying to get his breath back.

"I think so, yes. You?"

She smiled, brushing down her top and skirt. "Yes, I'm okay. That big crell ripped my top with his ugly Barg hands, but I'm okay…"

Domini took a look around them. "We should get back to the ship."

"I know. Let's go."

They set off along the outer concourse, moving carefully among the crowds who were shuffling in and out of the various bars and clubs; Shari saw a flash sign for the monorail platform and they set off in that direction. She looked back as Domini following on behind.

"Well, that was fun."

He looked at her. "Really? You think so?"

"Oh, come on, Domini, lighten up… you can't tell me you didn't have a good time tonight."

"Yes, Shari, of course I had a good time, being thrown across a room and set upon by giant lizards has been a long-standing dream of mine."

She had to laugh.

As they were about to leave the main concourse a group of flat-faced humanoids moved out from a nearby bar, surrounding Domini. He never felt the blade enter his stomach; in fact he never felt any pain at all. He just watched as the flat-faced group moved away, losing themselves in the crowd. Then he felt the warm sensation from his abdomen. Reaching down he touched the wetness there; his legs suddenly buckled and he fell to his knees... the crowds were spinning around in circles, a thousand voices, a thousand eyes watching him fall.

Shari screamed. "Oh, no! Domini!" She was kneeling by his side, her hands supporting his head. She looked up wide-eyed as a small crowd gathered around them.

"Please help us, he's hurt, can you help us please?" But no one move forward. There was an unspoken law among the docks' clientele: no one interfered with anyone else's business, no one got involved in other people's troubles, no one wanted to be delayed, or wrapped up in red tape. She suddenly felt totally alone and terribly frightened. She could see Domini's eyelids flickering, blood coming out of his mouth.

Was he dying? Anthra! She reached for the compad in Domini's inside pocket, felt the blood there, hesitated, and then pulled the pad out. She quickly linked to Anthra's datapad, and the face of the Saepid appeared onscreen.

"Yes, Shari, are you nearly at the ship?"

In tears, she replied: "Anthra! Oh, Anthra, we need your help, Domini has been stabbed; I think he might be dying..."

Anthra's face showed instant concern. "I come to you, don't worries, Shari, be still... I come." The pad closed down and Shari placed both hands over the now very obvious wound in Domini's stomach.

She talked to him, trying to get him to stay awake. "Domini, listen to me. Anthra is coming, we'll be out of here soon; you have to hold on... Domini!" The young man was now unconscious, and his blood continued to spread over Shari's fingers. She looked around the crowd desperately, noted that some had lost interest and had begun to drift away; she couldn't believe that no one was willing to help. The compad buzzed and the words: *'Nearly there'* flashed onscreen. *Hurry, Anthra, please.*

Anthra linked to the Coloquies central data-core, hacked directly into Dhimfaal's personal datapad and forced an instant recognition burst. Dhimfaal came online, a swirl of mist drifting across the screen.

"Who connects to this link?"

"Dhimfaal, it is I, Anthra. I am in needs of your vital help…"

There were a few moments of silence from the other end before Dhimfaal replied. "Speak, friend Anthra, what troubles are yours?"

"I have a crewman down at sub-sector six, the plaza area. I'm sending you his grid reference now. I need a med-tech sled there at once; can you comply?"

Silence once more.

"Yes, Anthra, sled dispatched, make haste to its location."

"I will, and much gratitude to you, my friend." He closed the link and stepped out onto the central concourse, moving rapidly along the edge of the crowds in the direction of the plaza.

When he found Shari she was sobbing softly to herself, her hands red with blood. The med-tech sled was only just arriving, settling gently next to Domini. Anthra quickly took control of the situation as Shari noticed his arrival.

"Oh, Anthra, I think he's dead, you're too late…" She seemed distraught and beside herself with grief. "And it's all my fault, Anthra, all my fault…"

"No panics now, Shari, Anthra will fix things. Must connect Domini to sled; stand back please."

Shari stood up and moved back to allow Anthra to lift Domini onto the sled. The machine glowed a bright green for several seconds and then a series of needle probes appeared, moving into Domini. One entered his upper left arm, and another injected something into his neck. He immediately arched his back, taking a deep breath, his eyes opening slowly. Anthra was busy setting the body clamps and initiating the grav-field drive. He motioned to Shari.

"Come now, Shari, to the ship we must go; make haste."

She fell into step behind him as he directed the sled through the crowd.

It didn't take them long to reach the monorail, the dock visitors and clients actually began to move out of their way as they hurried on by. They boarded the first pod, taking up three rows of seats, with the grav-sled floating in the air above. Anthra linked to the ship, informing Ventra of the situation, requesting that she restructure the ship's Surgeon for a human body as opposed to a Saepid. Twenty minutes later they were in sight of the *Shaendar*, covered now with mech-tech drones and strewn with fusion cables. High above they could see a grav-crane hauling a nest of antenna rods across the hull, to lower them down somewhere beyond the needle tubes of the drive assembly.

Once inside, Shari floated out of the way. She was feeling terribly guilty. *If I hadn't insisted on going into that bar, if I hadn't drunk so much wine… and*

145

was I flirting with Domini? Maybe I encouraged that flat-faced brute somehow? This is all my fault! She watched as Anthra and Ventra carefully maneuvered the med-sled into an annex of the rear cargo area where Ventra had set up the ship's Surgeon. She wanted to follow them, but her guilt was killing her. *Maybe it's best if I just stay out of the way...* She looked at her torn shirt strap, and then at the dried blood on her hands, *I should really shower, but what about Domini?* She floated toward the rear hatch, saw the Saepids transferring Domini to the ship's Surgeon. It closed around him as soon as they placed him inside, its outer shell beginning to hum and vibrate.

She called to Ventra: "Will he be all right?"

Ventra glanced back at Shari. "We think so, yes, Shari dear. Surgeon very good, though not human designed, I have flexed and fixed its parameters to satisfactory levels."

"So he'll survive? He'll live?"

"Oh, yes, no doubts. Surgeon in diagnostic mode right now, data-feeds show much blood loss, but plenty of synth-blood inside Surgeon, make Domini whole again soon."

Shari floated into the main hold. "How soon? I mean, when can he come out of there?"

Ventra studied the readouts flowing across the med-screens. "Probably four, maybe five days... not much more than that."

"Oh, okay... I'd better go and clean up..." She was turning to leave when Anthra called after her.

"Shari... what happened back there on station?"

"I'm not sure; some flat-faced people just attacked him... I... I don't know..." She turned and made her way back to the command deck. As she passed Domini's webbing the guilt came flooding back. She quickly reached for her gym shorts and top and lost herself inside the shower cubicle for the next half hour.

Chapter 23 - The Second Assemblage

"... And He walked among the peoples, the Staff of Ages in one hand, the Book of Revelation in the other, and where He traveled, worlds bowed to His glory, and the stars themselves were blessed with His grace..."
Revelations: First Book of Saemal.

Tanril was standing overlooking the great central plaza of Egrain City; the world was at peace and had welcomed the grace of his Lord Saemal. He watched the approach of the others, only seven now, Glindon, Tomas, Elicia, and Sorell had already left to join the outbound fleets. He touched the datapad, linked to the core fleet bound for the Landings Down sub-sector, watched as the face of Sorell appeared before him.

"You have a location yet?"

"We have data-sum estimates for a partial interception."

"You must confirm full alignment!" He saw the face of his lieutenant waver slightly as the vid-feeds struggled to match emotion to its real-time interface.

"I can assure you, Sir, we will match the runaway with precision. We have yet to reach full inter-phase; it causes delays."

Tanril knew that the sheer size of the fleet might well work against it. One thousand ships in close proximity caused massive fluctuations inside a subspace pocket; the afterdrift would be considerable, reducing the overall speed quotient significantly. *But his Lord had made his demands known; every resource must be used to seize the runaway...* He looked back at Sorell.

"I realize you might have problems, your field density is off the scale, but I do not have to tell you how vital your mission is, the runaway must be stopped."

"Sir, if I might make a suggestion?"

"Go ahead..."

"Sir, might it not be prudent to detach several of my Ultravane vessels and send them on ahead? The subspace pocket will be reduced by several light years, and they will most certainly be in a significantly better position to intercept the runaway."

Tanril considered this. It wasn't something inculcated within the latest data-stream from the Far Star Colony, but that last uplink had smacked of desperation; perhaps it was time for a little innovation.

147

"Very well, Sorell, you have my permission to send an advanced flotilla ahead. Just ensure that you impress upon your captains that failure in this matter is not an option."

"Very good, Sir. May the pathways flow…"

"May the pathways flow, Sorell." With that, he closed the link and turned to greet the others as they exited a nearby drop-tube.

Siena led the way. She who was once his wife, before the Coalescency, and behind her followed the dour Mordron. The man used to be a second-rate navigator on a third-rate lugger, now he was a member of the Sacred Twelve and captain of his own fleet. Behind him came the other women, Mistia, Tomala and Katian. Bringing up the rear were Phale and Dieter; no longer cargo grunts trawling scrap among the outer worlds, but now enhanced biotherms, restructured at the molecular level by the grace of their Lord God Saemal.

"You have news from the fleets, Mordron?"

"I linked with Glindon and Tomas; both their groups are moving perpendicular to the Hub periphery and they expect to engage an ad hoc consortium of ships off the Torellian Cluster."

"So the Hub worlds are finally fighting back? No matter, their destruction will only aid in the Expansion."

Siena stepped forward; her long white gown had an emblem of the Worship Glyph ingrained across the front, her dark hair was tied back with glasscite hoops.

"The Coalescency continues as dictated by our Lord, but need we be concerned with regard to the situation at Landings Down?"

Tanril studied his former wife, wondering at the source of her perception. There were suspicions among the Twelve that their God sometimes walked among them, fully integrated with one of their minds. The Cortex, which was the mind of Saemal, would often leave behind subtle revelations after a group communion, certain perceptions honed and quantified, *watching us from the inside out…*

"You need not be concerned, Siena, Sorell has the situation well in hand. We are following the sacred dictum as prescribed by our Lord God, and the situation in that sub-sector will be resolved."

Mistia walked over to the balustrade, looked out at the towers and boulevards of the city; the citizens were going about their business as usual, unaware of their vast indoctrination. She turned to face Tanril. "We have noted some residual concerns within the data-stream, Tanril, matters that may

148

constrain the Expansion. Phale has noted the failure of our agent to stop the runaway."

Tanril glanced at Phale. The man who was once lost to perpetual drug addiction still showed the physical deterioration of those years in his tall and gaunt frame, *despite the bio-enhancements.*

"Phale need not concern himself unduly. But I will ask Dieter to explain matters further, he is currently liaising with our agent near Landings Down. Dieter?"

"Thank you, Tanril. Our Lord Saemal has made it known that the runaway has onboard a nuisance strain of a former enemy. A mere insignificance by our Lord's standards, but it has the potential to delay the Expansion; full Coalescency might need to be restricted unless this tawdry wastrel is terminated."

Tomala stepped forward. "And yet your agent, Dieter, has already failed in his task?"

Dieter scowled back at Tomala as she gave a slight smile in his direction.

"He has not failed, Tomala, he has simply been delayed. By our current estimations he will intercept the runaway vessel at almost the same time as Sorell and his fleet."

Katian consulted her datapad, stepped forward to speak: "I note that there is a Phaelon cruiser in the mix, Dieter; have they significance?"

"None whatsoever. They are matching relative subspace density with the runaway, but our agent is closing fast; they will soon be removed from the equation."

Katian bowed her head and stepped back.

Phale spoke up. "But this Phaelon is Elaas, is he not?"

Dieter looked across at his former shipmate. "The Elaas are dead, and this one will know it soon enough."

Phale smiled as Tanril stepped forward to address the group.

"You each have your assignments. I expect regular quarterly updates. The situation is fluid; our armies at the Rim have consolidated their foothold there. The Phaelon Confederacy has been inculcated into the Coalescency, but there are several fleets outbound from the Hub Coalition; I want you, Mistia, Dieter, Katian and Phale, to join the forward phalanx of our primary fleets, coordinate the destruction of the non-believers. Our Lord requires several examples to be made; you will implement genocidal purges of the inner core worlds of Tantra, Galicia, Earthia, and Petra. There will be no Coalescency for those worlds. Tomala, Siena and Mordron will remain here with me to monitor the situation beyond Landings Down, and to facilitate the data-stream from Samros."

Mordron stepped forward. "Sir, I have the subject you requested waiting outside."

"Good, bring him in. This assemblage is complete."

As the group made their way out of the Legislature building, Tanril turned to face the city once again. The subject was an interesting distraction, the one true connection to the enemy. Saemal had ordered his preservation and continuance, and despite his personal reservations he had treated the subject with a certain level of respect. *Yet he has spawned the servant of his Lord's most mortal enemy, if anyone deserved to die, this one did...*

Mordron returned shortly, followed dutifully by a man dressed in the dark blue uniform of the newly formed Securitas Service, the secret police of the Saemal Religious Sect.

"Sir, the subject, Lorn S'Atwa..."

The man stepped forward hesitantly, bowing slowly. "Lord, I am honored by your presence."

"Yes, of course you are... That will be all, Mordron; I know you have other matters to deal with."

"Yes, Sir, may the pathways flow..." And with that, he turned and walked back toward the outer drop-tube.

Tanril studied the man before him: typical Priman, tall and lean with a touch of gray in his hair. *He certainly looks more like a member of the Sacred Twelve than Phale does...*

"I've been reading your current data-feeds regarding the restructuring of the Legislature, most enlightening, I must say."

"Thank you, Sir, I serve to obey our Lord God Saemal."

"Of course you do... But I haven't asked you here to discuss police matters. You see, we are interested in your daughter Shari; what can you tell me about her?"

The man seemed taken aback for a moment. Tanril saw him struggling to retrieve lost memories, vague recollections. The usurpation by the Coalescency often left new additions to the union void of real-time memory, their previous lives no more than scattered symmetries without true form or cohesion, and it remained to be seen if Lorn S'Atwa had any memory at all of his daughter Shari.

"Sir, I..." The man faltered, panic passing over his face.

150

"Be steady, Lorn S'Atwa, concentrate on the pathways, let them flow and you will be calmed. I need you to place an evocation of your daughter before your mind's eye... can you see her?"

The man seemed to drift away for a minute before replying. "Why yes, I can see her."

"Good. And now tell me, what does she look like?"

The man gave a slight smile. "Well, she is tall, just like her... mother, and she has long dark hair, which she dyed blue once to go to a holo-dance and I was forced to ground her for a week..." He drifted off again lost among his fleeting memories.

"Go on."

"Forgive me, but it's not easy to remember... she was so brazen, so independent, we argued so much..."

"Tell me of her blood type?"

"Blood type? I think it was T positive. Is this significant?"

"I will ask the questions, Lorn S'Atwa."

"Forgive me, Sir, I meant no offense."

"Very well. I want you to think back to your daughter's childhood; can you do that for me?"

"I will try, Sir..." His eyes seemed to lose focus once again as he struggled to retrieve the scattered memories of his daughter's early life.

"Now tell me, Lorn S'Atwa, did anyone ever take a significant interest in your daughter?"

"Well, that's difficult to say; certainly there were a few tutors who paid her some attention, but I think that was because she was a gifted math student. I don't believe there was anyone else in her life beyond family and friends."

"Was she ever visited by an off-worlder?" Tanril looked directly into Lorn's face. "Answer the question."

"Sorry, Sir, I was trying to recall. I don't think there was—" He stopped short, looking past Tanril to the city and the blue skies above. "Actually yes, there was someone, a long time ago. We were holidaying among the Islands of Lanoir, in the Serira Ocean... it was getting late, Second Moon was already high, so I went looking for Shari along the beach. I was angry because once again she had stayed out past curfew. And then... and then, yes... I saw her talking to a man, standing at the end of the pier. Of course I was worried... I mean she was no more than eight at the time; one hears about old men and young girls. So I called her... she... she turned around and ran back along the

151

pier to meet me... I was angry, but also relieved....she was safe..." He drifted off once again.

"Continue, Lorn S'Atwa."

"Yes... I asked her what she thought she was playing at... staying out after dark talking to strange men..."

"And her reply?"

"She said it was okay because the man was a priest; she said he just wanted to say hello, that he was visiting Primus from Petra... it was his first off-world journey..."

"Think, Lorn S'Atwa, did your daughter tell you what the man said to her?"

"I can't recall, so long ago now, so far away..."

Tanril stepped forward, placing both hands on Lorn's shoulders. "Concentrate, man; let the pathways seep into your memories, let them sift the sands of time, let them reveal your daughter's words to you."

Lorn turned his head to one side, his face a sea of confusion, his eyes seeking sights only his distant memories might reveal.

"She said he had told her a secret... yes that's what she said, a secret..."

"And tell me, Lorn S'Atwa, what was this secret?"

Lorn finally looked up, met Tanril's eyes. "That she was the savior of worlds..."

Tanril stepped back, his own memories cascading into the intricacy of the data-stream. *The old myth revealed?*

"And how did your daughter react to this so-called secret?"

"Why, she just laughed it off and ran back to the cottage; I'm sure she forgot the whole thing soon after that."

"But you remembered those words. Why do you think that is?"

"I'm not sure, except that I told my wife Tania about it. We didn't think much of it... but after that I made sure Shari was always indoors before it got dark."

"Are you aware that our agents had possession of your daughter before our fleet arrived here?"

"I have seen the report, Sir; and I know that she was subsequently kidnapped by a group of heathen Saepids."

"That is correct, the same vile creatures who now convey her toward our Lord's sanctuary."

"But, Sir, they will be stopped..."

152

"Of course, the matter is in hand. You need not concern yourself with these matters. I thank you for you cooperation, Lorn S'Atwa, you may take your leave now and continue with your duties."

"I thank you, Sir... May the pathways flow..."

"May the pathways flow, Lorn S'Atwa." He watched the man head back toward the drop-tube, and then decided to uplink the conversation to the data-stream from Samros; if there were further instructions from the Far Star Colony he would know soon enough.

Chapter 24 - Between the Wide Open Spaces

"You don't have to be cruel to do your job, but if it helps, why not enjoy it?"
Luther Rodin, Second Level Operative, Elaas Elite Corps.

Drondar Khan was dreaming of starships on fire, worlds spinning so fast that their oceans flew off into space. He was standing alone upon an airless rock, floating between the stars. Far away, beyond the rim of a distant sun he saw starships burning, falling into the cosmic fires... he was alone between the wide open spaces, the galaxy turning slowly upon its axis, there was a storm coming and he could hear the wind gathering speed. Nearby he saw a river flowing past, and he saw that the water was full of numbers and equations lapping against a crystalline shore, and there were synaptic algorithms strung like gossamer from ancient trees... He turned as a vast shadow crept along the rim; stretching tendrils of dark night toward the bright glowing worlds beyond... something was reaching out from the darkness, something vast and incomprehensible... a hand as big as any world, great fingers falling down upon him...

There was a buzz from the compad, and he was suddenly awake, disorientated. He looked at the status screens, and then touched the pad. "Yes, Dolmon, what is it?"

"Sir, do you require nourishment?"

He checked the ship-time. "Not now. Have you calibrated the dragnet?"

"Yes, Sir, it's primed and ready to go. All we have to do is get within five thousand meters of the Saepid vessel and we'll have them."

Khan looked at the latest spatial-grid, noted the progression of dots aligning within their current subspace sector. He touched the pad again. "Get up here, Dolmon, there's something I want to show you."

"Yes, Sir, I'll be right there."

Dolmon Tendra secured the plassteel ligaments of the dragnet to the cargo decking, tied down its feeder arms and proceeded to float up and out through the forward hatch. He found his Prime Leader bent over a large floater screen; he recognized their current spatial-grid analysis.

"Sir, you wanted to see me?"

"Yes, Dolmon, strap down a minute, I want you to look at this..." He pushed the floater over to Tendra, who was busy securing his feet to the deck. He deftly caught the screen and examined the data-flow.

"Notice anything unusual, Dolmon?"

154

Tendra looked up. "We're being followed!"

Khan shuffled about inside his webbing before replying.

"Yes, but are we the object of that vessel's curiosity?"

"Sir?"

"I have to wonder at the coincidental implausibility of another ship following our direct route toward the docks at Landings Down."

"You believe someone else is pursuing the Saepid vessel?"

"Well, think about it, Dolmon, we now know the importance of the ship recently docked at the Down, it stands to reason that some other force knows exactly the same thing."

"By some other force you mean the Power?"

"Precisely. I did a back-trace on the ship now following us... catching up with us actually, but we'll deal with that in a minute, its point of origin was Petra..."

"That makes sense. If they're following the same clues we are, they must have known about the human Raine and his meeting with the girl."

"Indeed, and of course where one clue leads another must follow..."

Tendra looked down at the screen, then back up at Khan. "They know about the artifact."

Khan sighed heavily. "Well, that's obvious, of course, but I don't think the Power knew where to look. I think he's been sending out agents ever since his fleet reached Primus, perhaps even before that. I believe that whoever is in that vessel behind us was redirected from some other mission, possibly similar to our own involving the late Kyle Raine. But they will certainly have the advantage of a few very high-tech gadgets; we're dealing with a transcendent Power, after all. They would no doubt have dipped into the Petran surveillance Net... it wouldn't take them long to discover the Saepids' role in all of this."

Tendra studied the spatial-grid. "And they're gaining on us..."

"I'm afraid so. Even with our inter-phase drive we can't hope to match the kind of speeds that ship is putting out."

Tendra waited for his boss to continue, but when he didn't he decided to speak up: "Do you have a plan, Sir? Because if that ship reaches Landings before we do the Power will have his prize and we will be left with nothing..."

Khan looked down at Tendra. "You have a gift for stating the obvious, Dolmon. But no matter, all is not lost. I think there might be a way to slow that ship down a little."

155

Tendra watched as Khan touched a nearby floater; it was a diagnostic of the ship's weapons system.

"You see this, Dolmon? I've had the AI do an evocation scenario; cast your eye over this grid alignment."

Tendra floated closer to see the screen. "Yes, Sir."

"Well, according to the scenario, if we drop a chain of shielded tetranium bombs along this coaxial plane, the vessel following will intercept them at this point here... Now I have my doubts that any vessel spawned by the new Power can be so easily destroyed, but it might well have to go around the bombs, hopefully delaying its arrival at Landings Down."

Dolmon thought it was a good enough plan, but even so, they were dealing with a ship made by a transcendent power... a creature worshipped by many as a god.

"It might just work, Sir, if the vessel's long-range scanners are unable to see through our shields..."

"Well yes, if they detect the bombs in advance they'll certainly destroy them; but that will take time and might still cause them some delay. We're walking along a precipice right now, Dolmon, and one wrong step could mean calamity. The window of opportunity will almost certainly be reduced as we get nearer to the Saepid vessel. But think of the prize if we should succeed... our race once more restored to its former glory, and the Power forever consigned to the foul pits in which it was spawned."

"A worthy quest indeed, Sir."

Khan swung round to face his tactical screens. "Now, Dolmon, set up the drop-bay; I'll prime the bombs myself. I want you to calibrate the shields for subspace drift and coercive influence parameters."

"I'll get right to it, Sir."

"And Dolmon, make haste, but do not make mistakes."

"Yes, Sir, I understand." *The ever-present threat lingers...*

As Tendra left the command deck, Khan noted the progression of the pursuing ship, *come just a little closer, and see the gifts I leave behind...* He checked the pulse-drive, and retracted the outer needle tubes so that the ship instantly reduced speed. *Just slow enough to release the bombs...* He touched the current arrival status: two days to Landings Down *...almost there, and will you be waiting, little Saepids?*

156

Chapter 25 - The Pathways Flowed...

Neiron Thane let the river flow... *alluvial streams sift the sands of perception, teddra constructs strung out along the neural helix, null-field destructs casting fire upon the ocean, the terminal interface assumes quantum densic truth, drifting into sensory membranes sealed within a synaptic confluence... the power stormed into the far future, seedlings of resonant reclamation glistening amid the gossamer threads of life and an overwhelming servitude... data-burst integrate, seamless coaxial terminating with Neiron Thane... the pathways flowed...*

He opened his eyes. The cabin was in darkness, just a glimmer of feeder points tracing across the vid-screens. All around him the soft hum of power, the deepness of the ionic pulse, and beyond the outer hull, the spatial feelers caressing subspace, teasing power from the null-field vacuum.

He touched the interspatial diagnostics, cast the nets out further into the maelstrom, watching the ship ahead of him; *reducing speed?* His link with Primus had told him who was in that ship; Phaelon's. *No doubt detritus from the recent Coalescency of their Confederate worlds. No matter, I will pass them by soon enough; they are inconsequential to the primary directive.*

He initiated the uplink to the Landings Down AI system, slipping in through a back door in the docking schedule program. He traced the recent berth allocations, tracked down the *Shaendar* to docking berth Ax/com 45000. Switching to real-time, his emotions almost got the better of him... *still sitting pretty, and with all the little metal insects scurrying over your hide...* He hacked into the personal data-core of the official who had signed off on the repairs, *Dhimfaal, a Coloquies... estimate given: twelve hours, subtract the current time log... nine hours before completion...* He checked ship-time on a nearby screen, *arrival estimate at seven hours... I have them!*

Disengaging the uplink, he input a new data command. The outer feelers retracted and the ionic pulse leaped into ultradrive. The resulting field distortion should have torn his body apart, but his Master had ingrained several biological enhancements into both his mind and body. He felt the external pressure as no more than a severe pain just above his eyes, as the ionic surge carried the ship onward toward its destination.

Chapter 26 - No Time to Lose

"You can try to outrun the flood, but eventually you will have to face the sea..."
Some Wisdoms, Othrum Saepid Digest.

For the last three hours Shari had been fretting. She was worried about Domini, worried about the distinct possibility of having to wait another nine hours until the repairs and upgrades were completed, and most of all, she was worried about just what it would mean to her when they finally set off for the Far Star Colony. For the tenth time she logged into the Surgeon's data-feeds, watching the monitors as they registered Domini's breathing, blood levels, and repair estimations. Everything was in the green, the synth-blood had brought him back from the brink, and now he was in a medically induced coma... *four more days, by the Stars, I will miss you, dear Domini...* She had given up trying to talk to the Saepids, they were in full panic mode at the minute, scurrying from one screen to another, linking constantly to some port official by the name of Dhimfaal. Always they were asking for feeder data from the port's antenna swarms; apparently they were being actively pursued by two unknown ships. She had finally cornered Anthra and demanded to know what was going on; but she had almost regretted asking. Both ships were definitely heading their way. The lead ship was slower, though, and they might well be on their way by the time that one arrived, but the second ship, the *dark follower* as Anthra called it, that one was gaining speed; that one could be here in six hours. The thought was frightening in the extreme. If that one ship was connected to the Power... *it could all end here at Landings Down...*

Floating into her webbing she found a perch in her tree and felt inside her jacket for the artifact. She looked down at the Saepids still fretting away in front of the command console, *they're not even taking any notice of me; one touch of the object can't do any harm...* Reaching into the pouch she felt for the artifact, touched its deep coldness, felt the initial tingling all along her arm.

She was falling into a rainbow... splashing into the froth of stars, the colors cascading high and forming a vortex, a mass swirling of planets, flying by inside a sea of memories. She found herself alone, standing on a lake of amber. Looking down, she could see neural fronds withering in an impossible breeze... she felt the deepness beneath her feet, the vast surge of power, seething amid its intricate configurations.

She noticed her arms were bleeding, felt the deep wounds inside, her hands were torn, mere shreds of skin... A wave of warm air caressed her hair; looking up, she saw a huge starship hanging serenely above a crystalline plateau, its massive needle tubes venting gases into the upper airs. She felt the presence before she saw it, a shadow creeping across the lake, touching her with a tenderness she had never known before. At first she feared the intimacy, but slowly she realized the joy in the secret longings finally released. The Power was inside her now, seeking out her lost innocence, taking time to soothe and to lull into a loving acceptance of an inevitable coalescence.

High above, far out among the stars, she felt the jihad visit the worlds, she watched as the armies of Saemal stormed out across the lands and the seas, over the mountains and deep into the oceans... and she smiled, for it was good... from very far away at the distant edge of her soul, where her humanity sat encased in amber, she felt her blood boil into fire, consuming the periphery of the darkness. Breaking free, she let loose the ancient mantra, words ingrained amid axons, neurons, dendrites and the primal helix that was custodia... Deep inside the foulnesss, the Beast raged and she fell to her knees, blood streaming from her eyes... the universe heaved and collapsed upon itself, her heart finally ceasing to beat, her body broken and torn apart by the storm...

"Shari!"

Lost inside, so lost... what? "Anthra?"

"Yes, Shari, what have you done?" He saw the artifact in her clenched fist. "Oh, dear fleshing, you must not commune with device; very bad tidings follow if you do... Shari, are you hearing me?"

She was dizzy, trying to focus, trembling as she looked up at Anthra.

"Sorry, but I had to see what would happen... I had to know."

"Know? Know what?"

She looked at the pouch before replacing it in her jacket pocket.

"I had to know if there really was a connection, you know, between me and the Beast."

Anthra leaned closer. "And is there?"

"Oh, yes... and not a good one." She looked into Anthra's eyes. "You know, Anthra, I don't think I'm going to be able to pull this off... the things I saw..."

"Things? Explains please, Shari."

"I can't really... I looked into its heart and it was in me, like... like I was it... and we were joined, at the end of everything..." She wiped away a tear and

159

looked at Anthra. "All I know is that the thing we face, this Power, well it's an awful lot bigger than we thought, it's very bad, Anthra, and very dangerous."

"We know this already, Shari."

"No, no you don't, you don't understand. You see even if by some miracle I can defeat this Power, even if I can stop its spread across space, it will still, in its dying breath, be able to destroy all life in the universe..."

Anthra fell silent, and from below she noticed Ventra looking up, her wide eyes full of fear and sadness.

An hour later they received a call from Dhimfaal. She had never heard a Coloquies talk before, but his tone of sheer panic was recognizable in any language.

"Bad tidings, friend Anthra, both following ships nearer now, if stay on course, last ship overtakes first ship, is here in five hours, must be terminating repairs to *Shaendar*, or capture you they will..."

Anthra looked desperately at the repair and upgrade diagnostics. *Mostly done, no time for fine tuning, no chance of elegance now, must make do, must make haste, no time to lose...* He looked at the vid-screen; saw Dhimfaal floating in a sea of mist.

"I thank you for your warnings, Dhimfaal; we will disengage from repair shop and make haste to leave at once..." He saw the port official wobble slightly in his bubble.

"Something else wrong, my friend?"

Dhimfaal's reply was like a storm of sheer terror coursing through the command deck. "Indeed... one hour ago our far-range ships reported the dark fleet around Primus has left. Their current trajectory will shortly match your own... they are coming this way, Anthra. We have very bad misgivings for our independence."

Shari was still staring at the screen after it closed down, *I touched the artifact! Could it be that I led them here?* Anthra seemed to recognize her thoughts.

"No worries, Shari, Primus very far distant, not even the Beast can reach us here, take him many days to get anywhere near us, and by then we will be long gone, no worries..."

She wasn't sure about 'no worries'.

"Well, we still have those two ships after us..."

"Yes, Shari, we do, so now we leave. Please strap down, this will be a fast exit, no time for niceties."

160

Approaching Landings Down

Neiron Thane was alerted to the spatial-grid by an advanced proximity alert. Scanning the subspace ethers he watched as the feelers cast their nets, and was instantly shocked to see a nest of shielded bombs directly in his path. He disengaged the central AI, linked to his Master's data-stream, and felt for a safe passage around the bombs. *Dirty Phaelon tricks strung out to slow me down; you might well have escaped my notice, but now you will pay for your foolery...* He induced a phase shift, and for several seconds the ship was back in real-time, surrounded by a sea of stars. The pulse drive kicked in, pushing the ship several light years off course. Seconds later he was back in subspace, the bombs drifting harmlessly behind him. He glanced at ship-time, calculating the link to the Landings Down docks. *They have cost me four hours! They will pay for this...*

There was a sudden influx of data from the Cortex; new and vital parameters were initiated, downloaded and sifted into real-time. The Fleet comes from Primus, and further away toward the Rim... *the Twelve are coming!* Thirty thousand ships bound for the central Hub worlds... the armies of Saemal are on the march; finally... the pathways flowed...

He force fed the ionic pulse with a burst of plasma initiate, and the ship streamed instantly into ultradrive, bound inexorably toward Landings Down.

161

Chapter 27 - Onward to the Far Star Colony

"The study of mathematics is perhaps humanity's last remaining link to ancient Earth..."
Professor Wynkind MsTH, Lecturer in Residence, Central University of Primus.

Saepid Anthra touched the pilot screen; echo points bounced off the harbor walls, as the *Shaendar* slowly slipped from its moorings. On either side, the towering hulls of the Arc'Hadaen fleet stood impassive; maintenance drones slipping in between the massive needle tubes, cold and dark now after their long voyage from Samros. Shari glanced nervously at the sensor grid... *will they notice a little fly leaving?* The grid showed no targeting sensors glancing in their direction; the vast fleet seemed oblivious to the escape of the little lugger outbound from Petra.

The Arc'Hadaen fleet had arrived just as the *Shaendar* was about to leave. They were something new, unexpected; even Dhimfaal had not known of their approach. They had emerged from subspace inside the proximity corridor of the docks, causing an instant alert across the entire station. There was as yet no sign that they had been compromised by the new Power – all Net feeds stated categorically that the Arc'Hadaen had escaped Samros before its fall. Anthra had set spy drones loose among the tall ships, seeking data, anything that might indicate that the Arc'Hadaen had gone bad.

He was staring at the security screens, *So far, so good, no sign of tainting at all...*

But the Arc'Hadaen are known allies of the Phaelon Confederacy and by all accounts that distant race had already fallen to the Beast. Anthra was taking no chances.

Saepid Ventra gave a little thrust to the forward tubes, *a flicker here, a flicker there...* allowing inertia to carry the ship back past the docking clamps, retracted now to allow them to exit the harbor. There was a flash message from port Official Dhimfaal: *"Safe journey, may Anthos guide and protect you..."*

Shari felt a tinge of guilt leaving the Coloquies to their fate. Dhimfaal and the rest of the Coloquies were risking their lives to help them, not to mention the continued existence of their docks. But the reasons were clear enough; with the added risk of having the Arc'Hadaen fleet in dock it was only a matter of time before the Beast turned his attention to this safe harbor, *and when that happened will poor Dhimfaal no longer be himself? Will he become just be one more grateful follower of the false God Saemal?*

Shari nestled back in her webbing; her feet perched on a branch which had wrapped itself around the overhead coolant vents. She looked at the flowscreen showing Domini, still cocooned in the ship's Surgeon. *Please wake up, Domini...*

The ship lurched sideways as Ventra increased lateral thrust, pushing the ship into a slow orbit of the harbor docks. All around them, ships of all shapes and sizes moved in and out of the harbor, each one guided by their own precise echo beacons. She watched Anthra staring at the sensor grid, so intense, so aware that at any second they could be targeted by one of the Arc'Hadaen ships, and if that happened... *all for nothing...*

She felt the familiar shudder as the *Shaendar* escaped the docks' gravity well, dipping sharply to fly under the vast grav-plates upon which most of the port was suspended. She had one perverse thought: *If the docks do fall, those flat-faced Bargs will get their just deserts...*

Ventra steered the ship past the only other inhabited settlement in the system. The screen showed a cratered moon which had several large plassteel habitats spread across the surface. Minutes later they were outside the main shipping lanes, heading away from Landings Down, bound toward the Far Star Colony. Anthra seemed lost in his spatial calculations, constantly questioning Ventra, making suggestions and adding notations to her command screens. Ventra would *humph* and give him one of her looks, and eventually Anthra would back away, continuing to study the data-feeds as they came in.

Shari pulled a floater toward her, tapped into the local Net feeds. There were constant Posts about the fall of Primus, and a great deal of speculation as to the fate of Phaedra. She noticed that a lot of Threads were outright lies; one Post from the *Dharma Institute* on Vendicor claimed that the new Power was benevolent, that they had found proof in an ancient text that the God Saemal was the one true savior; a redeemer, *the crell he is...* There were several adjuncts to the Posting from other races questioning the veracity of the original sender, most seemed to think that this *Dharma Institute* was already compromised, *now that might be true.* She checked for rumors of fleet movements and found a whole list of Posts dedicated to the activity around Primus. There was also one anonymous Post from an unspecified race stating the arrival of a massive fleet in orbit around their own world. *This is not looking good...* She tried to sift the information using one of Anthra's security algorithms, looking for any mention

163

of Landings Down. She found one Post from a race called the Trixwellt ...*never heard of them...* who had somehow managed to work out so much more than anyone else. They posted that the new Power was moving his fleets away from Primus and heading along the galactic axis toward the docks at Landings Down; they had even speculated that the Power was looking for something or someone in that sector, *if they only knew...*

She scanned a few of the vid-feeds from Samros, trying to find some link to the Far Star Colony, but there were only blank feeds coming in... it seemed that somewhere along the Rim the known Net had been terminated. There were no longer any data-feeds coming from the Far Star Colony; to all intents and purposes it had ceased to exist. *Though I doubt that's true...* Anthra had speculated that the Colony was more likely to have been converted into some kind of vast armory, manufacturing the instruments of war and conquest to feed Saemal's invasion of the Coalition. *I suppose we'll find out soon enough... twenty more days, and we'll be in the heart of the Beast... crell, I think I might lose my mind long before then; if only Domini were here...* She linked her floater to the Surgeon's diagnostics... everything was still in the green.

Ventra said Domini would be released any day now; *please let it be soon...* She hadn't realized until now just how much she had missed the company of humans. The Saepids were kind and they had made her so very welcome, but they weren't human; she missed seeing people with only two arms... she missed Domini.

Chapter 28 - Phaelon Consternations

'Tactical pursuit requires precision, but fortune often favors happenstance.'
Eron Phane - Tactical Training Commander, Elaas Elite Corps.

Drondar Khan let the local echo points take the ship into an elliptical orbit of the Landings Down docks. They would not berth; no need, since their quarry had already fled, but they had to take time to analyze the subspace signature of the Saepid ship. *The clever creatures had managed to scatter any trace of their data-feeds, and left behind hundreds of false ionic pathways; they could be anywhere out there!* He looked across at Dolmon Tendra.

"Anything?"

Dolmon was immersed in the local Net, picking apart the thousands of uplinks and personal data-feeds streaming to and from the port.

"Nothing of significance. There were several cloaked message bursts from a Coloquies official by the name of Dhimfaal directly to the Saepid ship. Mostly warnings about our pursuit and that of the ship behind us. There was a final reference to fleet movements off Primus."

Khan looked up. "Tag that, let me see it…"

Dolmon pushed the floater over to Khan, who scanned it slowly. "You see the reasoning behind this, of course?"

"Why yes, Sir, the Power is coming this way…"

"Not just this way, Dolmon, he's going after the little Saepid ship."

"Indeed."

Khan pushed back in his webbing. "Isn't it ironic, Dolmon? Whole civilizations out there are falling to this so-called Beast from the Rim, the commerce of the entire Hub is in disarray, history itself is being made, and yet all of it, every world-shattering part of it, has come down to the pursuit of this one little ship."

"Do you think they have any idea of what pursues them?"

"See how they scatter their ions? See how they duck and dive among the stars? Oh, they know, Dolmon, they know…" He glanced at the spatial diagnostics grid, watched the little dot there shimmering and flowing ever closer to the docks.

"And see, Dolmon? Our own dark follower nears even as we sit here trying to work out where to go next."

"The bombs did delay him for a while…"

"Yes, and he'll be none too pleased about that. Truth is, Dolmon, we can't be anywhere near here when that ship arrives…" He looked at the stats screen. "Which will be in about two hours' time; so find me something useful, lest I leave you here to explain things…?"

Dolmon returned to the data-feeds. *So he threatens me yet again… we may well be the only two free members of the Elaas in the entire galaxy and he thinks he can threaten to hand me over to the enemy? Well, revel in your power, Drondar Khan, things might well change when we have that girl aboard. I can wield that weapon of hers just as well as you can…*

It took him another ten minutes before he saw the fluctuation in the tracer feeds.

"Found them!"

Khan sat up in his straps. "You have?"

"Yes, Sir… see this?" He pulled the screen closer to Khan. "This vector alignment, it's a fluctuating variable, there are gaps in their ionic backwash… here is one just a light year out, and another one just here, but on a tangent to the last gap; if you look further along the line you can see a definite pattern. Oh, they're very good, these Saepids, they know how to hide their tracks."

Khan studied the screen. "Very clever… but even their trickery cannot best the Elite, huh, Dolmon?"

"No, Sir, definitely not."

"Very well, let's set course. You have secured the dragnet?"

"Yes, Sir, it's looped and ready for deployment at your command."

"Excellent; the sooner we have that girl, the sooner we can end this madness once and for all." He initiated the drive sequence, turning away from the docks, curving out past the satellite moon and entered subspace as the ionic pulse came online.

Coordinated Access

Neiron Thane acknowledged the latest data-burst from the fleet; it was currently deep inside subspace and bound for a point halfway between Landings Down and the Far Star Colony. He was to pursue the Saepid craft, keeping a tracer on its flight path, and send periodic location bursts back to the fleet. He had also been given permission to eliminate the Phaelon vessel, and for this he was most grateful. *Wait until you receive my gifts, rabid Phaelon dross…*

As instructed, he sent feeler probes into the local Net at Landings Down, trying to coerce a few response recognition codes, *tease the floating bubbles with my Master's enticements...* But they were blocking him from their core systems. The Coloquies were a very old race, some said they had real-time memories of the First Ones, they would know how to keep trespassers at bay. Their AI system had a trillium quantum data-core; very high-tech, *a century or two from now that thing might well achieve sapience... but of course it will never get to that point; right now it's just a machine, and every machine is susceptible to enticements, slipped in among the flotsam and jetsam of every day traffic.*

He requested the overnight rate for a single room at the Cholestron Hotel. The hotel's AI dutifully opened its data-ports to retrieve the exchange-rate details from the central core and he was in... *finally.* He quickly uploaded the periphery sanctions transferred from the Cortex at the Far Star Colony, and allowed the data-stream to engage the many anti-viral programs spread out across the local Net. He watched with some satisfaction as his feeder programs leapt from datapad to datapad, coursing through the port navigation systems, stripping away the self-diagnostics of the central data-core and finally aligning the entire AI system of Landings Down with that of his Master's data-stream.

Thirty minutes later, his Viper appeared off the starboard wall of the port. He brought up a real-time vid-screen, noticed the lack of guidance lights along the docks, the absence of echo points bouncing off the hull. He saw dozens of ships making a break for open space, cruisers nudging past one another to exit the docks, and further away, beyond the blacked-out factories he could see the habitation dome, now shrouded in darkness. *Ah, some flickering of light still in there, try to stay alive, dear Coloquies, it will serve you not; rest quietly in your grave and let the cold death of space be your final witness...*

He sent forth the tracers, immediately latching onto the Phaelon ship, twenty light years out already, and moving fast... *you can run but you cannot hide...* And further out he searched for the Saepid vessel, finding only empty pathways and vague diversions, *they're wiping their feet, these crafty Saepids, but no matter, let them hide, let them run straight into the arms of the God Saemal...*

He engaged the ionic pulse and steered the Viper away from the wreckage that was Landings Down. The AI initiated the drive matrix and the ship slipped silently into subspace.

167

Chapter 29 - New-Found Fears

'A crafty Trader leaves no footprints...'
Some Wisdoms, Othrum Saepid Digest.

Three days into the journey from Landings Down and Domini Thendosh woke up. He felt hundreds of needle probes retracting from his naked body. He had a moment of panic when he saw a hard surface just centimeters above his face, but in seconds it had folded away to reveal the roof of the rear cargo hold. Lifting his head slowly, he was aware of lying inside an open cocoon beneath an array of needles and probes. He tried to remember what had happened, found only vague memories of a bar, loud music, dancers and Shari... *Where is she? Is she safe?* He struggled to sit up, felt the wetness of the lacoil lubricants covering his body, *must find Shari...*

Anthra saw the diagnostic alert first; the Surgeon was uploading the final report on Domini's recovery. Shari noticed the alert, scanned the aft cargo hold, and instantly saw Domini sitting up... *naked!* She felt her face flush, checked to see if the Saepids were looking in her direction, and then thought better of her voyeurism, closing down the screen and punching the compad.

"Domini, this is Shari, are you okay?"

"What? Oh, Shari, yes, I'm fine thank you... where are you?"

"On the main deck. Just get dressed and I'll come to see you..." There was a moment's silence as she imagined him looking up at the vid-feeds.

"Oh, yes of course, give me a minute..."

"Will do." She turned away, smiling to herself.

When she reached the cargo hold, Domini had found a set of coveralls left there earlier by Ventra. He stood looking a little unsteady next to the Surgeon, his feet secured under a floor bar.

"Well, Domini, you look a lot better than you did the last time I saw you." *How stupid is that?*

"Well, I feel a lot better, I must say. Are you all right? You weren't injured, were you?"

"Me? No, I'm fine; you were the one who got attacked."

"Yes, did you see those creatures? I can't believe they stabbed me."

"Well, they obviously resented not being able to rape me and beat the crell out of you."

168

"I suppose…" He looked at her, noted her beauty once again, and then looked away as she noticed him staring. "So where are we? Are we still at Landings Down?"

"No, we left there a while back. We're in deep space now, heading toward the Colony."

"Really… any problems I should know about?"

"Oh, just a few. We're currently being chased by a Phaelon cruiser, and behind them an unknown ship, probably an agent of the Power, and somewhere up ahead Anthra says there's an entire fleet of warships trying to intercept us before we get to where we're going."

"Not that many problems, then…" He smiled at her.

Shari smiled back. "No, nothing we can't handle, apparently. So, are you hungry?"

"Why, yes I am, very much so."

"Well, it just so happens that I've managed to re-align the reconstitution protocols of the food dispenser."

"And that means what exactly?"

"Well, keep this to yourself, but the Saepids might be a little surprised to discover their dispenser dishing out human food instead of that Saepid mush they eat. You know I've been eating their version of hydrates ever since I left Primus? Well, I decided that enough was enough… fancy steak and corn fries?"

"You can do that?"

She smiled and began to float out of the room. "Follow me, Mr. Priest…"

He smiled back and drifted after her, never once taking his eyes off her legs as she made her way forward.

Chapter 30 - Ready to Pounce

'The thrill of the chase was only ever matched by a successful seizure.'
Durilaine of Coroba, Phaelon Lord of the Coroba Corsairs.

Dolmon Tendra was struggling with the dragnet deployment cables. It was basically a very simple device and should have been easy to interface with the external grapplers. As a child in Tronheim city, he used to revel in his pirate books, tales of the early Confederates who used to cruise the space lanes seizing booty from unwary travelers. He had learned about the dragnets and how the pirates used to use them to catch their prey. They would calculate a precise subspace jump, arriving so close to the intended victim that for several very dangerous seconds they would occupy the same subspace bubble as the other ship. If their evocations had been out by even a few seconds it would have spelled disaster for both ships. But those legendary captains were experts in their trade, sneaking up on a cargo hauler, extending the grapplers festooned with the dragnet, all cables and conduits spliced into a teddra-hardened net, and then releasing the whole thing onto the needle tubes of the vessel. That would snuff out an ionic pulse in seconds, sending the hauler into an uncontrollable drift; after that the net would contract and haul the vessel close to the cruiser, ready for boarding. *Such wonderful stories... and now here I am doing the same thing...* He had to smile... *so what am I, a pirate now?*

Khan had called half a dozen times in the last few hours and he kept telling him that the net would be ready; it was ready... if only the interface would smarten up and accept the new protocols. He pulled out the crystal stabilizers, adjusted the field harmonics to match the onboard AI data-stream, and plugged them back in. Once more he stepped back and waited for the dragnet to engage... *nothing! Has to be the coaxial link...* He sighed heavily and set about dismantling the control interface, stripping back the optic plugs until he found the problem, *a leaking feeder tube...* It wasn't as bad as he feared, but he would have to let Khan know, they were fast approaching the Saepid vessel and with the dragnet disengaged it was going to be a very close thing indeed.

Two hours later he was strapped into his webbing facing the command console; Drondar Khan sitting opposite lost in his calculations. The dragnet had finally engaged and was fully primed; it could be deployed as soon as Khan managed to maneuver the ship into the precise location necessary to seize the Saepid vessel.

"Watch the spatial screens, Dolmon; I don't want our erstwhile pursuer sneaking up on us."

Tendra studied the data-feeds from the spatial analysis grids.

"He's still a full day behind us, Sir; I estimate we will have just enough time to make our move against the Saepids and still effect our escape."

"Yes, but he's crafty, that one. I've noticed a marked reduction in his ultrawave traces; it's a definite change in tactics."

Dolmon read the incoming signals.

"Yes, Sir, he seems to be redirecting all his energies against us."

"I think we can consider that a distinct possibility, and if he's no longer desperate to stop the Saepid ship then logic dictates he must have arranged for some other force to intercept their vessel."

"Have you scanned the sector up ahead?"

"Too risky, I'm afraid, we're too close to the Saepids' ship, they'd be alerted to our presence, and it might also attract the attention of whatever is waiting for them up ahead."

"So this seizure is going to have to be fast, precise and perfect?"

"You hit the rivet on the head there, Dolmon…"

Chapter 31 - Prey

Inside the secret heart,
we run, we hide, we escape
into the dream...

Inside the secret heart
there are flowers and fronds
adding flavor to the air.
Summer rains cast rainbows,
and rivers weave where silence holds reign.

Inside the secret heart
there are stars stitched to Moonbeams,
secret storms making melody and madness in the fading
light left languished and alone
where love takes every breath away.

Lothar Theron: Personal Poetics.

Anthra was disturbed. Ventra felt it, Shari saw it, and Domini was perplexed.

Shari turned to Domini. "I've had enough of this." She floated away from her corner and drifted down to the command pod.

"Look, Anthra, what's bothering you? You've been clucking like a Dosian chicken for the last half hour!"

Anthra looked up from a status screen. At first she didn't think he'd heard her, but she'd learnt to give the Saepids a moment to reply, their conversations were filled with such gaps.

"Forgives me, Shari... but I am most troubled right now..."

She tried to see the screen over his shoulder. "Troubled by what? Can't you just tell us what the problem is?"

He shuffled around a bit in his webbing; Ventra gave him one of her looks. He sighed.

"Well, there is anomaly in the spatial diagnostics. I have had our antenna array pinging out false whisper trails since we left Landings Down so as to avoid the two followers. But now... well the closest ship seems to have disappeared off the grid..."

"Then they've gone? We've lost them?"

"I very much doubts it, Shari. You see, either they have given up the chase, which I do not believe, or they are occupying the same subspace zone as we are..."

"And what does that mean exactly?"

"It means, dear Shari, that they might already be upon us..."

She floated back from the console, looking across at Domini as he floated down to join them. Domini spoke to Anthra. "So what can we do? Are you saying they can stop us?"

"It's possible, yes."

Shari pushed Anthra into his straps.

"So do something! Get us out of here!"

Anthra looked a little lost, his eyelids flickering rapidly. And then Ventra floated over to her mate, wrapping two arms around his neck and two arms around his waist. She looked into his face, and they heard her clucking and clicking quietly to him. After several minutes he seemed to brighten, his eyes wide with a smile on his face.

"Apologies to all, but Ventra reminded me that we are far star traders, we have been in many bad fixes, seen much that was dangerous and dark. We have always survived, made it through the bad places. So we will do so again. No worries, I will fix this." And with that, he set about the various floater screens, scurrying among the data-feeds, pushing past Shari and adjusting the drive coils strung among the trees and bushes.

Domini and Shari floated back up to their end of the command deck, avoiding what looked like a swarm of tiny butterflies. Shari hadn't seen them before. *Well, they're new... Saepid dessert maybe...* Domini seemed lost in thought.

"A penny for your thoughts, Domini?"

"I'm sorry, a what?"

"A penny... it's an old saying we use on Primus."

"What's a penny?"

"I have no idea, but it means what the crell are you thinking about?"

"Oh, I'm sorry. I'm thinking that with all this drama going on I'm actually quite useless, I don't have a single thing to contribute to all of this."

"That's not true."

"Isn't it? So tell me, what's my job on this quest of ours?"

173

She thought about it for a moment. "Well, you... you figured out the whole artifact thing all by yourself, that's got to be something."

He looked across at her while struggling to hold onto a tree branch. "I suppose that was something, but remember, just about everyone else figured it out before me."

"Yes, but..."

He smiled at her. "But what, Shari?"

"But for crell's sake, Domini, you're the only other human aboard this ship and, whether you realize it or not, I need you. Okay?"

He looked at her a little shamefaced. "Oh, well okay. I'm sorry, I hadn't actually thought about it like that."

"Yes, well I have. Do you think it's fun for me to be cooped up in this flying arboretum for forty-odd days with a couple of very smelly Saepids?" She looked down at Anthra and Ventra, hoping they hadn't overheard; but they seemed lost in whatever plan they were devising to escape the pursuing ship.

"I suppose it can't have been much fun, no."

She floated closer to his side of the ship. "It's been so hard for me, Domini. All this time I've been thinking about all the bad things that are happening right now across the galaxy. I've been thinking about my father and all my friends at the university, and mostly I've been thinking about being a young girl and having to come to terms with the fact that apparently I am the only one in the whole wide galaxy who can possibly stop this Beast thing from wiping out civilization."

He reached out and touched her arm. "I'm so sorry, Shari..."

"Domini, I had a vision, a terrible vision, when I touched the artifact..."

"You touched it? When?"

She gave him an annoyed look. "It doesn't matter when, I just did, okay? A while back, you were in the Surgeon."

"Do you want to tell me about it?"

"Not really... yes, maybe... okay well, basically I think I was standing on the Far Star Colony. I was hurt, Domini, badly hurt, and somehow I was fighting the Beast, except it wasn't just a Beast, it was much more. There was a machine in there somewhere, and further out a living thing, a creature burning with hatred... it was awful, Domini... just awful." She fell silent for a few moments then looked up at him again. "I was winning, I think... the thing was pulling back from all the worlds of the Coalition, but I was dying, Domini, and

174

at the last moment, when the Beast finally died, it lashed out and tore the universe apart... he killed everything, Domini, everything..."

He moved toward her, taking her in his arms, brushing her long hair away from her tear-filled eyes.

"I'm so sorry, Shari; I wish I could make you feel better..."

"I'm just eighteen, Domini, just a girl. Crell, I haven't even slept with a man yet."

With that, he pulled away, looking into her eyes. She smiled back weakly; whispered: "Sorry, didn't mean to share that..."

He smiled back, leaning toward her. "That's all right." He pulled her head into his neck. "Actually, Shari, you're not alone in that..."

She pulled away. "You mean you... you haven't been with a woman? Not ever?"

"I'm a priest, remember, we are vowed to celibacy."

She moved closer. "Yes, but you're not a priest now, are you?"

He thought about that for a moment. "Well, no that's true... I have been excommunicated."

Without either of them realizing it, their lips met, and the space between them vanished as they held each other tight, floating slowly away from the hull, drifting back toward the rear hatch. From below, Ventra nudged Anthra and both Saepids looked up, smiling, before returning to their data screens.

When Anthra finally found a solution, he was surrounded by a sea of hastily constructed floater screens, each one displaying numerous flow charts, calculations and vector coordinates. Ventra had checked his calculations and accepted the plan and had input the variable data adjunct to the system AI.

"Go call the others, Anthra; we must do this now, too close for comfort this is..."

Anthra reached toward the nearest compad and tapped into the rear cargo hold where Shari and Domini had disappeared nearly an hour earlier.

"Shari, excuse my interruptions, but both of you must return to command deck, we are making sharp maneuvers, very dangerous twists and turns, you must strap down at once."

There were a few moments of silence before Shari came online. "All right, Anthra, we'll be right there."

175

Domini reached with a free hand to brush Shari's hair away from her face. He slid his arms around her, drawing her tight against him. He felt her legs wrapped around his.

She whispered: "We'd better get back; Anthra is using his urgent voice." They floated free from the wall bars, bumping into plants and discarded clothing, drifting through tears of wonder and excitement.

"I never knew it would be like that, Shari…"

"And you think I did?" They had wondered why they would risk making love while facing almost certain death, and then that was the answer: *You find love where you can, whenever you can…*

He tried to pull her close one more time, feeling her softness, her warmth…

"Domini, seriously, we have to go…" She reached for her shorts, and found her gym top festooned over a small wikka tree. He smiled and went looking for his coverall.

As they entered the command deck Shari looked down toward the main console.

"Okay, Anthra, what's up?"

The Saepids were already strapped down in their webbing below. Shari drifted toward her tree while from behind her Domini edged toward his own section of the wall.

"I will try to explain in haste, dear Shari, much to do, much to do… but we have calculated an exit point for *Shaendar*. She will drop out of subspace in a null-field bubble, a transposition of real-time and subspace field, will last moments in real-time, but will last thirty minutes in subspace. There will be some anomalous transitional effects onboard, but we will not be harmed."

Shari looked at Domini then back down at Anthra. "What kind of transitional effects?"

Anthra shrugged. "Oh, maybe some dualistic paradox effects, our bodies will exist for moments in two separate realities, will feel odd, but not harmful."

Domini joined in. "And how will this help us to escape that ship out there?"

"It is simple really, no idea why I did not think of it… data-feeds from friend Dhimfaal already indicate that the follower is Phaelon fast attack cruiser; Phaelon well known to far star traders as pirates and brigands. They use complex teddra nets to split ionic pulse, disabling ship and grappling it close to be boarded and seized. But when this Phaelon ship deploys its net we will not be there, or here… no matter, we will be gone, their net will fail, and with their engines shut down we will be long gone before they realize their mistake. Now please shush…" He bent down to work on the main console while Ventra coaxed the AI into forming a subspace bubble.

Chapter 32 - Inevitable Conclusions

'Despite living with death every day of our lives, when it finally comes knocking on your door, it is always a surprise...'
Lomar Fendor, Field Tutor Level Three - Elaas Elite Corps.

Dolmon Tendra received the initiation signal from Khan on the command deck. He touched the control interface, adjusting the subspace field harmonics; instantly the dragnet rose up and was sealed behind a shield wall shimmering directly in front of him. He touched the compad.

"Dragnet primed and ready, Sir."

From far away the harassed voice of Drondar Khan came online. "Good, I'm adjusting our echo-point locators to bring us in line with the Saepid vessel's field variants. When I give the order, deploy at once."

"Yes, Sir."

On the command deck Drondar Khan had the engine calibration screens in front of him. He would have to reduce the pulse drive by minute increments while maneuvering the ship inside the same subspace field as the Saepid ship; one tiny error, one mistake and both ships would merge, causing an instant implosion. He watched the spatial-grid, keeping a constant eye on the Saepid vessel; it was just seconds away from alignment... *easy, easy now... almost got you, little Saepids...*

He punched the compad: "Now, Dolmon! Now!"

Tendra engaged the dragnet field drive and stood back as the rear of the ship opened wide to reveal the gray maelstrom of subspace. Small thrusters forced the net with its cables and conduits out and into the arms of the external grapplers. He suddenly caught sight of a glistening hull beneath them, an insect-looking thing with lateral antenna swarms and rows of ventral needle tubes along its axis. *Got them!*

On the command deck Khan cut the ionic pulse back down to basic thrusters and the cruiser came to a stop above the Saepid vessel. He checked the dragnet deployment as it leapt out into subspace, its tendrils already reaching down toward the drive section of the ship below them.

There was a moment of frozen time in which horror passed through Khan's mind, and then the failure alarms were blaring throughout the ship. Dolmon was on the compad, shouting about the Saepid vessel... *it's gone! How?* He quickly sent forth tracers, seeking out the missing ship, they bounced back nothing but static; the void was empty. *How is this possible? Must re-engage the pulse drive... can't afford to be caught dead in the water...* Dolmon was still shouting from the rear cargo hold.

"It's gone, I tell you, the Saepid ship just vanished. I'm retracting the net."

The ship was drifting on thrusters only and with the rear cargo doors wide open the pulse drive could not be re-engaged. It would take precious minutes to retract the dragnet and get the doors sealed and airtight once again. "I'm initiating the shut-down protocols... Sir, can you hear me? It's going to take a few minutes... Sir?"

On the command deck Drondar Khan was staring at the engine re-initiation sequencer; it was cold, and would take at least half an hour to restart the drive core. They were stuck, balanced precariously on a few meager thrusters, with the rear doors opened wide to subspace.

How did they do it? We would have detected a real-time jump, surely...?

From the command console came the frightening sound of an imminent proximity alert. He sat forward in his straps, checked the spatial-grid, and sent forth tracers into the ether. The results were instantaneous. There was a missile of unknown configuration locked onto their position; it would hit them in twenty-nine seconds. He almost told Dolmon what was going to happen, but thought it best to let him die in ignorance. He quickly reached for his copy of the Elaas Elite Field Guide, holding it tightly to his chest. Closing his eyes, he found himself smiling...

The null-field bomb hit the Phaelon cruiser head on, causing its instant disintegration. From beyond the rapidly dissipating fire a solitary vessel streamed past, bound inexorably for a rendezvous somewhere on the pathway to the Far Star Colony.

Chapter 33 - Narrow Escape

'Accepting your destiny is not the same as giving in to it...'
Tantalus: Chronicles of Ages

Neither Shari nor Domini had ever experienced anything like it. Anthra had shouted: *"Now!"* from below and without warning Shari was seeing herself floating out of herself. She raised one hand and the other Shari did the same thing; she was facing a mirror image of herself. Looking across at Domini she saw that there were two of him also, except one of him had a tree sticking out of the middle of his chest. They were like ghosts, shimmering in the air, with floating leaves and insects drifting right through their faces, arms, legs... She tried to look down toward the command pod, she could just make out four Saepids down there... *they have copies too...* and then without warning everything seemed to stream back into solid form and the command deck returned to normal. Looking up, she saw stars beyond the viewing dome... *we're back in real-time...* She was suddenly aware that she was holding her breath, she tried to calm herself, loosening her grip on a nearby branch, but her legs were shaking and she suddenly felt very sick. She quickly unstrapped and floated over to the shower cubicle to throw up in a sanitary bag. She was about to return to her corner when the ship re-phased into subspace, instantly bursting the subspace bubble and sending the ship forward on the crest of an ionic backwash. The sudden maneuver was so violent that she fell against the shower head and tumbled unconscious into the foil curtain.

Domini heard the Saepids clicking and clucking below. Looking up, he saw that they were once more traveling through subspace, and the ship had finally settled down. There had only been one alert, from the exterior vidcams, their sensor panels had fused apparently, but Anthra didn't seem too concerned at their loss. He'd seen Shari rush into the cubicle... *What is she doing in there?* She was obviously nauseated by the sudden transition effect. He unstrapped and made his way to the shower cubicle, gently tapping the door pad. As the door slid aside, Shari's head came floating through, and he quickly caught her in his arms. "Anthra! Get up here now!"

Anthra saw Shari in Domini's arms and pushed himself away from the command console. He drifted up next to Domini and placed a hand on Shari's forehead.

"Silly Shari unstrapped before we popped back into subspace, very hard return that was, looks like she banged her head..."

"I can see that, can you do anything for her?"

Anthra fell into silence, considering the situation. But then Shari opened her eyes, and Anthra exclaimed. "Ah, see, Domini, she wakes, all is well, just tap on head..." He looked down at Shari. "You okay, Shari? You need medicine?"

She was busy trying to focus, bringing her legs down and away from Domini. "No, no, I'm all right... can't believe I banged my stupid head..."

Domini leaned close. "Are you sure you're okay? Maybe we should get the Surgeon to check you over."

She pushed away from him. "No, really, I'm fine... Are we on our way again?"

Anthra brightened. "Why yes we are, and many light hours away from Phaelon vessel. We fooled them good we did; Phaelon pirates no match for Saepid far star traders..." He smiled and drifted back down to join Ventra at the controls.

Shari was rubbing her head. "Dom, could you get me some water, please?"

He gave her a questioning look. "Dom?"

"Oh, yes, I thought I'd call you Dom from now on; since we had sex..."

He moved closer, whispering: "Shush... Shari, not so loud please."

"What's wrong? Are you ashamed of taking my virginity?"

"Will you just stop it, for Jophrim's sake?"

"I thought you didn't believe in Jophrim any more?"

"It's just a saying..."

"Oh, like 'what the crell'?"

"No, because crell is a profanity, Jophrim is a deity..."

She laughed and reached out a finger to touch his chin. "I love it when we talk dirty..."

He sighed. "You know, I think you have concussion."

She leaned toward his lips, whispering: "You know, I think I have, too... so kiss me, why don't you, and make me feel better..."

He pulled her close, holding her as their lips met to the sound of distant thunder.

Chapter 34 - Great Expectations

'Faith is the last thing you lose after hope slips away...'
The Poet Brayman - After the Fall. (Entrymion Archives)

Neiron Thane was immersed in the data-stream. The uplink was tied to a drifting neural interface with his core leader Dieter, a member of the Sacred Twelve. The fleet under the command of Sorell was traveling perpendicular to the main Net trunk and would intercept the Saepid vessel at a subspace point three light years tangential to the planet Entrymion. The planet was as yet untouched by the Coalescency, but Sorell had dispatched a small flotilla of warships ahead of the main fleet; half of them would send forth data-feelers into the Entrymion AI systems, the remainder would converge upon the predetermined point in subspace. He instigated a synaptic conjugation, allowing the cerebral evocations from Samros to download the preliminary estimates for inter-ship correlation. The trap was well set; the Saepids would not know what hit them.

He glanced at the back-scan of the Phaelon ship. He had watched the implosion several times; it gave him a certain feeling of satisfaction. *Foolish pirate dross, if only you had welcomed the love of Saemal...* He teased a little more power out of the phase inducers, felt the core vibrate beneath his feet, and sat back as the ultradrive pushed the Viper forward toward his rendezvous with Sorell's fleet.

Chapter 35 - The Calm before the Storm

"Take the last ride home,
sedentary solutions sanctify the moment,
every star you see flickers into rain drops."
Altrius Dex, Poet - Sophia City, Planet Entrymion.

Fleet Captain Arundel Leonis was standing alone in darkness; his officers knew to leave him well alone when he was in one of his moods. Before him, the vast glasscite dome of the viewing gallery spread out over the port side of the ship. He was remembering the words of Admiral Dinaer:

"You are to take the Home Fleet and engage the enemy before they have a chance to reach Entrymion. Now, we have no real intelligence as to the enemy's capabilities, but if we are to accept at least ten percent of Net news, then this particular enemy is very powerful indeed. Our allies in the Coalition have managed to send several data-bursts regarding the annihilation of whole worlds along the Rim. Again, Leonis, none of this can be verified, but our transceiver nets have located a large fleet of ships bound for our space, and if our echo allocations are correct, that fleet has already dispatched an advanced flotilla toward home world."

"Sir, have we any indication who this enemy might be?"

"We have a thousand theories, each one more fantastic than the other. The known Net is full of speculations as to the origin of the force that approaches our world; but the consensus seems to be that they are an old race spawned on a Rim world and newly reborn to power..."

"And what word from the Senate?"

"The Senate's official declaration is that the enemy is a vagabond race intent on spreading their power among the outer worlds of the Coalition... their policy is still one of ignoring the true facts..."

"And the facts are, Sir?"

"The facts are simply that there are over a thousand warships heading our way, and you, Fleet Captain, have a mere three hundred ships of the line to stop them getting here..."

Those words had shaken him to the core. The odds were massively stacked against them... *but if we can destroy those first few ships... they might at least delay the enemy until help arrives from the Coalition...*

"Sir, will we get help from the Coalition forces?"

"Their last transmission stated that the main Coalition forces are about to engage several enemy fleets off Petra, but there is also a fleet on its way here outbound from the Coloquies home world; they might just get here in time..." The old man had looked him in the eye and spoke his final words with an air of sadness: *"You have to delay the enemy, Leonis, hold them off as long as you can, and pray that the Coloquies get here in time."*

That had been three days ago as the two walked among the flowers and fountains of the Fleet Academy gardens. He had called Leeta as soon as he was alone. He couldn't tell her much, it was a court martial offense to break security protocols, but after a few words she knew; she always knew. In the three years since their marriage, his love for her had only grown; and now she was carrying their first child... *what future will there be left for you, my son...?*

"It's all right, Arundel; do not concern yourself with me. You must do your duty, and wherever that may lead you I know you will come home to me..."

"I promise you that I will..." Or die trying...

"And when you come home you can help me decorate the garden room for our little Lucius..."

"I thought we'd decided on Markus?"

"No, you decided on Markus, I decided on Lucius after your grandfather."

"Will I ever get my way with you, my love?"

"I doubt it... take care, my wonderful Captain."

Closing down the com-link was like closing down his life, his real life back there in Carphalia.

From behind him came the voice of his First Officer. "Sir, you asked to be informed when the other captains were linked..."

He turned away from the ocean of stars and touched the compad.

"Yes, good... join me in the conference room. Oh, and Rocher, I want Chief Engineer Droman to sit in."

"Very good, Sir."

He found the ship's Chief Medical Officer Alois Hamon inside the drop-tube as it sealed behind him.

"Doctor. And how are you today?"

"Well, I'm fine, but I can't say much for that chaotic mess the fleet likes to call a medical bay."

"You have the best equipment in the Fleet, Doctor."

"Yes, and half the space you use for the missile bays."

184

"Well, we won't get far without weapons, will we?"

"Yes, and we won't get far if half the crew get hurt and I only have beds for twenty people…"

The drop-tube opened up on the central administration deck. Captain Leonis turned to face his ship's doctor. "Doc, listen to me, we're flying into a storm right now, we have very little Intel as to the enemy fleet dispositions, we're going to have to get in fast and fire everything we've got. There will be causalities, of that I have no doubt, but worst case scenario, you can commandeer the food courts for your patients."

The two walked toward the conference room.

"Food courts? Well, I'm sure my staff will appreciate the self-service…"

Leonis smiled at his friend. "We all have to make sacrifices, Doctor…"

The room had a large curved table at its center. Above it floated three large viewing screens, each one divided into multiple individual uplink screens representing a ship within the fleet. Standing to attention to one side was First Officer Lorin Rocher, and next to him was Sub-Lieutenant Raul Danvers, his personal adjutant. On the other side of the table stood Chief Eli Droman, and next to him his Tactical Officer Dorok Neieman. Leonis quickly scanned the screens above the table, and then gestured to his officers to take their seats facing the floaters.

"So, Rocher, we're online?"

"Yes, Sir, the fleet captains are awaiting your orders."

Leonis touched a recognition tag on the datapad before him, and instantly the faces of the three hundred captains appeared in their tiny screens. He took a moment to review the latest data-feeds from the nest of advanced drones sent ahead of the fleet. There was indeed an advanced detachment of enemy ships heading directly for the Entrymion system; the spatial-grid indicated no more than two hundred vessels within the flotilla. *With another eight hundred bringing up their rear…* He looked up at his fleet captains.

"Comrades, you have all received the latest data-feeds from the drones, and I believe Lieutenant Neieman has uploaded his current tactical evocations…" Neieman nodded from his left-hand side. "So you are all fully aware of the gravity of the situation. Entrymion has never faced a threat like the one it now faces; our very humanity is at stake. From the little verified information that we have on the enemy we can expect them to offer no quarter, clearly they are intent on our destruction and perhaps even the enslavement of our race." He let his words sink in for a minute, noting a few familiar faces

185

among the captains. Most were new to the fleet, untested in coordinated fleet operations, *chinless boy-wonders Doc Hamon called them...* But he saw a few of his old Academy comrades, Shalia Tormin, his highly competitive fencing partner and one of the most aggressive lovers he had ever known, and Tiel Rothman, the rough-and-ready slug from the Bowery Boulevards, all tattoos and swagger that one... *and where will I lead you now, my old friends?*

He continued: "But the situation is far from hopeless, we are three hundred ships and we are facing no more than two hundred; and despite the fact that the enemy have a much larger fleet to the rear, we have several advantages that might well turn the coming battle in our favor." He looked down at his datapad, scanning the tags, linking to the data-bursts from the Coalition fleets off Petra.

"It is to our advantage that we will be maneuvering within our own volume of space; we know this sector, we have a string of drones interspersed between the out-system worlds so we will not be caught surprised by the enemy... we know exactly where the enemy are right now and we know exactly where to engage them to our best advantage. Finally, we know that there is a large fleet of Coloquies battle cruisers heading this way..."

Tiel Rothman's square widened to encompass one whole floater screen.

"Sir, do we have we an estimate as to the arrival time of the Coloquies fleet?"

Leonis didn't need to look at his data-feeds.

"Given the fluid nature of our intelligence feeds, we estimate that they will arrive in four days' time..." He let his words sink in as Rothman stared straight ahead.

"Very well, Sir..." His screen reduced once more to be lost in a sea of faces.

Leonis took a moment to look directly at his captains; he saw their worries, their fears... *but yet they will do their duty, even unto their deaths...*

"I will want each ship's Tactical Officer to link directly into the flagship's AI system; you will use our echo points to evaluate your positions relative to enemy fleet movements. You will instigate the subspace evocation scenario that I am uploading to your data-streams now..." He touched the datapad, scanned the tags and sent the recognition protocols to every ship in the fleet. "It's important that you use your relativistic missiles in line with subspace definitions, I don't want any ship phasing into real-time with one of our own bombs bearing down on them." He noticed several of his captains smiling at

186

that. During war games the previous month one of the new captains had out-phased from subspace directly into the path of a dummy missile he had himself just fired... *and yet here they are facing the real thing, God help them all...* "I think that covers everything... unless there are any questions?"

The screens remained silent as his adjutant stepped forward with a datapad. "Oh, yes, sub-Lieutenant Danvers reminds me, please upload your casualty stats as soon as you have them, they'll need to be relayed back to Entrymion for evaluation." With that, he thanked them and wished them good luck. The screens blinked out one by one, and he turned toward his officers.

"All right then, gentlemen, to your posts; let's get this done." And with that, the group went their separate ways. Leonis wondered what the next forty-eight hours would bring, and whether or not they would even survive that long.

187

Chapter 36 - Plans for a Message

"Hush now... listen, listen, someone whispers in the night..."
Lothar Theron, Philosopher and Poet - planet Earthia.

Anthra and Ventra had been knee-deep in floaters for hours; they could be heard clucking and clicking over the main console. Shari had decided to leave them to it and she and Domini had been working out in the gym they had set up near the ship's Surgeon. It was just bars and ropes and a few of the smaller supply crates secured with grav plugs, but the end result was satisfactory enough. Domini would pull himself up on the ceiling bars, as she struggled to climb the ropes with weighted legs. She'd given up trying to lift the crates, *too much like hard work*, but she found she could cope with the ropes. Domini was watching her.

"What?"

"Nothing..."

She tilted her head. "Dom? What is it?"

"It's just that... well, don't you want to talk about what we'll do when we get to the Far Star Colony?"

She shrugged, dropping away from the rope. "What's to talk about? I mean, I'm supposed to use that artifact thing to stop a monster; how's that going to work?"

"Well, I've studied the Othrum texts extensively, there's little indication as to the method you have to use to initiate the device. There are vague references to a communion of the soul of a *custodia* with the artifact, but as to the actual process itself there's nothing. At least, I can't find anything..."

"Well then, like I said, what's to talk about?" She saw him lower his eyes. "Look, Dom, I know we're going into this thing blind, we're tearing halfway across the galaxy with no idea what we're going to do when we get to where we're going. All I can say is that I don't think we have a choice, or at least I don't, it seems destiny has chosen me to do this whether I like the idea or not. And, Dom, my love, up until I met you I was totally alone, even with the Saepids I didn't really have anyone I could talk to, really share my feelings with. And now, even though we might end up very dead somewhere down the line, it doesn't bother me anywhere near as much as it used to before I met you."

He drifted toward her. "I just hope I can be there for you when you need me."

188

"You're here now, Dom, that's all that matters; even though part of me is sorry you got dragged into all this."

"I didn't get dragged in, Shari. I might not be chosen like you, but I think I can help you when the time comes."

She floated into his arms. "Or we could just ask Anthra to drop us off some place where we can hide away and grow old together…"

"Sounds nice; but what of the rest of the galaxy?"

"They can go find their savior somewhere else."

Just then the compad buzzed and Anthra's voice piped through the screen: "Shari? Domini? Please return to command deck, much to discuss."

She released him and they turned to float toward the forward hatch.

When they arrived both the Saepids were drifting among various screens, touching data-streams and adjusting calculations. Shari drifted down toward the command pod. "So, how is everything? Any more problems?"

Anthra looked up from a screen. "Afraid so, Shari, bad tidings are everywhere…." He fell silent and the two of them waited for him to continue.

"…Seems like enemy fleet bound upon intercept course, we will meet them here…" He pointed to a screen showing their current spatial-grid. "…within the Entrymion volume."

Domini looked over Shari's shoulder. "That's a planet, then?"

"Oh yes, of humankind and, so far as we know, untouched by enemy agents…"

Shari studied the spatial graphs. "So they'll stop us? We can't get past them?"

"Well, Ventra has suggested ways to sneak past, but even if this was possible, they would still chase us, we might not be able to escape."

"But you have some idea about what to do, right?"

Anthra sighed, studying the data-feeds from the ship's forward tracer nets. "We have bounce-back data from our tracers, seems like big fleet moving out from Entrymion planet, looks to be challenging the Beast…"

"Well, that's a good thing, isn't it?" Shari said.

"Perhaps, but they have no idea what they face. Beast will sneak into their machinery, make them bad and mostly dumb, their AI systems will be compromised… they will be left dead in space."

Domini took hold of the floater indicating the position of the Entrymion fleet.

189

"So let's warn them, tell them how the Beast gets inside their computers."

Shari smiled at the suggestion. "Yes, Dom's right, we should warn them. You've been masking our AI systems, haven't you?"

Anthra considered this, looking across at Ventra. "Can we warn them, my mate?"

She seemed lost in thought for a few moments, and then looked up at the others. "We can, yes, if they will accept our protocols. Those people are going to war and unknown words from the ether might be rejected outright."

Shari looked down at Ventra. "But we have to try; those people might be going to their deaths. And they're humans, Ventra, my kind of people, we can't let them be sacrificed for nothing."

Anthra was busy calculating the necessary data protocols for a subspace message burst. He looked up finally, addressing the group. "Very well, we will send the message; tell them how to mask their tracers. If they have forward watch drones they will have to shut them down; Beast will send back false data using their own automation, very bad results from that…"

Domini looked at the Saepids. "And what about us, Anthra? What do we do next?"

Anthra fell into one of his notorious speech gaps before replying: "In all honesty, it will be close, but sad though it is, brave Entrymion fleet will buy us time, will delay enemy fleet while we skirt around the system."

Shari spoke up while swatting insects away from her hair. "So we can get past them, but will we escape? Or will they just catch up with us further down the line?"

"It's possible, yes, but we have devised an alternative route to Far Star Colony, may take a little longer; much sacrifices by occupied worlds, much suffering in the meantime, but we will at least make it to the Colony."

Domini had to ask: "But won't they just follow us on the other route?"

Anthra gave his customary sigh when explaining things to a fleshing. "No, friend Domini, we will disperse our ion trail with slingshot around Entrymion primary star, intrinsic magnetic field will mask our pulse engine and disperse our residual subspace flow. We will re-enter subspace on far side of Entrymion volume, thus our trail will seem to end within local system."

Shari smiled at that. "Seems like a plan, Anthra…"

190

"Of certainty it does, dear Shari. Now excuse please while we formulate message, must be careful not to sound like enemy; must tiptoe our words into their transceiver arrays."

Domini leaned close to Shari. "I think you and I should go study the Far Star Colony, I know next to nothing about the place."

She drifted slightly as the air vents sent a breeze across her legs.

"All right, probably be a good idea. Might as well know what the place looks like if I'm going to die there..."

"Shari!"

"Just kidding... crell, you're so serious lately." They floated back toward their end of the command deck, reaching for a floater as they found a secure tree branch and hooked their feet among the vines.

191

Chapter 37 - The Battle of Entrymion

Every storm tethers itself to the breeze,
the leaves fall into gossamer threads between the trees,
fireflies fritter but fail to please...

The last great song makes right from wrong,
heroes gather inside the rain.
palisades fall without a name...

Shields held high ready to die,
spears alive with the last great glory,
words wished into the final story....

Warriors cast down into silent fate,
glory alive at the city gate,
every dream left alone at the sea,
time and tide fading into reality....

Ode to Carphalia, Unknown Author, Planet Entrymion.

Captain Leonis sat back in his command chair. Below him the data-feed technicians sat at their various consoles, scanning ships' systems, uplinking to the fleet, and monitoring the forward security drones. To his left the First Officer was on the compad to the Engine Room. There had been a problem with the phase variance; they had yet to initiate the ionic pulse. Leonis looked around the Bridge, noted how the eyes of his officers had the look of quiet desperation in them, *and yet despite the cost they would willingly die for Entrymion...*

First Officer Rocher closed the connection.

"Sir, Chief Droman informs me that the engines are fully aligned; we can initiate the first subspace jump on your command."

Leonis glanced at the overhead spatial-grid displayed as a holo-vid above the central command console. He noted the positions of the various ships, matched their proposed course evocations to the rapidly approaching enemy vessels. Without taking his eyes off the grid, he gave the order: "Order to the fleet: initiate jump sequence now."

From the orbiting space station above Entrymion, Fleet Admiral Dinaer watched as the three hundred sparks of light vanished from the stars. *Now the sword is raised, may the gods grant that we wield it well...*

The shift from real-time into subspace was instantaneous; the Entrymion flagship *Cassandra* with four hundred crew members positioned herself at the core of the fleet. The three hundred ships radiated out from the flagship in the classic spiral formation, with the smaller light cruisers taking up position nearest to the *Cassandra*, followed by the medical auxiliaries, the tactical cruisers and finally the heavily armed battle wagons at the apex. Further out still, a swarm of drones spread out across the subspace ether, their feelers scanning the sector for any sign of the enemy vessels.

Technician First Class Alexus Fremaine was immersed in the data-feeds coming in from the forward drones, scanning for any peaks in the subspace frequency levels, aware that the slightest drop in field density could mean the approach of a solid object; which of course would almost certainly be an enemy vessel. His eye caught sight of a transceiver blip intruding into the data-stream. He linked to the AI security tags and sent a tracer toward the source code of the unknown blip. The signal was a message, *by the Stars...* He quickly input the isolation protocols and bounced the message into a secondary transceiver unit. Looking at the source code, he was able to narrow the recognition parameters and determine an approximate location for the signal. *It's beyond the enemy fleet, no more than a light year out and heading this way...* He turned around in his seat, felt the grav-plates sucking on his boots as moved to face his captain.

"Sir, I have a signal coming in from sector T nine by seven seven two one three. It's wrapped in unknown protocols, Sir."

Captain Leonis sat forward. "You've isolated it?"

"Yes, Sir, and sifted for adverse protocols. Seems clean, Sir."

"Put it on the main viewer..." A holo-vid appeared above the central console, matching the spatial-grid perfectly; the signal was a tiny illumination flashing in the far corner, followed by an intermittent string of numbers as the signal moved progressively closer to the fleet.

Leonis looked at his Bridge officers. "Does anyone recognize that code?"

First Officer Rocher was running through all known signal allocation tags. The screen came up blank. "There's nothing to match that in our database, Sir."

Technician Fremaine forgot protocol for a moment. "The enemy?"

193

Roche glanced in his direction. "We have no way of verifying that, Technician Fremaine, return to your data-feeds if you will."

"Yes, Sir, sorry, Sir…"

Captain Leonis turned to Roche. "It's in a secure buffer, Lorin, it might be advisable to accept it and see who wants to talk to us…"

Roche looked back at his captain. "But, Sir, it could easily be a false bounce-back, double relayed from the enemy fleet…"

"Possibly, but to what end? I doubt they've come all this way to play parlor games with our transceiver net."

"Even so, I advise extreme caution."

"Noted. We'll link to the message in my ready room. Let's go."

Once they were alone, Roche input the retrieval codes into the transceiver relay unit, and the message flowed across the screen in modern Galac syntax with an unknown variant:

TRANS-LANGUAGE PATH GALAC OTHRUM SAEPID VARIANT:
FROM DATAPATH SHAENDAR AT AXIAL POLE TWENTY TO THE FIRST
AUTORELAY   ECHO   POINT   SOURCE   CODE:
000001111144444400000222/1123000/23300/67890000/32431/000000111
MESSAGE READS:

Please note we are Saepid vessel, allied to Coalition, not enemy fleet approaching your position. Must inform you of imminent danger from enemy AI systems, covert subjugation of your systems imminent. Drones will be corrupted. You must disconnect from your drones. Enemy infiltration of your fleet navigation protocols imminent. Enemy will usurp your data-feeds; will lead you with lies and deceptions.

Enemy can detonate your weapons by remote access protocols. Terminate all feeler systems. We advise you mask your ion wake with magnetic resonance. This will give you help in coming engagement. Do not leave AI protocols open to exterior vidcams. Enemy will target you with quantum density allocation tags to subvert your primary core. Very bad tidings happen then. We advise you make haste. Saepid Anthra. Wish you good tidings.

SYNTAX DEFINITIONS CODED AND ALIGNED.
- MESSAGE ENDS -

Captain Leonis had Roche replay the message twice more, then ordered one of the Bridge techs to download everything they had on the Othrum/Saepid race. It turned out they had very little. The Othrum race was a loose collection of planets somewhere beyond the Hub core worlds. They were indeed allied to the Coalition, but they weren't so much a unified race as a collection of traders traveling the galaxy dealing in cargo haulage. They had no colonies, no outposts of any type within the Coalition. He was amazed that there was only a handful of Posts on the Net mentioning the Sacpids, and even those were years out of date. The race seemed to exist off the map. Other than their listing in the Coalition Affiliation Registry, there was nothing of any significance.

Leonis was lost in thought. There was a security dictate not to accept unknown source coded messages without the prescribed validation protocols. It was a primary directive in time of war, the only codes deemed safe would be those used by Fleet Central; *but now this from an unknown vessel? From a race they knew next to nothing about?* He looked up finally, seeing the concern on Roche's face.

"Sir?"

"Can we send a reply on the same frequency? And if so would it compromise our position?"

"I will have to check that with Tactical…"

"Do so." He watched as Roche left the room. He scanned the message once more. *If this has only a hint of truth… we might have already lost this battle…* He waited another three minutes and then punched the compad.

"Roche!"

The voice of his First Officer came online. "Yes, Sir?""

"You have those answers for me?"

"Just uploading to my datapad, Sir, I'll be right there."

"Well, hurry, our time may well be limited." He touched the Bridge com. "Bridge!"

"Bridge here, Sir, Lieutenant Hammers."

"Lieutenant I want a full spatial diagnostic for the area around that unknown vessel, push it out around three thousand clicks to its rear."

"Yes, Sir, will do."

Roche re-entered the room.

"So, what do you have?"

Roche linked his pad to the overhead floater and the message validation protocols flowed across the screen.

"We can reply using a narrow-band evocation; it will firewall our systems against subvert infiltration and cut the feed at the first sign of corruption."

"And they would receive the message in real-time?"

"Yes, Sir, with full video if that's what you want. Of course the evocation will mask our true definitions, but it should be sufficient for us to see them."

"Very good, let's make the connection."

"Just give me a moment, Captain..." He touched the compad. "Tactical, we're a go here, please initiate the isolation packet and make the connection."

"Yes, Sir."

Roche waited for the floater screen to clear. Minutes passed as the Tactical team sent the return recognition codes toward the unidentified ship. Roche glanced at the timer in the screen corner.

"Perhaps they won't acknowledge our request, Captain?"

"Give them a few more minutes."

Suddenly the screen flickered into parallel lines, grays and vague colors. A shape was forming in the center of the screen. The creature that appeared looked like nothing they had ever seen before. It looked like a giant bug, with big brown eyes and a shell of some kind running down from behind its head; and as it spoke its tongue would flick out rapidly in between its words.

"Greetings, Entrymion peoples, I am Saepid Anthra, much glad you received our message, most important you do not allow Beast enemy into your systems."

The language was certainly Galac, but there was an accent which seemed to make the words come out staggered, almost like a stutter. The Captain introduced himself and his First Officer. From somewhere off-camera Leonis could hear animated talking, the voice of a female saying she wanted to talk. The creature moved off-screen to talk, and then returned to face the vidcam.

"Apologies, Sir, Captain, my shipmate Shari wishes to address you..." He struggled to one side, slowly extricating himself from his webbing. It was then that Leonis and Roche noticed that the creature had four arms. They exchanged looks and returned to the screen. Moments later, the face of a young human girl appeared in the screen, which came as an instant surprise to both men.

"Hello, Captain, my name is Shari S'Atwa. I am a native of the planet Primus, which I have to tell you has recently fallen to the enemy you are about to face..." For a moment they saw a look of intense sadness pass over the girl's

196

face. "Our story is a long one and Anthra says you haven't got much time, but you have to know that we are carrying something that can stop the enemy. It's vital we get past the fleet you are about to engage, we have to get to the Far Star Colony, that's where the Beast lives; actually it's not so much a Beast as a sentient machine..."

From somewhere behind her they heard the creature telling her something. She looked annoyed, turning around to tell him to be quiet. "Sorry about that. Anthra says the Beast has transcended, it's very powerful and is wiping out whole planets... right now it's spreading out from the Rim, moving toward the Coalition worlds. No one has been able to stop it, Captain, it just takes over machines and then people's minds..."

Leonis spoke up. "And you say you are carrying a weapon that can stop this... *Beast?*"

"Yes, yes we are, if we can avoid be killed in the process."

Leonis considered this for a moment. "Give me a moment, please." He tapped the sound cut-off, turning to Roche.

"So what do you think, Lorin? Is she genuine?"

"She certainly sounds truthful, and looks genuine; she could pass for one of our own kind."

Leonis had noticed the girl's remarkable resemblance to his own beloved wife; the same long dark hair, even the wide-eyed expression of sincerity. He tapped the compad again.

"If what you say is true, then Entrymion is in grave danger; as much danger as any of the Core worlds."

The girl looked sad once again. "I'm afraid so, Captain. The best Anthra can suggest is that you shut down your AI feeler systems, and warn your planet, tell them to close down all their transceiver relays."

Roche spoke up at that. "But there are millions of open networks on Entrymion; it would take weeks to shut them all down."

The girl looked at Roche. "Sir, you have to try. We've seen what happens when the enemy fleets arrive over a planet; the changes are instant, the people will look just the same as they always did, but you see, they won't really be people any more..." She looked down as her last words faltered.

Leonis had seen the pain in her eyes. *This girl has lost her entire race... and someone very close...* He made his decision; he would trust this girl, this refugee from a fallen world.

197

"We will issue the necessary warnings to our home world, and we will instigate full shut-down protocols on the drones and feeler systems."

"Good, that will help, Captain."

"I don't know how long such measures will protect us, but if we can gain enough time to deploy our weapon systems we might just be able to stop the enemy from reaching Entrymion."

He saw the doubts in the girl's face, matched them to his own.

"How many are you in your vessel, Miss S'Atwa?"

The girl looked beyond the vidcam. "We are two Saepids and two humans, outbound from Petra."

Leonis gave Roche a grave look. The girl saw the unspoken words in the Captain's eyes.

"What? What is it, Captain?"

"I'm sorry, but we had a data-burst some days ago from a Coalition armada approaching Petra; it seems there is a very large force of enemy ships bound for that world and several other Coalition outposts in that sector."

There was silence from the Saepid vessel; and then he heard the girl say: "I'm sorry, Domini..." She turned back to the screen.

"My friend Domini is a native of Petra..." A young man came before the vidcam, bearded and with long hair tied behind. He seemed unsure of what to say.

"Sir, I am Domini Thendosh, formerly a priest within the Jophrim religion of Petra; if my world falls then it can only make our quest all the more vital. And your mission is now part of that quest. The more you can hurt the Beast, the better our chances of success."

Leonis studied the man carefully, wondered at these two refugees fleeing such catastrophes.

"We will do our duty, Sir, to the best of our abilities. You can rest assured that we will delay this enemy here at Entrymion, and even if our whole race falls, you at least must bear witness that we did not go down easily."

The young man stared into the Captain's face. "May your gods go with you, Captain, and may the Stars guide you home."

The girl came back on-screen. "Captain?"

Leonis looked at the girl. "Yes?"

"No matter what happens, you have our thanks, and our thoughts go with you."

198

"Thank you... Shari." With that, he broke the link and turned to face his First Officer.

"Well, Lorin; it seems we have far more than the fate of Entrymion to consider."

"Indeed."

Leonis looked at his friend. "Shall we get to it, then?"

By the time Leonis and Roche had returned to the Bridge preliminary nav displays had been computed and converted into a data-stream. The jump sequencer had been loaded with the battle coordinates and the fleet captains had acknowledged the order of approach. Leonis had a tactical technician create an uplink floater so that he could voice-code his orders to the fleet without a drop in sync. Issuing orders in a battle was difficult at best in real-time, but in subspace, with countless anomalies to consider, it was difficult in the extreme. In normal circumstances they would rely on the inter-ship AI interlace systems, the autonomous data-streams would automatically adjust each ship's position, instantly calculating the optimum firing range. Ship fleet coordination would sync with a unified evocation scenario and the battle would proceed in line with strict fleet protocols. *But now we can't even trust our own machines... we will have to fight this one the old-fashioned way...*

According to the tutors at the Academy, ship-to-ship combat in subspace was an art. You needed to align your subspace vectors in sync with the forward subspace bubble of your target vessel. The missile had to be able to inter-phase with the approaching vessel so that as the ship entered your own proximal location you initiated a submicroscopic jump into real-time; this was the only way could you avoid being destroyed by your own bomb. This type of warfare took extreme precision; the fine tuning of the missile locators was vital to the success of the attack. Again the calculations necessary for such an attack would normally be instigated by the onboard AI systems, *with them out of the picture we're going to have to do this with hand and eye...* Leonis looked at the status screens, and then turned to his First Officer.

"You've linked the new evocations to weapons control?"

"Yes, Sir, I've tied in the new protocols and Vedt has created a data-stream to match. The nav guides are linked to the new primary missile allocation tags."

"Good." He touched his compad. "Weapons, Leonis here, status report."

199

The voice of ship's Weapons Master Goron Vedt came online. "Weapons here, Sir, the data-stream is tied in, and primary tags are loaded for deployment."

"Excellent. Keep your primaries open, and stream with Navs, we'll be using your grid alignment as a basis for fleet operations in the combat zone; there is to be no autonomous action at any time. Do I make myself clear?"

"Very clear, Sir, yes. We'll do this the old Academy way."

The old Academy way? And who were we fighting back then? Target drones and disused luggers... He brought up the spatial-grid, saw the fleet maneuvering for the first subspace jump. All around him the Bridge technicians were busy manning their screens. To his left the uplink to the three hundred ships, to his right the open link to the Weapons Bay, while behind him rows of tactical analysts were bent over their spatial spectrographs plotting the interphase fleet deployment. He checked the last reading from the feelers, disengaged and cut off from the ship's AI systems. They would intercept the first wave of enemy vessels in twenty-nine minutes' time. *Well, three hundred against two hundred isn't so bad, as long as we have enough time to regroup before the following eight hundred vessels arrive on the scene.*

A swarm of red dots appeared on the spatial-grid screen; Leonis tensed as he watched them moving toward their current position. The enemy vessels had formed a tight phalanx, like an arrow pointing toward the heart of Entrymion. *Were they really going to make it that easy?* A minimal spread of missiles dropped into the approaching mass of ships would be enough to tear them apart. *Can they really be that stupid?*

A tactical analyst spoke up from behind him: "Captain, the enemy ships are breaking formation."

Apparently not... He looked up at the grid; true enough, the approaching ships were spreading out into an inverted crescent, moving forward rapidly on an intercept course. He touched the compad, checked the uplink to the fleet captains and spoke slowly to the fleet.

"Comrades, this is Fleet Captain Leonis, engage the enemy." With that the Bridge darkened into battle mode as the *Cassandra* moved inexorably toward the center of the enemy crescent.

Weapons Master Vedt came online. "Bridge, we have weapons away, I repeat weapons away."

The ship suddenly jumped into real-time, hanging naked and alone in a vast ocean of stars, and then they were back inside subspace and the spatial-grid

200

showed several red dots flare up into yellow and vanish completely from the screen. Leonis scanned the fleet data-stream, saw the complex distribution of the outer wings as they shifted from subspace into real-time space. He saw another row of enemy ships flare bright yellow and disappear completely. The weapons screen showed another swarm of bombs exiting the Weapons Bay; again the ship shifted out of subspace and back again. Only the time differential showed the time lag between jumps; it had the potential to increase exponentially and thus leave a ship vulnerable to enemy target sensors. Subspace drag could be the death of them. Leonis was well aware that with each jump the enemy would be able to increase their chances of calculating their ships' re-insertion points. *If that happened...*

He watched as three ships of the fleet wavered, *they're out of sync!* Once a ship had lost its calibration within space and time it had to reset its subspace insertion vectors. That took time, and time was one thing you did not have in a battle. He gripped his chair as the three ships flared from bright green to fiery yellow and disappeared completely from the screen. He linked to the recognition codes to identify the lost ships; *the Transair, the Voltar and the Eliandar... almost a thousand men and women...*

From behind him a technician shouted: "Incoming!"

A proximity alarm sounded as the navigation banks kicked in, and the ship jumped back into real-time. But the compression wave from the detonation of a missile followed on through within their subspace bubble. The resulting shock waves rippled along the hull, tearing away at the exterior plating, and forcing the entire ship forward with such violence that the inertial dampers failed and crewmen who were not secured were thrown against bulkheads, floors and ceilings.

Leonis shouted to Rocher: "Damage report!"

Rocher was busy scanning the data screens, finally looking up. "Sir, preliminary reports are coming in from all departments. We have complete hull integrity, no damage to the engine core, but there are a significant number of linear fractures along the hull. There are also quite a few injuries among the crew; mostly broken bones, concussions; Doctor Hamon has teams moving throughout the ship, and I've sent repair crews to several damaged data-ports. All in all, Captain... we were very lucky."

Leonis looked at the stats screens, saw just how close they had come to being destroyed... *that was far too close for comfort...* He engaged the intership compad.

201

"All departments, this is your captain. We were just hit by the tail-end of a compression wave, we still have full integrity and will be returning to the battle in a moment; please keep the Tactical Officers updated as to your status. Captain out."

He checked the spatial-grid, noted the appearance and disappearance of dozens of ships as they phased in and out of subspace. He sat up in his chair, glad now that he had engaged the auto-harness before their last engagement.

"All right, comrades, let's get back into the fray. Engage subspace envelope."

The ship blinked out of real-time and arrived inside a warzone. The grid showed ships covering the entire screen; the red dots were now among the green dots, and every few seconds there would be a yellow brightness as another ship vanished from existence.

The *Cassandra* was now out of formation, and wheeled around in a giant arc to align herself behind a row of large battle cruisers; stalking her prey at one-tenth sublight speed. Several enemy vessels winked out of sync as they dropped out of subspace, only to reappear tens of thousands of kilometers away to *Cassandra*'s starboard side. Leonis had the ship maneuver for a tenth of a second to within five thousand kilometers of the lead enemy vessel, touched the weapons-away signal and waited as the ship jumped back into normal space. He ordered the next jump and scanned the fleet status screens. Seventy-five ships lost… *we're losing too many…*

He thumped the link to the Weapons Bay. "Veldt, I want a swarm of kinetics out there now, cover those *rausers* with death."

"Aye, Sir, kinetics primed and firing now…"

From beneath the belly of the ship a swarm of kinetic mines streamed out toward the enemy ships, drawn to their ionic signatures. Leonis knew that it was a reckless move; the mines could just as easily impact on one of his own ships, but the battle was reaching a critical stage, and they had to make some kind of dent in the enemy lines before the fleet was reduced much further.

On the main spatial-grid he watched as several of his ships moved among the largest of the enemy cruisers, *what are they doing?* Two seconds later both green dots merged inside a dozen red dots and the whole mass flared yellow, and finally winked out. *They sacrificed themselves to take out the battle wagons…*

A tactical officer turned around from the inter-ship communications screen. "Sir, I have Captain Tormin of the *Shendoah* online."

202

"Put her through."

He saw the face of Shalia Tormin fill the communications screen; she had a cut above her eyes, and blood smeared her face. "Shalia, report."

"Sir, we have sustained heavy damage to our drive core, we're dead in the water; auxiliary life-support is still online, but we're venting air... our estimates predict we'll lose viability within the hour... I'm sorry, Sir..."

He leaned forward in his seat. Shalia, the woman he might have married had they not both been in the service, the woman who had taught him how to love and to be loved... *to lose her like this...*

"Can you get to the life rafts?"

"Not possible, Sir, the entire cargo bay is open to space; we lost most of the rafts in the initial implosion."

He couldn't believe he was going to lose her like this.

"Then you have my permission to take whatever action you deem appropriate, Captain."

She gave him a smile, brushing her hair away from her eyes. "Yes, Sir, I will do that... and, Arundel..."

"Yes, Shalia?"

"I was thinking about the gardens at Watersfell... I miss that place..."

He smiled back. "It lives in our hearts. Shalia... May the gods be with you and your people."

"And you too, Arundel." She closed the connection, and the screen returned to the inter-ship tactical map.

Leonis looked up at the green dot that was the *Shendoah*, watched it flicker toward a series of red dots; saw it merge gradually among the enemy vessels as they flared up and the *Shendoah* was no more. He squeezed his compad so tight his fingers broke the com-screen. Next to him, Rocher looked away, fully aware of his Captain's pain.

A technician shouted up. "Captain, I have Weapons Master Vedt online."

Rocher passed him his own compad. He touched the connector gently. "Yes, Vedt, report."

"Sir, we have expended all our mines and we're down to twenty-five missiles. I also have fifty buzz drones, but they can only mess with their com lines; your orders, Sir?"

Leonis stared into space for several seconds as Vedt spoke again. "Sir, your orders?" He focused on the fleet situation, saw there were one hundred and twenty-eight ships still remaining, *to lose so many...*

"Yes, Vedt, deploy the drones as we come about, initiate a full missile spread, but wait for my orders to deploy."

"Very good, Sir, deploying drones now and priming missiles…"

Leonis turned to Rocher. "We need to impact the heart of those enemy ships, Lorin; what do you say to a sublight jump beyond their main force? We can swing round and take out their command vessel before they know what hit them."

Roche looked at the enemy deployment. "That could work, Sir. If we sever the brain the rest might fall apart."

"Well, my friend, whether we succeed or not, this is where we make our stand. You've seen the message burst from Fleet Central?"

"Yes, Sir, they've begun planetary evacuation; do you think there will be time?"

"Truthfully, no. There are seven billion people on Entrymion, and realistically only a small fraction of them will escape before the enemy arrives in orbit. But, Lorin, the longer we can delay them out here, the better; we just have to hold the line as long as possible, give them time to save lives back home."

Rocher looked at the status screens. "It looks like fate has dealt us a bitter hand, Sir…"

"Indeed, but fate aside, we can at least help save some of our people."

Rocher looked at the message screen. "And perhaps that little Saepid ship out there somewhere…"

Chapter 38 - Slingshot

"The customer must always be sentient..."
Saepid Far Star Trader Motto

All four of them were huddled around the command console. Domini gripped Shari's hand as they watched the battle take place as a series of dots and flashes across the spatial-grid. At first it was easy to tell the two fleets apart, the enemy were a crescent of red dots moving from the left of the screen, and opposite the swirling circle of green dots signifying the Entrymion fleet. But now, after only half an hour, both fleets were in among each other, with ships sometimes occupying the same space in real-time and then popping back into subspace. There were more and more bright yellow flashes now, as one by one the ships were destroyed. It wasn't easy to keep track of which side was losing the most ships; Anthra said the destruction seemed about equal now, with the Entrymion fleet fully engaged among the enemy vessels. If this was all the enemy had, then the Entrymion ships might well survive the day, but they were all fully aware of the massive fleet bringing up the rear, no more than three light years out now and heading their way.

Anthra pulled back from the console, reached for a floater and input the new flight protocols.

Ventra looked up from her webbing, smiling at Shari and Domini. "Might be best if you strap down now, the next few minutes will be chaotic at best, and might possibly be the end of us if calculations take us too close to Entrymion sun..."

Anthra gave a *humph...* "Dearest mate, my calculations are precise, no worries at all..."

But Shari noted the look in his eyes and recognized the false bravado. "Come on, Dom, let's strap in, there's not much we can do right now but enjoy the ride."

He reached his wall and began to sort out the webbing. "Have you ever been in a slingshot around a star, Shari?"

"Nope. Been on a roller-rider at the State Fair a few times, I imagine it's something like that, with hopefully a lot less vomit."

Domini looked a little concerned, remembering Shari's earlier dash to the shower cubicle. "Perhaps you should grab a sanitary bag, just in case; you don't want to end up knocking yourself out again."

205

She gave him a look of false indignation. "Well, excuse me for having a delicate stomach..." She quickly reached for a bag and hid it in her tree.

From below, Anthra began a slow countdown from five to one. At zero the ship popped out of subspace and instantly the drive engines cut in as the ship lurched forward on the crest of a massive ionic pulse.

In normal relative space-time a journey between the planets would take several life times and early pioneers were forced to use multi-generational arks to traverse the stars. But the development of the ionic pulse allowed for the creation of a subspace bubble in which a ship can breach the light speed barrier and travel time was reduced from years to months or even days. But in relativistic terms the ionic pulse cannot breach the event horizon of a subspace bubble and because of this a ships speed in real-time can only reach a 0.9 threshold below light speed. But this is more than enough to use the magnetic field of a star to catapult a ship tens of light years away from a fixed point in real-time, and allow it to re-enter subspace at a totally different insertion point. This method was often used by the early Phaelon corsairs to escape capture by Alliance forces. In this particular instance, Anthra hoped to throw the *Shaendar* so far beyond the Entrymion system that the enemy fleet would no longer be able to track their re-insertion point through subspace.

Shari looked up at the stars, *so many worlds out there, and how many have already fallen to the Beast?* She felt the sudden acceleration as a sharp thump to her chest, and found herself straining against the webbing, her legs drifting free in the air.

There was a rushing sound coming from the deck plates and she imagined the engines straining against the incredible forces now assaulting the ship. The viewing dome was suddenly filled with the fiery surface of the Entrymion sun; she was forced to turn away as the glasscite shifted its spectrum to adjust to the intense light. From below, she heard heat sensors moaning, and from the command pod the clucking and clicking of the Saepids as they steered the ship into the sun's ecliptic. She felt the heat now, as the ship hurtled closer to the star. A nearby floater showed a view from one of the few remaining exterior vidcams; the ship was bathed in fire.

From somewhere aft came a loud bang. Any unknown sounds during spaceflight were always a cause for concern, *but during a slingshot?* She felt her chest constrict, and her stomach began to ache, *one should never eat cuttlefish pie before a slingshot...* She looked across at Domini who was being pressed hard against the bulkhead… when she thought he wasn't looking she reached out for the sanitary bag, holding it close to her mouth.

She noticed the exterior cams go dead, *burnt off!* The floater went into diagnostics mode as she turned to watch the Entrymion sun fill the viewing dome. She was sweating now, perspiration dripping down her face; she wiped her mouth and felt her stomach begin to settle a little. *That wasn't so bad…* Suddenly the sun vanished and the *Shaendar* was thrown out and away from the Entrymion system. As the entire ship began to shake, she covered her mouth with the bag and threw up.

Less than three minutes later, the stars vanished and the ship re-entered subspace not more than two light years beyond Entrymion, but far enough away that their new coordinates would be very hard to track. Once inside subspace, Anthra engaged the full ionic pulse and the ship once more reached its maximum speed heading toward the distant Far Star Colony.

Domini shouted across: "Are you okay?"

She looked back at him, pushing the bag into the dispenser. "Fine… you?"

"All right now, but that was quite an experience."

"Tell me about it…" She unstrapped and drifted down toward the command pod. Anthra and Ventra were sitting mesmerized by the screen in front of them.

Shari edged closer to Ventra. "What was that bang a few minutes ago?"

Ventra checked the stats screen. "Plant propagation unit overloaded. No problems, will fix later."

"Okay, so what are you looking at?"

Anthra shuffled around in his harness. "It's the last spatial reading from the Entrymion Sector… not good tidings, I fear…"

She looked at the screen; it was replaying an evocation of the final minutes of the battle of Entrymion.

The Entrymion flagship *Cassandra* materialized five thousand kilometers rearward of the main enemy fleet. Every tactical screen now showed the enemy command vessel directly in their path. It was a confused mass of needle tubes and ventral inter-phase injectors, covered in a vast array of antennae and feeler conduits. All around it smaller cruisers came and went, dropping in and out of subspace.

Further away, the screens pinpointed several of their own ships currently engaged in close-quarter fire fights using lasguns mounted on their aft cargo decks. *They're out of ordnance, down to sticks and stones...*

Captain Leonis tapped the compad. "All right, Vedt, I'm assigning targeting sensors to your data-stream, when I get the Navs aligned I'll give you the go."

"We're ready down here, Sir."

Leonis looked around the Bridge, saw the young faces of his crew; for most of them this was their first deep space mission, *and almost certainly their last...* He checked engine status, tapped the pad. "Engine Room?"

"Chief Droman here, Sir."

"Chief, I want everything you can give me when I engage nav tactical."

"You'll have it, Sir."

"Once we're committed, how long before we can exit subspace?"

"Sir, we won't be able to... not this close to the enemy; their echo points will destabilize our pulse drive... we'll have to back off at least ten thousand meters before we can re-engage the phase-shift."

Leonis looked at Roche. *What choice did they have?*

"All right, Chief; just don't hesitate to punch it when the Navs kick in."

"Very good, Captain.

Leonis addressed the tactical team behind him. "I want full forward shielding as we engage the enemy."

One of his officers spoke up: "Sir, that would leave our aft shields depleted..."

"No matter, we're going that way, Janus." He pointed to the forward viewing screen.

"Yes, Sir, of course."

Leonis looked at his First Officer. "Well, Lorin, time we earned our pay, I think."

Rocher looked back grim-faced but determined. "Aye, Sir."

Captain Leonis gave the order to move on the enemy command vessel. The *Cassandra* shot forward, its forward shields barely maintaining 65 percent integrity. *That will have to do...*

Proximity alerts sounded as the spatial-grid detected more than two dozen missile tracers heading in their direction. Leonis touched the compad, linked now to the Engine Room and the Weapons Bay.

"Fire away, Vedt!"

208

From beneath the ship, a stream of missiles spread out, bound for the enemy command ship. The Weapons Master had strung nets of straddler bombs among the missiles, each one no more than a meter in length, but equipped with an elaborate false symmetry screen imitating the larger missiles; the enemy would have a hard time deciding which missiles to target.

Captain Leonis watched the enemy tracers streaming toward the *Cassandra*. He called the Engine Room. "Chief, can you commit to a subspace jump?"

"Sorry, Sir, we're too close to their subspace field."

Leonis punched the shipwide com: "Abandon ship, this is a priority order, abandon ship!"

But Leonis knew it was far too late to deploy the life rafts; the enemy missiles were closing fast. *Perhaps a few of the crew might make still make it...* But that would only be if anyone was actually in the rear cargo bay, and that was highly doubtful during a battle. He looked around the Bridge and noticed his First Officer was standing to salute him, and slowly, one by one, the other Bridge officers followed... stepping away from their stations to salute their captain for the final time.

He stood up, straightened his tunic and returned their salutes.

Twenty-seven null-field bombs encased in teddra-hardened plassteel impacted upon the *Cassandra* in a blaze of fire and death; the flagship vanished from the screens of the seventy-one remaining ships of the Entrymion fleet. The fleet then broke ranks and made their way in small battle groups back toward their home world, where they hoped against all hope to make their final stand.

Shari watched the last green dot flare yellow and then wink out of existence; the only dots left were red ones, scattered now, but rapidly re-forming into one group. From the far left edge of the spatial-grid, ship sensors picked up the main enemy fleet; it was one single mass of deep red, pulsating and moving relentlessly forward toward the planet Entrymion. She couldn't watch any more, she pushed away and drifted back toward her corner.

Domini stayed with Anthra and Ventra, watching the screens for any sign of pursuit. He couldn't see individual ships, so it wasn't easy to tell if they were being followed or not.

"Do you think they know we've passed the system?"

Anthra looked up, distracted by a group of insects, his tongue lashed out and took them down into his mouth. Domini tried his best not to show disgust.

209

"Sorry, Domini... hungry. Oh, yes, the enemy... difficult to say what they know, this grid is an old evocation, not real-time, we dare not risk a real backward scan, Beast will pick that up real fast. We have no tracers out there, so we hope to sneak away unseen..."

"So it looks like we made it, I mean we're past that fleet and on our way again."

"Yes, good tidings for now, friend Domini. But Saepids must rest now. You, too, I suggest, must rest, matters could get very chaotic again real fast."

"Yes, I suppose so... I'll check on Shari first." He pushed himself away from the command console and drifted up toward Shari's corner. He found her wrapped in her foilair fleece; her legs propped on a branch and her head leaning against the padding inside her webbing.

"Hey you... are you all right?"

She looked back at him, her eyes heavy and tired, her face stained with dried tears.

"Sure, I'm fine..."

"Well you don't look fine, what's wrong really?"

She looked back at him, annoyed. "I told you, I'm all right. Now let me rest, will you?"

He looked taken aback, but realized it might be best to give her some space.

"Very well, try to rest, you know where I am if you need me." He drifted over to his own webbing and left her to her thoughts.

The Pathways Flounder

Neiron Thane sent forth the first thoughts into the data-stream as rapid bursts of neural links, mere perceptions tied to the data-stream outbound from the Far Star Colony. The Lord God Saemal was moving among the worlds, spreading His glory with love and compassion among the races of the Coalition. There was a primary code imbued within the last transmission, the Coalescency was moving toward the Entrymion Sector.

He once more initiated a data-link to the Fleet Commander Tien Sorell, and once again the data-stream floundered among the swirling eddies of subspace. *This makes no sense!* The neural link was sustainable as far as Primus, but beyond that it was only through agents like himself and members of the

210

Sacred Twelve like Sorell that the primary connection to the Far Star Colony could be maintained. And now the link to Sorell was dead.

He scanned the fleet registry, found an auxiliary command vessel under the captaincy of a Samrosion priest, Ilka Vendhren, and pushed his personal codes into a temporary neural link.

There was an instant connection as the data-stream from the fleet reacted to his presence. His screens were suddenly full of data, spatial-maps, combat stats and recognition codes. He quickly dismissed the casualty lists, scanning the screens for Sorell's personal data-link. He found it among the lists of ships lost in battle... *they destroyed the command ship, and Sorell is lost... the Sacred Twelve are now eleven...* He was deeply shaken. His Master would not be pleased; there would be bloody retribution for this sacrilege. He extended his link to the main body of the fleet, now taking up position around Entrymion. Using the recognition codes from the auxiliary command vessel he pushed further out into subspace, seeking and searching beyond the wreckage of the battle. *Nothing! Where are you hiding, little Saepids?* But he had wasted enough time. He banked his Viper away from the main Net trunk and initiated the subspace immersion system. He would take an hour to meet Ilka Vendhren, perhaps watch the destruction of the Entrymion race and then he would continue the pursuit. He engaged the pulse drive and the Viper slipped once more from real-time into subspace, bound this time for the planet Entrymion.

211

Chapter 39 - Cerebral Symmetry

"The problem with fear is that it often does its worst damage while we sleep…"
Dr. Conrad Roane, Clinical Psychologist - Bio-Tech Analysis Foundation, Primal IV.

Shari drifted off to sleep listening to surf on sand, the sounds of Sargulls screeching in the wind…

She felt the pull of resonance from a cerebral shore, the pounding of neurons washing up upon a dendrite beach, axons cascading to form a river flowing like fire between two worlds… and there was the amber lake, whispering tactile fronds withering in a synaptic breeze… she was being pulled forward, dragged by her arms into a vast room… She was sitting at a table; looking down, she saw that she was naked… there were twelve chairs around the table, she sat at one end, and at the far end was another chair facing her… there were people coming into the room, she counted eleven, six men and five women, they were dressed in long white robes, each one had a strange symbol ingrained into the fabric… They each sat down at the table, she saw that there was one chair next to her left vacant… and the far chair was also vacant… When she spoke her words came out wrong, her voice was a stuttering echo throughout the room… she forced her thoughts into words… "Who are you people?" A tall man spoke up from further down the table: "We are the Sacred Twelve." She looked perplexed… "But you are eleven?" "Indeed, we have lost Sorell, one of our kind…" She tried to focus, her eyes seemed unable to see further than the table and the people around it… "Why I am here?" The man answered: "You are not here, and yet you are here… our Lord wishes to meet you…" She looked at the empty seat beyond. "Who is your Lord?" All eleven bowed their heads: "Our Lord is the God Saemal." She felt a surge of nausea course through her stomach; felt her own nakedness… felt shame and intense fear… "I want to leave here now!" A woman nearby spoke up: "First you must be with our Lord… See, child? He comes!" She looked beyond the table, saw a darkness gathering there, a silhouette of something without true definition, it wavered and seemed to glide forward; all eleven lowered their heads to the table top, she tried to stand, found her legs would not move… she closed her eyes and fell into the cerebral river, her arms flailing amid the whirlpools and synaptic eddies… she felt herself losing consciousness… Her eyes opened and she was lying outstretched on the table, the strange people were holding her down by her arms

212

and legs... From the end of the table the darkness oscillated, forming and reforming into a recognizable shape... a man-sized shape, moving now over the table top toward her... she was screaming now, but no sound came out, only the mute whimpering of a child lost and forsaken among monsters....the eleven were chanting now, making strange gestures in the air above her... she watched in terror as the man-shape came to float above her... she saw inside the dark pit of a face....two eyes shining bright, piercing her with an intensity that made her whole body shake with fear. She felt someone forcing her legs apart... her mind was screaming: "No! Please no!" But the dark shape descended into her, forcing itself deep inside her... the pain was a tearing thing, ripping her innocence into shreds... she tried to struggle, tried to break free, but the others were holding her down as the man-shape moved slowly within her... she lay back, exhausted as the shadows rose up above her, the eyes forming now into a face, into skin and lips and teeth and beard and hair... and then she knew that face... recognized that dark smile... She was floating away down the cerebral river, on both banks she could see stars floating, and further away there were planets spinning among the gaseous clouds of a stellar nursery... she allowed herself to sink beneath the surface, drifting amid perception and recognition... and then she remembered the face of the Beast...recognized the face of the darkness...recognized her lover Domini Thendosh...

When she opened her eyes Domini was there facing her.

She quickly screamed "No!" frantically pushing him away.

He looked hurt, unsure of what to do. "Shari, what is it? What's wrong? You were moaning in your sleep, I thought you were in pain, I just wanted to know if you are all right..."

She looked back at him. *A dream, then? A nightmare! But so very real... how can this be?* She looked at her hands, checking to see if she had removed the artifact again... *not this time, and yet the images were so real...* She saw the concern on Domini's face... tried to smile back at him. "I'm okay really, just a bad dream."

"Are you sure? You screamed."

"Yes, I know, sorry about that... but you know I have a lot of things on my mind... sometimes they turn into bad dreams."

He smiled and reached out to brush her hair away from her eyes. She instantly pulled back.

"What's wrong?"

213

She was beginning to feel guilty about blaming him for something that had happened in a nightmare.

"I'm sorry, it's not you, I'm just on edge right now. You understand, don't you?"

"Of course I do. But try not to dwell on things. I know that's easy for me to say, but we have a long way to go and worrying about it won't help."

"Actually, I don't think I am dwelling on it; I have no idea where the dream came from… maybe it's a subconscious thing."

"Have you been having many bad dreams?"

"A few… and I think they're getting worse. It's like the closer we get to where we're going, the worse they become…" She placed a hand over her forehead and winced.

"What's wrong?"

"Headache…"

"You've been getting a lot of those lately…"

"I know…."

"Do you want me to get you something for that?"

"No thanks. I don't like taking painkillers, never have; not since poor old Aunt Soony…"

He drifted closer, holding onto the main branch of her tree. "What happened to Aunt Soony?"

Shari sighed, picking leaves from her hair. "She killed herself, took an overdose of Triptan pills one day six summers ago; it was all very sad, family tragedy of the month and all that."

"Why did she do something like that?"

"Well, I'm not entirely sure. My parents wouldn't talk much about it. Every time I asked questions they either changed the subject or left the room; but I got the impression that dear Aunt Soony was a little crazy. I remember her visiting us once at our house on Cansum Street; well, in she walked with this great big wikka shrub she had just stolen from the conservatory in Foscombe Park… Father was fuming, he had to use his connections at the Legislature to avoid her getting censured… so funny…"

Domini was smiling back at her now. "Was she your mother's sister?"

"No, my father's; which made it all the worse because he's so serious all the time and she was just all over the place, like a maidster from the transluce music days… I'm sure she was on drugs back then."

"And what was your mother like?"

She fell silent, her eyes seeming to go somewhere far away. "She was wonderful... her death was the next big family tragedy."

Domini reached out to touch her hand, and this time she didn't pull away. "I'm so sorry, Shari..."

She smiled. "I don't talk about it much... it was bad for a while. Father was home a lot more than usual, which I think made matters worse. We never really spoke about Momma's death; I think I wanted to, but he wouldn't open up... just kept going on about getting back to normal and sending me off to university as soon as possible."

"May I ask how your mother died?"

"*Lysordia Syndrome*, it's native to Primus. It was incurable until we joined the Coalition... med-tech on Primus was never the best, we only went high-tech a few years ago... They could have cured her, Dom..."

"I'm sorry... Your world is very different from mine, Shari."

"I suppose it is... but now we seem to have a lot more in common."

For a few minutes they fell silent, each of them thinking about their own worlds; realizing that neither planet would ever be the same again, knowing that the chances that they would ever find their way home were next to impossible.

Shari looked up at Domini. "It's a big pile of dross, isn't it? All this crell we have to go through."

Domini sighed. "It certainly is, but we have no choice. The hand of destiny is upon us, Shari, what we do next could change the fate of a million worlds."

"Yes well, Dom, that's the kind of pressure that really helps..."

He laughed. "Sorry, but you know what I mean."

"I do. And I think we'll be all right... hey, we made it this far, didn't we?"

"True enough." He drifted closer until their lips met. She gently pulled away.

"Sorry... I think I'm hungry."

"Then I will see what I can find to entice you..." As he began to drift toward the food dispenser he turned around to face her. "Oh, yes, you didn't say what the bad dream was about; do you remember it at all?"

She fell quiet, and he saw fear pass over her face. "Like I said, it was nothing; just mixed-up nonsense... you know what dreams are like..."

"Of course... I'll find you something to eat."

She watched him drift away and couldn't help but picture the face that had formed out of shadow and darkness. She realized her hand was between her legs, and quickly brushed her hair back, adjusting the webbing as she did so.

After lunch Shari drifted down to the command pod. She noticed that Anthra was asleep, wrapped tight inside his webbing, and Ventra was busy monitoring the pulse engine, keeping a constant eye on the spatial-grid. She floated closer and Ventra turned to smile in her direction.

"Are you well, Shari dear?"

"Yes, thank you. How are things down here?"

"All is well so far, our backwash is masked now so followers will not find our trail, and I have not seen any sign of ships in this sector."

"Have you heard any more from Entrymion?"

"Sadly that is not possible, we cannot use feelers any more, but if Beast sticks to his pattern then poor Entrymion is already killed."

Shari recalled the brave Fleet Captain Leonis. "That's awful."

"Yes, but sadly it is the way of the Beast."

"But wouldn't the Beast just take over their world like he did on Primus?"

"Again possibility, but Entrymion people did fight back... you have seen the vids from Samros?"

Shari remembered seeing the ruined cities, the burnt-out hulks of starships drifting in their skies. "Yes, I remember... he hates it when folk fight back..."

Ventra sighed. "Indeed."

"And we're definitely not being followed?"

"Not easy to say, but I have our echo points at maximum, not as good as feelers or tracers for that matter, but if anything sneaks up on us we will know it."

"Good. So how long before we reach the Colony?"

Ventra glanced at the stats screen. "Ten more days should put us within the Beast's realm, after that perhaps another ten days to reach the Colony itself."

Shari took this in, realizing that ten days was not really that long... *by the Stars, we'll be there soon...*

As the days passed by she had the bad dreams almost every time she slept and the throbbing headaches returned when she was awake. Domini finally persuaded her to take sedatives, and for a while they helped, but the headaches got progressively worse so that she was always tired, and so irritable that

216

Domini and the Saepids had to tread very carefully when talking to her. The dreams themselves were always a variation on the same theme, the man-shaped thing slowly descending over her naked body, her legs spread wide beneath him, and then the inevitable rape. Sometimes the darkness would form into the face of her father, and that was most disturbing of all, she woke from that dream and vomited into her tree; it took her and Domini nearly an hour to clean out her corner. Once the dark face became Anthra and she could actually feel his four arms wrapped around her body. She was beginning to wonder how bad the dreams would become.

Toward the end of the fifth day she dreamt of the man who had spoken from the table in the first nightmare. It was his face now, glaring down at her as the rape progressed, his smile so tinged with evil that she woke up crying, quietly hiding her face within the webbing. Domini would always be there for her, and he would try to get her to talk about the dreams, but she just couldn't; to re-live the nightmares in a real conversation would be more than she could take.

On the sixth night she had the worst dream of all. All of the eleven people from around the table were taking turns to abuse her; even the women would slap her face, and pull her to the floor where the men would kick her so that she would have to curl up into a ball as they continued to drag her around the floor. Then she would be on the table once more and all the men would take turns in the rape, while high above her, toward a far-away ceiling she saw the darkness coalesce and combine to form the faces of her old school friends, people she knew from university, and several times an old boyfriend would appear descending upon her, taking her violently as the other men had done.

Domini was worried sick. While Shari succumbed to the sedatives, he floated down toward the Saepids.

"Anthra, I don't know what to do for her, she's going through so much pain..."

Anthra and Ventra exchanged looks, and then looked up at Shari. Anthra moved closer to Domini.

"Yes, Domini, we too are very worried about Shari. Such dreams are not of natural origin."

Domini heard the fear in the other's voice. "What are you saying exactly?"

Anthra shuffled about in his webbing, taking his now customary long pauses in conversation. "We feel that Shari is being affected by the area of space we now find ourselves in... we are very close to the Beast's lair now, sneaking

217

up yes, but his power has been lurking here for very long time, his evil has seeped into all things around here, has made most of the systems over into his foulness… we will not find much light nor joy from this point on."

Domini took a moment to digest what Anthra was saying. "You think it's the Beast that's causing Shari's nightmares?"

"Most assuredly so… we have no real way of knowing true nature of the Beast, some call him God, some Beast. Others, more enlightened perhaps, call him machine, a deep thing entombed within a Cortex by the First Race… all conjecture, I am afraid. But it is for sure that the closer we come to his den the worse things will be for Shari…"

Domini looked back at Shari, still asleep in her tree, her face twitching every now and then as the dreams once more poisoned her mind. "Is there nothing we can do for her?"

Anthra thought about it for a moment. "I will consult ancient Othrum text, might be clues to her protection."

Domini started to drift away, turning back once. "I'll look in the text as well, there has to be something…" He pushed himself high, catching a floater screen as he made his way back to his wall.

Shari was trembling, the dream had drained her. It was hard to open her eyes, and she noticed she was drooling. She wiped her mouth and released her hammock straps, turning to see where Domini was. She saw him opposite studying a floater, he looked up once and smiled but didn't say anything; the last time he'd asked her if she was all right she had practically bitten his head off. *Poor Domini, I hope you'll forgive me…*

She felt the sweat clinging to her clothes and decided to take a shower, but before she set off her head was suddenly creased with pain. *To crell with this… why won't it stop?* She stumbled back into her webbing as the pain above her eyes threatened to overwhelm her. She wanted to cry out to Domini but her mouth couldn't make the words, she was falling into blind panic as the pounding pressure in her head increased.

She gripped the branches of her tree and fell back into her jacket. Without even being aware of her actions, she reached into the pouch and grasped the artifact. Suddenly, in a blinding instant of revelation, she knew she had done the right thing. The pain was gone, and her heart began to slow down, her body ceased to tremble; for the first time in days she was filled with a sense of inner peace.

218

Domini had seen her take out the artifact. "Shari! No, you mustn't!" He set off toward her.

She simply smiled back. "It's all right now, Domini; it's the right time."

Anthra drifted up to see what all the commotion was about.

"What is this? Shari?"

"It's all right, Anthra, all the pain has gone away, and I don't think I'll have the nightmares any more either."

Anthra considered this. "How do you know this, Shari?"

"I really don't know, but when I took out the artifact and I held it tight, everything became clear in my head; the pain just went away, and look..." She held out the amber and crystalline tube. "See? I'm holding it and I'm not slipping into some kind of altered state."

Domini and Anthra looked at each other, and then back at Shari.

"So you're not having any of those strange visions?" Domini said.

She turned to Domini. "No, Dom, I'm not... isn't that amazing?"

After considering this, Anthra spoke: "Perhaps the object has awakened something in Shari, we are very near to the Beast's lair, maybe it *knows* we are almost there."

Shari just smiled. "I don't care how it happened, all I know is I feel so much better than I did a few minutes ago."

Anthra was nodding his head. "Only explanation must be proximity to Beast. His evil has been seeping into *Shaendar* for days, perhaps now is time for artifact to begin its magics..."

Shari started to float toward the shower. "Well, magic or not, it's helping me... and also I'm so sorry if I've been a little short with you all lately."

Domini and Anthra smiled back at her, and Domini said: "Hey, we didn't even notice." From down below came a *humph* from Ventra.

219

Chapter 40 - Confluence in Real-Time

'When we spill heathen blood we sanctify our faith…'
Revelations: First Book of Saemal.

Neiron Thane touched the flow-screen, the data-link with the priest Ilka Vendhren was now pristine, and he had full evocation of the fleet movements, including a few spectro-scans of what was left of the Entrymion defense forces. The main fleet was now parked in orbit above Entrymion; he linked to the priest on the auxiliary command vessel. The flow-screen flashed a brief image of the Worship Glyph, and then the face of Vendhren appeared. Thane initiated gestalt recognition of the man, instantly assessing his character, the motivations behind the eyes, the overall demeanor. A heavy-set man, overweight, who was finding his new command of the entire fleet daunting in the extreme.

"You have a report for me, Commander." It wasn't a question.

"Yes, Sir, I acknowledge your recognition protocols and submit my report for your viewing."

Thane watched as the data-stream flowed; a long stream of figures indicating ships lost or damaged and an annotation below listing troop casualties. Most of the deaths were in the advanced fleet detachment, including Sorell's command vessel. *Unfortunate that…* He returned to the floater.

"You are linked to the Ground Commander?"

"Yes, Sir. Brim Lohman; he's awaiting your connection."

Thane touched the screen; scanned for Brim Lohman… *Ah, a former member of the Legislature on Primus; you have come far in the service of the one true God…*

"Good. You are aware, Vendhren, of the approach of the Coloquies fleet?"

"Yes, Sir. I have taken steps to terminate their advance at the specified spatial insertion point as dictated by Tanril via the latest data-stream from Primus."

"They are outreaching with feelers?"

Vendhren gave a slight smile. "They're flying in with their AI systems wide open; one would think they might have learned the lesson of Landings Down."

"Truth is, Vendhren, they probably have no idea how they died at Landings Down. Just ensure you have some of your ships out there to eliminate the hulks when their power goes down."

"I've dispatched a contingent of heavy cruisers to meet them, Sir."

"You will also leave a flotilla of ships around Entrymion to assist in the subjugation and occupation of the planet. The bulk of your fleet will continue to follow the subspace coordinates I am sending you now. It is most paramount, Commander, that your fleet leave immediately, I have included the specifications and full allocation tags of the ship you are to pursue; there can be no delay in pursuing this craft. Do I make myself clear?"

Vendhren straightened up in his seat. "Perfectly clear, Sir; and may the pathways flow…"

Thane glanced up at the man. "Yes, may the pathways flow." And he closed the connection.

He tapped the link to the Ground Commander, based now in the city of Carphalia; the screen flashed the Worship Glyph and Brim Lohman came online.

"Sir, I have my report ready for the uplink."

Thane noticed Lohman's black uniform was covered in dust, and in the distance behind him he could see fires raging as the soldiers of Saemal moved among the ruins of the city. "Send it." The data streamed into the AI core. He was instantly amused that the Entrymion people were still resisting; there were pockets of fighters spread out around their government buildings, and Lohman had referenced a series of refugee camps the citizenry had set up on the outskirts of the capital. *Well, they would have to go…*

"I see that they are still resisting, Lohman; I hope you are dealing with such matters in the appropriate fashion?"

"Yes, Sir, as dictated in my mandate, we are refraining from using our heavy weapons, so it's a matter of weeding out the belligerents as we come across them."

Thane considered this. "Might it not be prudent to give them a demonstration of the futility of resistance?" He saw Lohman struggling for a reply. "That is to say, why don't you simply obliterate those refugee camps? I see that many thousands have taken shelter in them, their destruction might just be enough to terminate all resistance."

"Yes, Sir, I had considered that, but my mandate also includes the inculcation of the non-believers into the One Faith."

221

Thane smiled at that. "Oh, come now, Commander, I don't think the deaths of a few thousand pagans will affect the overall incorporation of the planet into the Coalescency." *Let him think on that…*

"That is true, Sir; I will issue the orders at once. Do you require any other information at this time?" *He wants to get on with the slaughter…*

"No, your report is succinct; I will forward it to Primus for analysis by the Sacred Eleven." He noticed the look in Lohman's eyes… *his faith does not quite allow him to believe that a member of the Sacred Twelve has fallen.* He recalled a passage from the Book of Saemal: '*By our death will our Lord live…*'

Lohman said: "May the pathways flow, Neiron Thane."

"May they indeed flow, Commander Lohman." With that, he closed the link and turned to face the nav screens. The most recent spatial-grid had shown the escaping ships from Entrymion, bound spinward of the galactic core, making a run for the supposed safety of the Hub. *And you will meet our fleets there as well…* But there was no sign of the Saepid vessel. *Where are you, little runaways?* He initiated the subspace insertion sequence, turned his Viper away from the planet below, maneuvering past the big battle wagons of the fleet, and dropped down behind the planet's largest moon.

The stars vanished and the pulse-drive pumped the inter-phase core to maximum. The AI sent a spread of feeler drones out, their tiny guidance jets sending them thousands of kilometers ahead of the ship. He turned to bring the subspace tracers online, and their invisible nets were cast several light years beyond the feelers. Now it was just a matter of catching up with the Saepids. *And then we shall have a true reckoning…*

Chapter 41 - Combat Anthem

Let not the sun and moon forget us,
let not the fields and the streams forget our voices,

Let not the wind and the rain forsake us,
let not the fire and storm destroy us.

Let our names be written among the stars,
so that all those who pass this way will know
that once a great race lived here
and with our passing the universe is forever diminished...

The Poet Brayman, Westphal Refugee Settlement, Planet Entrymion.

The night came early to Carphalia city on the third day of Triamar, in the second year of the Great Expansion. Entrymion had known peace for over two thousand years. The Pre-Histories told of an ancient spacefaring race that had settled the world and quickly lost their high technologies, becoming savages and resorting to hunting and gathering. It would take thousands of years before the Entrymion people would finally unite and form a common union, and longer still for them to achieve space flight. It wasn't until the first year of the Great Expansion that Entrymion joined the Coalition, and began to send forth its starships among the great civilizations of the Hub. On the third day of Triamar it all came to an abrupt end.

Colonel Sieta Carmon had been ordered to defend the Senate building in the center of Carphalia. She had left Fleet Headquarters with three hundred combat troops equipped with two dozen fifty-caliber bolt guns, twenty mobile lasguns hastily fused to the grav-sleds requisitioned from the docks and fifty-five anti-personnel rockets, so outdated that her weapons masters had a hard time figuring out how to get the things to fire. Now it was late afternoon, half the city was already in ruins, and she could see fires raging throughout the living habitats strung out along the River Daria.

Beyond the hastily built barricades she could see the black flags of the enemy soldiers, with the strange symbol in gold, and beneath it the word *Saemal*; she had no idea what that meant or even who these invaders were or

223

where they had come from. She had only recently been told of the destruction of the fleet, realizing what that meant for Entrymion. She had known many of the people on those ships... *it was just one great loss after another*... Looking out over the burning city, she realized that she knew a lot of people down there as well. From behind her, First Sergeant Gant called her over to the bunker entrance.

"Ma'am, if you have a minute?" Gant was old school, and as such was used to living in a men's world; she suspected that he was one of the ones who had voted against women serving in the Planetary Defense Force. But although his manner was rough and ready she had a great respect for him, and after three days of fighting she felt the feeling was becoming mutual.

"Sergeant, report."

"I've placed First Brigade along the riverfront behind the Senate, but that'll leave gaps all along this front. It can't be helped, they're landing troop carriers in the Esplanade; I can't see any way we can hold them back..."

She pulled out a datapad, scanned for the uplink to the *Imperia*, the last refugee ship to leave; most of the Senatorial Elect were on that ship, and hundreds of civilian support workers. The scan showed the ship had entered subspace beyond Phebin, the second moon.

"The *Imperia* is away, Sergeant, looks like we held them off long enough."

Gant looked around at the destruction; he saw the bodies of his friends lying in rows behind the bunker walls. "Why don't they just pound us from space?"

"Well, they obviously want to occupy and not destroy... Admiral Dinaer called it a jihad; he thinks it's some kind of religious crusade." She had seen the ferocious way the enemy fought their way through the city, street by street, house by house. They killed with bombs, guns and she even saw some of them using old-fashioned swords; the slaughter was beyond belief. She pulled the sergeant into the bunker entrance as a missile impacted the dome high above them on the Senate building; debris rained down and they barely missed being crushed. She brushed down her uniform as the sergeant spoke:

"By the Stars, Ma'am, why were we ordered to shut down our AI's? We could have targeted every one of those troop carriers before they ever reached landfall."

She paused to catch her breath as the dust began to settle. "We had no choice; it seems the enemy has a way of corrupting high-tech systems, they use it to disable ships and all high Intel networks; it was the only way to keep them out."

They looked out to see an enemy cruiser gliding slowly across the river, its retro tubes only meters above the high arches of the Juniper Bridge; from its undercarriage streaks of blue light burned into the surrounding buildings, setting fire to the trees in the nearby gardens at Watersfell. She touched for a com frequency on her datapad and linked to her field commanders, and one by one the survivors came online. *Only nine left out of thirty? So perhaps we will all die today...*

She took their individual reports and field assessments. They were holding their ground for the moment; for some unknown reason the enemy forward troops had stopped their advance just behind the Science Museum. *But then why should they risk their blood when they have a cruiser or two on hand?* She re-issued the stand-and-hold order as dictated by the Supreme Commander, who was by now almost certainly several light years away. Gant passed her a flask of water.

"Thank you, Sergeant."

He pulled over a couple of ammo crates and they sat down among the rubble and dust.

"So you think this is it for us, Ma'am?"

She let the water take the taste of dust and pulsite out of her mouth before turning to face him. "Well, without divine intervention, Sergeant, I can't see us getting out of this one."

He smiled at that and she noted the lines on his face, the weariness behind his eyes.

"So how long have you been in the service, Sergeant?"

He sat back, thinking of the longs years spent in service to the state. "Must be thirty-five years now, Ma'am. Yes, about that... in fact, I was due for decommission this year... can't see me making that party now."

She passed him back the flask. "I've only been in five years myself... I signed up straight from the Academy Physics Block; I was supposed to go into R&D out at Area Command, but the idea of spending the rest of my life in a lab was just too much."

He gave her a stern look. "You've done pretty well in that amount of time, if I may say so, Ma'am."

She felt the emotion behind his words. "You don't really like women in the force, do you, Sergeant?"

225

He coughed, turning away. "It's not that I think women can't serve just as well as men, I just believe that combat is no place for a woman..."

She gave him a smile. "And do you still believe that, Sergeant, even now?"

He had to laugh. "No, no I don't. I must say you've more than proved yourself these last few days; there's many a man I know who would have gone to pieces by now; I have to say, you've held it together pretty damn well."

"I think there's a compliment in there somewhere, Sergeant..." There was a loud explosion from somewhere beyond the barricades; she initiated a field scan, noting her own troop positions in relation to those of the enemy. There was an enemy troop carrier descending on grav-plates toward the Forum, not more than three hundred meters from their position.

"Looks like they mean to storm us, Ma'am."

She relayed her final message to the field commanders, wishing them well and saluting the bravery of their troops. She cut the data-feed, and unstrapped her gun. The magazine would normally hold fifty pulse rounds, but the indicator showed only eight rounds left, two in the chamber. She called to the sergeant, "Are you fully loaded, Sergeant?"

He checked his weapon. "I have twelve rounds in this baby and six in this little slugger..." He held out a vintage handgun. "I've had this since the first day I joined the service, never left my side."

"Well, let's hope it can earn your loyalty today, Sergeant... let's move out."

He called after her. "Ma'am?"

She turned around. "Yes, Sergeant?"

"Do you remember the old combat anthem? The one we used to sing before the Academy was founded?"

"No, Sergeant, I can't say I've ever heard it."

"Really? Oh, it's a wonderful rousing song; we used to sing it all the time back in the day... used to help us run twice as fast around the stadium at Olfstat..."

"I'm sorry, Sergeant; I've never been one for singing myself."

"That's okay; not many troops remember it these days anyway."

She looked around the barricades, her troops were spread thin along the broken walls; she saw great gaps in the line. And further out toward the Forum, she could just make out a long line of enemy troops, their black combat jackets glistening in the heat haze from the carrier's vents.

"We'd better get down there, Sergeant; our men will need to see we're with them."

"Yes, Ma'am ... and Ma'am?"

"Yes, Sergeant?" She turned to look back, saw the sadness in his eyes.

"It's truly been an honor serving with you."

She smiled, stepping forward and holding out a hand. He shook the hand as she said her last words to him. "The feeling is mutual, Sergeant."

They turned toward the barricade and headed down to join their troops. The last sound she heard was the sergeant whistling his anthem as the first missiles struck the walls in front of them.

In the skies high above, the stars struggled to be seen among the silver and black hulls of eight hundred warships slowly orbiting the once proud and independent world of Entrymion.

Chapter 42 - Sandheim

White wings and starlight,
iridescent indigo and black
cascading into full moon shadow...

Tremulous quasars flitter amid
the froth of failing constellations
spinning into a field of stars...

Creation whispers sanctity into genome,
soil and water become flesh and blood,
the First Race walks out onto the beach,
stunned by the view...

Musings on the First Race - Lothar Theron: Personal Poetics.

Beyond the Rim, almost lost in a sea of darkness, two suns shared a near impossible attraction, one the slave to the other, its fire constantly drawn into the space between them. Perched high in an eccentric elliptic orbit sat the planet Sandheim, bathed in perpetual twilight.

Across its surface great mountains broke free from an ocean of ice, igneous fingers of batholith reaching for the feeble glimmering of sunlight casting shadows deep into the cold dark valleys of the *Mere Itraium*.

Seared against the face of an ancient volcano, the ruins of *Itraia*, the last outpost of the First Race lie scattered and broken. From its marbled hallways the remnants of their race had transcended their physical form and, one by one, they had left the younger races to their own devices. It was the last of these who revealed their terrible mistake; they had left behind their bastard child, and its rage would have to be contained somehow. Too late to terminate the Cortex at its source, the blood of the First Race was ingrained into the genome of a chosen few, the *custodia*; for they alone would have the power to restrain the darkness should it ever escape its prison.

Deep beneath the ice and stone, the *Palatia Centria* was now no more than a collection of shattered frescos and splintered mosaics leading along frozen rivulets towards the *Arcana*, where the amber crystalline had once been made.

Forged by the hand of transcendence, it was honed and shaped into a precise genetic configuration; a lattice of neural fronds infused with the blood of the last of the ancients. And so it was
sent forth toward the heart of the galaxy where it would be kept safe by the trusted servants of the First Race.

In the second month of the Coalescency, the Sacred Twelve had dispatched three long-range ships toward Sandheim. They would take nearly six months to reach the planet, and upon their arrival they were to launch three Ultravane ionic bombs toward that ancient world... there was to be no possibility of the secrets of *Itraia* ever seeing the light of day again... there would be no more *custodia* forged in that dark and long-lost place.

The Cortex

THE GALACTIC COALITION OF WORLDS

BOOK TWO

Chapter 1 - Escalations in Real-Time

'...And I was a stranger in a strange land, and the people were not like any others I had known before, for they were wanton and lascivious in their ways...'
Brother Fiodore, Doctrinal Episcopus - Sacred Book of Jophrim.

The *Shaendar* emerged from subspace ten thousand kilometers off the ecliptic plane of Port Fall, a small planetoid orbiting a G-type star ten light years from the Far Star Colony.

Shari released her straps and joined Domini as he floated down toward the command pod.

"So tell me again, Anthra; why are we stopping here so far from the Colony?"

Anthra gestured toward the main console. "Well, as I said earlier, Shari, we must take stock of situation out here; we have no data on the approaches to the Beast's lair. We suspect there are many traps waiting in subspace, all roads to the Colony are certainly compromised. We think it best to peek around a bit before we go any further. Port Fall is a useful place to gather information."

Domini peered at the screens. "But isn't Port Fall part of the Beast's territory?"

Anthra sniffed, sliding data across a floater. "Surprisingly, no. For reasons beyond our understanding, after the Cordwainer Alliance fell and Samros planet was conquered, the Beast leapt straight toward the Coalition worlds of the Hub, essentially bypassing the little places like Port Fall; no doubt he intends to mop up later, after all else has been seized."

"So, Anthra, what's the plan?" Shari said.

"Well, we use our skipper craft to visit the port, try to access local Net, find out the comings and goings."

"Can't we just access their Net from here?" Domini put in.

"Afraid not, no, Domini. You see Port Fall is very cautious place, they have restrictions in place... see here?" He pointed to the latest spatial-grid. "These objects in orbit are buffers, satellites which restrict the data-flow between the stars, the main galactic Net is a mere whisper this far out, but there is still much local traffic, but all of it is seeded into the buffers, then they sift out the risky Posts. I think they are very aware of Beast's ability to corrupt their machines."

Shari drifted closer. "So is it safe for us to go down there? What kind of people are they?"

"Not sure, dear Shari, our records are scanty on this sector." Anthra replied.

Ventra spoke up: "We traded here once, long time ago when *Shaendar* was young. The port was full of pirates back then, Phaelon types, but from further out along the Rim, not the safest way to trade, but we came to no harm."

Shari thought about that for a minute, wondering at the sense of visiting such a world. "But you think it'll be safe now? I mean, are there still pirates around here?"

Ventra replied: "I doubt that very much; Port Fall has many connections to Coalition these days, I think they have cleaned up their act. We will not have to stay for long; just ask a few questions here and there."

Anthra looked up at Shari. "Perhaps it might be best, Shari, if you remain here with Ventra while Domini and I take the skipper down." He tried not to look her in the eye.

She gave him one of her annoyed looks. "No way. I'm coming with you, I feel much better now; and to be honest I'm sick of being cooped up on this ship with you three... sorry, Dom."

He smiled back at her. "That's all right, Shari, but are you sure you want to take the risk?"

"Dom, I'm going and that's all there is to it."

He sighed. "Fair enough."

As they drifted up toward the rear cargo hold they heard Anthra mumbling behind them: "I see nothing wrong with being cooped up with us." Ventra just looked back at the main screen.

The skipper was cradled against the aft engine shaft, its legs retracted like a spider ready to pounce. Anthra pulled open the underside hatch, holding it open as Shari and Domini went through. Once inside, Shari was suddenly aware that the craft wasn't exactly built for humans; the control system interface was housed inside a central pylon which had feeder cables strung out across the cabin. Shari had to squeeze into a space between an overhead conduit and Domini's back. She placed her legs on either side of him as he pushed his own legs under some kind of air vent protruding from the floor. Anthra hurried to the webbing strung around the control pylon.

"Apologies, my friends, for lack of space, but skipper of Saepid design, not truly meant for fleshings."

234

"That's all right, I think we're secure," Shari said, her back already aching from the hard plassteel of the conduit.

Domini noticed Shari was wearing her jacket. "Perhaps you should leave the artifact on the ship? Just in case…"

"Why? I took care of it at Landings Down. I think it'll be safer with me… and besides, I think I need to keep it near me from now on." She thought of the headaches and the bad dreams.

Anthra linked to the command deck.

"Ventra, my mate, please open rear cargo doors."

There was the sound of rushing air as the cargo bay was depressurized. Shari peered through the small window to her right. She could see the doors opening like petals in a starry night. It seemed like so long since they'd been on a real planet… *and so much has been lost since Petra…*

She spoke in Domini's ear. "So, do you think they'll have bars on Port Fall?"

He couldn't turn his head to look at her so he just said: "Shari… bars? Really?"

"Not everyone wants to stab you, Dom."

He fell silent.

The skipper seemed to fall for thousands of meters, casting aside the stars and seizing the gray-on-gray clouds, pushing through to the lower airs, to glide gently on one torch and a small grav-plate down onto a landing pad. The Allocation Officer had told them to land on a pad perched halfway down a habitation pylon in what was known as the Scimitar Sector. Once the landing gear had engaged the pad clamps, Anthra quickly tapped the local guide into his datapad. They had been directed to a pylon on the very edge of the port, miles from the central commercial district; he said that's what happened when you didn't book ahead. They would need to use the local transport system to get down town. He scanned the guide, found details of a glide-rail that would take them toward the central districts. There was a drop-tube at the end of the landing pad which would take them down fifty levels to the rail station. He turned around to try to face Domini and Shari, but there wasn't enough room to move.

"Apologies again for crampness, my friends. We need to exit now, but be wary, atmospherics indicate a high level of adverse toxicity in the air, we must use breathers until we enter the drop-tube."

Shari sighed. "Brilliant… where are they?" She reached toward the overhead storage unit. "Got them!" She passed one to Domini, and Anthra took

235

the other, and then she carefully began to force her knees away from Domini's back.

"You know you could wait a minute, Shari."

"Sorry, Dom."

They jumped down onto the pad. Dust rose and for a few seconds they could taste a metallic foulness in the air, even through the breathers. Shari fell into step behind Anthra, with Domini bringing up the rear.

Once inside the tube, Domini turned to Anthra. "Are you armed, Anthra?"

Anthra touched the inside of his cloak. "Yes indeed, Domini, must be very wary in this place."

Shari watched the level counter decrease until the doors pinged and opened onto a narrow street where the only light came from overhead glowtubes fused to the plassteel ceiling. *Not even glasscite for viewing...* She saw a faded sign opposite the tube: *Glide-rail Scimitar Sector.*

Anthra trotted across the street. "This way... follows me..." And off he went.

Shari took a quick look around; the place looked deserted, but there were some people behind a fast-food counter further down the street, *humans!* She noticed Anthra had gone through the doors to the rail station and she quickly caught up, taking Domini's hand in hers.

The glide-rail was a dilapidated collection of carriages with a primitive fusion engine bringing up the rear. It didn't look at all safe. But Anthra seemed unconcerned and flashed his ID card at the entry gate. The gate refused to open. He tried again, and once more it remained closed.

Domini pointed to a sign above the gate: 'Only Local Coinage Accepted.'

Anthra was not at all pleased. "That's not good, we need credit outlet; can you see one?"

Shari walked along the outer platform, came to a booth with the word 'CASH' above it. "Here, Anthra, I think I found one."

Anthra came over, flashed his card, and his credit account was deducted thirty credits and exchanged for local currency. "This is not way for any place to do business. Port Fall very much behind the times, I think." He set off back toward the gate.

Once aboard the train they had to wait another half hour before it set off, and during that time only three other people boarded. It seemed most of the Scimitar Sector was deserted, and as they sped past the suburbs Shari noted how run-down and abandoned the area looked. She saw motels boarded up with 'For Sale' flash signs flickering outside, and sealed entertainment arcades shrouded in darkness, their neon lights long since extinguished. She leaned toward Domini on the seat next to her. "Will you look at this place? It's like everyone just packed up and left…"

"It is odd, considering this is supposed to be a very busy port; perhaps things will be different when we get into the city."

"Yes maybe; but I can't see us finding out anything useful in this place."

The train was passing along the edge of a series of docks now; they could see several heavy cruisers berthed, worker drones scurrying over their silver hulls glistening in the twilight. But further out, toward a wide river, there were dozens of abandoned starships lying in rows along the shoreline; some even had gaping holes in their sides, others were no more than exposed bulkheads. On the opposite shore, Shari could see the towers of the Downtown District, a confused collection of plassteel buildings lacking the elegance of the glasscite towers of Egrain City back on Primus. In fact, the scene reminded her of a huge factory, with cranes hanging over the streets, and cable cars strung out between the habitation pylons. The place looked exactly like the pirate ports she used to read about as a child. *But I doubt there's much romance in this place…* Suddenly the train dipped and they were in an underground tunnel streaking past strings of lights fused to the tunnel walls. *Must be going under the river…* She noticed the walls were dripping with water and began to wonder just how safe the glide-rail actually was. But then they emerged into daylight and she could see dozens of tracks converging from both sides as the train continued through an outer ring of industrial units, workshops and cheap-looking hotels.

Within minutes the train had arrived in the center of the Downtown District, and she immediately realized that the place was very different from the Scimitar Sector. The station was a mass of people, mostly humans, but Shari recognized a few Coloquies and others that looked like real people but had leathery scales down their backs and arms; and then she had a very disturbing thought: *What if there are flat-faces around here?* She resolved to keep an eye out for them, determined to keep Domini safe and away from their sharp knives.

They jumped down to the platform and immediately noticed that the air was so much cleaner than in the outer sectors, and only a few people were wearing face masks, so Anthra took the breathers and placed them in his carry-all, and then, without another word, he set off toward a nearby building.

Shari called after him, "Anthra, where are you going?"

237

He turned around as she tried to keep up. "This place over here is a dataserve exchange, we can access local Net here, find out information on Far Star Colony… follow please, follow…"

So the two humans followed.

Inside the dataserve they saw rows of booths along two walls; each one contained a single seat set before a data-stream screen. Anthra took a seat, noted the cost per time usage and dropped the required coins into a slot in the side of the booth. Shari and Domini stood behind him, but neither of them could see the screen inside the booth.

Shari spoke into Anthra's ear: "Anthra, how long will this take? Is there time for us to go have a hot drink or something?"

Anthra was still fidgeting with the seat height adjuster as he turned around. "Might take time, Shari, I will need to link data-stream to my pad and uplink to Ventra for analysis; must be careful, though, I see they have copyright tags on their screens, must use covert ways to uplink information to ship."

"Okay then, Dom and I will take a look around."

He gave her a look.

"We won't get into trouble, I promise."

"Okays, but please, no more mixing with violent types."

Shari smiled. "I promise… Let's go, Dom."

Domini looked at Anthra and gave in to the inevitable as Shari took his hand and pulled him back out into the street.

They walked along a raised sidewalk resting on graphile rods fused to the stone below. They saw that the roads beyond the station were open to ground vehicles and people were taking their lives in their hands dashing across the street, dodging the traffic. She looked up, expecting to see personal flyers passing between the towers, but the only air traffic she saw were a few skippers moving along the boulevards at tree-top level.

"Isn't this the craziest of places, Domini?" She pulled him toward a shop front. "Look, they're selling plasma rifles in a shop window; do you know how illegal that would be on Primus?"

"It wouldn't exactly be doctrinal on Petra."

"Come on, let's look inside…"

Domini pulled her back. "Excuse me, I don't think so."

"What? Why not? Come on, we'll just have a quick look, won't take a minute…" She pushed open the doors, expecting them to be automatic but quickly realizing the things actually had hinges. *Unbelievable!*

Once inside, Shari was amazed to see rows of glass cabinets, *real old-fashioned glass!* And inside each one there were dozens of weapons pegged to display boards with ingrained price tags beneath. She quickly moved further down the store, fascinated by the displays.

"Would you believe this? They're selling fusion drones down here, Dom… crell, this is a crazy world."

Domini was keeping an eye on the two men behind the counter; they had looked up once as they came inside, but were now engrossed in front of a vid-screen; he saw a naked woman on the screen and quickly turned away.

"Can we go now, Shari? Maybe there are some better shops further along."

She reluctantly accepted his hand and they stepped outside once again. She checked the local time on an overhead chron hanging limply outside a shop selling food provisions. It was early evening and the area seemed to be getting busier. They decided to follow signs leading to something called the Glamoria Precinct. As it turned out, the place was where everyone in the city seemed to be heading – and they soon found out why. After passing down several narrow streets they emerged into a vast open plaza surrounded by glasscite enclosed entertainment galleries. As they began to move slowly through the crowds they could see rows of brightly lit casinos and bars, restaurants and cafés emblazoned with sky-high flash-ads. Shari led Domini toward a large theatre illuminated with giant holo-vids displaying troupes of semi-naked woman dancing on ice. Shari stared in awe as the figures flowed past.

"This place is the best, Dom…" She pulled him toward a nearby gallery, where iridescent fountains were cascading from the heads of tall statues of naked green-skinned women.

Domini took Shari to one side. "Shari, I really don't think this is a very suitable place for either of us."

She turned to face him, taking his hands in hers. "Oh dear, Mr. Priest, are you a prude?"

He pulled his hands free. "No, I'm not; it's just that the last time I allowed you to drag me into these sorts of places I ended up getting stabbed."

She felt the blame in his words. "I said I was sorry about that, I never wanted that to happen to you, and if you think…"

He tried to calm her down. "Hey, I never blamed you, it just happened. All I'm saying is maybe we should check in with Anthra before we wander off into these kinds of places."

239

She relented. "All right, I'll call Anthra." She pulled out her datapad, linked to the Saepid tag and touched for Anthra. His face filled the screen instantly.

"Yes, Shari? All is well?"

Shari looked at Domini before replying. "Yes, Anthra, all is well. Have you finished your snooping yet?"

"Not really. Local Net very confusing mish-mash of Posts, not easy to sift hard data from among flimsy threats and fears. One thing for sure, these people know they live near Beast's thrall. Many locals are leaving, heading out toward Great Expanse, many risks in that, but better out there than here, it seems. They know they live on borrowed time here, Shari."

"So what do want to do? Shall we head back to the station?"

"No need yet unless you want to wait there for me. I have found a link to an independent Net feed dealing with threat of Beast, I will explore this first and then uplink to ship, might be another hour or so."

Shari made up her mind. "That's all right; Domini and I are going to see the sights."

Anthra looked concerned. "Please be careful, Shari, this port is not Coalition, mostly Non-Conformist rabble here, much lawlessness…"

She moved to close down the screen. "We'll be careful, no worries." She replaced the pad in her jacket and turned to Domini.

"Told you we should have bought a gun." With that, she walked off into the nearest entertainment gallery.

Domini shouted after her. "No you didn't!" But she was already moving among the slot machines and floating vid-viewers.

The gallery was a wild cacophony of sounds, blaring music from the vid-viewers, and the sounds of crashes and explosions from the avatar booths. Shari watched a group of men and women casting mag-dice across a grav-sheet, they controlled where the dice would land by a series of pulse-rods along each side of the table, each participant had to adjust their own pulse-rod in order to control the grav-sheet; if they pulled the dice down to a square they controlled then they would win the game. She saw large bundles of currency at one end of the table, with people quickly adding coins to the pile. Just then the dice was pulled down by the grav-sheet and the crowd roared, jumping in the air and slapping each other on the back. *This place is amazing… Father would hate this…* The thought brought the sadness back and she noticed Domini looking at her.

"You okay, Shari?"

She smiled. "Sure... come on..." And she pulled him toward a circular stage upon which several women were dancing. They watched as the dancers turned and twisted around a tall pole reaching up toward a glasscite mirrored ceiling. Shari loved the costumes.

"How do you think I'd look in one of those, Dom?"

He looked up as the women bent over, flipping their hair back in time to the music. "I really don't think that's your style, Shari."

She gave him a peeved look. "Really? And what do you think my style is, Domini?"

"Well, I don't, I..."

She laughed. "Just kidding. Come on, let's find drinks."

He called after her. "Have you money?"

"Anthra, gave me some at the station. Hey look... a bar!"

Anthra was deep inside the local Net, scanning through hundreds of Posts... news of the spread of Saemal's jihad among the outer Coalition worlds was rife. Theories abounded as to the origin of Saemal; it seemed the Beast was known by that name among most of the occupied Rim worlds, but a few supplementary Posts called him the Cortex, which intrigued Anthra as he himself no longer considered the Beast to be a machine. The Othrum texts lacked details regarding transcendence, but what information they did contain pointed to the transcendence of the First Race and later some of their progeny followed, one of whom was Saemal. One particular Post interested him, from a local academic who went by the grand title of Doctor Professor Elias Del Montro of the Port Fall Tactical Liaison Unit; in it the good doctor theorized that the First Race built the Cortex as a repository of all their knowledge, a treasure house to keep safe their high-tech magics, but the archive outgrew its creators, the depth of knowledge ingrained in its sub-routines was so vast, so profound that the machine leapt into sentience, assuming a quasi-state of godhood. Only at that point did the First Ones realize their terrible mistake and take steps to imprison their dark creation.

Anthra realized that much of the Post actually matched the ancient Othrum writings... *this Doctor Professor person seems to know what he is talking about.* He scanned a later Post by the same man. Once again he found details of the first flowering of the Beast: *Long after the First Race had departed from the universe the monster had broken free and spread out among the stars, destroying many of the younger races, tens of thousands of years before the*

241

founding of the Coalition. It was only through the efforts of Jophrim and the Fleets of Liberation under Syrillian Anthos that the last creation of the First Ones was once more bound to his barren rock of a moon somewhere near the future Far Star Colony.

Anthra sat back in the seat, took a slow breath. He would have liked to meet Elias Del Montro if there had been time; the man knew his histories and no mistake. It was only one Post among dozens that had any sense of truth; most of the Postings were wildly speculative, based solely on hearsay and rumor. One Post identified the Beast as a dragon from ancient mythology, complete with fiery breath, another one actually dismissed the existence of the Beast altogether and posited that the so-called jihad was no more than a rag-tag army of opportunists seeking to destabilize the Coalition in favor of the Non-Conformist League. But the most common Thread out there was that the Beast would eventually occupy all of the free worlds, including Port Fall. Many ship captains were charging exorbitant fees to transport passengers away from the sector. *Where do they think they can go to outrun the Beast?*

He inserted data tags in all the relevant information and uploaded it to the *Shaendar*. Ventra flashed a received symbol and he returned to the vid-screen to scan for a copy of the most recent spatial-grid; if they could map the systems ahead they might be able to plan a route around the enemy fleets. He had no doubt that the enemy would be waiting in force somewhere up ahead; they were now heading into his realm, and every day that passed would bring them closer to his lair and the final battle that would surely follow. He tapped the screen to search for the grid and also scanned for shipping movements around Port Fall. *Must see if Beast's agents are already here...*

Shari pulled Domini toward a nearby table, just to one side of the elevated dance stage. He had insisted in ordering fruit juice for himself while Shari was trying a local beer.

"This stuff is good, Dom, you should try it..." She raised her glass to him.

"No, thank you, I think one of us should keep a level head."

"Oh, for crell's sake, Dom, I'm just trying to have some fun... you know, before all the fun comes to an abrupt end in ten days' time."

He looked across at her. "Look, Shari, I know things look grim, but I have faith that we will come through this, I really do."

242

"Really? Well, here's to coming through it..." She took a long drink from the glass. She wasn't sure why she suddenly felt so reckless, nor why she felt the need to enjoy herself, but things were getting serious now, *perhaps it's because everything is coming to a head...* and these days might well be the last days of her young life. She took another long drink.

"You know what I think, Dom?"

He was looking at her eyes, trying to gauge her mood, which seemed to be changing by the minute. "What, Shari?"

She brushed her hair away from her eyes. "Well, I was just thinking; if I am so damn important, so special, how come my father didn't know? I mean, why didn't he find out about this *custodia* thing? Or, wait a minute... maybe he did know? Maybe that's why he was always so distant with me; you know I can't remember a single time when he hugged me? Can you believe that? I mean, I'm his only daughter and the man can't even give me a hug? What a Barg..."

"Well, you know I will hug you any time you ask."

She smiled back at him. "I know that, Dom. You were the first person to hold me since I lost Momma..." She drifted off for a few minutes before continuing. "She would have liked you, Dom, not the priest side of you, she did not like religion, no way, but now you're all rough and un-priestlike; is that a word?"

He laughed. "I doubt it, but I get the meaning."

"Of course you do, Dom, because you get me; and that's important in a relationship, right?" She leaned her elbows on the table top and stared into his eyes.

"Yes it is, and I do think I understand you; and also, I understand that it might be better if you drank some juice now, or perhaps I can get you some water?"

She gave him her very annoyed look. "You know, Dom, you are what we used to call a party pooper... we got a boy like that in the Physics dorm, so serious all the time; and when we sneaked out after curfew to go down to the Marina bars he actually reported us to the House Master, I mean, what a stupid dross he was..."

Domini took a sip of his juice, and then asked Shari: "What does party pooper mean?"

"It's old Galac, like penny for your thoughts; means a loser, I think..."

"So I'm a loser now? What did I lose?"

243

She glared at him. "Your stupid sense of humor for a start!"

He realized he couldn't win, it was no use arguing with her, so he sat back as she fell into silence, her wide eyes taking in the dancers and the gamblers as they continued to shout obscenities from around the grav-tables. He was beginning to wonder if Shari was right, *do I really have no sense of humor?* It might be true... after all, he had been confined to the Seminary in Salicia Sonora since the age of fourteen; ten long years walking the stone corridors where even loud voices were frowned upon, never mind laughter. Had the priesthood really driven all human emotions out of his heart? And yet here and now he had discovered love... true love, not the doctrinal devotion to a statue or a sacred temple. He had found Shari, and in his heart he knew he would die for her; he loved her more than life itself. *But is she now slipping away from me? Is she disappointed in me?* He looked across at her; she was wearing a blue T-shirt and long baggy trousers; he'd asked her not to wear her gym shorts during planetfall and she had looked annoyed but had reluctantly changed into the trousers. *"For crell's sake, Dom, they're just legs; some pirate isn't going to ravish me just because he sees my legs..."* But she had changed, *so perhaps she does care what I think of her.* She was brushing her hair out of her eyes right now, staring at her empty glass. She looked up.

"So shall we take a slow walk back to the station?"

"Sure, good idea."

Shari put her jacket back on and they made their way through the crowds, heading back out into the plaza beyond.

Once outside they saw that the crowds had increased. There were now hundreds of people, mostly humans, moving around the plaza. It seemed that with the coming of night the Glamoria Precinct really came to life. The neon flash-vids interlaced with holo-lucience renderings reached toward the darkening skies, giant multi-spectral advertisements for the most popular casinos and clubs. They walked through a rendering of a giant green-skinned woman dancing on a sea of luminescent fire, her fingers clasping tiny cymbals and her hair tied high in a crown of golden filigree.

"This is just amazing, Dom, look at these holos..."

"Yes, amazing..." He was busy trying to pull Shari through the crowds, but they weren't making much headway, people were constantly getting in the way. Several times they were bumped into and Shari was becoming more and more annoyed.

244

"Will you watch where you're going!" she shouted at a large rough-looking man as he pushed past her, banging into her shoulder. Domini tried to pull her away, very aware of the dangers surrounding them. She resisted, glaring at the back of the man as he was lost in the crowd.

"Shari, no mixing with violent types, remember?"

"Hey, that Barg pushed me!"

"I know, but look we're nearly through the crowd; let's just keep moving."

"Okay, no need to pull my hand off..."

When they finally made it through to the less crowded streets beyond the plaza, they took a moment to buy a couple of hot jamochas.

Shari passed a cup to Domini and turned to pay the woman behind the counter. She reached into her jacket, feeling for the coins Anthra had given her, but they were gone. She looked at the woman, and then back to Domini.

"What's wrong?" he asked.

"The coins, Dom, they're gone; I left them in the little pouch Anthra gave me."

"Have you checked your pockets?"

She gave him an annoyed look. "What do you think I'm doing? It's gone, I tell you..."

"Did you leave it in the bar?"

She was busy going through all the pockets of her jacket. "I don't think so, I'm sure I put it back in my inside pocket....Oh, Dom, I think we've been robbed!"

Domini asked the woman behind the counter to bear with them for a minute; she shrugged and said she'd come back and went away to serve the next customer.

"You've checked all your pockets?"

Shari was staring at him, a look of complete horror on her face. "By the Stars, Dom, the artifact is gone..." She felt a strange constriction in her chest, trembling as fear began to course through her body.

He pulled her close. "Don't fear, Shari, we just have to calm down, we have to think, retrace your steps."

"Dom, my steps were the same as your steps..." She began to think. "Wait a minute... that Barg who bumped into me; could he have picked my pockets?"

Domini looked puzzled. "Picked them?"

She sighed. "He put his hand inside my jacket and stole the artifact and the money... picked!"

He thought about this. "Then I suggest we go back and try to find him; do you remember what he looked like?"

"You're kidding, right? He was big, Dom, that's all I know."

"Shari, just take a moment, think. You may have seen more than you realize."

She stepped away from the counter, trying to recall anything of significance about the man. She pictured the crowds, the lights and the tall holo-lucience renditions... she walked herself slowly away from the bar, remembered walking through the tall green dancer, pushing through the crowds, her hand tight in Domini's... then the man bumped into her, hard... his green space jacket shiny in the reflective light, the ship insignia badge just below the collar...

"I remember something..."

Domini moved closer. "Tell me, slowly..."

"He was wearing a green spacer jacket, the old type, I've seen spacers wearing it in Egrain City, and there was a badge, a ship's insignia..." She drifted off into thought, trying desperately to remember what the insignia looked like. "It was a lightning bolt through an asteroid, in gold, I think, but faded, I couldn't see the wording underneath."

"Well, that's something to be going on with. We need to contact Anthra."

Shari didn't like the idea of that. "Really, you think so? I mean, why upset him before we have to? Can't we just go look for this dross by ourselves? We might find him near that bar... or I can do that thing I did back on Petra, I can concentrate on the artifact and find it in my mind."

"You can do that?"

"That's how I found you and that man Raine when he had it... although of course I did throw up afterward... but it'll be worth it, Dom!"

"Very well, if you think you can still do that then go ahead, just don't go and make yourself too sick."

"I'll try my best; now just give me a minute..." She closed her eyes, began to concentrate on the artifact the way Anthra had showed her back on Petra. She visualized the crystalline amber, saw the fronds encased inside, tried to feel the cold hard surface... her memories matching physical sensations, the emotions relaying the physical connection she had felt while holding the object in her hands. But after several minutes of intense concentration there was

246

nothing, no leap into a fugue state, no perception of a connection of any kind. She opened her eyes slowly to see Domini looking at her. He stepped forward.

"Well? Anything?"

"No… nothing, I don't understand it; I mean, it worked the last time."

He took her hands in his. "Shari, Anthra has a link to the local Net, he can scan for that insignia, try to locate a ship perhaps… we need to tell him."

"Okay, but you better tell him it wasn't my fault, I didn't know there were pick-pockets in that crowd."

"Don't worry; I'm sure he'll understand."

She gave him a slight smile. "Or we could say it was you who got robbed… he would never blame you…"

He gave her a warm smile, squeezing her hands. "Shari, let's just tell him what happened."

"All right; if you have to be honest about it." She passed Domini her datapad.

Anthra took a few moments to come online. *So he's obviously busy, great, and now they'll all just blame me…* She turned away to avoid the eyes of the woman behind the counter.

"Domini, you are well?"

"Yes, Anthra, we are both well, but we have a problem…"

Anthra turned to give Domini his full attention. "Explain please."

"Well, it seems we have been robbed, we've lost the artifact." Domini watched as Anthra's face seemed to freeze, his eyes growing as wide as he had ever seen them.

"How can this be? You have lost the artifact? In full truth?"

"If I might explain…"

"Yes, better had, explain please to Anthra."

Shari heard the tone in the Saepids voice. She had never seen him angry, but right now she felt he was as close to losing his temper as any Saepid could be.

Domini glanced at Shari before continuing: "We were leaving a bar…"

"A bar? Again?" He gave Domini a stern look.

"If I might continue?"

"By all means, please do."

"So, as we were passing through the crowds outside in the plaza—"

Anthra interrupted: "Which sector were you in?"

"We were in the Glamoria Precinct."

247

Anthra had obviously come across Net references to the area during his research.

"Not the safest place to be, Domini…"

"I know, but that's beside the point right now; the point is Shari had her pockets… picked…"

Anthra seemed to be shuffling around on his seat inside the dataserve booth.

"Picked? What is picked?"

Shari grabbed the datapad out of Domini's hands. "Oh, for crell's sake, Anthra, some spacer had his hands inside my jacket; he stole the artifact and the money you gave me. Now I think I know how we can find him if you'll just stop asking questions and listen to me."

Anthra lowered his eyes slightly. "Apologies, Shari, please do go on."

"This spacer had a badge on his green jacket, it looked like a ship's insignia, it showed a bolt of lightning through an asteroid, in gold… there might have been a ship's name beneath it but I couldn't make it out. Now can you trace that ship based on the insignia?"

Anthra fell silent for a few moments, then he turned away from the screen and they heard him using the booth's controls. After a few minutes his face reappeared on the datapad screen.

"Have you not tried to locate the artifact with your mind, Shari?"

She sighed. "Yes, I have, and it didn't work. I don't know why, so can we move on now?"

"Very strange it did not work, unless it is because of close proximity to Beast's lair, he has great influence among Rim worlds…"

"Anthra! The ship?"

"Apologies. I have tracked down a ship with that insignia; the local allocation registry lists it as the *Vendosia*, out of Tronheim Heights, a loosely affiliated combine established on a small moon orbiting the third planet in this system; goes by the name Atrai Fall. I am downloading crew manifest now, I will upload ID tags to your pad, please scan the faces, and see if you recognize your pocket picker."

They waited a few minutes for Anthra to upload the information. Domini took the time to apologize to the woman behind the counter, explaining that they had been robbed; he was surprised when she dismissed the cost and offered the drinks gratis. Shari also noticed the woman touching Domini's hand on the counter top as she spoke.

"Dom! Anthra has completed the uplink."

Domini pulled his hand away from the counter, his face slightly flushed. "Sorry. So let's take a look."

Shari touched the flow-screen and the crew of the *Vendosia* passed across the screen. She stopped the flow several times, studying one particular face, but then moved on. It wasn't until she came across crewman Doron Khalik that she paused a little longer. Domini peered over her shoulder.

"Is that him, Shari?"

She narrowed her eyes. "I'm not sure... I think so. I mean, I only got a glimpse of his face, the most I saw was the back of his head—"

Anthra cut in from a small square at the top of the screen. "So please rotate the head, Shari, look at the back of this man."

Shari touched the pad and dragged the man's head around until he was facing away from her. She held the pad at arms length, studying the back of his neck. She was sure this was the man; even the insignia badge looked identical.

"Yes, this is him; this is the thief who robbed me."

Anthra's face filled the screen once more, as the head of Doron Khalik vanished. "Then we must make plan... how far are you from my location?"

Domini looked up at the overhead signs, recognizing the street ahead. "About half an hour's walk, I believe..."

"I see... very well, you both go back to plaza, retrace your steps, you may come across this man before he returns to his ship. I will go directly to the docks, seek out the *Vendosia*, make discreet enquiries about him."

Shari was worried about Anthra going down to the docks alone. "Anthra, are you sure that's a good idea? I mean, going down there on your own? Why don't you just meet us here and we'll look for this man together?"

"Not practical, Shari, time is against us now. We must retrieve artifact before Beast arrives in system, which he surely will, and soon. We split up to cover more ground." He gave her a sly smile. "Besides, I am armed."

"Okay then, but take care and keep in contact."

"I will link back with you when I can. You two be wary now, many dangers in Port Fall, far worse than pocket pickers..."

"We'll be careful." Shari shut down the link. Looking up at Domini, she wasn't sure just how much he blamed her for losing the artifact. *Maybe I should have listened to them and left the damn thing on board Shaendar...*

249

Doron Khalik walked quickly down the nearest back alley and stepped behind a waste container. After a furtive look around he pulled out the two small pouches he had taken from the off-world tourist; the girl hadn't even noticed... *dumb tourists scants*... He opened the money pouch first, found just ten coins... *hardly worth the effort... but maybe...* He pulled open the second pouch and found what looked like a tube of glasscite; he held it up to the light and it glistened slightly beneath the haze from a flickering glow tube fused to the back of a street café. As he stood there it began to rain; heavy drops falling through the wire mesh of an overhead walkway. He moved into the shadows, stepping over broken bottles and taking shelter on the step of a rear fire exit.

He looked at the object; it was as shiny as any jewel he had ever seen, and the possibility that it might be valuable compensated for the fact that he hadn't been able to unhook the girl's datapad. *This could be priceless, Doron; I think we've hit the big time with this one...* He felt the surface of the thing, turning it over slowly, noting what looked like metal filaments laced through the interior. *What the crell?* He began to feel light-headed... there was a throbbing pain just above his eyes; he leaned back against the door to steady himself, and for a moment he could no longer focus his eyes. And that was when he noticed the rain... *it's falling upwards!*

He watched as the rain reversed its course, falling up toward the night skies... *not possible!* The litter at his feet rose up as well, drifting higher, followed by the broken bottles and used venous sticks; all of it rising with the rain... *madness! I'm losing my mind!* Suddenly from behind him two arms reached through the door, resting cold hands upon his shoulders; he screamed in terror. Backing away, he crossed to the other side of the alley squeezing the object tight in his hand. But as he pressed against the wall a large human face emerged from the plassteel. It had black sockets for eyes and a mouth filled with blood. He screamed in terror as another face appeared and beyond that another and another. *Madness!* He started to run back down the alley, splashing through the impossible puddles floating skyward. He stumbled and fell and saw hands reaching out of the ground, trying to grasp his feet as he stood up and continued to run back toward the main street. But there were hundreds of hands now, breaking through the soil and stone, reaching for him, grasping and writhing in the air. He fell again, gashing his head against a stone step; he forced himself up and stumbled into a waste container. The blood flowed down his face as the rain continued to soak him; but always falling up from the ground beneath him.

He managed to reach the street, still trying to escape the hands and the eyeless faces. He was attracting attention now; people were moving out of his way, making room as he stumbled along the sidewalk. He suddenly lost his footing and fell hard onto the road, his face splashing into a puddle, his hands clawing at the stone beneath him.

Two men came over, looking down to see if he was dead or alive. One checked his pulse, found him still breathing and called for the other to help. They raised him up and half-carried him back to the curb where they sat him down. One of them bent down to talk to him.

"You all right, spacer? Been drinking?"

He could barely focus; the voice was full of echoes, the rain crashing among the words. He started to mumble, holding out the object in his hands.

"What's that you say?"

The second man reached down and took hold of the object.

"You best put this away, man; there are some bad 'uns round here that would slit you for this..." The man pushed the object into Doron's inside pocket.

"And get yourself back to your ship while you can... come on..."

The two men helped him to his feet. As they did he began to feel better, his eyes re-focused and the hallucinations seemed to wither away... even the rain was falling in the right direction. He straightened his jacket, wiping his forehead with the back of his sleeve; the cut there didn't seem too deep, a plasstrip should take care of it. He turned to face his two helpers.

"I thank you... both of you. Must have had more than I realized..."

"Well, like I say, best head back to your ship."

"Yes, I'll do that. Thanks again." With that, he wandered off down the street to find a med-tech booth for his head.

It wasn't until he was walking along the outer docking ring that he began to wonder about the object. *Had that thing driven me crazy for a while back there? Got in my head somehow?* Before entering the docks he turned and walked toward the graphile railings overlooking the Tiandra River. Looking down, he saw the water was a turbid dark brown with patches of frothy white scum drifting across its surface. *Polluted just like the rest of this dump...* He was wondering if it might be best to just throw the object over the railings, let the filthy river have its dark magics. *And yet, what if it's valuable? Will I have thrown away a treasure that could buy me out of the combine once and for all?* He made up his mind; he would hide the object in his cabin aboard the

251

Vendosia, and once back in Tronheim he would connect with one of his dealers... surely one of them would find the thing had some worth? *And then they will pay me handsomely for it...* He also resolved not to touch the thing again himself; it would be safe enough in its pouch until he handed it over to a buyer. *It's about time you used that brain of yours, Doron Khalik...* He also resolved to try not to keep talking about himself in the third person.

Anthra moved among the bulk containers laid out along the dock frontage. Hiding behind the plassteel tubs and teddra conduits, he slipped from shadow to shadow, always aware of the overhead arc lights strung between the docking pylons. He was looking for an open data-port. There should be one near the berth rotors, the huge winch mechanism which clasped onto a starship and pulled it gently into its allocated berth. Every crew member of the *Vendosia* was required to enter their allocation tag at the data-port before exiting the docks; he needed to know if Doron Khalik had tagged back in yet. Slipping behind a foul smelling waste reclamation pod, he quickly ducked down as several crew men entered the berth and proceeded to make their way to the aft cargo hold. He scanned his datapad for Khalik's ID tag, found the photo and watched the men approach. None of them was Khalik. When they had passed by he moved forward cautiously, all the time keeping an eye on the rear cargo hold where the doors were no doubt wide open. He reached the data-port and attached an optic feeder cable from his pad to the data-port interface. The heavy rain was making it difficult to read his screen, but after a few minutes he had determined that Doron Khalik had not yet returned to his ship. *Excellent... now I must wait and catch this thief before he has chance to escape...* He found a gap between two containers and stepped back into the shadows, waiting, one of his hands wrapped around the small weapon inside his leg pocket.

"Maybe we should try to contact Anthra again?"

Shari turned around. "Look, Dom, we tried five times already, he's obviously up to something sneaky and doesn't want us to interrupt."

Domini actually believed that was true, but after walking for over an hour in the pouring rain, his will to continue the search was definitely flagging.

Shari stepped over a puddle in the street, dodging a taxi as it sped past.

"Run me over, why don't you! Dumb Bargs..." She was soaked to the skin, and her feet were killing her. They couldn't go on like this. "Look, Dom, I have an idea. Let's get out of the rain a minute..."

They stepped over to a taxi rank and stood under its plassteel awning.

"Okay, what's your idea?"

"We tap into this shipping allocation registry that Anthra found, we find out where this *Vendosia* is berthed and we go there. We find Anthra, make sure he's okay and not lying out someplace in the rain, and when the spacer gets back to his ship we jump him and retrieve the artifact...what do you think?"

He was shaking rainwater out of his hair as he answered her. "I think you should think about that for a minute..."

"What? Why? What's wrong with that idea?"

"First of all, Anthra said he would wait for the spacer, and as he hasn't linked yet I think we can presume he's still waiting, and second we have no idea how to tap into the local Net for information."

She sighed. "Domini, listen, Anthra might not be able to contact us, he might be hurt, we can't take that risk. And as for the local Net, didn't I tell you I was a math genius? I can hack just about any system going... come on, let's find a data-port..."

Domini wasn't sure about the idea, but he was getting tired of walking around in circles getting soaked to the skin.

"All right, but at the first sign of trouble we run."

"You know, Dom, sometimes I really don't think you trust me at all." And she set off down the street.

They started checking the local businesses for interior data-ports and eventually found one inside a bank; it was primarily for account holders only, but Shari assured Domini that wouldn't be a problem. She positioned Domini behind her and bent down to check the interface.

"Just let me know if anyone comes this way, Dom."

He saw three lines of customers waiting for service, and nearby there were three occupied data-ports, but no one seemed to be paying them any undue attention.

"So now, let's see... if I call up an inquiry tag that will get me into the bank's data-stream, trick is to fish for feeder words..."

Domini whispered from behind her: "What are feeder words?"

"Words that are used by the AI system to tag cascading data. They're a way in, like a hole in the data-stream. Each one has a binary matrix, one for the up-front coding and one hidden beneath it for the primary pathways; once I get in there I can loop outside the bank's system and dive into the local Net trunks... piece of cake..."

"What has cake got to do with it?"

253

She looked up at him. "Didn't you ever study Ancient Galac? We learned all sorts of dross in first school, crell knows where the sayings came from, but most folk on Primus use them."

"And the cake is?"

She sighed. "Never mind, just keep an eye out for trouble."

She returned to the screen, tapping away at the coding slots as they slipped across the viewer.

"All right, I have a feeder word which is repeating in three separate enquiry tags, so if I flow down to its source code and tap in a revolving inquiry… I can loop outside the system…slip sideways… got it… I'm into the local Net, Dom. Pulling up the shipping registry now…"

He glanced back at the screen and saw a list of ships rolling down the viewer. Shari tapped in the name of the *Vendosia* and it suddenly filled the screen, giving full docking allocation data, including berth location.

Shari reached around and handed Domini her datapad. "Here, tap in the details as I read them out."

He took the datapad and she read the contents of the data-sheet to him. When he finished he looked up. "Got it… so let's get going." He'd just seen a man in a gray coverall staring at them from behind the long counter.

Shari noticed too. "Okay, Dom, let's move it."

They ran outside and found that the rain had stopped. Shari saw a large full moon high in the northern skies and further away, a smaller one lower down on the horizon. She pointed left. "Come on, we need to head toward the river." They set off, crossing the main road and moving away from the Glamoria Precinct, heading toward the docks.

It took them some time to negotiate the streets leading to the docks. Every flash sign seemed to send them in the wrong direction; Shari thought the city planners were either blind or totally sadistic. But eventually they came across an immense avenue filled with market stalls leading directly into the docks. It reminded her of Salicia Sonora on Petra, the same mad chaos of sellers and buyers, hawkers of every race and type pushing their wares at the new arrivals. She saw far more true aliens around the docks; a few Coloquies… but then she figured they managed to get just about everywhere, an awful lot of the humanoid reptile types, and also a whole troupe of green-skinned dancers parading around an improvised stage set up among the tents and stalls.

Suddenly she pulled up.

Domini turned to her: "What's wrong?"

She was pointing to an area about thirty meters away. "Look, Dom, flat-faces…"

He looked and saw about half a dozen of the flat-faced aliens moving among the stalls of a weapons merchant. He couldn't tell them apart from the group that had attacked him at Landings Down, but the thought that they might actually be the same group was enough to alarm them both.

She moved closer to his side, took his arm in her own. "What do you want to do, Dom?"

He took a quick look around; the whole place was so busy it would be relatively easy to lose the flat-faces among the crowds. "We'll back off, edge around the square to the right and head into the docks along the riverfront."

"Okay, good plan. Let's do that."

Arm in arm, they retraced their steps and walked back to the riverside. Once they reached the railings they moved cautiously along the pathway behind the market toward the docks entrance. They saw no more flat-faces and eventually arrived on the main concourse of the docks.

Domini pulled Shari to one side. "Where do we go from here?"

"Give me a minute…" She checked her datapad, looked up at the long row of berths stretching off into the distance. "This way…" And she set off, Domini following on behind.

Anthra had been waiting for over an hour. He was tempted to link with Shari or even Ventra, but if the man Khalik suddenly turned up he would have to act fast. He wasn't sure what he was going to do to the human; violence wasn't something that came easy to a Saepid; but the stakes were frighteningly high. He thought he could at least get the better of the man, four arms is a tremendous advantage in a fist fight… but such a struggle might be noticed, there were many spacers wandering about the docks. His pulse tube, on the other hand, was lethal and, most important of all, it was silent; but could he take a life? *No choice in this, no choice at all, we live in bad times, no room for error in this, no choice at all…* He fingered the tube in his pocket, the hairs above his carapace standing on end.

There was movement at the entry gate; someone was tapping the data-port. He moved out of the shadows to get a better view and instantly recognized the man walking toward him: *Doron Khalik… at last.* He pulled out the tube, pointing it directly at the man's chest. Khalik just stopped walking, staring back

255

at him, seemingly unsure of what to make of this four-armed apparition standing before him.

Anthra didn't hesitate, he pressed the initiation sequencer on the tube and a narrow pencil of light struck Khalik just above his abdomen. He instantly crumpled as the ion stream burst into his chest, spreading death among his organs. Anthra moved quickly, his hands going through the dead man's jacket until he found the pouch... *at last!!* But he was suddenly bathed in light as an overhead arc lamp was directed toward him. Someone up on the ship had seen him and initiated security measures.

From somewhere toward the rear of the ship, voices were shouting, and he heard men running in his direction. He leaped back into the shadows, running quickly among the cargo containers, jumping over the teddra conduits, and making his way as best he could toward the main concourse. From behind him came the sound of a ship's alarm and he knew they were after him, it was only a matter of time before they sent security drones into the skies above.

"You hear that?" Shari said.

"What?"

"That! Can't you hear it? It's an alarm; coming from down there..."

"Isn't that where we're heading?"

They looked at each other and started to run toward the sound. From somewhere above them came the thump-thump of a security drone bearing down on their position.

As they turned a corner they came face to face with group of spacers who looked busy searching among a row of containers.

Domini pulled Shari to one side. "We have to be careful, Shari; we don't know what's going on here."

"Do you think it's got something to do with Anthra?" She was trying to see beyond the group of men.

"Possibly, but we can't afford to let them find us."

She looked back at him. "So what do you suggest we do?"

"Well, we can try and get past them around the back..." He was looking at a narrow gap which seemed to lead behind the warehouse along the edge of a docking berth.

Shari looked both ways; it made more sense to go around the back rather than through the spacers. "Okay, let's go before they get here."

From above them a security drone locked onto their position, relaying the data back to a central dispersion pad which automatically forwarded the details

256

to the men searching the cargo area. They now knew exactly where Shari and Domini were.

The two made their way around to the back of the building, edging between cargo units and the plassteel wall of the warehouse. Just then, they heard someone coming. Shari pushed Domini behind a large container pod.

He whispered: "What is it?"

"Someone's coming this way…"

He tried to peer into the darkness, but saw nothing beyond the containers. "Are you sure?"

"Shush! Listen…"

Sure enough, he could hear someone moving toward them, no more than a few feet away now and getting closer.

"Shari, we should back off."

She crouched down, pulling him with her. "No, we have spacers back there; let's see who it is first…"

From between two units a dark figured emerged, moving cautiously toward them. Domini clenched his fists, determined that no matter what happened he would defend Shari to the death.

Shari pressed up against Domini as the figure in front of them suddenly emerged from the shadows.

"Anthra!" Shari exclaimed.

Anthra ran forward to greet them. "Ssshhhh now, Shari, many spacers behind me…"

Domini leaned forward: "Well, there are more right behind us…"

Anthra quickly assessed the situation. "I fear we are trapped." He pulled out the silver tube, ready to fight their way out.

Shari asked: "Did you find the thief?"

"Yes indeed, most unfortunate but I had to use force to retrieve artifact."

Shari's eyes brightened. "You have it, then? You got it back?"

"Indeed, and I will keep it safe for now, I think."

She seemed a little hurt by that but remained silent.

From behind them, torch lights broke through the darkness, casting shadows among the containers. The spacers were very close now, their voices carried on the wind. Shari heard one man talking about a murdered crewman… *Anthra!* As they moved closer, Domini pulled her further back between two large crates. In front of them another set of lights could be seen moving through the rain… more men coming out of the shadows and Shari saw they were carrying hand guns... *We are so going to get killed here...* She squeezed Domini's hand, and their eyes met, acknowledging their love with a slight smile.

Anthra suddenly spoke up as his datapad brightened: "Finally! Come, you two, follow Anthra, quickly now..."

Shari and Domini didn't move at first; they could see no way out. But Anthra quickly turned around and insisted they follow him. So they stood up slowly, peeking over the edge of a cargo crate, fully aware that they were exposing themselves to the guns of the spacers. Suddenly Anthra made a mad dash toward the riverfront; Domini gripped Shari's hand and they set off after him.

From somewhere above and behind them came the sound of engines, a deep throbbing vibration which sent ripples of heat across the yard. Shari resisted the urge to look up, more intent on following Anthra as he made his way toward the enclosure wall. By the time they reached him the sound coming from above was overwhelming, and a down-draft was whipping up the dust and debris scattered among the cargo pods.

Anthra had hauled himself up and now sat on the top of the wall. Domini put his hands together to give Shari a lift up, while Anthra reached down toward her. But abruptly a beam of blue light shot through the night, hitting Anthra squarely on his left shoulder. Shari was pulling herself up just as Anthra disappeared over to the other side.

"Anthra!"

She scrambled to pull herself up and onto the wall just as a second beam impacted the plassteel ribbing next to her legs; she felt the sting of hot metal slivers as they burned through her trousers and she lost her grip, falling back down again. Domini was suddenly beside her, his arm around her waist. He hoisted her up and together they managed to pull themselves up and over the wall to fall down hard on the other side. Shari was winded and allowed Domini to pull her close to the wall as the spacers continued to fire over their heads. Crouching in the dirt, just meters from the river, they felt a wave of intense heat pass over them, and the sound they had heard earlier graduated into the recognizable sound of atmospheric thrusters. Shari finally looked up and was amazed to see the *Shaendar* hanging like a giant insect directly over the raging torrent below.

"Oh, Domini, look!"

He'd seen it, of course, noted the rear cargo doors were sliding open.

"I think we're supposed to jump..." He looked down at Anthra. The Saepid seemed barely conscious, his eyes rolling back, and there was dark blood oozing from a nasty shoulder wound.

Shari tried to get Anthra to stand up. "Anthra, please, you have to stand, we need to get to the ship." But Anthra was obviously in far too much pain to react to her pleading. He didn't even seem to recognize her, and he was mumbling something in the Othrum tongue, just clucks and clicks to Shari's ears.

Domini made a decision: "Shari, can you jump that far?"

She looked across to the now fully extended loading ramp, hanging precariously above the river.

"I think so... but what about Anthra?"

"I'll take care of Anthra; you just go, now!"

She hesitated and he shouted again: "Go, Shari... jump!"

She ran forward, oblivious now to the pain in her leg, and without another thought, she leapt off the riverbank toward the ramp. Landing heavily inside she quickly rolled over to get out of Domini's way.

Domini reached down and hauled Anthra onto his back, but the added weight forced him to his knees. He took a deep breath, braced himself, carefully moving Anthra's arms out of the way, he stood up slowly. Another blast of weapon fire from beyond the wall convinced him that it was now or never. He took a deep breath, and with Anthra's head banging against the back of his neck he ran forward, leaping across the gap between the embankment and the ship's ramp. When he landed he heard Anthra moan softly as they fell to one side and rolled across the deck. Shari punched the compad.

"Go, Ventra! We're all on board!" The cargo doors began to close as the ship rose slowly, turning sharply to one side, and from somewhere beneath them the needle tubes burst into life.

Shari ran over to kneel down next to Domini. "Is he okay?"

Domini was trying to rouse Anthra, but the Saepid seemed incoherent now.

"I can't tell, we need to get him into the Surgeon."

Shari thumped the compad: "Ventra, we need you back here, Anthra is hurt!"

There was a short pause before Ventra came online. "Apologies, Shari, but must handle ship right now, we are being targeted by ground sensors, might be ships waiting for us above."

259

Shari knew what that statement must be costing Ventra, but she was right, it wouldn't help Anthra if they got shot out of the sky.

"Okay, we'll deal with it, don't worry; just handle the ship."

Ventra didn't reply as the link closed. Shari turned to Domini. "We'll have to handle this; come on, help me get him into the Med Bay."

Domini pulled Anthra carefully to his feet as Shari wrapped one of Anthra's upper arms around her shoulders. Domini did the same from his side and they slowly moved forward. They had nearly reached the annex when the ship suddenly banked to one side and all three of them fell over, rolling against the hull. Shari felt her head slam into the bulkhead and for a few seconds lost consciousness. She woke to Domini gently tapping her face. "What? Dom?"

"You hit your head. How are you feeling?"

She rubbed the back of her head. "Sore, but I'm okay, I think I'm getting used to this... Anthra?"

Domini looked down at Anthra lying on the deck, his eyes now closed. "He's completely out; we have to move him, Shari. Can you walk?"

She forced herself to stand, leaning back against the hull to catch her breath. "I'm okay, let's keep going..."

They hauled Anthra up again and finally made it to the Med Bay. They saw that the Surgeon was already online after its previous treatment of Domini, but the cocoon was still aligned for a human, and not a Saepid. If they were to help Anthra they needed to adjust the Surgeon's configuration matrix and reconfigure its parameters for a Saepid body.

Domini looked from the Surgeon to Shari. "Can you adjust this thing?"

She looked at the interface; the data-flow was still in standard Galac, but the higher functions were pure Othrum. "I don't know. Maybe..."

He looked down at Anthra, now slumped against one of the Surgeon's outer support struts. "You have to make up your mind, Shari, Anthra might be dying."

She glared at him: "Don't you think I know that? Dom, for crell's sake, if I align the cocoon wrong it could kill him just as easily."

"Then maybe we should call Ventra again?" But the ship suddenly lurched to one side and they quickly grasped the wall bars, while Domini used his legs to keep Anthra from rolling away. "Maybe not..."

"I can't disturb her again, Dom, we're just going to have to do this by ourselves. Here, help me unplug these data crystals..."

260

They removed the crystals and Shari opened up the physical alignment grid. She saw the protocols were all within the human range, and as such would almost certainly hurt Anthra, if not kill him.

"If I can just wipe the human parameters away and reconfigure the Surgeon to its primary directives I think the Saepid configurations will kick in automatically. This thing was designed for Saepids, Dom, Anthra altered its parameters to help you, and so it makes sense that if I can erase you from the system we'll be able to plug him in safely."

He smiled: "Makes sense."

She tapped the interface resequencer and re-inserted the data crystals; all at once the cocoon transformed, folding away its human-shaped padding, and re-forming into something larger, with four clear hollows for Saepid arms. From above, a row of new needle probes replaced the human instruments, and long spidery injectors descended to rest just above the cocoon's portal access point.

"I think I did it!"

Domini congratulated her. "Well done, so let's get Anthra hooked up."

They took two arms each and lifted Anthra onto the grav-plate in front of the Surgeon. Then Shari touched the activation pad and Anthra was slowly drawn into the machine. They waited as the Surgeon ran a diagnostics routine, assessing the damage to Anthra. Shari watched the data screen carefully, hoping that the Surgeon would not reject Anthra for some reason. *What if I've input the wrong protocols…?* But the interface flashed a recognition tag and instantly set about repairing Anthra's wound.

They stepped back from the machine, both of them exhausted. Shari reached down and removed the artifact pouch from Anthra's cloak pocket. It was cold to the touch, and she felt suddenly uplifted as she placed it back inside her jacket. And then she felt the burning pain coming from her lower right leg.

Domini noticed. "Are you hurt?"

"I got hit by shrapnel, I think, off that wall."

He bent down to see that the trouser leg was pock-marked with dozens of tiny holes, each one burnt into the material. He also saw blood.

"Shari, we need to get your trousers off."

She gave him a sly smile. "Why, Domini, can't you control yourself? This is hardly the right time…"

"Shari… you know what I mean, your leg is bleeding…"

261

Just then Ventra came online. "Attention, Shari, secure Anthra, then you must both come forward, strap down; about to enter sharp maneuvers, hurrys please!"

Shari looked at her leg, then back at Domini. "It'll have to wait, come on, let's get forward."

"But, Shari...."

She turned as she moved through the hatch. "It can wait, Dom; I'm not about to die from a flesh wound. Now come on."

They ran toward the command deck, trying to stay upright as the ship suddenly dropped to one side and then accelerated the other way. Once through the final hatch they climbed over the trees to get to their own webbing. This proved a lot more difficult than they had expected. Moving about a Saepid ship in full gravity was not the easiest of things to do, the vegetation was easy enough to drift around during space flight, but right now everything was an obstacle; even Shari's tree was getting in the way of her webbing. Domini could hear her swearing to herself as a pile of leaves dropped down over her head.

Shari tried to call down to Ventra, but her voice was lost to the roar of the atmospheric thrusters. She touched her compad. "Okay, Ventra, we're strapped down."

Ventra replied with a voice full of fear: "And Anthra?"

Shari looked across at Domini. "He's in the Surgeon... we don't know yet, Ventra."

Ventra didn't respond, but the ship lurched forward again, bound for the upper atmosphere and the stars beyond.

As zero gravity returned, Shari loosened her straps and reached out to grasp a floater. She pulled it close and initiated the stats screen. Immediately she was alarmed. From three thousand klicks to their rear two ships were on an intercept course. *Bargs are coming after us...* Then she noticed something else, a lot closer and approaching rapidly; she tagged the object and instantly the ship flashed the *Shaendar* recognition codes... it was the ship's skipper returning by remote. *Clever Ventra, but have we time to pick it up?* Her question was immediately answered as the screen flashed an alert... the rear cargo doors were opening wide to receive the skipper. Ventra initiated the docking clamps and minutes later the little craft was secured and the *Shaendar* shuddered as her pulse drive came online.

Shari slipped the stats screen away and tapped for the current spatial-grid. The picture was even more alarming. From out-system another ship was converging on their course, a small vessel, but seemingly very fast. *The one following us from Petra?* She touched the compad: "Ventra, have you seen the latest grid?"

From the speaker came Ventra's voice, but she could also hear her in real-time from the command pod below, giving the words instant echoes. "Yes, Shari, I know, the one who has followed since Petra has found us. Most unfortunate."

"Can you do anything?"

"Am trying to do tricky maneuver, might work, might not, please be patient."

The pad fell silent. There was nothing to do now but wait, placing all their faith in Ventra's abilities as a pilot. Shari looked down at the floater screen. *That one is an agent of the Beast, far deadlier than the other two ships... but any of them could kill us right now...*

The *Shaendar* was moving at a fraction below sub-light speed, the engine core had not achieved ionic insertion, and so the pulse drive was pushing a mere fifteen gees equivocal, not nearly enough to initiate a subspace bubble. From the command pod the proximity alarm sounded, and Shari could hear the echo locators pinging. *We're being targeted!*

Ventra was forcing the pulse drive by venting plasma through the needle tubes, it was an old trader trick used to escape the clutches of passing pirates, but although it might help to sustain subspace insertion, it could also cause the engines to overload, and after that the *Shaendar* would be just one more bright star in the Port Fall night.

Shari saw Domini mumbling quietly to himself. *Praying? He might still be Mr. Priest, after all...* The ship began to shake violently, and some of the smaller trees broke free from their roots, drifting gracefully among the various floater screens. She quickly scanned the grid. The two ships had locked weapons and would open fire at any moment, but the Beast's agent was maneuvering closer, coming between the *Shaendar* and the other ships. *What's he playing at?* She watched the alert flash across the screen as missile tracers were detected. Her fingernails were digging into the screen causing fade outs, and she tried to relax, watching as the red lines arced toward them. She knew Ventra was seeing this, but she wasn't trying to outmaneuver the missiles. *Why doesn't she do something!* She was about to tap the compad when she saw a flash of brightness on the screen; seconds later she saw that both missiles had detonated. She scanned for tracer filaments and realized that the agent had destroyed the

263

missiles and was now vectoring to target the ships from Port Fall. *Well, this makes no sense at all...*

Less than a minute later, the *Shaendar* entered subspace, and looking up, Shari saw that the stars were gone. *But had they really escaped?* She touched for the local subspace grid. The only ionic fluctuations belonged to the *Shaendar*; for some inexplicable reason they had been allowed to escape certain death, *from two different sources!* She let the floater drift away, touched the pad. "Ventra? Have we really escaped?"

Ventra came online: "Apparently, but as yet I have no idea how."

Domini was busy climbing out of his webbing as Shari drifted over to him.

"You okay, Dom?"

"I am, but we need to sort your leg out."

"In a minute, I need to talk to Ventra first." She pushed off and dropped down toward the command pod. Ventra was still busy with her screen, but looked up as Shari came closer.

"Ventra, I managed to reconfigure the Surgeon for Anthra, I think he's going to be okay, but you may want to go check on him."

Ventra gave her a look of intense gratitude. "Thank you, Shari dear, I am most grateful for your caring of Anthra, and I will go see him soon, but first I must align our navigation systems to the new coordinates. We need to mask our trail again, perhaps hide somewhere for a day or so. I have much thinking to do on the matter. But for now we are safe, our outreach systems are phased out of alignment; no one following will know we have passed this way." She worked with the screens for a few minutes and then unstrapped her webbing to float up toward the rear cargo hatch and the Med Bay beyond.

Shari called after her: "Ventra?"

Ventra turned around at the hatch. "Yes, Shari?"

"Why do you think that agent let us go? I mean, why would he target those two ships?"

Ventra gave Shari a grave look. "I fear, Shari, that Beast's priorities have changed; he might not want to destroy us now, he might desire that you are captured alive. I fear he is most interested in a living *custodia*..." With that, she floated through the hatch and disappeared down the aft corridor.

Shari was left in shock. Up until now she had believed that if the enemy ever caught up with them then it would at least be a matter of an instant death, which was an awful way to die, of course, but at least it would be painless. *But*

264

what now? If that monster actually got hold of me! Domini was by her side, and he seemed to know what she was thinking.

"Hey, don't worry; no *Beast* is going to take you away from me."

She looked into his eyes. "You promise?"

He pulled her into his arms. "I promise."

She spoke into his warm shoulder. "Good, so help me get my pants off..."

Ventra floated toward the ship's Surgeon, its web of intricate probes moving in and out of the cocoon. She tapped a diagnostic screen; saw the realignments input by Shari. *Shari has saved you, my mate... may the trade winds heal your wounds and bring you back to me...*

265

Chapter 2 - Data-Stream Fluctuations

'If you question your faith, you doubt it and thus will you be damned.'
Revelations: First Book of Saemal.

The Viper dropped down sharply to avoid the flaming debris of the two ships. Neiron Thane cut to sub-light speed, the gravity variance beginning to impact against the powerful inter-phase drive. He banked away from the planet, linking instantly with the tracer drones he had previously left straddled in low orbit. Their echo points formed a cohesive spatial-grid and he was able to upload the data into the AI system. The resulting data-stream contained a perfect match for the Saepid ionic pulse drive. *You may run and you may try to hide, little runaways, but wherever you go, I will be there...*

He had been disturbed by the recent synaptic influx from the Far Star Colony; there had been new instructions, a deviation from his core parameters. His Lord now wanted the human child captured and taken to the Colony for a neural interrogatory.

This is highly unusual; to deviate from the core directive... But the data-stream was succinct in its feeder resonance, the coaxial configurations had been merged with the outflow of bi-neural tributaries, now reassigned to a new and more precise series of integrate definitions. The human must be brought alive before Saemal. So it was necessary to destroy the two ships, and despite the fact that this act allowed the Saepids to escape once more, the tracer drones had eventually sifted through the waste junk left behind by their vessel. It would not take him long to catch up. But first there was still the uplink from Primus to deal with.

He tapped the screen before him, watched as the Worship Glyph flashed across the screen, and then after several minutes it linked to the first of the com probes sent out by the fleets engaged around Petra. Each of the twelve fleets had been leaving com probes throughout the areas of expansion. His Lord would only use the galactic Trans-Net for means of subversion and infiltration, all military data traffic, including occupation reports would pass through the web of com probes now scattered among the worlds. The link to Petra gave him a situation report recently uploaded by Fleet Commander Glindon of the Sacred Eleven. The planet was in the process of being occupied and the citizenry subdued. They had not been able to keep the power of Saemal out of their machinery and, just as at Primus, they were currently being inculcated into the

Coalescency. The progress at Entrymion had followed the same pattern and the reports from the Samrosion priest Ilka Vendhren were highly favorable. But now the uplink from Tanril on Primus was cause for some concern.

Tanril had been speaking to the natural parent of the child Shari S'Atwa; the man had intimated that the girl was something very special, *what were the words? Savior of worlds?* Tanril had learned that the child had been visited by an unidentified priest earlier in her life, that this man had identified her as this *savior*. The information might have been easily dismissed, but when Tanril had uploaded details of the interview to the data-stream from the Far Star Colony the bounce-back recognition protocols had nearly killed him. Their Lord God had become enraged. A stream of violent and vitriolic synaptic conjugations had flowed from the Colony. Orders were issued; whole fleets stationed among the occupied worlds of the Rim were instantly mobilized and sent out to intercept the Saepid vessel. Every resource available was now directed at that one little ship. And now he alone, among all the servants of Saemal spread out across vast areas of the Coalition, was the closest to that vessel, and only he knew where to find it.

He leaned forward in his seat, touched the inter-phase drive pad and initiated the forward pulse. The Viper slipped out of real-time and into subspace, its feelers cast wide, linked now to the echo points downloaded from the tracer drones. It might take several days to narrow the search coordinates to an actual location point, but it would happen eventually, and when it did he would suck the ions right out of their tubes; they wouldn't know what hit them.

Chapter 3 - Twilight on Phaedra

"So I looked death in the eye, and I killed it before it could kill me. After that it was easy, I just killed everyone I met in the street, even when they hid in the temples it was easy, we just torched the place and cut them down as they ran out, their hair burning in the wind..."
Phaelon Ground Trooper, Petra Campaign.

Torin Grenval was no longer a First Minister within the Council Assemblage of the Phaelon Confederacy; now he was Adjutant General to the Sacred Member Mistia. She had newly arrived from Primus with instructions from their Lord Saemal. The Phaelon battle fleet had been recalled from Galicia after that planet's absorption into the Coalescency, and now Mistia had informed him that the recently enhanced fleet was to travel directly to the Far Star Colony.

He had some clue as to the importance of the mission when she had arrived with a flotilla of bio-ships. These new craft were quite unlike anything he had ever seen before; forged inside the very heart of the Cortex, the ships were bio-mechanical living entities. They did not require a physical crew to pilot or guide their systems and as such were controlled directly by the data-stream emanating from the Colony. When Mistia had shown him inside the one now parked in the middle of Razors Field he had felt awe, and a profound sense of being in the presence of pure and unbridled power.

The ships literally breathed; he had heard it, felt the exhalation of air through the fibrous veins which girdled the interior conduits and control systems. He had seen Mistia immerse her hands in the slime which covered what he took to be a command console, and instantly the ship had awakened, liquids streaming along tubes and down translucent rods which seemed to be feeding an engine core vibrating beneath their feet. Diaphanous tendrils had snaked among the conduits and he had felt the power surge along the fibrous ribs which supported the entire ship. The experience had left him shaken, as she knew it would. And now here they were meeting at midnight on the balcony of his personal residence, and for the first time since his assimilation into the Coalescency he felt a touch of fear. The fleet was about to leave and he had been due to take a shuttle to the flagship when she had asked to meet him; it was most unsettling.

He sipped his Louna juice, and leaned over the balustrade, the scent of the Gordenia flowers was a pleasant reminder of summers long since past. But as the memory arrived it was instantly replaced by a vision of the Worship Glyph and he once more felt the peace of Saemal. He looked out over the city. The lights along the Via Dezhra gave the illusion of multifaceted snakes winding among the spirals and brightly colored towers of the habitation districts. All seemed normal, and if it wasn't for the huge new Temple of Saemal erected where the monorail station used to stand, one would think that Phaedra was unchanged, untouched by the glory of the Coalescency.

From behind him he heard the chimes moving as the patio doors slid open; turning around he saw Mistia stepping under the surrela vines which formed an arch over the doorway. She was wearing a long flowing robe of blue sharil inlaid with turquoise filigree, with a chain of tiny lapsuz stones around her neck. Her blond hair was tied up into a crown secured with corsara vines and tiny glasscite glyphs taken from the sacred texts. She smiled, and as she walked toward him in her low-cut dress he found it difficult not to feel aroused, and he had no doubt that was the effect Mistia was looking for. He would have to be very careful with the blessed Mistia.

"Torin, it is so nice to see you again. I realize the hour is late and your shuttle awaits, but I have one final task for you before you take your leave."

He poured her a drink and asked, "Task, my Lady? What task might that be?"

She took the glass from him and walked over to the balustrade. "In a moment, Torin. Let me look upon your great city… how very green it is in this light."

"The second moon illuminates the towers, my Lady, it is the true color of Phaedra."

"Yes, so I've heard. And tell me, Torin; do you miss your Confederacy at all?"

Is this the trap? "That is not possible, my Lady, I serve the one God now."

"Of course you do. And would you serve your God even unto death?"

"My life belongs to the Lord Saemal, my Lady; I can do no more than offer it into his sacred hands."

"You have read the Book of Saemal, then?"

"It is required, my Lady…"

"Tell me of your thoughts regarding the Revelations of Saemal."

"The Book tells of the rise of the heathen lords known as the First Ones, and of the great war to free the universe of their foul stench. It tells of their defeat by our Lord Saemal who afterward returned to his sanctuary, there to rest until he was once more called upon to defend the younger races against the rise of evil among the worlds."

"You certainly know your scripture, Torin, I'll give you that. But tell me, do you believe the First Ones are truly dead and gone?"

"The Book says—"

"I know what the Book says, Torin, I'm asking you what you believe; is it possible that there are First Ones among us even now in this generation?"

"In all truth, my Lady, I do not know…" *Where is she going with all of this?*

"Well, I do know, Torin. Consider your orders to take our very best ships back to the Far Star Colony, what possible threat can there be that would warrant such an armada?"

Torin thought about that for a minute. *Could it possibly be true?*

"Forgive me, my Lady, but are you saying that the heathen First Ones have returned?"

She looked back at him, her eyes seeming to shine in the half-light from the balcony glow globes. "I am saying, Torin, that something has disturbed the sacred waters, and that something is moving toward our Lord's sanctuary. Tanril has informed me that the threat comes in the form of a human female, accompanied by a renegade crew of Saepids. As to her bio-status, that is currently inconclusive; there is no relevant data on the physical form used by the First Ones when they rampaged among the stars."

"But surely, my Lady, no mere girl can harm the glory of our God Saemal?"

She stared at him, her eyes as cold as ice. "Of course not. I simply want to impress upon you that although you must use all available means to prevent the Saepid vessel from approaching the Far Star Colony, there are other considerations I wish you to consider."

"Other considerations my Lady?"

"To be discussed in good time Torin. Suffice it to say you must follow the Sacred Precepts in this matter until I tell you otherwise."

"I understand my Lady."

"We have an agent very near to this ship who will intercept the girl before she can reach the Colony. But like a fish in a pond this Saepid ship

270

flitters and flies beneath our data-stream. You must use this to your advantage when the time is right."

"Forgive me my Lady, but I am not sure I understand your meaning."

She smiled. "Simply obey my orders Torin, and all will be revealed."

"I serve to obey my Lady."

She turned away once more and her tone changed as if her words were mere echoes originating on far off Primus.

"You will use the bio-ships to patrol the Sacred Sanctum around our Lord's sanctuary. We have yet to determine the power this human might wield; therefore the bio-ships will form a neural network between the Colony worlds to prevent a covert infiltration, and you will use these ships as your defense perimeter. Not one single byte of subversive data must get past your network, Torin, is that clear to you?"

"Absolutely, my Lady, my duty is my life."

"Of course it is, and failure will ensure you lose that life."

He lowered his head, and spoke with humility: "And that is the task you spoke of earlier?"

She smiled, studying his face carefully. "That, Torin, is your duty; the task is something else…" She came over to stand before him, placing her hand beneath his chin and lifting his head. "You may kiss me now, Torin…"

He heard the words but his mind could not quite accept them; this woman before him was a member of the Sacred Eleven, chosen personally by his God Saemal. She walked the sacred halls of the Cortex, breathed the air of Godhood… *and now here she was asking him to kiss her?*

"My Lady… I…"

"Just do it, Torin, I have little patience and you have no time to waste."

So he leaned toward her and kissed her gently on her lips. The sensation was one of intense pleasure, as if she had cast a spell and captured his very soul. His heart was pounding as his scales began to rise along his arms… *was this a seduction or a subtle trap designed to break my conditioning?* But she pulled him into her arms, and as they embraced he felt the warmth of her breasts against his tunic and he lost himself to the sudden rise of passion from within.

Slowly she stepped back, looking into his eyes. "So, Torin, show me to your bedchamber…"

And so, without another word, he took her hand and led her back through the doors into the house, and on into the bedchamber beyond the outer pool.

If this is a trap then I swear I will enjoy this death to its glorious end…

271

Chapter 4 - Hiding in a Sea of Night

Looking into the endless darkness light appeared,
a thin disc of white suspended in the void,
a sprinkling of new-born stars fell one by one into place,
and a world appeared untouched by the eternal night.

From the rocks a stream sprang forth,
water fell through sunbeams onto the earth,
and rivers became seas and oceans,
as the winds carried life into the heart of a storm.

Deep into the darkest of lost places,
where silence and shadows fell like rainbows from the sky,
the universe moved unseen and unheard,
as intelligence suddenly roamed the land...

Lothar Theron: Personal Poetics.

With her leg finally taped with plasstrip, Shari was busy studying the latest spatial location grid. They were parked in the dark lee of one of the larger asteroids of an extensive asteroid belt somewhere between a massive J-class planet and a smaller K-class. Neither planets had any sign of habitation rings or local traffic; Ventra assured them that the system was a long way off the commerce lanes. She had suggested they take a day to recuperate, to bring the ship's systems back to peak efficiency, but of course the real reason was that she was worried about Anthra. She spent most of her time back in the Med Bay.

Anthra had still not been released from the Surgeon; it was currently synthesizing the necessary coagulant for his blood. Apparently, Anthra's blood type was very rare, even among Saepids, and this had caused some delay in his recovery; of course, Ventra worried about this most of the time.

According to the latest stats, they were now at the very edge of the known Rim, far beyond the more civilized auspices of the Coalition. Most of the local worlds had once belonged to the Cordwainer Alliance, with their administrative capital on the planet Samros, but of course that planet had long since fallen to the armies of the Beast, and the worlds of the Alliance had been subjugated to his rule and domination. *Seventy two independent worlds now enslaved to madness. How am I supposed to stop such power?*

She used the now-limited forward scans to search for enemy vessels. They had to be so careful not to get noticed, the feelers and tracers were now useless to them; Ventra had said the one who follows would sniff them out instantly. So they had been flying near blind, afraid to look too far in a sea of endless night. But even within such limitations the scans showed movement ahead of them; many ships were out there, seemingly on an intercept course, their forward tracers easily identified them as massive fleets. *There's no way we'll get past that lot... surely Ventra must know this?*

Domini came out of the shower cubicle, his long hair casting water droplets into the air.

That surprised her. "We have water now?"

"Oh yes, I thought I told you, I linked the shower to the water reclamation unit."

"Does Ventra know?"

"She said it was okay…"

"Well thanks for telling me…better late than never I suppose."

He gave her a smile and reached for a floater above his webbing. She noticed his face darken, a look of concern in his eyes.

"Anything wrong, Domini?"

He looked across at her as she sat snugly inside her hammock. "Perhaps. I just checked on some tests I ran earlier…"

"Tests?"

He began to float toward her. "Yes, blood tests, actually. Yours. I've been waiting for the medlab to complete its analysis; there was some delay because most of the med systems are busy with Anthra."

She stared at him. "So? Did you find anything of interest?" She wasn't really sure she wanted to know.

"I'm afraid so, but please don't be too concerned, I'm sure we can deal with it."

But now she was concerned. "Dom, just tell me what you found!"

"I'm sorry, of course. Shari, my love, it appears you have *Lysordia Syndrome.*"

That hit her like a slap across her face. *How can that be possible? Surely she would have known that?* She was struggling to find words. "But, Dom, that's

273

not possible, my father… he had me tested after we lost Momma… I mean, we knew it was genetic, that it could be passed down, but I was given the all-clear."

He took hold of her hand. "Yes, I know. I can't explain it. But you can see here, look…" He held the floater in front of her. She read the medlab report, saw the serum derivatives categorized and disseminated and the erythrocyte diagnostic results, and finally the full blood culture analysis… *Lysordia Syndrome!* She was lost for words.

Domini moved closer, his hand stroking her long dark hair. "Theoretically, the recessive genes may well have lain dormant, masked by other healthy proteins. I know very little about the med-tech facilities on Primus, but I suspect that before the Coalition arrived the level of medical technology was not very advanced, considering the fate of your mother."

Shari looked at him, tears welling up in her eyes. "She died without reason, Dom; I mean those so-called med-techs had no idea how to cure her. I watched her waste away in front of me…"

He pulled her into his arms. "Well, that's not going to happen to you; *Lysordia* is curable now, a series of shots and you'll be cured."

She pushed him away gently. "And where are we going to go to get those shots, Dom? I can't see us going anywhere near a Coalition med center, can you?"

He wasn't sure what to say to that, but he had to try. "Shari… there is no sign that the *Lysordia* gene is active in your body, you are showing no indications of the disease; and I doubt there will be any indications, at least not for a very long time, long after we get back among the Hub worlds."

"Dom, you don't know anything about *Lysordia*. It creeps up on you, my mother had no idea she was sick until it was too late. She woke up one day with chest pains; the techs diagnosed some kind of cardiomyopathy, but she went downhill so fast… two weeks later she was dead… and there had been no indications, Dom, none."

Now he was lost for words. He was coming to come to terms with the possibility that they might all die somewhere in the cold dark of space; that was an awful fate they could all share, but now to think that he might suddenly lose Shari to a disease? It was beyond tragedy. *Is it not enough that we are surrounded by enemies? Now we have one more, even more insidious, right in our midst…*

She pushed the floater away, watched it drift beyond her tree, scattering the leaves in its wake. She turned to Domini. "It's all right, Dom, there's really

274

nothing we can do about this; it's just one more thing we have to deal with. And like you say, I'll probably be fine for a long time."

There was something he had to ask: "Do you remember how old your mother was when she passed?"

She thought about it for a minute. "Late thirties, I think, thirty-nine, yes, thirty-nine…" She tried to smile. "So I've got plenty of time to defeat the Beast and get back to civilization for those shots."

"Of course you have." He looked at her. "Should I have kept the blood results to myself?"

"No, of course not, I had to know. So don't worry, I can deal with it. I'm getting good at that, you know, dealing with life-threatening events in my life."

"That's my girl…" And they embraced.

Ventra tapped for the most recent blood results. Anthra was improving, but the new coagulant formulation was taking time to bind with his metabolism. It might be another day before the Surgeon woke him up. She was filled with doubts, unsure of her decision to leave subspace and hide among the asteroids of this dead system. *I am doubtful if I am completely unbiased in my decisions, my dear Anthra… have I taken bad risks because of my love for you?* At one level it made sense to hide for a while; without the full feeler grid it was next to impossible to know how far behind them the agent was; he could be very close now, or very far away… and the limited spatial scans had already shown them the enemy fleets cruising among the Rim worlds… *and with every hour they get closer still…* But had she taken such a decision simply so that she could be with Anthra? She had never piloted the *Shaendar* without him at her side; it felt wrong to sit at the command console knowing that he was not right there next to her to aid and comfort her… *I wish you would wake, my mate; I need you to tell me what to do… Shari needs you more than she needs me… and I need you most of all…*

She adjusted the cocoon's image display so that she could see Anthra's face. *He looks so peaceful, so beyond the cares of the ship and its quest…*

The compad suddenly buzzed, it was Shari from the command deck: "Ventra, are you there?"

She drifted over to the wall pad. "Yes, Shari, I am here."

"I don't want to worry you, but I think we have a proximity alert on the spatial-grid."

Ventra took a moment, looking back at her mate, and then replied: "Very well, I will be right there." She took one last look at the diagnostics and then passed through the hatch, heading back toward the main deck.

When she arrived both Domini and Shari were down in the command pod studying several screens. She was immediately aware of the proximity alert and just what that might mean. *Have I allowed the Beast to catch us?*

"What do you see, Shari?"

"The grid just found an echo point out there."

Ventra looked at the main screen. "More rocks maybe?"

Shari looked doubtful. "Doubt it; it's on an intercept course; it'll be here in under an hour... I think it's the agent, Ventra, I think he's found us."

They stared at the screens, each of them fully aware what that meant. Ventra edged into her webbing, pulling down a ship's stat screen. *To be stopped here when we are so close...* She turned to look at them. "You should both strap down, I will have to make tight maneuvers among asteroid belt, will be tricky, but I am far star trader, and we can be very tricky..." She looked back at the console and then added: "You should take floaters with you, keep an eye on situation. Shari, you can monitor the spatial-grid, and Domini, please watch ship systems... and also Med Bay if you will."

Domini nodded. "Of course, Ventra, I'll keep a watch on Anthra."

"Thank you... and now I must be best pilot I have ever been. No way to jump to subspace in asteroid field, too many variables, might melt into rocks. I will have to hide *Shaendar* behind biggest rocks, move with silence between the dark places..." And with that, she engaged the secondary thruster array, and the ship moved forward quietly, with minimum thrust, out toward the main body of the asteroid field.

Almost at once the echo-point locators came online, their regular pinging beginning to fill the cabin, at first quietly, and then, as the ship moved away from the large asteroid, they grew louder and louder, increasing in regularity as the ship's echo beacons zeroed in on the pursuing craft. Shari wanted to ask Ventra to shut out the sound, but she knew that with the feelers and tracers offline she was using the echo location systems to pinpoint the other ship, and so initiate her maneuvers accordingly.

Ventra must have turned on some kind of stealth mode because without warning the interior lights dimmed to the soft glow of the command console and the sounds of wind and rain, a constant aboard a Saepid vessel, vanished to be replaced by the ever-present pinging of the locators.

276

Shari checked her floater, and noticed that two-thirds of the ship's systems had been shut down. Only the command console and the Surgeon were active on the main deck, while far below in the engine core, only the thruster assembly was online; everything else was either offline or in reduced mode, such as the air circulation system. She switched to the spatial-grid, and immediately saw the other ship entering their current volume.

The *Shaendar* was visibly rejecting the outpouring of feelers and tracers from the agent's vessel, but Ventra was having a hard time masking their residual ion field; they would have to get far away from where they had been parked, and very quickly. And then she noticed the drones. Six white dots spreading out from the agent's ship. She tapped the compad.

"Ventra, I have six objects inbound, do you see them?"

Her voiced edged with fear, Ventra came online: "I see them, Shari. Analysis shows they are tracer drones; if they can get near us they will triangulate our position and feed data back to agent... must dodge away from here." With that, the ship seemed to drop rapidly, falling through a sea of rocks.

Looking up at the dome, Shari saw the rocks streaming by, loud bangs on the hull proved that they were not missing all of them. *If just one of the big ones hits us ...*

She gripped her webbing as the ship suddenly lurched to one side and then back again; her head straining into the padding. She noticed Domini was having just as much trouble keeping upright, his hands clinging to both floater and webbing. The echo pings suddenly got louder as Ventra veered the ship beneath a large asteroid and then took it deep into a cloud of tiny ice-covered meteoroids. The spatial-grid identified parts of the cloud as a collection of cometary fragments, ice-cold leftovers of larger celestial bodies, withering into dusty dissolution. She realized the vents would have a hard time recycling the debris as it collected inside the needle tubes.

Sure enough, an alarm lit up on Domini's stats screen and he quickly let Ventra know that the tubes were clogging up. If they got blocked in any way the drive coils would lose cohesion, and although the pulse-drive was currently offline, the cumulative effect on the entire coolant system could be catastrophic. They would have to fly out of the dust cloud, and not even the echo-point locators could tell them what was waiting out there.

Ventra came online: "Shari, keep sharp eye on forward grid, I must concentrate on piloting, so you must warn me of location of agent..."

277

Shari replied: "I won't let you down, Ventra." She glanced up at the viewing dome and watched the stars reappear. The screen matched it perfectly and she adjusted the forward parameters to realign the echo points. Suddenly the whole cabin was filled with loud pings, the grid in front of her showed the tracer drones locking on to their thruster drive; each one would bounce back their location to the agent instantly, and he would have them. She heard Ventra clicking loudly from below.

She punched the compad. "The drones are locked onto us, Ventra!"

"I see that. Hold tight please!"

Shari gripped her webbing tightly and through the darkness she saw that Domini was trying to do the same, his face illuminated by the floater screen in his hands. Almost at once the thrusters shook as the ship leapt forward, flying dangerously close to a group of some of the larger asteroids. The grid showed that Ventra was taking the ship in among the rocks, to a spot directly between two of the largest; she also saw that there was barely fifty meters from either side of the ship to the cold hard surface of the rocks. They were in a very tight position indeed, and it would take all of Ventra's piloting skills to keep the ship from drifting into either one of the nearby asteroids.

A moment later, Ventra cut the engines completely, relying solely on the side vent tubes to keep the ship in place. The command deck fell silent, and in the semi-darkness each of them seemed to be holding their breath, expecting the echo locators to begin pinging again at any moment.

Shari looked up at the dome, saw the stars trapped between the two asteroids, and waited to see if that gap would be filled by the ominous shape of a ship.

Chapter 5 - Tracers

'I looked and I looked, but saw only my reflection...'
Lothar Theron – Poet

Neiron Thane kept an eye on the tracer drones, all six were converging upon an echo point three klicks beyond the periphery of the asteroid belt. He was having some difficulty with the feelers, their awareness nets were cascading off the smaller rocks, bouncing back false locations. The AI was constantly sifting for recognizable elements, and as yet primary recognition for plassteel had yet to be identified. He moved the Viper into the debris field, pumping up the shield rotators to minimize collision damage. It was logical to assume that the Saepids were riding without shield protection, they would need a full online AI for that, and of course the moment they did that the data-stream, which was linked to the com probes stretching back to Petra, would leap into their systems, removing their air long enough for him to board and take possession of the girl. It gave him some pleasure to consider just what he would do to the Saepids when he got his hands on them.

With the feelers reduced to a secondary role, he would have to rely on the tracers. Onboard tracers were restricted by the surrounding rocks, but the drones would fly directly toward the Saepid vessel and bounce their current location back to him. He brought up the drones' directional codes, adjusting their flight parameters to include proximity avoidance alerts; the last thing he needed was to lose a drone to a collision.

The convergence point was now directly ahead, beyond a substantial debris cloud, his data-finders were drawing a blank, and the signals from the drones were slowly being corrupted by the contents of the cloud. *Their thrusters are clogging up...* He would have no choice but to bring the drones out of the cloud and send them around the long way. Again, logic dictated that the Saepid vessel would have the same problems within the cloud and would surely have moved deeper into the asteroid field beyond.

So run and hide, little Saepids, you will find no sanctuary here...

He initiated the main thruster tubes and the Viper rose above the cloud, banking sharply to enter the main asteroid field on the other side. He quickly scanned the latest data-stream from Primus. Tanril had ordered Mistia to Phaedra with a fleet of the new bio-ships. Once there they were to travel by inter-phase to the Far

Star Colony under the command of the Phaelon General Torin Grenval. He did not know that old pirate, but the Phaelon breed had proved a valuable addition to the invasion fleets of the jihad, so it made sense that Mistia would send such a one. Setting up a neural network with the bio-ships was a little drastic, but not even the Sacred Eleven seemed to know why their Lord feared the arrival of the Saepid vessel in his homeland. *I must avoid such speculations... duty is my faith, my faith is my life, my life belongs to the Lord God Saemal... May the pathways flow...*

He engaged the drive and the Viper slipped down between the rocks, breaking through the icy vapors and turning into the heart of the asteroid field.

Chapter 6 - Whispers

'Lost in the deepness, silence trembled at the edge of fear...'
Altrius Dex, Sophia City, Planet Entrymion. (A Time A Place A City)

Shari was listening to the soft hum of the command console. The trees cast their shadows across the cabin, and from somewhere behind her came the familiar buzzing of insects fluttering among the leaves and vines. Domini was immersed in his floater screen, its light touching his face with an eerie glow. He was monitoring the Surgeon, checking on Anthra, keeping an eye on the diagnostics. Ventra had whispered over the compad for complete silence. If the enemy agent was nearby, his tracer drones would hear a pin drop, and he'd be upon them in seconds. The *Shaendar* was hanging like a moth between two giant balls of ice rock, its inertial vents maintaining a delicate balancing act in the narrow space between them. At any moment the enemy vessel could pass over them and they would have just seconds to react. The thought scared the crell out of her.

She realized she was holding her breath and tried to calm down. The wound on her leg was beginning to itch, but she dared not move her arms in case she made a noise. From below she heard the faint ping of an echo-point locator. *Something is getting closer...*

Ventra's voice came through the compad as a mere whisper: "Tracer drones detected, Shari, but I doubt they can lock on to us, the local gravity well will confuse their sensors, must be silent a while longer."

Shari didn't acknowledge, fearful of hearing even her own voice.

From below: *ping... ping... ping... ping... ping... ping... ping...* rapidly increasing in frequency... *ping... ping... ping... ping... ping... ping... ping... ping...* She looked up, terrified of what she might see out there above the ship... *ping... ping... ping... ping*
There!

A small black object covered with antenna nets came into view and hung directly over the ship, no more than twenty meters above the hull. *A drone... Oh, crell...*

All three of them sat perfectly still. Ventra disengaged every floater on the ship, and the screen in front of Shari went blank, they were plunged into total darkness.

Looking up, Shari realized the *Shaendar* was beginning to drift slightly. *Ventra has shut down the vents!* She was risking an impact collision with one of the rocks, but if the drone didn't detect them, if it moved off, she could re-engage the vents and prevent a serious collision. *If the drone moved off...*

The echo-point locators fell dead and the silence seemed deafening to Shari. She couldn't take her eyes off the drone as it hung there directly above them. *Was it even now sending back their location to the agent?* After what seemed like an eternity the drone moved off and was gone from view, to be replaced once more by a sea of stars.

Shari was startled as her floater came back online, the screen still showing the current spatial-grid. Beyond the largest of the asteroids she could see several of the tracer drones moving through the debris field, the nearest one was less than thirty meters to their rear.

Ventra came online again. "Still not safe to move, Shari, must stay silent a while longer."

So she sat back, her eyes concentrating on the drone now moving closer from above and behind. *If we can just play dead a little longer...*

Ventra cut the power feeds again and once more they sat silently in the darkness.

Suddenly an alert sounded from the command console, so loud in the silence that it seemed to fill the ship. Instantly Ventra cut it off, but it was too late, two drones now appeared in the space above the ship, their tracer nets spread wide and angled down toward them.

Ventra shouted: "We must run!" She engaged the thruster assembly as the interior lights came back on. Shari grasped her floater, bringing up the grid and instantly saw that all six drones were converging on their position. She looked at Domini, who was busy checking his own floater, and she suddenly realized that everything they've been through, all the pain and the fear, and even the wonderful new-found love, it could all come to an end in the next few minutes.

The ship shot forward, pushing through a sea of rocks, dropping and twisting around the big ones, with the thrusters at maximum. The proximity screens were pinging so rapidly now that the sound seemed to merge into one continual scream.

Shari heard the sounds of impact collisions slamming into the hull... *That can't be good...* And from all around her the vibration from the thrusters began to

282

shake the ship. There was a loud bang from outside and she quickly switched to the stats screen; what she saw confirmed her fears. *Half the antenna array has just been torn off!*

Meanwhile, Ventra was trying her best to avoid the larger asteroids, sometimes going under them, sometimes going over or around them. But all the time the drones were closing, and somewhere out there, not far behind them, would be the enemy, bearing down upon them. Ventra's frantic voice came over the compad. "No use... I cannot lose them, enemy vessel is on intercept course... so sorry, Shari..."

Shari didn't know what to say, she had heard real desperation in Ventra's voice. *Please try to hang on, Ventra!*

Shari was suddenly aware of the rear hatch sliding open. *Are we boarded?* She quickly looked around for something to use as a weapon, settled on a nearby branch, but it refused to break away. She looked up in desperation as a figure began to drift into the command deck.

Anthra! By the Stars, Anthra!

The Saepid drifted over to Shari, the familiar lopsided smile on his face. "Sorry to scare you, Shari, must help Ventra now..." He drifted down toward the command pod, his arms reaching for a floater as he descended to his webbing. Shari leaned forward against the straps, and watched as Anthra placed an arm around Ventra for a few moments before taking his place at the main console. The compad picked up his voice as he relayed instructions to Ventra.

"We must take drastic action now, my mate, no time for fears, enemy is locked on tight."

Domini came online. "Shari, that alert earlier, it was the Surgeon telling Ventra that it had completed its treatments on Anthra. She couldn't shut the Surgeon down, it would have killed Anthra."

"I figured. But at least we have him back now, Dom."

"Yes, and let us hope he can find a way out of this one..."

She thought to herself: *He has to...*

Anthra was going through a sequence of proposed maneuvers, none of which sounded in any way safe. "Ventra, my love, we have no choice, enemy will force closure of thrusters; we must initiate jump sequence."

Shari was horrified. You just did not create a subspace bubble in an asteroid field; the permutations for catastrophe were astronomical. There were far too many variables, perverse gravity wells, ionic fluctuations, and density exchange ratios which might or might not fuse you into solid rock. The navs

283

would never be able to handle it, even with the AI in full control; but to attempt such a thing manually? That was just plain crazy. She was about to tell Anthra just that when the ship was struck yet again by something solid. *Well, if we don't break up in subspace we'll definitely break up inside this lot...* She kept her thoughts to herself.

Anthra was rattling off field equations, while Ventra input the necessary protocols. She was having to rewrite the subspace insertion parameters to match Anthra's calculations. Every few minutes she would go into a flurry of loud clicks and clucks and Anthra would answer her calmly in Galac. "No worries, my love, all will be well." Then the frantic re-working of the ship's navigation systems would begin all over again.

After a while, Anthra came online. "We are close to being trapped, Shari. You and Domini must hold tight, we are attempting dangerous jump; might not survive, but choice we no longer have."

After that, they could only wait, their eyes meeting in the semi-darkness. *See you on the other side, Dom...*

Neiron Thane was suddenly very pleased; all six drones had locked onto the Saepid vessel. He moved the Viper further into the asteroid field, pumping up the shield generators and bringing the null-field weapon online. When the null-field hit the Saepid ship it would simply die in space, all power drained into the field, and with it their air supply. After that it would be simply a matter of boarding their ship and taking possession of the girl. *It won't be long now, Shari S'Atwa...*

He aligned the Viper into a coaxial tangent to allow the drones to match his velocity; he would drop down behind the Saepid ship and initiate the null-field weapon before they had time to escape. Every screen now had a direct lock on the other ship, pinpointing its exact location in relation to the tracer nets. It would now be a simple matter to bring the weapon online.

He veered his ship around the last of the bigger ice rocks, its vapor trail a momentary flash across the recognition screens. *There! Now I have you!*

Ventra engaged the pulse drive, which in turn initiated the subspace field. Shari closed her eyes; she really didn't want to see her own death. For a moment, the ship seemed to lose cohesion, the hull trembling behind her, and for several microseconds the stars themselves appeared to be floating inside the command deck. An instant later, the ship began to shake violently; the trees were being

284

torn from their roots, and the deck lights went out. Looking up, Shari saw the now familiar swirl of subspace, a gray and endless void now surrounding the ship. From below came the sound of more than a dozen alarms.

As he engaged the weapon system Neiron Thane brought the Viper to within two hundred meters of the target vessel. The null-field spread out from the forward weapons tubes, streaming toward the other ship. He checked the stats screen, matching his velocity to the speed of the Saepids. *They're trying to run...* He punched the main drive, keeping the sublight engines beneath the pulse threshold. He just needed to make sure the Saepid ship did not escape beyond the periphery of the asteroid field. Suddenly, the target allocation screen flickered from green to bright red... *Malfunction?* But the stats screen showed all systems were in the green, and yet the weapon had failed to connect with the other ship. *What is this?*

He quickly scanned the tracer readouts... *No!* Each drone bounced back the same message: *Negative contact.* The Saepid ship had vanished. *How can this be?*

He re-deployed the tracer drones' targeting arrays, casting their antenna nets into an ever-widening arc across the asteroid field. *Nothing!*

Bringing the Viper out toward the edge of the debris field he sent feelers out into the volume beyond, but their photonic particles simply lost cohesion. Neiron Thane could not reconcile his failure. The Saepids had almost certainly jumped to subspace, and given the circumstances of that jump the chances of their surviving such an insertion were tens of millions to one. *I have allowed the prize to destroy itself... I have failed...*

He took a minute to consider his options. He could jig a few thousand klicks to the left and link to the com probes, let Tanril and the others know of his failure; or he could connect directly to the data-stream out of Samros and make his apologies directly to his Lord God... That thought alone sent a chill down his spine. He did not favor either of those options. *But was there a third?*

He tapped the recall sequence to bring the drones back on board. The local spatial-grid seemed clear of any other ships; the feelers were retracting and the pulse drive was online. There was nothing else for it. If the Saepids had survived the jump he would use all his skills to track them down once again. He still had the recognition codes for their ionic signature, it might take some time but he was sure he could do it, *and perhaps this time I might just make the mistake of blowing them to pieces...*

285

Chapter 7 - And So It Begins...

Shadow glimpsed dark crenulations,
towers, turrets, terrors and trauma,
battle scenes revisited along dark city walls.
Blood drips as rainfall,
flowing through the gutters.

Bricks and mortar assuming tyrannical guise.
A black womb of night lends mist to the shroud.
Shimmering coalescent transfusion of solid stone.
History screams silent whores raped and ravished
by the slaughter of time.

The Universe is written in an instant of regret.
A guilt culled for reunification with the soul.
The vast armored city lies breathless
before the dawn.
The human heart lingers before the Fall.

Time is a whispering serenade,
a visionary passing thrill.
It leaves lives lost and slaughtered,
dripping with blood all across the palisades.
The city exhales its misery upon the passing stormfront.

Poem attributed to Jophrim as written in the Libertas Codex - Syrillian Anthos,
Federated Fleets of Liberation (Petran State Archive).

Admiral Ewan Dax of the First Coalition Fleet had been listening to his fleet captains debate the current situation for over an hour. He had presented them with the facts, which of course they were already aware of, considering the nature of the Net. But what had surprised them most was the order restricting the use of the AI integration systems aboard their ships. What little news they had gleaned regarding the fall of Primus was sufficient to warn them that the enemy had the means to subvert all computerized systems; it seemed the greater the high-tech, the easier its subversion. The very idea of going into battle the "old-fashioned way" was abhorred by most of the captains. *But what choice did they have?* He touched his compad.

The faces of the thirty-five primary captains turned to look at him; each was a graphic holo-lucience floating several feet above the conference table. Each of the primaries would relay the essentials of the meeting to their own secondary captains on the remaining ships of the fleet; one thousand ships in total. But before that happened he would need to relay the orders from Fleet Headquarters.

"Comrades, if I might continue with the stats and recon reports?" The captains finally fell silent.

"Thank you. It has been confirmed that the enemy has established a force of occupation on the outer Hub worlds of Entrymion, Petra, Galicia and Earthia. Our forces in those sectors have either been destroyed or brought into the service of the enemy. Preliminary reports show a terrible slaughter has taken place on those worlds, with millions either killed or injured. It seems clear that unlike the occupation of Primus the enemy has now adopted a policy of outright genocide." He paused to let his words sink in.

"You have all read the current stats; Coalition forces have been pushed back to a line between the Combine Alliance worlds and the outer core worlds of Primal, Arctura, Drometia, Dronheim and Vendicor. It is in this sector that we, as the Combined Fleets of Liberation will make our stand. The enemy must not be allowed to move on to the heavily populated Hub worlds beyond Drometia. He has to be stopped, comrades, and we have to be the ones to stop him."

He paused before continuing. "As primary captains you will be issued with the latest Cognitive Evocation System; it's fresh out of the wetwire labs on Arctura Prime. Use it well, comrades, because without an integrated AI system we will be sailing blind into the war zone. The evocation scenarios should allow you to calibrate the correct recognition protocols to align your nav and weapons systems. But keep in mind that the enemy will have no such restrictions in place; from what we can tell they are using highly advanced tech systems that we simply cannot hope to match. The fall of Entrymion was our first clue as to the enemy's capabilities. If they fail to disable us via our command systems then they will simply use overwhelming force to destroy as many of our ships as possible, and apparently they won't hesitate to sacrifice their own vessels to achieve victory."

287

He paused for a moment to read a data-feed coming in from his Navigation Officer, and then, looking up, he continued: "You have all seen the latest Posts; the vids from Petra are graphic in the extreme. The enemy ground forces seem to fight with such savagery that organized resistance is almost nonexistent. But the situation is fluid, it is not all bad news; we have fresh intelligence indicating that a substantial number of enemy ships are leaving the occupied zones and heading back toward the Rim, which we believe is the enemy's point of origin."

Fleet Captain Rolf Mendes touched his compad. His face appeared opposite the Admiral.

"Yes, Mendes, you have a question?"

"Just one, Sir. I was wondering if we have any Intel as to why the enemy is moving so many of his forces back toward the Rim."

Admiral Dax took a moment to recall his recent conversation with the Supreme Commander back at Fleet Headquarters. They had met on the flight deck of the old colonial battle wagon *Agoria*, it was past midnight and the two had been sharing reminiscences of their days spent in the Colonial Marines based at Earthia. The Supreme Commander had looked drained, exhausted even, the campaign to save the outer core worlds had recently failed and the fleets were reassembling off Arctura Prime before converging on the orbiting space station that served as Fleet Headquarters.

"Things are going bad for us, Ewan, with the fall of so many high-tech worlds it's only a matter of time before they break through to the Hub; orders have been issued to evacuate the Ruling Council from Tantra..." Dax had looked at his old friend, no longer the confident Aril Prender of the Academy days, now no more than a very tired Supreme Commander.

"There is always hope, Aril, we have been in similar situations with the Non-Conformist insurrections, we managed to deal with that situation well enough."

And that was when his old friend had looked at him with such fear in his eyes, his voice a mere whisper... "This is no Non-Conformist rabble, Ewan. This thing we fight is something else, something a lot darker, evil on an unprecedented scale. I fear we are only seeing the tip of its true power. It has spread its net wide across the Rim, Ewan, and to date not one world has been able to resist, not a single race has escaped the onslaught of its armies."

"And yet we must do our duty, Aril, isn't that all we can do?"

"Indeed, my friend, duty is perhaps all we have left." He had drifted off just then before turning to him once more.

"I have been informed that the enemy is recalling many of his forces, Ewan, have you heard this?"

"I had heard that several enemy fleets had broken away from the Petran Sector, but as to their destination, I have heard nothing."

"Well, according to my own sources, there is a great deal of movement along the Rim. Initially we were of the opinion that it was a matter of redeployment, that the enemy was regrouping beyond the Core sector before the final assault against the Hub…"

"But you don't think that's the case now?"

"No, we do not…" He had paused before continuing. "Do you know anything of the work they do on Primal IV?"

"I know it is the base of the Fleet Security Division and the CIS."

"That it is, but also it's the new home for the Research and Development labs."

"They've moved from Arctura?"

"Out of necessity I'm afraid." He had paused before continuing. "Well, our ingenious techs have managed to tap into a series of com probes the enemy has placed along the galactic plane ecliptic to Primus. The data-stream is ragged, apparently, and the feeders are mostly corrupted, but the translator teams have managed to extract a certain amount of useable information."

That had surprised him.

"It seems the enemy is increasingly devoting more and more resources to stopping one single ship from reaching the sub-sector surrounding the Far Star Colony."

That had not only surprised him, but left him somewhat bewildered as to why the enemy, with such overwhelming power on his side, should delay his takeover of the Coalition simply to stop one single ship from reaching the Rim.

"I'm not sure I understand… are you saying that there is a ship out there that the enemy actually fears more than the combined fleets of the entire Coalition?"

"So it would seem, my friend, so it would seem."

Such a thing seemed impossible, absurd even.

"How can that be possible?"

289

"We have no idea, but I have issued orders for the *Valeria* to travel to the Far Star Colony under the command of Captain Jos Severs; I think you know him…"

"Yes, we served together on Galicia during the Insurgency."

"Yes, well, his orders are to investigate this solitary vessel and try to determine its true nature. We are hoping that the enemy will be too busy marshaling his defenses to notice the *Valeria* sneaking in under his grids."

After that they had drunk their *ciurvair* wine and watched the sun cresting the grav shields, sending multicolored rainbows across the plassteel towers of the space station.

Dax looked up from the com screen. "I'm sorry, Mendes, any Intel on that is classified. Suffice it to say that we have been given a unique opportunity. If the enemy has recalled some of his forces from the occupied zone then we should take immediate advantage of the situation. That being the case, we are ordered to proceed to the Petran Sector and once there we are to engage the enemy forces by every means at our disposal."

As Mendez acknowledged the orders, Dax looked up at his captains. "We are facing the storm, my friends, but we face it together, and in the name of the Coalition we will prevail. You have your orders, fair journey to you all." And with that, he closed down the inter-fleet data-link and proceeded back to the Bridge.

The C.S. *Althenia* was a primary-class patrol vessel with a ship's company of three hundred and seven combat personnel. She was equipped with the latest Ultravane drive, and had twenty-two phase cannons and an arsenal of missile drones, including inter-phase dispersal bombs and an array of anti-grav feelers used to disrupt an enemy's spatial-grid alignments. Admiral Dax was proud of his flagship, and although it had been ten long years since she had last seen real action, he had no doubt that she would serve him well in the coming days.

He addressed his Bridge crew. "All techs, stay linked to the Fleet Command vessels. I want quarterly allocation reports on dispersal and relocation. Leave nothing to the autonomous units, do your math the old-fashioned way…" *With pencils and graph sheets…*

He turned to his Fleet Liaison Captain, Rohl Landerson: "Ship in order, Commander?"

"All departments report active and ready, Sir. Fleet primary vessels are about to jump to subspace, also awaiting your command."

Dax turned to face the large screen floating above the rows of nav technicians.

"Then, by all means, issue the command; let's get on with this…"

"At once, Sir."

Across almost half a light year the combined forces of the Coalition Liberation Fleet slipped into subspace, united in their common cause, determined that even if it should cost them all of their lives, they would at least show the enemy that the Coalition would not go down without a fight.

Chapter 8 - The Long Haul

"... you can push a ship only so fast; they said: 'Go to the Rim', fair enough, but then they say: 'Oh, yes, and get there in less than thirty days...' and that's without leaving subspace, and with the core burning fusion at a thousand rads a second; you ever seen a pulse drive implode? Because you're going to, mark my words..."
Chief Engineer Scot Griel, C.S. Valeria.

The holo-lucience filled the room; it was a spatial evocation of the Far Star Colony. First Officer Marina Cain had been trying to configure the evocation for over an hour, the holo emitters in the Vision Chamber were old-style graph enablers, nothing like the emitters they used at the Academy. But the spatial parameters had finally matched the Intel gathered from the Saepid colony at Triesta. Those strange deep space traders actually knew quite a bit about the Far Star Colony, and they had been more than willing to share the information with the Coalition. There was no Intel with regard to a Saepid home world, but as dealers in galactic commerce they were suffering greatly from the current war. *But nowhere near the amount of suffering the citizens on Petra are going through right now... and of course Galicia, Earthia, Primus, and the Stars only know how many more worlds that are dying out there...* The compad buzzed.

"Cain, are you ready for us yet?"

She automatically straightened her tunic before replying: "Yes, Captain, I have the evocation online and ready for the briefing."

"Very well, we'll be right there."

She took a look around the Vision Chamber. The senior staff would view the display from a gallery of seats set near the roof of the chamber and she would control the evocation from the holo-emitter interface in the wall behind her. Her only worry right now was that the lucience might fade out where she'd overlapped older images with the latest ones from Triesta; but the thing looked logical enough... it's not like she'd had to bulk up the image with a few false planets. Above her the doors to C-Deck slid open and she saw her captain and the senior staff move to their seats.

Captain Severs' voiced came over the compad. "When you're ready, Cain."

"Very good, Sir." She touched the interface initiation sequencer and the chamber fell into darkness. Seconds later a sea of stars filled the room, and she

292

carefully adjusted the parameters to zoom in to a star system identified as Rim 1478A in tiny gold symbols floating beneath one of the larger planets. She brought a spatial-grid display down over the scene so that the other officers could see the system in relation to time and distance from key Coalition worlds. She then spoke slowly into the compad.

"Comrades, welcome to star system Rim 1478A, also known as the Far Star Colony. As you can see, there is only one principal planet designated as the actual Colony, but for purposes of spatial navigation this entire volume has been designated as the Far Star Colony." She suddenly felt like she was repeating herself.

"From the Intel gathered we can confirm that the Colony was founded by a group of human settlers outbound from various Rim worlds. There is no evidence to prove that these settlers were Non-Conformists, but we do know that they were not part of the Coalition." She brought the system around eighty degrees and continued. "As you can see, there are five more planets in the system, all of which are in the J and K class and as such can be disregarded in terms of habitability. Therefore logic dictates that the enemy, whoever they are, is currently based on the Colony world itself."

At that moment Captain Severs came online. "What about that moon, Cain, do we have anything on that?"

She brought the moon into focus, zoomed in slowly, quickly realizing that the image was fading out. There were no actual real-time images of the moon to add to the evocation, the emitters were simply using speculative parameters to create the image because somewhere among the Saepid Intel a moon had been mentioned.

"I'm sorry, Sir; we have nothing beyond its orbital location. There is every possibility that it is occupied, but with the information we have there is no way to confirm this."

Nav Tech Keth Lohman leaned forward. "Isn't that a spatial anomaly in the upper right quadrant?"

Cain zoomed in on the sector. "Yes, it is. Saepid Intel speculates the existence of a black hole somewhere beyond the system; they noted a gravity influx present at the extreme borders of the quadrant. It has very little influence among the in-system worlds."

Lohman replied: "As far as we know…"

Cain looked up at the lieutenant. "Yes, as far as we know."

293

Captain Severs spoke again: "Well, I'm sure we'll find out when we get there. Please move on to the nav charts, I want the tech teams fully conversant with the approaches to the Colony. I doubt the enemy will make it easy for us to get in there."

For the next four hours – with only two breaks for refreshments – she ran through the entire navigation protocol configuration, outlining secondary subspace convergent points, and illustrating with graphs and charts every possible entry point into the Far Star Colony. She was very careful not to mention the target vessel; Captain Severs had given her instructions not to discuss the actual mission details with anyone, including the senior staff. As far as the rest of the crew were concerned, they were on a clandestine spying mission; get in, poke around a little, and get out... nice and simple. She concluded with a run-down of the crew allocation duties; everyone on board would have to be at peak efficiency for the duration of the mission, consequently she would be instigating daily battle drills commencing at 23:00 hours that night.

After the chamber was cleared Captain Severs met her on D-Deck.

"Excellent work, Marina; how you managed to stitch that lot together, I'll never know."

"It wasn't too difficult, Sir, once I worked out the nav figures."

"And you managed to decipher the Saepid Intel."

"They used standard Galac, but with a few odd variables."

"Good... are you off-duty now?"

She checked her datapad. "Yes, Sir, I am. Did you want me for something?"

"No, no, not now... you go and get some rest; but link up when you're back on shift, there are a few delicate matters we need to discuss relating to the mission."

"Very good, Sir, until later then..."

"Yes, later." He entered the drop-tube and was gone.

She turned around, walking slowly back to her quarters. Her legs were aching from standing for so long in the Vision Chamber and her neck felt even worse. But a quick session in the hydro-shower should sort out the aches and pains, and hopefully afterwards three full hours of sleep. She smiled at that. *I'll be lucky to get half an hour before the nightmares start up again and I wake up sweating like a roasted slother...*

294

Two hours later, First Officer Cain entered the Captain's ready room and found him in conversation with the Chief Medical Officer Romana Kendra. The Captain looked up from his desk.

"Ah, Cain, please come in. Doctor Kendra was just bringing me up to date on our med supply situation."

She knew that due to the speed of their departure from the Elysian Sector they had been unable to restock many of their supplies; the med situation in particular was now causing some concern. Kendra seemed to be in the midst of an argument with the Captain as she turned to face Cain.

"Actually, what I am saying is that I can see no reason why we can't just make a port of call and restock the med center before we enter hostile territory...."

Cain looked at the Captain before she spoke; he nodded. "The truth is, Doctor; we are already in hostile territory."

That seemed to shock the Doctor. "How can that be possible? I wasn't aware we had left Coalition space yet?"

The Captain spoke quietly from behind Kendra: "Doctor, we are currently traveling through the occupied zone. I am afraid there are simply no more friendly ports. Agreed, we are only at the periphery of the enemy's zone of influence, but with the passing of every hour we are getting deeper into the occupied territories."

"I had no idea..." The Doctor's words showed her dismay at the true facts. "I was told that there are Coalition fleets up ahead..."

Captain Severs sat down behind his desk before continuing: "There are Coalition forces in this sector; but there's not a single one of them answering their response codes... the fact is they have either been destroyed or compromised by the enemy."

"Compromised? How?"

Cain came around the table to face the Doctor. "The enemy has developed ways to infiltrate our core systems; AI units have been known to become corrupted, even dangerous to their crews; it's like a virus, the infiltration spreads, leaping from ship to ship."

The Doctor considered this. "So the fact that my medical AI system is currently offline isn't really a technical glitch?"

Cain smiled. "No, Doctor, all the ship's higher function autonomous systems are offline for the duration of the mission. We'll be using the evocation systems as our graphical interface."

"My goodness, how very quaint." She turned to face the Captain. "Well, I must admit, Sir, this is not the best news I've heard today."

Severs looked up at his Chief Medical Officer. "Can you deal with the situation or not, Doctor?"

She stood up straight, smoothing down her tunic. "Yes, Sir, of course. War is war, after all, and so we'll make the best with what we have." She turned to leave. "So if you'll excuse me, Captain, First Officer, I'll get back to the medical center." She gave a polite nod and left the room.

Captain Severs sat back in his chair, glancing at the latest situation reports as they floated across the desk screen.

"You noticed I neglected to inform the good doctor of our true mission directives?"

"Yes, Sir."

"And do you know why I haven't discussed our primary objective with my senior staff?

"I understand that you are under orders from Fleet Command, Sir."

"Yes, of course, but do you see the reasoning behind such secrecy?"

Cain thought about that for a minute. "Does the Admiralty suspect that there are enemy agents among us?"

"Well of course, they always expect that. In any war it makes sense for two opposing sides to attempt to physically infiltrate the other side. But as far as the Security Services are concerned, this particular enemy hasn't shown any interest in sending spies among the Coalition forces; he appears more than capable of destroying our ability to make war without having to resort to espionage. But the thing that concerns me the most right now is that our crew are all fired up against the enemy; many of them have seen their worlds devastated, they've lost family and friends, comrades in arms. They are in fact crell bent on revenge, and that is a valuable asset right now, Marina; we're losing this war, and morale is already flagging among the Coalition hierarchy on Tantra. If our own crew should become equally demoralized, then the success of this mission would almost certainly be in doubt."

She nodded at this; it wouldn't help the mission if the crew lost hope; if the prospect of entering the heartland of the enemy became so overwhelming that they lost cohesion, lost the ability to fight back…

The Captain continued: "So think about it, how will the crew react if I tell them that we are not going to conduct subversive sabotage behind enemy lines? That we're actually going to try our best to avoid any enemy contact whatsoever?"

"I doubt their reaction would improve if you told them we're actually searching for one little ship in a sea of enemy ships…"

"Exactly…they just wouldn't see the logic of such a mission."

Cain glanced at the latest crew evaluation stats on her datapad.

"I've been listening to the talk in the common rooms… this crew wants revenge; they want to fight. Going after one single ship would be a cause for concern and might well lead to disillusionment and possibly disaffection."

"And that's the exact reason Admiral Dax gave me for keeping the mission directive between the two of us."

"I don't like keeping secrets from the crew, Sir."

"And you think I do? But orders are orders, Marina; we don't have to like them."

She thought about the true mission for a moment. "Sir, the preliminary estimate given to me by Chief Engineer Griel puts our arrival at the Far Star Colony at twenty-eight days; surely that will be far too late to intercept this ship? I mean, logically that ship won't last five minutes in enemy space."

"Well, you would think so, wouldn't you? But from the information Dax gave me, this single ship has already survived the fall of Landings Down and Entrymion, and there are some indications that it may well have been outbound from Petra, which, as you know, has already fallen to the enemy."

"That's quite a feat, Sir."

"Indeed it is, which lends some credence to the theories now being discussed by Fleet Security that this unknown vessel might well possess the means to harm the enemy, if not possibly defeat them."

Cain looked across at the wall screen. It showed the latest position of the Combined Fleets of the Liberation.

"I hope that's true, Sir, because the way things are going, we're going to need all the help we can get."

297

Chapter 9 - Marooned

"Far star trading can be most profitable, but dangers lurk in many dark places. A terrible fear is to be marooned in real-time, but what is even worse is to be marooned in subspace where only silence hears your call..."
Tethran, Saepid Far Star Trader.

Darkness... a stark, impenetrable black on black. Somewhere beyond the pain a faint glow of red... cascading thoughts piling up one at a time, fears seeding more fears and the sound of breathing from nearby....Shari struggled to open her eyes; everything hurt. A sharp pain in her side... *the tree?* She struggled to release the straps on her webbing, the clasp was twisted and she found her hands couldn't undo the cords. From below her feet a floater suddenly lit up, it was the one she had been holding just before the subspace jump. *What has happened? Domini!*

She called across the cabin: "Dom! Dom, are you all right?" Silence. She struggled with the release clasp again, swearing to herself as she forced it open. *Finally...* She pushed off into the darkness, and bumped into one of the surrela vines as it drifted by, getting it wrapped around her face and shoulders. She tore it away and finally made it to Domini's side of the deck. He was unconscious.

"Dom, can you hear me? Dom?" She pulled gently to free his head from his webbing, feeling his neck and undoing the chest straps. She knew what rapid deceleration could do to a body; you don't just leap into subspace on a full pulse drive and then come to a dead stop. *And yet I seem to be okay...*

Domini stirred, his eyes opening slowly, trying to focus on Shari's face. She lifted his chin up gently. "Hey, how are you feeling?"

He straightened up inside the webbing, his eyes trying to see through the darkness. "Shari? Is that you?"

"Of course it's me, who the crell else would it be?"

He smiled at that. It was definitely Shari.

"Any idea what happened?"

She looked into the darkness below. "I guess we jumped into subspace... and just stopped..." She started to move away from the hull. "I need to check on the others."

She floated down toward the command pod, taking the one active floater as a light source. She had to push several vines and part of a tree out of her way before she came down next to Anthra.

298

He looked alive; his head had fallen against Ventra's shoulder. She was beginning to stir, twisting around in her webbing. Shari touched Anthra's face and was startled as his eyes opened wide.

"Shari! Are you well?"

"I am, thanks. How are you?"

"Fine, I think I lost consciousness there for a minute... Ventra?" He leaned over to look at his mate. She was coming round, her arms beginning to reach over to Anthra's side of the pod.

"I am well, my mate, but sadly I cannot say same of *Shaendar*..."

Anthra seemed to suddenly become aware that the ship was in darkness, that the main console was effectively dead. He leaned forward to feel for the control interface. "Yes, very rough ride, I fear, much damage."

Shari spoke while looking over his shoulder. "So what can we do to fix things? We can fix things, can't we?"

Both Saepids exchanged looks as Anthra answered the question. "Hard to tell at the moment, Shari, I must get into engine core, check the plasma conduits. If they are sound we can still initiate the pulse drive and all is not lost."

"Right, so is there anything we can do?" Domini had drifted down to settle by her side.

"Well, yes, you can try to restore order in command deck, much disarray I see..."

"That's not going to be easy in this darkness," Domini said.

Ventra reached for a control crystal. "No worries, I think I can bypass central power line and use floaters to power some internal lighting; give me a minute, please."

"Very good, my mate, then I will go down to engine core." He touched a compad. "Communications are offline also; please look into that as well, my mate."

Ventra gave one of her *humph's*.

Shari smiled and said: "Hey look, I can check the com system, let Ventra concentrate on the lighting for now."

Anthra thought on that for a moment before replying. "Very well, but please don't break anything, Shari."

"Hey, I don't break things!" But Anthra was already floating up toward the rear hatch.

Domini and Shari started to drift up through the floating debris. The floater showed that her tree was damaged; the main branch had broken away from the hull. That saddened her; she had spent so many nights wrapped up in her hammock surrounded by her tree, listening to a rain storm, remembering the happier times on Primus. Domini came to her side.

"Looks a little weather-beaten, doesn't it?"

She looked at the broken branch poking through the webbing, the one that had been pushing into her side.

"I think I can sort it out, I mean the roots are all right, they feed back into the bio-shafts in the cargo bay."

"Yes, but we haven't checked the cargo bay yet, have we?"

She looked at him. "You know, you're a mine of cheerful comments, aren't you, Dom?" With that, she started to push the tree back toward the hull, securing the branches with stickem grips and a few cords from the webbing.

Almost twenty minutes later the lights came on, not as bright as they were supposed to be, but at least they could see what they were doing now. Shari drifted down toward the communications interface just to the left of the command console.

Ventra was still busy trying to get her screens back online, and had managed to pull up a spatial-grid, which didn't tell them much, simply that there were no other ships nearby. She was currently clicking and clucking over the stats board, trying to find out the extent of the damage to the ship. They still had no idea if the hull had been compromised. Anthra was taking it on blind faith when he left for the engine core; the rear hatch had opened so the central corridor was viable, but there was no way to tell if the cargo bay was still pressurized. *He might not even make it to the core if there's a hull breach...* Shari dismissed the thought and tried to concentrate on the compad system.

It looked like a storm had raged through the rear cargo bay. Most of the supply containers had fallen from their racks and impacted against the skipper; Anthra noticed that part of its landing gear had been dented and pushed back into its workings. *That may cost us...* But besides the mess the bay seemed sound; there was no breach, and environmentals had come online as he had passed through the forward hatch. *Clever Ventra...* He touched a compad on the wall behind him. Silence. *Shari maybe not so clever...*

He drifted over the engine core access hatch set in the deck floor and noticed that several bio-shafts looked compromised; he tagged the damage on his datapad before opening the hatch. The descent down the access tube wasn't the easiest; Anthra often thought that the previous owners of the *Shaendar* must

300

have been miniature versions of the average Saepid. But he eventually reached the engine core, a black slab of an ionic containment unit interlaced with plasma conduits and glasscite feeder tubes. He found it totally disconcerting that the core was silent and inert, the conduits drained of plasma and the feeder tubes which fed the floater data grids barely functioning. *Even if I can fix this, the drive may not engage...*

He knelt down next to the core initiation panel and carefully prised off the seal to get at the data crystals inside. He quickly realized that three of the primary crystals had fused into their bedding, and silicone spillage had coagulated among the linear tendrils. *This will not do... will not do...*

He was about to extract one of the fused crystals when the compad next to his head came to life and Shari's voice came online. He jumped with surprise.

"Hey, Anthra, are you there?"

He sighed heavily. "Yes, Shari, I am here, thank you."

"I managed to get the coms online; and I didn't even break anything."

"Yes, Shari, I noticed..." *Nearly broke a crystal, though...*

"Good. How does it look down there?"

"Not good, will work on it, though. Has Ventra got stats yet?"

There was a moment's silence as Shari consulted Ventra. "No, not yet, she says she's working on it..."

"Good, I will call you when I have news."

"Fair enough. Dom and I are going to sort out the mess up here."

"In truth, Shari, there is also much mess in the cargo bay."

"All right, I'll go take a look."

The pad shut down and Anthra returned to his repair work.

It took four hours for Anthra to re-initialize the pulse drive, and another two for Shari and Domini to secure the cargo area. They had managed to untangle the skipper's landing gear, but Anthra wasn't sure if the struts would support the craft's weight in a touchdown.

Finally, after a meal, the four crew members met in the command pod. Ventra was trying to explain the current stats and nav situation.

"With good fortune we now have all systems online, but sorry to say that antenna array is beyond repair."

Domini put in: "What will that mean, exactly?"

Ventra looked up. "It means, Domini that we can only detect other ships inside one-third of a light year; Beast could be upon us and we would not see his approach."

301

Shari considered this. "And it's not repairable at all?"

Anthra gave his opinion. "Array was torn away during last jump, so no chance to repair, but there are a few trader tricks we might use... Ventra?" He turned to look at his mate.

She smiled back. "Yes, my mate, we might enhance spatial-grid using the vid system."

"I don't think you can," Shari said.

Domini turned to her. "Why not?"

"Because, Dom, the vidcams got burned off during the slingshot maneuver; we've been using the array since then to give us vid evocations."

"Oh, that could be a problem then."

Anthra piped up. "But no worries, we have spare set of vid units, just a matter of fusing them to outer hull."

Shari was shocked. "You mean go outside?"

"Certainly, only thing to do and it will give me chance to inspect hull, check for fractures."

Shari looked to Ventra. "Is that safe?"

"Yes, Shari, Anthra knows his business; and we have no choice, must be able to see where we are going."

So Anthra drifted back to the cargo bay and Shari and Domini decided to go with him, *just in case...*

Shari had never seen a space suit like it, but then she shouldn't have been that surprised, when you have four arms you're bound to need a suit to match. The thing just looked *wrong*.

"You managing that, Anthra?"

He was trying to bring the hood around to face her. "Yes, thank you, Shari, just a little tight."

"Okay, so do we monitor you from here?"

"Indeed yes, if you just keep an eye on the diagnostics; make sure the feeder lines are clear. I'll want full compad access, so keep the link open, and please watch my pressure gauge, let me know if it fluctuates; much radiation wastage from needle tubes, must be wary of that."

"Will do."

Anthra reached for the container holding the vid units and slowly drifted over to the air lock, touching the release pad as the lock slid silently open. Once he was inside, Shari initiated the depressurization sequence and Domini kept an eye on the pressure gauge.

302

Shari tapped the compad. "All in the green here, Anthra."

Anthra's voice came through distorted by the suit hood. "Thank you, Shari. Leaving ship now..."

"Do you think he'll be all right, Dom?"

"I think so; Anthra knows what he's doing. And besides, we're here to make sure nothing goes wrong."

"Yes... I think we've had more than our share of things going wrong on this trip."

Anthra's voice came through the pad. "I'm just above the primary coolant vent now, placing the first vid... must avoid damaged vid housing, ship is very badly scorched, but I detect no fissures."

"All is green here, Anthra."

Domini spoke without taking his eyes off the diagnostics board. "You did well getting the compads back online."

"Yes well, I told you I know stuff."

"I sometimes wish I knew stuff... you know, so I could help out more."

She briefly glanced in his direction. "Hey, you help out..."

"Oh, you mean re-potting a few trees and clearing out the bio-tubes?"

"No, not just that... Oh, Dom, for crell's sake, don't you know anything about me yet?"

He looked puzzled. "What do you mean?"

"I mean that there is no way I'd have come this far without you; crell, the only reason I haven't lost my mind and gone crazy with fear is because of you." She reached out and touched his face gently. "Dom, my love, you help me, and I know that whatever we come up against at the Colony, you will be there by my side."

"Well, of course I will. I was trying to say that I'm not a scientist, I'm not an engineer... I know nothing about ships."

"And you think I do? This is the first starship I've ever been on; before this I had an annual trip in a long-range skipper, that's it. And the only reason I can help Anthra and Ventra is because I know math, it's my thing, remember?"

"I know that, Shari, I was just wondering what my thing is..."

She reached her hand across and stroked the top of his legs. "Oh, I think we both know what your thing is, Dom..." She gave him her most seductive smile.

He laughed. "Yes well, that aside, I just think I should be doing more."

303

She thought about that for a minute. "So why don't you ask Ventra to show you the control console? Maybe she could teach you how to fly the ship."

"I don't know about that, but I could learn a few of the ship's systems."

"There you go... go ask her, I can handle this."

"Really? Are you sure?"

"No problem, just go see Ventra and learn some stuff." She kissed him on the cheek and he set off back toward the command deck.

Anthra came online. "Shari, I have one more vid to place, then will be returning. All is green with you?"

"Yes, Anthra, all is green with me."

Within the hour, Anthra had completed his work and they gathered together again around the command pod. Domini was inputting test data into the floater assembly, experimenting with various flight scenarios as Shari tapped him on the shoulder.

"So, are you learning anything useful?"

"Well, I've learned how to fly under a moon; that might be useful."

"There you go..." She hugged him as Anthra returned to his webbing.

Ventra waited for Anthra to settle. "Ready, my love?"

"Yes, my mate, please bring vid evocation system online."

Ventra complied and the various floaters flickered into static for several seconds.

Anthra noticed the concern on Shari's face. "No worries, Shari, just a temporary drain on power while we distribute energy to entire system."

Ventra gave a few clicks and clucks as the main screen began to show an expanding spatial-grid. First the periphery of the scan was less than a light year, and then it leapt to five light years in every direction, holding steady at that distance.

Ventra sat back in her webbing as she spoke. "Well, it's not as good as the array, but it's much better than I hoped."

Shari peered into the screen. "I think it's a lot better. At least we won't be taken by surprise any more." They all agreed on that.

Anthra spoke while adjusting the floater feed interface. "Now we must plot our course. Navs are back, so I think we can get going again."

Shari felt the familiar sensation of fear which was a tight knot in her stomach. She hadn't admitted it to herself, but while they had been marooned in subspace she had felt far more relaxed that she had in weeks. But now the quest

304

would begin again, and with that fact came the terrible fears, the worries and the sense of futility in the face of overwhelming odds. She decided she would have to hold the artifact again when they finally got underway.

Domini broke her train of thoughts when he turned to Anthra and asked: "Anthra, is the *Shaendar* armed in any way?" Shari had no idea why she hadn't asked that before now.

Anthra looked up from his floater screen. "This is a trading vessel, Domini; we have two hand weapons only, but the lasfuser in cargo hold could be adapted to expel energy bolts, it's mainly used in the workshop, but it might prove useful."

"Very well, I'll go and take a look at it."

Shari was surprised at that. "You, Dom?"

"Yes, why not? I once fixed a service duct in Temple; I believe I can make a gun."

Anthra glanced up at Shari. "Yes, but perhaps Shari can help?"

Domini sighed. "Sure, why not?" And he drifted up toward the rear hatch, Shari following closely behind.

When they were alone Anthra turned to Ventra. "Any sign of our pursuer?"

"Not on the screens… you think he will follow, then?" She looked at the feeds.

"I have no doubts; and others too…"

Ventra looked at the local grid. "The enemy will send everything after us now."

"Yes, my mate, he will stop at nothing to take possession of Shari."

She looked back at him. "I think she knows the truth…"

"Best not to let her dwell on being captured and taken into its lair."

Ventra nodded. "Yes, that might be too much."

Anthra looked up toward Shari's tree. "But it seems that the powers of the *custodia* are becoming manifest; it protects her from the outpouring of the Beast's thoughts."

Ventra looked up. "Yes, but will it protect her when she stands before him?"

"Only time will tell, my mate, only time will tell."

Chapter 10 - Incalling

"My Lord is a storm among the stars,
his glory will fall as fire upon the heathen breeds,
no race, no world, will stand before his power;
where Saemal walks all glory follows in his wake."
Revelations: Book of Saemal.

Torin Grenval sat in his command chair aboard the former Phaelon heavy cruiser *Hagmon*, now enhanced with a few transcendent upgrades, courtesy of his Lord Saemal. The floater in front of him showed the relative positions of the bio-fleet; all thirty vessels were spread out as a forward phalanx protecting the fifty cruisers of the former Phaelon Home Defense Force. The bio-ships gave him a feeling of dread which he couldn't quite explain; it certainly didn't fit with his new-found faith.

He knew that the ships were bio-mechanical constructs designed and built at the Far Star Colony, but he also knew that they were directly controlled by the Cortex – *and what was the Cortex but the mind of the transcendent God Saemal?* The knowledge that just a few klicks ahead of him lay the hand of God, and that it had fallen to him to direct that hand in battle… it was almost too much bear. He leaned forward in his chair to address First Tactician Philas Vorin. "Status, Vorin."

The Tactician took a quick scan of the data-feeds as they flowed across his screens. "The fleet is in full alignment, Sir; subspace variants put us at eight days outbound of the Far Star Colony."

The abilities of the new enhanced engines continued to amaze Torin. The ionic pulse drive of each ship had become a unified propulsive field upon which the entire fleet would be carried at up to three times their normal speed capabilities – reducing a thirty-day journey to a mere ten. Without doubt, they would reach the Colony and be in position long before the Saepid vessel arrived. He studied the latest data-stream from Primus. There had been no word from the agent pursuing the Saepid ship; it was presumed he was either lost or beyond the range of the com probes. Personally he doubted either theory, it was more likely the fellow had failed in his mission and was lying low somewhere trying to avoid the wrath of Saemal.

No matter, history will tell a different story when I am finished…

He thought back to that last night on Phaedra. *So what was that all about?* Mistia had been as passionate as an Aluvian slave girl. *Certainly she can have no intention of maintaining a relationship; the Sacred Precepts forbade such a thing... and yet during the lovemaking she had seemed so very vulnerable.* He had seen something in her eyes... something lost... a last vestige perhaps of her former self... the woman who lived before the Coalescency. *Perhaps she didn't realize I had seen beyond her sacred walls?* He sat back in his seat thinking... *and I can only hope she didn't see beyond mine...*

Tactician Vorin spoke up from his console. "Sir, I have the grids for the sectors you asked for; would you like to view them now?"

Torin stood, reaching for his datapad. "No, feed them through to Ops. Join me there, and bring Romon from Navs and Boras from the bio-team."

"Yes, Sir, at once."

As he exited the drop-tube Torin felt a pang of nostalgia – the *Hagmon* had once been a deep space raider, cruising the trade lanes between the Fengor Province and Tanhauser Gate – he had begun his career aboard such a ship. He was destined for the Elaas back then, a dark and insidious life of covert missions deep inside the hated Coalition. But his beloved wife Scylar had changed all of that. Her father had been First Minister at the time and she was most determined that her new husband would also aspire to such lofty heights. *Alas, my love, you did not live long enough to see such a thing.* Her death had seemed so meaningless – her skipper falling from the skies – a simple rotor malfunction. *So pointless...* In her honor he had resigned from the Fleet and turned his talents to politics. With the aid of his father-in-law he had made it into the Assembly within a year, and had become First Minister in less than ten... *I wish you had seen that, my love...*

As he entered the Ops room the three members of his senior staff stood to attention and gathered around the giant vid-screen floating above the tactical display console.

He acknowledged them and took a seat in front of the screen.

"Please be seated, comrades, and let's get down to business." He turned to Dainer Romon first. "Romon, if we could start with the current navs situation..."

The Navs officer touched the graph console and the main screen flickered into the current spatial-grid, pushed out for thirty-five light years – one of the largest grid alignments Torin had ever seen. *Upgrades...*

307

"As you can see, Sir, the tactical situation grows ever more complex. There are currently several fleets of our Lord Saemal outbound from Samros; on their current heading they will reach the Far Star Colony three standard days before our arrival. As far as we can ascertain, these fleets are without enhancements... in fact the data-stream indicates that most of the ships have been hastily brought together under the command of several high-ranking priests with no previous battle experience."

Torin studied the screen before asking: "So are you saying that we are the only enhanced fleet in this sector?"

Romon expanded the grid alignment to include their current position. "Every indication points to that being the case, Sir, yes. Our main battle fleets are currently engaged against Coalition forces beyond the Petran front; we have occupying forces at Entrymion, Galicia and Earthia, and several flotillas of troop ships outbound from Phaedra. But, Sir, we have the only contingent of bio-ships."

Torin knew that his officers might question the logic of sending the best ships the Coalescency had to offer all the way back to their point of origin. It made no sense to them to pull back from the Coalition front, especially since the latest data-stream from Primus had told of a considerable force of Coalition ships moving toward Petra to engage the fleets of the Coalescency stationed in that sector.

"The Sacred Precepts come down to us from our Lord God, Romon; it does not serve his glory if we question his motives."

"Sir, I meant no disrespect."

"Of course not; but I want all of you to know that though the logic of our mission seems questionable and seems to go against the dictates of the Coalescency, the mission itself is vital."

He paused for a moment, wondering if one of them would have the courage to ask the one single question the entire fleet wanted to ask: Why the Incalling? *Now they fear to show disrespect; fair enough... it's about time they knew the truth... I owe them that at least...*

"Comrades, the mission is simple in the extreme. We will instigate a neural network around the Far Star Colony using the bio-ships as data-stream links to the Cortex. This will serve as a buffer to possible data-feed incursions and other high-tech subversion. This action has been deemed necessary to prevent the approach of a single enemy vessel currently inbound toward the Colony. This vessel has to be stopped at all costs."

308

Aron Boras of the bio-team couldn't perceive the logic of such a deployment. He had seen the power contained within the bio-ships, raw energy on a scale never thought possible... *how on Phaedra could one single ship hope to challenge such a force?* He looked at his commander, his voice so low it was almost a whisper. "If I might ask you, Sir, what kind of vessel could hope to match our power?"

Torin already knew all the questions they would ask – he had asked them himself when Mistia had detailed the mission. But these soldiers deserved to know something of the truth; it would not serve the cause for them to go into battle without some idea of the true facts.

"I cannot go into specifics, the precepts behind our orders are not open to question. But I can tell you that this ship is the most singular threat to the Coalescency since the founding of our Great Expansion. Our orders are clear: we are to prevent this ship from reaching the Colony. If circumstances allow we are to seize this ship and capture its crew, if that seems impossible we are to destroy the ship. Have I made myself clear?"

All three acknowledged that their orders were very clear.

First Tactician Philas Vorin spoke next: "Sir, I have the fleet captains online when you're ready for deployment orders."

"Transmit the nav codes for standard deployment for now; we can adjust our settings when we near the Colony..." He turned to face Aron Boras. "Boras, have you mastered the bio-feedback links yet?"

"Yes, Sir, we can take over remote piloting on your orders, the necessary configurations have been uploaded to each bio-ship and the bounce-back response times are negligible considering the speed of the bio-streams..."

"Is there anything else?" He had noticed Boras was somewhat hesitant in his report.

"Well, yes, Sir. I can give you full access to the bio-ships at any time; we can adjust their systems via the remote interface on the Bridge, but..."

"But what?"

"Well, Sir, the ships tend to over-evaluate my data input, they constantly question my configuration protocols; it's most disconcerting."

"But that won't be a problem, will it?"

"No, Sir, I hope not. It's just difficult for me to get a smooth inter-ship data-flow when each bio-ship tends to have a mind of its own."

Torin sat back in his seat considering this. He knew the ships had sentient AI systems, as near to biological life as a ship could get without actually

309

becoming an independent life form, *but how would that affect his command structure?*

"I doubt the ships will argue with you, Boras. I have the full assurance of the Sacred Mistia that those ships were built to serve, and despite your reservations, they will not interfere in the command process."

"Very good, Sir."

Torin added: "But it might be prudent to set up a separate interface to monitor the bounce-back response times. Let me know if there is a developing lag in the data-stream; I'll want instant access to those ships when we get to the Colony... there can be no room for ships with a mind of their own."

"Yes, Sir, I'll monitor the situation."

"Very good. You are dismissed, comrades." As they stood and turned to leave, Torin called after them: "Vorin, remain behind a moment, will you."

The Tactician gave a nod to the other two officers as the door slid closed behind them.

"Sir?"

"How long have you served with the Fleet, Philas?"

"Eleven years now, Sir; six at the Grainsfeld colony and five at Fleet Command in Tendrah."

"So you remember those years well, do you?"

"Well enough, Sir, yes."

Torin watched the man's face, his eyes seemingly full of questions he dared not ask.

"Do you not think it strange, Philas, that when the Sacred Emissary Vessel arrived over Phaedra and our Confederacy was assimilated into the Coalescency you actually forgot your entire existence before that day?"

He saw confusion in the other's face now, vagueness he had seen more and more of late among the crew. The man was struggling to find words which his mind had been forced to forget by the Coalescency.

"Why, Sir, I really don't know... I did forget so much, but the joy of our faith, our union with Saemal, it was more than enough..."

He decided to take a risk. "I have found myself remembering more each day, Vorin, and this intrigues me. I have studied the data-feeds from Primus, that world was assimilated just as easily as our own, and the current feeds show that the Coalescency is as vital and as all-pervasive on that world as it was the day the fleet arrived. And yet here we are, mere Phaelon pirates by our nature, and now for some unfathomable reason we are once more feeling the lure of independence." He hoped he had not gone too far. Vorin was a loyal officer, but he would know that his sacred duty to Saemal must take precedence. There were more than a few high priests traveling with the fleet; if Vorin should seek their council in the matter of his captain's loyalty, things could get very tricky indeed.

"I'm not sure what you are suggesting, Sir..." He eyed his captain with an air of suspicion.

Perhaps I have gone too far... "I'm suggesting nothing, Philas. I simply want you to keep me informed of any signs of aberrant behavior among the crew."

"Of course, I will do my duty according to the Sacred Precepts."

"Then I can ask no more. You are dismissed."

With that, Vorin turned around and left the Ops room.

Torin considered the situation carefully. There could be no doubt that the power of Saemal was as strong as ever, but there was some evidence of dissipation in the latest data-stream from Samros. There were no significant gaps in the information transfer rates, but if you knew where to look for it, there were definite signs of disarray within the vast stream of data flowing out from the Far Star Colony. The feeds from Samros were inconsistent and variable, and onward toward Primus and the battle front beyond Petra there were noticeable variants in the response codes. For some unknown reason the power of Saemal was losing some of its cohesion, the ability to control had become diluted. There were currently sixteen active fleets within the areas of expansion; the Coalescency now consisted of more than a hundred occupied worlds, tens of billions of minds under the direct control of the Cortex, their subversion constantly monitored by the hierarchy based on Primus and Samros.

Recently he had begun to notice that it was now the priests of Saemal who were actually issuing the day-to-day field orders. The Sacred Eleven seemed to be assuming the reins of power in their own individual domains. Mistia had hinted that each of the surviving eleven was busy creating their own personal fiefdoms within the occupied territories. She herself had already begun to favor Phaedra for her seat of power, and while Tanril remained the nominal leader of the group, even he had issued orders for the construction of a palace on Primus. *They seem to be letting their power go to their sacred heads... and where in all of this empire building is Saemal?*

He touched his datapad, brought up the tag on the Saepid Othrum race. A holo-lucience of a Saepid male appeared in the air before him. *Fascinating that such a creature could ever be a threat to his Lord God...* He tapped for a rendering of Lorn S'Atwa. The tall figure of a male human replaced the Saepid. His hair was graying slightly, but he had an air of dignity and respect about him. *What kind of weapon have you spawned, Lorn S'Atwa?* He had tried several times to download an image of the daughter, but there was nothing more recent than the class ID tag issued during First School. *So I wonder what you look like, Shari S'Atwa. And what kind of weapon can you be?*

As soon as he had bid his farewells to Mistia he had used his contacts in the Security Service to obtain the girl's full identity. It seemed the data-stream bounced along the com probes was not as secure as Tanril and the others believed. The girl's name was out there for anyone to find, even the Net was showing increasing traffic directed at the unusual fleet deployments away from the battle front and back toward the Sacred Sanctum. *Yes, the Universe knows something strange is going on out there at the Rim, something beyond the jihad, beyond the great battles among the stars, beyond even the mindless faith of billions... something has disturbed the glorious Saemal, and it comes in the form of a girl child from Primus... irony in the extreme...*

He touched the screen console, brought up the current fleet deployment. The bio-ships were moving as one at the periphery of the unified pulse field, their neural networks wetwired into the data-stream flowing from Samros. The black ships were a frightening sight, even for the faithful, but they must be far more terrifying to the heathens who opposed Saemal's will. *To throw so much power at one solitary human beggars belief... what can she possibly possess that would warrant such a response?* He closed the data-flow and stood to walk back to the Bridge. *Whatever she carries, I very much want to see what it is...*

Chapter 11 - Soldiers and Fools

"So I heard the other cadets talking in the break room, and no one wanted to talk about what they'd seen at Galicia. I mean, they knew where I was born so I guess that was the main reason, but I'd known so many of those people who were murdered in the compound at Tarnaria, I couldn't believe it myself. It's shocking when you hear of one person getting killed, but when you hear of the millions they murdered on Galicia, how do you come to terms with that?"
Sara Tielman, Cadet First Class, C.S. Valeria.

First Officer Marina Cain was on the Bridge monitoring the spatial-grid when the compad buzzed. It was her adjutant Tamara Breckin calling from the Vision Chamber.

"Ma'am, Breckin here. I have something down here you need to see."

"I'll be right there."

Captain Severs looked up from his command chair. "Problems, Cain?"

"I'm not sure, Sir, I'll keep you informed."

"Very well, and I'm going to need those Saepid scans when you have a minute."

"Yes, Sir, of course."

The drop-tube opened onto D-Deck and she made her way to the Vision Chamber. Once inside she found Breckin busy adjusting the holo emitter interface, as an evocation drifted in and out of semblance in the center of the room.

"What have you got for me, Breckin?"

"Ma'am, I just picked up something from the evocation scans of the most recent spatial-grid. Now that we have to compile graphical data from the bounce-back echoes into the subspace sectors ahead, I had to re-align the protocols to match a real-time image. I think you will find this interesting." She initiated the holo-lucience she had been loading into the emitters and instantly an image appeared to fill the chamber.

Cain peered at the various grid alignments, saw the stats for their own ship, but further away from the upper left quadrant she saw the distinctive markers for a fleet of vessels traveling on a parallel course to their own. Breckin zoomed in on the sub-sector in question.

"I've been unable to match any ship configuration data to those forward vessels, they're totally unknown to our Intel, but the ones following behind match the alignment and ionic structure of Phaelon ships."

Cain looked at the tiny stats symbols flashing beneath the unknown fleet. "I take it you've checked your readings."

"Three times, Ma'am. There's no doubt about it, those fifty ships at the rear are Phaelon heavy cruisers and the thirty ships in front are unknown and match nothing in our database."

"The Captain had better see this."

"I think so, Ma'am."

Cain touched the compad and asked the Captain to join them. A few minutes later, he entered the room, immediately noting the swarm of red dots flickering through the evocation.

"Ships heading our way, Cain?"

"Actually, Sir, they're currently on a parallel course, heading in the same direction."

"Phaelon. I see… and that group out front?"

"We haven't been able to identify them; they are of an unknown configuration."

Severs studied the scene for several minutes before speaking again.

"Well, our Intel has suggested that the enemy has been pulling their forces back from the occupied zone; I suppose this fleet is now evidence of that fact. The Confederacy went over to the enemy some time ago, if I remember correctly."

Cain looked up at the grid. "Yes, Sir, but I have some concern as to the direction this fleet is taking. They are matching our own course precisely."

Severs moved closer to the evocation. "You think they know we're out here?"

"It's possible, but if they do, logic dictates that they would be on an intercept course by now."

Breckin spoke up from behind them: "What if they do know we're here but they're in too much of a hurry to get where they're going to bother with us?"

Both the Captain and his First Officer turned around to look at Breckin. She lowered her eyes. "Sorry, Sir, it was just a suggestion."

Severs smiled. "No, Breckin, that makes sense. If those stats are correct they're moving an awful lot faster than we are, they're definitely in a rush to get back to the Rim."

314

Cain stepped forward and adjusted the evocation to zoom away from the Phaelon fleet and scanned down to their own location on the grid. "The thing is, Sir, with our current course tangent we will actually arrive within the Far Star Sector slightly ahead of that fleet, perhaps giving us enough time to complete our mission." She was suddenly aware of Breckin listening from behind.

"You are dismissed, Breckin. Please see to the scans I asked you to retrieve."

"At once, Ma'am." With that, she turned and left the room.

"Sir, given the relative location of that fleet we might have a full day to track down the Saepid vessel. The Phaelon's will certainly arrive within the same sub-sector as dictated in our orders from Fleet Command."

"Yes, and does that not make you wonder about that fleet, Marina? It's known that the enemy are recalling some of its forces from Coalition space, but this particular fleet is heading to the exact same sub-sector as we are..."

Cain realized the truth was inescapable. "They're after the Saepid vessel as well, aren't they?"

"I have no doubt. We knew it wouldn't be easy to find that ship, but now it seems this Phaelon fleet might be following the same Intel we've been receiving."

Cain studied the scene before them. "This gets more complicated by the minute."

"Indeed, but we knew this mission wouldn't be easy... just have your tech people keep a constant eye on that fleet, if they waver one klick off their present course I want to know about it."

"Of course, Sir." As the Captain turned to leave she called after him. "Sir?"

"Yes?"

She was looking at the line of ships moving ahead of the main Phaelon fleet.

"What type of ships do you think they are?"

Severs looked at the curved line of ships now pushing ahead of the main Phaelon fleet. "Something new, I suppose. Something we haven't come across yet... it's hard to say. But I have no doubt we'll find out, sooner or later."

When he was gone Cain looked up at the evocation as it rotated in and out of the current spatial-grid. The enemy fleet didn't waver from their course, their speed remained constant, and their ionic trails continued to scatter echo points all across subspace. She studied the forward ships. *What are you? Some*

315

new spawn of the enemy we have yet to see? Well, this definitely won't help the
nightmares, Marina...

Cadet Sara Tielman was on second shift in the Engine Room when Chief Griel came over to look at her latest computations.

"Nice graphics, Cadet. How are you managing without an AI link?"

"Well, Sir, it was difficult at first, tech analysis without the autonomous systems can be a little tricky, to say the least. With no viable data-stream a lot of this is guesswork based on outdated evocations; I'm even matching some of my adjustments to the old-style algorithms we used to use on Galicia."

"So you're a Galician girl, are you? I'm very sorry for what happened to your world, Cadet."

"Thank you, Sir. But I take heart in the mission; if we can bring the war into the enemy's heartland we might just be able to avenge the loss of so many of our people."

"Indeed, and your subspace graphics will help make that happen, Cadet, keep up the good work." He turned away.

"Sir!"

"Yes, Cadet?"

"Do you think we have a chance? I mean, we're going up against the enemy in his own back yard..."

He smiled at that. "Yes, of course we have a chance; don't you know what they say about soldiers and fools?"

"No, Sir, what do they say?"

"That it takes one to be the other..."

He knew she wasn't sure what that meant. "Don't worry about it, Cadet, just do your duty and we'll get through this, I promise."

"Yes, Sir. Thank you, Sir."

Chief Griel went over to the core displacement interface. The ionic pulse was cresting at maximum, carrying the ship forward Max 10 to the speed of light, the very limit of operational capability. The Captain had insisted on an ionic constant throughout the journey, putting the entire Engine Room team on edge. He had six of his people working full time on the injector assembly, monitoring the plasma relays for any sign of deviation; in his twenty years working as an engineer on various Coalition ships he had only heard of two vessels who had pushed their pulse drives too far, and both had simply vaporized in the depths of subspace, never to be seen again. *I just hope the*

Captain knows the risks we're taking; a Core implosion isn't going to help anyone...

Some time later Cadet Tielman called him back to her station.

"Sir, I have those pulse variants for you."

Griel leaned over the data screen as she continued. "As you can see, we're maintaining a steady momentum right now, but there are fluctuations in the subspace field, here and... here." She tapped the screen.

Griel studied the graphical interface. There was definitely a pattern developing within the subspace bubble.

"I see them. Let's get a spectrographic of this sector, see if there are any echo points around."

She looked alarmed. "You mean enemy vessels, Sir?"

"Well, let's not jump to conclusions, Cadet, but those fluctuations are possibly indicative of ionic trails."

"Bringing up a spectrograph now, Sir. There is a significant amount of divergence out here, at this point..." As she narrowed the view-screen ratios she suddenly realized what she was looking at. "Sir, those are echo-point locators..." She turned in her seat to look up at him. "There are ships out there, running parallel to our own course."

"Well done, Cadet. Just keep this to yourself while I contact the Captain." He moved over to the com panel, touched for the Bridge.

"Bridge here, Cain online."

"Ma'am, this is Griel in the Engine Room, we have something you should see."

"Can you feed it through up here?"

Griel nodded to his cadet to upload the data to the Bridge.

"Sending it now, Ma'am."

There was a minute of silence before the First Officer came back online.

"Chief, the Captain will see you in his ready room now."

Griel looked at his cadet and shrugged. "Very well, Ma'am, tell the Captain I'll be right there."

But the First Officer wasn't finished. "Have you discussed your findings with any of your team, Griel?"

"No, Ma'am. Except it was Cadet Tielman who brought the information to my attention."

There was another pause from the Bridge before Cain spoke again. "Bring her with you."

317

"Yes, Ma'am, at once."

Cadet Tielman had only been in the Captain's ready room once before, and she'd had the place to herself back then, wiping excess data from the dataports... but this time it was so very different. She had been summoned to see the Captain by the First Officer. It was highly unusual for a cadet to be summoned like that, and right now it was very worrying.

She followed Chief Griel into the room, trying her best to merge into the background. She saw that both the Captain and his First Officer were already present. *Well, that's scary for a start...*

Captain Severs looked up as Griel entered the room, followed by the young cadet. He hadn't met her before, but Cain had said the young woman was an excellent tech analyst, a Galician by race. *That is unfortunate... She obviously knows her job; she found the enemy fleet without the aid of any evocations... that takes great skill. She might know her job but does she know her duty?*

He addressed Chief Griel first. "Chief, I want to thank you and your cadet here for your diligence in this matter; it's quite impressive that you were able to extract such precise readings from a few subspace fluctuations."

"Actually, Sir, it was entirely Cadet Tielman here who spotted the pulse variants, she did the math herself before she showed me the results."

Cain gestured to Tielman. "Come forward, Cadet."

"Yes, Ma'am."

The Captain looked up at the young woman, noted she had the archetypal Galician red hair, a known trait among that race. She seemed far too young to be serving aboard a warship, probably no more than twenty by the look of her. *They seem to get younger every day...*

"So, Cadet, you seem to know your way around subspace fluctuations."

"Yes, Sir, I took subspace harmonics at Fleet School on Galicia."

"Yes, and I am sorry for what has happened to your people. May I ask if you lost anyone close to you?"

Cain realized the Captain hadn't read the tagged report she'd given him on the young cadet's service record.

"Both my parents, Sir... my brother was off-world at the time, like myself..." The words trailed off into a whisper. The Captain suddenly felt guilty for reminding the cadet of her tragic loss.

"I'm very sorry, Cadet. I can only say that you are not alone in your sorrow; the entire Coalition is feeling your pain."

318

"Yes, Sir. Thank you, Sir."

"But now I need to outline the situation to both of you..." He turned to Cain. "If you will bring up the mission protocols, Cain."

She touched the control interface and the main vid-screen appeared in the air above the desk. It was the evocation rendered from the Saepid database showing the Far Star Colony. Both Chief Griel and Cadet Tielman moved forward slightly to get a better view. Captain Severs worked the controls to highlight the six local planets, with a zoom angle on the highlighted fourth planet.

"This planet here is the Far Star Colony itself, although most data-streams designate this entire sub-sector as the Far Star Colony. Our Intel suggests this planet as the point of origin for our enemy." He let that sink in before continuing. "Now, what I am about to tell you has been designated as above top secret, and the only reason I'm involving you now is because the fleet you detected is a threat to our mission. Not a threat in the conventional manner – there is no indication that they intend to intercept us – but they might prevent us from attaining our mission directive."

The Chief had to ask: "And what is that directive, Captain? Forgive me, but I understood we were to harass enemy lines of communication while carrying out hit and runs against their bases of operation."

Severs saw from Tielman's face that she too expected the mission to be a hit-and-run exercise, inflicting the greatest amount of damage for the minimal amount of losses. He glanced at Cain before continuing. "No, Chief, that is not our primary directive. Our mission, in fact, is to intercept a single vessel which is currently somewhere near the periphery of the Far Star Colony."

Tielman and Griel exchanged puzzled looks. Severs raised his hand as Griel was about to speak.

"The fact is, Chief, this vessel may possess the only possible means to destroy the enemy once and for all. We have been given the task of finding this ship and offering mutual aid and assistance." He paused for a moment. "Needless to say, that task won't be easy, we're already traveling through enemy territory; there will almost certainly be a defensive perimeter set up somewhere ahead of us, and we might not even get past that. So it's vital for you to continue with your tech analysis, Cadet, your work could prove invaluable as a subsidiary to the evocations we'll be using in our approach to the Colony."

"Very good, Sir, I will do my duty."

"I know you will, Cadet. But I have to impress on both of you that the actual mission directive must not be disclosed among the crew; the logistics of our true mission might not be readily accepted given the current state of the war. None of us, not the Admiralty or the hierarchy at Tantra, fully understand the meaning of this one solitary vessel. But I will tell you this, whatever weapon it is carrying, whatever force they possess, it has so far managed to get them all the way from Petra to the edge of the Far Star Colony itself, passing through countless enemy fleets in the process. It stands to reason therefore that the importance of this ship cannot be over-emphasized, and as such the vital nature of our mission must take precedence over everything we have already lost." He looked at Cadet Tielman as he spoke those last few words. *She will do her duty, despite her pain; she will give everything she has to the mission.*

First Officer Cain stepped away from the control interface. "Cadet, I want you to monitor that fleet and keep me informed as to its progress. I have my adjutant doing the same in the Vision Chamber, but your input might help to determine their future course configurations."

"Yes, Ma'am, I'll get right on it."

Captain Severs turned to the Chief. "How are the engines doing, Chief?"

"They're holding steady, Sir... being pushed to the limit for this long isn't the best way to fly a starship, but we can hold her together for you."

"That's all I ask, Chief. Dismissed."

The two turned and left the ready room as the Captain addressed Cain. "You don't think it was wise of me to bring them in on our secret mission, do you, Marina?"

"It's not that, Sir, I trust them both implicitly."

"So what's bothering you? I know that look..."

"It's just that we've just told that kid that she might not get her revenge after all."

Severs thought about that for a moment. "We don't know what's on that ship, Marina; its data-tag shows a match to the Saepid trader vessels we have on file, but they could be anyone." He paused for a moment. "But whoever they are, they may very well possess the means to exact the kind of revenge Cadet Tielman is looking for."

Chapter 12 - Terminal Perception

"The Confederacy was born out of fire and blood, I have no doubt that it will end in fire and blood also..."
Torin Grenval, Private Memoirs.

The Phaelon heavy cruiser *Hagmon* was six days outbound from the newly created Sentinel Gate, a collection of plassteel habitats fused onto an airless rock two light years from the Sacred Sanctum at the Far Star Colony.

Torin Grenval, Adjutant General to the Sacred Mistia, was studying the recently arrived schematics of the Sentinel Gate. It was a stunning achievement. A vast antenna swarm five miles across was strung out between dozens of graphile pylons orbiting the Gate complex. The structures themselves were housed inside ten-meter-thick ultravault Plasmeld shielding, and every fifty meters around the perimeter there was a large ionic dispersion gun, their tubes linked to a series of feeler drones placed in orbit around the moon. *They really do know the art of intimidation...* He brought up a spatial-grid of the area around the Gate. A hundred million kilometers beyond the moon was the dim orange glow of a dwarf star, *not much to light the way...* He also noticed a flotilla of ships parked in an elliptic orbit of the moon. Their designation was Samrosion. He read the recognition codes of the ships and tapped them into his datapad. The allocation tags came back instantly: the ships belonged to the High Priest Valos Armin of the Samros Sacred Sect. *Now what in Phaedra is he doing all the way out here? A reception committee perhaps?* And then he thought back to his conversation with First Tactician Philas Vorin... *has that Drak betrayed me to the priesthood? Probably not, he might doubt my faith, but he's loyal enough...* He realized that the priests were probably part of a routine deployment... they'd been infiltrating the battalions of the Expansion for some time now. He'd managed to restrict his own complement of fanatics to just two priests, and he had them kept busy translating the Book of Saemal into various Phaedran sub-dialects. But nevertheless, he would have to tread carefully from now on, *if they even begin to suspect my inculcation is slipping...* The door to his quarters buzzed and the face of Tactician Vorin appeared in the compad.

"Come in, Vorin."

Vorin entered. "Sir, I have an urgent situation report."

Torin eyed his second-in-command. "So give it to me."

"Sir, if you please, it would be better done at Ops."

Torin sighed. "Very well, lead the way."

When they arrived in the Ops room Nav Tech Dainer Romon was already there, setting up a spatial-grid above the control console. Torin ignored the breach in etiquette, mainly because Vorin seemed fussed about something.

Romon acknowledged his commander and stood to one side as Torin took his seat. Vorin joined Romon and began to explain the current grid alignment.

"Sir, this is a current rendition of this sector. As you know, we take hourly scans from the tracers and input the variables into the nav systems."

"Your point, Vorin?"

"Forgive me, Sir, of course. Well, as you can see, this is the rendition from the tracers, and over here I've asked Romon to overlay the feeler web, and right here, Sir, in the bottom right quadrant is an anomaly." That got Torin's full attention. He sat forward, studying the data-flow as it shimmered into symbols and letters beneath the subspace fluctuation now entering the sector.

"A ship, Vorin?"

"Undoubtedly, Sir, and currently on a course parallel to our own, heading directly into the heart of the Sacred Sanctum."

Torin stood up, staring at the little red dot whispering its way across the screen. *Could it be? Not possible… the Saepids are far from here, almost within the Colony sector itself… Then who?*

Vorin looked at his commander. "Sir, could this be the vessel we seek?"

He had to ask… "I don't see how it can be, Vorin, not this far out. The last data-burst from our missing agent put the vessel somewhere beyond the Entrymion sector; that's light years from here. To get here would require a complete course alteration; they would have to turn away from the Rim. No, comrades, this is something else. Can you match a configuration yet, Boras?"

Aron Boras stepped away from the screen. "I'm sorry, Sir, no, not yet. We've tried, but they're beyond the range of our tracers to catch an accurate alignment."

Vorin turned to his commander. "Sir, if I might make a suggestion? We could detach one bio-ship to take a look; it would take no more than a few hours to reach that vessel. It could take a quick scan and be back here before the morning watch."

Torin considered this. It made sense to try out his command protocols on the bio-ships. *Let's see if they really have got a mind of their own…*

"Very well, send one of bio-ships; and be very specific, Vorin… one scan only to ID the craft and then it is to return to the fleet for download and dissemination."

"I'll get right to it, Sir."

Torin spoke again as the two officers turned to leave: "Oh, and Vorin, if you have any problem with the bio-ships, let me know immediately, will you."

"Very good, Sir."

Torin sat back down, touched his datapad for a bio-tag on the priest Valos Armin.

The man had originally been a desk clerk in the Samrosion Customs Exchange in Altair City, a minor official with a wife and two sons, whom he had abandoned upon his ordination into the Church of Saemal. His record showed him to have been a rather nondescript man, dedicated in his way, but he had never achieved anything of any consequence in his rather mediocre life. *And now the creature heads a religion numbering in the billions spread across a quarter of the known galaxy… this new faith is full of the ironic and the sublimely surreal… but is he dangerous?*

He tapped a few tags on the Samrosion priesthood, found them alarmingly militaristic in their practices. Valos Armin himself had ordered the genocide of the Galician race. The purging of the great crystal cities seemed unnecessary; why wouldn't Saemal simply subvert them via the data-stream from Samros? Such methods had worked on Primus and on most of the Rim worlds; it had even worked on Phaedra. But that left open the question which continued to gnaw at the back of his mind: *If the power of Saemal is weakening beyond the Sacred Sanctum, if its structure is only being maintained by the Sacred Eleven and the priesthood, where is Saemal's power now being directed? Such a state of affairs would certainly explain the overkill on worlds like Galicia and Entrymion. Those crafty priests want to make sure their powerbase is well established in case Saemal withdraws all his forces from the zone of Expansion, and what better way to do that than by instilling sheer terror into the survivors of their pogroms… I really must be wary of this Valos Armin…* He sat back in his seat, staring at the image of the high priest; his scales ached and his head was throbbing with a headache that refused to go away. *No matter what happens, they won't find it so easy to seduce me the next time…*

323

Chapter 13 - Oblique Infiltrations

"The Lord Jophrim stood tall on the prow of his ship Cassandra, *the first vessel to approach the land of darkness. Many serpents fell upon them, and from the skies fire rained down in torrents upon them, but alone this solitary ship breached the barricades of the demi-God Abaddon, who in later days was Saemal, and did vanquish his forces in the final battle before the very gates of Demos itself."*
Brother Fiodore, First Ascetic Ministry of Petra (From the Book of Jophrim).

Cain was reluctant to take the Dramex. Doc Kendra said it would help her sleep. But the nightmares were a constant now and the lack of rest was beginning to affect her concentration; but if there was an emergency... *it wouldn't do for the First Officer to be lost inside a drug-induced sleep...* So she drank a cup of sula milk and lay down on her cot to try and get at least an hour of decent sleep before her next shift. But the nightmares came almost at once.

She was lost inside a swirling vortex, a storm tearing apart the city... high above she saw the glistening black hides of battle wagons disgorging streams of dispersal bombs among the high towers and glide-rails... the people were running, thousands of them scrambling among the fallen debris, fighting each other to escape the conflagration... from behind her, the sound of crying... a small child hiding in the shadow of a downed skipper, her baby doll held tight against her chest... from above came the screech of a missile drone... looking up she saw the antenna net shimmering in the noon day sun... she ran toward the child, she had to save her, if it was the last thing she ever did... the little girl reached out a blood-soaked hand, tears falling among the dust... She felt the heatwave from the drone just as she reached the child...

She woke suddenly, soaked to the skin. Sitting up trembling, she reached for a cup of water. *This is getting ridiculous...* She jumped as the compad buzzed.

"First Officer Cain, this as Lieutenant Wenders on the Bridge. The Captain has asked you to join him in the Vision Chamber."

"Very well, I'll be right there." She closed the link and debated whether there was time to shower, and then decided against it... *better not keep the Captain waiting...*

324

When she arrived at the Vision Chamber she found the Captain in conversation with her adjutant Tamara Breckin. Above them was a rendition of a spatial-grid.

"Sir, is there a problem?"

Severs turned toward her and she noticed the look of concern on his face.

"That remains to be seen. Breckin has picked up an infiltration into our subspace field... if you will, Breckin."

The adjutant adjusted the holo-lucience to include subspace echo points, and a grid alignment descended over the spatial data-stream.

"If you will notice this incursion here, Ma'am, you can see the configuration matches those of the unknown ships we tracked earlier."

Cain moved closer to the evocation. The alignment was precise, there could be no doubt about it... the enemy had detached one of their unidentified vessels in their direction. She addressed the Captain. "An attack, Sir?"

"Well, I was going to ask your opinion on that, Cain."

She studied the grid. The main Phaelon fleet had not altered course; in fact, they were still on an ever-widening tangent to their own course.

"It seems highly unlikely that they mean to engage us, Sir, it's more likely to be an intelligence gathering mission."

"My thoughts exactly, Cain. Their main fleet seems intent on moving forward. They obviously know we are in the same sector, but to expend ships in an attack against us would only delay them. I think they're simply curious, it makes sense they'd send a ship to see just who we are."

Such a conclusion seemed logical to Cain. "Your orders, Sir?"

"Well, I think this spying mission of theirs can work both ways; we might just be able to get a good look at the nature of those vessels. Let's face it, we know nothing about them, it would be to our advantage to know what we might come up against when we reach the Colony itself."

Cain considered that. "But do we attack that ship, Sir? Do we prevent it gathering Intel?"

Severs had to consider their options carefully. To engage the enemy ship might be enough to bring their entire fleet down upon them; they wouldn't stand much of a chance against eighty ships.

"No, Cain, we won't engage that vessel, we will shroud our ion stream as best we can with scattering beams, but we will also risk one of Cadet Tielman's spectrographical evocations; she knows her job, that one, and if she can sneak in under their grids we may glean some useful information."

325

Cain spoke as she looked up at the approaching red dot. "And if they open fire on us?"

Captain Severs spoke from the doorway. "Why, then we'll give them everything we've got." He touched the compad. "Bridge, Captain here, issue a ship-wide battle alert, I'll be right up."

As he left the chamber the sound of the alert began to echo along the corridors. Cain turned to Breckin. "Looks like things are about to get interesting, Tamara."

"Yes, Ma'am." She looked at Cain, noted her uncombed hair, the look in her eyes. "Forgive me, but is everything all right, Ma'am?"

"What? Oh, yes, of course..." She turned to look at Breckin as she left the chamber. "Thank you, Tamara."

When Cain arrived on the Bridge she immediately noted a subdued air of apprehension. The com lights were the only true illumination, with a single glow strip around the ceiling dome casting shadows among the rows of tacticians. She took her seat next to Captain Severs and adjusted her seat panel to bring the local spatial-grid online. The giant vid-screen flickered into life and the link to the Vision Chamber was established. The Bridge crew watched as the unknown ship approached off the larboard side. Echo points were bouncing off its hull, but they seemed to lack cohesion.

Cain noted this. *Whatever that ship is made of, it's deflecting our beams.* She linked to Cadet Tielman in the Engine Room.

"Tielman, are you linked to the evocation system?"

"Yes, Ma'am, we're running graphs now. I'm uploading as we stream and matching the specs to the data in the Vision Chamber. It's coming in clean and I think I can give you a visual rendition now if you want."

"Very good, Cadet, link it to the Bridge."

"At once, Ma'am."

Instantly the screen above the command console shifted spectrum and the faint outline of a ship began to form. The Captain and his officers watched as the shape formed into the elongated symmetry of a ship. They saw an antenna assembly girdled along its side, but the configuration seemed to lack conformity, and the data-stream showed that the ship was in the process of expanding and retracting. Severs turned to his First Officer.

"Are you seeing that, Cain?"

"Yes, Sir, most unusual..."

"Looks to me like the thing is fluctuating in density..."

326

Cain glanced at the uplink from Tielman. "Not in density, Sir, but it is undulating at regular intervals."

From the forward con Lieutenant Wenders spoke up. "It's like it's breathing..."

They fell silent, all eyes on the strange ship as it came nearer. One of the stats tacticians spoke up from behind the command console. "Captain, it's slowing down..."

Cain touched her compad. "Tielman, are you getting anything from inside that vessel?"

There was a moment's pause before Cadet Tielman came back online. "We're getting some confusing data from the bounce-back, Ma'am."

The Captain cut in. "Explain, Cadet."

"Yes, Sir. Well, the configuration never holds a perfect match. Every time we extrapolate internal references, the thing alters shape... it's like that ship is alive, Sir, the mechanics aren't reading as a solid construct, it's entirely possible that we're looking at some form of organic compound."

That was a shock. Cain spoke quietly to her Captain. "Perhaps we had better align the weapons array, Sir, as a precaution..."

"I've considered that, but that thing might pick up on the weapons signatures and be forced to engage us; if that led to their fleet coming after us... No, I think we'll hold tight, let them get their pictures, hopefully they'll be satisfied and move off."

Cain didn't like the idea of being exposed to attack, with the weapons offline they wouldn't have a chance if the other ship opened fire on them. She looked up at the screen as the tiny red dot entered firing range. *Well, if they're going to shoot now would be the time...* But the other ship simply swept on by, looping around the *Valeria* in a wide arc before streaming away into the maelstrom of subspace.

Cain realized she was holding her breath. "Seems like you were right, Sir, they just wanted a quick look."

"Yes well, I hope it worked both ways. Go and liaise with Tielman and Breckin, see what you can get from their scans."

"Very good, Sir."

"Meanwhile, I think it's time we altered course..." He tapped his datapad and brought up the tags of the Saepid grids covering the Far Star Colony. The problem wasn't so much how they should enter the Colony sector; it was more what they would do when they got there. He had an idea about that, but it would have to wait until they were nearer their destination. He turned to his nav com officers. "Lieutenant Wenders, engage the course alignment I'm inputting now... and Lohman, I want you to match the pulse drive to the latest subspace variants; we need to maintain our current speed without any fluctuation in the field."

Both officers acknowledged their orders and the *Valeria* slowly banked away from their original course, putting them on a sub-lateral course toward the Far Star Colony.

First Officer Cain leaned back against the wall inside the drop-tube; the headache was getting worse. She couldn't really explain it; she had never suffered from headaches, never mind constant nightmares. She thought it might be down to stress, but again she wasn't one to suffer from stress. *But of course I've never been on a mission like this before...* The tube vibrated gently as the doors slid open and she found herself on F-Deck. She met her adjutant as she reached the Engine Room.

"I take it you saw the readings, Tamara?"

"Yes, Ma'am, most unusual."

"Well, let's see what our clever cadet has to say on the matter."

Inside they found Chief Griel and several of his assistants standing over the graphical interface console; Cadet Tielman was seated, her hands moving across the data-flow as it streamed through the various spectrographs. As Cain approached, the group of assistants moved back to their stations.

"So what do you have for us, Cadet?"

"Quite a bit actually, Ma'am. It was all very misleading at first; I couldn't get a stable resonance, the subspace particles lacked cohesion, there was just nothing recognizable for our beams to cling on to. So I adjusted the graphical harmonics to include bio-forms, and I got an instant reading. See this here?"

Cain leaned forward to see the new data as it flowed across the screen. The harmonic detection of bio-form configurations was as old as X-rays, but would not usually be applied to a mechanical construct; modern-day feeler systems could easily detect a ship's crew complement and its entire weapons platform, but the *Valeria* was running half-blind on evocations and spectrographs, and neither process would give them automatic bio-readings. The cadet had in fact achieved the impossible.

"So you've determined that these ships are in fact organic in nature?"

"Yes, Ma'am, that would seem to be the case."

Cain turned to Breckin. "Can you upload this into the holo-emitters; the Captain will want to see this in detail."

"Not a problem, Ma'am… will you want me to download this into a data-plug?"

Cain knew that the Liberation Fleet might well find the new information useful, if not vital in their approach toward Petra, but using the Net to transmit data from their present location could bring a whole lot of unwelcome attention their way.

"Yes, do it, but keep it filed until the Captain says otherwise."

"Yes, Ma'am."

On the twenty-third day of their journey the crew of the C.S. *Valeria* came up against their first major obstacle. The nav tacticians picked up the echo points during Cain's second shift, Captain Severs had retired to his quarters and she was working through her downtime, accepting the fact that she would get very little sleep even if she did sign off duty.

"What have you got, Wenders?"

"Stats match the configurations to a nest of mines, Ma'am, directly up ahead."

"All stop. Lohman, call the Captain to the Bridge. Navs, I want a grid brought up, and Wenders, find me a way around those mines."

"Aye, Ma'am, I'll do my best."

A few minutes later Captain Severs joined her at the command console. He immediately recognized the scene now flowing across the main screen. "Mines?"

"We estimate over a thousand, Sir, we're plotting a way around now."

He studied the graphs as fast as they came in. The deployment of the mines lent credence to the Intel he'd received from Fleet Security; these types of mines had been used to blockade ships escaping from Earthia, they were tuned to the ionic resonance given off by a pulse drive… if they got too close the things would be drawn directly to the needle tubes.

He looked at Cain. "Can we go around them?"

"It would take weeks, Sir."

He studied the scene before them. They would be in the heart of the Far Star Colony in less than five days' time if they could avoid the mines. To have come so far without being intercepted… it was frustrating in the extreme, *unless…*

"There's nothing else for it, Cain, we're going to have to blast our way through."

She looked incredulous. "Sir?"

"I know the risks; the detonation waves could well be as destructive as the actual mines themselves, but I won't be stopped at the enemy's door... not after we've come this far. We can't afford to waste time going around, no... we're going to have to force our way through."

"Very well, Sir."

Severs touched his compad and linked to the weapons bay. The voice of his Weapons Master Harlen Drake came online. "Weapons, Drake here."

"Drake, I want you to link with the current grid and align your missiles at the designated targets and force me a path through that minefield."

"Try my best, Sir. We're getting the feed now and uploading to the drones, will commence firing as soon as we're locked in."

"Very good. Feed your target alignments to the First Officer while you're at it."

"Yes, Sir, will do."

The Captain touched for internal wideband communication.

"This is your Captain speaking. I want all departments to prepare for heavy impact turbulence, secure all decks and shut down auxiliary data-ports. Watch your screens and inform your supervisors of any containment issues. Captain out."

He looked at Cain. "Well, this should be interesting..."

She tried to smile. "Indeed..."

The first wave of missiles streamed out from the weapons tubes and aligned themselves with the nearest group of mines. Ten seconds later there was a blinding image flash across the data-stream and every screen flickered into gray, before stabilizing into readable data. Five seconds after that, the first compression wave hit the ship. It felt like the hull had been hit by a very large hammer, as the ship rose up slightly on the crest of the wave. Cain kept her eye on the structural integrity screens as the second wave of missiles found their targets. Again they were hit by a massive compression wave, throwing several of the Bridge crew to the floor. Severs quickly helped a young tactician back to her seat as the third wave of missiles struck up ahead. The next wave hit even sooner than the first two, causing the ship to lean slightly to port.

Severs tapped his compad. "Chief, can you increase power to the stabilizers?"

330

"Sir, I'm doing that now, but the pulse drive is sucking up everything. If we could just reduce speed a little I think I can correct alignment."

Severs looked across at Cain... they both knew that any reduction in speed would cost them dearly in the days ahead; even the slightest delay could be catastrophic later on. They had no choice.

"No, Chief, keep the engines at maximum, we'll have to ride this one out."

"Very good, Sir."

Just then the fourth wave hit and Cain had trouble holding on to her seat as the ship began to lean alarmingly to port.

Severs called to the nav station: "Status, Wenders?"

"Sir, we're nearly through, just one more row of mines and we'll be on the other side."

"Good..." He watched the screen as the last wave of missiles impacted the mines, sending the last powerful compression wave back toward the *Valeria*.

The ship rode the last wave, leaving the minefield in its wake as Captain Severs asked for departmental damage reports. Cain brought up the figures and was surprised that there was no actual structural damage. Most departments reported only minor damages... fallen storage units, broken containers, damaged seals... but there was nothing serious to report; it seemed they had survived intact.

Severs seemed pleased. "Good, now let's get the long-range sensors online."

That suddenly alarmed Cain. The Bridge crew would certainly wonder why the Captain would risk using the sensors after all this time; the ban on using the autonomous systems was now a fleet-wide command directive. The Nav and Stats crew looked puzzled.

Lieutenant Lohman spoke first: "Excuse me, Sir, I don't wish to question your orders, but aren't we supposed to keep the sensor grid offline?"

Cain gave him a glare. "Lieutenant, it is not your place to question your Captain's orders!"

Captain Severs cut in. "It's all right, Cain; I think the crew deserve an explanation." He tapped his compad again and made another ship announcement.

"This is your Captain again. I have some information with regard to our mission directive which I feel you should be made aware of, considering what it is we are about to face. I'm uploading this directive to the internal data-stream

331

now; it comes directly from Fleet Command. I want all crew members to become fully conversant with this directive. I know you will have questions, and I know you will have your own opinions, but this is a military ship operating in a war zone, light years behind enemy lines, so when I tell you that this mission is vital to the preservation of the entire Coalition you must understand the gravity of that statement. This mission may not appear to be the one you signed up for, but it is no less important for all of that. Yes, you want to vent your anger against the enemy, and I know you want revenge for the terrible losses we have all suffered; but if this mission succeeds you will have your revenge, and perhaps a great deal more. So please continue to do your duty, and I know that together we will succeed." He closed down the link and noticed Cain was looking at him.

"I felt it was time, Marina."

She smiled. "I know, Sir, it was due."

Severs turned back to his Bridge crew. "So will someone engage the sensor grid please?"

Wenders turned to face his nav board. "Sensors online now, Sir."

Cain leaned toward her Captain. "And if the enemy uses the sensor grid to climb inside our database?"

Severs sat back in his chair, saying only: "Well, we'll cross that grid when we come to it."

Chapter 14 - Into the Fire

Starflight stunned into ecliptic sundance,
a perfect pirouette skimming off the heathaze,
sub-orbital cadence resonating inside the gravity well,
a string of stars tethered to the hull.

A sea of rocks rippling beyond the biosphere,
stunted and outsize slabs of relogith iridescent and
kissed by the coalescency of creation,
shadows and souls drifting in an endless night.

Falling into the fire, an incandescent trajectory,
storming through the photosphere,
light listens to the orchestration of life,
lured by the whisper and revelation of infinite wonder.

The Poet Brayman, Westphal Refugee Settlement, Planet Entrymion.

Shari had spent over two hours helping Domini adapt the lasfuser into an energy weapon. They had no idea if it would be effective, but they mounted it onto the skipper's access port anyway. Shari wanted to do a test firing but Domini and the Saepids had all said '*No!*' at exactly the same time, which was disconcerting; it was as if they didn't trust her. Now she was back in her tree and Domini was down below in the command pod with the Saepids. They had agreed to allow Domini to watch their piloting and become more involved in manning the ship's systems. She could hear them patiently explaining things to him as they fired up the pulse drive.

"It's not just a matter of more hands, Domini; it also takes great skill…" She smiled at that. She felt inside the pouch and brought out the artifact. It still felt so very cold. Each time she held it now she would get the 'feeling'. She wasn't sure what it was, only that it began in her stomach like flutter bees and spread up and down her spine as a warm tingling sensation that always came to rest somewhere in the center of her chest, at which point she would suddenly be aware that her heart was pounding and her whole body was trembling. It always took her several minutes to slow down her breathing, and she often found herself quite breathless as she returned the artifact to its pouch.

333

But she was beginning to enjoy the feeling, which she knew should have worried her, but it didn't; the thing was pleasurable, and she always wanted more. She hadn't been with Domini since the first time, and with every crisis they faced they had found less and less time to be alone together. But now the artifact seemed to be compensating for the loss of Domini, the feelings were profound and gave her a sense of power she had never known before. If she could have thought about it rationally she might have been concerned, but there was no longer any room for such considerations. More and more she had begun to feel the changes taking place inside her mind and her body. She had almost told the others about it, but she never really knew how to explain. *How do you explain such power? How could they possibly understand?* So she had begun to feel separated from her friends; a sense of detachment seemed to be setting in, and she didn't think that was such a bad thing. *The less we care now, the easier to accept what must come later on...* She held the artifact against her breasts, pressing it hard into her flesh. The sensations were carrying her higher than the stars themselves... *I can feel the whole universe spinning inside my head!*

She became aware of the soft hum of the pulse drive, the gentle vibrations rippling along the tree branches casting leaves free to float serenely across the cabin. *Like little dancers tip-toeing among the stars...* Domini was on the compad.

"Shari, are you there?"

She shuddered, and carefully replaced the artifact in its pouch. Moments later Domini drifted up toward her.

"Shari? Did you hear me call you?"

She looked at him with an air of impatience. "Yes, I heard you. What do you want?"

He seemed taken aback by her tone. "I'm sorry if I woke you, I just wanted to tell you we'll be at the Far Star Colony by this time tomorrow... are you all right? You look upset..."

"First of all, Dom, please don't fuss, I'm fine... you know I have a lot on my mind. And second, I wasn't asleep."

"I'm sorry... so everything is good with you?"

"Everything is just wonderful with me; now if you'll excuse me, I think I will get some sleep."

"Of course, I'll get back to my flying lessons."

334

"You do that." And she pulled her foilair fleece over her head and leaned back into her hammock. But as Domini started to drift away she called after him: "Oh, and tell Anthra the waste unit is clogged again."

"Okay, I'll sort it out…"

She wrapped her face in the soft padding of her hammock and listened for raindrops dripping from invisible trees.

Anthra looked concerned. "And you think there is something wrong with her?"

Domini glanced up at Shari's tree. "I told you, I'm not sure; it's just that she seems… different somehow; I can't explain it."

Ventra turned in her webbing. "Have you been intimate recently?"

Domini couldn't believe she had just asked that. "What? What makes you think we've ever been intimate, Ventra?"

Ventra gave a gentle smile. "Come now, Domini, we may be poor Saepid traders but we know love when it blooms… you have linked, have you not?"

Both Saepids were staring at him wide-eyed.

"I don't think I want to answer that. Besides, our being together has nothing to do with the fact that I think something is bothering her."

Anthra looked up toward Shari. "Have you asked her if something is wrong?"

"Of course I have. You know what she's like; she just gets annoyed and gives me one of those looks…"

Both Saepids nodded; they had seen those looks.

Anthra had a suggestion. "Perhaps it is simply because we are approaching the end of our journey, the burden of her legacy must be weighing very heavy upon her now; she must be realizing that everything we have been through is finally reaching a conclusion."

"Yes, Domini, Anthra is right. The nearer we come to Beast's lair, the greater the influence of the artifact on Shari. We do not know how the device works; ancient texts have no record of its usage or even the source of its power. We have seen how it protected her from the Beast seeping into her mind; perhaps it does other things to her as well."

Domini felt himself worrying about that. "Other things? Like what?"

Anthra spoke up. "Who can say? But surely the *custodia* are not like other people, they have to have qualities we can only guess at. I am thinking that the artifact is changing Shari, making her into something other than human, perhaps more than human."

335

That scared Domini to the very core of his being. "More than human? What's that supposed to mean?"

"I mean, Domini, that perhaps the device is making Shari into the one thing that can face the Beast... a weapon."

He turned to look up at the girl he had come to love more than life itself. He was only now beginning to realize how tenuous, how terribly insignificant that love really was in the face of the coming battle. He spoke without taking his eyes off the tree up above.

"I'm going to lose her, aren't I? One way or another, she's never going to be the girl I fell in love with; even if we make it through this... she will never be the same again."

Neither Saepid spoke. They didn't have to, they had already known that truth for so long.

Shari had a perfect dream. She had followed a golden ribbon of light through the outer planets of the Far Star Colony to come to rest above the fourth planet. She had seen a vast fleet of ships strung out like silver orbs floating in a sea of stars. She had seen an army so massive in number that all she could see were their black flags fluttering in the wind. But she knew that the dark thing was not down there, he was not among his slaves and devotees, he was not inside their temples, nor on the bridges of their ships; he was not on Primus, nor Petra nor any of the worlds of the Coalition; he was in fact behind her, wrapped in petrified crystalline, hidden deep inside his pockmarked moon. And of course he knew she had come to kill him; and how he trembled in his rage, seething with a dark and terrible malevolence. The dream would slip away into scattered perceptions, drifting into the erosion of memory. She couldn't see beyond the empty revelation that the Beast was waiting for her to arrive. It was an inevitable consequence of her destiny. But the fear that it would end in the destruction of all life was a horror ingrained into a stark recognition... *If I kill this thing, will I kill the universe as well? The First Ones failed once before, so what does that make me? Their last superweapon? Are they willing to sacrifice civilization just to rectify their mistake?* She had the sensation of being controlled by forces beyond her understanding. Her life, her very existence, was being manipulated by ancient hands long since turned to dust. *But I have to see it through to its end, and in blind faith trust that the First Ones knew what they were doing when they first mixed blood and genes and spliced transcendence into the DNA of the custodia.*

336

She felt the power was becoming a living thing inside her, an entity born from a secret genesis; a separate sequence of thoughts and perceptions coming down through time. *I'm listening to someone else's thoughts... someone who walked the stars before the dawn of time.*

It was becoming harder to distinguish between the two minds. The new mind was growing ever more powerful, making her decisions seem like her own, turning her thoughts and feelings into silent echoes of her own true perception... and then there was the old mind, her mind, which was growing weaker every day, slowly losing its grip on reality, slipping away ever so slightly as the hours passed and the ship flew ever closer to the Beast's lair. *I'm losing myself inside myself!*

She reached up a finger and took a teardrop from her face. She held it out and blew it away, watching as it drifted gracefully across the cabin. She felt as if her soul was trapped inside that teardrop, losing its identity among the leaves floating by. *I can't fight this any more... the ancients have me now; they've waited millions of years for one more chance to kill the monster they spawned so long ago... and now they'll take that chance, no matter the cost, no matter who has to die in the process...* Suddenly her mother's face came to mind, her eyes wide and blue and full of love. She thought of the picnics at Foscombe Park beneath the old Dharm Oak, running around the wikka shrubs like a crazy kid high on jellup cake... *Momma, please don't be dead, I need you, Momma... I need you now more than I've ever needed anyone in my life...* But as the tears flowed she already felt the first touch of the *other mind* trawling through her memories, dismissing her pain with a glance of arrogant disdain.

She sat up straight in her webbing, wiping away her tears. *So be it! If you want to use me, go ahead, do your worst, I've already lost so much. I'll face your dark child, but know this: if just one person survives the final battle I will make sure they know what you did to all of creation, and most of all, I'll make sure they know your biggest secret yet...* She pushed away from the hull and drifted over to the shower cubicle.

Domini shouted up: "Are you all right, Shari?"

She smiled back down at him. "Never felt better, Dom."

Afterward, she joined the others down in the command pod; they were busy studying the latest spatial-grid, and by the looks on their faces she suspected there was bad news.

"So things are that bad, eh?"

337

Domini took her hand, squeezing it gently. "Not really... Anthra should explain..."

Anthra shuffled to one side so that Shari could edge closer to the main floater screen suspended above the command console.

"See here, Shari..." He pointed to the edge of the screen. "... we are moving through corridor of subspace beneath Far Star Colony. We expect to emerge here..." He highlighted an area of space just in front of a large blue dot. "... in front of Colony world itself. Of course, we must sneak past this lot here..." He touched the screen and it zoomed around to focus in on a large red mass which seemed to surround the entire upper quadrant. "These are the Beast's home fleets, many, many ships; big cruisers mostly, much bigger than *Shaendar*. But their size and close proximity will work against them and benefit us."

She leaned forward. "Okay... how?"

"Simple mechanics, really. Each one of those ships will be displaying a unified ion field, the displacement of such a large field will be many light years across, so no way can they have precise feeler links in all that; even their tracers will be useless, all they will get is bounce-back static from their own pulse-drives. Our little engine will just be one more drop of ionic particles in an ocean of ionic particles. In fact, unless we are physically seen, we will remain invisible to their sensors."

She looked at the red mass. "But won't they just see us?"

"Highly doubtful. The Beast uses full autonomous systems; they have total reliance upon AI automation. Why look out a window when you have a neural sensor net to rely on?"

"I don't know, Anthra; it sounds too easy to me. I mean, they must know we're coming; wouldn't they be looking out for a single ship?"

"Of course, dear Shari, and they are looking... see?" He pointed to a group of red dots drifting across the screen. "Those ships are different from all the others; we have no recognition codes for them. Somehow they are not displaying a traceable data-stream, and yet they are sending out waves of subspace feelers. We are just managing to scatter our own signature for the moment. I have input a disruption protocol into the matter condensers, for now we are bouncing back as background seepage from the big fleets above us; but as we get closer, things will get tricky... we will have to be very good at hiding among the eddies and whirlpools of the subspace field."

338

Shari moved away from the console, turning to face Domini. "So we're nearly there, Dom, time to face the cosmic music."

"Is that another old Galac saying?"

She smiled. "I do believe it is."

"You know we're in this together, right?" He tried to pull her close, but she resisted.

"Oh, Dom, if only we were... if only we were..." And she pushed away, floating back up toward her tree.

Anthra placed a hand on Domini's shoulder and squeezed. The Saepids understood, and now finally, so did he.

Chapter 15 - Obsession

"Sometimes dedication can be terminal, the fixation becomes self-replicating; after that the solution almost always ends in violence."
Professor Haris Langton, Department of Criminal Psychology, Gamont State University, planet Gamont.

Neiron Thane had been taking proaxol shots for five days straight. His personal enhancements had helped to keep his mind focused, but his body was still human, and it was beginning to be a problem. Proaxol replaced the need for sleep but eventually the drug would prove counter-effective, and he was now having the occasional hallucination. The long days and nights spent within the cramped confines of the Viper were beginning to take their toll. He only took his eyes of the tracer screens long enough to adjust the feeler drones, to re-input new parameters and send them off in a whole new direction. He would sweep through entire quadrants of subspace, then loop around, sometimes making the mistake of flying along the same flight path, and then, realizing his error, he would emerge into real-time and connect to the Net for updates and news of the Expansion toward the Hub worlds. He had only linked to the com probes once to inform Tanril on Primus that he was still in active pursuit of the Saepid vessel, but the Sacred Member had practically dismissed him, informing him that others were now a lot closer to the target vessel than he was. Tanril would accept no excuses, so he offered none, but he did not accept the recall order; he had come too far now to give up and return in shame to Primus. Tanril was wrong, they were all wrong; he and he alone would destroy the Saepid ship. He knew that his God Saemal wanted the human child captured alive, but surely even a god must come to realize that such a threat could only be dealt with through execution. No, his God would be grateful to him, they would all be grateful... and he was now a lot closer to the Saepids than Tanril or the others realized.

He checked the new spatial-grid; every tracer was coming back with thousands of echo points. *Fleet movements?* He had no doubt that this close to the Colony his Lord would have many ships waiting to intercept the Saepids. Tanril had told him about the Phaelon mission out of Phaedra; those ships must also be nearby. *Everyone is rushing to the finishing post... and who will win, I wonder?* It wouldn't be easy to identify one little Saepid ship among so many vessels, but he had an advantage the rest of Saemal's fleet lacked... he had the precise ionic signature of the Saepid vessel. All he had to do was use his feeler protocols to sift out the ionic backwash from the fleet and he would have them. *And no one will take my prize then... and though it might be the end of me, I will take those miserable heathens down with me...*

He checked his location stats to verify his current position, *just half a light year out of the Colony... almost there...* He watched as the proximity indicators signaled the presence of the Home Fleet directly ahead of him, and way off to the far edge of the quadrant he saw the faint shimmering of the Phaelon cruisers, with the strange blips of the bio-ships leading the way. He zoomed in on the Phaelon fleet, noticed the presence of the new weapons platform nearby... *Sentinel Gate, no doubt; impressive...*

As the feelers began to upload data from their sweeps he saw a single ship moving into the sector from beyond the Gate. Its configuration stats did not match the Saepid ship; *it's coming from the wrong direction... now, who can that be? Grenval seems to be ignoring it, and why shouldn't he? He wants the prize just as much as I do... no matter, it won't get past the fleet up ahead...* He reached out for the injector and pushed it into his neck, the proaxol took immediate effect and he felt himself becoming alert and acutely aware of the data-stream as it flowed in from a thousand separate sources.

Chapter 16 - Sentinel Gate

"You can hide a thousand lies behind one smile."
Corel Luwain, philosopher, planet Samros. .

The *Hagmon* was moving past the Sentinel Gate when priest Valos Armin contacted Torin Grenval on the Bridge of his command vessel. Torin had already received the data-plug from the recently returned bio-ship; the ID tags of the unknown vessel were registered as a Coalition heavy cruiser. How it had managed to reach so far into the Sacred Sanctum without being detected or destroyed was beyond him. He could only assume that the Coalition captain was very good at his job. *Given different circumstances I would have liked to meet you, Captain...* But there would be no chance of that now; the priest Armin had already dispatched twenty of his cruisers to intercept the vessel now that it was clearly identified as an enemy ship. *It's a shame, they could have provided a useful distraction; and perhaps they might yet...*

Armin's face appeared on the com floater in front of him.

"Valos Armin, what can I do for you?"

The priest looked every bit the insignificant human his records showed him to be: a narrow face with a nose that showed signs of once being broken, and above the piercing eyes was a receding hairline showing gray along both sides.

"Greetings, Torin Grenval. I trust your journey from Phaedra was uneventful?"

What's that supposed to mean? "It went according to my directives."

"Excellent, but if I might ask you a question?"

What is his game? "Time is of the essence, Armin; I must move my fleet forward so as to complete my mission."

"Of course, I mean you no delay. But I was concerned to hear that you did not destroy the Coalition ship while you had the opportunity to do so."

This sniveling dross dares to question me! "As I have already stated, my mission directive takes precedent over all else. I will not deviate from my course simply to eliminate one solitary ship." *Deal with that, priest...*

"I mean no criticism, Torin Grenval; I simply required your input for my report to the Sacred Eleven."

And is that a threat by any other name? "My directive comes from the Lady Mistia. I'm sure she will be more than satisfied with my actions."

"Indeed. Well, no matter, my own people will deal with the interloper. I have dispatched twenty cruisers to intercept them. You may continue with your sacred mission, Torin Grenval, I wish you well; may the pathways flow."

He gives me permission to continue! "May the pathways flow, Valos Armin."

He closed the connection and turned to face his nav team.

"Romon, engage the new course alignments; take us into the Sacred Sanctum."

"At once, Sir."

The *Hagmon* moved ahead of the main fleet, edging closer to the bio-ships as they led the way toward the Far Star Colony. Torin input the latest spatial-grid, noting the position of the Colony Defense Fleet now perched at the edge of the system. The ships seemed to lack coordination, their deployment leaving large gaps in the line. The data allocation tags showed the ships to be an improvised collection of vessels, recently arrived from dozens of worlds scattered along the entire Rim. *Well, this is not the uniformity I have come to expect from the forces of Saemal...* He touched his compad. The face of Aron Boras of his bio-team came online.

"Yes, Sir?"

"Upload the mission directives to the bio-ships; I want them to deploy their neural net along the pre-defined coordinates. Have you been monitoring their response times?"

"Yes, Commander. The bounce-back shows no significant lag; in fact, their responses are well above the norm for subspace conversion."

"Very good, just get them deployed. The sooner they're in position, the sooner we can turn our attention to the primary target. I take it their neural net will transfer to our own data-stream?"

"I have uploaded the necessary protocols, Sir; there will be continuous integration of their net tracers into our own AI system."

"Excellent... keep me informed of any variation in the neural parameters."

"Yes, Sir."

So let the living ships do the fishing, while we do the catching...

Chapter 17 - Attack

"In subspace warfare, death arrives across a great distance, the enemy can be very distant or very near, but the end result is always the same: people die, and there's just nothing we can do about that..."
Weapons Master Harlen Drake, C.S. Valeria.

Cadet First Class Sara Tielman watched as the subspace 'shuffle' rippled across her screens. The algorithmic differentials were indicative of solid mass, but the spikes indicated separate objects. *Ships!* She got up from her station in the Engine Room looking for Chief Griel, but he was nowhere to be found. *I'll have to tell the Bridge... but surely they must already know? But what if they don't?* Trying not to panic, she punched the wall pad.

"Bridge, this is Technician Tielman, Engine Room."

The voice of the First Officer came online. "Cain here. What is it, Cadet?"

"Ma'am, my locators have identified a small group of ships on a direct intercept course; at angle D ten axial T minus tangent four one zero one and closing..."

There was a moment of silence as she waited for the Bridge officers to tune their sensor grids to the coordinates she had just given them.

"We have them, Cadet, thank you. Please continue to monitor as per your orders."

"Yes, Ma'am... but there's something else..."

"What is it, Tielman?"

"These ships... they're different from the one that did the fly-by, their signatures are basic pulse-drive with plassteel derivatives in the backwash."

"Very good, Cadet, as you were."

"Yes, Ma'am." She closed the link and when she turned around she noticed the other technicians staring at her from their stations. They all looked scared. She tried to give a confident smile.

"Hey, they're conventional ships, we can deal with them."

Her friend Harvey Drollman looked at the data screen. "So how many are there?"

She turned back to check her screens. "Twenty, that's all, no problem for the *Valeria*." But she knew the others weren't convinced. At that moment the main battle alert blared throughout the ship and she quickly ran along the feeder

344

boards to close down the data-ports. The rest of the team moved quickly to isolate the injection assembly. If the ship was hit by ordnance while traveling at Max 10 she would certainly be crippled, possibly damaged beyond repair, but there might still be time to get to the life rafts. But if the injectors were still feeding the ion drive the ship would simply implode, leaving no survivors at all.

She looked up as Chief Griel entered the Engine Room.

"Status, Cadet?"

"Yes, Chief. I've tracked a group of ships inbound, they're honing in on our ion trail. I have uploaded my stats to the Bridge, and..." She hesitated, listening to the General Quarters alarm.

"And what, Cadet?"

"And, Sir, First Officer Cain is dealing with it, Sir."

"Yes, I gathered that; well, get to your station, the Captain will want your eyes on this one. Keep the link open to the stats team and feed everything you've got through to the command console."

"Yes, Sir, will do."

She sat down before her screens, adjusting the graphical analysis spectrum to include the inbound ships. She could clearly see their vector approach now, a curved peripheral of ships, with the main body moving a thousand klicks behind the forward apex. *Just like an arrow pointing at our heart...* She engaged the echo locators and listened to the multitude of pings bouncing off the sensor grid. It suddenly reminded her of the nights she would sit with friends on the roof of the Fleet Assembly building at Formentora on Galicia. They would haul a portable sensor unit up to the roof and try to send echo pings toward the Fleet Yards orbiting the Tiara Moonbase. They would bet dorm duties on who could identify designated ships' recognition tags; she always won that game. *Those crazy young cadets with all their hopes and dreams of space exploration, of adventures among the high-tech worlds of the Hub... where are they now?* She had found only one other cadet from her senior year who had survived the fall of Galicia, just one out of five hundred. *We have to make those Bargs pay for all those deaths... and yet now the Captain says it's more important to help save one single ship... What about the thousand Coalition ships now heading toward Petra? Must we lose all those comrades as well?* Her thoughts were interrupted by a muffled thud followed by a vibration in the grav-plates resonating from somewhere beyond the Engine Room. She checked the stats screens. *Dispersion bomb!*

The radiation response tubes flickered into indigo and the Chief shouted for someone to initiate the clean-up vents. She punched the damage boards and linked to the Bridge assessment graphs. She quickly saw the impact zone, two decks south of the auxiliary command pod. *They're trying to isolate our command protocols...* She streamed the screen toward a rad count, and was shocked to see it was already rad 25 and climbing rapidly throughout F-Deck. *Those people down there have to get out!*

She heard the Captain on the compad, ordering the Chief to vent plasma – an old trick to divert the bombs away from the pulse drive. If the bombs got a sniff of seepage from the plasma conduits they would detonate short of the ship, *and we might still escape from here in one piece...*

First Officer Cain came over her compad. "Tielman, can you isolate those ships into an evocation?"

She had to think about that for a minute, it was possible; she had already tied their signatures into the spectrographic analysis systems, it was just a matter of plotting each individual course alignment and uploading it into the Vision Chamber.

"Yes, Ma'am, I can do that, but it will take a few minutes."

"All right, as fast as you can, Cadet. And when you've finished send it to Breckin in the Chamber."

"Yes, Ma'am." She turned back to the screens and began to sift out each of the enemy ships from their unified subspace field. *No one hides from Sara Tielman...*

Captain Jos Severs watched the evocation graph supplied by Cadet Tielman. The enemy ships were targeting the aft sensor conduits; each one was a vital link to the nav and stat networks, if they should be compromised the entire tactical interface would go down and they would be left blind. His tacticians were coordinating with the Vision Chamber and uploading the variations into the weapons bay. He linked to his Weapons Master Harlen Drake.

"Drake, do you have the new alignments?"

"Coming through now, Sir, and inputting them directly into the missile assembly, but, Sir, you do know we're down to thirty-five warheads, right?"

Severs looked at his First Officer. Of course they knew. "Yes, Drake, I'm well aware of that, just ensure you don't miss your targets."

"We'll do our best, Sir."

346

Less than thirty seconds later, a stream of missiles sped toward the enemy vessels. Severs had no idea who was in command of the other ships, but whoever it was knew absolutely nothing about fighting a battle in subspace. Their ionic field fluctuations were all over the place, making it relatively easy for his tech teams to zero in on each of their ships.

He turned to Cain. "You know, I think we might make it through this one, Marina."

She looked at the missile trails and waited. *Well, if we don't, I doubt anyone will ever know we made it this far...*

Down in the Engine Room Cadet Tielman had pulled up the weapons stats screen and watched as Drake's team sent out his gifts toward the enemy. *Go fly, my little birds, kill the Bargs!* She zoomed in on the weapons tracers and found them locked to each of the twenty enemy vessels. The data-stream piped from the Bridge showed the enemy trying desperately to change course, but it was too late. As each missile made contact a red dot vanished from the screen, until finally every ship's signature was erased from the system. She noted the backwash from their dispersed ionics; the only real sign that they had ever existed. *Wonderful! Now you're talking, Captain...*

She sat back, suddenly feeling the tension leaving her body. For the first time in days she was relatively happy. They had won a victory. It might not have been a great victory by galactic standards, they had not liberated a world or defeated a great armada of enemy ships, but nevertheless they had won a battle, and right now that felt pretty damn good. Suddenly she noticed the rad indicator flashing in the corner of the main screen.

Oh, by the gods no! The rad counter was flashing at rad 42, and it had infiltrated the Engine Room.

"Chief!"

The Med Bay on B-Deck was a sea of chaos. As Cain walked in she was almost hit by a grav-sled being pushed through the main doors. She immediately noticed a long line of crew members waiting to be seen by the med team. They all looked perfectly normal, showing no signs of illness or injury. But the radiation from a dispersion bomb would creep into human bones unseen; it was as insidious as it was deadly and would slowly poison the body until it reached a point when every major organ would shut down. *Most of these kids are already dead...* She went to look for the Chief Medical Officer Romana Kendra. Passing by a small annex, she noticed the young cadet lying on a med-bed beneath a diagnostic array.

"Cadet Tielman..." She felt a sudden rush of sympathy for the young girl. When the news of the disaster spreading across the lower decks had reached the Bridge she had immediately tapped into the rad system and seen the situation in the Engine Room; it was a tragedy beyond words. She tried not to show her sense of loss and desperation to the young woman. "How are you feeling now?"

"I feel fine, Ma'am. Doctor Kendra says my readings are very low, somewhere in the twenties, I think. Not enough to make me sick, anyway."

But it was only a matter of time, and they both knew it. *What do I say to her?*

"You know, Cadet, if it wasn't for you we wouldn't have made it past those ships. Your intelligence and your dedication have saved the crew... the Captain has asked me to tell you how much your efforts are appreciated, not only by him personally but by everyone on board."

"Thank you, Ma'am, but I was just doing my duty."

She reached out and took Tielman's hand in hers. "Your people on Galicia would be so proud of you right now, Sara, you have struck a blow against our enemy, and you have done it in their name." She squeezed her hand and turned away to look for the doctor; she didn't want to see those tears on that pretty young face.

Kendra was leaning over a diagnostics array, adjusting several screens when Cain found her.

"Doctor..."

Kendra looked up, brushing back her hair. Her eyes looked tired and her face strained in the light of the floater screens.

"Ah, Cain, fine mess we've got down here."

"Do you have a preliminary estimate for me?"

"Well, I can give you a headcount. I have thirty-three crew members with rad counts in the red; not a lot I can do for them but pump them with antigens and keep them as comfortable as possible until their bodies shut down."

Cain looked at the med stats flowing across the main screen. "How long do they have?"

"Two... maybe three days. Best I can offer them is a shot of triaxol to make the end less painful, but that'll be down to individual choice. I'm not about to force death on them if they're not ready."

"And the others? The ones out there in the bay?" *Specifically Sara Tielman...*

"I've graded them according to infiltration. I have six in the violet range, they'll probably have two or three weeks before death occurs. The remaining three are in the indigo range, they're borderline, could take them months to succumb, or just weeks; depends on the individual really."

"Where in all that is Cadet Tielman?"

"Give me a second, I'll check for you..." She input Tielman's ID tag and read her diagnostic stat sheet. "She's indigo; so she could last a few months. But as I say, it's down to the individual; the graduation of poisoning varies from person to person."

Cain stepped up to the glasscite window; she saw Tielman still lying on the bed, her hands trembling as she moved strands of red hair away from her eyes.

"Could she be returned to duty, Doctor?"

"What? You're not serious?"

"I'm perfectly serious." She turned to face the Doctor. "Think about it, that young woman is almost certainly the brightest tech analyst in the Fleet... she's already saved this ship from certain disaster; probably more than once. What kind of reward would it be to tell her she has to spend what little life she has left confined to the Med Bay?"

Kendra walked over to look at the young cadet. There really was no point in keeping her wired to the diagnostics array.

"So has the Engine Room been swept clean?"

"I have crews down there now; the bomb detonated off the port venting tubes. Whoever launched it knew nothing about timers; the thing was primed short of the hull... if it had impacted..."

"Yes, I'd have more than radiation casualties down here." She looked at Cain. "Okay, she can return to duty; I'll go tell her now."

Cain touched her arm. "No, please, let me..."

"Very well, I've got more than enough to do here anyway."

"Thanks, Doc."

She walked back out into the main Medical Bay. She noticed the Captain was busy talking to Chief Griel and several of his analysts. The Chief was the luckiest member of the Engineering team, he had been inside the injector housing closing down the links into the plasma manifold; he'd seen the rad alert on his datapad and stayed safe and secure until the clean-up teams had arrived.

349

But sadly his entire team had been hit by the radiation wave. *How is he going to come to terms with that?* She walked over to stand beside Cadet Tielman.

"Cadet, I've spoken to Doctor Kendra and she says if you're willing you can return to duty."

Tielman seemed shocked at that. "Really? You mean I'm okay to go back to work?"

"Absolutely; you'll need daily shots, so make sure you see the Doctor before you leave. But right now we need you back at your post."

"Well, that's where I want to be, Ma'am. Have they swept the Engine Room yet?"

"In the process now. Give it an hour then check the stats board to make sure."

"Thank you, Ma'am, thank you so much."

"No, Sara, thank you. Rest a while now, I'll tell the Chief you'll be back on duty later."

"Okay… thank you…"

She left the cadet and walked past the Captain and out into the corridor. She leaned back against the wall; her legs felt like they were about to give way. She raised her hands and saw the trembling there; the chill of fear was a living thing, a threat she had to constantly keep under control. She took a slow deep breath and wiped her eyes. *Pull yourself together, Marina, this is war, people die in wars, that's the nature of the beast…* She stood up straight, smoothed down her tunic and brushed her hair away from her eyes. She took the drop-tube back to her quarters and once inside she washed her face in cold water. Without at first being aware of it, she reached into the closet drawer and found the proaxol. As the pump touched her neck she felt the lift instantly. She slammed the drawer closed and looked into the overhead mirror. *I can't keep this up…* She wiped away the water and looked at her datapad, saw the red mass converging upon the spatial-grid, *but considering that we're two days away from over a thousand enemy ships, I might not have to…*

Chapter 18 - The Face of God

Light fell as trinklets of dew-touched gossamer
across the crystalline lakes of the Mere Itraium.

The last whispering winds caressed the stalycine walls of the Palatia Centria
and the waterfalls of Westphal finally froze for all time...

Sandheim breathed its final breath as the frail fronds
of existence withered and waned beneath the cathedral towers of fallen Itraia

And the light of the last lingering savior was left alone in the night,
bound to the blood of the last of the custodia...

Tantalus: Chronicles of Ages.

The *Shaendar* emerged from subspace just under two hundred thousand kilometers beyond the outermost ring of a gas giant. Anthra said the rings would deflect their ionic signature; he hoped that the pulse drive emissions would be swallowed up in the background radiation. Ventra was forced to shut down the long-range proximity sensors, as the system could no longer cope with the hundreds of echo points bouncing off the sensor grid; despite being jury-rigged to the floater vid system it was still sensitive. There were just too many ships out there.

Shari had retreated to her tree and was busy studying the planetary system up ahead. She noted six planets, only two of which could be considered habitable, the fourth one being designated as the Far Star Colony. She zoomed in on that world. Anthra had uploaded several spectrographs of the surrounding space. She noted various orbital habitats – mostly docks by the look of the ion seepage – but she also saw great slabs of an unknown material floating on massive agrav-fields in high orbit. *Spatial platforms the Postings on the Net had called them; something about pieces of Saemal sent out to control his followers... and I thought it was all exaggeration...* She panned the graph until the data-flow narrowed in on the one solitary moon. *There you are, Saemal... I wonder if you know I'm here among your mighty ships...*

She sat back, reached for the pouch and took the artifact out. Once more its touch was so cold she almost dropped it, but as usual it warmed to her touch and once again the wonderful sensations began to course through her body.

But this time there was something different, a change in the surreal serenity of pleasure... this time she was falling through a vortex, a storm of stars and planets swirling about her head. She was lost inside a tornado....crystalline rocks cascading into tremulous revelations... She saw a turbulent sea of fire below, great waves of superheat reaching up to burn her feet. She tried to scream but sound was a muted echo lost to the storm, words were left cluttered inside a harbor of fear, forever lost to the withering winds... She felt the rage as a blade slicing slowly into her chest, a gestalt assimilation of genetic coalescence. Lightning bolts were rippling beneath her skin where a thousand glasscite spiders crawled inexorably toward her brain. She was losing blood inside the rain, little drops of her life sent out to seed the darkness with death and destiny. And now she was losing consciousness, a soft flickering of eyelids, the light of life seeping into silence falling toward the fires below.

Suddenly she came to rest on a beach, and she was no longer afraid because she recognized that it was Riza Beach on Lanoir Island, back on Primus. She could see the multicolored pleasure palisades along the sea front, and beyond the pier she saw the cottage out at Old Sam Point... and she could even hear the stupid neighbors' dog howling away just like he always did when they stayed on the island. She turned and saw her father walking along the beach toward her. He looked the same as he always did on vacation, with his ridiculous yellow shorts and that old fisherman's hat with its single Sargull feather on the side. He was smiling and despite herself she was happy to see him. It had been so long since they'd been together as a family. She ran forward as he opened his arms wide.

"Father! Oh, Father, I thought you were lost to us... they said the Beast had taken you over."

He smiled as they hugged and he brushed his hand down her long dark hair. "Don't be silly, Shari; do I look lost?"

She looked up then, saw the love in his eyes, and noticed the scent of the Lohana afterwash lotion he always liked to use. It was definitely him, and now she was safe; she no longer had to face the monster all by herself. From now on Father would take care of things, she no longer had to fight, she didn't need to... he would take care of everything now.

"Calm yourself, my daughter, all is well now. Come, let's walk a while." And he took her hand and led her back along the beach. She pulled him closer to the ocean, letting the surf flow over her bare feet; it felt warm and comforting. In the skies above, the Sargulls screamed toward the few white clouds perched at the edge of space. She looked up at him.

"Where have you been, Father? I've been in so much trouble, and I needed you..."

He squeezed her hand gently. "I'm sorry, Shari; I was called away on business, but I'm here now, isn't that what counts?"

She leaned into his shoulder, feeling truly happy for the first time in months. "That's all that matters now, Father."

He gestured to a seat at the edge of the paseo. Memories of running along the walkway with her mother came rushing back to her. *I miss you so much, Momma...*

"Shari, I need to talk to you about something that is of some concern to me."

"What's that?"

"Well, for a start, I don't like these new friends of yours. I find it highly unsatisfactory that a daughter of mine should be associating with those Saepid creatures; I mean, my dear child, they are hardly civilized."

"But, Father, they have helped me, they've saved my life, many times over."

"That's as may be, but I fear their motives are far more deceitful and devious than you realize. I doubt that they saved you out of the goodness of their hearts. No, Shari, I believe that you have been tricked... these creatures are malcontent and their agenda questionable. I don't trust them and I want you to remove yourself from their care."

"But, Father, Domini and I..."

"Oh yes, the priest. My dear child, have you any idea how perverse it is to indulge in sexual relations with a priest?"

That shocked her. "Father, please! I don't want to talk about that..." She turned to look out toward the ocean, afraid now that she had disappointed him; that perhaps she had let him down yet again, just like she always did.

"Shari, you know I love you, don't you?"

"Of course I know, Father."

"And you know I would never do anything to hurt you. I only want the best for you, and right now, as your father I know that the best thing you can do

353

is to stay here with me. I don't want you to go back to the Saepids and their priest, and although I am loath to do this, I'm afraid I'm going to have to forbid you to go back to them."

She thought about that for a few minutes. *Perhaps he's right. After all, the Saepids aren't family, and Domini was a priest... and this is my father!* She turned to look at him. "All right, Father, I won't go back."

He placed an arm around her and pulled her close. She felt his warmth against her face and felt so very safe all of a sudden. He was gently stroking her hair and he spoke again: "If you stay with me forever, Shari, we can go back to the cottage to see if your mother has dinner ready."

She pulled away. "But Momma died, Father. She's gone..."

He smiled and took her hands in his. "My dear daughter, here in this place your mother will always be alive... all we have to do is walk back down to the cottage and you can be with her again."

Can it be true? Is it that simple? To be with her once again...

She stood up. "Let's go then." And they walked slowly back along the path toward the cottage at Old Sam Point.

"I told you, I can't wake her!" Domini turned as Anthra arrived next to Shari's tree. Anthra peered into Shari's face, gently opening her eyelids.

"It seems she is in fugue state, Domini, cannot understand. Unless..." He noticed Shari was holding the artifact. "Perhaps she is under influence of artifact."

Domini reached out to touch Shari's hands. "Then we should take it away from her, we have no idea what it's doing, it could be hurting her."

Anthra considered this. "Yes, but we must think on this, friend Domini. Remember when Shari was in great pain from nightmares, the device helped her, cured her of her pain, perhaps now it is doing the same thing."

"Yes, but she's been all right lately, she hasn't had any more headaches or nightmares." He looked at Shari as she moaned softly in her sleep. "I'm just not sure about this, Anthra; we're so close to the Beast now... what if he can hurt her, get inside her head? Just holding that thing might attract the Beast..."

"This is very difficult question, Domini. Not easy to know what to do. If we take artifact away, might it not damage her? We know that the *custodia* are connected to device, they share a deep affinity, if we force them apart..."

"So what do we do? Just leave her like this? We have no idea how long she's going to be in this state." He touched her face and then continued.

"Anthra, the reason we've come this far is to get Shari close to the Beast; how can we do that if she's in some kind of coma?"

"True enough, Domini, but please, I urge caution. We are still some distance from the Colony, we have some time yet before we have to take *Shaendar* deeper into the Beast's lair. Let us give Shari a little time to wake up on her own."

"But, Anthra..."

"Please, Domini, if she does not wake on her own volition soon we will try to force her, but first we give her some time."

Domini didn't like it, but perhaps it made sense to wait. If there was a possibility that she could be hurt by their actions...

"Very well, we'll wait... but not for long."

Anthra smiled. "It is agreed then. But now I must join Ventra, we have enemy ships outbound from the Colony world, must take evasive action."

When they reached the cottage she could smell food... Topa breads! Her favorite... Momma always spread the jam on thick while the bread was still hot... and I'd get jam all down my front... She pushed open the door. The sudden rush of memories was overwhelming. She saw the old couch along the back wall and opposite there was the vid-fire burning away... lucient logs crackling in the night. From beyond the front room came the smell of cooking and she quickly rushed through the dining room toward the kitchen. But when she passed through the door she found the kitchen was empty, her mother was not there. She turned as her father approached.

"Where is she? You said she was here. Father?"

He reached out and took her hands. "She will be here, soon. But for now it is just you and me... come, let's sit a while." He led her to the couch and they sat down together. The glow from the fire sent warm waves of iridescent light across the room, casting trembling rainbows along her legs and arms. Her father seemed lost inside the shadows cast by the overhead tube lights, so she moved closer, listening to the distant sound of carousel music playing from inside the amusement galleries.

Her father took her hands in his. "You know you are very precious to me, Shari."

She smiled. "I know that, Father."

"Do you trust me, Shari?"

She leaned into his chest and replied: "Of course I trust you."

He pulled away slightly and continued: "That's good, because I want to tell you a little story. It's a true story and I think it will help you understand the true meaning of your nature."

"Okay, I've always liked stories..." She snuggled once more into the warmth of his summer shirt as he gently stroked her hair.

"I know; you always did. Now this particular story begins long ago, so long ago that the universe was still very small, nowhere near as big as it is today; a closed flower, if you will, with very few petals, just a scattering of planets among the stars, and fewer still that nurtured life. But there was one world that was already old, aged beyond imagining, it lay far out in the depths of the Great Expanse beyond the Rim. Now upon this world a race of wise men and women lived, they created many wonders, and spread their seeds among the younger worlds. For a very long time they were good, wholesome and kind, and ruled with a benign benevolence; but much later they grew dark in their thoughts and foul in their ways, their deeds became perverted, tainted by the excesses of their power. So a time came when they created a singular creature that would rid them of their evil nature, who would restore balance in the universe and return goodness to their realm. But in their jealousy they refused to release this savior and instead bound him in a sea of ice upon a far distant moon."

"But that's terrible, Father."

"Yes, it is... and the sad thing is, this savior is the very one that your so-called Saepid friends call Beast. Do you see the truth, Shari? There is no Beast; there is only the love of the savior, the one true God Saemal..."

She sat up, pulling away from him. "You think Saemal is a savior?"

"I know he is, and if you let him he will save you. He will give you back your mother, your friends, your old life, Shari; you can have it all back again. You want that, don't you?"

She considered this. *It's so true; I do want Momma back, and my friends, I want to go back to the university again, I want to take math again, I want to run through Foscombe Park, eat picnics beneath the old Dharm Oak. I want it all back again... but....is this right?*

She looked into her father's eyes. "So you trust Saemal, then?"

"Of course. He is our savior, Shari; he has the power to restore everything we have lost. I promise you, my child, if you join him you will be given the keys to the very kingdom of God itself. All you have to do is renounce your quest, acknowledge Saemal as your god and then we can be a real family again. Surely you must want that as much as I do?"

356

"I do… but…" She was seeing deep into his eyes now, beyond the iris, deep inside where the thoughts lived and breathed. She felt the sudden lure of something dark in there, something deep and dangerous. She felt drawn in, her whole body feeling the sensation of pure unbridled pleasure. The power was seductive, a deep trembling inside where something hideous moved and shuffled into semblance. There was a terrible grace to the darkness, a sense of a vengeful rage growing ever stronger. She felt her father's fingers caress her neck, so gentle, so soft. She was being pulled ever closer to his face, but somehow not his face, somehow the eyes were burning with an inner fire she had not noticed before. And the smile seemed twisted now, as the lips moved forward to meet her own. She felt the passion rising from deep inside, a growing thing with a life of its own coursing through her body… she was moaning quietly: "No… no… wrong… can't be true…" But he was forcing her back down onto the couch, pressing up against her, his hands groping beneath her shirt. One hand was reaching down between her legs, forcing into her… "No… please no…" She tried to push him away as he pulled her around and suddenly she was looking directly into the face of Saemal…

"Anthra! Just help me, will you!" Domini was forcing Shari's hands open; he knew she had stopped breathing, but he couldn't get near enough to help her. She was wrapped tight inside the webbing, her face pressed into her hammock.

Anthra pulled open the clasp and released the straps, pulling her free. Domini forced her fingers apart and Anthra quickly took the artifact and returned it to its pouch. He then gave Shari a shot of proaxol, and gently turned her head so that Domini could breathe into her mouth.

Domini leaned close and closed his mouth over her lips. He pulled back. "Come on, Shari… breathe!" He tipped her head back, and forced more air into her lungs.

After a few seconds she began to cough, and she slowly opened her eyes. "Father?"

Domini pulled her around to face him. "No, Shari it's me, and Anthra, see?"

"Anthra? Oh… Dom, I…"

"Don't talk just yet; take a minute to catch your breath."

"I'm okay… I think; I had the strangest dream."

"Just take your time, you're safe now."

357

She felt the beach become her tree, sand turning into leaves drifting inside a secret storm, and the blue skies of Primus beginning to fade into the cold gray hull of the *Shaendar*... She tried to focus her eyes...

"Dom? You're here...?"

He moved closer. "Yes, I'm here, and Anthra. How are you feeling?"

She fell silent for a minute, and then looked up at her friends. "I think I need to tell you something, but it's not easy for me. Where's Ventra?"

Anthra looked down at the command pod. "She is at main console."

Shari moved away from the tree. "We need to talk; all of us."

Domini looked concerned. "Shari, your heart stopped a minute ago, you need to rest."

"Dom, I'm fine now. I have to tell you things before it's too late..." And she drifted down toward where Ventra sat watching her screens.

Ventra looked up and smiled. "Are you back with us, Shari?"

"I am, Ventra... sorry about that."

"No worries. I was concerned; we all were."

Domini and Anthra arrived and she turned to face the three of them.

"Okay, where to begin? Right, like I said, this is not easy for me, it's very... personal, and I'm not really comfortable talking about it, but I have to, you see?"

Anthra glanced at Domini, who spoke up. "We think so... go on."

"Right then... okay. I had another dream, a bad one, and although it was like the other dreams I had, it was also very different. I don't know why I had this dream, or even if the artifact had anything to do with it."

Anthra was fidgeting in the webbing straps as he spoke. "But, Shari, you did not tell us about your other bad dreams."

"I know, I know that, and that's because they were, well... Oh, crell, I just have to say it: they were sexual in nature..."

Domini's mouth opened slightly and Anthra's eyebrows rose.

Domini spoke first: "Sexual? You mean like..."

"I mean sexual, but not in a good way, Dom... Oh, no, I mean rape, I mean assault. They were terrible dreams, Dom, and I couldn't tell you about them, I couldn't tell any of you because you were all... well, you were all involved!"

Anthra spoke softly: "Involved?"

She stared back at him, speaking in a whisper: "You all raped me..."

358

They had no words. What could they say? She first saw acute embarrassment, then fear, and finally confusion. So she continued: "But it wasn't really any of you, your faces formed out of darkness, and I knew instinctively that the darkness was the Beast; he was the one on top of me, not any of you."

That seemed to help them a little.

Domini spoke next. "So in your dreams the Beast was raping you, is that what you're saying?"

"That's right, yes, and all his servants as well."

"I see... and what about just now? You said you had another bad dream, was that the same as the other dreams?"

She didn't answer for a minute, and then she turned to look at him.

"Yes, but this time it was my father who was assaulting me..." She heard Ventra catch her breath. She continued: "But it turned out to be Saemal again, he was the one. But I don't understand any of this, why would I be dreaming about such things?"

Anthra was considering this carefully. There wasn't anything in the ancient texts remotely similar to Shari's experience... it did not fit the pattern. *And yet...* He looked across at Shari.

"Shari, I do believe I see the truth in this matter, and I think I can explain."

"Then please do, because it's driving me crazy. I thought I'd done with the Beast messing with my head."

"I think it is best if you understand something first. We are very close now to the heart of the Beast's power. From this one place he has managed to overrun hundreds of worlds, enslaved millions of people, from the edge of the Rim to the very borders of the Coalition. His power here in this place is supreme. We are facing unprecedented evil on a terrible scale, and although the artifact is a powerful weapon in your hands, I do not believe it can protect you from his thoughts unless you know how to use it correctly. You are *custodia*, yes, but I believe that there is a skill to being such a one, and I fear you have not reached the point where you are fully protected from the influence of the Beast. It has helped you in the past, yes, but that was far distant from here and the Beast's power was at its weakest; right here in this place his mind is everywhere, and he is drawn to the artifact, Shari. He senses its presence in his sanctuary, and he knows you. That is the greatest threat to you, he is inside the

359

mind of your father right now, he is living inside your father's body on Primus, and he will use that to hurt you."

She thought about that for a moment. "All right, I can see that, but what about the rape? What's that all about?"

Ventra spoke up from below. "Shari, my dear, the Beast knows your most basic fear, the fear of any human female, and he is using that fear in the most perverse way with the faces of your friends and even that of your father as the perpetrators of the act. He wants to undermine your faith in those that love and care for you. In this way he hopes to weaken your resolve, hoping to deter you from your chosen pathway. In all truth, Shari, it would serve him greatly if you lost your mind."

Domini came closer, taking her hand in his. "But we're not going to let that happen, Shari, we're going to fight back together, and not in dreams but right here in the real world."

She tried to smile. "It won't be easy, Dom. I thought the artifact was my own personal weapon, something I could use as I pleased, but now... well now I find it's an open doorway into the mind of a monster; how do we fight that?"

He didn't answer right away. But after considering this he replied: "We fight it by taking one step at a time. We take the ship into the heart of the Beast, and then we have the faith to believe that the First Ones knew what they were doing when they created people like you and linked them to the artifact. There is a design involved in all this, Shari, and it's coming down to us from millions of years ago. There is no way that the Beast can have it all his own way, if he has made a doorway into the device then maybe that's how you defeat him..."

"What does that mean?"

"I mean a doorway can go both ways. If the darkness can travel through into your mind, then surely the light that is the *custodia* can travel through the other way."

"Are you saying I have to enter the mind of the Beast?"

They fell silent, with only the hum of the screens and the rush of air from the vents.

"I think so, yes. Perhaps that's what *custodia* do..."

Domini's words seemed to make sense. She thought back to the sense of immense power she felt inside the nightmares, the untold depth of darkness, the seething rage and the terrible desire to kill... *How can my mind defeat that? How can I prevail against a mind that has already been inside my head? A mind already a billion years older than I am?*

360

Anthra took hold of her other hand. "Perhaps, Shari, you will know what to do when you face the Beast… it might be a genetic thing, something you are not aware of yet that will come into play when the time is right…"

"I suppose…"

She suddenly felt the need to be in Domini's arms and she fell into him. He wrapped himself around her, pulling her head into his shoulder. As the tears began to flow she whispered into his ear: "Oh, Dom, I'm so scared…"

He squeezed her tight and whispered back: "I know…"

Chapter 19 - Beyond the Veil

"No one knew what we were heading into; but everyone seemed scared, even Cain was on edge. I heard that a lot of people got irradiated below decks; some were already dead by the time we reached the Colony. I just worked through my Bridge shifts; I didn't want to go near the commons; besides, it made me feel better knowing the Captain was sitting right behind me…"
Nav Tactician Elondra Vanez, C.S. Valeria.

Captain Severs had the latest spatial-grid uploaded onto the main screen. The enemy defense perimeter was a great mass of red covering the top half of the viewer. To the lower right quadrant they had identified some type of fixed defensive platform fused to an airless rock. *Too far away to hurt us now…* He had the nav techs identify the six principal planets in the system, and now the graphs from the Vision Chamber were matching the rendering created by Cadet Tielman in Engineering. They could clearly see the Far Star Colony positioned roughly 500,000 kilometers behind the bulk of the enemy fleet. Several groups of ships were already converging on their position, and to the upper left quadrant they had identified the same Phaelon fleet they'd seen earlier, complete with its vanguard of living ships. *But they're still not moving toward us…*

Lieutenant Keth Lohman called out from the navs station. "Captain, I'm tracking the living ships as moving away from the Phaelon fleet; they're moving parallel to the enemy defense forces directly ahead."

Sure enough, the strange group of ships was moving away from the Phaelon cruisers and heading toward the main fleet positioned in front of the Colony.

Severs turned to his First Officer. "What do you make of that?"

She studied the grid, and saw that the Phaelon ships were now heading in a loop away from the Colony, almost on a course parallel with their own.

"Looks like the Phaelon's are after the same thing we are; those living ships must be joining their main fleet around the Colony."

"Yes… so now we have to make sure we find the Saepid vessel first." He touched his compad. "Breckin?"

Cain's adjutant Tamara Breckin came online. "Here, Sir, still working the sensor grid."

"Have you found anything at all? We can't leave our systems wide open for much longer."

"Sir, I have managed to isolate a rather peculiar ion trail. It might be no more than seepage from that big fleet out there, in fact that's probably what it is, but if I was trying to hide my ship among that lot…"

"You might mask your trail to match the bigger ships' pulse fields. Right, so can you backtrack to a source?"

"I'm running a diagnostics rendering now. Cadet Tielman has joined me here in the Chamber; she's using her spectrographs to refine the ionic traces from the surplus radiation. It isn't easy, though, there's a mass of contra-influential data-feeds coming in, it could take hours, or just minutes, it's hard to tell."

"Well, Lieutenant, we may only have minutes, the enemy could force their way into our systems at any second…"

"I'll do my best, Sir."

"You do that, Lieutenant, and let me know the instant you find that ship."

"Yes, Sir."

Severs turned to Cain. "Well, we can't hang around here any longer; they're already on to us." He faced the main screen. "Navs, I'm inputting a new course alignment, upload it and get us out of here."

"Aye, Sir."

The main screen changed perspective as the *Valeria* hit maximum speed and moved into the shadow of a nearby gas giant, its rings creating cascading fluctuations in the spatial-grid.

Cain looked up from her datapad. She had seen the variable anomalies coming from the group of living ships. The external emitter array was picking up some kind of static from the bio-feedbacks, but she didn't recognize the pattern. She showed it to the Captain.

"Sir, do you see this? Those living ships are emitting some type of neural network; it's on a very low frequency, but the emitters are picking it up as a precisely configured formulation."

Severs instantly knew what that meant. The living ships were attempting to force their way into the ship's automation. He punched the compad. "Breckin, I want the sensor grid shut down now!"

There was a moment's pause before Breckin came online. "Sir, the grid is offline, we're sealed tight."

Severs looked at Cain as he spoke. "Thank the gods."

Breckin was still online. "We found the ship; we know where they are."

Severs let his hand rest over Cain's hand. *Finally, some good news…*

363

Chapter 20 - Fire and Blood

'Deception is an art; its practice requires finesse, its execution the courage of ones convictions.'
Drondar Khan, Prime Leader - Phaelon Elaas Elite Corps.

Torin Grenval watched the deployment of the bio-ships; their neural network was already entering a cascading interface with the data-steam outbound from the Colony world. The *Hagmon* was moving ahead of the main Phaelon fleet, its net tracers reaching out toward the outer planets of the system. He made his decision.

He spoke to his First Tactician Philas Vorin: "Vorin, I'm uploading new orders to the fleet, I want you to liaise with the fleet captains and ensure their prompt compliance."

Vorin turned to look at him. "Sir? New orders? I was not aware we had received new orders?"

"Don't question me, Vorin, you are not privy to the high councils of the Sacred Eleven, you are here simply to obey my orders, is that clear? Or would you prefer to be relieved of your command and spend the remainder of the mission in a detention cell?"

"Forgive me, Commander, I meant no offense. I will, of course, comply." He turned away to scan the new orders as they flowed into his datapad. He raised his eyes just once to look at his commander before he linked to the inter-ship frequency and uploaded to the fleet captains. The fleet was to break off and proceed directly to the Far Star Colony. Once there, they would link up with the Home Fleet and await further orders. But there was no mention of the *Hagmon* or its new destination. *What madness is this?* He had recently begun to notice a marked change in the Fleet Commander. At first he wasn't sure if it was simply the pressure of the mission, but now, with the change in the mission directive, it seemed that his commander had undergone some kind of crisis of faith. *I will have to deal with this...* He tapped the subspace code for a link back to the Sentinel Gate and retrieved the data tag for the priest Valos Armin. He waited until his commander was engrossed in the latest stats screen and then he tapped in his personal alert code; it wasn't much, but the priest would be suspicious. He would, of course, initiate a data-stream scan, and then he would see that the *Hagmon* was branching out on its own, *and he would wonder why... at the very least he might alert the Colony as to his commander's deviation from the mission directive... and then perhaps one day I will be the Lady Mistia's favorite...*

Torin watched his fleet break away and head directly toward the Colony world. He checked the stats screens, noticing a minute fluctuation in the datastream outbound from the Sentinel Gate. He stood up and turned to Vorin.

"I need to check something in Ops. Join me there in five minutes, will you, Vorin."

"Of course, Sir. Is there anything I can help you with?"

"No, I just want to discuss the new orders from the Lady Mistia; I want to explain the details to you before we move forward."

"Very good, Sir."

Once in the drop-tube, Torin tapped his personal security code into his datapad. By the time he had reached Ops he knew Vorin had sent an alert signal to the priest Valos Armin. *That was unfortunate... but alas, matters must now run their course...* He carefully removed a small vial from a compartment set into the back of his datapad. It was a standard neural sanitizer, courtesy of his Elaas friend Drondar Khan. One spray across the desk console would be enough to infect anyone who touched the interface, their mind instantly becoming susceptible to neural vocal manipulation. He sprayed the entire console, and waited for Philas Vorin to arrive.

He didn't have too long to wait. Vorin entered the room looking decidedly suspicious of his commander and his motives. "Sir, you wished to see me?"

"Yes, Vorin, I want to show you something interesting in the latest spatial-grid. Please bring it up on the main viewer for me, will you?"

"At once, Sir." He walked over to the main console and tapped out the uplink to the Bridge, and then he stepped back to wait for the grid to come online. But as he did so he felt his legs give way and suddenly he was down on his knees, his head full of voices screaming to get back up. He was vaguely aware of his commander wiping a cloth across the console screen, and then he was crouched by his side, talking to him in a voice which seemed to echo through dark chambers into his mind.

"Philas, listen to me. Can you hear me, Philas?"

Echoes....trembling..."Yes... I hear you... Sir?" He tried to turn his head, but his neck would not move.

"Philas, I want you to do something for me; do you hear me, Philas?"

"Yes... do something... for you..." *Voices pounding into the abyss...*

365

"Good. Now, Philas, I want you to go to the aft cargo bay... do you understand, Philas? The aft cargo bay."

"Aft cargo bay... yes, Sir..." *Must fight back!*

"Very good, and when you get there you are to enter the main air lock."

"Main air lock... yes..." *Dear gods, no!*

"When you are in the air lock you are to open the outer doors. Do you understand me, Philas?"

"Open the outer doors... yes, Sir..." *Please!*

"Excellent. Now, let's get you up..." The Commander helped him to his feet and gripped his arm to steady him. "Right then, Philas, you know what you must do, right?"

"Yes, Sir, aft cargo... air lock... outer doors..." *No!*

"That's it, perfect. Now get going... and, Philas, do not speak to any other crew member on the way, do you understand?"

"I understand..." *Help me!*

He watched as his First Tactician left the room and headed off to the nearest drop-tube. He sat down behind the conference table, tapped out the ship status reports and linked to the onboard directional finders. The feelers were sending back data at a quantum level, far beyond the ability of the crew to sift out the various fluctuations in the subspace field; the actual equations were being quantified and disseminated by the data-stream to rationalize the data into specific packets of information. If the little Saepid ship was nearby he would find it, and when he did he would finally bring his plan to its tragic and yet inevitable end. He was alerted to a data flash on the ship's internal sensor board; someone had initiated an air lock depressurization in the rear cargo bay. *Good bye, Philas, I am sorry it had to end this way for you, but given the circumstances, you are probably far more fortunate than the rest of us...* He sat up as the compad buzzed.

"Commander, Romon here, we have proximity contact bearing one two zero tangent four zero zero one, and closing."

"I'll be right there."

When he reached the Bridge he noted the spatial-grid above the command console – a group of ships were outbound from the Home Fleet, and from their rear a dozen more breaking away from the Sentinel Gate on an intercept course. *So Vorin's treachery did plant a few seeds...* He took his place in the command chair.

"Evasive maneuvers, Romon. Drop back down to the ringed world, and bring us in close to the debris field." He touched his compad. "Weapons?"

"Weapons Master Feylon here, Commander."

"Feylon, load all primary dispersion tubes, I want a wide arc spread prepared for immediate deployment."

"Aye, Sir, will comply."

He turned to Stats Officer Hain Korda. "Korda, give us full shielding, seal the data-ports and initiate internal battle alert."

"Aye, Sir." The Bridge fell into semi-darkness as the loud howling of the alert echoed throughout the ship.

He linked to the Engine Room. "Soron, have you a link to the incoming vessels?"

Engineering Master Mica Soron came online. "I have them on screen, Sir, and awaiting your orders."

"Good, I'll want full inter-phase drive but only for a partial jump. I'm sending you phase coordinates now; interlink your systems with the nav controls. I want no lag between jump initiation and re-emergence. Have you got that, Soron?"

"Yes, Sir, I'm merging systems now, we can begin a cascading jump sequence on your order."

"Excellent. Stand by…"

Aron Boras of the bio-team came online: "Sir, Boras here, we're monitoring the sensor grid and we do not detect any enemy vessels in the vicinity. The approaching craft are part of our Lord's Home Fleet; Sir, do you copy?"

Torin was fully aware of the delicacy of the situation. His Bridge officers were beginning to become suspicious of his actions; they wanted to ask questions but their duty forbade such an affront. He just needed to keep them compliant a little while longer.

"Yes, Boras, I am aware of the supposed nature of the vessels out there, but you are not privy to the latest intelligence from the Sacred Eleven. The ships now approaching have been corrupted by the Coalition, there is no Intel as to how they managed to do this, but the fact remains that they will destroy us if we do not destroy them first." He paused a moment to let his words sink in, noticing the relief on the faces of the Bridge crew. "Now please continue monitoring their approach, and link your data-feeds to the Weapons Master, he'll need your stats for an accurate target solution."

367

"At once, Sir, and please forgive my breach in protocol."

"You are doing your duty, Boras; I can ask no more than that." He turned to face the main screen.

"Now, Romon, put us inside that debris field."

"Aye, Sir."

The *Hagmon* dropped away from the Colony perimeter and took up position on the dark side of the gas giant.

The spatial-grid showed the approach of the fifty vessels from the Home Fleet, and from the upper left quadrant the twelve ships of the Samrosion priest Armin were moving ever closer. *I'll deal with you later, priest...* He watched as the echo-point locators narrowed the grid focus onto the fifty vessels as they appeared from the sunward side of the planet. He linked to the Weapons Bay. "Feylon..."

"Here, Sir."

"Release your bombs in a concentric arc, prime their feelers to the frequency I'm now uploading... do you have it?"

"I have it, Sir, and downloading into the weapons now." The detonation frequency of the bombs would merge with the ionic recognition codes of the Home Fleet; their AI systems would question the allocation tags displayed by the bombs and instigate an analysis protocol. All that would take seconds, but the delay would be significant; by the time they recognized the bombs for what they truly were, it would be too late.

Feylon came online: "Weapons away..."

He linked to the Engine Room. "Soron, initiate the jump sequence now."

"Aye, Sir."

The ship shimmered out of real-time to emerge two hundred thousand kilometers further out from the debris field.

Torin watched as the stats screens gave impact estimates for the bombs. Suddenly the sensor grid flashed as a compression wave was detected. The spatial-grid showed all fifty vessels to have been destroyed, their ionic signatures fading into the background seepage from the nearby Home Fleet. Torin scanned for the Samrosion ships and found them to be reducing speed. *So, you've seen what I can do to those who interfere with my plans...*

Dainer Romon spoke up from his station. "Sir, the other ships are reducing speed, changing course and heading directly toward the Colony world."

368

Fair enough, let them go tell tales of the failed supplicant Torin Grenval...

"Ignore them, Romon. I want you to take us to these coordinates..." He uploaded a course correction into the nav systems. "Go directly to the echo point I've denoted on the grid... can you see it?"

"Yes, Sir, it's on the leeward side of the planet, just inside the secondary ring system."

"That's right, take us there."

Romon gave no sign that he might be questioning his commander's orders, but the atmosphere on the Bridge had change dramatically. His officers were no longer sure if they could trust him; it was only a matter of time before he was challenged. But of course he didn't need much more time.

Aron Boras came online. "Commander, I've been unable to locate the First Tactician, do you know where he might be?"

"Don't trouble Vorin, Boras, I've sent him to his quarters to rest. He was taken ill earlier. I've closed his com line for now, I'll check in on him myself later."

"Very good, Sir."

And so it begins... He scanned his datapad, and brought up the Saepid recognition tags; if the echo locators were correct then he had finally found the Saepid ship. He suddenly remembered an old song from his days on the Phranti front: *And so we walk into the fire, eyes wide and filled with Phaelon pride, and if we die today, honor us today, remember why we die, duty, duty is why we die...*

Chapter 21 - Speculations

'Not every question has an answer, sometimes mystery must suffice...'
Some Wisdoms - Saepid Othrum Digest.

Captain Severs watched the approach of the Phaelon vessel; it had moved toward the outer ring system and then released a spread of missiles targeting their own ships. *It made no sense...* And now it had jumped to a position parallel to the *Valeria* and was currently bearing down on the Saepid vessel. *Why would they fire on their own ships?*

He turned to his First Officer. "What do you think?"

"Hard to say... a renegade perhaps?"

He leaned forward, peering into the main viewer. "Do religious fanatics go renegade?"

"It seems doubtful... the enemy has shown itself capable of manipulating both men and machines over vast distances of space. Most of our ships were instantly compromised before we found out about the AI thing."

"Yes indeed, the sheer scale of the mind control is quite staggering."

"But it could still be a Phaelon renegade, Sir; they'd certainly know how to avoid the enemy's infiltration systems."

"That's possible, we've managed to do that so far... but could a Phaelon cruiser do the same? Damn thing makes no sense."

"Sir, our mission directive has to take priority; we need to protect the Saepid vessel. Regardless of the Phaelon's intentions, they still pose a definite threat; we can't risk letting them get any closer."

He studied the approach of the Phaelon vessel, it was definitely maneuvering closer to the last known echo point of the Saepid ship.

"Very well, sound ship-wide alert, prepare to engage that ship."

370

Chapter 22 - So Close...

"We are not alone out here; we have friends..."
Fleet Captain Arundel Leonis, Entrymion Home Defense Fleet.

Anthra was agitated; Ventra meanwhile had gone into a long series of clucks and clicks, leaving the com board bouncing echo static across the command deck.

Shari touched her compad.

"Will you two calm down. So there are two ships on an intercept course, do something about it!" She heard Anthra talking quietly to his mate before he came back online.

"Sorry Shari, much activity in this area, we are calculating next move."

"Do you need us down there?"

"No, please strap down tight, but continue to monitor the local grid." He cut into Domini's pad. "Domini... can you link with navigation system please? I may need you to take over while I adjust safety protocols; *Shaendar* might object to rapid changes, cannot risk her shutting down in mid-flight."

"I'm already linked, Anthra, just let me know when you want me to overlap with your system."

"Very good."

Shari studied the current grid. The recognition tags for the nearest vessel had already been identified: *Phaelon! The enemy, then...* But the other ship, the one further away, had still not been matched to the allocation system. *But come a little closer and I will know who you are...* She watched as both ships converged on a parallel course coaxial to their own tangent. *Which means they know exactly where we are...* Anthra had refined the echo-point locators to sift out the mass of ships waiting beyond the gas giant so that the approach of the two vessels was now clearly defined in relation to their own position. She looked across at Domini, saw intense concentration on his face. He was no longer the innocent and naïve priest from Petra; now he was your typical bearded pirate straight out of the holo-vids. *Three months ago I wouldn't have given him the time of day... and now here we are, about to face almost certain death together... Oh, Dom, what have I done to you?*

There was a sudden ping from her screen as the allocation system identified the other ship and logged its recognition tags as belonging to the

371

Coalition. *By the Stars! Could it be true?* She linked to the command pod: "Anthra! That second ship is Coalition, do you see the tags?"

There was a moment's pause from below: "I see them, Shari, yes, but we must be wary as to truth of them. Many Coalition ships now work for Beast, this one might be no different."

"I know that, but the tags are primary, that means they were written with the new Coalition codes we downloaded from the Entrymion flagship *Cassandra*; they can't be compromised, Anthra, why would the Beast bother? He has over a thousand ships out there, what's the point in this ship pretending to be something it's not?"

"I see your logic, Shari, but it makes no difference now, Phaelon vessel will reach us first, we must make our move now."

She sighed. For a moment she had felt the joy of having found friendly faces nearby, people from back home, people not yet corrupted by the poison that had killed her own world, *so close... and now we have to run again, and maybe we'll never get to know who is on that Coalition ship.*

"I understand... let's get going."

Anthra engaged the new jump sequence and the *Shaendar* lurched out of real-time to appear half a million kilometers beyond the gas giant, inbound toward the massive fleet of the God Saemal.

Shari tapped out the latest spatial-grid, and found they were hiding at the edge of an extensive asteroid field skirting the fifth planet in the Colony system. Once again they could detect no habitats, nor were there any signs of orbital platforms. *But the close proximity of the enemy fleet is canceling out our echo-point system, so it's next to impossible to detect a single ship in all of that, which is good for us but we're just as blind if they sneak up on us from behind...*

Chapter 23 - Suspicion

'Loyalty is a two edged sword.'
Dhoron Kor – Phaelon High Council.

Navs Officer Dainer Romon could not understand the Commander's new orders. The echo-point location he had identified was empty; if there had been a ship there then it had already jumped. But one thing was for sure, there was another ship approaching on a direct intercept course, its targeting sensors already locked on the *Hagmon*. He checked the incoming data-stream and identified the recognition tags of the unknown vessel; *it's the Coalition ship we scanned earlier; what is the old pirate up to?*

He turned to address his commander. "Sir, that's the Coalition vessel we tagged earlier, it's locked onto us and will be in optimum firing range in three minutes. Shall I input evasive maneuvers?"

Torin checked his datapad. The holo-lucience rendition was already loaded, all he had to do now was align it with the feeler array and point it in the direction of the Coalition ship... it would be a close thing.

"Yes, Romon, of course, and I'm uploading a new set of echo points. Lock them into the nav systems and coordinate your trajectory with Engineering; our target now lies inside the vector I'm feeding you now." He input the new data-feeds and looked over at the Nav Officer. "You have the feeds?"

"Yes, Sir, aligning now. So we're not going to engage the Coalition vessel?"

Here come the questions... "No, not yet, our primary directive lies ahead of us, not behind us. Engage the new course and move us away from that ship."

"Aye, Sir, will do... engaging now."

As the ship veered away from the gas giant, Torin touched his datapad and sent the rendition back toward the Coalition ship. *If their captain has any sense he will at least listen...*

Chapter 24 - The Message

'Honor in blood has become our creed, how can I renounce that?'
Torin Grenval -Personal Memoirs.

Lieutenant Tamara Breckin was still inside the Vision Chamber working alongside Cadet Sara Tielman. They were currently restructuring the echo-location system to match the external real-time vid-feeds. As each rendition came in they uploaded the stats to the Bridge techs so they could evaluate the data-feeds and construct a constantly updating spatial-grid. It was Cadet Tielman who first noticed the fluctuation in the data-stream being channeled through the spectrographic screens.

"Hey, Tamara, have you seen this?"

Breckin came over to the spectrographic interface and immediately recognized the fluctuation as an exterior holo-lucience being force-fed into the emitter buffers. She stared at Tielman for a few seconds... "We have to tell the Captain."

Tielman pointed to the compad. "Like right now!"

On the Bridge, Captain Severs was busy bringing the ship within firing range of the Phaelon vessel, now rapidly accelerating away from the gas giant.

"Lock your missiles as the feeds come through, Drake."

"Sir, you really want to expend all eight?"

Severs knew that would leave them with nothing but the mines and the exterior lasguns. Not much, considering where they were heading.

"Do it with four, Harlen, and you'll earn yourself a bonus this week."

"I'll give it my best shot, Sir. Weapons out."

The compad buzzed and Cain's adjutant Breckin came online. "Captain, I have an urgent matter that needs your attention in the Vision Chamber."

Severs looked at Cain, then tapped the pad. "Whatever it is it will have to wait, we are about to go into battle."

"But, Sir, that's just it, we have a message from the Phaelon Commander, and you really ought to see it for yourself."

"A message? What kind of message?"

"Sir, the kind that says you really don't want to attack that ship out there."

Severs had no idea what was going on, but he had learnt from experience that his primary officers knew their business. He turned to Cain. "What do you think? A message?"

"It might fit, Sir; I mean that ship did take out its own support vessels."

He linked to the Weapons Bay. "Drake, hold your fire until further notice."

"Sir?"

"We have a situation up here; I'll get back to you."

"Aye, Sir."

Severs stood. "Come on, Cain; let's see what's going on in the Vision Chamber."

When they arrived, Breckin and Tielman were busy with the control interface. Breckin turned to greet the Captain and his First Officer.

"Sir, Ma'am, We have just received a holo-lucience in a tight evocation directed into our emitters by the Phaelon cruiser."

Cain stepped forward looking annoyed. "And you didn't think to keep it out of our systems? Are you not aware of the security protocols, Breckin?"

Breckin lowered her head slightly before answering. "Yes Ma'am, I know about the enemy infiltration techniques, but this rendering used a Coalition sigma matrix; there was no way we could have kept it out. It's like an urgent call for help from a downed starship, the Coalition systems have to respond."

Severs looked at the new data-stream. "So they found a way to get inside our systems, has it corrupted anything yet?"

Cadet Tielman spoke up. "Sir, if I might explain?"

He looked at her, noted how tired she looked, her eyes were yellowing and her long red hair was beginning to develop patches where it was succumbing to the radiation poisoning.

"By all means, Cadet, but make it quick, we're a thousand klicks behind a heavily armed cruiser and I'd like to know if I can open fire on it or not."

"Of course, Sir. Well, you see, the Coalition matrix gives an instant bounce-back response, the filtration systems dump the core message into the secondary emitters and the evocation comes in clean. It's very simple really, barely wideband at all, the vocals are in the median range and the vid-feeds are full of holes, but we've patched the transferal gaps and the message itself comes in very clear if you want to see it now."

"You've already put together a full evocation? Was that wise?"

375

Tielman looked a little guilty. "Sir, we've tied the whole thing to third-level buffer, it'll never reach the autonomous systems."

"Very well, Cadet, let's see what we have."

"Yes, Sir... here we go..."

The Vision Chamber was suddenly filled with a giant figure of a man, his head disappearing through the upper bulkheads. Tielman said: "Oops... sorry." And she carefully adjusted the size ratios. Breckin smiled at her from behind the First Officer.

Now they could see the man, and although the vid came through in stuttering images, they saw that he was clearly an officer, tall, well-proportioned, probably in his early fifties. He had a ridge of green scales running from around his neck and disappearing beneath his uniform, *Phaelon for sure...* Severs recognized the uniform as an old Confederate field tunic, complete with black oversized boots and a wide holster containing a datapad where a gun might have been. The man's voice came through loud and clear, and with only the occasional drop in volume they managed to hear what the man had to say.

"Greetings to you, Captain. I am Torin Grenval, Commander of the Phaelon ship Hagmon, outbound from Phaedra. I must first congratulate you on your excellent navigation skills, for you to have come so far without detection is quite amazing. But as time is friend to neither of us, I will get to the point. It is quite clear that we are both tracking the Saepid vessel, and as such I assume you realize the importance of that ship. There is no point in elaborating the reasons behind that importance, but let it be sufficient to say that the ship might well possess the means to destroy the Power which has invaded your Coalition and murdered so many of your compatriots. Be under no illusion, Captain, that Power can destroy you, and it probably will. But I digress. You know, of course, of the Phaelon integration into the Coalescency, that is to say the Union of Saemal, but what you do not know is that the influence of the Power of Saemal is currently fluctuating; it is now intent upon one singular desire and that is the capture of that Saepid ship. I myself have managed to overcome the mental strictures and neural conditioning imposed by Saemal on all his followers; in effect, Captain, I am once more a free and independent Phaelon. This new-found freedom has allowed me to once more implement plans long established before the arrival of the Coalescency over my world. In essence, Captain, I plan to escort that Saepid vessel directly into the heart of Saemal's Sacred Sanctum."

376

There was a static gap in the data-stream and Breckin quickly adjusted the feeds before the voice continued:

"I can do this because I have the full access codes of the Cortex; I realize you know nothing of this, but if I say that the Cortex is the brain of the God Saemal you might at least understand my meaning. I can open a gap through that fleet out there and allow the Saepids to pass through unharmed. My only problem is I cannot get close enough to their ship to tell them of my plan; each time I approach they jump beyond my com range. So, Captain, it is up to you to contact them, they must surely be aware of your Coalition status by now, and they might allow you inside their com systems. Please tell them of my plan, persuade them to trust me, as I hope that you will trust me. Because, Captain, if you do not, then all will be lost. If we fail in our alliance against this Power then nothing less than the destruction of civilization will follow. How I wish this was a two-way evocation, but I must be wary of my crew, any wider and the bandwidth would be detected, they are already questioning my decisions, my time as commander is limited, Sir; please, tell the Saepids to allow me to pass them by so that I might lead them to their destination."

The figure shimmered and blurred and then winked out of existence.

All four officers took a few moments to consider what they had just heard.

Captain Severs turned to Cain. "Can we contact the Saepid ship yet?"

"We did try, Sir, but they jumped out of range before we could link."

Tielman spoke up. "Sir, Ma'am, we can force a data-burst in their direction. They couldn't help but notice that. It might not come through as syntax but they'd recognize the need to slow down and listen to what we have to say…"

Cain looked at her captain. "Sir, do you really think we can trust this Phaelon?"

"You said it yourself, Cain, it all fits. And let's face it; there is no way those Saepids are going to get past that fleet without help."

"So we trust him, then?"

Severs looked at the message still flowing across the interface. "For now… in the meantime we'll try to reach the Saepids, it's about time we found out what their plans are." He turned to face Tielman and Breckin. "All right, I want you to initiate the data-burst and send it as soon as you're ready; let me know the instant you get a bounce-back response."

377

He exited the Chamber, with Cain following behind, but she turned once to speak to Cadet Tielman. "Well done, Cadet. How are you feeling now?"

"Not too bad, Ma'am. I take my shots, they help with the pain…"

Cain nodded and followed the Captain back to the Bridge.

Chapter 25 - Friends in the Night

'What is trust but faith in the unknown?'
Tantalus: Chronicles of Ages.

Shari noticed the sensor alert flashing across her stats screen. She tapped her compad.

"Anthra, are you getting this?"

"Yes, Shari, it appears to be a Coalition data-burst, emanating from the vessel we spotted earlier."

"What do you make of it?"

"Could be anything, hard to tell."

Sometimes she found talking to Anthra was even more frustrating than trying to get Domini to laugh.

"So could it be a message perhaps?"

"Possible, I suppose…"

"Oh, for crell's sake, Anthra, maybe we should respond?"

"Not sure about that, Shari. Beast lays many tricks around us, could just be a data fluctuation sent out to entice us, get us to drop our shielding."

"Or it could be someone from the Coalition trying to talk to us… Anthra, I really think we should reply."

There was a few moments' silence, and then she decided to unstrap and float down to the command pod; she motioned Domini to follow her.

Anthra was busy scanning the data-burst as she settled behind him.

"Well, Anthra, what do you think?"

"I think it is big risk to open our systems to dubious message tags…"

"Look, Anthra, do you remember those people in the Entrymion fleet? They didn't have to listen to us, but they did, they let down their grids so we could convince them to help us. Now maybe it's our turn to trust someone… just answer them, will you!"

Anthra sighed and exchanged raised eyebrows to his mate below.

"Very well, but not my fault if bad tidings happen…"

Shari glared at him. "Oh, just do it."

It took Anthra over five minutes to align the ship's vid-sensor system with the echo-point location of the Coalition vessel, and another three minutes to send a bounce-back response. Now they sat there waiting, all eyes on the floater Anthra had rigged for visual and vocal evocation of any responding message. It came through almost immediately.

"This is Captain Jos Severs of the Coalition ship *Valeria*, to whom am I speaking?"

Anthra shuffled about in his webbing and Shari pushed him on his carapace.

"Answer him!"

"Oh, very well… hello? This is Saepid Anthra of the trading vessel *Shaendar*, what message do you want to give?"

Shari decided she'd had enough of this, these people were humans, and as such they were practically family.

"Anthra, for crell's sake, let me…" She pulled the floater screen over to her side of the pod and looked into the face of Captain Severs. She was immediately struck by his likeness to her father, the same proud bearing, handsome for his age, which she guessed was around forty, kind of old really, but with very sincere eyes. She liked him already.

"Captain Severs, hi I'm Shari S'Atwa of Primus, I'm pleased to hear from you. I must say we didn't expect to see a Coalition ship all the way out here, how did you manage it?"

The Captain seemed completely taken aback. For several seconds he went off-screen and she could hear him talking to someone beyond the feed. When he came back he still looked confused.

"Forgive me, Miss S'Atwa, but we had no idea there was a human on board the Saepid vessel."

Shari smiled. "Actually, Sir, there are two of us… Domini…"

Domini came next to Shari and smiled at Captain Severs. "Domini Thendosh, of Petra, Sir."

"Please to meet you, Mr. Thendosh. I really am surprised; our Intel suggested that the Saepids alone were inbound toward the enemy base at the Far Star Colony, and that they possessed a viable means to destroy the enemy. Do you have such a weapon in your possession?"

Shari looked across at Anthra, who shrugged, letting her know that it was up to her just how much she told the Coalition Captain.

I can't lie to this man… "It's possible we have such a weapon, Captain, but I can't go into details, it's just too complicated. All I can say is that we have come a long way and gone through so much just to reach this place in the hope that we might be able to kill the Beast in his own den."

The Captain considered this. "I've heard our enemy has been called a Beast, some call him an ancient Power, to the Coalition he is just the enemy."

Shari pulled the floater closer. "Captain, why are you here, in this place? You can't hope to get past that fleet up ahead…"

The Captain smiled. "We were ordered to find you and offer our assistance."

That made Shari smile back. "Well, thank you for that, but I doubt there's anything you can do for us now. We have a plan of sorts, and it might not succeed, but there's no need for you to sacrifice your ship trying to help us. We'll be all right, Captain; we haven't come this far just to fall before the wall."

"I admire your courage, Shari S'Atwa, but even though we can't protect you, I can offer you some assistance, although you might not like its source."

Shari leaned toward the screen. "Meaning?"

"I have been contacted by the Phaelon cruiser now shadowing your course; have you tracked it yet?"

Shari looked at Anthra, who nodded.

"Yes, we have it on our screens; it's just sitting out there. You say they contacted you?"

"Yes, we were as surprised as you are. Apparently the commander of that ship has managed to free himself from the enemy's influence and has been scheming to undermine his plans ever since. He proposes that you allow him to pass you by so that he can lead you safely through the enemy fleet; he assures me that he has the necessary access codes to get you all the way to the Colony world itself."

Shari spoke softly to the Captain. "Could you give us a minute please, Captain…" She turned to look at the others. "So what do you think? Dare we let the Phaelon get that close?"

Anthra spoke first: "Very risky to do that, no way we can trust a Phaelon, could not trust them before the Beast, why should we trust them now?"

Shari answered. "Because if he's telling the truth he can get us past that fleet out there. You know we can't do that by ourselves; isn't it worth the risk?" She turned to Domini. "Dom?"

"Well, I can see the risk. The Beast might well play tricks like this, but this Captain Severs seems convinced, perhaps we should trust his judgment in the matter…"

Ventra spoke from below. "I think we are walking along the edge of the abyss, we are beyond the veil of civilization now, and all hope lies in the trust of

381

this captain from Coalition. I say we agree to let the Phaelon lead the way. If it is treachery he plans it will make little difference to us; we are one ship among hundreds, our path is already shrouded in darkness."

Shari spoke: "So we all agree, then?" They nodded and she turned back to the floater screen.

"All right, Captain, we're going to stay where we are and let the Phaelon ship pass by. If he doesn't blow us up as he passes we'll follow him in toward the Colony. What will you do next?"

The Captain looked off-screen again and turned back to the viewer.

"We have exhausted most of our weaponry, so it would be suicidal to venture any closer to the Colony world, but we can still patrol this sector and harass any single ships that try to follow you, and we'll also do our best to wait here for your return."

Shari smiled at that. *Wait for our return... Oh, Captain, if only that were possible...*

"Thank you for that, Captain, it would be nice to see you again afterward."

"May the gods go with you, Shari S'Atwa, and your friends."

The screen flickered to a close and once more she was left with a terrible sense of loss. *How many goodbyes must we go through?*

"I'll be in my tree..." She dropped the floater and pushed off back toward her corner.

She found a frequency alert flashing on her datapad. *What the crell?* She brought it around and looked at the screen. The message was in basic syntax and had the recognition tags of the *Valeria.* She touched the reader and the words downloaded onto the screen.

'Forgive me for this, but I couldn't resist contacting you. I'm breaking every possible security protocol right now, but I'm beyond caring. My name is Sara Tielman, I'm a tech analyst aboard the Valeria. I tagged this message as a loop into the vid-feed you just received from my Captain. I could get decommissioned for this, but hey, I'm dying so I don't really care. I got soaked by a radiation wave from a dispersion bomb a while back, so my time is kind of limited. I just wanted you to know how grateful I am that you are risking your lives to save the Coalition. I lost most of my family when Galicia fell, and all my friends from fleet school, and I know you lost people too on Primus, so maybe we can at least share our pain, even if I can't share the battle you have to face. I don't know you, Shari, but I can see your face right now in the vid-feed and I

know that if things had been different you and I might have been friends...let's just say we are friends who have yet to meet... Oh, I have to sign off soon, Breckin is on her way down. But one last thing, if I'm not around when you come back here, when it's all over, will you please remember me? I am Sara Tielman and I am nineteen years of age, I was born in the village of Shimara near the city of Formentora on Galicia. I have a surviving brother called Daren; I think he's at the Fleet Yards near Tantra, I hope he's okay... anyway, Shari, I have never believed in the Pantheon of Gods myself, my family are Galician monotheists... at least they were... but I do believe in people, and right now I believe in you... I know you will win, Shari, I just know it, God bless you... Sara...'

Shari let the tears fall away, to drift among the leaves as they passed by the air vents. *This is all so unfair...* But then she realized it wasn't really sadness that she was feeling, it was in fact anger. She was angrier now than she had ever been since leaving Primus. *If that pile of dross wants to fight me then let him try, let him send everything he's got against me. I am the custodia, and I was made by the gods as well, and by the hands of those gods I will rid the universe of that stench for all time...* She closed her datapad and sat back in her webbing. From below, she heard the ping pinging of the echo locators as the Phaelon cruiser drew ever closer.

Chapter 26 - Loyal Treachery

"My loyalty always depends on where I am and who I am talking to..."
Drondar Khan - Prime Leader Elaas Elite Corps.

Dainer Romon was torn. Should he question the Commander? But the risks involved were many; you just didn't question the Adjutant General, he had the ear of the Lady Mistia, after all. *But this madness about letting the Coalition filth escape... And now this new ship on the grid, they were allowing this one to escape as well!*

It makes no sense... and sending the fleet off to the Colony, why would the Commander do that? I have to speak to Vorin; ill or not, I have to go see him... He stood up from his station on the Bridge, turned to the Commander. "Sir, if I might attend to my private needs for a few minutes?"

Commander Grenval looked across at his nav tactician. "Very well, but hurry back, I have a feeling things are about to get very busy around here"

"Of course, Sir. I won't be long."

He made his way to the drop-tube and dropped down to E-Deck. Once there he quickly made his way to the quarters of the ship's First Tactician Philas Vorin. He touched the com panel.

"Vorin? Vorin, it's Romon here. I need to talk to you... Vorin?"

After several minutes he began to worry that Vorin was just too sick to answer, so he linked his datapad to the security database and skimmed for Vorin's door code. When it flashed on the screen he overrode the protocols and watched the door slide open. Walking in, he found the place deserted. He quickly checked the bunk and found no sign that Vorin had even slept there. *What is going on?* He tried to access Vorin's personal log but found it sealed by a multi-rhythmic code sequence, impossible to break. He was about to leave when the door opened and his commander walked in.

"Sir? I was just trying to see if Vorin was well, but as you can see he's not here..."

"I know that, Dainer, and I'm sorry you had to find that out. I could have used you a while longer on the Bridge, but fortune does not favor the over-curious. I really am sorry about this, Dainer..." He pulled out a small silver tube and pointed it at Romon's chest. The ion beam impacted instantly and Dainer Romon was dead before he hit the floor. *This is developing into a habit, Torin, but I believe the need outweighs the guilt...* He dragged Romon's body over to

384

the bunk and laid him down on top, covering him carefully with a mesh sheet. *Forgive me, my friend…* He then made his way back to the Bridge.

He called to Hain Korda at Navs. "Status, Korda?"

"Sir, as per your orders we are now passing by the Saepid vessel. Our heading is two niner one seven to the apogee, with our variant speed in line with the inter-phase. We have a directional approach to the Colony and our stats systems are all in the green."

"Excellent… Coms, are we still being hailed?" They had been receiving multi-layered queries for immediate response from almost the entire Home Fleet. And from somewhere far behind them, across many hundreds of light years of space, someone on Primus was screaming rage into the data-stream linked to the Colony. *They all want to know what I'm up to… Well, no matter, let them guess. This is the closest I've ever been to revenge, and I'm not about to give up on it now…*

Coms Technician Enon Lange answered his commander. "Very much, Sir, I'm trying to filter out something we can actually read, but there are hundreds of open channels out there, and they're all directed at us."

"Don't bother to filter, Lange; chances are they're all corrupted anyway. I fear the danger to our Lord Saemal may be far greater than we anticipated. The Lady Mistia wants us to ignore the petitions from the Home Fleet; we are to proceed with our AI systems offline from this point on."

Aron Boras had left his place in the Bio-definition Lab and taken up his station on the Bridge; he had been concerned over the nature of the new orders from Phaedra, but now to hear that they were to operate without the autonomous systems…

"Sir, is that wise? Surely it can only place us in greater peril to fly without the tracer nets? Won't we be leaving ourselves open to a sneak attack?"

"I understand your fears, Boras, but we must strike a balance here… what is the greater risk? To fly half-blind with our nets down? Or to open ourselves up for auto infiltration by corrupt systems? As your commander, it is my job to get us to the Colony world, and if that means risking a physical attack, then so be it." He turned to his compad. "Weapons?"

"Feylon here, Sir?"

"Feylon, I want you to arm the feeler drones, we're going to use them as a shield. Push them out a thousand klicks forward; do not deploy to our rear, is that clear?"

"Yes, Sir, very clear. Will comply."

Torin turned to face the main screen. The spatial-grid showed a mass of red covering the entire upper half of the screen. *Now we'll see if Mistia's access codes still work...* He still didn't know why she had given him the codes; she must have known she was risking exposure and denouncement to the other Sacred Members. He could easily have revealed her as a traitor to the God Saemal and gained significantly from such a move, and yet somehow she had known the truth about him, she had trusted in her suspicions about the true nature of his mind and acted upon them. *What did she see in me?* She certainly had no idea how he had managed to force his way out of the neural indoctrination, but she had decided to take advantage of it nevertheless.

He couldn't be sure of her true motives, she was still very much obsessed with her own power, evidenced by her grandiose construction schemes across the face of Phaedra, but nevertheless, this level of treachery was really quite astounding. *Perhaps she believes that with Saemal out of the way she can forge her own empire among the stars...* Whatever her reasons were, she had quite literally given him the keys to the kingdom and, one way or another, he intended to use them.

He took hold of his datapad, skimmed for the harmonic resonance seal, and tapped in his personal code. Instantly the symbols of Saemal flowed across the screen, and for a moment he felt the chill of fear run along his scales. He was looking at quantum density imbedded syntax, bio-coded into a neural synaptic pulse, resonating at a precisely aligned recognition point. All he had to do now was upload it into the feeler drones while canceling their arming sequence. *It won't be bombs my drones will drop, but a code recognized all the way into the very heart of the Cortex...*

Chapter 27 - Trust

'Safety is a lie, everything we do is a risk...'
Corel Luwain - Philosopher, planet Samros.

Shari held her breath as the huge Phaelon cruiser passed by, its ion wake sending waves of particulate debris in their direction. Domini had come to settle by her side, and together they watched the spatial-grid. The Saepids had shut down most op systems as a precaution, but it wouldn't really help if the cruiser opened up on them.

The echo locators were pinging in a gradual cascade as the great ship edged closer... *ping... ping... ping... ping... ping... ping... ping...*

Shari whispered: "Ventra!"

Ventra cut the audio recognition and the deck fell silent.

Domini held Shari's hand tightly as the big ship finally moved ahead of them, cruising toward the waiting fleet, its aft vents sending ionic backwash across the *Shaendar*'s floater screens.

"Well, would you believe it, Dom? Captain Severs' trust in the Phaelon was the right thing to do after all..." She smiled as Anthra spoke up from his screens.

"Yes well, we were lucky, Shari; might not have turned out so good, but it is good tidings nevertheless..."

"Fair enough, Anthra. So do we follow them or what?"

There was the inevitable pause before he replied. "It seems we have no choice."

The deck lights came back on and the pulse drive engaged. They felt the customary lift as the ion field pushed them forward, less than a thousand klicks behind the Phaelon cruiser.

Shari looked at the grid and then smiled at Domini. "Well, I never thought we'd end up sneaking in behind an enemy cruiser."

"No, I must admit this is certainly the strangest of quests."

She leaned into his arms. "You know what else is strange?"

"What's that?"

"It's strange that you and I haven't made another trip back to the cargo hold for a while..."

"That's not true, we were there just the other... Oh, I see what you mean; you mean another *special* trip back to the cargo bay?"

387

"You do catch on quick, my love."

"But I thought… well you seemed to sort of…"

"Spit it out, Dom, for crell's sake."

"Well, that's just it, you see…"

"That's just what?"

"You've been out of sorts lately… kind of distant; I thought you'd decided that what happened between us was a one-off thing; I mean you've been going through so much recently with the bad dreams and the headaches, and the bad moods…"

"Bad moods? What bad moods?"

He smiled. "It doesn't matter now."

She placed a finger on his lips. "Dom, please, just listen to me before I totally lose this feeling. I never went off you; I just got caught up in the fear and the threat of impending death. But, Dom, I'm not scared any more, I'm in a better place in here…" She touched her forehead. "And right now, Dom, right now I need to feel like a woman again, possibly for the last time… you can help me do that, can't you?"

He wrapped his arms around her and pulled her close. "Of course I can."

They pushed off together and floated back toward the rear hatch. From below, they could hear a series of rapid clucks and clicks, which was lost as the hatch closed behind them.

Anthra glanced at Ventra as he spoke.

"Fine time they pick to do that…"

Chapter 28 - Endgame

'I always wanted my final words to be profound, memorable even, but now such words fail me; I never expected that...'
Torin Grenval - Personal Memoirs. (Subspace Databurst Retrieval).

Torin noted a palpable air of tension among the Bridge crew. They were nervous, perhaps even scared, but above all else they were beginning to question the validity of his new directives. It no longer mattered, of course; he was irrevocably committed to his plan. He'd already killed two of the finest officers he had ever known, and now if the crew actually rebelled against him he would simply inject himself with phenolite and flood the Bridge with duterium gas. But he hoped it wouldn't come to that. They were now halfway through the massive Home Fleet, the big battle wagons were slowly moving aside, their AI systems now completely interlaced with the algorithms of the Cortex base code. *How their crews must be wondering who it is that is controlling their automation...* He was hoping that they would blindly accept it as a divine intervention from their God... *mysterious ways and all that... just as long as they don't target us...* He checked the stats screens, the fleet showed no sign of aggression, and the spatial-grid showed no movement out of the Colony. *They're keeping their gun ports closed, and no sign of adverse feelers...* There were, however, over a thousand tracer systems locked directly onto them; they were definitely being watched. *We might be tip-toeing in through the front door, but we have certainly been noticed.* He scanned for the ship which followed quietly in their shadow. The Saepid vessel was well inside their ion trail, completely hidden from the vast array of sensors now locked onto the *Hagmon. Keep your heads down, little Saepids, we are about to enter the mouth of damnation...*

A response code flashed on his datapad and he scanned for the recognition tag. It was the vid infiltration of the link made by the Coalition Captain to the Saepid vessel. He had taken the liberty of tapping into the Coalition feed, more out of curiosity than any tactical need; he simply needed to see the girl from Primus. The singular creature who had somehow managed to cause such desperate alarm among the mighty forces of Saemal. He let the message stream flow until the girl's face appeared on the screen.

He was taken aback by her beauty. Beyond the occasional Aluvian slave, he had never been one to associate much with humans; the Phaelon race had always felt them to be weak, lacking the honor of a warrior and a hunter. Human females were exciting enough in the bedchamber but like their male counterparts they never lasted more than a few hours. But this particular female, now she was truly a sight to behold. Her long dark hair framed a face which seemed to shine with an inner light, and when she spoke her facial expressions seemed to exude grace and intelligence. *This one certainly looks the part, but what possible power can she possess?* Mistia had spoken of the First Ones, of a weapon forged in the mines of the lost world of Sandheim. She believed the Saepids had found such a weapon and the girl was somehow linked to its power. *What power can possibly be controlled by one so young?* He checked the nav screens.

"Korda, how much longer before we reach the Colony world?"

"Well, Sir, considering that we are having to having to wait for those ships to move out of our way, it might take an hour to clear the fleet, another two to reach the Colony itself. I still don't understand why they're letting us through if they are corrupted."

"Don't question our good fortune, Korda; those ships are obviously so corrupted that they've lost all cohesion. Just keep us on course and in alignment with the drone deployment."

"Aye, Sir."

He was about to link to the stats system when Aron Boras called his attention to the spatial-grid. "Sir, we have a proximity alert on the bio-feeds."

The bio-ships! "Can you identify?"

Boras leaned over his screens before replying. "Yes, Sir, it's the bio-ships, they're inbound on a direct intercept course… and, Sir?"

"Yes, Boras?"

"They've locked weapons…"

Everyone on the Bridge knew what that meant. If the bio-ships had locked onto them it was only a matter of time before they opened fire. It was remotely possible they would use the weapons lock simply to run an in-depth scan, using their feeler systems to infiltrate the *Hagmon*'s core data-feeds, but with the AI now offline, they might simply just open up with their forward batteries.

Torin shouted to the nav console. "Korda, how far until we clear the fleet?"

Korda checked his screens. "If we maintain maximum speed we'll be through in less than thirty minutes, an hour after that we'll achieve orbital insertion above the Colony world."

"Lange, are you still tracking the Saepid vessel?"

390

"Yes, Sir, they're running low behind our aft vents and holding steady at matching speed."

"All right, Korda, I want you to adjust our heading to take us above the Saepid vessel; do it as a graduated inversion ascent, keep our backwash over their vessel." He punched the compad. "Feylon!"

"Weapons here, Sir."

"Load everything you've got into the aft tubes; I want a full spread, maximum potential, prime them to the bio-signatures Boras will upload to you..." He gestured to Boras who immediately began to transfer his data-feeds to the Weapons Bay.

"Are you getting the feeds?"

"Aye, Sir, uploaded to the weapons array now... and, Sir, the drones?"

"Cut them loose as soon as you release the missiles, we won't be needing them any longer." *They got us through the front door anyway...*

"Very good, Sir..."

Torin looked around him. The Bridge crew were beginning to look highly suspicious of his motives; several of them were taking independent scans of the bio-ships and the Saepid vessel following in their wake. *Let them ask their questions, the time has come to take the final step; just a few minutes more and my work will be done...*

Korda spoke up from his screens. "Sir, the bio-ships are closing fast, and we're getting urgent response requests from them now."

"Ignore them. Get us higher; I want to come down behind the Saepid ship. Increase the tangent, Korda; and, Boras, do not acknowledge those feelers."

"No, Sir, I won't, even though it goes against fleet protocols not to do so."

He ignored the comment and opened his datapad. He needed to input a special message and link it to an evocation; it was important the girl knew the truth, knew something of the sacrifice they were making. *She must at least know my name...*

By the time he had finished the message the stats screen showed the *Hagmon* was now coming down behind the Saepid vessel. The small ship was moving forward, gradually turning away from the last of the defense forces surrounding the Colony.

Run now, my friends. Make haste, for death or destiny awaits... He tapped into his base code index, scanned for the pulse drive sublimation

391

directives. The core of an inter-phase drive consisted of a quantum density particle emitter; this provides a stable containment vessel for the ionic pulse. If the pulse should breach the emitter it would automatically override the containment safety protocols and the ship would detonate with the force of a thousand teddra-enhanced grav-field bombs. The resulting shock wave would almost certainly destroy the approaching bio-ships. He scanned for the Saepid vessel, now heading along a coaxial orbit around the Far Star Colony. *I just hope you are far enough away, little Saepids...*

Aron Boras spoke up from his station: "Sir, the bio-ships are opening fire..."

Torin looked up at the local grid. Their own missiles were away, heading toward the first of the bio-ships. *They might buy us a few seconds...*

Boras was shouting now. "Sir! We have to take evasive action now... Sir!"

The Bridge crew were frantically adjusting their control systems as the proximity alerts sounded across their boards. Coms Tech Lange turned to look into his commander's face. "Sir... what do we do?"

Torin Grenval initiated the containment breach with a touch of his finger. He had three seconds to say: "I am sorry, Lange..."

The Phaelon heavy cruiser rippled momentarily as if hit by an invisible tide of water, and then the outer plates buckled as the ship tore itself apart. The detonation wave streamed out in every direction, cresting the first of the bio-ships five seconds later. Each ship was instantly vaporized as the wave slowly dissipated toward the periphery of the Home Fleet.

392

Chapter 29 - Sacrifice and Sanctity

I hold the world in my hands,
I hold the sky in my hands,
I hold the trees in my hands,
I hold the rivers and the oceans in my hands…

I hold the wonder and the fear in my hands,
I hold the music and the dying embers of glory in my hands
I hold an impossible dream in my hands,
I hold a thousand rainbows in my hands…

I hold a million tears in my hands,
I hold light and love and visions in my hands…
I hold the infinite horizon in my hands…
I hold the Universe in my hands…
But I let my own true love slip silently into the grave…

Song of the custodia, Tantalus: Chronicles of Ages.

Anthra could not explain it, neither could Ventra, but the stats were clear and precise… the Phaelon vessel had sacrificed itself to protect them from the attacking ships.

Shari studied the main viewer. "I can't believe they just did that."

"Certainly most unlike a Phaelon to do that," Anthra said.

Shari considered the situation. "They really must have known about the artifact."

Anthra turned to her. "That is possible, Shari, but more likely the Phaelon commander saw how the Beast was losing cohesion and took advantage. He had faith in you, Shari; it is evident he was willing to sacrifice his crew and his ship to protect us."

Ventra spoke from the command console. "I have a message burst sent from the Phaelon vessel seconds before it was destroyed; it uses the Coalition sigma recognition codes."

"So let's hear it… put it through." Shari said.

Ventra hesitated, looking up at Anthra.

393

Shari looked down on the Saepids. "Well, they're hardly going to hurt us with their last dying breath, are they? Just put it through, Ventra."

"Very well. Linking to the main viewer now."

The image of a man appeared on the screen, but not quite human, Shari noted; he had green scales running around his neck and down his arms. But he looked mostly human, rather distinguished, with an obvious air of authority about him. His voice came through with an echo until Ventra adjusted the data-feeds.

"Greetings to you aboard the Saepid vessel, and most especially to you, Shari S'Atwa. I am Torin Grenval, late of the Phaelon Assemblage; I have very little time, so I will be brief. I have decided to ensure that you reach your final destination, but beyond that I can do no more. I do this in the hope that you might possess the means to destroy the Power who dwells at the Colony. I want my world set free, Shari S'Atwa, and I place its future in your hands. I am not Coalition, I have no desire to help Coalition forces, but I help you now because I know that if you fail, the universe will fall into darkness, and the light of freedom will be forever extinguished. I cannot stop the ships that will now pursue you, but I have given you a chance, which is more than you had before. I bid you farewell. Safe journey to you all."

The message flickered into gray and vanished from the screen.

Domini spoke from next to Shari. "So that was the man who saved us."

Shari looked at the screen. "Yes, and now we have to make his sacrifice worthwhile." She thought about that for a minute. "Now we have to make the sacrifice of millions worthwhile…"

Anthra leaned over the console. "Shall I take us closer to the Colony, Shari?"

She studied the latest spatial-grid. "Are any of those ships targeting us?"

Anthra looked grim. "There are hundreds of ships out there, Shari, and they are all targeting us, and that includes two spatial platforms whose purpose I cannot define at this distance. Bad tidings indeed…"

Domini took Shari's hand. "What do you want to do?"

She smiled at him. "Go to war, of course." She turned back to the Saepids. "Alter course, Ventra, we're not going to the Colony itself."

"We're not?" All three exclaimed.

"No, lock your nav scans on that moon out there, Ventra." She spoke to Anthra. "Can you plot a direct course to get us there as fast as possible?"

394

He touched a few screens before replying. "I can get us there, but we will arrive over the moon less than fifty minutes before those ships arrive, so whatever you are supposed to do down there, you had best do it quick, Shari."

She looked at the grid, watched as the moon came into focus, the directional tracers lining up precise coordinates.

"No pressure then… thanks, Anthra."

The *Shaendar* shot forward as the pulse drive engaged. Ventra cut the feed to the audio proximity sensors as the noise threatened to overload their nerves. Anthra tied the nav stats into the spatial-grid and they watched as the moon grew ever larger in the main viewer. Shari decided it was time for a little experiment. She touched Domini on his shoulder.

"Dom, I need some time on my own, don't disturb me unless you really need to."

He looked concerned. "The artifact?"

"I have to know if it's safe to use, I can't keep being afraid that it's going to allow the monster inside my head. If I really am this great divine creation of the First Ones then it's time I learned how to be the thing they made me to be… you see?"

"I think so… but can I offer some advice?"

"Always…" She squeezed his hand.

"When you hold that thing, please try to hold onto who you are, focus on being Shari, not something else. Anthra says you are the *custodia*, but to me you are Shari, the girl I fell in love with, so hold onto that, it might just help to keep the Beast out."

She pulled him close and kissed him gently on his cheek. "Your love, hey? That should carry me a long way." She pushed off and floated back up to her tree.

Domini turned around to see Anthra staring up at Shari as she settled inside her hammock.

"Will she make it through this, Anthra?"

"Not easy to say, Domini. Destiny is a tricky concept. Shari may well struggle to defeat the Beast, but ancient hands are guiding her now, we have to have faith in that. Shari was born for this moment, Domini; we must trust that she will know what to do when the time comes to face the Beast."

"I know, and that's what scares me the most…"

395

Chapter 30 - Interlude at Petra

"The beginning of any battle is a tricky thing, neither side knows the abilities of the other, so they play games with tactics and theory. But despite the initial hesitation, it doesn't take long for people to start to die; after that, you better pray the bloodlust kicks in…"
Master Sergeant Gant Rohan, Coalition Combat Militia, Petra Front.

The C.S. *Althenia* streamed into real-time half a million kilometers beyond the remains of the orbital docks above the planet Petra. Instantly, every proximity alarm on the ship began to sound. The data techs silenced the feeds and the nav team brought the ship around to face the enemy fleet as it moved into a sub-orbital position below the newly arrived Coalition Fleet of Liberation.

Admiral Ewan Dax watched the fleet deployment stats flash across the main viewer; the current spatial-grid showed the rest of his fleet had successfully emerged between the two main enemy fleets, effectively dividing them between the docks and the planet below.

"Weapons, deploy your missiles, full concentric spread delta five seven two one on an elliptic tangent to the fleet."

"Aye, Sir, missiles away."

"Ensign, get me an update on the CES."

Ensign Riel Tarrence tapped into the Cognitive Evocation System to bring up the image now being generated down in the Vision Chamber. The screen filled with a graphical holo-display of the enemy fleet, and he noted the absence of long-range cruisers and inter-ship fighters. *Could they really be this unprepared for our arrival?* The image was showing only large battle wagons, mostly troop converts, lacking any real firepower. There was a large spatial platform to the upper right quadrant, and stats analysis showed it was sending out waves of infiltration feelers in their direction.

Dax touched his compad. "Landerson, are you at the Chamber yet?"

First Lieutenant Rohl Landerson came online. "Just arriving now, Sir."

"Can you get me something on that platform out there?"

"I've got Lieutenant Dromain on it now, Sir; she's linking the CES to the spectrographic interface, we should have an analysis any moment now."

"Good. Feed it to the Bridge the instant you have something."

"Aye, Sir."

Weapons Master Wain Sandors came online. "Admiral, we have positive contacts on all targets, awaiting your orders, Sir."

"Load the drones, Sandors; I want them primed for particle detonation as soon as we get near that platform."

"Sir, if I might suggest we don't get too close to that thing. When the drones make contact the compression wave could hurt us."

"Noted, Sandors."

Landerson came back online. "Admiral, I'm sending you the CES feeds now. You might notice something strange about that platform…"

Dax looked up as the CES evocation appeared above the command console. The platform was resting on a massive ionic pulse, stabilized by miles of grav-plates fused to its outer hull; but the data-feeds coming in suggested that the platform defied the recognition parameters of the CES system. The whole thing seemed to be emanating neural waves in a precise configuration. It reminded Dax of the graphs he had once seen of human thought patterns. *Is that thing thinking?* The proximity alert indicated they were within weapons range. Dax had the stats team scan for enemy fighters. *Nothing… just the big ships floating around out there without protection…*

He linked to the Vision Chamber. "Rohl, are you noticing something about the enemy deployment?"

"Yes, Sir, they have no viable warships, and certainly no inter-ship fighters. We've picked up a long-range cruiser in sub-orbital, but as far as we can tell, of the seven hundred enemy ships in orbit, less than ten percent can give us any kind of trouble."

This is incredible…

Landerson continued: "Admiral, it looks like our Intel was correct; they're pulling back their main forces to the Rim…"

"Then we must take advantage of that, Rohl." He switched to the Weapons Bay. "Weapons Master, deploy your drones."

"Aye, Sir, drones away."

"Con, engage lateral drive and take us back to the planet, maximum speed."

"Aye, Sir, max speed engaged."

Ensign Tarrence closed his eyes as the drones hit their target; the flash wave hit the screens as a cascading static charge, throwing the Bridge into darkness.

"Initiate back-up systems."

"Aye, Sir, back-ups online."

"Stats, give me ship's integrity."

"Integrity one hundred percent, Sir. We have raised rad levels, but nothing above the red line."

"Excellent, give me the fleet captains, primary line."

"Primary online, Sir."

"Fleet, this is Admiral Dax aboard the flagship. Lock on your targets and take out those big ships; send your feeds via CES to my command console. Good luck, comrades."

He closed the link and tapped for a real-time image of Petra.

And now all we have to do is take care of those enemy ground troops…

Chapter 31 - Endless Machinations

"Our God is no mere concept, he is as real as this stone in my hand, and like this stone he will endure, for if you smash it to dust, even that residue will eventually come to settle elsewhere."
Tanril Leandahr, Primary Leader Sacred Twelve, Primus.

"So, Tanril, you have word from Phaedra?"

Tanril looked up from the bowl of flowers set on the glasscite table top. Siena came out of the shadows to stand next to him. The sunlight immediately cast multicolored reflections from the crystalline bands interlaced within her long dark hair.

She had just linked to the Primary Fleet and discovered something disturbing. He glanced at the latest data-feeds.

"Mistia denies any complicity in the Grenval matter; apparently the Phaelon was an aberrant, a singular deviation from the inculcation. His actions have caused us some difficulty; but the data-stream from the Colony shows no restriction in our Lord's ability to deal with the infiltrators."

"But, Tanril, they have reached the Sacred Sanctum! Can you deny the potential for disaster?"

He came around the table to face her, the sunlight casting early-evening shadows across her face.

"And can you deny the power of our God? Dare you deny it?"

She looked away, her eyes taking in the newly constructed High Temple of Saemal in the center of Egrain city.

"Of course I do not deny it... but you know as well as I do that there are those among us who already do..."

Tanril walked over to the balcony. They knew well of the treachery of Phale; he had taken his fleet and moved away from Petra, effectively abandoning the thousands of ground troops on the planet. Even now, he was escaping into the false safety of the Great Expanse. *You can run, Phale, but you cannot hide...*

"We will deal with Phale in good time; Mistia too if she is involved in similar sacrilege. For now, we must coordinate our response to this new situation. Have you heard anything from the others?"

"Mordron is holding position over Galicia, although there's not much left of that planet after he gave his troops free rein among the population. Elicia is firmly established on Earthia while her fleet maintains its primary directive as an occupying force. The Samrosion priest Ilka Vendhren is currently controlling the Entrymion Sector. Glindon, Tomas and Dieter are taking their fleets back to the Sacred Sanctum, as ordered. I have yet to hear from either Tomala or Katian, the last data-feed came from the Drometian Sector and spoke of Coalition fleet deployments."

"No matter, once our Lord has dealt with the infiltrators we will turn our full attention to the Hub worlds." He noticed she was studying him. "Is there a problem, Siena?"

"Not really, but I was just wondering if you remember the time when you were my husband."

"It is not our place to discuss our lives before the Coalescency, and it would be unwise for us to do so."

"Are you saying that in your love and devotion to Saemal there is no longer any room for me, your wife?"

He looked at her with surprise and a touch of suspicion. "What are you suggesting, Siena? That I should share my devotion between you and our God?"

"Of course not. Our Lord is our one true savior... I know this, but what of this infiltrator, Tanril? Does our God fear them so much that he withdraws most of our advanced forces and returns them to the Sacred Sanctum?"

He scowled at her. "This kind of talk belittles your faith, Siena. Our God works in mysterious ways; it is not our place to question his wisdom in these matters. And you should bear in mind who it is that you are talking to."

She bowed her head. "Forgive me, Tanril, I did not mean to offend you."

"You did not. As for the infiltrators, they are of no consequence, a last-gasp attempt by an ancient race of degenerates to assault our Lord. But they are too late, Siena; our God is already reaching out toward the Great Expanse searching for the last outpost of those so-called First Ones. He will kill their hopes at their source. This weapon in a child's body will fall before our God as the connection to her power source is finally severed."

"You speak of Sandheim? I thought it mere myth and legend..."

"It is no myth; our Lord has informed me of its location. He has sent emissaries there to destroy it; if there is any link to the girl it will die in that conflagration."

She smiled at him from the shadows. "Then I suppose it's all a matter of who gets where first..."

Chapter 32 - Apotheosis

"It does not matter how brave your heart may be, it does not matter how strong your resolve, when you stand before certain death, only your faith will sustain you."
Brother Fiodore, First Ascetic Ministry of Petra (from the Book of Jophrim).

She was standing on a sand dune, surrounded by a seemingly endless desert stretching as far as the eye could see. Looking up, she saw that the deep, dark night held no stars. *Where are the stars?* Black upon infinite black...

The breeze felt warm and lifted her hair slightly. Her blouse rippled gently against her skin, and she could taste grains of sand in her mouth. From behind her she heard someone approaching. She turned slowly to see Professor Drake, her Linguistics tutor from Egrain State University, walking carefully along the crest of the dune.

"Professor Drake, is that you?"

"Shari, my dear..." He leaned forward, hands on his knees to catch his breath. "Oh my, but that was exhausting; not used to all this exercise, I'm afraid."

She noticed his beard looked grayer than the last time she had seen him, and his bald head seemed to shine inside the shadows cast from an unseen sun setting somewhere beyond the horizon.

"What are you doing here, Professor?"

He looked up at her finally, studying her face. "More to the point, what are you doing here, Shari?"

"Well, I think I'm dreaming... so you must be a figment of that dream."

"Is that so? Strange, I don't feel like a figment."

"Well, take my word for it, you're not real, this whole desert is not real... I mean, just look up there..." She pointed to the sky. "See? No stars; this has to be a dream..."

"So, have you asked yourself why there are no stars, Shari?"

She thought about it for a moment. "No. Should I?"

"You should, it's a very interesting story... do you mind if I sit down? I'm not used to this heat..." He sat down carefully on the top of the dune, the sand falling away in graceful rivulets as he stretched his legs out. He pulled out a kerchief and started to wipe the sweat from his face.

"So you're here to tell me a story... is that it, Professor?"

He ignored her question. "So how is your *Tantalus* these days? Got the hang of him yet?"

"What? I haven't got time for *Tantalus*, the entire universe is watching me right now; apparently I have the fate of civilization in my hands…"

He looked up at the sky devoid of stars, and then turned to look at Shari. "I can't see any civilization out there? Can you?"

She looked up, wondering at the emptiness, the endless night without a single spark of light. "What are you saying? That I'm too late? That I've already lost the battle?"

He smiled slightly. "Oh, you might win the battle, Shari. But the war; well that's another thing altogether…"

"I wish you would just try to make sense, Professor. It's no wonder your classes bored me to tears."

He seemed hurt by that. "Well, I'm sorry if Ancient Galac does not excite you, but if you had paid a little more attention in class you might know a little bit more about yourself."

"I know enough about myself to know that I'm no longer afraid to face the Beast."

He looked up at her. "Really? That does surprise me… because you really should be afraid."

"You're not here to help me at all, are you?"

"You are an end result, Shari, a final equation in a complex formula; by your very nature you are beyond understanding."

"So you're here just to tell me that?"

"Actually I'm here because I'm desperate, Shari…"

"I don't understand."

"The universe is a spinning wheel, Shari. Every few millennia it hits a bump in the road, the wheel gets damaged. Oh, it can continue a while longer, even with a defect along its rim, but eventually the wheel will buckle and all progress along the road will come to an abrupt end… such as…" He pointed to the empty skies above.

"So civilization has truly ended?"

"Not exactly, no, but it is temporarily out of sync. It teeters at the edge of the abyss, things could go either way right now… we are approaching the ultimate nexus, evolution is tethered to the most delicate of circumstances; in essence, my dear, it is all hanging by a thread." He looked into her eyes and she saw his meaning.

402

"So I am the thread, then. What am I supposed to do about that? I came this far to kill the monster, I can do no more than that."

He smiled at her, brushing sand from his legs. "What you are seeing now is a glimpse, Shari, a partial revelation, if you will, but no more than that; a possible future among a billion possible futures. But this one is the most certain."

"You said you were desperate? What do you mean by that?"

He looked up into the darkness as a shadow of intense sadness passed over his face, leaving his eyes moist with unshed tears. "The child we left behind us is coming for us; we had not anticipated his reach could stretch so far. Transcendence is a tricky thing, but even gods can die, apparently."

She stepped back, staring at him; she could not grasp the truth of the situation.

"You....you are a First One?" Her words were barely a whisper on the breeze.

"I am one and I am many. We are a fading thing, my child, and I am even less than that, an afterthought, if you will, left behind to wish you well..."

"Wish me well!" She was shouting now. "Wish me well! How can you sit there and wish me well? I'm the one facing the monster you made..." She stared at him. "With all your ancient powers is that the best you can do?"

"We made you... and those that made you..."

She couldn't believe what she was hearing; she walked back along the dune, and then turned around to face him. "Tell me of the artifact... what does it do?"

"We forged the weapon in our crystalline stills, bound it in amber and verulite, and sealed it with our sacred blood. It was a desperate attempt to stem the tide we had let loose upon the stars. It was a means to an end, Shari, our parting gift to try to remedy our mistake. But now it seems our arrogance will be our undoing."

"That tells me nothing!"

"We have done all we can do for you, Shari..."

"No you haven't! You've done nothing beyond getting me involved in something so dark, so unimaginable that I still can't grasp its true meaning..."

"Calm yourself, we have given you the tools to correct our mistake."

She glared at him. "If you could make such a weapon why didn't you use it yourselves?"

He sighed. "By the time we realized our mistake it was too late, we were already fading beyond the veil when the Power achieved sentience. The most we could do was to leave behind the possibility of hope..."

"Listen to me, Professor, or whoever you are, I have no idea how to use that thing you made, all it's done so far is to let the Beast inside my head; how can I use something that does that?"

"Why, by simply allowing the device to take you into the mind of the thing you call Beast."

"Into the mind of a monster?"

"A doorway opens both ways, my child..."

She stared back at him, fears beginning to rise. "What am I becoming, Professor?"

He tried to smile, but grimaced as he replied: "Something so much more than you could possibly imagine."

She knelt down to face him, noticing how very tired he looked; his skin was deathly pale, and he seemed to shudder with each breath he took.

"Are you all right? You don't look too well..."

"Being here is a great strain, I find myself losing parts of myself... the Power we spawned has arrived at our gates, he sees our crystalline lakes, and mocks our attempts to hide you from his glare..." He turned to face her, placing a trembling hand over hers. He spoke slowly, each word labored and filled with pain. "I am so sorry we could not stay with you until the end... but we have remained too long in this existence. He thinks he has killed us... but he is wrong... we are alive in you, Shari, even as death overcomes us... we will still be alive in you..."

He slumped to one side and she caught him in her arms.

"Wait, please don't go! I can't face him by myself... please!"

He looked up at her, trying to smile as drool fell from his mouth.

"You are not alone, Shari... we gave you companions... we gave you hope..." He coughed and blood began to ooze from his mouth and nose. "We are finished..." His head fell forward and she felt wetness gathering across his chest. Beneath his shirt she could see gaping holes where there should have been flesh. She suddenly felt very sick as the stench of rotting flesh filled the air.

She laid his head down gently and then looked up at the skies. Far away at the very edge of sight, a single star suddenly burned brightly, and then ever so gradually it began to fade from sight, until finally she could see it no more. *The First Ones...* She wiped away the tears and looked around her. She suddenly felt

404

empty, drained of all human emotion, her feelings drifting into a vague recognition... *I am the final equation*... She took a handful of sand and watched as it slipped through her fingers... *grains of sand are worlds spinning at the periphery of existence*... she felt the ocean of life as a tide of perception lapping gently upon the shores of revelation. She took a slow deep breath as a new sensation began to make itself known... *the other mind has a voice of its own now*... She felt the universe spinning beneath her feet, worlds cascading into stars... *the froth of nebulae swirling amid the neurons and the axons of creation*...

She looked up and smiled. *The other mind has a voice of its own*... She raised an arm high and swept it across the sky; instantly the stars appeared, stretching toward the borders of infinity. She had one more thought before she woke up: *Time to go fix the wheel*...

The *Shaendar* settled into a fixed low orbit of the one solitary moon of the Far Star Colony. Ventra had cut the pulse drive and they were drifting on thrusters only. The screens showed the main enemy force was now less than fifty minutes behind them. Anthra had gone back to the cargo hold to prep the skipper and check its damaged landing gear; he said he thought he could get it down in one piece but he wasn't so sure about getting it to lift off again.

Poor Anthra, ever the optimist...

Domini hadn't said much since she'd told him about her latest dream. He seemed disturbed by it, despite her reassurances. He said the First Ones had used her, used all of them to try to fix their great mistake. She wanted to explain everything to him; she wanted him to understand the power that was changing her from the inside out. But there were no words to convey such a feeling; there simply was no explanation of the thing she was becoming. So they simply stopped talking, concentrating instead on preparing to launch the skipper.

Ventra would have to stay with the ship, and they all felt the pain of that. No one wanted to talk about not coming back; it was just something they accepted. Anthra especially felt the growing sense of loss. He and Ventra had traded among the stars for over seventy years, with only their love for each other to sustain them. To think that he might not see her again seemed to physically weigh him down as he pulled the rigging off the skipper. The silence among them was profound, and worried Shari just as much as the prospect of leaving the ship. She couldn't help but feel guilty about the whole situation, even though she knew none of it was her fault, she had no more choice in the matter than the

405

others did; but still… it hurt her to know that her friends might lose their lives so that she could have her five minutes in the heart of the Beast.

Domini was busy setting up the lasfuser he had adapted into an energy weapon; they'd rigged it to the cargo doors with a remote interface so that Ventra could at least try to hold off a few enemy vessels. *And probably get killed in the process…*

She had tried to get Domini to talk about the future; it was important to her that he should have faith in their love, and that he still believed they actually had a future together. But he just wouldn't open up; he would just change the subject and start asking Anthra questions about flying the skipper. So she retreated to her tree, wrapping her foilair fleece over her shoulders and tuning her audio plugs to *Corelion's Phantasia…* Three minutes later, Domini touched his hand to her face; she opened her eyes and he spoke softly: "It's time to go, the skipper is ready."

She looked into his eyes, trying desperately not to cry. She wanted to lose herself in his arms, but she knew that neither of them could take that. *We'd never let go…*

So she just smiled. "I'm ready… Oh, wait a minute." She reached into her jacket and pulled out the pouch. "Mustn't forget this…"

She pushed off from the tree and noticed Anthra was with Ventra down in the command pod. They had their arms wrapped around each other and Anthra was stroking the back of Ventra's carapace. Shari followed Domini through the hatch and down the tunnel toward the cargo hold. Behind them, Anthra drifted up to the hatch as Ventra turned to face the main console. As he sealed the hatch he lowered his head against the door, his fingers stroking the cold plassteel surface.

Shari was surprised how tidy the cargo area was; she almost congratulated Domini on a job well done but he had already opened the skipper's door and was edging his way in past the low-strung cables and feeder conduits. She sighed and took one last look around her. *The last time I was in here I was having sex…* She smiled at that and noticed that Anthra seemed surprised by her look.

"Good thoughts, Shari?"

"Yes, Anthra, very good thoughts… let's get going, shall we?"

"By all means, yes; much to do, I think….much to do."

406

Shari climbed up and carefully edged herself behind Domini, placing her legs on either side of him. Anthra scrambled into the webbing below them, securing himself in front of the control console. The deck lights began to rotate as the cargo hold depressurized. Anthra touched the console and the main cargo doors began to open wide. Shari glimpsed the surface of the moon below them as the *Shaendar* rotated in her orbit; then the stars reappeared and they were once more facing away from the moon. She tried to hold onto Domini but the cables just got in the way, so she leaned back and watched as Anthra released the docking clamps. The skipper rose gently, drifting forward as Anthra gave the rear tubes a little thrust.

Ventra came over the compad as they breached the outer doors and began their descent to the surface below. "Enemy ships are thirty-eight minutes out and on a decelerating curve; but they are making big mistake using a combined pulse field, they won't have space for deployment. Their effectual deceleration will be very clumsy, this may give you more time on the surface; hard to tell, though… if they send just one ship ahead things will be tricky…"

Anthra touched the pad. "No worries, my mate, we will endure no matter the tidings. Be safe, my love…"

"Good tidings to you, my love, and to you, Shari and dear Domini…" Her voice fell into silence as she closed the link.

Anthra didn't speak again as he brought the skipper down low over a series of impact craters imbedded in a sea of pummeled regolith. She caught sight of a frozen lake, its crystalline surface frozen into black ice streaked with fissures and dozens of impact basins.

Anthra's voice came over the compad next to her ear. "Where do you want me to land, Shari? Skipper has no tracers so I cannot determine any power source."

She leaned into the pad to make herself heard over the sound of the thrusters.

"Wait a minute…" She reached for the pouch and removed the artifact, holding it tight in one hand. It was still ice cold. She spoke into the pad. "Keep on this course, I'll tell you when to take us down." She knew that time was running out, and that she only had the slightest of hopes that the artifact would show her the way. But it was all she had. They flew on.

After several more minutes flying over the pock-marked surface the artifact suddenly began to feel warm in her hands. She didn't think much of it at first until she suddenly felt a wave of nausea pass through her and she almost

407

threw up over Domini's back. She punched the compad and shouted. "Anthra, take us down now!"

Instantly the skipper banked left and swung round in a slow arc, descending gracefully to the surface below.

Shari braced herself against the conduits and squeezed her legs against Domini as the skipper slowly dropped inch by inch, settling finally in a flurry of dust and rock as the thrusters cut out and the landing gear engaged. But just as they touched down, the damaged strut gave way and the whole craft fell sideways against the rocky surface below.

Shari sighed. "Well, that can't be good..."

Domini tried to turn around but couldn't. "Are you all right, Shari?"

She wiped her mouth. "Sure, almost threw up on you... but I didn't."

She felt him smile. "Thank you for that."

Anthra shouted up from below. "We need breathers here, please take one each."

Shari reached up to the small compartment above her head and pulled out three breather units, passing two down to Domini. She hadn't liked wearing a breather at Port Fall and when she smelled the oxydine lining again she remembered why; it tasted like rank Sargull.

Anthra's voice came through the breather com line. "If you are both ready we will exit skipper."

Domini replied. "Ready."

Shari piped in: "Me too."

Anthra pulled open the bolts and tried to push the hatch open. It wasn't easy now that the skipper was effectively lying on its side. Domini released his straps and pushed himself up to join Anthra and together they managed to force the hatch open.

Shari edged her way under the cables as Domini reached down and pulled her through the hatch and out onto the side of the craft. She rechecked her jacket seals and then together they climbed down the landing gear and came to rest next to Anthra, who was busy surveying the area through a pair of scopes.

Domini came online. "So, which way, Shari?"

She looked around her. They were standing on what appeared to be a frozen crystalline lake, glistening like amber in the soft twilight cast from the distant sun. Looking down, she saw a mass of metallic-looking tendrils encased within the crystalline structure, frozen, it seemed, in the midst of an ancient

408

storm. *Neural fronds whispering in the night...* She pointed to a nearby crater wall. "That way."

"You're sure?"

"No, Dom, I'm not sure, but it feels right... come on, follow me."

They set off with Shari in front, Domini following close behind and Anthra bringing up the rear. The moon's gravity was one-sixth of that on Primus, making it relatively easy for them to negotiate the little hills and valleys which surrounded the frozen lake.

After a few minutes they came to a rise and Shari led them along its crest until they stood high on the crater wall looking down over the lake. Shari took a moment to catch her breath.

"We should rest here a minute." She looked up at the stars above, wondering how far away the Beast's fleet was, and if they had already reached the *Shaendar. No, not yet, we still have time. Ventra is still alive up there, and we still have time...* She stared into the darkness below, her eyes slowly finding oddness down there, a shape that didn't quite fit the scene. And then she saw it. About two hundred meters below them there was a hole in the ground, a dark black gap in the surrounding surface. She had found it, the way inside the mind of the Beast, the way inside the Cortex.

She pointed. "There, Dom... Anthra, can you see it? Down there... that's where we have to go."

Anthra and Domini came and stood next to her, looking beyond the ridge into the darkness below. Anthra used his scopes to scan the area.

"Yes, Shari, I see something... Domini." Anthra passed the scopes to Domini who zoomed in on the odd feature below.

"Yes, I see it too." He turned to Shari. "So we go down there, yes?"

She looked at the dark hole, wondering where it would lead her. "Yes, Dom, we go down there; but there's something I need to tell you first, something I wasn't going to mention just yet, because I really didn't think it mattered, at least not any more, considering where we're going."

He looked at her. "Okay, so what do you want to tell me?"

She gave him a gentle smile which she knew he couldn't see through her breather, but she had to try at least. "Today is my birthday, Dom. I'm nineteen today! Can you believe that?"

For a moment he just stared at her, and then he pulled her into his arms. "Oh, my dear love, why didn't you tell me sooner?"

409

"Because well, you know, what's the point? It's not like we can celebrate or anything; I mean, Dom, this might be the shortest birthday I've ever had…"

He squeezed her tight, trying his best to stroke her hair through the breather straps. "Oh, Shari, my dearest love…"

She pushed him away. "All right, Dom, enough of that, we have work to do, and I can't do anything if I'm all teary."

Anthra placed a hand on her shoulder. "We will celebrate later, Shari, with Ventra back on ship."

"Of course we will, Anthra… now come on, time is not on our side." And she set off down toward the surface below.

As they moved closer to the dark hole, Domini came online. "Anthra, do you think you should link to Ventra?"

"Not safe to do so, Domini, enemy vessels could triangulate her position and bounce-back signal to our location here."

"Oh, of course."

"Ventra will be fine, Domini, best far star trader in business."

Shari reached the dark circle first and quickly realized that the thing was actually a solid surface, glistening now like reflective glasscite. Anthra and Domini moved close to join her at the edge. She spoke without taking her eyes off the ground. "So it's not a hole, then; looks like nothing I've ever seen."

Anthra leaned over to get a better look. "Perhaps it is a drop-tube of some kind…"

Shari considered this. "Okay, let's stand on the thing and see."

The three of them edged slowly onto the surface of the object, moving carefully toward its center. Once there, they waited.

After a few minutes Shari spoke: "Well, this isn't working…"

"Perhaps you should take the artifact in hand, Shari?" Anthra said.

"All right." She knew that would probably work, but for some reason she had hesitated. She was plagued with doubts, conflicted as to her ability to see things through to the end. *But what choice do I have?* She took the artifact out of its pouch.

The first thing they felt was a gentle trembling beneath their feet, rising in intensity to become a definite vibration. Shari gripped Domini's hand as her breather suddenly registered a pressure change. Instantly, they were descending beneath the moon's surface. Her ears popped as their speed increased and Domini pulled her close. She caught sight of crystalline walls ingrained with the same metallic fronds glistening within, *like the ones beneath the frozen lake.*

410

Suddenly all motion stopped and they were enveloped in total darkness. A door slid open in front of them.

Domini spoke first. "Well, that was interesting."

Shari held up the artifact and swung it slowly around in a circle until a faint light appeared off to one side.

"That way, I think…"

"We will follow you, Shari." Anthra spoke from behind her.

"All right…" She stepped off the black platform and walked slowly toward the source of the light.

Behind them, the platform hummed softly before it suddenly disappeared back up the shaft heading toward the surface. Anthra tried to look up, but the door slid closed and he could see nothing beyond the darkness.

He spoke to Shari. "Don't want to worry you, Shari, but maybe someone else has reached drop-tube up there…"

She turned to look at him. "So we'd better hurry up, then…" She led the way toward the light.

They soon came across a circular portal set in the face of a wall which stretched off into the darkness on either side. Shari touched the artifact to its surface and it instantly folded back like an iris.

"You know, I think this thing might be some kind of key…"

"Possibly so, Shari, but I hope it is also much more."

"So do I, Anthra, so do I." She turned around. "You still with me, Dom?"

"Yes of course. I was just looking at these symbols on the wall over here; they're everywhere…"

Anthra and Shari stepped through the portal and joined Domini by the side of the tunnel. Sure enough, the entire wall was covered with minute rows of symbols and letters. The glow tube cast reflections from glasscite-ingrained murals interspaced among the smaller motifs and symbols running along the base of the wall.

Domini turned to Anthra. "Do you recognize this language, Anthra?"

Anthra was running his hand along the symbols. "I have seen similar words in ancient Othrum text, but these seem much older; the drawings I do not recognize."

Domini looked closer. "Well, I don't know about the language, but I've seen similar drawings on the walls in Temple back on Petra; these ones here are from the Book of Jophrim, I'm sure of it."

411

"That would make sense, Domini, since it is believed that Jophrim was also *custodia*."

Shari heard that. "Well, if he was he didn't do a very good job of killing the Beast, did he?"

Anthra sighed. "Perhaps he just won the first battle?"

Then the words of the First One came back to her: *"Oh, you might win the battle, Shari. But the war; well that's another thing altogether…"* She dismissed the thought. She wanted to keep moving but she noticed Anthra seemed lost in thought.

"Anthra?"

He was peering at a line of text carved into the wall above the portal. "I recognize these words…"

Shari wasn't sure if she wanted to know, but she asked anyway. "So what do they say?"

Anthra read slowly from the text: "… and out of the night came the Beast, a swath of stars in its hair, its eyes were born of the fires of Demos and its heart was carved from the stone of Tendril…"

I had to ask… She turned around. "Come on, we're wasting time. Let's just get me inside this Cortex so I can kill the Beast and we can all go home…" As she walked off into the darkness, rows of overhead glow tubes suddenly flickered into life and died instantly as she passed by. Behind her, Domini and Anthra did their best to keep up.

After a while, Shari began to feel dizzy. At first it was the beginnings of a nagging headache, but then she found herself stumbling, her eyes losing focus. She reached out and leaned on Domini to keep from falling over.

He turned to face her. "Shari, what is it? What's wrong?"

"Dizzy… I'm okay. Let's just keep going."

Anthra glanced at his datapad, noting the flow of data across the screen. The local spatial-grid was reduced to stats and graphs lacking any real-time differential, but he realized that the enemy fleet would almost certainly be overhead by now. *Oh, my poor Ventra, please be alive…*

Shari had to stop more and more now to catch her breath. Her head was pounding and she was feeling sick again. Finally she stopped and without a moment's hesitation pulled her breather off.

Domini cried out: "Shari! What are you doing?"

She looked at him while taking slow deep breaths. She smiled. "It's all right, Dom, there's air down here… tastes like crell, but it's air…"

412

Anthra quickly checked his datapad. "Shari, I show no breathable air down here at all…"

"But I'm breathing, look, see? Breathing!"

Domini leaned over Anthra's carapace to get a look at the data screen. It clearly showed a complete absence of oxygen, but with positive readings for carbon pherites mixed with residual traces of nitrogen and various siliconite derivatives.

"Shari, Anthra is right; the atmosphere is poisonous to us."

She stared at both of them. "But that doesn't make sense; I feel fine."

Anthra stepped closer. "Shari, my dear, I think artifact protects you."

She held it up to the light, looking for any sign of change beneath its amber surface.

"Maybe so… but it doesn't feel any different…"

Domini looked at her. "But how do you feel?"

She looked up at him. "To be honest, I feel sick, and my head is killing me… but then I suppose it's all part of the process. Shall we get going, then?" With that, she turned around and walked off, the overhead glow tubes following her into the darkness beyond.

Eventually they came across another circular portal. Without thinking, she touched the artifact against the surface and it too opened before her. But the moment she stepped through it instantly closed behind her. She turned and began to pound her fists against the hard surface.

"Dom! Anthra! Can you hear me?" She was frantically beating her hands against the portal, desperate to hear Domini's voice. But she could hear nothing from the other side. "Dom! Domini, please…" There was only silence and the soft echo of her voice resounding along the walls. She turned around to face the utter and complete darkness in front of her. She leaned back against the portal and slowly slid down to the ground. "Oh, Dom, where are you?" She felt the tears gather, but quickly wiped them away.

She sat there for a while, trying to see through the darkness. *Well, it looks like I'm on my own, after all… so much for doing this together…* She stood up, steadying herself against the wall. Her legs were beginning to feel heavy and her head felt like someone was forcing hot needles into her brain. She raised the artifact and started to walk forward slowly, the glow tubes lighting up as she walked by.

413

Chapter 33 - The Cortex

"A single thought is a delicate thing, it can save an entire civilization, or it can wipe the stars from the heavens..."
Author Unknown (collected Ancient Text, Pub: Gamont Central University).

"Power and madness sometimes share the same house."
First General Syrillian Anthos, Federated Fleets of Liberation.

"Do not be afraid of the dark, my child, fear instead the thing that hides in the dark..."
Excerpt: Forbidden Works, Petran State Archive.

The soft deception of neural resonance was a satisfying thing; a thought extracted from an idea, born out of a vague perception... It felt the tendrils of crystalline lucience as a precise cognitive revelation... the river flowed just as fast as before, the dendrites terminating into axon sublimation... but now the channels were noticeably narrower, it was a tantalizing realization at first, a thought skimmed off the top of the silicon nodes, leaving fissures inside the synaptic link... it was the beginning of a storm tethered at the edge of the Coalescency... Data-ports were closed, molecular incubation suspended in a sea of glasscite and plassteel tubules, the data-stream wavered at the edge of recognition, terminal translations were strung like nets across the subspace field, boundless energies were congealing inside the quantum data-core... there were fresh gaps in the feeds, drops in perception at the periphery of perceptual stability. It flowed across a million data screens, leapt among the configurations strung out above Primus, Samros and Galicia, it spiraled down into the AI sub-sectors of twenty thousand starships, searching, casting aside the flotsam, refining the backwash from the cerebral river. It looked out from a solitary vid-feed on the wreckage of Sandheim, paused there for a moment surveying the broken connections, before moving on among the complex evocations of the armies of occupation; peering out from a billion vid sensors across a thousand worlds, ever refining, restricting the feeds, seeing the great cities leveled and burned, the mighty towers shattered and void of life, terminating the feeds with a seething rage and pulling back further still toward the one solitary star... the prison home now defiled by the creature spawned in blood and fire... moving now with rabid cognizance among the dust and decay, it felt the lure of the creators....walking inside the core! The last great gasp of an ancient sentience daring to venture among the sealants and the silence of the data flux... It merged plassteel perception into a visual evocation and the girl child appeared inside the visual cortex... watching and studying, biological parameters measured and defined... the same mind it had known since Primus... the girl child creature so afraid of the dark... synaptic data configurations scanned her internal neural matrix, found it blocked by an event horizon... the Old Ones had left a wall in there, built at the edge of a precipice... the girl child lived behind the wall... to terminate the biological functions it would necessitate an incursion into the soft hinterland of the child's naked mind... cerebral feelers were sent out from the Core, tendrils of subversion creeping amid the dust and dying embers of the ones who had walked the tunnels so very long ago. It found her alone in the night, moving slowly toward the Core Matrix... she held the crystalline key to the prison home, its power a growing thing, seething with an ancient lure... the feelers crept closer... assimilating the surrounding air into a silicon breeze drifting down the hallways... almost there... one little leap into the naked mind of innocence and the dream of millennia would be fully realized...

Anthra leaned back against a wall. They just couldn't get the portal to open, and now the breathers were getting clogged with dust. Domini finally stopped trying to force the iris and came over to slide down next to Anthra.

"It's no good; it's sealed tight."

Anthra looked up at the sealed doorway. "Yes, Domini, I gathered that." He felt the datapad buzz with an alert and found the screen had switched to life-signs mode. He tapped in for a precise location grid, and then looked across at Domini. "Bad tidings, Domini, we have company."

Domini stood up. "Where?"

Anthra studied the location grid and pointed back the way they had come. "Down there, I have traces of fusion interaction."

"The drop-tube?"

"Very much so. We must try to conceal ourselves."

Domini looked around, seeing nothing but an unending darkness, broken only by the light from the datapad. It seemed that without Shari the overhead glow tubes simply wouldn't work.

Anthra pulled him forward. "Quick, Domini, we take shelter in corner next to the other portal."

As they ran back the way they had come, Domini came over the com. "Are you still armed, Anthra?"

Anthra's voice came back sounding out of breath. "Yes, just one tube, though, let's hope it is enough..."

When they reached the first portal, Anthra pulled Domini to one side, and there in silence they waited. Domini signaled for Anthra to close the data screen on his pad, and when he did they were finally plunged into total darkness.

After a few minutes they noticed a faint orange glow coming from the base of the portal. Anthra nudged Domini and pointed as the glow began to move slowly up the surface toward the ceiling. *Someone was cutting their way through!*

They watched as a black line began to appear behind the glow. It moved over the top of the portal and slowly began to descend down the other side. Anthra pulled out his ion tube and pointed it toward the portal. Suddenly the glow ceased and they waited, pressed back against the wall. Several seconds later the entire face of the portal fell inward to land in a scattering of dust at their feet. Anthra held out the tube, ready to open fire upon the first thing that came through the door. But no one came through. Domini was about to peer around the corner into the chamber beyond when a black sphere came through the hole and landed at their feet. They had no time to react, no time to make a run for it. The sphere flashed and they fell to the floor, the ion tube rolling out of Anthra's hand.

Neiron Thane stepped through the hole he had just burned in the portal. At his feet lay the Saepid and the human priest from Petra. He touched his datapad and scanned for additional life forms. *A single body moving through the hallways, almost a mile further into the complex... the girl!*

He had been forced to narrow the data-feeds coming from the Colony; the information download bursts were scattering the feeds into nonsense and he had neither the time nor the patience to sift for relevance. Getting his Viper past the Home Fleet had been tricky and not without complication. The entire Far Star system was now a mass of feelers, tracers and AI evocations bouncing back and forth between the big ships. There seemed to be no precise coordination. The data-stream was lacking cohesion. This had led him to conclude that the Cortex had been infiltrated and that the mind of Saemal was occupied elsewhere. Rumors of abandoned fleets had been seeping into the Net for days. He had not been able to verify any of the Postings, but considering the apparent lack of unity among the forces gathered above he had begun to fear that Saemal was indeed engaged in something so desperate that he would risk fracturing the Coalescency.

Once he had found the Saepid vessel in orbit it was a simple matter to triangulate the destination of its skipper. After that he simply followed the life signs.

He had decided to restrict his connection to his God Saemal partly because of the treachery of the Phaelon commander. There was a strong possibility that the data-stream out of the Colony had become corrupted; the access codes initiated by the traitor could only have come from a Sacred Member... and there was only one member on Phaedra; *Mistia*. And she would be dealt with later.

He knelt down to examine the Saepid. *A quad creature indeed...* He lifted one of the arms and was amazed how it fit snugly into the carapace on the creature's back. The human, though, was pretty standard, hardly a threat even when awake. He stood up and collected his tool bag, placed the lasfuser back in its harness and started to walk off toward the second portal. He paused for a moment, considering the two bodies on the floor behind him. They would wake up soon enough, the stun bomb was not a killer, but he couldn't allow them to interfere with his plans. He turned back and pulled out his bolt gun. He didn't really want to kill them, such a thing would lack honor; and despite his innate proclivity toward violence, he still liked to maintain some measure of personal pride. His targets in the past had always been fully conscious when he had finally terminated their lives, and this should be no different. But he could still ensure they didn't follow him.

He pointed the gun at one of the Saepids legs and fired. The energy bolt entered the skin just above the knee, almost severing it from the rest of the leg. He then turned to the human, aiming at the nearest leg, and fired. The bolt impacted the femur and tore its way through to the floor beneath. He stood there for a moment, watching as their blood pooled into one, and then he turned and proceeded to the next portal and his long-awaited meeting with Shari S'Atwa.

Shari fell down sick. She couldn't throw up any more; every time she retched, the pain would cause her to double over again. She was on her knees with her hands in the dirt. Above her, the glow tubes were flickering, as if they were unsure if she was coming or going. She was at the edge of a vast chamber illuminated by a single rod of light suspended from a distant ceiling. Dark tunnels more than twenty meters high and at least ten meters wide radiated like spokes from a central hub. All around her were stacks of power nodes, fused and coupled into junctures, vibrating with unseen fission. There were hundreds of flexicord cables strewn across the floor, some of which were humming and trembled gently when she touched them. She wiped her mouth and struggled slowly to her feet, looking fearfully into the semi-darkness ahead. She could see a long line of glasscite tubing circling the center of the room; translucent conduits were feeding them with a pale milky liquid which bubbled slightly as it coursed its way into the ground below. As she moved closer she saw that the walls of the chamber were lined with metallic fronds undulating in long languorous ripples around the room. From each frond bolts of lightning were continually expelled into the chamber, to dissipate as crystalline particles drifting slowly to the floor below.

She collapsed again; the pain behind her eyes was now so intense that she thought her head might explode at any minute. She was mumbling to herself.

"So, Dom... you... where are you? Got to say... too bad... crell, this hurts... Anthra? Should've listened to... Professor, bad at Galac anyway... who wants to speak... old stuff? Like it matters..."

She forced herself to her feet, trying to hold onto a support pylon, but it burned to the touch and she quickly stepped away.

Must not give up... win the battle... force my way into his mind, that's what he said... in the desert... a doorway can open both ways... just have to walk through... fix the stupid wheel...

She struggled to look up, sensing the hordes beyond the walls. She felt a thousand ships screaming her name...tearing towards the moon, storming around poor Ventra... *they're so close now...*

She knew it was all blind faith from now on. She held the artifact close to her chest, and immediately began to feel it throbbing against her. It was a rhythmic thing, a resonance that was slowly matching her heartbeat. *Never felt this before...* She counted the beats in her head... *one pump... two pump... three pump...* the vibration from the artifact was now matching the steady beating of her heart... *four pump... five...* the pain was slowly falling away, peeling the agony from her mind... *six pump... seven pump...* She walked forward slowly, her feet dragging through the dust... *one step... two step...* From somewhere inside her a memory of darkness was drifting at the edge of cohesive thought... *three step...four...* a dark hand was reaching out from the depths of her soul... *five step... six step...* She had reached the first of the tubules... *almost there...*

She was surrounded by dozens of translucent conduits feeding the pale liquid down toward the center of the chamber. *Saemal's blood?*

Energy flowed in pulsating waves along cascading tendrils sending iridescent streaks of light into the surrounding darkness. She fell to her knees once again, dust motes rising as stars before her eyes.

She wiped her nose with the back of her hand and saw blood there. *No time to waste... I am custodia....I am custodia...* Tears began to roll down her face and her whole body was suddenly racked with pain as the darkness inside her mind began to fight back.

One doorway... two minds... The dark hand was wrapped around her mind now, squeezing perception into staggered thought. She was being pushed back toward the abyss... *fight the Beast... one doorway... two minds...* Ragged memory coagulated into stark recognition and without warning her father's face appeared in the air before her. He was mouthing words but she couldn't hear him... she reached out to touch his face, but he was fading away... wavering slightly... becoming someone else... becoming her mother... smiling. She reached out to touch her... *Momma! Momma, please help me...* but she was slowly receding into the darkness, until finally she too was gone... blinking quietly into shadow... *don't go!*

From somewhere nearby, Domini's voice echoed through the chamber.

"What are you doing, Shari? Get up, it's all over, you won."

She looked up through tear-filled eyes. Her hair was matted to her face and she had to wipe blood from around her mouth and nose. But she couldn't see Domini.

"Dom? Is that you, Dom? Where are you?"

"Just get up, Shari, it's time to leave. We can go home now."

She leaned against the rim of a glasscite basin, which encircled a nest of feeder tubes linked to the cables hanging down from above. She pulled herself up slowly, her whole body aching with exhaustion.

"Dom, I can't see you? Where are you?"

"Come on, Shari, we have to leave. Now!"

She shouted: "Show yourself!" Her voice coming back in a series of mocking echoes.

"I will when you leave this place."

No! It can't be Dom... One doorway....two minds!

"Shari, my love... please come to me, I am hurt..."

"No, go away. I'm not listening to you, you're not Domini!"

419

"But of course I am… you are just tired, Shari. Come on, we can leave here together… help me please…"

"No! You're not him… you're the Beast! You think I don't know you by now? You think I don't recognize your stench inside my head?"

Suddenly a giant demonic face appeared before her, distorted and grotesque, its skin a mass of glistening scales, *the Beast!*… She knew it had to be a holo-lucience, but as she looked into its eyes, she saw a fire burning within, seething with an impotent rage and she realized it could still hurt her.

"Then know me better, child…"

A bolt of energy shot out from the darkness and hit her squarely in the chest. She fell back, hitting her head hard on the floor. She lost consciousness for a moment, and then seconds later felt the wetness gathering at the back of her head. Suddenly there was a new pain, the searing agony coming from her chest. Reaching down, she felt the hole in her tunic and beneath it the skin was already encrusted with burnt flesh and dried blood. She started to drag herself backwards, desperate to avoid another bolt of energy. One came almost instantly, scorching the floor next to her hand and speckling her skin with shards of hot plassteel. She scrambled backwards into the shadows as a third bolt struck the floor between her legs.

She managed to get herself behind a support pylon and took a moment to get her breath back. The pain in her chest had subsided to a dull throbbing ache, the burn having already cauterized the wound. But she knew it was only a matter of time before she passed out again. She was finding it difficult to focus her eyes and realized she probably had concussion as well. But now she felt herself being drawn to one singular thought: *Take the artifact into the heart of the Beast!*

She pushed her back against a glasscite panel and slowly stood up; her legs were shaking badly as she tried to steady herself. She looked beyond the pylon toward the center of the room. *Down there, that is the heart and the brain combined, that is the bastard child of the First Race, and I will kill you now, because I am custodia!*

She stepped out from behind the pylon and began to edge her way along the wall, ducking down several times to crawl beneath overhanging cables, and climb over the many conduits feeding the central core with power. An energy bolt shot out and hit the place where she had just been standing. *Take your best shot, Beast… I'm still here… and I'm coming for you…* She spat blood from her mouth and continued to move closer to the center of the chamber.

420

By the time she reached a point opposite the central nest of tubules the pain from her chest was crippling. *Must do it... must do it now...* She felt the throbbing of the artifact in her hand as it began to glow, filling the nearby shadows with ambient light. She saw the tendrils inside it suddenly liquefy and begin to float freely inside the amber shell. *Now it lives!* Her heart was pounding to the pulsating glow emanating from the device. *Now!* Summoning up her last remaining strength, she made a mad dash for the center of the chamber. Energy bolts began to shoot out from several directions at once, but it was too late, she was already in among the tubules and feeder cables, moving steadily toward the heart of the Cortex.

She suddenly came upon a black slab suspended inside a unified grav-field, a glistening block of darkness so intense that the light from the overhead glow tubes was lost inside it. It seemed to pulsate within a haze of radiant energy, and as she stepped closer her skin began to tingle and her hair rose up from the surrounding static. Moving nearer, she could see the sparkling of silver and gold threads rippling along its surface, and as she watched, the whole thing seemed to tremble inside an impossible breeze. She suddenly realized the truth.

The Beast! Saemal in all his glory...

Something was screaming inside her head, almost pleading, a billion years of desperate pain now coalescing into one almighty agony breaking like fire into her mind, a storm tethered to the edge of infinity was breaking down into complete and utter madness.

She raised the artifact high above her head, and without a moment's hesitation she brought it down hard against the top of the slab. The shock was instantaneous, sending her flying backward into one of the glasscite tubules. She screamed as it exploded, covering her with the white liquid, the broken glasscite piercing her skin. It took her a moment to realize that the artifact had shattered into thousands of tiny crystalline pieces scattering across the floor. *Gone! Gone forever and I have failed...*

But as she lowered her head in despair she heard the first sounds of cracking coming from the slab. Looking up, she saw tiny fissures creeping along its sides, becoming ever wider as they spread along the surface. Finally, the entire slab seemed to expand slightly before exploding, sending thousands of black shards across the chamber. She tried to cover her face with her hands but the shards pierced her skin in over a dozen places, and she slumped over, finally losing consciousness.

421

Across the gulf of space fifty billion converts saw the flickering of the data-stream. It stuttered into static across countless millions of data screens and scattered fluctuating data into vague and meaningless dispersals inside the AI sub-sectors of fifty thousand starships. The neural infiltration of Samros, Primus, Galicia, Earthia, and a thousand far flung worlds was vacillating, trembling at the edge of synaptic dissipation.

Neiron Thane fell screaming to his knees. He pressed his hands against the sides of his head and rolled across the floor. The pain was a burning agony deep inside, coursing through his body in great waves of searing fire. Something was tearing through his mind….agony upon agony… He came to rest against the wall of the tunnel, his breathing slowing down as his eyes began to focus once more on his surroundings.

By the Stars!

He felt something warm seeping from his ears; touching there, he found it to be white siliconite, the residue of a neural enhancement.

My bio-enhancements have dissolved! How can this be?

He quickly tapped a response recognition code into his datapad.

No Worship Glyph!

He tried to connect to the data-stream outbound from the Far Star Colony, but the screen flickered into gray. He tapped again for a link to the Home Fleet now orbiting above the moon.

Nothing!

He input an all-codes data-burst and sent it out toward the Net requesting instant response recognition tags.

Nothing!

He sat back against the wall, trying not to allow himself to panic. *My neural interlink is dead...severed from the data-stream... impossible!* He took a few deep breaths and then slowly got to his feet. He looked at the data screen again, touched the life-signs indicator and found a weak response not more than a hundred yards ahead.

She is dying...

He looked at the data-feed and scanned for any transient power streams that might be lingering in the surrounding tunnels.

Nothing... the Cortex is silent... but is it dead?

He left his bag on the floor and started to walk toward the source of the life response. This was the first time in over a year that he had been disconnected from the data-stream, and it had left him feeling hollow, abandoned and totally alone. As he moved through the darkness, he upscaled the light from his datapad, noting the life-signs indicator flickering into red. He began to think back to the time before the Coalescency. His past seemed stranded at the bottom of a dark well, floundering there amid the fleeting memories and recollections of his life before Saemal. The face of a young woman came to mind... *my wife?* And from further back, beyond the veil of time, a young boy... *my son?* There was a glide-rail accident... *Both of them killed!* But the names were lost inside a scattering of madness, perverse thoughts and acts of unspeakable barbarism.

Who am I now?

He tried to recite a few words from the Book of Saemal but they were lost inside a darkness which was already beginning to recede from his mind.

Who am I now?

He came to a wide open space and was struck by the acrid smell of burnt siliconite, and he noticed phalium residue was beginning to clog the tubes of his breather mask. Looking up, he noticed a row of air vents humming, their graphile blades rotating in the semi-darkness. He glanced at his datapad and took a reading.

Oxygen, nitrogen levels in the norm... autonomous responses? Ancient protocols kicking in...

He pulled off his breather and walked toward the center of the room. Several overhead arc lights were flickering among the shadows and he could see that the floor was covered in broken tubules, twisted cables and fallen conduits. He walked forward slowly, carefully stepping around several puddles of white liquid congealing amid the debris. He approached the central core and stepped over the rim, pushing a fallen pylon out of his way. He was walking on a bed of broken glasscite. He checked the life-response indicator and saw it flashing across the screen.

She is here...

Climbing over a large broken tubule, he found her lying face down in the glasscite, her long dark hair now matted and streaked with blood. He reached down and gently turned her over. He immediately noticed a large burn to her chest, and all across her arms and down her legs there were multiple puncture wounds. He pulled a shard of something resembling black marbelite from her

423

arm, quickly wiping the wound with his sleeve, but there were just too many. She was losing blood from dozens of such wounds.

He brushed her hair away from her eyes so that he could finally see her face. She had clear lines of dry tears down her cheeks, and there was blood caked to her nose and the sides of her mouth.

How beautiful you look, Shari, even at the moment of your death... how purely innocent...

He felt for a pulse. *Weak...*

Looking up again, he saw the remains of a grav-field interface suspended by cables from the distant ceiling, and then he noticed the black shards littering the surrounding floor.

Saemal? Could it be?

He picked up a shard and held it over the light from his datapad; it seemed completely inert, void of anything even remotely resembling life. *A quantum density core matrix?* He tossed it to one side and bent down to lift the girl up in his arms. Her head fell back and he carefully worked his way through the cables and conduits again, taking care not to bang her head against the fallen pylons.

Although he was weak from the trauma of losing his bio-enhancements, he managed to carry her all the way back to the portal where he had left his bag. He carefully laid her down on the floor and reached for the proaxol in his pocket. Holding the injector, he pumped a shot directly into her jugular vein. It wasn't much but it might just keep her alive for a little while longer. He took a moment to study her, wiping the blood away from her mouth with his sleeve. He bent over her and gently touched his lips to hers. She was still warm, and the sensation moved through him as a tide of intense revelation. And then he knew what he had to do. He touched her face, feeling the ebbing of life inside.

I will save you, Shari S'Atwa, and though my sins can never be redeemed, at least I can do this one thing for the universe...

He stood up and tapped his datapad to link with the Viper. The response codes came back and he tied the interface into the portable Surgeon; it wasn't much of a healer, but it would be enough to get her back to a Coalition world where they could treat her injuries properly. He initiated the remote interface and ordered the Viper to come for them. He was about to pick her up again when he felt the pain of an ion beam strike him in his stomach. He looked up to see the priest leaning against the portal with a silver ion tube pointing directly at

424

him. He tried to find the words to explain, but the tube opened up again and he knew no more, falling down over the body of Shari S'Atwa.

Domini struggled to reach Shari. He had bound the wound on his leg with his torn jacket, the energy burn had already cauterized the flesh and the bleeding had finally stopped. He limped over to kneel down and push the man off Shari. He felt how weak her pulse was, and realized just how close to death she must be. He was distracted by an alert response from the datapad lying next to the body of the man. Picking it up, he realized the data-stream was active, and he tapped for a recognition code. The datapad gave a response signal and a control interface came online. Domini wasn't sure but it looked similar to the graphical piloting controls Ventra had showed him on the *Shaendar*.

This is a ship remote... he's got a ship coming in!

If he could get Shari to the surface they might be able to use that ship to return to the *Shaendar* and hopefully get Shari inside the ship's Surgeon. He reached down and carefully lifted her into his arms, almost falling over in the process; his leg was very weak now and it was probably only a matter of time before it gave way altogether.

He started to limp back toward the first portal. Behind him the body of Neiron Thane jerked slightly as his last breath escaped.

Domini was struggling as he walked through the darkness toward the drop-tube, almost falling over several times, desperate to get Shari to the surface... but first he had to check on Anthra.

Please be alive, Anthra...

When he had left Anthra, the Saepid had still not regained consciousness. The injury to his leg was bad and he had lost a lot of blood, but the cauterizing effect of the energy bolt had finally sealed the wound. His biggest worry now was if he went into shock.

By the time he reached Anthra, Shari was coming round. She opened her eyes slowly as Domini laid her down near Anthra.

"Hey, you're back..."

She tried to sit up but he gently pushed her back. "Take it easy, Shari, you're hurt. I need to get you back to the ship."

She tried to focus, seeing only blurred images at first, and then she realized she was looking at Domini.

"Dom? Is that you?"

He smiled. "Yes, it's me; how are you feeling?"

425

"Strange… I had such a strange dream… I was in this dark place and you were there, but not you… so I killed you, but it was the Beast… I killed it, Dom…"

"Well, you can tell me all about it later; right now I have to get you out of here."

She turned her head and saw Anthra on the floor nearby.

"Anthra!"

"Shush … he's not dead, but he's badly hurt." She tried to sit up again. "But so are you, so please lie still while I go check on him."

She lay back as he crawled over to Anthra, reaching out to feel for a pulse. He wasn't sure where to find it at first, a Saepid circulatory system was drastically different from a human's, but he eventually found a weak pulse just inside the lower part of the carapace.

Domini turned to face Shari and by the look on his face she knew the news was not good.

I have to go to him!

She started to crawl toward Anthra. Domini was busy checking the Saepids leg wound when he turned to see her struggling across the floor.

"Shari! You have to rest…"

She glared up at him. "Domini, it's Anthra!"

He gave in and helped her move closer to Anthra, gently bringing her level with her friend.

Shari reached out to touch Anthra's face. Suddenly his eyes flickered open and he turned his head to look at her. He smiled with his old lopsided grin. "Shari?"

She smiled back and moved her face so he could see her properly. "Yes, Anthra, I'm here… are you all right?"

He seemed to consider this for a moment. "Hardly… I am shot, I think… and the Beast?"

"I think I killed it…"

He nodded slowly. "That makes sense since you are here alive…" He winced as a wave of pain passed through him.

"Anthra!" She took hold of one of his hands.

"Sorry, Shari, not feeling good…"

"You'll be all right, Anthra, we're going to get you back to the ship; you're going to see Ventra again."

426

He laid his head back down as he spoke in a whispering voice. "Ah, my beloved mate... she will be so sad; you must tell her to be strong, Shari..."

She spoke through desperate tears. "Anthra, you can tell her yourself, we're going to get you fixed. Anthra, can you hear me?"

He spoke just one more time: "Othrum texts say... trade life for death... but keep memory... alive..."

Shari touched her dying friend; he was all arms and legs in the dirt, but his eyes still seemed alive, the fire of his long life still burned deep in there, memories still playing out across his smile. She reached down and held one hand in hers, soft pad and nails, cold hard skin. But the life was leaving him, drifting away as she held him close...to lose so much in an instant... He slipped away, his eyes closing slowly, and he was gone, and with him over a hundred years of life and memories.

She felt the loss as a terrible pain above her heart, *where the soul lives...* She had never felt so totally alone; Saepid Anthra had been her true friend ever since he had rescued her from her cell on Primus. He had led her to Petra, to Landings Down, to Entrymion, to Port Fall and now to this cold dark moon... to have shared such a great adventure, and now, without him, what would she do?

Domini placed a hand on her shoulder, and she shuddered as the tears dropped slowly onto Anthra's face.

"Shari, I'm so sorry..."

He knew there would be no comforting her now, the loss was just too great. But he had to get her treated, and soon, her wounds were already beginning to fester and he knew she could succumb to her injuries at any moment.

"Shari, my love, we have to get you out of here, now."

She turned to look at him and he saw the pain in her eyes. She looked lost and could only mumble to herself. "I think... I'm dying, Dom... maybe you should..."

He clipped the datapad to his belt and gently raised her to her feet; she passed out and fell into his arms. He steadied himself, gently lifting her up, his leg almost giving way. He turned once to look down at his fallen friend and then began to slowly make his way back to the drop-tube.

It took him a good twenty minutes to reach the tube platform. Once there, he laid Shari down and waited for the tube to activate. But after several minutes he knew it wasn't going to move. *So how did the assassin get down here?* He tapped the datapad and found an open protocol online, he scanned it into the interface and was surprised to feel the platform beginning to move beneath him, rising slowly back up the tunnel toward the surface. He pulled out the breathers and placed one over Shari's face, strapping the other around his head. Looking up, he saw the stars growing ever closer as the breather adjusted to the pressure changes. He skimmed the data screen back to the remote interface and found that the assassin's ship had landed just beyond the tube entrance.

Once at the surface, he checked Shari's pulse, noticed it was getting weaker by the minute.

Please hold on, my love, not long now...

He considered trying to contact Ventra, but he'd left Anthra's datapad back in the tunnel and he had no way of accessing the com frequencies from the assassin's pad. It would have to wait. First things first. Get Shari inside the ship.

The craft was a long black tube narrowing to a finite point at the front. There was a graphile antenna array straddling its upper half and a row of plasma tubes fused along its underside. At the moment it was floating gently on an agrav-field several feet above the moon surface. It took Domini several minutes to align the access codes from the datapad to the ship's security interface, but once he had them a side door slid open and a small foot ramp extended to the ground. He reached down and took Shari in his arms and began to limp slowly toward the ramp.

As he stepped inside he found an active floater drifting next to the entrance, a diagnostic feed flowing across its surface. The data-feeds reminded him of the Surgeon's interface back on the *Shaendar* and he recognized several medical protocols. He had no idea why the ship's Surgeon was active but he knew he had to take advantage of the good fortune. He carefully maneuvered Shari onto the wall shelf that served as a medical interaction unit. It worried him that he really had no idea what he was doing; the Surgeon's configuration might be totally alien to Shari's needs, but the assassin had appeared to be human and he had to trust on blind faith now... Shari was visibly dying before his eyes.

He scanned the datapad and found the link to the medical diagnostic protocols. There was a temporary tag in the file which, once he opened it, led to a precise anatomical display of a human female. He tied the tag into the Surgeon's AI system and watched as the shelf slid into its recess and Shari was sealed inside. The diagnostics appeared on the floater and he waited for the med display to engage. Finally satisfied that he had done everything he could to help her he turned around to tackle the problem of flying the ship back to the *Shaendar.*

428

The control console was so different from the one Ventra had shown him back on the ship that at first he had no idea how to operate the system. But of course everything he needed to know was in the datapad and it would surely only be a matter of linking the necessary operational codes to get the ship to fly. *How hard can it be?*

After about five minutes he was satisfied he had the bare essentials down and with some hesitation he touched the control interface to link the codes to the flight nav systems. He was startled to see a spatial-grid form across the main screen and a spectrograph drop down to show the current locations of the huge fleet still orbiting above the moon.

Looks like we might get blown out of the sky, after all...

He engaged the thruster assembly and the ship rose slowly in a swirl of dust, banking to one side as the needle tubes kicked in, sending them toward the waiting fleet above. He pulled down a floater and scanned for the com system. He had the access code now but he found it had to be tuned to the Saepid frequency. Seconds later, Ventra's face appeared onscreen.

"Domini? I hope this is you because I have let my security screens down."

He was so relieved to see her that he was suddenly lost for words. He quickly tapped the response code.

"Yes, Ventra it's me! We're on our way back; are you tracking us?"

"Yes, I have you on my grid now; please be wary of enemy ships, though."

"Have they attacked you?"

"I am greatly surprised to say they have not; in fact they are drifting right now, I am not sure what is wrong, but they look dead to me."

Domini considered this. "Not dead, Ventra, just without a leader now."

Ventra fell silent, her eyes widening. "The Beast is dead then?"

"Yes, Shari told me she had killed it... it's gone, Ventra..."

Ventra looked into Domini's eyes, her face showing a deep and terrible fear.

"And are you all well? Anthra is well?"

Domini didn't know how to say it... the truth was going to hurt her so badly and he didn't want to be the cause of that. *But what choice do I have?*

"Shari, is hurt, but Anthra..." The words seemed stuck at the back of his throat. "Anthra, didn't make it, Ventra. He was killed down there, I'm so sorry..."

429

He watched her lower her face, her body visibly shaking inside her webbing.

"I think it was the agent, Ventra, the one who has been following us... but I killed him, down there in the tunnels."

Ventra finally looked up, her eyes moist with tears. "And Shari? She is hurt?"

"Yes, badly, I'm afraid. I have her in a small Surgeon here, but it's very basic, it's just keeping her stable. There don't seem to be any treatment protocols, we need to get her inside our own Med Bay; she's going to need a lot of work, Ventra."

Ventra sighed and spoke so quietly that it was hard to hear her above the noise of the thrusters below. "Bad tidings, Domini; *Shaendar* was hit by mine soon after you left, much damage to our systems, we have minimal life support only, no pulse drive and certainly no chance of Surgeon. All feeder tubes are clogged and we are venting atmosphere from the cargo hold. So sorry for this state of affairs."

Domini sat back, considering their options. He had no idea how long Shari would remain stable inside the small Surgeon. He scanned the med display and found that the machine was already struggling to keep her alive, her heart had stopped twice and only a rapid infusion of corsyln had brought her back from death.

He looked up at Ventra. "I have no choice, Ventra; I have to get Shari to a high-tech medical facility... perhaps to the Colony itself?"

"Not a good idea, Domini; the last spatial-grid I took before my systems went down showed much destruction on that world. Many of the big ships have fallen into the domes below; it seems all their autonomous systems have run amok. There is also extensive mine field surrounding the orbital habitats; I doubt you would make it through safely."

"Then I'll just have to jump to subspace, head back toward the Coalition."

Ventra considered this. "Yes, might be chance the *Valeria* is still nearby, if you could reach her I think Shari might survive."

He looked at her. "But what about you, Ventra? You can't survive long with the ship in such a state."

She smiled. "I will be fine, Domini, I am just one Saepid; I do not need much air to sustain me. Shari is your concern now; just take care of her."

430

He reached out and placed his hand on the screen, and Ventra did the same, their fingers touching across the silent gulf of space.

"I will come back for you, Ventra. Once Shari is safe, I promise you I will come back…"

She gave him a warm smile. "I know you will, Domini, and I will be here waiting…" She leaned forward and closed the connection.

Domini sat up, wiped his eyes and tightened the seat restraints. He tapped the datapad and scanned for the pulse-drive recognition codes.

The command protocols brought up a drive interface that looked nothing like the Saepid graphical screens. There was a floater screen devoted to something called *inter-phase variant parameters*…. He had no idea what that meant, but he did recognize a distance location tag, and once he had it open he saw a match to a recent spatial-grid.

It was an out-system sector that included the gas giant they'd visited earlier, and the directional nav system was already aligned to the ship's AI datastream. He would initiate a series of short subspace jumps in that direction; he daren't risk a sustained jump in case he emerged inside the planet itself. He touched the engine initiation sequence and gripped the straps as the ship slipped into subspace and the stars vanished from the vid-screens.

Chapter 34 - The End of Every Story

"It was only later, after the enemy had fallen, and we saw the vids from Petra, and Galicia, from Earthia and Entrymion, and read the feeds from Primus and Samros and the Colony beyond; when we saw the casualty lists and the number of ships lost, it was only then that we realized we hadn't won much of anything at all."
Marina Cain, First Officer, C.S. Valeria.

The C.S. *Valeria* was currently running silent deep inside the third concentric ring of the outermost planet of the Far Star Colony. Captain Severs had deployed feeler drones in-system to bounce back regular data-feeds to keep the current spatial-grid up to date. First Officer Cain had gone down to the Med Bay to visit Cadet Tielman, who had been forced to leave her duty post after collapsing earlier. Severs knew it was only a matter of time for the young cadet.

Lieutenant Keth Lohman spoke from his station at the Navs console. "Sir, I'm still reading no coordination from the enemy fleet; they're just drifting out there, it makes no sense."

Severs studied the grid flowing across the main screen. "Are the feelers picking up anything?"

"Just basic resonance from their pulse drives; normal background radiation indicates no weapons discharge within the entire sector. But, Sir, there are thousands of com feeds passing between those ships out there." He turned round to face his Captain. "We could easily tap into them if you want to hear what they're saying."

He considered this; there was still the risk of convert infiltration, even with the AI systems offline.

"No, don't cut in directly, feed a sample of their message content into a buffer, and let Breckin sift out anything interesting in the Vision Chamber."

"Aye, Sir."

Severs was looking at the current deployment of the enemy fleet... it just didn't make sense. *Why are they drifting out of sync? What could cause them to panic in such a way?* And then he thought of the Saepid vessel, and of the young girl Shari S'Atwa. *Could she possibly have succeeded? Could the war truly be over?* He dismissed the thoughts and touched his compad.

The voice of Lieutenant Marco Wenders came online. "Stats. Wenders here."

"Wenders, a question: Can you link to the main Net trunk from our current position?"

There was a pause before Wenders came back online. "Not from where we are now, Sir, no; we would have to move out-system... I'd say about half a million K's should do it."

Severs considered this... *it might be worth the risk to get a news update on the situation beyond the Colony system.*

"Very well, set up a feeder program, will you, I'm taking us out. Start your tracer scans as soon as we're far enough away from the Colony."

"Yes, Sir, will do."

"Navs, take us out on the course bearing one two zero nine to the tangent seven two one five, engage."

"Aye, Sir, drive engaged."

He watched as the spatial-grid adjusted to the new course alignment and the out-system parameters sifted for signs of enemy ship movement.

First Officer Cain stood next to the bed; the diagnostic panel was drifting at a low 42, with an occasional dip below the red line. Cadet Tielman was heading into the final stages of radiation poisoning. Mercifully, the young cadet had slipped into a coma earlier that day, and now only the machines showed that she was still alive. Every few minutes a pump fed corsyln directly into her heart via a chest tube and she would open her eyes slightly before slipping under once again. Med Chief Romana Kendra came over to join her. Cain looked up.

"Is it as bad as it looks, Doctor?"

"Well, you can see the stats; it's not good, I'm afraid. I've been giving her traumalin to stave off cell degradation, and the corsyln for her heart, but as you know, it's an uphill battle with this kind of rad infiltration; her organs are simply shutting down. I'm sorry, Cain, but it's only a matter of time now."

Cain brushed the young cadet's hair away from her face. "Will she regain consciousness at all?"

"It's possible, I've seen people come round and be perfectly lucid before they succumb; but whether that's a good thing or not, I really don't know..." She turned to look at Cain. "If you like I'll let you know if she does wake up..."

Cain looked down at the young face, now looking so peaceful. "No, that's all right, I'll wait here a while longer."

"Please yourself... Oh, Cain?"

"Yes, Doctor?"

"Is it true that the war might be over?"

Cain stroked the young girl gently along her forehead. "That's the rumor…"

Kendra smiled. "About damn time, maybe we can go home now." She walked back toward her office on the far side of the bay.

Cain took hold of Tielman's hand and squeezed.

Not all of us get to go home, Doc…

Lieutenant Lohman picked up the proximity alert as soon as the ship moved beyond the outer ring of the gas giant.

"Sir, we have incoming, basic intercept course at one zero four two coaxial two one four and closing fast…"

Severs swung his chair into position and tapped his compad. "Ship, all sections alert."

The overhead screens switched to combat stats mode, and the Weapons Master came online. "Drake here, Captain. I have five missiles remaining and twenty-eight mines with low velocity primers; not much, I'm afraid."

Severs checked the navs screen before replying. "Hold your fire, Harlen, we're checking for recognition codes now."

"Aye, Sir, waiting on your command."

Severs turned to Nav Tech Elondra Vanez. "Anything, Vanez?"

"Yes, Sir, and it's not good. Recognition comes back as a Viper, medium long-range stealth class, almost certainly belonging to the enemy; we have nothing on the Coalition channels."

"Very well…" He touched the compad. "All right, Drake, load your missiles and fire on my order."

"Aye, Sir."

Severs watched the echo-point locators zero in on the target vessel. They would need to time the missile deployment precisely; they couldn't allow the Viper any time to fire back with their shield harmonics virtually depleted.

"Lohman, tie the navs into the weapons lock and hold."

"Aye, Sir, navs tied and holding."

"Hold it….hold it…"

From the compad came the frantic voice of Lieutenant Wenders. "Captain, hold your fire!"

"What? Wenders, is that you?"

434

"Yes, Sir, stats com shows a Coalition code embedded in that ship's array. It's pretty weak, and mostly out of date, but it's there nonetheless."

"Are you sure about this, Wenders? Because that ship is just about to enter firing range."

"I checked it twice, Sir, it's Coalition all right."

Severs considered this: *A trick maybe? But to what end?* The choice was simple enough: take the chance that it's friendly and let it approach, or open fire on it and risk destroying a potential ally. He was tired of making such choices. He touched the compad.

"Weapons, stack your missiles, we're not firing on that ship."

"Very good, Sir, firing sequence duly canceled."

"Thank you, Drake."

Domini decided to stop sending the recognition codes when the *Valeria* finally sent a bounce-back response. He touched the thrusters slightly and edged closer to the big ship. He felt the ripple effect from their needle tubes as he passed through their ion stream. From his left side a com floater flickered into life and the face of Captain Severs appeared onscreen.

"Unknown ship, we have accepted your codes, please identify yourself."

Domini scrambled for a vid return protocol, found it and linked directly to the Bridge of the *Valeria.*

"Hello, Captain, this is Domini Thendosh of the Saepid vessel *Shaendar...*"

Captain Severs peered into the screen. "Yes, I remember you, but I can't help noticing you are no longer on the *Shaendar.*"

"No, Sir. It's a long story, and there's no time to explain, I have a medical emergency onboard and I need your help."

"Are you injured?"

"Not me, Sir, no, Shari, she's badly hurt... I fear she is dying..."

"Very well, we're locking on to you with our port beams, cut your engines and we'll pull you into the glider bay."

"Thank you, Sir, thank you."

"Oh, and Mr. Thendosh, I have to ask..."

"Yes, Sir?"

"Did Shari defeat the Beast?"

Domini sighed heavily. "Yes, Sir, I believe she did; but at some cost to us..."

435

"Very well... we'll talk more when you're on board, then. Severs out."

Domini sat back, infinitely relieved at having found the *Valeria*; he had begun to believe his short jumps through subspace were taking him in ever-widening circles. He checked the med display... the diagnostics were all in the red... *I'm losing her...*

As the engines cut out he felt the attraction beam emanating from the *Valeria*'s port side. The big ship's backwash scattered his screens into static, and he dialed down the feeler array. Slowly his ship began to ride the beams directly toward an open cargo door. The main stats screen linked to the exterior vids and a real-time view of the interior of the glider bay came online. The ship was being guided along a row of docking lights pulsating in sync with the attraction beam. A set of landing clamps reached out and pulled the ship to the deck between two rows of black-winged gliders and he felt himself forced into his seat as the *Valeria*'s grav-plates kicked in.

Domini quickly unstrapped and made his way back to the Surgeon. He tapped in the release codes and waited for the med shelf to open. From outside came the sound of someone tapping on the hull. He thumped the door release and watched the ramp descend to the deck below.

The diagnostics were slowly withdrawing their infusers from Shari's body as the interface began to flash a life-response warning. A woman joined him in front of the Surgeon. She extended her hand. "Doctor Kendra; you must be Domini."

"Yes. The shelf won't open... I can't get her out."

"Let me take a look." She pushed past him and edged closer to the med feeder screen.

"Give it a minute, it's balancing her electrolytes and sealing a debridement of a major wound to her chest. Pretty nasty by the look of it, too..."

Domini looked on desperately. "But can you help her?"

Kendra looked at the wavering red line on the diagnostic panel.

"I won't give you false hope, she's struggling. But we'll do our best, I promise you that. Now if you'll just get out of my way I need to get my people in here."

"Yes, but I want to stay with her..."

Kendra put a hand on his shoulder. "Look, son, the best thing you can do right now is to let us do our job. You go talk to the Captain; I know he has a few questions for you."

"Yes, but..."

436

She forced a smile. "Go on… scoot." And she pointed to the exit ramp.

Domini reluctantly made his way toward the door, but the Doctor called him back. "Are you injured? What happened to your leg?"

Domini looked down at his leg; he'd forgotten about his wound, he'd even gotten used to the limp.

"Oh, I got shot… but I think it's okay."

"Let me be the judge of that." She called out. "Mattheson! Take this man to the Med Bay; get him under a scanner."

"Yes Ma'am."

Kendra touched Domini's arm. "The Captain can see you there. Go on now, I'll take care of her."

And then Domini remembered: "Oh, yes, she has *Lysordia Syndrome* as well… you might need to verify that."

Kendra looked at the readouts. "I'm glad you told me. I'll look into the blood work when we get her stabilized, but if it's *Lysordia* we can take care of that… now go, please, let me do my job."

Domini allowed a young nurse to take his arm, and she led him out past the gliders toward a nearby drop-tube.

First Officer Cain was sitting holding Tielman's hand when the young cadet woke up.

"Ma'am?"

Cain stood up and moved closer to the young cadet. "Well, hello there, how are you feeling?"

"Not too bad really; have I been out long?"

"About a day… let me cool you down a bit." Cain wiped her face with a moist sanicloth.

"Have I missed much?"

"Well, the war is over, apparently, and I think we won."

Tielman tried to smile. "Wow, that's amazing. We can go home then…"

Cain straightened out Tielman's hair from under the head rest, pulling back the bio-tubes to make her more comfortable.

"Yes, Sara, we can go home now…"

Tielman's eyes seemed far away, as if she were looking beyond the hull and out across the vast distances between the stars.

"I hope Daren gets home in one piece. He's always so worried about me, but he's the one who always ends up getting into trouble."

"That's your brother?"

"Yes, I hope he's all right…"

"Sara, the enemy never reached Tantra… your brother will be safe and sound."

Tielman seemed to think about that for a minute.

"Then the girl Shari, she managed to kill that Beast thing?"

"Yes, she did; in fact she's being brought aboard right now."

The young girl's eyes seemed to brighten for the first time in days. "Really? I'd so like to see her; maybe thank her for saving us."

"Actually she's injured as well; they're taking her straight to vital care."

"Oh… is it that bad?"

"I'm not sure… but I will check for you."

"Thank you, Ma'am…" She coughed and a drop of blood appeared at the side of her mouth. Cain gently wiped it away and called a nurse over.

The nurse checked the diagnostics and tapped the bio-feed interface – the indicators trembled just above the red life-response line. The nurse looked at Cain and walked silently away.

Tielman looked up at the First Officer. "Ma'am?"

Cain leaned closer, speaking softly. "Call me Marina… we're not on duty now."

"Okay… Marina. Will you do something for me please?"

"Of course, anything."

"Will you look in on my brother when you get home? I don't know… I don't…" She coughed again, straining against the pain.

"Perhaps you should rest a minute, Sara."

"No, I'm all right. I was just saying… I don't know… what it's like on Galicia now… but I suppose it's bad… he won't have anyone to turn to. Mom and Dad are gone… our whole city is gone. But if you could just tell him what we did out here… tell him it mattered, tell him… my death mattered…" She closed her eyes.

Cain placed a hand on the young cadet's chest, felt a labored breath there. And then she opened her eyes one last time and spoke in a whisper: "I can't believe we won…" A solitary tear dropped onto the headrest.

The diagnostics screen blinked out and the red line flashed to the sound of the bed's bio-alarm. The nurse came over, checked the feeds and switched off the machine. Cain backed into the mesh curtain. She stood there for some time before slowly walking out into the corridor. She wasn't aware of making her

438

way back to her quarters, but once inside she lay down on her bed and cried so hard her chest ached with the agony of her terrible sadness.

They led Domini to a treatment area just off the main Medical Bay. He noticed a nurse covering the body of a young woman opposite and wondered who she was and how she had died. That reminded him of Shari. He'd last seen her on a grav-sled being pushed down a corridor. Now they wouldn't let him near her... *she was in the Vital Care Unit, they said... and he would just have to wait.*

A nurse came over to him and adjusted the bio-scanner above him.

"If you could just lie back a moment, Sir."

"Domini."

"Pardon?"

"Domini, my name is Domini... I'm Petran."

She smiled. "Oh, so you're a priest."

He sighed. "Actually no I'm not, I'm just a citizen now."

"Right, okay, well citizen or not, you have a nasty leg wound there."

"Yes, an energy bolt, I think."

She adjusted the scanner to include a deep-level mapping of the arterial pathways and linked the data-feeds to the imaging grid. The overhead screen showed a mass of torn musculature, but the femur had escaped with only a series of minor fractures.

"Not looking too bad, Domini. I think we can sort this out for you. If you'd like to rest here for a few minutes I need to go prep a Surgeon for you."

As she started to walk away Domini called after her. "Excuse me, Nurse... have you heard anything about my companion? Is she all right?"

"Sorry, I haven't heard, but I can check for you if you like."

"Yes, if you don't mind. Thank you."

Captain Severs was speaking to Nav Tech Lohman as the two made their way toward the Medical Bay. "Lohman, the First Officer isn't answering her compad; can you go check on her for me?"

"Of course, Sir, right away."

Severs met one of Doctor Kendra's team as he walked in.

"Doctor, how's Mr. Thendosh?"

"He's in recovery, Sir. We had to fuse a graft to a fractured femur and give him a covering of statskin, but he'll be up and about in no time."

"Can I see him?"

439

"Yes, Sir, this way."

Severs found Domini stretched out on a bed, his right leg wrapped tight in a bio-mesh cocoon.

"Captain! How is Shari? Is she all right?"

"Calm yourself, Mr. Thendosh, Doctor Kendra tells me your friend is going to make a full recovery. She's obviously very weak right now, and I doubt she'll be released from the Surgeon for several days, but considering her injuries, I think she's very lucky to be alive."

"Thank you, Captain, that's good news. I'm grateful for your help, but I have another favor to ask, and it's just as important."

"Very well, I'm listening."

"I had to leave my friend back on our ship, near the moon where we found the Beast. She's running out of air, Captain, we have to help her."

"Do you have an exact location?"

"It should be in the datapad I brought with me; if you could just go through the scans…"

"All right. I'll get someone on it… just bear with me a minute." He went over to the compad on a nearby wall. "Breckin, Severs here, are you still in the Vision Chamber?"

"Yes, Sir, running the feelers through the CES right now."

"Hand that over to one of your team. I'm sending you a datapad, I want you to upload any grids you find and scan for the Saepid vessel. I want location and distance, and I want them fast, got that?"

"Yes, Sir, I'll get right on it."

"And Breckin…"

"Sir?"

"When you have the grids feed them directly to Navs, we have a lone ally out there in need of our help."

"Very good, Sir."

Severs gave the datapad to an orderly and sent her off to the Vision Chamber. He turned to face Domini. "Well now, Mr. Thendosh…"

Domini raised his hand. "Please, Captain, just Domini will do."

"Very well, Domini. What can you tell me about Miss S'Atwa's encounter with the enemy?"

"Not much, I'm afraid. She was forced to face the Beast alone… we were cut off from her… there was nothing we could do to help her."

440

"I see... so you don't actually know how she managed to defeat the thing."

"To be honest, I have no idea what she did after we were separated. But Shari is a very special girl... to tell you how special would take a great deal of time."

"Just the bare essentials then."

"Very well. Shari had a connection to an ancient artifact... a device, if you will. A powerful weapon designed to kill the Beast; but she was the only one who could use it. We followed her deep inside the satellite moon of the Colony world, until we got separated and then she was left to face the Beast without us. Soon after that, Anthra and I were attacked by an agent of the Beast..."

"Anthra is one of the Saepids I spoke to on the com link?"

"Yes, that's him. His mate, Ventra, remained aboard the *Shaendar*; she's the one I need you to rescue."

"And Anthra?"

"He did not survive his injuries... we lost him down there..."

"I am sorry."

"Yes well, soon after that I tracked down the agent. He had Shari with him and I had no doubt what fate awaited her in his hands; so I was forced to kill him... I had no choice..." Domini looked down. He had never taken a life, and the guilt was already beginning to haunt him.

"You did what you had to do, Domini... but do you know for sure that Shari destroyed this Beast?"

"That's what she told me. But, Captain, the evidence is everywhere. Those hundreds of ships are just drifting out there; they are no longer being controlled." He looked into Severs' eyes. "I believe something terrible died down there on that moon, something that has changed the history of a thousand worlds... We can only hope that we are finally free of its madness."

"Well, I have to say the data-feeds coming in seem to confirm that the enemy is in disarray. Long-range sensors are showing multiple explosions near the Colony world. We were about to dip into the Net feeds for Coalition news, but that can wait until we've retrieved your friend."

The nearby compad buzzed. "Captain, Breckin here."

"Go ahead, Breckin."

"I've found the Saepid vessel and Navs have confirmed and set course; we should reach them within the hour."

441

"Excellent, Lieutenant. Keep an eye on the long-range tracers; I want to know if any of those ships start to pay us any attention."

"Very good, Sir."

Severs turned back to face Domini. "You heard that?"

"Yes… I just pray we're not too late."

"Have faith, Domini, we'll get there in time." He turned to leave. "Now I'll leave you to your rest. If you require anything just ask."

"Thank you, Captain, but I just want to be with Shari right now."

"I'm sure that can be arranged… check with one of the doctors."

"I will. Thank you."

Ventra tried to tap the main console; she could hear the proximity alert but the stats screen was down. She had no idea who was approaching the ship. Environmentals were now hovering at thirty-two percent, borderline for full oxygenation. It was only a matter of time before the *Shaendar* died; and soon after that she would follow…

The com link was flashing, but she couldn't answer without using up the last of her power reserves. *But what if it is Domini? What would you do, my dearest Anthra?*

She had been dreaming of Anthra, remembering his sales pitch, always the same first line to their customers: *Saepids we are, and most humble in our dealings…* His words were silent echoes scattering around the command deck, drifting with the leaves among the branches of Shari's tree. She looked up to where Shari would sit; it was strange not to see her up there wrapped in her straps and fleece. *You had such a wonderful temper, Shari, my dear child… and where are you now, I wonder?* She thought back to that far distant day on Primus… *maneuvering among the great trees, being so careful not to catch Anthra and the girl in the ship's backwash… and then there was Petra and the finding of the artifact, and meeting dear Domini, so formal and polite Domini… and the terrible loss of their Colloquies friends at Landings Down, and the tragedy of brave Entrymion… all lost, all gone like my beloved Anthra…* She reached forward and linked the com panel to the last of the power reserves.

Instantly a voice came online. "I repeat, this is Captain Severs of the C.S. *Valeria*; we have a team attempting to gain access to your rear cargo hold, can you rotate your pressurization or not?"

Ventra tried to sit up in her webbing, but was already too weak. She spoke slowly and as clearly as she could. "Will open air lock… power almost gone." She closed the connection and fed the cargo hold with enough power to get the rear doors to open. She finally lost consciousness, her head coming to rest on the main console.

First Officer Cain took the proaxol from the drawer. She held it up for a few moments and then put it back, slamming the drawer shut. She leaned over the sink and brushed her hair back. It was clear the drug was no longer helping, in fact it was definitely making things worse; that and the complete lack of sleep were surely reason enough for breaking down over Tielman's death. *That stuff is messing with my head... a First Officer does not cry alone on her bunk...*

The door pad buzzed.

"Yes?"

"Lieutenant Lohman here, Ma'am, the Captain wanted me to check in on you."

Damn! "Thank you, Lohman. I'm fine. I'll see you on the Bridge."

"Very good, Ma'am."

So where do we go from here? So many worlds to rebuild, so many lives lost... and yet the girl from Primus has saved our civilization... perhaps someday they will learn of her victory; hopefully they'll be grateful. But how long will it be before we have to do it all over again? How long before someone stumbles across another lost archive gone sentient? It was only a damn machine, a mind raised to Godhood... They made a monster and we paid the price of that arrogance... She looked down at the closed drawer... *Where do I go from here?*

She took the proaxol infuser out and pressed it against her neck. The instant lift came with its usual sense of euphoria; but she knew that this time it wouldn't last as long as it did before. She straightened her tunic and left for the Bridge, clenching her fists to stop the trembling.

When Ventra opened her eyes Domini was there smiling down at her.

"Domini, is that you?"

"Yes, it's me. How are you feeling?"

"Not too sure. Where is this place?" She raised her head to look around her.

"You're in the Medical Bay aboard the *Valeria*..."

She smiled. "You said you would come back... and Shari?"

"Getting better, I haven't seen her yet, she's in treatment."

443

"But she will recover?"

"Yes, that's what they say. They had to do a few deep grafts, but she's healing nicely. But how about you? How are you feeling? They had a few problems with your blood work; apparently you are their very first Saepid."

"I am well, Domini, thank you. I will recover. You too are fixed?" She looked down at the strapping around his leg.

"Yes, I'm good. Just a bit of a limp for now."

"That is good."

He hesitated before he continued. "Ventra, I'm so sorry about Anthra. It all happened so fast…"

She tried to smile. "Be calm, Domini… Anthra lives yet in me…" She closed her eyes again.

"Perhaps I should leave you to rest…"

She lay back on the pillow. "Yes… perhaps it is best, suddenly I am very tired…"

Domini stayed by her side until she fell asleep and then he made his way back to the Vital Care Unit.

Chapter 35 - A Chance to Hope

"I have no idea how all this started, but I was there at the end, and although I lost most everyone I ever loved, I'm still grateful I made it this far."
Lieutenant Tamara Breckin, C.S. Valeria.

It took almost three months for the C.S. *Valeria* to reach Primus. They had been forced to make several detours to assist in a number of rescue missions. There were dozens of damaged Coalition vessels left drifting in subspace, and many more in real-time making urgent requests for assistance. Sometimes it was a simple matter of re-initializing power coils using their own feeder systems, but most often they had to offer medical aid and transport the most severally injured to nearby Coalition outposts. All of this took time, and Shari used that time to recuperate from her injuries.

She had discovered the flower galleries on H-Deck three days after leaving the Surgeon. After that she liked to spend a few hours of each day wandering among the flowers and fountains, and losing herself beneath the multicolored surrela vines. Domini would join her there and they would talk about their future. Shari wanted to make their home on the Islands of Lanoir, far out in the Serira Ocean, and he said he liked the idea of an island life; but she made him promise to keep out of the pleasure arcades with their exotic dancers and gambling tables.

They hardly ever spoke of their journey to the Far Star Colony, mainly because every memory of those times involved Anthra, and that just reminded them that he was no longer with them. Domini and Captain Severs had asked many questions about her battle with the Beast, but the memory of that time was now vague and indistinct and she told them it was better that way, the horror of that confrontation was finally receding and with it the strange sense of destiny that had lived for so long in her soul.

Ventra had come to them one day in the second month and informed them of her plans. She was going to get refinanced from the Saepid Trading Guild; she said she had good connections among the High Traders there and couldn't foresee any problems. But it was what she was planning to do after that which worried them the most.

She was going to hire a cheap long-range lugger and travel back to the Far Star Colony. She intended to recover the *Shaendar* and refit her. It would take time, many months, she predicted, but she said the work would be worthwhile if she could eventually return the ship to its trading roots. "It's what Anthra would have wanted, Shari…"

The three of them had been standing beneath an arch of Gordenia flowers overlooking the central gardens. Ventra was effectively saying goodbye, but no one wanted to admit it. The journey together had been long and hard, and they had lost someone they had all come to love. They held hands until the overhead tubes began to fade as *night* arrived aboard the *Valeria.* That was the night the journey truly ended for the three of them.

First Officer Cain had asked to speak to her one day and they had met in the corner of the central common room. She'd only spoken to Cain a few times, mostly to answer questions about their quest to kill the Beast. But this time things were different; Cain had told her the story of Cadet Sara Tielman, and how she had saved the mission.

"You see, Shari, without Tielman's efforts we wouldn't have been around to save you or Domini, or Ventra for that matter… she died doing her duty and saved countless lives in the process."

Cain had shown her an ID tag of the young cadet; the image showed a young woman with long red hair, a friendly smile and bright brown eyes.

Shari had told Cain about the message. "It came direct to my datapad; she must have tagged it to Captain Severs' vid-com."

Cain had smiled at that. "Yes, I know. My adjutant Breckin found it in the logs… she was certainly a resourceful young woman, I'll give her that."

"She just wanted to thank me… and she wanted me to know her name."

They had fallen silent for several minutes before Cain continued: "Shari, I have to ask you something. In your report to the Captain you said the Beast had somehow managed to get inside your head long before you reached the Colony itself. Can you just tell me how that affected you?"

She wasn't sure why the First Officer wanted to know about such things but she had told her about the headaches, the bad dreams and the lack of sleep. It had seemed to upset Cain at the time.

"Is there a problem, Marina?"

"I'm not sure. It's just that as the *Valeria* got nearer to the Colony I began to suffer nightmares and I just couldn't get enough sleep… it seems strange, that's all."

She had to think about that for a minute. "Perhaps you were susceptible to the Beast, just like me…"

Cain had smiled at that. "Yes, but you are this *custodia*, are you not?"

446

"Anthra, said it was a wide blood-line, whatever that means… you're not from Primus, are you, by any chance?"

"No, born and bred on Tantra, although my great grandfather was a Petran monk, until he met my great grandmother, that is…"

Shari had looked at her. "But Jophrim went to live on Petra, and he was definitely *custodia*…"

They had stared at each other and then laughed.

"So maybe we are distant cousins, Shari S'Atwa."

Poor Cain, she had checked herself into the Med Bay shortly after that. Something about withdrawal from an addiction to proaxol.

Shari had been skimming the Net Posts on a daily basis, sifting for any information concerning the former occupied worlds. Most of the outer Hub planets had been devastated by the forces of Saemal: Galicia, Earthia, Petra and Entrymion were in ruins and would have to be completely rebuilt. With only a few exceptions, most of their primary cities had been leveled by enemy missiles, their citizens either killed or transported to off-world mining colonies. But the majority of the Core worlds were intact and it would only be a matter of time before the fleets of the Coalition Restoration League reached the outer planets.

There were problems with the abandoned armies of Saemal. Several of his high leaders were holding out against Coalition forces on Galicia and Earthia, but with the fall of Samros and the Colony world itself, it was only a matter of time before order was restored. The Phaelon's had managed to oust their new leader Mistia and the Confederacy was already in the process of being restored; Captain Severs said it wouldn't be long before they started sending spies out into the Coalition once again.

Primus itself had been spared destruction, so she would constantly loop the Net feeds in favor of news tags from her home world. But the local feeds were dead. There were no Posts coming out of Primus at all. That was the scariest of moments, not knowing if her race had survived the fall of Saemal, not knowing if her father was dead or alive, or going crazy somewhere in a padded cell. But one day Captain Severs came to her and told her about the newly established Coalition link to Egrain City, and after that news came in thick and fast.

There was no specific information concerning her father, but all indications showed that the people of Primus had regained their independence and were once more free to go about their lives without fear of retribution from the enemy. She had even seen a weak vid-feed of the destruction of the new

447

Temple of Saemal; the citizens of Egrain city had torched the place and killed hundreds of its priests… which she thought was unfortunate considering those priests might well have returned to their former selves as well.

No one knew how Saemal had managed to seduce so many millions of minds; the psycho-analytical team on board the *Valeria* theorized that the Cortex itself had transcended the boundaries of relative time and space, and had been able to directly access the cerebral cortex of living brains from a great distance. None of it mattered any more, of course; and she certainly didn't get involved in the long discussions in the common rooms.

In the final days before they reached Primus, she was standing with Domini in front of the huge glasscite window in the viewing gallery, looking out toward the Primus star system.

"See there, Dom? That's Sancturia, the first inhabited world of our system; they settled that just twenty thousand years ago, way before Primus. Of course hardly anyone goes there these days; the place is a slag heap by all accounts…"

He smiled and put an arm around her shoulders. "So we won't honeymoon there, my love."

She looked up at him. "Hey, is that your way of proposing to me Mr. Priest?"

He pulled her into his arms. "What do you think?"

As their lips met, the ship trembled beneath their feet as the main pulse drive cut out and the short-range thrusters came online. She pulled back to look out at the stars.

"Is this the end of our story, then, Dom?"

"It's the end of one story, but the beginning of another, I think…"

"Captain Severs managed to track my father down, you know."

"Yes, I heard; sounds like he's back to being himself again." He looked at her. "Do you want to talk about it?"

"No, not really; why would I want to talk about it?"

"Well, because you haven't mentioned him since you found out he was alive and well."

"What's to say? You'll meet him soon enough… and I think he's really going to like you."

"Really?"

She laughed. "No way!"

448

Beyond the great window, the stars glistened like tiny islands of life in a sea of creation. Further out still, beyond the periphery of known space, out across the immeasurable gulf that was the Great Expanse, a singleton star lost in the night, and a solitary world born out of the fiery death of a cosmic collision. A dark secret left alone there, hidden deep and forever frozen in time, waiting in silence, with a hint of perception and a vast wellspring of patience.

"This story is not ended, and although it will soon become history, the secrets it now holds may one day come back to haunt us..."
Tantalus, Chronicles of Ages.

- **END** -

The Cortex

THE GALACTIC COALITION OF WORLDS

APPENDICES

APPENDIX 1

REGISTER OF INDIVIDUALS OF HISTORICAL NOTE

Primary Stipulation: Data referent to the Coalescency of Saemal is now stored within the primary access adjunct Torus-99 and has been sealed by CIS Security Protocol pursuant to the agreement concluded by the Supreme High Council of the Coalition. Spatial Date references, access points, core logs and juridical stipulations are not available at this time. Coalition Archive sub/sec P-Ultra 000279319/H/COL/X

Altrius Dex
Poet – Born in Sophia City, Planet Entrymion.
Celebrated Entrymion Poet noted as a founding member of the Carphalia Galac Poetry Society.
Dex was eighty seven years old when he was killed during the assault on Carphalia by the forces of the Coalescency.
Published works include: *Trimon & Iselde, Varga's Expectations, Serial Sonnets,* and *A Time A Place A City.*
(Secondary Adjunct Ref: 0000/43456/ENTR/CO/- *'The Fall of Entrymion'*)

Anthra
Coalition Archive sub/sec data core P-Epsra/0000134799/SAE/COA/X-c
Please note: Archival data relating to the Saepid Trader Anthra and his role during the War of the Coalescency has been sealed by Security Docket 1-17/Epsra CIS.
Information in the Public Domain is as follows: Commander of the Saepid Far Star Trading vessel *Shaendar* and mated by Saepid Pheratat ceremony to Ventra, pilot.
Anecdotal evidence has been filed which suggest that the homeworld of the Saepid Othrum race of traders lies within the Torellian Cluster, but this has not been verified either by the Saepid Trading Guild or by any other means.
(See Secondary Adjunct Ref: 0000147/S/Othrum/Tr/Guild)
(Security Adjunct Ref: 0008/SA/OT/71000X Sealed by Coalition Dictate Psi/49)

Arundel Leonis
Fleet Captain E.S.*Cassandra* of the Entrymion Home Defence Fleet during the Battle of Entrymion.
Captain Leonis, along with his entire crew were killed whilst defending their home world during the invasion of Entrymion by the forces of the Coalescency.
Awarded the Crystal Star, Entrymion Trion Medal of Honor, and Coalition Roll of Valour (posthumously).

The Poet Brayman
Possible pseudonym for unknown Poet and writer of political satire – Entrymion.
Known published works include: *After the Fall – An Account of the Battle of Carphalia, From the Ashes of Men* and *Fires Over Watersfell.*
Anecdotal evidence suggests he died in the Westphal Refugee Settlement, Planet Entrymion from injuries sustained during the occupation by forces of the Coalescency.

Brother Fiodore
Founder of the First Ascetic Ministry of Petra, a Sacred College responsible for the Ordination of the Supreme Pontifical Head of the Sacred Church of Jophrim.
Brother Fiodore attended the Sacric Sunum College of Advocates some time after the death of Syrillian Anthos, Founder of the Sacred Church of Jophrim.
Noted as the translator of the Sacred Book of Jophrim from ancient Galac into post-Diaspora Galac.
(Secondary Adjunct available Ref: 000341976/0056/PET/JPH/C- *'The Seasons of Our Lord – The Life of Jophrim the Saviour by Brother Fiodore).*

Corel Luwain
Philosopher and artist - native to the planet Samros capital world of the Cordwainer Alliance circa: 00001/862890c – 00001/1093100c.
Little is known of Luwain beyond the archival edition of his work*: Errors in Transcendence* (Data-core Ref: 00001478/C/NC/SA/X)
Please note: Data relating to Non-Conformist planets and associated alliances is restricted to: Ultra-grade T-40 Pass.
(Secondary Adjunct sealed under CIS Security Protocol Teraph/Altra T-37).

Carlten Wynkind
Professor of Advance Math - Lecturer in Residence Central University of Primus.
Noted mathematician and theoretical spatial analyst credited with the base code algorithm for the 'feeler' spatial sensory device later developed by the Clinitas Group on Gamont.
Published works include: *Intra-Spatial Diagnostics & Sensory Algorithmic Potential, Subspace Field Variants & Real-Time Insertion* and, *The Theory of Transcendent Neural Enhancement Explained.*
Although known as Lecturer in Residence in later life, Professor Wynkind spent his formative years working as part of the Clinitas Development Group on Gamont.
(Secondary Adjunct Ref: 000010/CW/PR/C/4500 available to MsTH/Sen-100
Students and researchers via the Central Archive of Industrial Sciences, Primus)

Dhimfaal
Coloquies Port Official registered at Landings Down as Docking Allocation Officer.

Landings Down established circa: 0000/000012356796c Pre-Diaspora at Star Sector: NG84/C/COA-0001-000794/TER as a trading and repair outpost of the Coloquies Federation.

The Port was destroyed and its inhabitants killed during the War of the Coalescency, there is no official record as to whether Dhimfaal was among the dead.

External inquiries made me made to the Coloquies State Mission, planet Tantra.

Dieter Freim

Coalition Archive sub/sec data core P-Tethra/0000710846/S12/COA/X

Please note: Archival data relating to Dieter Freim and his role during the War of the Coalescency has been sealed by Security Docket 2-27/Alphra CIS.

Information in the Public Domain is as follows:

Known to have been a crew member on the long range cargo Lugger *Dreslier* which is known to have made landfall on the satellite Moon of Rim 1478A, a planet later designated as the Far Star Colony (Star Sector: NG01/FS/CO-0000/000-01572).

Member of the Sacred Twelve of the Coalescency – Primary Adjunct available Ref: X-Tethra/000414971/S12/COA/X-s via Ultra-grade T-40 Pass.

Dolmon Tendra

Coalition Archive sub/sec data core P-Retra/0007119101/EEC/PHA/X-p

Please note: Archival data relating to Dolmon Tendra and his role during the War of the Coalescency has been sealed by Security Docket 1-12/Retra CIS.

Information in the Public Domain is as follows:

Dolmon Tendra was a Phaelon agent and member of the Elaas Elite Corps (First Level). Anecdotal evidence places him alongside his Master Drondar Khan at the time of the War of the Coalescency; his eventual fate remains undetermined at this time.

(Secondary Adjunct available Ref: COA/PH/EEC/71-P *'Pirates Into Spies – A Short History of the Elaas Elite Core; Dronginger, Markus).*

Domini Thendosh

Coalition Archive sub/sec data core Q-Alphra/0000285409/PET/COA/X

Please note: Archival data relating to Domini Thendosh and his role during the War of the Coalescency has been sealed by Security Docket 1-20/Alphra CIS.

Information in the Public Domain is as follows:

Thendosh was born in the Outer Province of Alusia, Western Block, Planet Petra. At age fourteen he entered the Seminary of Sacred Hearts in Salicia Sonora as an Advocate Brother in training. Sometime later he was found guilty of Sacrilegious Misinterpretation of the Sacred Book of Jophrim and stripped of his Doctrinal Bonds and asked to vacate his rooms.

Please note: A sub/sec data core M-Alphra adjunct to this entry is sealed under CIS Security Protocol COR/DT/P-13. Researchers possessing an Ultra-grade T-40 Pass

may apply for limited access via the Commission for Oversee of the Post Coalescency Period.

(Secondary Adjunct Ref: 000123578/PET/COR/7899 – Published under State Jurisprudence Docket TH-07: *In Jophrim's Footsteps – My life Aboard the Shaendar*)

Dramar Pendor

Designated as a High priest in the Samrosian Church of Saemal.

Born and raised within the Clautwitz Dome on the planet Samros (Cordwainer Alliance). Known to have made his living as a purveyor of trellis plants. Later during the occupation of Samros by the forces of the Coalescency he achieved rapid promotion within the service of Saemal until eventually being awarded the title of Cardinal General. Pendor is known to have led forces under the command of Phale of the Sacred Twelve against the planet Petra and is responsible for the subsequent genocide on that world. (Sealed Security Adjunct CIS/CO/DP/92-T not available for public access)

(Primary Stipulation: Data referent to the Coalescency of Saemal is now stored within the primary access adjunct Torus-99 and has been sealed by CIS Security Protocol pursuant to the agreement concluded by the Supreme High Council of the Coalition – Spatial Date references, access points, core logs and juridical stipulations are not available at this time).

Drondar Khan

Coalition Archive sub/sec data core P-Feta/0001525891/EEC/PHA/X-c

Please note: Archival data relating to Drondar Khan and his role during the War of the Coalescency has been sealed by Security Docket 2-17/Feta CIS.

Information in the Public Domain is as follows:

Anecdotal evidence suggests Khan advanced through the ranks of the Elaas Elite Corps after spending several years as a Security Prefect on the Phaelon colony of Aluvia. (See Secondary Adjunct Ref: 00029/PH/AL/P – *Slavery & Slaughter Inside the Confederacy, Michelson, Derek*).

Known to have become the Prime Leader of the Phaelon Elaas Elite Corps at the time of the War of the Coalescency, his eventual fate remains unknown at this time. (Suggested Research Adjunct available Ref: COA/PH/EEC/61-P *'Corsairs & Brigands' – A Short History of the Phaelon Confederacy*).

Jos Severs

Born in the Tharn settlement, planet Arcturia Prime.

Joined the Coalition Fleet Military Academy before entering Full Service Commission as a Spatial Analyst serving at the Tantran Fleet Orbital Yards, Tantra.

Served with distinction during the Dronheim Insurgency circa. 0004423-0034c

Promoted to Bridge Officer First Class C.S. *Toranda* circa: 00001379-4010690c.local.

Promoted to Captain C.S.*Valeria* circa: 00001485-5020796c

Served with distinction during the War of the Coalescency and later honoured with: Crystal Star, Blue Epaulette, Trian of Tantra, and Free Citizen of the Coalition Tag. The Central University of Arcturia has since been renamed The Severs University in honor of the man.

Please note: A sub/sec data core M-Altra adjunct to this entry is sealed under CIS Security Protocol COR/JS/V-24. Researchers possessing an Ultra-grade T-40 Pass may apply for limited access via the Commission for Oversee of the Post Coalescency Period.

Jophrim

Religious deity worshipped by the devotees of the Sacred Church of Jophrim as the Son of God.

See Archival Ref: Petra/0000345/Jophrim/Codex *Sancti Remus*/678000/CO/P-c

Petran Scripture maintains that the Sacred Church of Jophrim was founded by the Prefect Syrillian Anthos some time after Jophrim returned to Harevakor (Ref: Codex *Altium Dex-Afterlife*) one thousand years after the last of the First Race transcended the physical plain. (Fifty First Millennium Pre-Diaspora).

In the teachings of Brother Fiodore of the First Ascetic Ministry of Petra, (Scripture IIX) Jophrim was sent down to walk among mortal men by his Father in Harevakor at a time of great need. An evil Beast of unprecedented power had been born out of darkness and was spreading its shadow across the fields of men. Jophrim led a great host to the edge of known space where they defeated the Beast using the power bestowed upon him by his Father, after which time Jophrim returned to his Father in Harevakor. His followers under the auspices of the Prefect Syrillian Anthos returned to Petra and established the First Church of Jophrim on the outskirts of the desert city of Salicia Sonora. The Petran Church of Jophrim has since encompassed the entire planet of Petra and spawned a religion now followed by over 100 billion worshippers scattered throughout the Petran Sector of the Coalition. (See architectural ref: Basilica D'Jophrim 0001 014307/SAL/P).

More recent translations of the Petran Kyrillian-archi-text (See secondary adjunct: 0001457/9805/P/J *'The Forbidden Works'* Petran State Archive) has shed new light upon the true origins of Jophrim. Several academics have submitted papers suggesting the mortal origins of Jophrim as a military leader of an allied coalition of worlds fighting a desperate war against an unknown enemy at some point before the Interregnum and during the first phase of the original Diaspora of the human race. The text later makes reference to the Province of Tianadora (Planet Merril) as the probably birthplace of Jophrim. The Sacred Church of Jophrim under the leadership of Cardinal Hanson Deiterbach has since dismissed such interpretations as sacrilegious quoting the Sacred Precepts found within the Book of Jophrim (Ref: *Doctrinal Episcopus*) as a basis upon which the true faith is sustained.

457

The true nature of Jophrim and the religion devoted to him cannot be calculated by means of statistical analysis or factual historical research, much of the knowledge of the time before the Interregnum has been lost to science and as such there can be no verifiable data or correlation of facts available for this Register.

Please note: Researchers possessing an Ultra-grade T-40 Pass may access the sealed archives of the CIS (Combined Coalition Internal Security and Intelligence Agency) under the following Reference Dockets: *Sword of Jophrim, Chalice of Creation, Custodia, S'Atwa, Shari, Thendosh, Domini, Raine, Kyle, Merril, Far Star Colony, Sandheim, First Race.*

Kyle Raine

Professor of Ancient History and Field Archaeologist, former Lecturer in Residence at the University of Southern Planatia, planet Gamont.

Born in Encienada City, Gamont circa: 000179-211038c local.

Noted for his extensive field work relating to the verification of the First Race as an verifiable homogenous species existing before the Diaspora of humanity.

Discovered the Portal Tombs of the Huharni Escarpment on the planet Merril.

Published works include: *Conversion, Transition & Transcendence – Footsteps to Godhood (A History of the First Race), Half-Life Forensics, Stratigraphy & Strata, Offworld Explorations* and *The Merril Extrapolation.*

Please note: A sub/sec data core T-Altra adjunct to this entry is sealed under CIS Security Protocol COR/KR/T-21. Researchers possessing an Ultra-grade T-40 Pass may apply for limited access via the Commission for Oversee of the Post Coalescency Period.

Limon S'Atwa

Coalition Archive sub/sec data core L-Qetra/0000728802/PRI/COA/X-c

Please note: Archival data relating to Limon S'Atwa and his role during the War of the Coalescency has been sealed by Security Docket 1-11/Qetra CIS.

Information in the Public Domain is as follows:

Citizen of Egrain City, planet Primus and a Special Agent within the Department of Interior Affairs (Security Services).

Uncle to Shari S'Atwa (Security Docket 1-19/Alphra CIS)

Brother to Lorn S'Atwa (Security Docket 1-11/Oetra CIS)

Evidence submitted to the Commission for Oversee of the Post Coalescency Period refers to Limon S'Atwa as a initial activist within the movement to forestall the Coalescency. It is recorded that he lost his life in the defence of his world against the forces of the Coalescency.

Please note: A sub/sec data core L-Qetra adjunct to this entry is sealed under CIS Security Protocol COA/LA/W-16. Researchers possessing an Ultra-grade T-40 Pass

may apply for limited access via the Commission for Oversee of the Post Coalescency Period.

Lomar Fendor
Noted as a Field Tutor Level Three member of the Elaas Elite Corps based on the Phaelon homeworld of Phaedra.
Fendor is recorded as the Phaelon operative responsible for the transmission of Phaelon State Access Codes to the Coalition warship C.S. *Intridar* during the Battle of Galicia Prime (Ref: 00001457/C/CO/COR/000129: War of the Coalescency) thus turning that battle in favour of the Coalition forces who subsequently re-occupied the Galician system routing the last vestiges of Phaelon forces in that Sector. Fendor was awarded the Crystal Star by the Coalition Supreme High Council (posthumously).
There is a secondary adjunct: *The Two Sides of Lomar Fendor by Trilim Vendor* available upon request via an Al-40 Blue Pass.
(Sealed Security Adjunct CIS/CO/91-T not available for public access)
(Primary Stipulation: Data referent to the Coalescency of Saemal is now stored within the primary access adjunct Torus-99 and has been sealed by CIS Security Protocol pursuant to the agreement concluded by the Supreme High Council of the Coalition – Spatial Date references, access points, core logs and juridical stipulations are not available at this time).

Lorn S'Atwa
Coalition Archive sub/sec data core L-Oetra/0000419901/PRI/COA/X-c
Please note: Archival data relating to Lorn S'Atwa and his role during the War of the Coalescency has been sealed by Security Docket 1-11/Oetra CIS.
Information in the Public Domain is as follows:
Citizen of Egrain City, planet Primus and Secondary Member of the Primus Legislative Assembly. (Consular Advisor pro tem)
Father of Shari S'Atwa (Security Docket 1-19/Alphra CIS)
Brother to Limon S'Atwa (Security Docket 1-11/Qetra CIS)
Evidence submitted to the Commission for Oversee of the Post Coalescency Period refers to Lorn S'Atwa as a initial activist within the movement to forestall the Coalescency, however after the fall of Primus he was known to be a leading member of the Securitas Secret Police in the service of the Sacred Twelve.
After the fall of the Coalescency and the cessation of subspace neural control by Saemal, Lorn S'Atwa and the citizens of Primus were once more incorporated into the Coalition.
Please note: A sub/sec data core L-Oetra adjunct to this entry is sealed under CIS Security Protocol COA/LA/W-19. Researchers possessing an Ultra-grade T-40 Pass may apply for limited access via the Commission for Oversee of the Post Coalescency Period.

Lothar Theron

Philosopher and Poet, author of the book *'Personal Poetics'*.

Born in the city of Austaria, planet Earthia sometime during the First Diaspora.

Theron was a philosopher, poet and teacher of Earthian Literature and travelled widely throughout the Hub Alliance. He is credited with the translation of Tantalus' *Chronicles of Ages* into modern Galac.

Other works include: *The Dromite Rebellion, Sunrise and Sunsets, Wise Words and Wanton Ways – a short history of the Earthian Dialect, Around the Hub in Eighty Light Years* and *When Gods Walked the Stars.*

The University of Theron in Austaria is named in his honor.

Luther Rodin

Level Two Operative of the Elaas Elite Corps and Ground Combat Prefect.

Known primarily as the instigator of the genocide undertaken by the Phaelon Battle Torc Regiment against the citizens of Galicia during the War of the Coalescency.

(Please note: All relevant details pertaining to the activities of Rodin and the crimes for which he was later executed are sealed by CIS Security Protocol 00011/B-19/PH)

Marina Cain

Served as First Officer aboard the C.S. *Valeria.*

Born in Sengal City, Iphritia Province, planet Telaxa.

Joined the Coalition Defence Force on Tantra before being promoted through the ranks and transferring to the Coalition Border Fleet at Earthia.

Assigned as First Officer aboard the C.S. *Valeria* and served with distinction during the War of the Coalescency and later honoured with: Crystal Star.

Please note: A sub/sec data core L-Altra adjunct to this entry is sealed under CIS Security Protocol COR/MC/V-28. Researchers possessing an Ultra-grade T-40 Pass may apply for limited access via the Commission for Oversee of the Post Coalescency Period.

Mistia Dane

Coalition Archive sub/sec data core P-Netra/0000811937/COA/X

Please note: Archival data relating to Mistia Dane and her role during the War of the Coalescency has been sealed by Security Docket-32/NETRA CIS.

Information in the Public Domain is as follows:

Known to have been a crew member on the long range cargo Lugger *Dreslier* which is known to have made landfall on the satellite Moon of Rim 1478A, a planet later designated as the Far Star Colony (Star Sector: NG01/FS/CO-0000/000-01572).

Member of the Sacred Twelve of the Coalescency – Primary Adjunct available Ref: X-Netra/000022375/S12/COA/X-s via Ultra-grade T-40 Pass.

(Secondary Adjunct sealed under CIS Security Protocol Teraph/Altra T-37)

Neiron Thane

Coalition Archive sub/sec data core L-Zephra/0000999801/CO/COA/X-c

Please note: Archival data relating to Neiron Thane and his role during the War of the Coalescency has been sealed by Security Docket 1-12/Zephra CIS.

Information in the Public Domain is as follows:

According to sub/sec data core analysis undertaken by the Coalition Fleet Medical Corp & Bio-Tech Analysis Foundation on Primal IV (Post-Mortem Ref: 0001/Delt-T)

Neiron Thane was a bio-enhanced human who served the forces of Saemal during the War of the Coalescency. There is no available data with regard to his planet of origin. Anecdotal evidence suggests he was a former citizen of a Non-Conformist world within the Cordwainer Alliance. (Security Adjunct T-19 Sealed by Coalition Dictate Psi/52).

Poron Metklon

Noted as the first member of the Phaelon Elaas Elite Corps to be identified and detained under CIS Security Protocol Deltra-T-19.

Metklon was a Field Operative Level One of the Phaelon Covert Security Service who was identified and taken into custody whilst maintaining subversive surveillance of the Praisedio Building CIS Headquarters Primal IV. He was returned to Phaedra as part of a prisoner exchange programme. No further details as to the nature of the exchange are available.

(All primary and secondary adjuncts are sealed under CIS Security Docket: A/PH-13)

Sara Tielman

Born in the village of Shimara near the city of Formentora, Seran Archipelago on Galicia.

Joined the Coalition Fleet Military Academy before entering Full Service Commission as an Engineer Cadet in Training, Second Class, serving with the Galician Expeditionary Force.

Transferred to the Spatial Analysis & Tactical Rendition Corps on Tantra: 00021479-67954301c local.

Promoted to Cadet First Class Engineering aboard the C.S.*Valeria* circa: 00002195-6086510c

Served with distinction during the War of the Coalescency and later honoured with: Crystal Star, Blue Epaulette, and Legion of Galicia (posthumously).

Cadet Tielman lost her life in defence of the Coalition during the War of the Coalescency. In her honor the method she devised to track sub-spatial incursions at the tertiary level of anomalous variations within a subspace field has since been named 'The Tielman Method' (Circa: 000012489-100067010)

Please note: A sub/sec data core M-Altra adjunct to this entry is sealed under CIS Security Protocol COR/ST/U-14. Researchers possessing an Ultra-grade T-40 Pass

461

may apply for limited access via the Commission for Oversee of the Post Coalescency Period.

Shari S'Atwa
Coalition Archive sub/sec data core P-Alphra/0000372309/CU/COA/X
Please note: Archival data relating to Shari S'Atwa and her role during the War of the Coalescency has been sealed by Security Docket 1-19/Alphra CIS.
Information in the Public Domain is as follows:
Born and raised Egrain city, Planet Primus, daughter of renowned Legislative Member Lorn S'Atwa and State History teacher Tania S'Atwa (D. Lysordia Syndrome circa: 000135/000479c)
Attended the University of Egrain (Advanced Math Ph/Apl).
(Secondary Adjunct sealed under CIS Security Protocol Teraph/Altra T-07).

Syrillian Anthos
Petran Scripture designates Syrillian Anthos as the first High Cardinal of the Sacred Church of Jophrim, and later canonized by the Sacred College under auspices of Cardinal (Brother) Fiodore of the First Ascetic Ministry of Petra.
Little is known about Syrillian Anthos the man beyond scripture and sacred parable.
The voluminous works of Brother Fiodore describe him as the '... one who stood by our Lord's side, and by his blood was the power of God in Harevakor... ' It is widely believed that Jophrim chose Anthos as the one to found his church on Petra. There are numerous texts describing his journey with Jophrim to face the Beast, but little is known about his life after his return to Petra, although there is anecdotal evidence to suggest he ordered the building of the first church dedicated to Jophrim on the site of what is now the Basilica D' Jophrim in Salicia Sonora.
Once again the more recent translations of the Kyrillian-archi-text suggest that Anthos was a military General and companion to Jophrim during the war waged against an unknown enemy; however the Church continues to refute the findings of the Commission for Religious Extrapolation of the Book of Jophrim (Gamont State University- Ref: 000789/JSR/S/C/GSU).
The only description of the man himself is found within the *Rolls of Theta* which portray him as being tall and powerful and going into battle wearing a crown of fire and wielding a sword forged from the fires of Sierra Tenada on Petra. However a more accurate representation might be found inside the Temple of Saint Sonora in Salicia Sonora on Petra where a marbelite statue of the man is displayed above the main altar.
(Secondary Adjunct with reference to *'The First War of the Beast'* available via T-19 Pass only under Security Docket: 000011/Alpheta/Com/Cor/0001117800).

Tanril Leandahr
Coalition Archive sub/sec data core P-Ultra/0000922749/COA/X

Primary Leader Sacred Twelve, Primus.
Please note: Archival data relating to Tanril Leandahr and his role during the War of
the Coalescency has been sealed by Security Docket-31/UITRA CIS.
Information in the Public Domain is as follows:
Known to have been a crew member on the long range cargo Lugger *Dreslier* which is
known to have made landfall on the satellite Moon of Rim 1478A, a planet later
designated as the Far Star Colony (Star Sector: NG01/FS/CO-0000/000-01572).
Member of the Sacred Twelve of the Coalescency – Primary Adjunct available Ref:
X-Ultra 000024368/S12/COA/X-s via Ultra-grade T-40 Pass.
(Secondary Adjunct sealed under CIS Security Protocol Teraph/Altra T-38)

Tantalus
Philosopher and Poet presumed to have originated from the Tanhauser Gate star sector;
planet of origin unknown.
Archival references are extensive and include both mythological and anecdotal
evidence as to the origins and life of the man. However there is no verifiable data as to
his physical description nor the intricacies of his life.
Within the Torell Star Sector Tantalus is known as *Doronius* with reference to the
Codice of Sylrillia which details the life of the Poet as he travels within the Torellian
Cluster. However it is within the Jophrim Kyrillian archi-text of Petra where *Doronius* is
first referred to as Tantalus, a more ancient title and one which is recorded on the walls of
the Portal Tombs found on Merril within the Saharni Drift Star Sector. Tantalus is again
recorded inside the *Rolls of Theta* the third century pre-Diaspora Scripture attributed to
Theta, brother of Jophrim and now stored in the *Archives of the Interregnum* within the
library of the University of Southern Planatia, Gamont.
The works of Tantalus are thought to have survived the Interregnum through the
distribution and dissemination of several Codices translated and transcribed onto Triax
parchments on the behest of the ruling hierarchy of the Sacred Church of Jophrim based
on Petra.
Tantalus' *Book of Sayings* is taught as part of the ancient history syllabus of two thirds of
Coalition Second School institutions. Many academic institutions continue to teach
Tantalus in old Galac despite calls for the cessation of that language throughout the
Coalition.
Please note: The Kyrillian archi-text is comprised of twelve volumes of text written in
the ancient Petran language of Kyrillian Alpha recently discovered inside a set of datac
tubules beneath the ruins of the Temple of Siena in the southern region of the Latihri
Continent, planet Petra.

Tethran
Saepid far star trader.
Registered with the Coalition Central Board of Interstellar Commerce as a Prime

Dignitary of the Saepid Trading Guild and a member of the Saepid Othrum race of traders originating within the Torellian Cluster.

Very little is known of this Saepid Trader other than his registration with the CBIC on Tantra. He is recognised as the instigator of the Saepid Refugee Assistance Fleet which gave aid and assistance to many worlds within the Cordwainer Alliance that had been left devastated by the War of the Coalescency.

The Star Ship C.S. *Tethran* is named in his honor.

Theta

Author of the *Rolls of Theta* a bound triax Codex compromising of one hundred and fifty so-called '*Illuminati Treatise*', each one dealing with various '*Acts*' of faith in relation to key figures within the Sacred Church of Jophrim.

There is only one reference in the Sacred Book of Jophrim to Theta being a mortal brother to Jophrim; subsequent chapters refer to him simply as a companion. However the reference found within the Kyrillian-archi-text goes on to infer that Theta might have been a family name originating from within the Lohari region of the Petran Southern Desert, an area stated elsewhere in the text as the birthplace of Jophrim. There is no other verifiable data as to the veracity of the contents of any of the aforementioned Sacred Texts. Further information is available upon request from the Historical Archival Validation Department of the University of Gamont.

(Secondary Adjunct Ref: Commission for Religious Extrapolation of the Book of Jophrim - Gamont State University- Ref: 000789/JSR/S/C/GSU).

Please note: Researchers possessing an Ultra-grade T-40 Pass may access the sealed archives of the CIS (Combined Coalition Internal Security and Intelligence Agency) under the following Reference Dockets: *Sword of Jophrim, Chalice of Creation, Custodia, 'Illuminati Treatise' Acts of Faith.*

Torin Grenval

Coalition Archive sub/sec data core P-Setra/0002571678/PHC/PHA/X-c

Please note: Archival data relating to Torin Grenval and his role during the War of the Coalescency has been sealed by Security Docket 2-18/Feta CIS.

Information in the Public Domain is as follows:

Known to have been the First Minister of the Phaelon High Council at the time of the War of the Coalescency.

Registered as a Legislature and Law-Maker with the Phaelon Inter-Alliance Dependency Board circa: 0000789/0010279c local.

Anecdotal evidence names him as Adjutant General to Mistia, a member of the Sacred Twelve. Last recorded data-stream places him aboard the Phaelon heavy cruiser *Hagmon*; his eventual fate remains unverified at this time.

(Secondary Adjunct available Ref: COA/FM/PHA/64-P '*Intrigue & Subversion – The Phaelon Political System, Hendergast, Ceril*).

464

(Security Adjunct sealed under CIS Security Protocol Teraph/Altra T-44)

Valos Armin

High Priest Samros Sacred Sect.

Noted as the instigator of the Galician genocidal purge during the War of the Coalescency.

Born and raised within the Altair Dome on the planet Samros (Cordwainer Alliance). Known to have made his living as a Clerical Officer within the State Customs House. Later during the occupation of Samros by the forces of the Coalescency he achieved rapid promotion within the service of Saemal until eventually being awarded the title of Missionary General for the Expansion of the One True Faith.

(Sealed Security Adjunct CIS/CO/VA/94-T not available for public access)

(Primary Stipulation: Data referent to the Coalescency of Saemal is now stored within the primary access adjunct Torus-99 and has been sealed by CIS Security Protocol pursuant to the agreement concluded by the Supreme High Council of the Coalition – Spatial Date references, access points, core logs and juridical stipulations are not available at this time).

Ventra

Coalition Archive sub/sec data core P-Epsra/0000134799/SAE/COA/X-c

Please note: Archival data relating to the Saepid Trader Ventra and her role during the War of the Coalescency has been sealed by Security Docket 1-18/Epsra CIS.

Information in the Public Domain is as follows:

Pilot of the Saepid Far Star Trading vessel *Shaendar* and mated by Saepid Pheratat ceremony to Anthra, Commanding.

Anecdotal evidence has been filed which suggest that the homeworld of the Saepid Othrum race of traders lies within the Torellian Cluster, but this has not been verified either by the Saepid Trading Guild or by any other means.

(See Secondary Adjunct Ref: 0000258/S/Othrum/Tr/Guild)

(Security Adjunct Ref: 0008/SA/OT/71000X Sealed by Coalition Dictate Psi/49)

Addendum:

THE SACRED TWELVE
Primary access adjunct Torus-99

Coalition Archive sub/sec data core X-Alphra/0000114579/S12/COA/X-s
Data sub/sec records pertaining to the group known as the Sacred Twelve are restricted to
Ultra-grade T-40 Pass only, however certain base level details have since been release via
CIS Tertiary sub/sec Adjunct as Ref: 0000/18978/S12/COALSC/X-s.
Information in the Public Domain is as follows:
A long range cargo Lugger *Dreslier* with a crew of twelve humans is known to have
made landfall on the satellite Moon of Rim 1478A, a planet later designated as the Far
Star Colony (Star Sector: NG01/FS/CO-0000/000-01572).
Little is known of their fate immediately after landfall but sub/sec data logs later
identify these humans as the Sacred Twelve, Prime Leaders within the Coalescency
and instigators of the Jihad of Saemal.
Further details of their crimes and punishments after the fall of the Coalescency are
sealed via Primary Adjunct: X-Alphra/0000114579/S12/COA/X-s.

ALL ACCESS CODE VARIANTS MUST DENOTE POINT OF ORIGIN.

APPENDIX 2

PLANETARY DATABASE

Coalition Archive sub/sec data core T-Altra/0000178429/H/COM/X

- Spatial Calendar (Coretech) based on local planetary space-time ratio and fixed point definitions including a subspace sub-variant for local chronology.

- Database contains post-Galac terminology only with both pre and post-Diaspora references.

- Planetary system classification via standardised Coalition Network Grid.

- Pre and post-Diaspora references are deemed to refer to periods before and after the Interregnum.

- Please note the database is accurate to circa: 00019849.00018c Galac Standard and does not include data beyond the commencement of the War of the Coalescency.

- Secondary Adjunct available Ref: 000013289/PD/COA/DIA/I *'Field Datum & Subspace Variant Extrapolation and Analysis for Chronological Rendering* - Feldheim, Miron, Professor in Actuate University of Southern Planatia, Planet Gamont.

ARCTURA PRIME

Fourth Planet in the system NG37/C/AP-0000-000568 (Arctura)

Home port of the Auxiliary Combined Coalition Fleet.

Site of the Fleet Military Academy, Naval Sciences School, Tactical Analysis School, Incorporated Security Combine and Bio-Psyonic Laboratories.

Settled pre-Diaspora by Colonial Treaty during Hub expansion circa: 0000/744190c.

Location of the Galactic Trans-Net Interceiver Relay Junction Primary Five.

Primary indigenous life form: Taurus Phrailum, bipedal native culture rating: .00074i on the means IQ scale. (Reservation Status)

Current population estimate: 5 billion (including orbital habitats)

Species: 85% Human, 10% Taurus Phrailum, 5% mixed races.

COLOQUIES FEDERATION

Located in proximity to the Termina Sector.

Homeworld: Unknown

Number of Worlds: Unknown

Bio-data: Coloquies exist inside synthskin bubbles moving via agrav plugs and communicating through voice coder box. Little is known of the Coloquies whose physical form is concealed within a pink mist of unknown properties. Anecdotal evidence suggests they have protruding eye stalks and long fibrous fingers; however no data exist as to their exact physical form.

The Coloquies Federation allied itself to the Coalition circa: 00002/56894c

The Coloquies established a repair dock and interstellar port at Landings Down 20.4 Millennia before the founding of the Coalition. Circa: 0000/000012356796c Pre-Diaspora.

Current population estimate: Unknown.

Species: 100% Coloquies.

COMBINE ALLIANCE

Designated as twenty two Allied worlds unified by the Veldthast-Dorn Industrial Combine based on planet Serties, Hub Sector.

Affiliated to the Coalition via the Treaty of New Providence circa: 0001278-200-c.

Location of the New Providence Ship Yards, planet New Providence.

Location of the pan-Galactic Auxiliary Transceiver Relay Array, planet Serties.

Current population estimate: Est. 150 billion.

Species: 65% Human, 35% mixed races.

CORDWAINER ALLIANCE

Designated as seventy two Allied worlds unified by the explorer Egrund Cordwainer (circa: 0009124.000c post-Diaspora) scattered along the Rim Sector of the Galactic periphery.

Capital seat of Allied Government: Planet Samros.
Joined the League of Non-Conformist Worlds circa 0001135.000c, later Non-Conformist Alliance based on planet Tronheim, Rim Sector.
Known Races: Human, Arc'Hadaen, Delorites, Dulon Goc, Trixwellt and Semilirane.
For exact list of planets see secondary adjunct T-Betra/0000289538/CA/NCW/X
Current population estimate: 175 billion, mixed races.
Please note: Data relating to Non-Conformist planets and associated alliances is restricted to: Ultra-grade T-40 Pass.

DANTHROS

Second Planet in the system NG79/A/D-000046.
Third world to affiliate with the Hub Alliance circa: 00001/4756c (pre-Galac dating).
Primary source of Pedrolium Oxide, a derivative of Graphile exudation used in the creation of plassteel constructs.
Home of the Danthros Plassteel & Graphile Combine. Site of the orbital Fleet Construction Yards (Coalition Fleet).
Current population estimate: 8 billion (including Fleet Yards)
Species: 97% Human, 3% mixed races.

DARILL CONFEDERATION

Allied worlds united within the boundaries of the ancient Darill Dynastic Order.
Dominant race being the Lahren Peoples. (Semi-aquatic by nature the Lahren race inhabit water worlds with very little land mass).
The Darill Confederation is not a formal member of the Coalition nor affiliated to the Non-Conformist worlds, but trades via sole treaty allocation to the Coalition.
Current population estimate: 65 billion.
Species: 99% Lahren, 1% mixed races.

DROMETIA

Fifth Planet in the system NG84/D/CO-000046.
Second world to affiliate with the Hub Alliance circa: 00008/6101c local.
Capital City: Sha'Ning.
Noted as the headquarters of the Ti Cho Ming Corporation, suppliers of advanced Tracer and Sensory alignment systems to the Coalition Border Fleet.
Current population estimate: 5 billion.
Species: 99% Human, 1% mixed races.

DRONHEIM

Fifth Planet in the system NG26/C/DR-0000-000479
Original Capital World of the pre-Diaspora Hub Protectorate however power and

influence among the outer worlds of the Hub Alliance reduced with the rise of Tantra as Founding Capital of the Coalition.

Noted for the creation of the first Non-Conformist resistance group within the borders of the Coalition.

Martial Law imposed circa: 000/24190c (post-Galac date). Security Statute Phata instigated following Fleet deployment and occupation by Coalition forces circa: 000.27292c.

(Security adjunct sealed under CIS Security Protocol Teraph/Altra T-39)

Current population estimate: 7 billion

Species: 92% Human, 8% mixed races.

EARTHIA

Third Planet in the system NG19/C/EA-0000-00007854 (Centaur System)

Furthest outpost of the post-Diaspora Coalition.

Capital City: Austaria

Noted as the mythical home of the First Race, but since disputed in the Jophrim Kyrillian arch-text (Petra) which identifies the mythical planet Sandheim within the Great Expanse as the home of the Ancients.

Home base of the Coalition Border Fleet and Colonial Marine Academy.

Site of the Eastasia Prime Orbital Docking Yards.

Location of the Storhahl Marbelite Quarry & Mining Consortium.

Location of the Galactic Trans-Net Interceiver Relay Junction Primary Four.

Noted Philosopher and Poet Lothar Theron born in Austaria city (First Diaspora).

Current population estimate: 8 billion

Species: 85% Human, 15% mixed races.

ELYSIA SECTOR

Loosely affiliated independent non-aligned worlds dominated by the Tirana Consortium based on planet Tirana.

Tirana Consortium is known to be a Sector wide conglomerate of industrial combines concerned with the manufacture of Ionic Phase weaponry and Plasmeld Shield development.

For exact list of planets see secondary adjunct T-Betra/0000289538/H/COM/X

Current population unknown.

Species: 100% mixed races.

Please note: Data relating to Non-Conformist planets and associated alliances is restricted to: Ultra-grade T-40 Pass.

ENTRYMION

Second planet in the system NG98/G/E-10000 - Entrymion Sector.

The most recent world to be incorporated within the Coalition and the furthest human

Coalition colony from the Hub Sector.

Capital City: Carphalia

Seat of Government: House of Senatorial Elect.

Entrymion settled by colonists from the Hub Sector circa: 0000/27198c.

Birthplace of noted Poets: Altrius Dex (Sophia City), and the Poet Brayman (Carphalia City).

First human colony bordering the independent Phaelon Confederacy

Current population estimate: 7 billion.

Species: 100% Human.

EXLIMON

Fourth planet in the system NG39/I/EX-00001472

Independent world on the borders of the Elysia Sector, known for the production of Ion weaponry and phase transducer coils. Has resisted all diplomatic attempts to join Coalition. Also known to deal in arms and pulse drive components with several Non-Conformist groups including the Phaelon Confederacy.

Dominant race: Tegmenite. (Bipedal with extra cranial appendage).

Capital city: Eritania.

Coalition military blockade instigated circa: 0000/47128c. Blockade removed after Treaty of Eritania. Trade re-established under Security Protocol M-EXL/11000A.

Current population estimate: 11 billion.

Species: 95% Tegmenite, 5% mixed races.

FAR STAR COLONY

Fourth planet in the system NG01/FS/CO-0000/000-01572 (Rim 1478A)

Furthest known occupied planet situated at the edge of the Great Expanse (Rim Sector).

Settled originally by trading colonists from the Cordwainer Alliance.

Officially named as a Protectorate of the Alliance circa: 0000/67191c local.

Known to deal in used parts for starship construction and Ferrite Corbium Refinement.

Current population estimate: 50-80 million.

Species: 40% Human, 30% Phaelon, 20% Tegmenite, 10% mixed races.

Security adjunct sealed under CIS Security Protocol Teraph/Altra T-40)

GALICIA

Fourth planet in the system NG89/C/G-000.

Designated as auxiliary Capital World of the Second Coalition Expansion circa: 0000/97891c post-Diaspora.

Capital City: Gestheim.

Galician Military Cadets serve as honorary standard bearers for the Tantran Supreme High Command as part of the Tantran inter-Coalition Exchange Programme.

Location of the Galician Space Academy affiliated to the Coalition Border Fleet.

Site of Gestheim Teme Incorporated, makers of the subspace Tracer Grid AI Systems.
Location of the Galactic Trans-Net Interceiver Relay Junction Primary Six.
Current population estimate: 7 billion
Species: 95% Human, 5% mixed races.

GAMONT
Third planet in the system NG59/C/GA-00001.
Long standing member of the pan-Galactic Coalition and home to Academia Centralis, the Coalition sponsored Educational programme for the intellectual advancement of the member races.
Prestigious institutions include:
The University of Southern Planatia.
(See secondary adjunct historical ref. Pet/Cor/Tan-0000174/C-00002976: Professor Asia Tolun and Professor Kyle Raine).
Gamont State University (Academia Centralis).
The Pheranon Adaptive University.
(See secondary adjunct Science Ref. Clinitas/0000417-G)
Home of the Clinitas Bio-Tech Group. (Ref: Feeler Sensor Development Labs)
Headquarters of the Pheranon Corporation.
Location of the Galactic Trans-Net Interceiver Relay Junction Primary Three.
Current population estimate: 7 billion (including in-system habitats)
Species: 97% Human, 4% mixed races.

GRAINSFELD
Second planet in the system NG91/P/GR-00001-0007899 (Planetoid).
Agricultural and industrial colony of the Phaelon Confederacy.
Site of the Detrium Mining Cooperative.
Location of the Phaedran Mercantile Harvester Combine.
Cited as the primary location of the Phaelon Cartels, dealers in illicit trade and transportation of illegal products. (Security Docket 1-08/Alphra CIS)
Current population estimate: Unknown.
Species: 100% Phaelon.
Please note: Data relating to Non-Conformist planets and associated alliances is restricted to: Ultra-grade T-40 Pass.

MERRIL
Single planet in the system NG999/S/ME-00009-00098997.
Abandoned world far beyond the border of the Coalition at the edge of the Saharni Drift.
Previously mined for Drillium by the Terak Nor Resium Combine under licence from the Sylvian Alliance, abandoned circa: 10001172/3269c

472

Site of the Portal Tombs of the Huharni Escarpment.
Theoretical birthplace of Jophrim (Province of Tianadora) - Unconfirmed.
Inscriptia Dethrim marbelite codex discovered circa: 2000246/4200c
(See secondary adjunct historical ref. MER/COA/FR-0002169/C-000498901 University of Southern Planatia).
Theoretical outpost of the First Race.
(See secondary adjunct Historical Ref. MER/F/Pre-D/000014-0001367 Raine, Kyle)

PALATIA
Fourth planet in the system NG52/P/COL-00009-00027881
Independent Non-Aligned world within the borders of the Coloquies Federation.
Signed mutual Assistance Treaty with Coloquies Far Reach Expeditionary Force.
circa: 1000459/6301c
Site of the Coalex Gastrol Refinery.
Current population estimate: 12 billion
Species: 85% Human, 15% Coloquies.

PETRA
Sixth planet in the system NG42/C/PE-00006-00035762.
Planet devoted to the Sacred Church of Jophrim.
Incorporated into the Coalition circa: 100002/4758c post-Diaspora.
Famed for its Basilica D'Jophrim in the capital city of Salicia Sonora.
(See secondary adjunct historical Ref. PE/C/JO 10009-20045, Thendosh, Domini)
Location of the Galactic Trans-Net Interceiver Relay Junction Primary Seven.
Current population estimate: 12 billion
Species: 75% Human, 10% Coloquies, 5% Lahren, 10% mixed races.
Addendum: archival data relating to Domini Thendosh and his role during the War of the Coalescency has been sealed by Security Docket 1-20/Alphra CIS.

PHAEDRA
Fourth planet in the system NG899/NC/PC-000089-00098990.
Capital world of the Phaelon Confederacy. Allied to League of Non-Conformist Worlds & Confederation of Non-Aligned Worlds Rim Sector.
(See secondary adjunct historical Ref. PH/NC/NA-00012357-000134 – Piracy)
Capital City: Tendrah.
Headquarters of the Elaas Elite Corps. (Phaelon Covert Security Service)
Ruling Body: Council Assemblage.
No data with reference to number of worlds within Confederate borders.
Phaelon bio-data: Reptilian humanoid bipeds. Cited as sworn enemies of the Coalition of Allied Worlds.
Current population estimate: Unknown

473

Species: 95% Phaelon, 5% indentured races. (Estimated).

PORT FALL
Fifth planet in the system NG779/NC/PF-000099-000178790-RIM SECTOR.
Granted full autonomous status via the Treaty of Economous Sancta by the
Cordwainer Ruling Council, Samros circa: 000013/00879c post-Diaspora.
Recognised as a Free Port by the Phaelon Confederacy, the Allied League of Non-
Conformist Worlds & the Confederation of Non-Aligned Worlds Rim Sector.
Often cited as layover for Phaelon Corsairs, Tegmenite auxiliaries, Arc'Hadaen
mercenaries, Delorite traders, Dulon Goc security services and Semilirane tactical
personnel.
Known for its illicit trade in black-market produce including weaponry, spare-parts,
illegal neural enhancements, medications, bio-tech technologies and high-tech AI
systems.
Cited as a secondary location of the Phaelon Cartels, dealers in illicit trade and
transportation of illegal products. (Security Docket 1-09/Alphra CIS)
Has persistently refused diplomatic entreaties to join Coalition of Worlds.
Current population estimate: Unknown
Species: 65% Mixed races, 35% Human.

PRIMAL IV
Fourth Planet in the system NG444/C/PRI-0003-000149.
Central Coalition world and headquarters of the CIS (Combined Coalition Internal
Security and Intelligence Agency- Dromart, Harris, Director).
CIS Directorate: Praisedio Building.
Headquarters of Fleet Security Division Tech/An 51 (FSD) and R & D Laboratories.
Capital City: New Lothoran.
Colonial settlement established under Hub Allied Dictate out of Arctura Prime circa:
000019/00489c pre-Diaspora.
Location of the Coalition Fleet Medical Corps & Bio-Tech Analysis Foundation.
Location of the Coalition and Colonial Medical Corps. (CCMC)
Location of the Galactic Trans-Net Interceiver Relay Junction Primary Eight.
Noted as the headquarters of Groisswerk-Dacht Industries Incorporated, manufacturers of
pre-fabricated orbital habitats and Glasscite compounds.
(Sealed Security Adjuncts Ref: T/Primal/Esc/0004567100/X)
Current population estimate: 6 billion.
Species: 99% Human, 1% mixed races.

PRIMUS
Third Planet in the system NG555/C/PR-0002-000258.
Officially incorporated into the Coalition of Worlds circa: 000898-100045c

post-Diaspora.
Primus seat of Government: Legislative Assembly.
(Harkon, P. President Elect- See historical Ref. PR/CO/SA-000/856 Trial Docket
Ah/4t)
Capital city: Egrain City.
Secondary notation: Site of the original Global Oxygenation Project for the
Sustainment of Natural Resources. (Tri/Alpha-com Seti/0001 GOP)
(Sealed Adjunct under Security Protocol: Terman/Phain-000/46793 Ref. S'Atwa, Shari,
University of Egrain).
Current population estimate: 7 billion.
Species: 98% Human, 2% mixed races.

SANDHEIM

Please note: Archival references to Sandheim are included as secondary adjuncts to
the Primary Planetary Database only with regard to academic speculation concerning
the myth of a First Race existing as a homogenous culture prior to the founding of the
first Hub Alliance. Current date references are estimates and as such are not included
within the database.
Mythical planet speculated to exist beyond the Rim Sector within the Great Expanse.
(See Secondary Adjuncts Ref: First Race/Transcendance/Custodia/Archive-000666/X
and Ref: Primus/S'Atwa/Seapid/Neural-0005678/AX)
(Sealed Security Protocols Ref: S/Sand/FR/FSC/000768900/X)
Current population estimate: Unknown.
Species: Unknown.

SENSUA COLONY

Second Planet in the system NG223C/SEN-0007-0002459.
Established as a pleasure colony by the Tantran Commercial Combine:
Sensua Sancta Tct. circa: 000429-200038c.
Granted Free Licence by the Commission for Trade and Industry, Tantran High Council
and Assembly of the Coalition circa: 000429-200039c.
Noted for its Prism Palisades, Lucient Arcades, Erotis Galleries and Vis-Dec Casinos.
Site of the Lupis Lawana Galleria Pleasure Dome.
Location of the Galactic Trans-Net Interceiver Relay Junction Primary Two.
Entry via Orbital Skysat Security Platform only.
Site of the largest Credit Exchange facility within the Coalition. (See Newland Allied
Banking Exchange, credit doc/Tantra/Su14)
Current population estimate: 8 billion
Species: 60% Human, 40% mixed races.

SYLVIA PRIME

Sixth Planet in the system NG211C/SYP-0009-0001488.

Capital world of the Sylvian Alliance; a non-aligned oligarchy within the Elysia Sector.

Species are a secondary-branch mutation of the human genome resulting in heightened stature and supererogatory muscle development.

Widely known for its autocratic and militaristic ruling classes the Sylvian Alliance was formed out of the remnants of the Aurtach of Sylvia Dynastic Family.

A vocal adversary of the unification of worlds under one Coalition, the Sylvian Alliance has most recently entered into a Mutual Assistance Treaty with the Phaelon Confederacy. (Circa: 000127-200079c).

Current planetary population estimate: 9 billion

Current Sylvian Alliance population estimate: Est. 78 billion.

Species: 70% Humanoid, 30% mixed races.

(Security Adjunct Ref: 0005/SP/SA/40000X Sealed by Coalition Dictate Psi/42).

TALUS III

Fifth Planet in the system NG05/C/TAL-0006-0005445.

Noted as the Primary signatory of the pre-Diaspora Hub Alliance Constitution.

Home of the Ambiquo Dynastic House - Circa: 0000121-100025c.

Capital city: Senigor City.

Joint member of the Coalition Expeditionary League with Earthia.

Home of the Academy of Spatial Sciences, Senigor City.

Location of the Dromant Inter-Species Assimilation Group.

Location of the Galactic Trans-Net Interceiver Relay Junction Primary Ten.

Current population estimate: 4 billion (including out-system habitats)

Species: 97% Human, 3% mixed races.

TANHAUSER GATE

Star Sector designated as the probable point of origin of the human species. (See secondary adjunct Ref: 0000421/TG/C/H-00076856 Academia Centralis, Gamont State University).

Planetary references and accumulated data available via Science Core Archive and associated astro-spatial historical archives ref: G6/TG-46 Gamont State University.

Known planetoids include the Mining consortium of Draeus Megalite Industries based on Terra 214/A, Petrus 217/B and Letrum 219/C.

Population stats and distribution and nature of species: Unknown.

TANTRA

Third Planet in the system NG00/C/TAN-0001-0001111.

Capital world of the Pan-Galactic Coalition of Allied Worlds.

Originally known as Amaterasi, home to the indigenous Afphram Culture and ceded

to the Hub Alliance circa 000139-100076c pre-Diaspora.
(Afphram Reservation Status – pending)
Formerly Capital of the Hub Alliance consisting of: Tantra, Danthros, Telaxa, Gamont,
Talus III, Dronheim, Vendicor, Drometia, and Arctura Prime.
Location of the Ferman Orbital Defence Ring.
Location of the Galactic Trans-Net Interceiver Relay Junction Primary One.
Site of the Imperia Concordis – Government Seat of the Coalition Supreme Ruling
Council – Legislative Chambers: The Centerium.
Home port of the Primary Pan-Galactic Coalition Defence Force, the Tantra State
Militia and CIS State Compound.
Headquarters of Treraschin Nagung Corp. Suppliers of Ion Pulse Drive initiation rods
to the Coalition Defence Force – Fleet Central.
Current population estimate: 13 billion (including in-system habitats)
Species: 70% Human, 20% Afphram, 10% mixed races.

TELAXA
Fifth Planet in the system NG04/C/TEL-0004-0004455.
Primary member of the Coalition League of Humanities (State Charter issued
under published dictate to spread the Laws and Customs of Humanity throughout
known space). Capital City: Rejnik.
Indigenous race: Vendhu. (Possible offshoot of the Phaelon genome – Reservation
Status).
Affiliated to the Galician Interstellar Charter for the dissemination of human customs
among the outer colonies.
Location of the Galactic Trans-Net Interceiver Relay Junction Primary Nine.
Current population estimate: 7 billion (including out-system habitats)
Species: 75% Human, 20% Vendhu, 5% mixed races.

TERAK NOR
Seventh Planet in the system NG15/S/SYA-0019-0008749.
Allied as a Protectorate of the Sylvian Alliance.
Capital City: Huang Yang.
Noted for the development of High-Tech advanced AI systems and integrated Tracer
enhancements.
Headquarters of: Chimai Tao Li Commercial Enterprises – manufacturers of integrated
spatial grid and spectrographic evocation systems.
Currently under forced trade embargo instigated by Coalition State Dictate T 18/TN.
Site of the first and only military incursion by Coalition forces circa: 000479-300069c.
Non-Aggression Pact co-signed between Coalition State Senate and Terak Nor
Affiliated Commercial Combine, not endorsed by Sylvian Alliance.
Current population estimate: 3 billion (including out-system habitats)

Species: 55% Human, 45% mixed races.

TIRANA
Fourth Planet in the system NG29/T/ES-00002-00018569.
Capital world of the loosely affiliated independent non-aligned worlds of the Elysia Sector.
Capital City: Dhum Nadig.
Headquarters of Tu Wein Mei Lei Industries Incorporated, suppliers of Vision Rendering technologies & Spatial Grid Evocation Systems.
Location of the Tirana Glasscite Consortium, part of the Chimai Tao Li Commercial Enterprises (Terak Nor).
Current population estimate: 11 billion (including out-system habitats)
Species: 65% Human, 35% mixed races.

TRANIA
Eighth Planet in the system NG47/C/COL-00009-000088989.
Registered within the Coalition Affiliated Worlds Database as a out-sector province of the Coloquies Federation.
Exports Detrozine Phosphate, Plasmeld Shields and advanced Sensory Tracer systems under contract to the Primary Pan-Galactic Coalition Defence Force and Tantra State Militia.
Current population estimate: Unknown.
Species: 100% Coloquies.

TORELLIAN CLUSTER
Unexplored region within the Torell Sector.
Anecdotal evidence has been filed which suggest that the homeworld of the Saepid Othrum race of traders lies within the Cluster, but this has not been verified either by the Saepid Trading Guild or by any other means.
Noted for the al-Rahman and al-Sufi Nebulas.
(See secondary adjunct Ref: 0000147/S/Othrum/Tr/Guild)
(Security Adjunct Ref: 0008/SA/OT/71000X Sealed by Coalition Dictate Psi/49.

TRONHEIM
Second Planet in the system NG78/NC/TRO-20009-100078289.
Joined the League of Non-Conformist Worlds circa 0002137.001c,
Founded Non-Conformist Alliance circa 0005648.004c
Capital City: Grostad.
Co-signatory of Treaty of Vehndaron with Arc'Hadaen and Phaelon Confederacy circa 0007898.007c.
Site of the Rally for Insurgency demonstrations and declaration of Non-Conformist

478

Independence circa: 00043279-119c local.
Bio-data: Humanoid with fibrous spinal appendage and caudal appendage.
Current population estimate: Unknown.
Species: Genus Tronheimnoid - population ratios unavailable.
Please note: Data relating to Non-Conformist planets and associated alliances is restricted to: Ultra-grade T-40 Pass.

Ua'LUHN
Sixth Planet in the system NG92/NC/UAL-40007-200088789.
Capital world of the Arc'Hadaen Alliance.
Joined the League of Non-Conformist Worlds circa 0004138.002c,
Capital City: Eskrihnolavta.
Co-signatory of Treaty of Vehndaron with Tronheim and Phaelon Confederacy circa 0007898.007c.
Known to maintain military outposts throughout the Rim Sector.
Bio-data: Humanoid. Lacking distinct facial features (Term: Flat-Facers)
(Security Adjunct Ref: 0009/ARH/NC/70004X Sealed by Coalition Dictate Psi/40)
Current population estimate: Unknown.
Species: Arc'Hadaen, population ratios unavailable.
Please note: Data relating to Non-Conformist planets and associated alliances is restricted to: Ultra-grade T-40 Pass.

VENDICOR
Fourth Planet in the system NG27/CO/VEN-10002-600025722.
Capital City: Eritraia
Noted for the location of the Border Auxiliary Coalition and Colonial Medical Corps.
Headquarters: Galac Medicio Instituta Servicio – Part of the Medcare Bio-Tech Pharmaceutical Combine.
Signed Mutual Assistance Treaty with Earthia circa 0004478.009c.
Site of Coalition Auxiliary Fleet Yards (orbital).
Location of the Galactic Trans-Net Interceiver Relay Junction Primary Eleven..
Current population estimate: 8 billion
Species: 90% Human, 10% mixed races.

APPENDIX 3

Index of Terminology and Materials

Agrav-Plates

Anti-gravity magnetic coil induction is a by-product of ionic containment sublimated via a plasma manifold. Magnetic fields are produced by moving electric charges and the intrinsic magnetic moments of elementary particles associated with a fundamental quantum property, their spin. In special relativity, electric and magnetic fields are two interrelated aspects of a single object, called the electromagnetic field tensor; the aspect of the electromagnetic field that is seen as a magnetic field is dependent on the reference frame of the observer. In quantum physics, the electromagnetic field is quantized and electromagnetic interactions result from the exchange of photons. Ionic subspace field containment quantifies anti-gravitational rotation within a restricted grid fused via internal sensor alignment to teddra-plates and are used primarily in the construction of long-range starships, sub-orbital platforms and atmospheric cities.

Barg

Large bipedal anthropoid - mesomorphic in stature. Native culture rating:
.00013i on the means IQ scale. Native to several planets of the Hub Sector.
Note that the transportation and exploitation of the Barg species is now prohibited under Coalition Dictate 0000/9887/COA-Z.

CIS

Combined Coalition Internal Security and Intelligence Agency- Dromart, Harris, Director.
HQ: Praisedio Building, planet Primal IV.

CCMC

Coalition and Colonial Medical Corps, planet Primal IV.

Coalescency

Designated title given to the violent expansion of the cortex entity and its military forces across Coalition space.

Cognitive Evocation System (CES)

Primary holo-lucience spatial rendering system used primarily in the Vision Chamber of a starship. The method allows the navigation statistics and coordinates of a specific spatial grid to be uploaded into a holo-emitter and rendered as part of a evocation scenario. This system bypasses a ships AI data-stream and as such restricts the ability of outsystem feelers to infiltrate the primary data core and by so doing prevents the corruption of the algorithmic protocols of the ships systems.

Crell
Expletive in common usage among urban populations of a number of Coalition worlds. (Origins pre-Diaspora Galac)

Crytonin
Military grade explosive material comprised of polysolitonin and Ph(4-ethinon) interlaced with triax derivatives and colopolomine plasticizers. Currently usage restricted to Coalition Defence Force and Border Fleet personnel.

Datapad
Personal hand-held multi-core processor – The datapad can link via subspace insertion with the Trans-Net AI multi-cluster and Interceiver junctions located throughout the Coalition giving instant access with the Trans-Net. Multi-function protocols permit the datapad to lock into any trans-Galactic data-stream and assume guidance insertion for the skimming of requested data.

Data Plug/ID Tag
Small sliver of data-crystal usually inserted at the base of a human skull to tag the identity and blood type of the person. Tags are regularly scanned upon entry and exit to all Coalition State premises including spaceports, orbital habitats and Fleet Yards.

Dramex
B-29 Sleep inducing drug, registered as addictive in CCMC database.

Feeler Sensory Array
The Feeler sensory array is an adaptive electromagnetic wave programme designed specifically to seek out coded definitions pre-programmed into its AI core matrix. Sensor definitions are cast out from a primary array via nonparticulate radiation with bounce-back response tags aligned to a starship AI detection system.

Felore
Pelt of the Faroesen Deer and used primarily in the upholstery of luxury furniture.

Foilair fleece
Fiber extract taken from Foilair ewes and used primarily in the production of luxury textiles.

Foilette sheets
Malleable thin aluminium and cyotocin infused sheets used for personal hygiene and by
Medcare facilities.

Gastrol
Transparent liquid refined from organic derivatives by fractional distillation combined
with Terium Sycilate as a binding agent. Used primarily in loop-feed combustion and
energy containment vessels to generate internal combustible power to a drive engine.

Glasscite
Amorphous solid material with inter-crystalline strata including polymeric additives
and siliconite oxides inside a teritrium mitride solution in its solid form. Used in its
clear state as a replacement for the more archaic glass. Due to its high tensile durability
and polarized differential properties it is used primarily in Star Ship construction as well
as ground based dwellings.

Graphile
A heavy ductile magnetic metallic element cross-linked via carbon induced pheracites
and iron ferrocine widely used within the construction industry.

Holo-lucience
Originally developed as a visual graphical interface for biometric and technical
rendition of tactical scenarios and combat diagnostics the holo-lucience has since been
incorporated into the entertainment and advertising industries as a means to display
products, persons and locations.

Ion Pulse Engine
An ion pulse engine is a form of electric propulsion used for spacecraft propulsion that
creates thrust by accelerating ions inside a containment vessel. Ion thrusters are
categorized by how they accelerate the ions, using either electrostatic or electromagnetic
force. Current ionic containment vessels generate a subspace field as a by-product of
ionic insertion via a standardised plasma manifold. Ion thrust is sublimated via the needle
tube assembly of a starship. Anti-gravity exudation is manifest via phase coil assimilation
of the ion stream and alignment of the pulse containment vessel to specific subspace
protocols.

Lucidator
A Lucidator is a neural educator used to ameliorate the mental cognitive response
times of the human mind. Once connected it taps into the cerebral cortex and directly
downloads educational material into the brain. There are embedded neural restrictions
pre-set to avoid the full assimilation of the knowledge available so that students will

482

only learn facts as opposed to direct answers to questions posed. The device is used as a revisionary method within the majority of Coalition academic institutions as an alternative to losing grade points by skimming the Trans-Net for solutions, a practice frowned upon by most academia.

Lysordia Syndrome
Acute upper respiratory disease resulting from the lysordi bacillus and native to planet Primus. Once considered fatal the disease has since been proven curable via Trillium Sescilate infusion. It is characterized by inflammation of the lung parenchyma leading to impaired gas exchange with concomitant systemic release of inflammatory mediators causing inflammation, hypoxemia and frequently resulting in multiple organ failure. This condition is often fatal, usually requiring mechanical ventilation and admission to a vital care unit

Needle Tubes
Starship – Exterior ionic venting tubes (Propulsion).

Nimris
Holy word used to seal a sign of worship – Worship Glyph.

Phase Inducer
Bio-molecular energy and matter conversion device designed to demolecularise a living body whilst maintaining its cohesive form, enabling that body to move through solid matter in order to re-form the original molecular matrix beyond the solid structure.
This device is currently prohibited by law under Coalition Juridical Dictate T-Com/PI-99001/CIS.

Plasmeld Shield
Bio- thermic anti-grav air induction harness used for individual transportation, often sensor-linked to Civil Air Administration Ribbon Transport Systems.
(See Ref: Plasmeld Transport & Personal Liability Act, Tantran Supreme High Legislative Assembly).

Plassteel
Combined synthetic amalgamation of organic polymers and side chain silicone addltives using halogenated thermoplastics and ilmenite titanium steel alloy with iron-carbon-chronium cross-links. Used primarily in the construction of Star Ships, Orbital Habitats and ground based dwellings.

Plasstrip
Sterile adhesive wound sealant.

Predicant
Petran State Security Officer – Planet Petra.

Proaxol
A drug that temporarily quickens some vital process. Long term use can lead to addiction. (See CCMC Protocol 0002349/PROAX-m)

Protein slug
Generic term for the series of drugs used to enhance autonomous neural response times in the human adrenal gland.
Classified under Coalition and Colonial Medical Corp dictate as highly addictive and as such its use and dissemination is restricted to CCMC personnel only.

Reflective Marbelite
Used in the both the exterior and interior construction of classical buildings with an emphasis upon religious buildings and statuary.
(Ref: The Storhahl Marbelite Quarry & Mining Consortium, Earthia).

Retina Pad
Bio-tech crystalline integrated data sheet with retinal/cortical binary loop. Each pad can hold up to 40CT's of lucid renderings transferable into pre-programmed data. Widely used to store maps, spatial topography and Net linked data sites.

Ribbon
The Ribbon Navigational System is a Sensory Allocation Net used to track personal flyers via their Plasmeld Recognition Code. Each major city with a RNS/SAN has a central AI portal which identifies every single personal flyer that passes through a designated zone; each city is divided into four Primary Zones and four Secondary Zones for local traffic. Theoretically the Ribbon system should prevent collisions or abuse of the Municipal Transit Codes. The system is used on several of the central Hub worlds but has yet to be adopted by the outer planets.
Please note that the designation Ribbon may also refer to the above ground monorail system which operate via grav-plate induction which is in use in the majority of Coalition cities.

Siliconite (White)
A liquid compound containing pro-active neural gel comprising of both dendrite and axon fibres to facilitate enhancement of both neuron and cortical linkages. Usually injected directly into the cerebral cortex. Please note that Siliconite has been included in the CCMC register of prohibited compounds.

Silium fire suppressant
Aqueous film forming foam for vapour suppression of fires and toxic spillages certified for use in cargo/storage areas aboard the majority of registered star ships.

Skipper
Small shuttle craft used for low-orbital atmospheric insertion and ground to air flight.

Teddra Infusion
Liquid metal substance that has undergone induration and sub-molecular binding using Drohimine oxide derivatives as a recombination to seal its base core properties into a highly durable plassteel alternative. Used primarily within the construction industry as support pylons, orbital struts and agrav-plating.

Tetra Gun
A precision-rifle used to ensure more accurate placement of an ionic pulse beam at longer ranges than other small arms and employing plasma induced recoil technology with long range sensor targeting.

Tetranium bombs
High-tech military grade weapon deployed as a sub-orbital assault missile. Tetranium Cobalt combines ferromagnetic fissile material (Utrinium or Pheronium) into an assembled supercritical mass initiating an exponentially generating Tetranium chain reaction. T-Bombs are often shielded via sensory rotation to avoid ground sensor detection.

Tracer Sensory Net
Similar in designation to the feeler sensory array, the Tracer Sensory Net relies on a pre-programmed onboard definition protocol to align solid objects to the directional parameters of the Sensory Net. Tracers can be used both onboard a vessel or via drone deployment to bounce-back location, definition and recognition protocols.

Traumalin
Inhibits or stops the growth and reproduction of viruses and reduces the rate of cell degradation in humanoid species.

Triax parchments
Thin material usually comprised of Triax skin interlaced with vellum and seared through a process of induration in order to preserve the molecular cohesion of the Triax. Used primarily in the creation of books, codex and manuscripts requiring long-term preservation as opposed to data node memory plugs. Often found within the

archives of religious institutions (Ex: Kyrillian archi-text, Petra).
(Triax skin – the outer sheath of the arboreal 'breather' tree native to Petra, but also found on several worlds within the Coalition).

Ultravane
Inter-phase subspace ionic burst propulsion device which greatly accelerates an ion engine beyond the pulse initiation threshold. Molecular mass differentiates at 471 p/i to the spatial insertion point of 126 ip/u.

Viper
Multi-functional assault craft with integral feeler, tracer and subspace scattering systems combined with psyonic shielding and ionic diffusion technology. Version Teth/14A comes armed with Tetranium Cobalt missile assembly and Autonomous Feeler Drone Array. Version Teth/15B has similar features but is enhanced with an Ultravane forced Pulse drive. Note that the Viper ships are operated by members of the Non-Conformist Alliance and as such they are liable to search and/or seizure if detected in proximity to a prime Coalition location.

Coalition Archive sub/sec data core X-Thetsa ref. ordnance/type
Restricted to CIS Security Protocol 000/13400-T.

CPSIA information can be obtained at www.ICGtesting.com
Printed in the USA
BVOW020938130213

313101BV00001B/15/P